I0831279

About the Author

Martin Roy Mortimer is a Cultural Anthropologist, having graduated with honours for field work performed through the University of Newcastle in Australia. A former high school teacher, he now resides in the NSW Riverina district and has plans to continue writing and publishing books into the future. Watch for his next book!

The Cinder Chronicles is a Fantasy series suitable for young adults and adults.

Visit the official website:

www.thecinderchronicles.com

Science Fiction by this author:

Suspended Earth

Starlight

Dance of Nevermind

Shades of Farthrow

Armada's Disciple

Longarm Severed

Short story collection by this author:

When History Fractures, Heroes Rise

Visit www.suspendedearth.com

for information about other SF releases.

The Cinder Chronicles

Rangers Trilogy Omnibus

Martin R Mortimer

Omnibus First published 2020
Flame Rangers 2016
Ice Rangers 2017
Sand Rangers 2017

ISBN-13: 978-0648956303

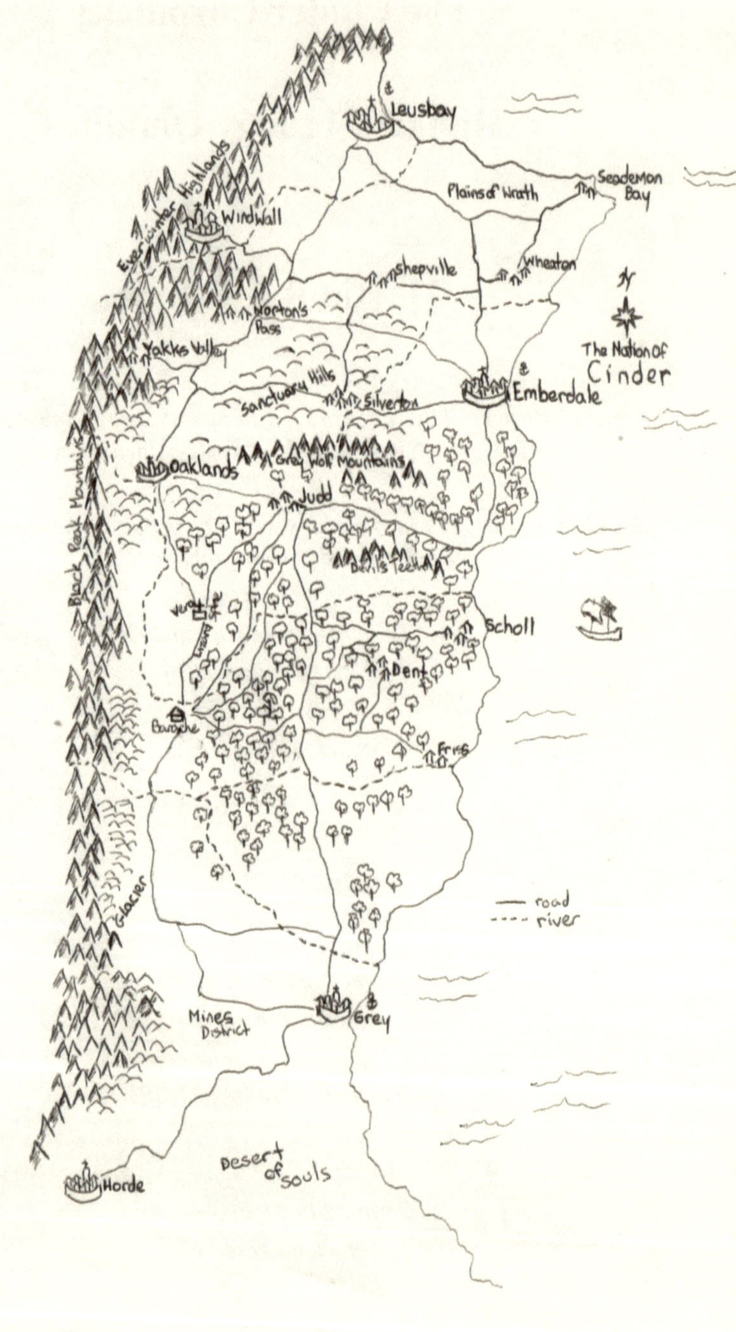

Leusbay
Evenwinter Highlands
Windwall
Plains of Wrath
Seademon Bay
Shepville
Wheaton
Norton's Pass
Yakks Valley
Sanctuary Hills
Silverton
Emberdale
The Nation Of Cinder
N
Black Peak Mountains
Oaklands
Grey Wolf Mountains
Judd
Devil's Teeth
Scholl
Dent
Baroche
Friss
Glacier
road
river
Mines District
Grey
Desert of souls
Horde

Book One
Flame Rangers

Chapter 1 – Children of fire

Red and menacing, the fire erupted from Fletcher's hands like the web from a spider. Treghan watched as his twin brother's flames skipped across the rocks. In response to the menacing heat, the foxes retreated into the cliffs, vanishing from sight. The grateful farmer rushed over, beaming his broadest grin at the pair, but favouring Fletcher with a congratulatory slap on the back.

"Lad, that was astonishing," the farmer said. "I doubt they'll be back any time tonight. The flock is safe, and it's all thanks to you. This village owes you a debt of gratitude, son. Tell your old man I'll drop the payment around first thing in the morning."

With that, the farmer turned to leave, casting a disapproving glare at Treghan. The farmer trudged off towards his flock, where his dog paced to keep them away from the rocks, and the foxes.

Treghan looked down at his hands, bereft in his uselessness. Focussing all his effort, he kindled a tiny, bright white spark in his palm. He pushed all his energy into that spark, but in spite of his best efforts, it failed to ignite into anything remotely like the fierce inferno his brother had sent roaring over the fields, and into the rocks, as they pursued their four legged prey.

Fletcher looked at him, a mix of pity and disdain in his eyes.

"You'll never be any use with that white rubbish," Fletcher said. "You should change your colour, then it might be bigger. Like mine."

"I know, but we can't change our colours, you know that. We're born with the talent, or without it, and we're born to a colour. No training can ever change that."

"Then you'll always be useless. Why bother trying if you can't even manage a flame?"

"Maybe it'll get bigger when I'm older," Treghan said with hope in his voice.

"Don't be stupid," Fletcher snapped. "We're fifteen, if it was going to get any bigger, it would have done so by now. You'll just never be as good as me. You should give up and go find something more suited to your feeble body."

Treghan had no reply. He never did any more. He tried to be useful, but he never managed to swing an axe with the force needed to split the hard wood they used for the fire. He never ran fast enough to be of use hunting, or chasing the livestock, and his eyes weren't sharp enough for the fine needlework his mother could teach him. Flame wielding was his only hope, and he couldn't even manage that.

"I just wish I wasn't so worthless," Treghan muttered.

"You'll always be worthless, so get used to it, and no complaining about your food when we get home. You get what you deserve. Ma and Pa supply what they can, and if I bring in a bit more, it's only right I should get more than you."

Turning, Fletcher began the long walk home. Treghan watched after his brother, the cruel words stinging his meagre pride. Fletcher never looked back, his disdain for his brother etched into his shoulders as the fading twilight licked at his ragged mane of sandy hair. Treghan slumped further, pushing his white hair away from his face as he drew in a long, steadying breath. He lurched to his feet, and trudged after his brother.

* * *

Corilai tossed and turned fitfully. In her dreams, the fire consumed everything it touched, jumping with malicious intent from person to person, slowly devouring her family and friends. She screamed for it to stop, but to no avail. Her screaming grew louder, and her parents woke in the next room, rushing to throw open her bedroom door.

They stood in fear as she threw herself about on the bed. The slim crescent moon hung in the sky, visible through the window behind her. Its light cast an eerie glow to the room, but it was not the thing that made the site so terrifying for her parents.

As she rolled and twitched on the bed, a black shadow writhed all around her body. It licked at the bed linen, like flames on a log, and it grew stronger. The black flames lept upwards, dimming the weak moon light as though a storm had obscured it. The moon's meagre glow seemed to be sucked into that sinister black flame, making it appear all the more terrible.

"It's the demon flame," the girl's mother screamed.

Corilai began to scream louder, and the linen began to smoulder, smoke quickly filling the small room. Her father ran to the kitchen, where he found a large cooking pot. He filled it from the tap, grateful they had been able to afford a large tank, mounted high on the outside of the house. Cursing as gravity fed the water too slowly, his anxious mind filled with dread. He waited until the pot almost overflowed before he turned off the tap and ran, sloshing the liquid as he rushed back to the girl's room. He threw the water over her face, waking her and dousing some of the demon flames in the process.

Corilai spluttered, catching her breath for a moment. Then she felt the heat as the linen around her burned. She screamed even louder, and scrambled out of the bed. She turned to face it, backing away in fear.

"How?" She stammered. "How's the flame here? How did it escape the dream?"

She began to cry, turning to her mother for support, but her mother shook her head and backed into the hallway, muttering.

"Stay back, demon child. Please, give me back my daughter!"

Corilai shook her head in confusion, reaching a hand towards her mother.

"But I am your daughter! Please, mother, I don't understand. What is all this?"

She moved towards her mother, but just then her father entered the room, shoving Corilai aside as he rushed to the bed, tossing another pot of water on the flames which still danced there, consuming the linen with gluttonous fervour. Corilai's mother took that opportunity to run from the house, screaming as she entered the street, shouting for the town to awake, and defend against the demon child, who had brought the flames of evil into their midst.

Soon, men began to arrive, carrying pots and buckets, to help douse the flames. Corilai was too stunned to help. She stood near the door and watched as they worked, but the flames were stubborn. By the time they had extinguished the fire, the bed was gone, the wooden floor badly burnt, and a gaping hole into the night replaced the wall, and the window. Her father turned to face her, hatred in his eyes.

"You, demon spawn, what have you done to our home? What did you do to our daughter? So kind and carefree, you turned her into this! How? What did you tempt her with? Speak, you filthy devil's whore!"

"But... but Father, please," she said. "Please, Father, I'm scared. Why are you talking that way?"

"Run, demon child," he said. "Look at the destruction you have wrought. Do you think your mother and I built this home simply for you to wreck it? I don't know who you are, and why you've possessed our only child, but now, just get out, or else we'll rip your flesh from your bones!"

The other men cheered, and lurched towards her, the anger and hatred in their eyes more terrifying than any black flames. Corilai held her hands before her face in a defensive reflex, and black flames erupted in a vicious burst, stunning the men long enough for her to escape the room.

Hoping the men were not hurt, Corilai bolted into the street to find the townspeople crowding around the house. Another burst erupted from her panicked mind, echoing in the air around her, and the people scattered, a screaming, confused mob.

Picking a direction at random, she ran, tears streaming from her eyes. Her miraculously unharmed night dress flapped about her legs, slowing her down as she heard the angry men slam the house door open and rush into the night, intent on their prey.

Corilai gathered up her nightdress to free her legs, and ran like she had never run before. In her fear, she left a wake of black charred bushes and trees as the demon flame took on its own life, driven by her emotions and the raw energy she could never contain.

Eventually, as her energy was drained, the flames flickered and died. In a moment of clarity, Corilai realised the townsmen were likely to follow the trail of destruction, to hunt her down and then who knew what horrors they would inflict. She altered her direction, and ran into the trees, deeper into the forest.

Corilai had no idea where she was running to, nor what she would do when she got there. But in all her fifteen years, she had never thought she would have the need of shelter in a situation like this.

After what seemed an eternity, she found her way to the top of a rocky cliff. The ocean stretched out before her, the dim rays of a beautiful sunrise just peering over the horizon.

Slumping onto the rocky ground, Corilai sobbed, allowing her emotion to win out, and screamed till she was hoarse, her wracking sobs echoing out across the still seas as she drained her eyes of tears.

*　　　*　　　*

The hearty breakfast was vanishing from the table as Treghan watched. He was not permitted to join them as they gorged on bacon, eggs, and fried tomatoes. The stale bread had been toasted, and thick butter melted into the bread like a soothing rain into soil.

"Please, can I eat now?" He asked, his pleading tone drawing an angry glare from his brother.

"No!" his father snapped. "You worthless boy, your twin is the one who earned this food for us, you earn us nothing. All you do is stuff your face for free, like a leach. We have a meeting to prepare for, and good fortune to celebrate, and it's all thanks to your twin brother. When you deserve better, you'll get it. But today, for you, if you're so damned hungry from doing nothing, there's a piece of stale bread left. Don't think I'll let you toast it, or take any more of our butter though! Take the bread, and get out of my sight!"

"Yes, sir," Treghan murmured as he took the bread and left the room, continuing under his breath. "I bet they won't take him anyway."

"What was that, boy?" his father yelled. "Your brother worked hard for this opportunity. He worked hard to help all the people of this village, keeping foxes and wolves at bay, and that has earned us this visit from the academy scout. He will get in and the academy will pay us handsomely in compensation for the loss of a good worker. And your brother will continue to send us money from the wages the academy pay, long into the future, so he deserves your respect! Give it to him, or else."

Treghan stopped, and returned to the room. He stood there, his filthy rags making for a pathetic sight. He stared at the floor as he spoke, hoping it would hide his expression of hatred.

"I am sorry, dear brother, for my impertinence. You are great, far greater than I, and you deserve this success. I wish you the best, and hope for your future to be bright, bringing good times to our loving parents."

"That's better, lad. Now get out of here. We can't have the academy scout thinking you reflect the talent in this family."

"Yes, Sir," Treghan replied, and left.

Dejected, Treghan sat on a miserable straw mattress in the room he shared with Fletcher. He shivered under his moth eaten and filthy blanket, staring the whole time across the room at the luxurious silken bedclothes gifted to his brother. He stewed with envy as he nibbled on the tasteless, dry bread. He stayed there for hours, sulking as he heard his brother and his parents talking, laughing, and enjoying themselves while they waited for the man from the academy.

After what seemed an eternity, he heard a pounding on the front door.

* * *

Symin approached the door with a confused thought. He had been told there was a powerful flame wielder here, but he sensed no such power now.

Surely this was a joke? The villagers were in awe of the lad, what was his name? Fletcher. But all Symin sensed here was a carnival level flame energy, nothing to warrant his presence. Oh well, best get it over with.

Stepping up, he knocked on the door.

"Answer the door, will you Son? I'll fetch the good fellow a drink," came a voice from inside.

"Yes, Papa," replied a boy.

Then the door was thrust open, and Symin looked at the lad, sandy, scruffy hair and fine clothes. Clearly the family were trying to impress him. Symin reached out with a tendril of yellow flame, so fine and controlled he was not sure the others could see it. He felt the boy's mind, and found the bright energy of a flame wielder. Not a strong one, but serviceable for the needs of the village.

"You must be Fletcher. I have heard talk of you from the villagers, it has reached us at the academy, and I am here to assess your skill. Please do not be afraid, I will not harm you."

Symin reached out a hand, and rested it on Fletcher's head.

"I may as well go through the motions," he thought.

He released the boy, and waved him inside, following.

"Now then, hold out your hand, and give me a flame."

The boy complied, and a tall red fire lept upwards to the ceiling. The boy panicked, then snuffed it out.

"You need better control," Symin clucked. "But your energy is reasonable. Please, sit at the table."

Fletcher did as he was told, and his parents beamed with pride as Symin ran through a series of mundane tasks, purporting to be an assessment of the lad, but Symin had already decided. This one was not for the academy. Not now. Perhaps if he matured a little, but he would be dangerous, if given greater power than his mind and his emotions were ready for.

This child was the spoiled one, Symin thought to himself. He looked around the room, sparsely furnished, clearly not a wealthy household, yet they had the boy dressed in finery befitting a merchant's son.

Symin looked to the door, where a rack held shoes of four people. Two obviously the parents, serviceable, honest farm ware, but in good condition. A third must have been this boy's. Also in good condition, though not suited for field work. And the fourth, ratty, bedraggled shoes of a child left with less than their sibling.

Symin fumed silently. He had seen this before. Greedy peasants who no longer wanted to work the farms, exploiting a child with talent, and neglecting the others who could not make them wealthy. Deplorable behaviour. These animals would never see his support.

But, where one talent exists, invariably another sleeps in the wings. Symin closed his eyes and reached out his tendril of seeking yellow flame. There was the red energy of the boy at the table. But what else?

"Ah!" Symin said, in a surprised tone.

He felt it, something bright, but weak, weak from hunger and suppressed by fear. And white! Symin jumped from the chair, and spun on his feet, seeking. A white! The rarest of talents. Often seen as weak. This one was weak, but through no fault of its own.

Weak, but with the greatest potential, a white flame child was a treasure nobody outside the academy understood. This one was close. Ignoring the protestations of the parents, Symin charged through a doorway, intent on his prize.

He turned at the end of a hallway, and burst into a bedroom, luxurious on one side, but barren on the other. On a ratty bundle of straw in the bare half of the room, the white child cowered under a threadbare blanket.

"There you are," Symin whispered. "There is something great in you, boy. Find me, when you escape this family. You are not ready yet, but one day, you will be."

With that, Symin slipped a small printed card into the trembling boy's hands, and backed out of the room, bumping into the father as he did so.

"Sorry you had to meet that worthless child," the father simpered. "Good sir. He has no talent of any use, It's Fletcher you need to see."

"Of course," Symin said. "My apologies, let us return to the table. I thought I had sensed something, but I must have been mistaken."

Symin returned to Fletcher, who had not moved from the table. He made a show of performing a final examination, then stood. He faced the father and bowed slightly.

"Thank you for your patience with me, Sir. But I must regretfully decline your son's application to the academy at this time. Perhaps when he matures somewhat, we can return and reconsider. Good day."

"But why? What's wrong? How is the boy lacking? You've seen his power!"

"Good day, Sir," Symin replied, and left in a rush.

Fletcher looked at his father, sorrow and fear in his eyes.

"Fletcher my boy," his father said. "Don't worry. We know your power, and you work hard for us."

"Thank you father, but I don't understand. How can I have failed?"

"You didn't fail, son. It was that other worthless boy's fault. Why did the academy man have to go and see him like that? He must have done something. Worked some feeble spell to catch the man's attention, and that's why the man discounted your skill. He thought to himself 'if this boy is so weak, then Fletcher is probably at his strongest now, so why bother training him?' Blame Treghan."

"You're right, Father! That little turd ruined everything!"

They rushed down the corridor and dragged Treghan from his room. Their father threw him across the table and removed a strap from the wall. There, on the table, flogged and beaten within an inch of his life, Treghan found his resolve.

Curled in the foetal position, Treghan endured as the beating continued for a long time, until they finally relented.

"Get back into that room," his father screeched. "And don't even think of showing your face for the next few days, worthless brat. You've cost this family far too much to be forgiven lightly this time."

Treghan scurried as fast as his battered body would allow, and wept in his pain as he fought for sleep on his straw bed. Pulling out the card the academy man had left him, he struggled through swollen eyes to read what it said.

"That's it," Treghan mumbled. "I know what I have to do."

His mind set, Treghan waited as his family caroused and swore and argued through the day, only breaking from their noise to eat, which they did a lot. His stomach grumbled, and he endured. Finally, late into the evening, his bones aching and his bruises sore, Treghan crept out of the room as quietly as he could. He watched his brother as he closed the door, snoring peacefully on the soft silk sheets, kept warm by luxurious blankets, and stifled his anger.

He heard his father snoring as he passed his room. His mother's presence was not evident, which was strange, but he thought nothing of it. He was intent on escape, and couldn't care less what was happening in the rest of the family.

As he entered the front room, Treghan saw copious left overs from a lavish meal on the table. In a final act of rebellion, he fetched a potato sack from the kitchen area, and scooped as much of the food as he could carry into it. Bones from a roast leg of lamb, still with enough meat for a few snacks, roast potatoes, and vegetables, foods he had always seen but never enjoyed.

Then he saw a gravy pot, still half full. Picking it up, he drank from the pot. The warm liquid filled him with renewed energy and hope as it oozed down his throat. Putting the pot down, Treghan picked up a half loaf of bread, tore off a chunk and dunked it in the gravy.

Throwing the rest of the loaf into his sack, Treghan ate the chunk as he pulled on his ratty old shoes, and then slipped quietly into the night.

Freedom, at last.

Chapter 2 – Running

Corilai awoke on the cliff top in mid afternoon, still feeling tired and sore. She sat up, and felt the warmth of the daylight baking her. She was pink from the burning sun, and a little tender.

Standing, she looked down at the ground, singed from the flames while she slept. The sight of the scorched ground brought the memory of what had happened, and she cried.

Turning, she looked along the coast, and noticed that there was a narrow animal trail along the rocks, leading down to a beach. Hitching up her night dress, Corilai began the long walk down from the cliff.

It was hard going, and twice she nearly fell. But Corilai was determined, and persevered until finally she felt the soft, warm sand of the beach beneath her feet. With a sigh, she sat and inspected her blisters and cuts, her bare feet torn up by the rocks.

"Salt water. I should wash my feet in it, to help them heal," she mumbled to herself as she stood and hobbled down to the water's edge.

Along the beach a way, a group of men left the tree line, dragging a small fishing boat down the sand. Children followed behind, laughing and giggling. Corilai watched them with suspicion.

"I'm still too close to the village," Corilai mumbled. "They've likely been told by now about the demon child in the woods. But I do need to find shoes and clothes."

The cool ocean offered no reply, but the gentle waves lapped against her legs in a comforting motion. On impulse, Corilai threw herself into the water, and lay there, afloat on the rippling sea, momentarily without worry. That feeling was short lived, as two pairs of footsteps ran towards her.

"Who are you, lady?" said a high pitched voice.

Corilai sat up in the water, and looked at them. Two children, a boy and a girl, probably about eight or nine years old.

"I'm nobody important," Corilai said.

"I bet you are!" the boy said. "Some poor princess, chased from the castle by an evil sister, and now stuck on the run with no clothes or shoes or anything!"

The girl gave him a stern look, slapping him on the shoulder.

"Don't be stupid, Allen!" the girl said. "I bet she's that demon child the other village chased off."

Corilai gasped, and jumped up in a panic, ready to run. As she strode from the water, the boy grabbed at her night dress, stopping her.

"Don't worry, lady. We won't tell, but you need some clothes, and some shoes. We can help you with that."

"Really?" Corilai said, not willing to believe it.

"Of course, but don't let the grown ups catch you," the girl replied. "Our mother's big sister was chased off for having the black flames. It was so unfair. She tells us the story sometimes. It was a long time ago, and she hates that it happened. She can give us a pair of shoes and some clothes, they'll be big, but it's better than that night dress."

"Oh, that would be wonderful," Corilai said, daring to hope this could work out.

"Just go back into the trees, near the rocks and wait for us there," Allen said, before he turned and ran across the sand, towards the place they had come from.

Following the boy's directions, Corilai went into the trees, found a small clearing, and waited.

* * *

Walking with a long stride, Treghan made his way through the quiet forest beside the road, each step taking him further away from his old life. He was avoiding being seen on the road, at least while he decided what he was going to do.

Reaching the crest of a hill, he heard the rapid pounding of hooves, getting louder. Treghan ducked low and hid, waiting as the hoof beats came closer. He watched through the foliage as six riders rushed by, cloaks billowing out behind them baring the Ranger Academy emblem.

The riders had their hoods drawn, but even so, Treghan felt certain one of them was likely the scout who had come to the house that morning. He wondered about that man, and what he had said. Pulling out the man's card, Treghan read it again, shook his head, then put it away in a secure pocket.

Treghan listened as the riders moved further away, their hoof beats disappearing into the east, following the narrow road probably as far as the sea. Once there, Treghan thought, they would turn north and head towards the academy in the port city of Emberdale.

"Well then, I know he said one day, and I wasn't ready yet, but that's where I'll go!" Treghan declared, striding out onto the road and following the direction of the horses. "When I get there, I'll convince them to let me stay. I don't know how, but I'll think of something. Won't that annoy my idiot brother and my father? After Fletcher was rejected out of hand, I'll be the one to become a ranger!"

* * *

"Oh you poor thing," Said a soft, feminine voice.

Corilai jumped at the sound, and looked up at the woman as blind panic swept over her. She climbed to her feet, thinking she could run back up the rocks into the trees above the cliffs, but the woman held her hands up in a gesture of good will.

"Please, do not be frightened, child. My little ones told me where to find you. Here, I brought you some things."

The woman held out a basket, placing it on the ground. Corilai could see a pair of nice, but worn, hiking boots in the top. She began to cry as she smiled her gratitude.

"Thank you so much! I really didn't dare hope..."

"Hush, child," the woman said. "My name is Uma, and I have the flame talent as well, though I hide it. Mine is orange, and easy to control. I never tried to do anything with it though. Not after my sister was run out of the village when I was a child. She had the black flame, like you."

"Did you never see her again?"

"No, though she did get word to me a few years ago. She has been living in Ranger Academy all these years. Had you thought about where you would go?"

"No..." Corilai admitted, reaching into the basket to pull out a brown tunic and slip it over her head.

"Well, perhaps you should think about the academy. They can teach you to control the flames, and who knows, maybe one day you could go home again?"

"I..." Corilai mumbled. "Don't ever want to go back there. Those people, I don't care if I never see them again."

"Oh, come now," Uma said. "I know it hurts, but please remember. Time heals. If you ever do make it to the academy, please tell my sister Loka I send my love. But for now, let's get you ready. Then we can sit and eat. I brought fresh bread, some roast meat, and a jug of fresh tea."

Corilai nodded, unable to speak through her emotions as she gratefully accepted the woman's help getting into a pair of sturdy riding slacks and an overcoat. Finally, she pulled on a warm pair of woollen socks and the boots, a little too big but good enough.

"You know," Uma said. "If you want to sneak past the men of the village, you really must be more careful. I could hear you from a short distance away when I found you."

"What do you mean?"

"I mean, you talk aloud, when you're alone. You talk to yourself."

"I do what?" Corilai exclaimed, "I don't do that! Do I?"

"Of course you do," Uma replied, like it was nothing. "And if you don't stop yourself, you'll be caught quickly."

"But I never, I mean, I didn't realise..."

"Don't worry, dear," Uma said, with a chuckle. "It's not your fault. All flame wielders talk to themselves. I don't know why. Some people say it's because the flames are like a spirit, which is always with you. So you're never really alone, and on some level, you realise this and talk to your flames."

"Talk to your flames?"

Uma laughed, then tousled Corilai's hair.

"Not that I really believe that, but it is true none the less, all flame wielders talk to themselves."

Uma took the jug, and sipped from it, before passing it back to Corilai. The girl accepted the jug, and sipped as well.

"How can I ever repay you?" Corilai said.

"Just greet my sister for me, if you ever cross paths with her. That is the greatest thanks you could ever bestow."

They ate together, until after a while Uma stood, collecting the now empty basket and jug.

"I'm sorry, I have to go now, before my husband gets suspicious. I wish there was more I could do, but I would advise you stay away from our village, the men are eager for a hunt. Stick to the shore line for a few more bays, and you will see the road where it skirts close to the coast. Get on the road there, and it will lead you all the way to Emberdale. Good luck, Corilai."

"Thank you, Uma," Corilai replied in a cheerful tone. "I will never forget you, or your kindness. I promise, I will find your sister, and I'll speak to her about you."

With a smile, Uma bowed slightly, and ran off into the trees. The men had long since returned with the catch and dragged their boat back up the sand. Corilai walked out to the beach and began making her way along it, sticking to the shadows of the trees, which stretched long and dark, like fingers reaching for the sea.

* * *

Treghan trudged up hill after hill, and down the other sides, in a pattern that seemed never ending. He rested the first evening in the shelter of an upturned oak, off the side of the road, and walked again at first light, determined to put as much distance between himself and his old life as he could.

At noon on that second day, he finally caught a glimpse of the gleaming ocean, far in the distance, as he crested a particularly tall rise. He smiled, this was good news. The time was passing quickly, but so were the miles beneath his feet.

"If only I had a horse," Treghan moaned, but he was enjoying the walk just the same. "This is the longest I've gone without a beating in years,"

Treghan marvelled at the thought, and relished the peace and quiet of his new life on the road. Even when it was in sight, the ocean was still a long way, and by the time night fell on that second day, it was still far in the distance.

The exuberance of earlier was gone, and with the darkness, the rain clouds came in from the sea, drenching the forest in a dismal, damp misery.

Treghan shivered through the night against the trunk of a sturdy old tree, his clothing quickly soaked, and no better shelter in evidence. It was a wet and miserable Treghan who greeted the sunrise and began to walk again, his step slow and his guise bedraggled.

"Perhaps running away wasn't so smart after all," he muttered.

Treghan rummaged in his sack, which was almost empty now, the bulk of the food having been eaten the day before, while his spirits were high. He found the last corner of the loaf of bread, stale and dry now, and nibbled on it in grim determination as he trudged through the early morning fog, which rested in the valleys like a blanket of damp.

With each rise, the sun was warmer than the last, and finally on the fourth such peak, he paused, finding a warm rock to the side of the road, and lay on it, letting the soaking rays of the sun warm his bones and dry his sodden clothes.

Treghan was dozing there, and failed to hear the approach of a horse until it was too late.

"You there!" bellowed the rider.

Treghan sleepily sat up and looked at the approaching man, dressed as a town guard from Oaklands, a two day ride to the west. Three others approached in the distance, clearly outpaced by their comrade.

"How can I help you, sergeant?" Treghan asked, observing the insignia on the man's shoulder.

"Son, I seek a troop of riders, who left our town some three days hence. They wore the garb of the Ranger Academy, but were impostors, and fleeced a good many citizens of their money in exchange for promises of preferential treatment for their youngsters in applying for admission."

"I saw them, yesterday morning, they passed me heading east along this road. I thought them headed for Emberdale, via the sea. There was one visited my home, but he was alone."

"One actual scout was in the area. He alerted us to the criminals when he told us he was travelling alone. Were you on foot lad?" he asked, as his companions finally arrived.

"Yes, sir. I have walked the daylight hours. I am heading for the academy myself."

"Oh, so you are another hopeful youngster are you? Well, I hope you were not victim to the bandits and their schemes."

"No sir, I have not encountered them myself, aside from watching them pass. They were riding a strong pace, like they were pursued."

"They are," The sergeant said. "By me. Good luck, son."

With that, the town guards rode away at a fast pace, scattering stones as they left. Treghan took the hint from the gods, and began walking east, wanting a horse more than ever after he quickly lost sight of the guards.

*　　　*　　　*

Even big as they were, Corilai adored the boots. They made the rocky hills between bays easier than she could have hoped earlier that day, and now she had a clear goal in mind. Ranger Academy was not something she had even dreamed she would go to, but now, life had changed.

In darkness, she climbed the second hill, and found a secluded overhang away from the trail. Once there, she lay down and was asleep in moments; a deep, peaceful sleep like she had not had in many months.

She was exhausted, and did not even have the energy to dream. There were no dark flames haunting Corilai that night, and when the morning sun splashed across her face, she awoke refreshed and cheerful, ready to continue her journey.

Chapter 3 - Encounters

Corilai reached the top of a headland, looking out over a long sweeping bay of glistening white sand. It was already mid afternoon, and she was feeling hot and tired. She sat on a rock and surveyed the area.

Out to sea, a small ship was at anchor. She searched its masts, but could see no flag to indicate who it might be. On the sand about half way along the beach was a long boat, which she assumed was from the ship.

She could see the road, sweeping down to the low plain which met the bay. There, it turned and followed the bay north.

"Emberdale is along that road," she said. "I should keep going, but it will take the rest of the day to reach the road, and I don't really want to risk being seen by the people from that boat, at least until I know who they are."

She rested there, on the rock, and soaked up the warm sun for some time. Eventually a chilly breeze blew in from the sea, so she stood and began walking again. She made sure to stay within the tree line, so as to reduce the risk of discovery as she cautiously worked her way down to the bay.

After what seemed an eternity, Corilai finally reached the sand. She pushed through long grasses and scrub until she was properly within the forest that lined the southern end of the bay. As she turned to head towards the road, strange sounds came echoing across the bay.

Clanging noises. Steel on steel. The cries of men. Corilai stopped, realising what it was she was hearing. Up ahead, there was some kind of battle raging.

The bay was likely not a safe place to be. At least one side of what ever battle was going on must come from that boat. Corilai began making her way further inland, regretful that she could not head directly north. She would aim for the road later, after the combatants had moved on.

*   *   *

Treghan climbed the final rise before the long, slow descent to the ocean. Stretched out before him was a low plain, and the road cut a brown line almost to the shore, before taking a sweeping bend and heading north.

At that bend, Treghan could see something. He stared for a long time, at the tiny figures rushing about in the distance, until finally it dawned on him that he was watching a battle.

"It must be those guards and the bandits they were chasing," he said. "I really don't want to get caught up in that mess."

Walking to the edge of the road, Treghan found a tree, and climbed it. Sitting on the first sturdy cross branch, he watched the distant fight. It wasn't long before the last surviving guardsman fled, mounting his horse and rushing as fast as it would carry him, back towards Treghan's perch.

Three of the bandits chased the lone man, and before long had run him down, a few hundred strides down the slope from Treghan. Far enough that he was not seen, but close enough that the sounds of the encounter drifted to his ears, including the sickening grunt of the attacker as the man was run through, and his strangled scream as he died.

Treghan sat in his tree and shuddered as the bandits began towards him. He could hear their conversation on the breeze.

"How far shall we go?" one of them said.

"Just about to that first rise. I doubt there'd be any others, but we gotta be sure."

That was all Treghan needed to hear. He climbed down from his tree as quickly as he could, crossed the road, and ran into the trees. He had to get as far away from that place as he could, before the bandits could find him, and do the same to him as they had done to that poor guard.

At first, the land sloped downwards, but after some time Treghan found himself winding his way up hill again. He turned and began walking towards the sea. He figured the bandits were not looking for him and by now would have returned to their comrades.

Unexpectedly, he found some citrus growing wild, small and firm, but nearly ripe. When he tore one open, it sprayed him with tangy juice. Taking his time to choose the best and most ripe of the fruit, he gathered a good supply from the tree and stowed them in his sack. Eating one as he walked, Treghan continued on his way.

Carefree and no longer paying such close attention to his surroundings, Treghan was shocked when, as the sunset cast long shadows ahead of him, he stumbled into a clearing with a small camp fire burning in the centre.

He stopped, looking around for the person responsible, but there was nobody there. Sitting just beyond the edge of the clearing, he waited. Surely whoever lit this fire would not be far away. If it wasn't a bandit, they might share the clearing for the night.

It was not long before somebody came. A figure entered the clearing from the opposite side, deposited a pile of sticks away from the fire, and set a handful of root vegetables on the coals. Then they stood, and for the first time, Treghan got a clear view of the person whose camp site he was about to invade.

It was a girl, about his own age, pretty but approachable. Her friendly face lifted his mood, and he stood. Holding his hands out and open, to show he was no threat, Treghan walked into the clearing.

* * *

Fletcher followed his father from the house, a small pack in hand.

"What's going on, Father?" he asked, for the third time.

"We're saving your mother, son. That's all you need to know."

"What are you talking about?"

"Just shut up, stop asking questions, and do as you're told. Then everything will be fine. They won't hurt her if we follow their instructions."

"Who's they?" Fletcher persisted.

"The same bastards your mother's been doing a lot of her needlework for recently. They took a liking to her, I guess. They're holding her hostage, and I want her back. Now, shut up boy!"

Shortly, they entered the village tavern, and Fletcher's father led him to a table in the corner, where a group of suspicious looking men waited.

"I brought the boy," Fletcher heard his father announce.

"This the one?" one of the men said. "Oh yeah, I remember seeing him in the fields, chasing foxes."

Fletcher stood at the end of the table, unsure what to do, as his father slumped into a chair.

"So, we had an agreement..." Fletcher's father said.

"Indeed we did. Don't worry, we will reward you handsomely for the boy's service," the man replied. "Boy, I'm Harv, but you'll call me boss. The boys and I are part of a, er, specialist organisation, and we have need of your skills."

"But my wife?" Fletcher's father said. "You said I could have her back if I brought you the boy."

"Your wife?" Harv said with a sneer. "Oh, of course, but you need to listen better, old fool. I said if you wanted to see her alive, you had best bring me the boy. Earl!"

The one named Earl went through a door to the back room of the tavern, and led Fletcher's mother out to the table. Her hands were bound, and her mouth gagged. Harv waved his hand, and Earl led her away again, back through the door. She screamed through the gag, but to no avail.

"I never said anything about returning her to you. You've had your payment, now get out of here. Your wife stays, as our insurance. Just in case the boy decides to misbehave."

Fletcher's father jumped to his feet, and made to lunge across the table at Harv.

"Why you, you dirty scoundrel! I'll kill you for this!"

He never got the chance to make good on his threat. Before his fist could reach the villainous Harv, another man's ham sized fist ploughed into Fletcher's father's face, sending him sprawling to the floor. Harv, Earl, and the third man set upon him, kicking and beating him until he was a bloodied mess. They tossed him, unconscious, into the street. Harv returned to face Fletcher.

"Do the wrong thing, and that'll be you next time. Betray us, and it'll be your precious mother. Am I clear?"

"Ye... Ye... Yes sir," Fletcher stammered.

*   *   *

"Who are you?" Corilai demanded.

"I'm just a runaway. Like you if I had to guess," Treghan said, emboldened by her sweet voice. "I wasn't good enough, or useful enough, for my parents, so they made it too hard to put up with living there. So I ran. My name's Treghan. You?"

"Something like that. I'm Corilai."

"Really? That all? OK, keep your secrets. Here," he said as he passed the sack to her. "I found fruit, got to taste better than those roots you gathered."

"But the roots will fill your belly and give you energy for tomorrow," she said. "How about we share both?"

"Deal," he said with a grin. "How did you get the fire lit?"

"I met a nice lady, who gave me these clothes. I found a flint in the pocket, so I used it."

"I wish I'd met a nice lady," Treghan moaned. "My shoes have had it. The blisters are starting to hurt bad."

"I had no shoes, until I met that lady, she gave me these. They're the wrong size, but hiking in them is heaven, after going bare foot for days. At least you have shoes, even if they are old and worn. I only had my nightdress when they chased me out of the village."

"You were run off? Why would anybody do that?"

"Well, there was a fire..."

Treghan jumped to his knees, lunging towards her in his excitement. She shied away.

"You're a flame wielder, aren't you?" he demanded.

She looked at her feet, and did not reply for some time. Treghan watched her, intrigued.

"Yes, I guess I am," she said finally. "But I can't control it. I never even knew I had the talent until recently, but I have no control. I dream flames, and then they're real. Torched my bedroom like that, and they said I was a demon child, with the demon flame, and ran me out of the village for it. I've been on the run ever since."

"Wow, the demon flame?" Treghan said. "I've heard they call the black flame that. It's supposed to be real powerful."

"Well, I'm sure it would be if I could just control it. That's why I decided, I'm going to the Ranger Academy in Emberdale."

"Really?" Treghan said. "That's awesome! I'm headed there as well. We should travel together! For safety, you know?"

"Oh yeah," she replied. "For safety."

She looked at her feet again, kicking at the ground, shuffling a small pile of dirt towards the fire. After a while, she looked at him again. She got the impression he had not taken his eyes off her the entire time.

"So, were you a demon flame wielder as well?"

"Well, not exactly," Treghan said. "My twin brother, he's really good at it. He has red flame, and he controls it pretty well. He was making money for my family by chasing foxes off the farms and stuff. But I'm a white, and really weak. I can barely make a spark. So my family branded me useless, and hated me as a free loader. I got beaten all the time, and never got enough food."

"That's terrible," she said.

"Well, I didn't bring any money in, and I wasn't strong enough for manual labour, so I was pretty useless. But I still think I can make something of myself, and of my flames, if I get to the academy."

"Why the academy?" Corilai asked. "If you can barely spark, won't they just turn you away?"

"I don't think so. Look," he said, remembering the card and passing it to her. “There was this man, you see, from the academy, he came to assess my brother. He rejected my brother, but he gave me that card, and he said something like, there's a great thing in you, come to the academy and find me when you're ready, so that's what I'm doing.”

“So you can flame now?” she asked, eyes wide as she passed the card back.

“Well, no...”

“So you're not ready are you?”

“But I will be, by the time I get there! I swear it!”

“Well,” Corilai said, giggling. “At least you're determined, that's something.”

“You bet I am!” he said with conviction. “I'll be the best damn white flame there is, then I can go back and rub it in those bastard's faces! My brother will be all look at me, I got flame, and I'll fry him! Ha! Just wait!”

Treghan beamed a wide grin at Corilai, laughing. She couldn't help but join in, and they both laughed for some time, until suddenly, she yawned.

“I'm getting tired. We should get some sleep, but promise you'll stay on that side of the fire OK?”

“Sure, I'll stay over here. What do you think I am? A pervert?”

“Perhaps, something like that. You and your wicked white sparks, you might do anything!”

“Shut up, demon girl,” He replied, and laughed.

She laughed with him again, then lay on the ground.

“Good night, Treghan,” she said.

“Good night, Corilai.”

* * *

Treghan woke with a start, Corilai's scream echoing in the night air. The fire was out, and it took him a while to see anything in the darkness. She screamed again, but this time, there was another voice screaming with her. A man. Treghan jumped to his feet and ran towards her.

“The damn bitch burnt me!” a man shouted.

Treghan heard a sickening sound, like meat being struck with a hammer, followed by the thud of something hitting the ground.

“She won't be doing that again,” the man said.

“Corilai!” Treghan shouted, stumbling in the dark, trying to find her.

The darkness suddenly intensified, as a sack was thrust over his head. Treghan struggled, and flailed his arms, trying to hit whoever had done it, but to no avail. As he twirled in the darkness, something heavy struck his jaw, and he fell to the ground.

'Right lads,” a gruff voice said. “Load these two on the cart, and get them back to the boat. Have the cap'n prepare the steel room for them. Can't have 'em sinkin' us on the way 'ome.”

Treghan felt himself being picked up, and struggled. A second blow to the jaw left him unconscious.

Chapter 4 – Bandits

Fletcher walked behind the boss, his hands and feet shackled to stop him from running. They were halfway to the next village before the boss stopped and left the road. They crossed a bare field, until they reached a low wooden fence.

On the other side of the fence, wheat grew in abundance, almost ready for harvest. It was a fine crop, probably one of the best yields in the area. The farmer must have been pleased. The boss looked at Fletcher for a moment, then released his hands from the shackles.

"Burn it," Harv said.

"But..." Fletcher said, hesitating.

Burning this field would hurt the entire village. Harv did not care about that at all.

"Do it. This farmer refuses to pay for protection, and he informed the Oaklands guards about our group's fake scouts. The real scout then told the guards in the town he was alone, and that caused us a lot of trouble."

Harv plucked a sprig of wheat from the edge of the field and chewed it thoughtfully before continuing.

"The bastard has to learn. We own this region. If he doesn't like it, he can leave. Or die. Otherwise, he has to cooperate with us."

Fletcher still hesitated. Harv smacked him across the top of the head, hard enough that his ears rang and the world danced.

"Do it, and hurry up about it. Or your mother gets it. One word from me, and she'll be screaming for weeks. You understand, boy?"

"Yes, Sir," Fletcher replied, raising his hands.

Closing his eyes, Fletcher calmed himself, then focused his energy. This was a large area. He wasn't used to such tasks. He felt the red flame begin, and poured more energy into it. The flames responded swiftly, and a large plume shot out from his hands, brushing across the top of the crop.

Lowering his arms, Fletcher aimed the fire at the stems of the wheat, igniting it quickly. Turning, he played the flame across the field, and soon a roaring fire had began to consume the crop nearest him.

"Perfect," Harv said. "I would've liked to see it all go up at once, but this will do nicely. That fire will spread quickly. Come, we have to go."

Harv turned and strode back towards the road. Still watching over his shoulder as the fire spread, Fletcher followed him without speaking. Soon, they reached the road and began walking back towards the village, and the tavern which Harv used as his base.

"You've done well today, boy. Keep it up, and soon you might be ready for your real job."

"My real job?"

"Of course. You didn't think we just wanted you for odd jobs did you?" Harv said.

"Well, I didn't know what I was here for, really..."

Harv laughed, the sound like a barking dog to Fletcher's ears, harsh and intimidating. The boss stopped, and tousled Fletcher's hair in a rough version of the usually affectionate act.

"Lad, we're gathering all the flame wielders we can find, and it ain't for burning fields I can tell you that. Get yourself a bit stronger and we'll be sending you away. I got bosses of my own, down south, and they'll be needing your services before long."

"You have bosses? I had no idea..."

"Best keep it that way, boy. The less you ask, the happier I'll be. Just do as you're told and we won't have a problem, got it?"

"Yes, Sir."

* * *

Treghan groaned as he came to. Sitting up, he felt hard steel beneath him. He looked around, but it was dark. A little light sneaked through the gaps around the door, and even that was dim to start with. He sat there, groaning as he reached a hand up to touch his head. It felt tender there, and sticky.

"Probably dried blood," he said.

"Treghan?" came a soft voice. "Are you there? I was so scared, I thought you might be dead. They must have hit you so hard. I saw your face when they opened the door to toss some bread in earlier, you were covered in blood."

"I still am," he replied. "Corilai, don't worry about me, I'm used to beatings. But how about you? Are you hurt?"

"No, not really. My head hurts like hell, but it's not bleeding, not like you."

"Good," he said, standing on wobbly legs.

He began walking towards the door, but then something strange happened. The floor moved! With his legs unsteady to begin with, the strange motion threw Treghan to the floor, and he slid until he hit the door, where he sat, propping himself against it.

"Damn it!" he exclaimed. "Where are we anyway?"

"Don't you know?" she said. "We're on a boat. I thought you might have seen it off the bay, given where we met."

"No, I hadn't seen it. I came from inland, remember?"

"Of course. Well, the ship was off the shore, and a long boat was on the sand, near where the road meets the sea."

"Must have been the bandits, then."

"The bandits?" she asked.

"Yeah, they were pretending to be academy scouts, trying to con people with promises of getting their kids into the academy as flame wielders."

"Why would they do that?" she asked.

"I don't know, but I saw a guardsman, he told me they had been doing that. It was them who were fighting."

"Of course," Corilai said. "And the bandits were the ones from the boat, so I guess we know who both sides of the battle were. I wonder who won?"

"The bandits. They killed all the guards. I saw them chase down the last one. The guards were hopelessly outnumbered. They should never have gone after them without getting help first."

"That's horrible. These men are real bastards," she said.

"Yeah, they really are," Treghan said, gingerly touching the wound on his head, wincing as the pain shot through him. "Ouch!"

His eyes had finally adjusted to the gloom, and he could see her sitting close in front of him. He reached a hand out and touched her face. If she was surprised by his boldness, she didn't show it. Carefully, he felt around her jaw, then her temples.

"No blood," he said.

"I told you that."

"I know you did, but I wanted to be sure. I'm glad they didn't hurt you too bad, or I'd have to do something stupid to them."

"So chivalrous, when you're already a prisoner," she chided him. "What were you going to do? Flame them with your terrifying white sparks?"

She could barely hold her mirth as she teased him, but he was quick to see it, and decided to play her game.

"No, I was going to put feathers in your clothes and throw you at them. You'd get so mad, you'd lose control and black flame them all to death! Demon girl."

She laughed, and it made him feel better, so he laughed too. After a while, he sighed.

"So, we're on a boat, we could burn our way out, but can you control it enough that we don't have to drown?"

"I don't think so. I've only had the flames a little while remember?"

"And the black are the hardest to control, they say," he replied.

"Yeah," she said, nodding. "And besides, didn't you notice what this room is?"

"No," he replied.

"It's steel. The whole room. Floor, walls, ceiling, even the door. They're all steel, to stop us burning our way out. If we flame, we'll just cook ourselves, like an oven."

He looked at her for a moment, thinking. Then it dawned on him.

"But, that means..."

"That's right," she interrupted. "They built this boat with the express purpose of transporting kidnapped flame wielders."

"Why kidnapped?" he asked.

"If they came along willingly, would they need to be stuck in the bowels of the ship, in a steel cell? Like prisoners?"

"Fair point," he said. "Hey, did you say there was bread? I'm getting hungry."

"Yeah, there is. And I'm glad you're hungry, that's a good sign," she said as she passed him a hunk of the stale loaf.

"Were you really that worried?" he asked as he ate.

"Of course I was. Wouldn't you be? Who knows how long we'll be in here for? A dead body would really start to stink up the place!"

He looked at her, his chewing stopped, the bread hanging from his mouth. Finally, he swallowed, pulled the bread out, and laughed.

"You really are a demon girl, aren't you Corilai?"
"Maybe. You'll just have to wait to find out," she said.

* * *

Symin wandered about the scene of carnage, not sure what to make of it. His two colleagues stood over one of the bodies, a guardsman from a town further inland. There were hoof prints and footprints, and even cart tracks, winding all over the site, which obviously had occurred after the battle that left these bodies.

Symin walked up the hill, following a set of hoof prints in the dirt, until he found the third guard.

"I guess they got him as he fled," Symin said. "The guards are the lesser part of the problem though."

Turning he walked back down the hill, to where the rest of the bodies were. Two guards, and two others. On the outside, at first appearance, they looked like rangers from the academy, but to Symin's trained eye, the similarity ended fast.

They wore the cloak, with the emblem, probably stolen, but underneath they wore chain mail and swords. No ranger from the academy in Emberdale would wear such things. The chain mail ran the risk of getting too hot, if a ranger was careless with his flames, or was simply caught in the wrong place. Rangers wore leather beneath the cloaks.

The sword was another mistake. It was rare for a ranger to carry such weapons, and usually then it was a dagger, or a steel baton. A flame ranger's weapon was always fire. Given that, why would they weigh themselves down with steel? Their speed was an advantage most rangers would not willingly give up.

"There's something much bigger than this fight going on here," Symin said, as he rolled one of the bodies with his foot. "These bandits are pretending to be us, and it would be for a specific reason. One of the bandit groups has been expanding, growing, and they are up to something big. Something long term. We have to find out what it is. And who they are."

Looking around, Symin wondered what he had stumbled into. He could see no clear tracks of the bandits, in either direction along the road, beyond those who chased down the third guard. But there were tracks leading off the road in two directions. Some down to the beach, and some into the forest beside the road.

"Jera, Miro," Symin said. "Go down to the beach. The bandits headed that way, if I'm reading the tracks right, and probably came from there as well. We're probably looking for a naval force, in which case there is little more we can do here. I'm going to check the surrounding forest, I'll meet you both back here in an hour."

"Yes, Sir," the two rangers said, then mounted their horses and rode off the road, towards the beach.

Symin entered the forest, slowly following tracks of horses and a cart. After about twenty minutes, the cart tracks stopped short of a clearing, while the rest of the tracks entered it. In the clearing, there was a camp fire, burnt out, and a lot of scuff marks in the ground.

"Another struggle," Symin said. "Though this time, nobody was killed. They took these ones away."

He dismounted, and walked through the scene, imagining the movements shown by each foot print. Two larger marks in the dirt indicated bodies had landed there. They were short, probably younger people, possibly mid teens.

"Why did they abduct these two?" Symin pondered. "Perhaps they thought they witnessed the battle, but why would they care?"

He paused, giving a last look around the site, then mounted his horse.

"No, these two sites are related. They took these two hostage for a reason, and it's related to the rest of it. Why would they dress as rangers and abduct young people?"

As he left the clearing, an idea began to form in his mind, but he didn't want to believe it.

"What would bandits be doing with abducted flame wielders?" he said. "That can't be it. I guess we need to take those guards home. Perhaps somebody there will know what's happening."

He rode back to the battle site, and waited. A short time later, Jera and Miro returned.

"They had a boat alright. It looks like they had a long boat," Jera said.

"It must have been a fair size," Miro continued. "To carry the cart and the horses, which implies a decent ship off the coast. There is no way they brought horses, a cart, themselves, their supplies, all that, without at least one decent ship, possibly two or three."

"Right, then we're dealing with a large, organised, and wealthy group of bandits," Symin said. "The suspicions we've had of a bandit group expanding, building an empire to the south, seem to be confirmed."

Dismounting, he pulled his blanket from his saddle bag. Carefully, he laid it out on the ground.

"Jera, help me lift this fellow onto the blanket," Symin said.

Together, they lifted one of the guards onto the blanket, and wrapped him in it. Carefully, they slung him over the back of Symin's horse, then did the same for the other two guards, one on each of Jera and Miro's horses.

"What about the bandits, Sir?" Jera asked.

"We leave them here for now, but we'll collect them later and take them to the academy. They may have clues on their clothing about where they came from, and who's pulling the strings. We should drag them off the road, though."

"Yes, Sir."

Together, the three men easily lifted the remaining two bodies and placed them beneath the shelter of the trees beside the road, then mounted up and began riding inland towards the home of the guards.

Chapter 5 – Steel and Fire

For days, the ship had pitched and rolled its way through the wild seas. Treghan was more than a little sea sick, and struggled to hold down even the meagre rations of bred and water they had been provided.

Corilai had used some of the drinking water to carefully clean his head wound, and found the cut to be smaller than she thought.

"I told you I was fine," Treghan explained at the time. "Head wounds bleed a lot."

Now though, after nearly four days, judging from the times they had been fed and watered, He was beginning to feel like perhaps there was something wrong. His stomach lurched with every change in the orientation of the floor, and his head spun with his hunger.

To make matters worse, when Corilai had complained about the smell of a dead body, she had not accounted for something potentially worse, and far more sickening. The bandits had given them a single, large chamber pot. And they refused to empty it. It slid from side to side across the room. It had a heavily weighted base, so until now it had not toppled over, but they were forced to use it, in the absence of any proper toilet facilities. It stank like nothing either of the youngsters had ever smelled before. Even with the sturdy steel lid they were provided with.

"If I get the chance, I'm tipping that thing out," she complained.

"Over their heads," Treghan replied, a wicked smirk on his face.

Corilai laughed.

"I'm glad you can still make light of the situation," she said.

A bell rang somewhere in the distance, and then a second, much closer, replied.

"That's the ship's bell. Do you suppose we're there?" Corilai asked.

"Wherever there is, I guess," Treghan replied.

The bells rang again, this time closer. The ship began to rock less as it came into port. After what felt like an eternity, there was a jostling of the ship and the sounds of men shouting as they tied it to the dockside.

After a long time it went quiet, and still they remained in their floating prison.

"Do you think they forgot about us?" Corilai asked.

"No," Treghan said. "I think they're probably trying to decide what to do with us. Clearly they're worried about us setting fire to the place. Maybe they have some way they're planning to transport us?"

"You're probably right."

They waited another hour, then they heard men climbing aboard, and heavy footsteps as they descended into the ship. The door was thrust open, letting in bright light from a flaming torch. There was a heavy thud with a resounding clang as two things landed on the floor.

"Put those on, and be quick about it," the man with the torch shouted.

Treghan picked one of the things up. It was a heavy pair of chain mail gloves, attached to shackles, with a matching tunic.

"What is this?" he asked.

"It's so you don't use your fire to burn us, or the docks. The chain mail will heat up and burn your skin, at least, that's what the boss said. Get it on, and hurry up."

Struggling, Treghan and Corilai helped each other get into the heavy mail, and then painfully, and awkwardly, they walked out of the cell. The man with the torch followed them, while a second man led the way. As they came out into the open air, the bright afternoon sunlight was blinding after being locked away for so so long.

"Welcome to the southern port of Grey," the man in front of them said. "The steel city. We run this town now, so you'd best remember, if you try to escape, ain't nobody here going to hide you away. You belong to us now. And the boss, he wants to meet you. Now get a move on, up on that cart. Now!"

They both climbed onto the cart, and the man with the torch hooked it into a sconce on the dock, then climbed up front, to drive. The second man climbed in the back with them, and hooked their shackles to the railings with heavy clamps.

"Righto, Beza, they's secure," he shouted, and the other man cracked the reins, the horses responding immediately and dragging the old cart, bouncing along the worn, bumpy cobblestone streets.

People in the streets mostly ignored them, though occasionally somebody would stop and stare as the cart rumbled past. The city was, like its name, grey and gloomy. Thick smoke hung in the air, from coal fires burning in many of the buildings to choke back the chill of the southern air.

Some of the buildings had smoke stacks towering above the roof tops, to lift the smoke from industrial fires above the streets, but it was not effective. Many buildings were obviously blacksmiths and foundries. Immense furnaces burned coal to smelter ore and produce all manner of materials, to be used by the various smiths around the town.

"I've heard of Grey, the steel city, but I never imagined it would be so dirty," Corilai said.

"But it's rich," Treghan replied. "They make so much steel, and other precious metals, and send it all over the country. I've heard they even send gold across the seas. Can you imagine how wealthy they must be?"

"Well, somebody here is, but I suspect it's not the working people," she said, watching a begging child as they passed, wishing she could offer something to the boy, even though she was in little better position. "Besides, nobody knows what's across the sea, so I doubt that's true."

"Keep quiet back there," the driver shouted, reaching back to swing a fist at Treghan's head.

With well worn instinct, Treghan ducked, and the driver grumbled, before turning back to face the road ahead. An imposing building was coming closer, some kind of immense, fortified factory, seven massive smoke stacks towering above it. Strangely, there was only the slightest of smoke coming from them, implying that this factory was either not burning coal, or not operating at all.

Nevertheless, the building was immense, and the fortifications impressive. As they arrived at the gate, a huge portcullis was raised, and a pair of wary guards looked them over, before waving them through.

The cart rattled to a stop in a courtyard just inside the gate, and their escort climbed down, before beckoning at them in angry gestures.

"Come on," Beza said. "You two, get down. Hurry up, we don't have all day."

With no point to rebellion in this situation, Treghan and Corilai complied, and followed close behind as Beza led them into the building.

"You'll be called to see the boss soon, but first you need to freshen up. You stink, the pair of you."

He led them down stairs into a basement, then opened a heavy steel door and stopped, unlocking their shackles.

"Get that mail off. You won't be needing it any more."

They did as they were told, and Beza tossed the mail and shackles against the wall, before waving them inside.

"Get in there, and hurry up about it. You'll find two cots, and a basin full of water. This is where you'll be living from now on. Get yourselves washed up and be ready within twenty minutes."

He didn't wait for any reply, closing the door and locking it from the outside. They heard his heavy foot steps returning up the stairs.

"Stand in that corner and don't look!" Corilai demanded, pointing to the place she was referring as she approached the deep basin, which was filled with fresh water as promised. In front of it, a steel grate covered a stone drain, so she stood on it, and began removing her soiled clothing. Picking up a large cup which rested beside the basin, she washed herself down, then washed down her clothes, before putting them back on, wet.

"OK, Your turn," she said. "I'll see if I can get my flames to dry me while you wash up."

Without saying anything, Treghan approached the basin, and stripped, before washing himself down just as she had done. He then washed his ragged clothes as best he could, before getting dressed. Turning, he looked at her, to see her surrounded in fierce black flames, which scorched the stone wall behind her.

"Come here, Treghan," she said. "I promise I'll be careful."

Tentatively, he approached her, and he felt the heat of the flames warming his face.

"Come closer, silly," she said. "If I go too long like this, I'll burn my clothes, and I don't know how long I can control it!"

The look of intense concentration on her face convinced him. Even with all her efforts, the flames were wild, bursting out and curling around her like a snake looking for a place to strike. She winced, and the flames burst outwards, engulfing the room for a moment in blackness.

Treghan moved closer, till he was almost touching her. Then she groaned as the effort became harder, and he stumbled as he tried to back away a little, instead falling forward, and crashing into her. They fell, a sprawling tangle, and her flames surged.

"Ouch! Dammit! It's too hot!" she screamed.

"I'm sorry," he said. "What can I do?"

Treghan smiled, as inspiration struck. He sat up, on the floor beside the girl, who was engulfed in the black flames and writhing against them, completely out of control. He looked at her. Maybe if he flamed too, somehow that would help. He couldn't say how, or why, it would help, but it was worth a try. Treghan held out a hand and focused his energy. The usual spark appeared, and nothing else.

Then, reaching his other hand, he grasped Corilai's shoulder. Instantly, her flames calmed, and she stopped struggling against them. She regained her look of composed concentration, and formed a tall, straight fire, roaring to the ceiling, erupting from the air just above her hands.

"Treghan!" she said, amazed, then looked at him, her eyes growing wide. "Treghan, you're doing it!"

"I didn't know if it would work, but it looks like we tamed your fire," he replied.

"Not only that! Treghan, look at your hand!" she said, excitement lending her voice an urgent tone.

He looked, as she told him, at his hand. The one on her shoulder. It looked normal. So he turned, to look at his other hand, which was held out behind him, and to the side, away from her. The hand he had been sparking in. From it, an enormous, pure white plume of fire, equal in size to her black one, reached like a questing frond to the ceiling. His eyes grew wide.

"Why?" he stammered. "How? How is this even possible? I've never even made a single little candle flame, just sparks, and now, suddenly this thing? It's incredible!"

"I'll say it is," she said, focussing her mind on quenching her own fire. "Let go of my shoulder, Treghan."

He did as he was told, and the white flame disappeared, replaced by the familiar sparks. Disappointed, he looked at her as she sat up. Her black flames also gone.

"I thought so," she said.

"What?" he asked, still confused by it all.

"I think you were drawing on my wild, uncontrolled energy, and using that to feed your flames. I bet it has something to do with what makes a white flame so pure and controlled, and what makes a black one so wild. But with you taking away my excess energy, I was able to control what was left. Treghan, we might make an awesome team, now we know this."

He grinned at her, his understanding exciting him as he realised the possibilities.

"You know what this means?" he said. "This is our way into the academy!"

"If we can ever get there," she said.

"We'll get there. Somehow, just as soon as we escape from these bastards. But Corilai, no matter what, we never show these guys what we've learned. You go wildfire on them, I'll go weak sparky boy. Got it?"

"Got it. I'll burn their eyebrows off and singe their backsides. All by accident."

He laughed.
"I'm sure you'll do worse than that, demon girl."

* * *

Symin led his men away from the town, the three guards now laid to rest, their widows and children weeping for the fallen men. It had been a disquieting visit, his worst suspicions confirmed.

"They were trying to find flame wielders," he said, summarising his own thoughts as they rode. "Youngsters, not yet in the training of the academy. They would seek to abduct them if necessary. But for what purpose? Are they trying to raise an army to oppose the rangers? That makes no sense. An untrained wielder is no match for a trained ranger. So why? There must be something I've missed."

"Sir," Jera said. "Whatever it is, it's going to be bad news, isn't it?"

"I have no doubt of that, Jera."

"Sir, I know we should get back to the academy fast, but why don't we head south, and see what we can find out? They might not have come from very far."

"They came by ship," Symin said. "That tells me they came some large distance on their task, and we don't have long enough to waste, travelling that far. We will return to Emberdale, and let the Chancellor make a decision. Perhaps we will lead a larger expedition south. I hope we do, but us three would be no match for an organised army of bandits, bent on our destruction. If that is what awaits us."

They rode in silence for many miles. Eventually, they arrived at the turn in the road, where they had left the two bandits' bodies. Carefully, they gathered them up, and took them the rest of the way to Emberdale.

"I'm glad these men had not been collected by their comrades," Symin said.

"Why is that, Sir?" Jera asked.

"Because they are the proof we will need to spur the less vigorous of those advising the Chancellor to action. Their caution and scepticism might be enough to quash our claims otherwise."

"But Sir, you are a respected scout, and accomplished ranger. Surely they would listen to you?"

"You would hope so. But Jera, surely you realise, as with any group of powerful men and women, the advisory council has not been entirely uncorrupted."

"That's a dangerous thing to say, Sir."

"I know this, Jera, but you two are beyond reproach. I trust you impeccably, and feel safe to speak my mind. The council has not always achieved the lofty ideals of the Ranger Academy, and there are always men in this world who thirst for power. Their greed will drive them to resist doing the right thing for the people, and for the rangers they represent."

"I wish I knew who it is you are speaking of, Sir; who on the council you suspect."

"I'm sorry, Jera, I will be keeping that information to myself. I could well be mistaken, and then I will have maligned an innocent man. Or woman."

"I understand, Sir. But nevertheless, on your suspicions, I will take extra care in dealing with the council."

Chapter 6 – Furnace and Fire

Beza led them from their cell, up the stairs and deeper into the building. The entire place was stone and steel. They did not see a single wooden or fabric fitting they might be able to burn.

"Where are we going?" Corilai asked.

"The Boss wants to see you. Just keep quiet, and make sure you listen to what he tells you. If you do the wrong thing because you didn't listen to his instructions, you'll be in a lot of trouble."

"Why would he want to see us?" Treghan asked.

"That'll be clear soon enough. Just stop asking questions, and do as you're told."

They walked in silence the rest of the way, and soon were led into a small office. A burly man sat in a chair, smoking a pipe and sipping an amber fluid from a tall, crystal goblet. He looked at them for a moment, then waved his hand. Beza left the room and closed the door.

"Before you get any ideas, your flames can't touch me," the man said. "My name is Yuri, and I am in charge around here. Do you have any questions?"

"What is this place?" Treghan asked.

"I see. I know Beza told you not to ask questions. Why did you ask one now?"

"I assessed the situation," Treghan said. "You're in charge. The boss. You outrank Beza, so when you ask if we have questions, that overrides his instruction not to ask any."

"So you're saying you respect my word as the boss?"

"Yes, Sir," Treghan said. "If you're in charge, your word is the most important."

"OK then," Yuri said. "This place is a foundry, and a smelter. It is also the headquarters of my organisation. We are the Mercenary Government of Grey. After we overthrew the corrupt government of the nobles, we were elevated from a small band of freelancers to the rulers of the city."

"So, with respect, Sir, you were bandits?" Corilai asked.

"I suppose you might have called us that. You have one more question."

"Why are we here?" Corilai asked.

"Ah! Good question, young lady," Yuri said. "Because we have need of flame wielders. We have a large project, requiring large amounts of steel to be processed. We will raise an army, and expand our lands to supply the resources we require, but our access to coal to drive our steel industry is limited. Without steel, we can't make our equipment for the soldiers. Our local mines have begun to run out of coal, and we already burnt the wood from the nearby forests. So we need to find alternative ways to heat our furnaces."

"So you want us to heat your furnaces directly?"

"No, not exactly," he said. "Follow me, it will be easier to show you."

He led them out into the corridor. Beza waited there, and he followed behind them, ensuring they could not simply run away.

"You could be an important part of our operation here," Yuri said. "If you just behave, cooperate, and never ask too many tricky questions, we will look after you quite well."

"How long will we be here?" Corilai asked.

"As long as it takes, and then as long as we need you, to produce the steel we need to support our ongoing operations."

"So there is no definite end in site," Treghan said.

"No, but as I say, you will be looked after."

"Looked after, in a steel cell, in the basement," Corilai said. "Pardon me for being sceptical, Sir."

Yuri spun on his heel and slapped her face, hard.

"Watch your tongue, insolent girl. Remember who is holding the key to your lives here."

She kept quiet from then on. Treghan stared at Yuri in mute rage, angry at the man for striking Corilai. Neither of the young flame wielders listened as he continued talking about his political beliefs like a true zealot.

Eventually, they entered a large chamber. Seven sturdy alcoves, open at one end for access, contained the smelters. Workers filled the hopper above with ore, while beneath was a space for the fire.

Four were still running on coal, which burned beneath the smelter. The others had young flame wielders standing beneath them, aiming their fire upwards. The ore seemed to not be melting effectively in those smelters.

"As you can see, using flame wielders directly to melt the ore is not as successful as we'd like. So we have another plan."

Yuri led them to the far end of the chamber, where he opened a door and led them through to a second, similar chamber.

"There are three of these chambers. It used to be that each had seven smelters, and any two chambers were running at all times. But now, we are converting this chamber to a new technology, and will convert the other two chambers to use what this one produces."

In this chamber, each alcove had a large water reservoir suspended in place of the smelter, and above those were mounted immense bladed wheels.

"We will use flame wielders, like you two, to heat the water, which creates steam. That steam then turns the wheels, which are called turbines. They generate a power, like lightning. We harness that power, and in the third chamber it is used by pumping it through enormous steal elements that generate heat, to operate the smelters. We have enormous banks of lead based devices which can store that lightning. So it takes less of you to create the same amount of heat to operate our facility. Ingenious, is it not?"

"I'd call it insane if I wasn't seeing it myself," Corilai said.

"That is often the nature of visionaries," Yuri said. "So, when you are rested, we will be assigning you both to a testing phase in one of these devices, and as your skills and control improve, we will roster you into the rotation of those who operate this equipment. Beza will take you to your cell. Please ensure you are rested and ready for the assessment in the morning."

Yuri walked away, as if expecting no further interaction. He postured arrogantly as he left, making grand gestures towards the workers as he passed.

"He has made his decision about you both, now follow me," Beza said, turning to lead them away.

Treghan and Corilai followed him without question. It was clear they would need a solid plan before taking any action to escape from this madhouse.

* * *

Fletcher watched as an enormous cauldron was propped onto a frame, enough room beneath it for him to stand. By bucket loads, the men slowly filled the cauldron with water, until it was spilling over the top as the thing wobbled on its precarious perch.

"Boy, get over here," Harv called.

Fletcher rushed over to where the man stood, beside the rickety structure.

"Get under there," Harv said. "I want to see if you can control your fire enough to boil the water, without ruining the stand."

"But what if I burn the stand?"

"Boy, if that happens, you'd better hope that thing ain't as heavy as it looks. But this is an important test, and it will decide your fate, so get on with it."

Stepping beneath the cauldron, Fletcher looked up. It seemed even bigger from underneath. The sturdy wooden frame covered a portion of the bottom of the cauldron, so this was going to be tricky. He raised his hands overhead, so that he was almost touching the cauldron, and focused his energy.

Red flames brushed across its surface, licking at the heavy iron like questing tendrils, seeking entrance. He kept the fire small, for fear of being crushed beneath the thing. Fletcher felt the warmth of his flames reflected back at him from the cauldron's base, but he could not see if he was having any effect on the contents.

"Hotter, boy! Don't hold back like that, you need more heat," Harv shouted.

Against his better judgement, Fletcher complied, pushing more energy into the flames, sending them into a frenzy across the cauldron, to lick at the wooden structure to the sides.

"That's it, boy, keep going!" Harv shouted. "More heat boy, more heat,"

Fletcher obliged, pushing the last of his reserves into the fire, and the iron base of the cauldron began to glow red. The flames were now engulfing the wooden beams. Fletcher started to worry about his position beneath the structure.

"Boss, we got boil, it's starting to form bubbles in the bottom!" yelled a man from atop the frame.

"Excellent," Harv said. "Keep going, boy. I want that water frothing like a witches brew before you stop."

"Yes, Sir," Fletcher grunted, squinting as he looked up into the reflected heat.

The moments crawled by, as the water became hotter. Fletcher became more worried as the wooden beams began to darken, and burned now with their own flames.

"Don't move, boy, stay there till it's done!" Harv shouted.

"We got boil," the man on top shouted. "We got boil, boss, the surface of the water is rolling about like crazy. It'll be making steam in no time!"

"Excellent, get down from there," Harv said to the man, before shouting. "Boy, don't you stop yet."

Fletcher stayed where he was, starting to feel his skin burn under the heat radiated by the cauldron, and the burning parts of the frame. Then, he heard a crack, as one of the beams started to give way, the one across the back.

That was enough for him, Fletcher dropped his arms, stopped his flames, and ran from beneath the cauldron.

"Idiot boy!" Harv shouted, catching Fletcher and smacking him across the side of his head. "I told you not to move! Get back in there and finish the job."

Fletcher turned back to face the structure, just as the frame gave way, tumbling the cauldron down behind, to spill its boiling contents on the ground.

"OK, good enough," Harv said. "We're done for today. Men, get that thing cleaned up, and rebuilt. I want a second test in the morning. And boy, next time, when I say to stay put, you stay put. No matter what. And I want to see that pot boiling faster than that as well. Am I clear?"

"Yes, Sir," Fletcher said, as the men set about their task, and Harv led him away.

*　　　*　　　*

Treghan and Corilai sat in their cell, a morbid tension in the air.

"We have to find a way to get out of here," he said.

"Is it really that urgent?" she said. "I mean, they need us, so they aren't going to hurt us, not really."

"But they won't let us go, either," Treghan said. "There's no way I want to be their prisoner."

"Fair point," Corilai replied. "And besides, we still have to get to the academy. It's clear these people don't have the knowledge to be able to help us with training as flame wielders, they're just using what they find in us, not trying to improve it."

"Exactly. Sure, we can learn by ourselves, but I suspect there won't be a lot of time for that."

"So how do we escape?" Corilai asked.

"First things first I think we make ourselves useless to them." Treghan said.

"But what if they kill us?"

"I don't think they will," Treghan explained. "I think they'll find somewhere else to use us if that happens, and that's when we find our chance to escape."

"I hope you're right, Treghan, but how do we make ourselves useless?"

"That's the easy part. We stick to our natural abilities, with no input from each other. I can barely spark at all, you have trouble controlling it. So you just go wild, total inferno on them, explode with your black flames so you damage the equipment, they'll hate that."

"So long as you're sure we'll be OK," she said, uncertain of the plan.

"I'm sure, I think these guys will find another way to use us, putting us in a mine, or on a boat, something like that, and that's when we get a chance to escape, out of this damn cell."

Treghan looked at her for a long while, his eyes narrowed, as he thought about his plan.

"One other thing," he said finally. "It's important, we have to seem like we're no danger. So you make a show of being scared to use your flames, before it all happens, so they don't think you'll just attack whoever we're sent to."

"OK, I can do that," Corilai said.

*   *   *

The next morning, they were awakened by a loud noise as the door to the cell was thrown open. Beza stood there, with two other guards.

"Come on, on your feet, you two," he shouted. "Time to get to work."

They stood and followed Beza as he led them up stairs. The other two guards fell in behind them, blocking any possible escape.

"You'd best hope you can be of some use to us, else it'll be a much less appealing job for the pair of you," Beza snarled.

Corilai cast a worried glance at Treghan, who simply shook his head slightly and smiled.

"Don't worry, Corilai, you'll be fine," Treghan said.

"Aww, ain't that sweet," Beza said. "Worried about your little girlfriend are you boy? Well, if she doesn't work out, I know a few brothels on the docks who'll buy her from us!"

Treghan lunged at Beza, who simply laughed and knocked him to the ground.

"Touchy subject is it boy?" Beza said. "Then you'd best aim to please us. Both of you. I'm sure we can find a place that would love to take a pretty boy like you off our hands, too!"

Both the youngsters stared at the big man, then at each other, the concern plain on their faces. Beza burst into laughter.

"Ha! It's just too easy with you two. Just get in there and do your best. You'll be fine if you prove useful."

"And if we don't?" Treghan asked.

"That'll be the boss's decision," Beza explained. "I dare say he won't be keeping you on around here. He has loads of places he can use a couple of youngsters like you. But it won't be the cushy life you'd get in the smelters."

They entered the first chamber and walked through to the second. Yuri was already there. A group of ten young people stood behind him, all looking warily about, clearly exhausted from their labours.

"Ah!" Yuri shouted. "Our latest recruits. I know you two were only found by accident, but I hope you can show a few of these night shift here how it's done. Are you both ready for your assessment?"

"Ye, yes sir," Treghan said.

Corilai shook her head, and backed away.

"No, I can't do it," she screamed, as she bumped into the guard behind her. "The flames will consume me!"

The guard picked her up by the shoulders, and tossed her forward, like a rag doll. She landed on her feet, stumbled, and fell forward, coming to a stop on hands and knees in front of Yuri. He knelt down and lifted her chin, staring into her face.

"What is it, child? Why do you disappoint me so?"

"I'm sorry, Sir," she said, tears rolling down her cheeks. "But, I'm scared. The flames, they're terrifying."

Yuri raised an eyebrow.

"Why is that, girl, mind you speak up, so we can all hear you."

"I can't control them, Sir," Corilai explained through her tears. "It takes all I have to hold them down, and if I let them out, their ferocity is overwhelming. I can't control it. I'm scared I'll kill somebody."

"Has that happened before?" Yuri said, sounding genuine in his curiosity.

"Well, no, I haven't killed anybody, but I destroyed my home, and the villagers chased me away. It took all their efforts to put out the fire that ruined my parent's house. They lost all the crops as well in the fire. They ran me out of town. It was after that your men found us. I'm just so scared of those flames, if they could do that, how can I know I will ever be able to use them safely?"

Yuri smiled, and helped her to her feet.

"You just have to try, child. But how about we let your boyfriend here go first."

"He's not... Yes, OK," she stammered.

Corilai stepped away from the intimidating man, her arms folded in front of her as she stared at the floor. Stealing a glance at Treghan, she winked, and he smiled.

Chapter 7 – Failure and Freedom

"I'm not sure I can do much, but I'll try, this stuff looks so cool!" Treghan exclaimed.

"I'm glad you think so, lad," Yuri said. "How much experience have you got wielding flames?"

"None at all, Sir, but I'll give it a shot!"

"Well at least you have a good attitude," Yuri said, turning to face the youngsters behind him. "Some of you night shift kids could learn a thing or two from this boy."

"So where do I stand?" Treghan asked.

"Just get right in there underneath, right in the middle, lad," Yuri said.

With a curt nod, Treghan stepped forward, an arrogant pride in his step as he reached his position, and held his hands up over his head. He focused his energy, concentrated, and let loose all he had in one enormous effort.

A tiny white spark danced between his fingers.

The night shift burst into raucous laughter, shouting out in their mirth.

"Oh no! Protect us from that evil boy, with his lethal powers of nothing!" one shouted.

"I think I'm learning something already!" another yelled.

"Yeah, how to be a useless slacker," a third replied.

Yuri strode forward, grabbed Treghan my the arm, and hauled him out from under the reservoir. Angry, Yuri tossed him to the side.

"You young fool, how dare you waste my time!" Yuri shouted, enraged. "Get the girl under there now. And girl, if you pull a trick like that, I'll beat you to within an inch of your life!"

"Ye, yes Sir," Corilai stammered. "I'll, I'll try. I hope it works out."

Walking into position, Corilai raised her hands, gulped in a lungful of air, and concentrated. Dust on the floor beneath her feet puffed outwards in a low cloud, then swirled around her. The flames began to seep out of her body, like oil oozing from an olive, being squeezed. The dust swirled faster, and the black flames lept out from her body, swallowing the dust cloud and obscuring her figure inside a maelstrom of fiery gloom.

"Aaaarrrrrr!" Corilai screamed, as the fire engulfed the area beneath the reservoir.

"It's the demon flame!" one of the night shift shouted, backing away.

The other night shift started to panic, and pushed back until they were against the wall. Still the black flames grew. The night shift screamed. Yuri looked around him, beginning to think there may be something to worry about.

The black flames engulfed the entire alcove, and began seeping out, questing for more space, more air to consume. Corilai's screams from within were now almost drowned out by the whooshing sound of the flames, and the screeching stone of the alcove under such intense heat. Yuri had retreated to the doorway.

"Stop her!" he shouted, but nobody was brave enough to enter that inferno.

Then an almighty crack echoed through the chamber. One stone wall of the alcove, holding the entire structure supporting the reservoir and the smelter above, split from the floor to the ceiling. Corilai's screams followed, in a macabre reminder of her presence in the heart of the disaster.

Hearing the sound, Corilai ran to the opposite wall, lowering her hands, just as the alcove gave way, and the reservoir dropped, crashing down with a terrible sound of rending steel and rushing water, as the contents spilled into the chamber.

Rapidly, the flames died, and Corilai, crying, wandered out from the rubble. Yuri, furious, ran to her, and slapped her, sending her sprawling to the ground.

"You evil little witch!" Yuri screamed. "Look what you've done!"

He kicked her ribs as she knelt up, sending her sprawling again.

"Worthless, demon child," Yuri muttered, then turned to Beza. "Get rid of them both. I never want to see these two worthless brats again. Take them to the docks, sell them for whatever you can get, I don't care, as long as they're out of this building within the hour. Oh, and if you're scared of that demon flame of hers, tie her hand to the lads. I doubt very much she has the heart to kill her little boyfriend. No need for the mail. See me when it's done."

"Yes, Sir," Beza said. "I warned you both. I guess it'll be the brothels for you two after all."

The burly man grabbed Treghan's wrist, then rushed to Corilai, and grasped her hair, pulling her to her feet. He shoved them both at the other guards.

"Tie them together, like the boss said. Then put them in the cart, and meet me in the courtyard. I'll be down in a moment."

"Yes, Sir," the two men said in unison, as they each grabbed one of the two youngsters by the wrist, and dragged them towards the door.

They led them to the courtyard near the gate and off to one side, where they entered a storage area, in which the cart sat. One of the men took some rope from the cart, and bound Treghan's right hand to Corilai's left.

Treghan looked at her, and winked. She smiled weakly, and grasped his hand for support.

"Aw, now ain't that sweet," one of the guards mocked. "Comforting each other by holding hands. Well, you might as well get it over with, it'll probably be the last chance you two get."

He grabbed Treghan's left hand, and used the rope to bind it to a wooden railing on the side of the cart. He walked around to the other side, and gabbed Corilai's right hand, and pulled her across, tying her wrist to the railing on that side.

"There'll be no funny business on this little trip, am I clear?"

Neither of them responded. The man looked angry, and scowled at them as he slammed a fist on the railing.

"I said, am I clear?"

"Yes, Sir," the pair said together.

"Good. Now you two wait there while I fetch the horses."

Treghan looked at Corilai as the man left, and whispered.

"This is perfect, but we wait until we're closer to the docks, agreed?"

She nodded her head in reply, as the second bandit guard entered, leading one of two palomino mares. Wordlessly, he hitched the horse to the front of the cart, then climbed into the driver's seat as the other man returned with the second horse.

Once the second horse was hitched up, he climbed up beside his colleague, who snapped the reins. The horses moved out, dragging the cart into the courtyard. Beza was there waiting for them. He climbed up with Treghan and Corilai, and waved an arm high.

The gates swung ponderously open, and they were on their way. Beza leaned in close. He glanced at Treghan, then Corilai.

"I understand if you two are a bit upset at the moment," Beza said. "If there was ever any chance for funny business, particularly an escape, this is it. But let's be sensible OK? I don't want to see anybody getting hurt, you get me?"

"Yes, Sir," Treghan said, as Corilai nodded.

"Good," Beza said, then sat back, on the tailgate of the cart.

They rattled through the streets, down hill towards the sea, where the slums of the docks awaited them.

"It'd be a shame if we lost you just this side of the docks," Beza said. "There are any number of rats dens you could hide in there. It would be a mighty pain in the backside trying to catch you again."

Treghan and Corilai simply looked at him. He glanced around, smiled, and shook his head, adding to their confusion. After a little while, he leaned forward again.

"Almost there. The streets will get busier up here, making it harder to move about. I'd say your chance is just about up."

"Right," Treghan said. "Corilai, now!"

With a nod at him, she released her flame, black and fierce. It cast a deep shadow over the cart, and set the rope on her right hand ablaze. Treghan drew on her excess energy, and white light shot from his left hand, an immense, blinding flash, which eviscerated the rope binding him to the railing. He stood, lifting her arm as he did so, and faced Beza, ready to hit him with a swift kick if necessary.

Beza jumped backwards, out of the cart, and pointed behind them. Treghan turned to see one of the guards coming at him. Narrowing his eyes, Treghan fired a blast of white fire at the man's face. Screaming, the guard ran, as Corilai did the same to the other man.

Untangling the rope that held them together, Treghan and Corilai made to run as well, but were stopped by a shout from behind.

Turning, they saw Beza, standing there with the horses unhitched, one bridle in each hand.

"You two can get a lot further a lot faster if you overpower me and take these," he said.

Without hesitation, the pair rushed forward and jumped at him, snatching a horse each and swinging onto their backs.

"But why?" Corilai asked.

"I may be a bandit," Beza said. "But I ain't no monster. I can't stand to see youngsters like you bought and sold into slavery. Especially that kind of slavery. Now get out of here. You'll find blankets and saddles behind a rock on the second hill outside town. I had my wife put them there this morning, just in case."

"Thank you, Sir," Corilai said, beaming him a beautiful smile.

"Don't be thankin' me yet, youngin, you gotta escape the city yet. Once you get the gear, I suggest you head inland till you hit the glaciers, then follow the edge of the ice north, till you enter the forests. That way you can avoid the roads, but the ground along there is still firm and level."

"Yes, Sir," Treghan said.

"I ain't no Sir to you no more, call me Beza."

"Yes, Beza. Thank you," Treghan said as he kicked the horse's side, spurring it into a fast gallop.

"Hey, Treghan, wait for me!" Corilai said, spurring her horse into a fast trot after her friend.

They rushed through the streets, heading generally north. Treghan led the way, not knowing his way around the city, but feeling certain that once they found the perimeter wall, they could follow it around until they reached the city gate.

His instincts proved correct, and before long they were galloping at speed through the outlying countryside of the steel city. Treghan slowed, allowing Corilai to ride up along side him.

"I've never been so scared in all my life!" she shouted. "I thought that smelter was going to crush me."

"But you played your part amazingly," Treghan replied. "And it all worked out, we're free"

"For now," she said. "But what about Beza? I never expected that."

"He's a good man."

"Do you suppose he's the reason there's nobody following us yet?"

"I have no doubt," Treghan said. "But his instructions did imply that we will be hunted. We should do as he suggested, and move north as fast as we can. We won't be safe until we reach Emberdale."

"Right," she said, as they rode down the back of the first hill, putting them out of sight of the city.

Climbing the second hill which was not as high as the first, they soon saw the rock Beza had mentioned, and headed for it. As they approached, a young woman stepped out from behind it. She raised her hands to show she was unarmed.

"Thank god you both made it," she said. "Quickly, let me help you down, so you can get these saddles on. Your bones must be rattled from that ride already."

"Are you Beza's wife?" Corilai said.

"Yes, lass. I'm Hono. Now quickly, he can only stall them for so long."

"I hope he won't be in trouble for all this," Corilai said.

"Don't you worry about my Beza, he knows what he's up to, and can look after himself. Though it is sweet of you to worry. Now quickly. There is not much time."

Accepting the lady's hand, Corilai swung down from the horse, then helped Treghan to do the same. Working fast, they got saddle blankets on the horses, then the saddles. Finally, the woman handed them saddle bags, full of supplies. Carefully, they hitched the bags to the saddles, and mounted.

"That's all I could spare," Hono said. "I hope it's enough. I wish you the best of luck. Now ride, fast and safe."

"Thank you, Hono," Treghan said. "This is far too generous. We will never forget your kindness. Corilai, we should go."

He turned and trotted over the road, heading inland. Corilai hesitated, turned and offered a hand to Hono. The gentle lady took it in both her own.

"Thank you, Hono, for everything. I promise, if there is ever a way I can repay your kindness, I will," Corilai said.

"I know you will, dear, now go. Before we're seen," Hono said, letting go of Corilai's hand and walking back behind the rock.

Not looking back, Corilai trotted over to meet Treghan, and they rushed off into the tundra, pushing the horses as hard as they dared.

It took nearly three hours to reach the edge of the glacier, a massive sheet of ice sliding down from the mountains. When they reached it, they rode along its edge a short way, till they found a green patch of grassy plants and weeds, where they dismounted, and allowed the horses to feed.

A stream ran through the area, providing icy cold water from the glacier. They drank their fill, though neither were hungry. Once the horses were watered, and had had a short break, Treghan and Corilai mounted up, and continued their journey.

There was a long way still to go. Many days of hard riding lay between them and their goal, and every step of the way there was the danger of discovery by their enemies.

They both knew in their hearts, this was only the beginning of the hardest journey of their young lives.

Chapter 8 – On the run

Just as Beza said, the ground was firm and level, and they made good distance the first day. As the dusk morphed into darkness, Treghan and Corilai pitched camp on a gravelled mound beside a trickling stream, and tied the horses to a tree near the water.

Searching through the saddle bags, they found soft padded bedrolls and warm blankets. Carefully, they laid them out then built a small fire. In the packs, they found preserved meats and dried vegetables, along with a small steel pot.

Fetching water from the stream, Treghan added some of the meat and vegetables and placed the pot on the edge of the fire, to heat.

A cold breeze blew down on them from the glacier, and they were thankful for the warmth of the fire. Treghan stirred the pot, watching the chunks in the liquid impatiently, feeling his hunger.

"We should take turns on watch," Treghan said. "We don't want a repeat of what happened at our last camp site."

"Good thinking," Corilai said. "Would you like me to go first?"

"OK," Treghan said. "Once we finish eating I'll go to sleep, while you keep watch. Anything happens, wake me up. When you feel too tired, we can swap."

"That's all good, but how much longer is that food going to take? I'm starved," Corilai said.

"I think it's ready now." Treghan said. "Do we have bowls?"

"I think so, and spoons," Corilai said as she went to the saddle bags and rummaged.

Corilai quickly found two small wooden bowls and a pair of steel spoons. She walked back to the fire and handed them to Treghan, who served the food. They ate in silence as the wind grew colder.

The warm food had the desired effect, and Treghan climbed into his bedroll more content than he had been in a long time.

Corilai watched the fire for a while, then turned her attention to the darkness. The sounds of the night told her there were all kinds of nocturnal animals out there, but the fire kept them at bay. The horses pulled at their ropes, moving as close to the fire as they could, seeming to be nervous of something in the dark.

Whatever was out there did not seem interested in bothering them, and Corilai's time on watch passed without incident. When finally she woke Treghan to take over, the clouds were clearing and a bright half moon was peaking through, casting its light on the area, to reveal small shapes dashing around in the rocks, occasionally running to the stream for water.

"What are they?" Corilai asked.

"Rats, I think," Treghan replied. "Get some sleep. They won't get at our supplies as long as we leave the bags on the horses."

"OK then," she said, climbing into her bed roll and yawning. "Good night, Treghan."

"Goodnight, Corilai."

Treghan sat watch for the following few hours, until the sun finally began to rise. As the light began to warm the air around him Treghan took the pot to the stream and collected water. He then put the pot on the coals of the dying fire, and went to the saddle bags.

Rummaging through the bags, he found a small paper satchel of tea leaves. Muttering thanks to Beza's wife, he dropped the tea leaves into the pot.

After moving the pot to let the tea brew without boiling, he took a walk around the perimeter, curious about the rats, but there was no evidence of their presence.

Returning to the fire, he collected their bowls from the previous night's meal, and washed them in the stream. He poured tea into the two bowls, and carried one to Corilai.

Kneeling beside her, he shook her shoulder and offered her the bowl. Sitting up, still groggy with sleep, she accepted the bowl without comment.

Once the tea had done its job, and they were both warm and awake, they packed up their things, doused the fire, and mounted their horses.

With a clear morning sky above they rode north, and by mid morning they had entered a dense forest. A narrow trail wandered into the trees, continuing the path they had been following. Without hesitation, Corilai and Treghan rode into the trees, glad to finally not be so exposed.

The ride was, by necessity, slower in the forest. They still made steady progress, until at midday they encountered a river crossing their path. Turning towards the hills, they picked their way slowly along the river until they reach a place where a shallow bar of gravel formed a crossing.

Carefully, they made their way across, and continued north through the forested hills. The journey became slower again as the terrain grew treacherous.

Ominous clouds began to close in overhead as the afternoon turned to evening. They pitched camp under a long overhang, tying the horses to a tree with enough rope to allow them under the meagre shelter.

The fire was going quickly, but the strong winds made it difficult to keep it going. They got their bedrolls set up under the shelter of the overhang, but then a driving rain began, quickly extinguishing the fire.

The wind drove the rain into their shelter, and before long everything was soaked. Treghan and Corilai huddled together, miserable in their sodden state. Then things got bad.

Lightning flashed, and thunder rumbled, as the temperature plummeted. Torrents of water rushed down the hills, and flushed over the edge of the overhang, and just as they thought it could not get worse, lightning struck the tree right beside the overhang, splitting it in a fiery explosion of wood and water.

That was too much for the horses, who had snapped their leads, and they bolted into the night.

“Well,” Treghan said. “I didn't want to suggest using our flames in case it spooked the horses, but now I guess there's no point.”

The split tree had dropped a branch just under the cover of the overhang, so Treghan, taking Corilai's hand, focused his energy, and hit the branch with a strong white flame. He held it there as the large branch dried, until eventually, it started to burn.

Treghan stopped his flame, but the branch continued to blaze, its warmth cutting through their sodden cold. They stayed there, huddled in front of the burning log, neither of them sleeping. A few hours before sunrise, the storm finally abated, and by morning the clouds had passed, leaving the wet earth under a warm clear sky.

Weary and on edge, they knew they had to keep moving, so Treghan and Corilai made their way slowly out of the hills, meandering north as they did so. As the rocks gave way to trees, and the morning wore on, the clouds began to return.

By mid morning, a depressing drizzle dampened their world, and their spirits. The grey sky cast a gloom to the forest which reflected their mood. Then, when they thought the day could get no worse, they stepped into a small clearing to hear a low growl from behind.

It was answered by another from their left, and then a third from the right. In seconds, they were surrounded completely. Six wolves, bigger than any Treghan had ever seen around the village, when Fletcher was chasing them away with his flames.

"Give me your hand!" Treghan said.

"Why?" Corilai said "Are you scared?"

"What? No! Just give me your hand!"

Treghan grabbed her hand, and she flared up in black flame.

"Thank you," Treghan said as he drew on her energy and fired a powerful blast of white flame at the wolf in front of them.

The wolf in front fled, however the wolf behind rushed in to attack. Turning her head to look at it, Corilai focused her energy, and her black flame surged to meet its approach, burning the animal's fur and sending it back into the trees with a yelp.

"Treghan!" She shouted. "I controlled it! Did you see?"

"Yeah, that was great," he said.

While they spoke, the remaining wolves had closed in from the sides, and one of them knocked Treghan to the ground. As he fell, Treghan lost his grip on Corilai's hand.

Landing hard, he looked up into the jaws of the beast, raised his hand and focused his energy. A tiny white flame flickered for a moment, then died. The wolf ignored it, and lunged for Treghan's face.

"No!" Corilai screamed, and flared again.

Her black flames swamped the small clearing with darkness and heat. With a scream, the wolf released Treghan, then ran, its fur smouldering. The rest of the wolves fled into the trees, convinced the two young humans were not the easy prey they had first appeared.

Corilai helped Treghan to his feet, and they continued walking. She looked at him, an odd sense of admiration in her eyes. He returned the look.

"What is it? Why are you looking at me like that?" he asked.

"You cast a flame," she said. "You cast a flame without my energy. It wasn't big, but you did it. You're getting better at flame wielding."

"So are you," Treghan said. "You controlled your black flames, and actually aimed them. You're amazing."

She smiled at the compliment, then grabbed his hand, not speaking any more as they walked on through the drizzling rain, their mood suddenly lifted in spite of the weather, and their lack of sleep.

The rain continued, as they hiked on through the forest, making good distance even without their horses, until on dusk they came across a small cottage, welcoming and warm.

"Should we avoid this place?" Corilai asked. "What if they're bandits?"

"I don't know, but a dry night would be nice..."

"Yeah, but a dry night with bandits would be terrible."

"Good point," Treghan said. "Perhaps we should just sneak by."

They began walking around the edge of the clearing, and were about half way around when the door the of cottage was flung open, and a tall man with a long salted beard and a stout cane was silhouetted in the light of the fireplace inside.

"OK you two," the man shouted. "You can stop sneaking around out there and get in here, before you catch your death in that rain."

The pair stopped where they were, indecision making them wait. As if to answer their questions, the old man lit a bright, yellow flame in the air above his hand.

"Don't worry, I'm a friend," he said.

Willing to trust him, and realising they had little other choice as the rain intensified in the growing darkness, Treghan and Corilai crossed the clearing and were ushered inside by the man, who closed the door behind himself, before hanging his cloak on a hook by the door.

It was then they noticed the symbol on its back.

"You," Treghan said, recognising the symbol from the clothing of the man who had visited his house so long ago. "You're a ranger, from the academy?"

"Well, I'm technically retired now, but yes, I spent my time with the academy, and that is why I am permitted to wear a ranger's cloak."

Chapter 9 – Meeting

Symin strode with purpose through the halls of the academy. Chancellor Howe had read his report, and the academy physician had examined the bodies of the bandits and submitted a report of his own.

Now, the Chancellor had called for him, and it was best not to be late to such an appointment. Reaching the sturdy wooden door to the Chancellor's office, Symin paused, took a deep breath, then knocked, one single loud rap on the polished mahogany panel.

"Enter," came a strong voice from inside.

Turning the handle, Symin entered, then closed the door behind himself.

"Please, ranger, take a seat."

Symin knew from the formal tone that this meeting was going to be a serious one.

"Yes, Chancellor," He said as he sat across the table from the wizened old man.

"I have read your report, and those of your subordinates," The Chancellor said. "You bring me reason to worry about the goings on to our south. Do you have any thoughts on how to proceed?"

"Sir, I believe there is something happening down there, I believe somebody has amassed great wealth and is building their organisation, and in so doing seeking to recruit, or conscript, young flame wielders. For what purpose, I do not know. We must send an expedition to find out."

The Chancellor nodded, picked up a small box, and pulled out a cigar. Clicking his fingers, the Chancellor sparked a small blue flame, and used it to light the densely wrapped tobacco. He puffed silently for a moment, before taking a long draft.

"Ranger, you echo my own thoughts," Chancellor Howe said, before taking another drag on the cigar. "I have been receiving many reports of suspicious activities to the south. Particularly around the port city, Grey."

"Reports, Sir? May I enquire as to what these other reports were about?"

Howe looked at Symin for a moment, then drew in a lung full of cigar smoke, before exhaling it towards the window.

"I have reason to believe the traditional government of that city has been removed, but I do not know for certain by whom, and for what purpose."

"Chancellor, Sir, that is indeed an extremely worrying report," Symin said.

"Yes, ranger, it is. But why would such a thing have happened?"

"I don't know, Sir."

The Chancellor looked at him again, put out the cigar, mostly unconsumed, and stood. He walked to the window, gazing out into the forested hills. Finally, he turned to face Symin again.

"Your report implies that the purpose is perhaps more sinister than I had previously suspected. We can not have bandits building empires, so we will do as you suggest. You will lead an expeditionary force south, take two dozen men, and ride for Grey. I will await your report. Meanwhile, I will send ranger Byron via ship. He will follow the coast, also to Grey, and report whatever he witnesses on that route."

"Yes Sir," Symin said. "I will select my men, and leave as soon as possible."

"Good. Go with haste, but take care," Chancellor Howe said.

* * *

"I am Barache, and yes, I am, or was, a ranger," the old man explained.

"You two are, I would guess, not rangers, as yet, but perhaps interested in that occupation. You are running from somebody, or some thing. You are both unusual among flame wielders, as you do not have any of the usual colours. You are a black flame, what the peasants call the demon flame, and a white flame, which some call the angel flame."

"Angel flame?" Treghan asked. "I've never heard of that before."

"Well, white is rare, and white which can use their talent is rarer still, so the stories do not get around as much as they do for other colours. Many whites never share their abilities with the world. Many black flames do not have that choice, so though they are only as common as white flames, their stories spread much further."

"But why angel flame?" Corilai asked.

"Because they are seen as the opposite of the demon flame. The demon flame is raw, powerful, uncontrolled. The white flames are usually seen as weak, which is not actually true, by the way. White flames are pure. They harvest the energy of all colours, and filter it. They purify it. And then they release it. The flame has great power, even in a minuscule state. Less flashy. White flames tend not to be show-offs, but they are certainly among the most powerful of flame wielders, if ever they can learn to produce their flames in a usable fashion. But this is why they are called angelic. They are quiet and their flames are pure."

"So that's why I can use your flames!" Treghan exclaimed.

"You can use her flames?" Barache asked.

"Yes! Here, I'll show you. Corilai, start your flames for me."

Corilai did as he asked, a burst of raw, uncontrolled black flame filling the room for a moment, before Treghan grabbed her hand, and used her energy to produce a long spear of blinding white flame. Corilai stopped her flames, smiling in pride at her new found control, and the white flame dwindled. Barache looked at them both, his eyes wide.

"That's most impressive, young ones. You discovered this by yourselves?"

"Yes, Sir," Treghan said. "I had never produced more than a spark, until we figured out this technique."

"And I had never controlled my flames until he took away the excess energy using this technique," Corilai added.

"This is verry Interesting," Barache said. "So individually, you were both incompetent as wielders, but with each other, you both become powerful. I would say more powerful by orders of magnitude, than you would normally be. You are to be commended for this self discovery, and I will recommend you to the academy without hesitation. Though once the Chancellor witnesses your combined abilities, that recommendation would not be needed."

"Thank you, Sir!" the youngsters said in unison.

"Now then, you are running. What from?"

"The bandits of Grey, we kind of ruined their fancy new machine before we ran from them."

Barache laughed.

"I think I like you two," he said. "I am sure that got those bastards a bit wound up. I've been watching their activities, as closely as I can. But I can't say I know exactly what they are up to."

"They're building an army, and are bent on conquest," Treghan said with scorn. "We ruined a machine they were using to create power to smelt ore without using coal."

"Without coal?" Barache said, raising an eyebrow. "Oh! I see. That's why they're rounding up flame wielders, is it?"

"Yes Sir," Corilai said. "They want to produce armour and weapons at a rapid rate, and they were finding it hard to supply enough coal, so they have these machines that create lightning..."

"Electricity," Barache interrupted. "I am aware of the theory behind it. But I was unaware of their progress in actually creating the machines. You must get all this information to the academy as quick as you can. I will send a bird with news of your coming, and a brief overview."

"A bird?" Corilai asked.

"I keep homing pigeons, and I use them to report to the Chancellor when something of import occurs to the south."

"Oh," Treghan said. "Is that how you knew about us?"

"No, son," Barache replied. "I am a yellow flame wielder."

"I don't know what that means," Treghan admitted.

"Son, a yellow flame is subtle, and can seek out information without burning. It can reach quite a distance, when trained properly. Our scouts, who assess potential recruits, are often yellow flames, because they are best suited to investigating the nature of young flame wielders without doing harm or letting those around them see what they are doing. That is how I knew a demon and an angel were passing my home."

"Wow, I really don't know a lot," Treghan said.

"You have many years in which to learn, lad," Barache said. "Now then, you both should freshen up, and get a good night's rest, before you continue. Do not worry, the bandits are not close, and when they do get here, I can hold them off for a while."

"What if they hurt you?" Corilai said.

"They can't touch me, young one. Do not fear. This old man has a few tricks. But to the bath with you, young ones. Through that door, you will find the bath, and a spigot to fill it from the tank outside. Use your flames to warm the water. When you have washed yourselves, wash your clothes as well. If they have dogs to track you, you'll be putting out a mighty scent by now. Take turns, one in there, one out here to help me get the evening meal ready."

They did as he suggested, and enjoyed a hearty stew of mutton, garden vegetables, and potatoes. It was the first real meal either had enjoyed in some time, and they left no seconds. He then directed them to set up their bedrolls in front of the warm fireplace, and retired for the evening into his bedroom.

Treghan and Corilai slept soundly, both asleep long before the old man, who wrote out in as much detail as he could the information they had given him, onto a tape he wound onto a pigeon's leg. It was a brief summary, but it would be enough. He wrote a second brief note, and wound it on the other leg, marking it with a green ink.

"Angel and demon, travel together, fleeing the bandits of Grey. Please find them fleeing, the forest from mine, they will be heading your way."

After he released the bird, Barache poured himself a small glass of whiskey, and sat sipping it. He watched through his window, as a gentle rain fell outside.

* * *

Dismayed at the lack of results searching for the two brats, Yuri led his men north along the road out of Grey. He was accompanied by a dozen strong men, and four of his best flame wielders.

"I'll catch those two mongrels myself," he kept muttering under his breath as they rode.

Finally, they saw something. Two palomino horses, by the side of the road. They had clearly run hard. Yuri signalled one of the men to check the beasts. Rushing ahead, one of the men dismounted, and approached the pair.

Walking slowly, and being careful not to spook the horses, the man worked his way around until he could see their left hand rear legs. There, on the thigh of the animals, was the distinctive branding. He returned to his horse, and mounted, riding back to Yuri.

"They're definitely ours, Sir," the bandit said. "They've been running hard, and have left a clear trail through the forest."

"Good," Yuri replied. "They must have been spooked by something and ran. Those blasted kids are done for now. Their misfortune is our gain. We follow the trail, once we find where the horses bolted from, we should be able to catch the kids before long."

"Yes, Sir," the bandit said.

"Wait, I have another idea. You ride ahead on this road. Eventually you should reach the village of Judd. Once you're there, go to the Tavern. Our man Harv is running things in that area, and he has a flame wielder too. Get him to march south through the forest. Those two can't escape us if we come at them from both sides."

"Yes, Sir!" the man replied, then turned and rode his horse at speed, soon disappearing into the distance as Yuri led his men into the forest.

* * *

Symin waited two days for some of his men to return from a trip to the north. He was annoyed by the delay, but he used the time planning, and asking questions of any who had been south recently. Finally, on the third day, he led his men south along the highway. They rode hard, until he saw the bay in the distance, where they would turn inland toward the village of Judd. Beyond Judd, in the hills, rested the town of Oaklands, where he had grown up. Symin smiled, reminiscing.

"I'll stop there, when this is over, for a visit," he promised. "But we don't have the time right now."

"Sir!" came a cry from behind. "We have a messenger approaching."

Symin raised his arm, indicating for the convoy of troops to halt, and turned to watch the messenger approach. After a long while, the man finally reached him, and passed Symin an envelope, before turning and riding back the way he had come.

Curious, Symin hurriedly opened the message, and read what the Chancellor had sent that was so urgent. He raised an eyebrow in surprise, then looked up to address his men.

"OK troops, change of plan. We will continue to Judd, and from there we will search the forest to the south. This just became a possible rescue mission. We're looking for an angel and a demon. But we aren't the only ones. Be sharp, you may well be facing great danger in coming days. Be ready for it."

"Yes, Sir," the men shouted in unison.

Satisfied, Symin turned his horse back to the road and trotted onwards, certain that this mission was going to be more interesting than he had first believed.

*   *   *

Harv rushed around, waking his men and shouting orders. Fletcher yawned as he walked into the front bar of the tavern, where a man sat nursing an ale, clearly tired from a long ride. He looked outside, where the man's horse stood, drinking. The horse was coated in froth around the chest and flanks, where the saddle and chest plate were rubbing. It shook briefly, then went back to drinking.

"That horse has been running hard," Fletcher said.

"Yes, boy," Harv said from behind him. "Now make sure you're ready to move out. We have a task at hand, and it will need your skills."

"Yes, Sir," Fletcher said.

The boy wished he didn't have to be involved, knowing that whatever it was, Harv would have him doing things that were wrong. Fletcher regretted his situation, and hoped that something would happen soon to change things.

He walked back inside and up to his small room. Gathering his things, which were sparse since he left his father's house, he packed them all into a satchel and slung it over his shoulder. Fletcher shook his head. So few possessions, after being the spoiled child for so long.

Perhaps this was what it had been like for Treghan. No. Fletcher shook his head. He couldn't fool himself any more. Treghan had things far worse than this. Treghan was beaten, and was never fed properly.

"I'm sorry, Brother," Fletcher whispered as he walked to the door. "I realise now what a fool I was, what a prideful idiot. But in the end, we're all just slaves to the bandits in Judd. Perhaps running was the best thing for you after all. Where ever you wound up has to be better than this dump."

The door burst open, and Harv was there.

"Quit your moping and get outside, boy! We're leaving. Now!"

"Yes, Sir," Fletcher said, walking out of the room and making his way outside, where he found Harv's entire group gathered, anxious and awaiting instructions.

"Right! Men, we have a mission from Grey. Yuri himself has requested our assistance, and we all know what that means. This task is an important one. There are two young flame wielders coming our way."

There were murmurs among the men. Some of them had only arrived in Judd recently, with the boat that came looking for possible flame wielder recruits.

"They are travelling through the forest," Harv continued. "Trying to avoid capture. They did a lot of damage to Yuri's machinery, and we are to catch them. We may beat them if necessary. He wants them alive, he doesn't care how healthy."

There was more murmuring. The recent arrivals knew well what the machinery that was damaged would be, and what it would mean if it was lost. They knew Yuri would pay handsomely for the men who captured the vandals.

"Are we ready, men?"

Harv's men cheered, and began to head out into the trees, forming a long line, so as to cover as much of the forest as they could. They were determined. Nobody was going to get past them.

"Boy!" Harv shouted. "You come with me. We are to be front and centre. I want you ready to light up those trees the instant we find them."

"Yes, Sir," Fletcher said, relieved there would hopefully be no killing on this trip.

Chapter 10 – The Chase

Treghan awoke to a bright sunrise and a clear sky. In good cheer, he gently rocked Corilai's shoulder, waking her.

"We should get going," he said.

"Yes," she replied. "What about Barache? Should we wake him up?"

"I don't think we need to," Treghan said. "He knows we have to run."

"Yes, I do know that," Barache said from his bedroom door. "But you should at least wait for a light breakfast and some tea. You can't run well on an empty stomach."

"OK then," Treghan said.

"You didn't take much convincing," Corilai quipped.

Barache went to his small kitchen, and prepared a simple breakfast of eggs, toasted bread with butter, and sausages. He also boiled a pot of water, then added a handful of green tea leaves to the water, and left it to brew while he served up three plates of food.

The three flame wielders sat and ate in silence, content and rested. Barache poured the tea, and they sipped the warming liquid in a happy mood. Barache enjoyed the chance for human company and the two youngsters enjoyed a chance for some civilised time with a new friend.

All too soon, they knew they had to leave. With a promise to return one day, Treghan and Corilai waved their fairwell to Barache, as they left his little clearing and made their way north once more.

The forest was thick, but they found a clear trail through, which Barache, or some other nearby resident, had maintained well. They hiked through the morning, and at mid afternoon, they paused for a rest.

"How far do you suppose we still have to go?" Corilai asked.

"It's hard to say. We were in that ship for days, but we don't know what the speed was like. Did they have a good headwind?"

"I know that trip was rough," Corilai replied.

"Regardless," Treghan said. "I've never been far to the south from Judd, so nothing here is familiar."

"My village was closer to the coast," Corilai said. "And I never really came inland all that much either. We really should have asked Barache about that. I think he sort of assumed we knew where we were going."

"Or perhaps he knew it was a long way and didn't want us giving up when we found out," Treghan said.

"Maybe you're right."

"But we made a good distance the first couple of days, with the horses," Treghan said.

"I wish we still had them," Corilai said.

"Well, we don't, and we probably have a long walk ahead. So we may as well make good use of the time," Treghan said, grabbing her hand and holding it tightly.

Corilai blushed a deep scarlet at the unexpected contact, but she did not complain. Instead, she looked at him. His white hair was stunningly bright with the morning sun, after his bath the night before. The breeze tousled it gently, and she smiled.

"You must have been teased for your hair as a child," she said.

"A little," he replied, surprised by the question. "Yours is so dark, but even then, it's not unusual to see black hair among people who don't have the talent for fire."

"Yes, that's true," she said. "Shall I start a flame?"

"Yes please," Treghan replied.

Holding her other hand out before her, Corilai focussed her energy and an immense burst of darkness flooded out of her, writhing and licking at the trees around them.

"It's not as wild as before," Treghan said, remembering the time at the smelter.

Treghan held his hand out in a similar fashion, and drew on her excess energy. Instantly, her flame subsided, growing tame and controlled. She held it there, a dark pillar of black before her, towering almost to the high forest canopy above.

He focussed the energy, streaming into him from her, and felt that there was a mix of energies now. It seemed that some of it was hers, and some was his. The balance was far from equal, but a small amount of the energy, he knew immediately, was his own.

"It feels like doing this is awakening my own energy as well as allowing me to use yours," he said.

"That's great," she said. "That must be why you were able to flame a little on your own when we met those wolves."

"Yeah. I mean, obviously I'll always be stronger with you, but if I can flame on my own, I'll never be helpless again. I won't be worthless any more."

She looked at him, shocked by his words.

"Treghan," she said softly. "You have never been worthless. At least, not to me."

"Thank you, Corilai," he said, pausing for a moment to look at her. "I'm so glad we met. Just think what we might be able to do in the future, now that we're learning to control our flames?"

Looking back at his hand, he took the reserve of energy he had been building, and pushed a small amount of it out through his upturned palm, creating a blinding white fire that reached upwards, equal to hers.

"It's beautiful," she said.

Facing him, she looked at his face, illuminated by his fire, the bright light casting their shadows long into the trees. She smiled, and turned her body towards him, bringing her other hand closer.

"What is it?" He said, looking to face her.

He stared at her pretty face, the white light and dark shadow complimentary to her features. He blushed, as he turned his body to face her, carried away in the moment. His hand moved closer to hers, and the flames almost touched.

Then, without warning, the flames jumped together and connected, calling forth an immense burst of unbidden energy from both of them. There was an intense explosion, and they were thrown apart.

The rapidly consumed energy left the air crackling with the dying fires they had ignited. Far above them, smoke billowed from the canopy where they had briefly ignited it. The birds above screeched and scattered, large amounts of charred leaves and twigs falling to the ground.

Treghan slammed into a tree, knocking his head. He sat up, feeling dizzy, and reached up to find his hair, washed last night, sticky with his own blood. Through blurred eyes, he looked for Corilai. She was slumped on the ground in front of a boulder, several meters away.

“Corilai!” he shouted.

Jumping up, he nearly fell as a wave of dizziness swept through him. Struggling to stay on his feet, Treghan stumbled to her side, and knelt beside her. He touched her neck, feeling her pulse, then breathed a heavy sigh of relief. Passing his hand above her mouth, he felt her softly exhaled breath.

“Thank god,” he whispered. “I thought I might have lost you.”

“What was that?” She said, groggily opening her eyes as she blushed again, certain she had heard his words correctly.

Looking at him, she saw the blood, running freely through his hair and onto his shoulder.

“That looks bad,” she said. “We should get you cleaned up. I hope it's better than it looks.”

“I'm sure it's not that bad,” he said, though it felt worse than he was willing to admit. “Remember what I told you? Head wounds always bleed a lot.”

“I know, but that's messed up your hair. It was so nice and clean before.”

“My hair?” he said, laughing at her. “I don't think that's the worst of our worries, Corilai.”

“I know, it's just that...” she paused, looking around. “Never mind. We should keep walking, maybe there's a stream or something nearby.”

She stood, wobbled for a moment as her head span a little, then helped him up.

“We must look a riot,” she said.

“A pathetic, sickly riot,” he replied.

Slowly, they began to make their way north again, neither suggesting any more flame practice for the rest of the day. At mid afternoon, they found a shallow stream crossing the path, and to one side, it formed a tranquil pool, before continuing off into the trees.

Treghan removed his shirt, and dove in, then Corilai helped him to carefully clean the blood from his hair. A small clump of his hair came away with the blood, revealing a shallow wound in his scalp. The wound was already beginning to scab over, but the washing released the scab and it began to bleed afresh.

“Wait here,” Corilai said, then disappeared into the trees.

She returned a short time later with a handful of leaves, which she dropped onto a rock near the edge of the pond. Finding a smaller stone, she began pounding and grinding the leaves. Adding water, she mashed them into a lumpy paste, then scooped it up with her hand.

"This is a poultice my mother taught me. It will stop the bleeding."

Carefully, she washed away the fresh blood, then applied the gooey stuff to his scalp, making sure to cover the entire wound.

"Thank you, Corilai," he said. "So, you coming in or not? The water's wonderful!"

She blushed deeply, and turned away.

"I have nothing suitable to swim in, and I'm not about to skinny dip right now. Besides, we have to keep moving."

"You're right," he said, climbing out of the water, and slipping his shirt on.

They returned to the trail, and continued northwards. As the sun began to set, the forest long since dark beneath the canopy, they still walked. Eventually the moon rose above them, casting its wan light between the leaves.

Owls hooted and wolves howled in the darkness, sending shivers down both their spines. An icy breeze blew down from the hills, rustling through the trees to chill the youngsters to the bone.

"We should stop for the night," Corilai said.

"We should," Treghan agreed. "But we should find a suitable spot to camp. Something sheltered from that wind. I don't think it safe to light a fire with all this foliage around, waiting to burn."

"You're right," she said. "Maybe there'll be something up ahead."

They continued walking, both beginning to tire badly. After nearly another hour of walking, the trail rounded a bend, to pass along the edge of a sudden drop. The ground swept down into the darkness, and as if plotting to stop them, clouds at that moment swept in to cover the moon, making vision along the trail impossible.

Treghan dropped to his hands and knees and felt his way along the trail, narrowly avoiding a deadly fall as he did so.

"Treghan," Corilai said. "This is too dangerous. We need to stop."

"I know, Corilai," he replied. "Please, we can make it. Just a little further. There has to be something along here."

His words proved prophetic, and a few meters further along they encountered a massive stone structure, crumbling and ancient, standing to the side of the trail. Its haunting facade gazed out over the edge of the cliff, giving its long lost occupants a clear view far into the distance.

Treghan found an entry into the building, its stout wooden door long since rotted away, and entered. It was dark, a little damp, and unoccupied. It featured a main hall, and several smaller chambers on either side.

The roof was gone, leaving it open to the sky, but the walls sheltered them from the wind. At one end of the hall, stood an altar, raised on a stone platform, and covered by a single immense stone archway, the only section of the ruin which remained under cover.

Treghan took Corilai's hand and led her to the platform, helping her up. Laying out their bedrolls beside each other, they climbed in and were soon fast asleep.

*   *   *

Barache hiked south from his cabin, following the same route Treghan and Corilai had followed the day before. Carefully, he did what he could to conceal their passing as he went, always aware the bandits could be approaching from the opposite direction. After some time, he found himself ascending into the rocky hills, the trees growing sparse.

Barache thought for a moment, then decided his chances of obscuring their trail through this region was slim, so he focussed his energy and set a blaze flooding out across the landscape, burning all the grasses and twigs, whose bent and broken remains might tell a searching tracker of their passage.

Walking forward, he ignored the flames as the grasses burned, stretching his flame far into the distance. Soon, the hills were ablaze with the glory of his power, and he smiled.

"If that doesn't confuse the bandits following their trail, nothing will," he said with satisfaction.

Leaving the fire to burn itself out, just as the clouds began to threaten with the afternoon rain fall the hills endured on a regular basis, Barache returned home, satisfied that he had bought his new friends some time.

From his home, he wandered into the trees, and made his way a good distance towards the road, being sure to leave broken branches and other evidence of his passing, before going home comfortable that things were adequately prepared.

*   *   *

Yuri rushed inland, following his tracker, as they traced the path taken by the fleeing horses. He was surprised how far from the road they were going, but he trusted his tracker, and his instinct said they would soon be on the trail of the little vandals.

Then, he smelled smoke, and he began to worry. They pushed on and after a long while, the trees began to thin out as they began to climb into the hills. The tracker stopped. Spreading out before them, and stretching as far as they could see in all directions, was a blackened, burned wasteland.

"Damn it," Yuri shouted, looking around and noticing a few straggling yellow flames. "They've had help. They must have. When I find out who did this, they'll burn like the hills they torched! Nobody comes between me and what I hunt. Nobody!"

They stood there as the rest of the men caught up, then Yuri called them together. He surveyed his men, his disappointment painted on his face.

"We go north. We don't know where they went in the hills, but we know they have to be headed north. There's nothing else in the hills for them but hiding places, and without supplies they'd starve in no time, so they have to be going north."

"Yes, Sir!" the men shouted in unison.

Marching into the forest, they trampled everything in their path, no longer taking care to follow a trail which had now gone cold. As the day grew old, they made slow but steady progress, and continued on into the night. Finally, they camped among the trees, and waited for sunrise.

At first light, they continued, and soon found a worn trail through the trees. Making use of it, they were able to make better speed, riding hard in the firm conviction that they were on the trail of the youngsters again, knowing they had to catch them soon.

Around mid morning, the men found themselves in a clearing, a small cottage to one side, and an old man digging a small patch of furrows, harvesting root vegetables as he worked.

"You there," shouted Yuri. "Who are you?"

Barache looked up at the man on the horse, and taking up a cane, hobbled over to him. Looking up at the strong man in the rich looking clothes, Barache smiled.

"I'd be guessin' you boys are up from the city then?" Barache said, slurring his words.

"I asked you a question, old fool," Yuri snapped.

"I'm nobody of consequence. Just an old peasant, minding his own in the forest. My wife left me for heaven some ten years past, and so I live here alone."

Yuri signalled two of the men to enter the cottage. They did so, and immediately could be heard smashing things around as they searched for any sign of the youngsters. Barache stared at the cottage, a forlorn expression on his face as he looked back to Yuri.

"Please, good Sir," Barache implored. "What is it your men seek? I have little of value, and live a simple life."

"Old man, have you seen a pair of youngsters come by here?"

Barache raised his eyebrows. And gasped.

"Why, of course, Yes, yes good sir. It was yesterday, in the mid afternoon I think it would have been. But there were three of them, two youngsters, and one a man, probably in his twenties, they walked out of the forest, the three of them on foot, the man leading a horse."

"Where did they go, old man?" Yuri asked.

"Oh, they asked if I had seen two horses, which I hadn't, and then which way to the road. I pointed them east, and they left, through the trees, though there is no real path. And it's a long hike through rough terrain. I shouted that they would be better taking the trail north, which is maintained by the men from the town two or three days ride along there, but they didn't listen, not even so much as a thank you, they just wandered off into the east."

"Tracker!" Yuri shouted. "Find the trail."

"Yes, Sir!" the tracker replied, and ran over to the trees, scouting along the perimeter of the clearing.

After a few minutes, the man shouted.

"Sir! They went through here."

At that moment, the two men returned from the cottage, and approached Yuri.

"Anything?" Yuri demanded.

"No Sir, no evidence of the brats in there, just an old fart with nothing of value at all."

"OK then," Yuri said, turning to face Barache again. "You're lucky, old fool. Had you sheltered them, I would have killed you on the spot. Remember that if you see them again."

Barache nodded, adding a little tremble to the act. Yuri smiled at the power he felt in that moment, then turned his horse and trotted to the tracker.

"Lead the way," Yuri commanded.

Barache stood and watched as the men wandered into the trees, and stayed there until he was sure the last of them was well out of earshot. Then, stooping down, he began to dig.

Shortly, he had uncovered a heavy steel crate, which he opened without removing it from the ground, and took out his ranger's cloak, along with several other artefacts that may have revealed his true identity during the search. Smiling, he kicked the crate closed, shoved the dirt back over it, and carried his things inside.

"Bloody fools," Barache said with a laugh. "Works every time."

Chapter 11 – Before the Storm

Corilai woke early, as the sunrise broke over the distant ocean. Walking out of the ruin, she stood on the trail at the edge of the cliff, and stared out over the valley below. Some distance away, she could see the road, winding its way north as it went around jagged rocks, and sought the narrowest points on multiple streams that ran down from the hills.

Looking north, she could see that the trail ran down an incline for several kilometres, until it met the floor of the valley, and then continued northwards, until it disappeared into the canopy of the dense growing rainforest. For the first time, she wondered about this country, and how it could go from glaciers to rainforest in such a short distance. Lacking any answer, she pushed it out of her mind.

There was no telling what dangers awaited them beneath that thick screen of foliage. Corilai knew they must face them, if they were ever to reach their goal. Looking out towards the ocean, Corilai realised that the next hill over, after the one opposite, was the same hill her home village rested on, albeit on the far side from her current location. She recognised, tiny in the distance, the bays she had travelled along when she first left her home.

Looking towards the north, she could barely make out the gaps in the trees where the road crossed the hills on its way east to the shore.

“Treghan's village must be somewhere up there,” she mumbled.

“Yeah, I think it is,” Treghan said, making her jump as she had not heard him approach. “Where's yours?”

“Straight to the east from here, on the other side of the second hill. Probably another days hike at least.”

“Well, we won't be going there. It looks like about two days walk to Judd, my home village, and from there we can follow the road east and then north, all the way to Emberdale.”

“And then, the Ranger Academy,” she said, awestruck. “It almost feels like we're going to make it, doesn't it?”

“Yes, but anything could happen still,” Treghan replied.

“I guess so. I hope Barache is OK.”

“He'll be fine. I'm sure he's done plenty to protect himself, and probably held up the bandits from Grey as well.”

“I hope so,” she said, turning and walking back into the ruin.

Carefully, they packed their gear, and carried it back to the trail. In silent agreement, they continued their long journey north, following the well worn trail down into the valley.

Even with such a good trail to follow, the going was slow on foot. Yet again, the youngsters both lamented the loss of their horses. They soon became tired, and hungry, as they made their way under the forest canopy.

Out of the direct sun, it was cool, which was a refreshing change after the morning hiking down the edge of the cliff, and they paused for a brief rest. Treghan sat beside the trail, and looked around in the leaf litter.

Before long, he found what he was looking for. Mushrooms, in great quantity, were thriving in the damp undergrowth. He plucked one, and turned it over.

"Corilai, these are edible mushrooms," he said.

"Are you sure?" she asked.

In answer, he took a bite out of one, and chewed. Grimacing at the bland flavour, he took a second bite, chewing and then swallowing the morsel.

"Yeah," he said finally. "You can tell by the gills underneath. See, when they are like this, it means a mushroom you can eat. But any other way, and they are some kind of toadstool or poisonous fungous. These ones are fine. A bit bland eaten raw, but safe, and nutritious."

"OK then," she said, taking one of the mushrooms, checking the underside, then eating it. "I really hope you're right about these things."

"Well, there are some deadly mushrooms that look very much like edible ones, so I wouldn't advise just grabbing them, but I'm sure these ones are fine. There are a few tiny differences, if you know what you're looking for. Most average people wouldn't be able to tell the difference."

"How did you learn?" she asked.

"When I lived at home, and I would often miss out on food because they thought I was worthless, I would go out the back and in the trees near the house there were a lot of different mushrooms growing. I asked the local medicine woman about them, and she taught me how to tell the difference. I basically lived on the things sometimes for weeks at a time. There were a few varieties growing there. I ate the wrong one once, but it wasn't a deadly one. Made me awful sick though."

"Even if they were only the good ones, it doesn't sound like a very good diet," Corilai said.

"It was better than starving to death."

"And once again," Corilai said with a smile. "You prove yourself not to be worthless. If you weren't clever with mushrooms, we'd still be hungry."

"I'll be right back," Treghan said, disappearing into the trees.

Shortly, he returned with two large tuber shaped fruits. Handing one to her, he cracked the other one open on a tree, quickly holding it upright so its watery contents did not run out.

"These are a type of melon, which seem to often grow in the same conditions as mushrooms. They form a ground cover, and hold a lot of moisture. They're a great source of water if you can't find a stream. I used to eat these a lot as well."

"You really do know about this stuff, don't you?" Corilai said, amazed.

"I had to."

Smiling at him, she struck the tree with her melon and sucked at the sweet juices that flowed from it. After a long drink, she looked at him.

"How could you ever have felt worthless?"

"Let's get going. We can finish these while we walk," Treghan said, blushing as he tried to ignore the compliment.

Holding the melon in her left hand, Corilai snaked the fingers of her right hand gently into his left. Blushing softly, she stole a glance at him, pleased to see the admiring look on his face as he stared at her.

This closeness was something she had never thought she would find, especially after she was run out of her home, but here he was, accepting her and watching over her.

Friendships like the one she felt with Treghan should always be nurtured, Corilai thought, happier than she had been for a long time. She thought she felt his hand squeeze hers in a gentle encouragement, as he tossed away his melon and held his hand out before them, lighting a small white flame to guide their way through the darkness of the rainforest.

* * *

Fletcher was sore and exhausted, seated on a horse behind Harv, who would not allow him any chance to escape. They had ridden all night, but so far had found no sign of their quarry. Entering a small clearing where an ancient tree had fallen, rending an immense gap in the forest canopy to let the sunlight in, Harv raised an arm high over his head.

"Fall in, men," Harv shouted. "We rest here for a short while."

Dismounting, Harv strode towards one of the other men, and began speaking softly to him. Fletcher could not hear what they were saying, but he assumed it was about their progress. Climbing down from the horse, Fletcher found a spot on the grass, against the fallen tree, and sat there, closing his eyes to snatch some rest.

"Boy!" Harv shouted. "Light us a fire, quickly now. The men would like some tea, and the damp of the night needs to be baked from their bones."

Standing, Fletcher scouted around for some twigs and smaller branches, scooping them into a pile. Carefully, he scraped the leaf litter and other combustibles from the ground, leaving a wide band of bare earth between his makeshift fire and anything that could catch and get out of control. Satisfied, he focussed his energy, and ignited the kindling with his red flames.

Once the fire was burning on its own, he started looking around for some bigger branches, and heaped them on top of the kindling. Before long, it was a roaring fire, casting its heat throughout the clearing. Harv approached, followed by a man carrying a heavy bundle.

"Good work, boy," Harv said as the other man began to set up his equipment to prepare hot tea and some basic breakfast for the men.

Another man approached, as Fletcher sat with his back to the fallen tree again. Harv ignored Fletcher, his usefulness over for the moment, and turned to speak with the newcomer.

"How do we proceed from here?" Harv asked.

"Well," the man replied. "We have in front of us dense rainforest. From here on, it gets much thicker than it has been. We may not be able to spread out like we have been doing, but then, the thickness of the forest will limit where the runaways can travel as well."

"So what options do they have?" Harv asked.

"There are three trails through the rainforest, all within earshot of one another, and of course the road, which is to the east of us. I suggest we split into four smaller groups, and travel in unison along the four routes, passing shouts of the status of our search at five minute intervals."

"Agreed," Harv replied. "And should anybody see the runaways, they shout immediately of the sighting, and all others push through the forest as fast as they can to help secure the enemy."

"I will inform the men, and assign the groups, Sir," the man said.

"Very good," Harv replied. "Tell them they have thirty minutes before we leave."

"Yes, Sir," the man replied, and walked away.

Harv looked around, then spotted Fletcher. Walking over, he sat next to him. Fletcher looked at him, unsure what he might want with him.

"Are you ready for this, boy?" Harv asked. "You may need to act fast, think on your feet. If these flame wielders are as good as you, or better, you'll have your work cut out for you keeping them held up while the men get in closer with the nets."

"I, I think so, Sir," Fletcher said.

"Good, we will be relying on you," Harv said, showing an unusual amount of respect for the youngster.

"I'll burn the entire forest if I have to, to stop them escaping."

"Good to hear," Harv said. "But be mindful you don't burn my men while you're at it."

"I will do my very best, Sir," Fletcher promised.

Harv stood and left him there, Fletcher confused by the man's change of attitude. Was this how he acted when he wanted something? Or was Harv genuinely warming to him? Fletcher wasn't sure, and decided it best not to make any assumptions. The man was not to be trusted, and Fletcher was still determined to be freed from this bondage.

As soon as he found a way to escape without putting his mother in danger, Fletcher promised himself, he would take whatever chance was necessary to achieve that goal.

* * *

Symin led his men through Judd and into the forest, heading south. They rode hard and fast, but even so he did not miss the signs as they entered the trees. A large force had recently travelled this same way. There were broken twigs, flattened grass, and well trampled sod all around them. It was a force at least equal in size to his own, and they were riding south. Probably in pursuit of the same people he was hoping to find.

"Men," Symin shouted. "Be alert. We will have company soon, and I would hazard a guess they will not be friendly."

* * *

Treghan and Corilai walked in happy silence, the trail ahead lit by his flame, the trail behind left in darkness. They were making easy progress now, in spite of the narrowness of the trail.

"It's like we aren't even being followed," Treghan said. "I would have thought that on horse back, they would have at least made some sign of their presence by now."

"I know. I'm a little worried about them, but it feels as if we have left them far behind. I hope Barache is OK."

"He's fine. He probably delayed them, sent them east instead of north, or maybe told them we ran into the hills or something."

"I hope you're right," she said.

He smiled his reassurance, and the pair continued on their way. The afternoon was passing them by, but so was the distance, which gave them confidence in spite of their tiredness.

"This time tomorrow, we'll probably reach Judd," Treghan said. "We should avoid going into the village, but in my mind, that feels like a major milestone in our journey."

"Yes," Corilai replied. "But at the same time, it's as though you will have done all this journeying, only to wind up back where you started."

"In location, yes, but in skills and knowledge, we are both already far beyond the place where we began," he said, trying to encourage her.

"That's true," she said.

"I know we were saying we felt safe, like we weren't being followed, but we should try to cover a bit of extra ground this evening," Treghan said. "I have a feeling we may need to."

"OK," Corilai said.

They walked for another few hours, the trail winding through the forest, until they crested a rise, and it stretched out before them, running in a long, straight line, down hill and onwards. The trail did not turn again for many kilometres, affording a long view into the distance, though the lack of light beneath the canopy made vision in those far off places hard even with the guidance of Treghan's fire.

"Lets run for a bit, it's a good downhill run," Corilai suggested.

"OK," Treghan said, dropping her hand. His flame wavered a moment, then he managed to stabilise it again.

"Treghan, you're getting so much better at it!"

"Thanks, Corilai," he said. "Last one to the bottom sneaks into Judd for food!"

Laughing, she ran after him as he bolted, the pair of them in good spirits as they rapidly closed the distance to the bottom of the slope.

* * *

Fletcher watched around Harv's broad shoulders as they trotted through the forest. The trail wound around like a giant snake through the thick undergrowth, until suddenly it crested a low hill and spread out before them, a long, straight and well kept track stretching off into the distance.

The gloom of the forest concealed much of what lay before them, but then, like a bolt of lightning, they saw it. A bright pinpoint of white light was advancing on them, rushing along the trail and closing the distance. It was them.

"Boy, get down, quickly now!" Harv shouted.

Fletcher did as he was told, then moved around to walk a few paces in front of the horse.

"Men, Fall in! Prey sighted. I repeat, prey sighted! All men to my side, now!"

Harv had a broad grin as the men rushed through the thick forest, crowding outwards on both sides of the trail. They settled in and waited, watching as the two they hunted approached from the distance, oblivious to the attack that awaited them.

"Finally," Harv murmured smugly. "We can round up these two, and Yuri will recognise my service with a comfortable post in Grey."

Chapter 12 – Confrontation

Treghan and Corilai walked down the hill, carefree and happy with each other's company. They reached the bottom, and continued without pause, Treghan's light guiding them.

Suddenly, red flames rushed down the edge of the trail, penning them in on both sides. They looked ahead, and saw two figures in the darkness, one smaller than the other.

"A flame wielder!" Corilai exclaimed.

"Who are you? What do you want?" Treghan shouted.

"We want you," shouted the larger of the two figures. "Preferably alive, though Yuri doesn't care how healthy you are when we turn you over to him. How badly you're hurt depends on how well you behave."

"We won't let you catch us!" Treghan shouted.

Giving Corilai's hand a squeeze, Treghan pushed out his flame, lighting the trail ahead clearly. In immediate response, Corilai pushed out her own flame, hoping to ensure he had enough energy. The smaller figure held his arms out high to his sides, and cast red flames in response, increasing the danger to the sides as the foliage ignited.

"Fletcher?" Treghan said, recognising his twin. "What the hell are you doing with these guys? Are you mad?"

"Shut up Treghan," Fletcher shouted back. "I don't want to hurt you. But if you don't cooperate, these guys won't hesitate."

"But why?" Treghan shouted. "Yuri's a lunatic. A madman, who will destroy this entire country."

"Ha!" Harv barked. "You young fool, you don't understand, do you?"

"Shut up you fat idiot," Treghan taunted, shooting a blinding flash at the man. "I'm trying to talk to my brother."

"I don't care, you aren't getting away from us, and regardless of how we treat you, Yuri will surely punish you for your crimes against him. Men, Close in!"

Treghan looked around, and realised the forest was alive with men on horses. They had circled around, and now closed in behind them. He panicked, and flared his white flames into the trees. Corilai groaned, surprised by her energy being drawn so strongly.

In the trees, where his flame had shot, a man shouted, and a horse screamed. Where the white flame had passed, the red flames were extinguished, all the oxygen having been sucked out of the air.

"You see, Fletcher," Treghan shouted, improvising his argument. "We can pass your flames without a problem! Stand down, these fools don't deserve you working for them!"

"Shut up, shut up, shut up!" Fletcher screamed back. "Stop talking like you know everything! You ran away, you coward, and now you have the gall to lecture me?"

"Silence, boy," Harv snapped at Fletcher. "No need to provoke them, you've done your part in springing the trap."

Harv turned to the trees, and drew a long, wicked blade from the bag on his horse. He strode forward, closing the distance between them by great strides as he shouted.

"You two are hereby under arrest, in the name of Yuri, ruler of the people of Grey, and commander of the bandit forces of the south. Do not resist, and perhaps you will live. Don't you get it? The great nation of Cinder is a rabble. Each village and town has its own chief, everything is a squabble between neighbours. Under Yuri's plan, we will rise again as a great nation, renewed, under a single leader. Yuri will rule the entire nation of Cinder, and his armies will march across the land, taking control from those bickering hoards. Too long, the rabble rangers from Emberdale's academy have run around as a mercenary force, dictating how we should live."

He paused, turned in full circle, the sword raised, eliciting a cheer from the men, many still hidden in the forest.

"Am I right, men?"

A roar from the darkness was their excited reply. Harv faced Treghan and Corilai again, levelling the sword at them, now only a few strides away.

"Yuri will lead us to victory," Harv shouted. "The reign of fire is coming to an end. We will rule over this land, with steel!"

Harv took a mighty stride towards the two fugitives, malice in his eyes, and in his heart.

"No!" screamed Treghan, firing a mighty burst of blinding white fire into the man's chest.

Harv jumped back, lucky for his reflexes, his hair smouldering, his clothing torched and billowing smoke.

"You bastard!" Harv shouted, and rushed at them.

This time, it was black fire that engulfed him. Corilai did not hold back, pushing as much energy into that flame as she could. Harv's screams as he fled back to the trees quickly died out as he ran, pouring water from his canteen over his face.

Treghan fired a bolt of white towards him, while Corilai played her black flame over the trees on the opposite side of the trail, killing the last of Fletcher's red fire. With a mighty boom, one of the tall, ancient trees cracked, then fell, across the place where Fletcher had been standing.

"Fletcher!" Treghan shouted, stopping his flames in shock and plunging the area into sudden darkness, before he lit a small white beacon.

It seemed the world had changed greatly in that moment of darkness. Treghan took a few hurried steps forward, filled with concern for his twin, but he was stopped in his tracks by Corilai's sudden scream. He turned to face her, his panic rising as he realised he had left her, and the bandits now had her surrounded, their swords pointed at her heart.

One of them leaned forward, and grasped a handful of her jet black hair, pulling her head backwards.

"Corilai!" Treghan screamed, rushing towards the group.

As he ran, a horse appeared from the trees, and he was knocked to the ground. Before he knew what had happened, he was surrounded. Men both on and off their horses had rushed in to attack, and one of them dragged him to his knees. Treghan thought his life was over, as a wicked knife appeared at his throat.

"Corilai," he whimpered, "I'm sorry."

"Don't be sorry," she grunted. "Just get us the hell out of here!"

As if on cue, the air was filled with flames. Fire of all colours, Flooding out of the trees. Greens, blues, yellows, reds, even a splash of white, the heat was unbearable, and the morale of the bandits broke in an instant.

Corilai and Treghan were released, dropped to the ground by their captors. They slowly crawled along the trail, beneath the flames and the billowing smoke from the exploding trees. Once they found each other, the pair clung to each other in the confusion, and waited for things to settle.

Treghan figured it was at least twenty men who strode into the area, wading through the bandits and wielding fire, like farmers harvesting wheat. It was over in moments. Some of the bandits escaped, but many were captured, and tied up.

Treghan was looking down when a pair of boots appeared in the dirt before him. He looked up, into the face of the ranger who had saved them.

"It's you," Treghan said, amazed.

"Yes, it's me," Symin said. "I'm glad we got here in time. It seems you have come a long way since I last saw you. And you appear to have greatly annoyed somebody, to be in the middle of this kind of scuffle. Can you stand?"

"Yes, I'm fine," Treghan said as he stood. "How about you, Corilai?"

"I'm Fine, Treghan," she said, standing and turning to greet their saviour.

"Good, follow me, I'll leave my men to clean up here, and take you both back to Emberdale, for entry to the academy. We'll take two of my men, Jera and Miro, as a guard. We can commandeer two of the enemy's horses, since we'll march the bandits to the city for trial."

They followed, and as they passed the fallen tree, Fletcher groaned, laying on the ground, his legs pinned under a branch.

"Wait, please, bring him," Treghan said.

Symin looked down at the boy, and his eyes grew wide.

"Your brother, is it not?"

"Yes," Treghan replied. "Please, I know he's not been the best of brother, but he's still my brother, and I'd like to know why he was with them. You know he's a flame wielder to, so perhaps, perhaps the academy could use him too..."

"I can't promise you that, but we will take him, as you wish. At any rate, he won't be running away, and certainly couldn't walk with the rest of them. Jera, Miro!"

"Yes, Sir?" said the two men in unison as they rushed over.

"Get this one out from under there, and put him on a horse," Symin instructed. "Find us two more horses, one for each of our young charges. You two will ride with us, we head for Emberdale immediately. The rest of the men know their tasks, they'll follow in their own time."

"Yes, Sir!"

The men moved quickly, and before long, six horses rode along the trail back towards Judd. Not far from the scene of the battle, they saw a man in smouldering clothes on the trail.

"That's their boss," Treghan said.

"Ignore him," Symin said. "If he escapes, he can tell their superiors what happened. Let it serve as a warning to those who flout the law."

Harv rushed into the trees as they approached. Doing as Symin instructed, they ignored him, and rode on into dusk. Treghan glanced at Corilai. She looked tired. But then, he figured, so did he, if he looked how he felt.

Looking behind, Treghan looked at his brother, strapped to the saddle, his horse being led by Jera, Miro behind them.

"He looks worse off than both of us," Treghan said.

"He's your twin," Corilai said. "Isn't he? The one who was so bad to you."

"Yeah, though I can't blame him. It was my father, really. Fletcher just took advantage of the situation. I can't say I wouldn't have done the same."

"Would you do the same, if it happened now?"

"No," Treghan said. "I don't think I would. A lot has changed since then."

"Is that why you saved him?"

"I don't know. But I want to understand. Or at least try."

They rode into the evening, and passed Judd as the last of the sunlight was dying on the horizon. Treghan was glad they didn't stop there. Symin led them out to the road, and headed east, towards the sea.

Stopping on the second hill from town, he dismounted, then led his horse off the road.

"We camp here. Jera, Miro, you two and I will take turns on watch," Symin said, then pointed at Fletcher. "Make sure that one is tied up. He's still a prisoner. But the youngsters need their rest. They've had a hard time these last few weeks."

"Yes Sir," Jera and Miro both said.

Almost falling from their saddles, Corilai and Treghan pulled out their bedrolls and laid them out beside each other. Climbing in, they were both asleep in moments. Meanwhile, Fletcher was laid out against a tree, his arms and feet bound together. They then tied him to the tree, with enough length to the rope that he could lie on the ground. He was given a small sack as a pillow, and a blanket.

Volunteering for the first watch, Symin lit a fire, and sat on the ground, facing away from it, staring out into the night as the owls hooted and the sounds of the forest echoed in the darkness.

* * *

Yuri and his men trudged through dense forest. After they lost the trail east from the old man's cottage, they had decided to turn and push north, spreading out in the hope they might pick up the trail again. It was slow going, and their direction not perfect, so eventually one of the men found himself stumbling onto the open road.

"That's it," Yuri shouted, exasperated. "This is pointless. We may as well take the road for a while, until we find a trail we can follow. Hopefully we can meet up with the men from Judd before they find the little bastards."

Moving out onto the road, Yuri and his men continued northwards. They made good time, but found no trail for a long while. Finally, the forest seemed to be thinning out a little. They could see a bluff in the distance, across a verdant valley.

"Spread back into the forest, men. We'll find these little blighters yet," Yuri instructed.

They did so, and continued for some hours, searching as they went. Then suddenly one of the men shouted. Yuri rushed over to him, and immediately understood. The ground, the trees, everything over a large area, was burnt. There were many footprints and hoof prints in the dust, as if many men and their horses had scuffled here.

"They found them, and there was a fight here," Yuri said. "We move on Judd, and find out what happened. With luck, they have our prey."

They rode in silence through the forest, and eventually came upon Judd. It was already clear that a long line of men had been marched straight past the village, and on towards Emberdale. Yuri knew what that meant, though he wanted to hear it from a witness. He dismounted, and strode into the tavern.

Seated alone, and badly singed, Harv looked up at his boss as he entered.

"Harv," Yuri said. "What do you have to tell me?"

"We had them. Really, boss, we did, but then we were ambushed by rangers. At least two dozen, maybe three. We didn't stand a chance. They took both the youngsters you wanted. And they took the third, the flame wielder I was preparing to send to Grey."

"What?" Yuri shouted, suddenly enraged. "Not only did you lose the two little bastards who we needed to punish, to make an example of, but you even lost a third flame wielder, one who was already recruited and working willingly with us? This will not stand! Harv, your incompetence will not go unpunished!"

"But Sir, please," Harv stammered. "It wasn't my fault, they burned us all, they even took my men, there was nothing I could do!"

"They took your men?" Yuri screamed. "You mean to tell me, that not only have you lost three valuable, if tiresome, flame wielders, but you also have lost an entire garrison of fighting men? You mean to tell me, my northern outpost, which I left in your care, has been essentially wiped out with this single event?"

"It wasn't my fault!" Harv whimpered.

"Then whose fault was it?" Yuri shouted, drawing a knife and advancing on Harv. "I can make no preferential treatment for you, Harv, and in this instance, I am not inclined to even try. You have failed me for the last time."

Yuri grabbed Harv's burnt collar, and hauled the man to his feet. Stepping forward, Yuri pushed Harv up against the wall, then shouted in his face.

"You have failed me, and your failure is catastrophic. In this utter defeat, you should have stayed there and died with your men. Instead, you die here!"

With that, Yuri stabbed forward with the knife, driving it between Harv's ribs and into his heart. The big man slumped, collapsing to the floor. Yuri left the knife there, and turned away from the body. Walking out of the tavern, he mounted his horse, his temper still simmering, and shouted to his men.

"We return to Grey. A year's wages to any man who kills a ranger on the way!"

Chapter 13 – Academy

Corilai and Treghan looked around in amazement as they entered the towering, stone gates of Emberdale. The evening sun was casting an orange hue over the western mountains, their long shadows dappling the streets in evening shade as a lone worker walked past, pulling a small cart and lighting street lanterns as he went, checking each for oil and refilling the ones which were low.

Carts, horses, and pedestrians passed in great numbers. The two youngsters were wide eyed. Neither had ever been to the city before.

"There's as many people at the gate as in my entire village!" Corilai said.

"I went to Oaklands once, but it was nothing like this," Treghan said. "It has a wall, but it's nothing like Emberdale in size."

"I spent my youth in Oaklands," Symin said. "Come. We should continue to the academy before dark. Once the night guards are on duty, we won't be able to assign you quarters until morning."

They rode through the streets, Treghan and Corilai quickly losing track of where they had gone, until finally Symin led them through a large open gate into an imposing complex of buildings. An immense curved sign over the gate read "Ranger Academy."

"The scout returns," Shouted a guard from atop the gate.

In answer to the call, a man in a leather suit emerged from the nearest building, a small hut behind the gate. He approached them and smiled.

"Welcome home, Scout."

"Thank you," Symin replied. "It is good to be home. I have brought two recruits, and a third, who is to face possible charges before joining them."

"It is good that you were successful," the man said, before turning to face Treghan and Corilai. "I am Barre, the bursar on duty this evening. The Chancellor had warned me of your possible arrival. I have quarters already prepared for you. Your assessment and initiations will commence in the morning."

Barre turned to face Fletcher, who had sat silent throughout the last three days on horseback. Feeling so much like a prisoner, his attitude had been one of defeat and dejection. His only words had been a curt apology whenever Treghan had pressed him to speak.

"You will have to be housed in the lock up, I'm afraid. But if your story meets with the approval of the Master at Arms, then you may have an application for clemency heard by the chancellor. Have you spoken to any of these people about your situation, or your motivations?"

"No, Sir," Fletcher said. "I felt that I should keep myself apart from them, in case I made a prejudicial impact on their admittance. Or my own."

"Well spoken," Barre said. "I hope your case is as sharp as your reasoning."

Symin dismounted. A second man came out and led the horse away as Symin turned to face the others.

"Treghan, Corilai, leave your belongings with the horses, they will be brought to us shortly. Jera, Miro, see that the lad is delivered to the lock up, and properly treated. Then you are dismissed for the evening. Rest well, you have earned it. Bursar, if you could please lead us to their quarters?"

"Certainly," Barre said, approaching and offering his hand to Corilai.

Grateful, she accepted the assistance and climbed down from the saddle. Barre then did the same for Treghan, before turning to walk towards a nearby building. He spoke in practised tones as they walked, pointing out buildings along the way.

"We are heading to the candidates' barracks. All new applicants are housed there, until they are assigned a house and moved into their student barracks. Those are the four stone buildings you can see to the north of the gates. First years share common barracks on the lower floor. Once you graduate to second year status, you will receive a choice of your own private room, or a shared suite. Most of these are on the upper floors of those buildings. Each building is a house, and you are to think of your house as family."

He turned to look at Corilai.

"I understand you are of the demon flame, miss. Depending on your progress, you might consider sharing, for safety. Most of your flame type do that, because their room mates will wake up if they don't."

"You mean, those like me all have trouble with the dreams?"

"If you mean, they flame in their sleep, yes. Though sometimes, that can happen with any colour of flame, but for those of the black flame, it happens with almost all wielders."

"Then I will remember your advice, when the time comes," Corilai said.

"Of course," Barre said. "This is why the first years have common barracks. It is rare that a first year who flames while asleep is not awoken soon enough to avert a disaster. The common barracks, as with the candidates' barracks, have no wood or other flammables in them. The furniture is stone or steel, the soft furnishings are wool, to reduce the hazard as much as possible. It makes for a barren feeling living space, but it makes for a safe one."

"What are the houses?" Treghan asked.

"Oh, those are Forest house, Plains house, Highlands house, and Hills house. They represent the areas of the land, from which our people come. It serves to remind us that we are one people, and no matter where we come from, we have no greater or less value than our fellow rangers."

"What house will we be assigned?" Corilai asked.

"I do not know. That will depend on your assessment, and which house has room for somebody with your skill level. We try to keep the students evenly placed among the houses, so one house is not unfairly disadvantaged in the support they are required to give."

"Do you think we can be placed together?" Treghan asked, stealing a furtive glance at Corilai.

"Together?" Barre said, then laughed. "It can probably be arranged. The Chancellor mentioned that it might be advisable, based on information he received from Barache."

Corilai and Treghan both stared at him.

"He spoke to Barache?"

"Not as such, but Barache is in regular communication with the academy. Did he not mention it?"

"The pigeons," Corilai said, suddenly remembering that Barache had spoken of them.

"That's correct," Barre said. "Now, be warned, the candidates' barracks will be cold, and quiet, as you two will be the only residents this evening. It used to be much busier, but not so much now."

"Why is that?" Treghan asked.

"Our scouts," Barre said, casting a disapproving glance at Symin. "Have not been bringing in as many recruits as they normally would, and besides that, our normal admission period ended for this semester a few weeks ago."

"So we missed it?" Corilai asked, despondent.

"Yes, but it is not so bad, fortunately," Barre said. "Usually, the new recruits would arrived anything up to three months before the assessments, and would reside in this barracks for the duration of that waiting period."

"So how is that not so bad?" Treghan said, "It sounds like we missed it, and that's that."

"Not quite," Barre said. "Classes for the first years commence in a week, so we can still push you through the assessment in time."

He turned to face Treghan, reached out and tapped the young man's shoulder encouragingly, then continued.

"But had you been a few more days, you would have needed to wait for the next admissions period, which would mean residing in these barracks for the duration. Our admissions periods are every six months, so you would have been there for quite some time, before your assessment."

"Symin, what house were you in?" Treghan asked.

"I was in Plains house," Symin replied. "Though I came from the hills. That served as a daily reminder of my purpose. I saw divisions in my community and I hoped, naively perhaps, to use my eventual position as a ranger to bring an end to such infighting in my home community. I am not so naive now, but I am just as resolved."

"So are you still in a house, as a ranger?" Corilai asked.

"As a graduate, we are all rangers. The four families are now one, though realistically, that was always the case. But working as a scout, I find myself working with rangers from all four academy houses. We are all family now, and look out for each other's welfare in all our actions. But I believe we all carry a soft spot in our hearts for the house which nurtured our talents. It would please me if you both entered Plains House, however I would do my best to support you both regardless of where you were assigned."

"That was well said, Scout." Barre said as he opened the door to the barracks. "You may select your own bunks in here. Boys in the chamber to the right, girls in the chamber to the left. Central hall is for meals, study, that sort of thing. The men will bring your possessions momentarily, and you will find two sets of clothing, in the style of the academy, and in the plain brown colours of the admissions candidate. I will be around to wake you at six in the morning. Your assessments will commence at nine o'clock. I leave you to settle in. Please, Symin, do not keep them up too late."

Corilai sat on a chair near the entry to the girls chamber, and Treghan sat on another, where they found the mentioned clothing. Symin stood just inside the doorway as Barre left. The man who had taken the horses was walking towards the building, carrying their packs, so Symin held the door open and waited for him to enter. He deposited the packs inside the door, offered a short salute to Symin, then left.

"Now then," Symin asked. "Before I leave you both for the evening, we should head to the mess hall for a quick meal. I can't leave you both to sleep on empty stomachs. I suggest you freshen up first. You will find men's and lady's wash rooms at the far end of the barracks. I'll be returning to my own quarters, and will be back here to collect you both in fifteen minutes."

"Yes, Sir," Corilai and Treghan both said as he left.

They looked around the barracks, and shortly found the wash rooms. They were basic, but functional, featuring a large basin, a bath, and a separate toilet cubicle. The water was fed by gravity from tanks mounted high on the outside of the building.

Collecting the offered clothes, a pair of long trousers and a tunic style shirt, with a belt and sandals, they returned to the wash rooms. Both were happy to remove the grime of days on horseback, added to the days on foot before that.

Treghan found the clothes hung a little loosely, but with the included belt, it was not a problem. He stood and admired them in the steel mirror which hung on the wall.

"Great clothes!" he called, not sure if Corilai would hear him. "I guess we get boots when we're admitted."

"They are," she replied. "Sturdy. Not the most feminine of outfits, but serviceable. I guess that's the life of a flame ranger."

"I've never had new clothes of this quality," Treghan said. "And this is just the basic stuff they give people who haven't even been admitted to the academy yet!"

"We certainly can't complain about the treatment," Corilai said as she left her wash room.

Treghan joined her, and they walked to the door, arriving just as Symin returned. He looked them over, then smiled. Both of them admired his uniform, fresh and tidy, it was a vibrant, forest green. A long sleeved tunic top hung loose over his sturdy trousers, also green. He wore a leather vest over the tunic, coloured to match the ensemble, and gloves, which while clean, seemed out of place as they were obviously recently worn.

"Why the gloves?" Corilai asked.

"They're my ranger's gloves, and an important part of my uniform. I was wearing them the entire time we travelled, but they were largely concealed, beneath my cloak and riding gloves."

"What makes them important?" Treghan asked.

"All flame rangers have gloves assigned to them on entry to the academy. You have one set, until they are worn out, and you can get them replaced. Your gloves are imbued with an element that would naturally burn in the colour of your flames, or otherwise has been found to enhance flames of your colour."

He took his right glove off, and turned it over in his hands, inspecting the fabric. Holding it up to the light, the colour appeared mottled, like the die had not taken evenly when they were made.

"Mine have fibres imbued with Sodium Chloride, which is table salt, and naturally burns with a yellow flame. They are treated so that the salt does not wash out."

"And you have to wear them all the time?" Corilai asked.

"You are expected to have them on, as part of the uniform, at any time you are wearing the uniform. That means all times on academy grounds, and all times when out on academy or ranger business."

"What will ours have in them?" Treghan asked.

"Treghan, yours would be imbued with Magnesium, which naturally burns with a bright white flame, and Corilai, yours would have onyx, a type of polished stone which comes in a variety that is black as the night sky and does not burn. This is because the black flame needs to be suppressed for the wielder to control it."

"They both sound so much more interesting than salt," Treghan said.

"Since your gloves are your own expense, I'm fortunate," Symin said, then laughed. "Salt is a lot cheaper than either magnesium or onyx. But don't worry, your first pair is supplied by the academy on admission."

Symin pulled the glove back onto his right hand, then turned to leave. Following, Treghan and Corilai were careful to stay close as he led them through a confusing sequence of twists and turns around the complex. Neither of them had any idea how to get back to their barracks by the time they arrived at the mess hall.

"I made sure there was still some food left for us before coming to get you," Symin said, as he led them to the serving counter.

A tall, pretty, blonde haired lady in her middle age smiled as she served them a mix of baked meats and vegetables, topped with a thick, dark gravy. Treghan's mouth hung open as he looked at the pile of delicious food before him. He looked up at the lady as she handed him his plate.

"Thank you so much," he said, almost looking like he was going to cry.

Corilai giggled at his obvious delight, as they followed Symin to a table. Sitting together, they ate voraciously until all the food was cleared. Then, the blonde lady delivered a round of tall drinks to their table.

Corilai sipped and squealed in delight. It was a freshly made orange drink, fruity and refreshing, infused with bubbles by some process she could not even begin to imagine.

"Treghan, you have to taste this," she whispered.

He took a tentative sip, then raised his eyebrows.

"This is amazing!" he enthused. "I've never tasted anything like it. I wonder how they put those bubbles in there?"

Symin smiled enigmatically, not giving them any answers to the mystery of the bubbles as he enjoyed his own. Once they had finished, the serving lady collected their plates, cutlery and cups.

"Have a nice evening," the lady said with a smile, before disappearing through a door behind the counter.

"We should get you back to your barracks," Symin said, standing and walking to the door.

Treghan and Corilai followed him, both content and feeling better fed than they had in a long time.

"What will the assessment be like?" Treghan asked.

"It's different for everybody that goes through it," Symin replied. "I suspect that for you two, it is going to be unlike anything we've witnessed before."

"Why is that?" Corilai asked.

"Because you two enter into an entirely different league, when you work together. That is something that no previous applicants have had. Your experiences and abilities are unique. We normally do our assessment alone, but I suspect the chancellor may have some other instructions for you two."

"But what will we have to do?" Treghan persisted.

"Nothing too difficult, I promise you. Don't worry about it. Just get some sleep, and you'll both be fine."

Symin fell silent for the remainder of the walk, depositing them at the barracks and then leaving them, to return to his quarters. Treghan and Corilai changed into their old clothes, then climbed into their bunks, and both were quickly asleep, to pass the night in comfortable warmth until Barre came to wake them in the morning.

Chapter 14 – Assessment

Corilai woke to the sound of a bang on the door of the barracks. Stumbling from the bed, she walked out of the girls' chamber, and to the door of the boys' area. Corilai looked at Treghan, still asleep on his bunk, and envied him.

"Thank you. We're awake," she shouted.

"OK Then," Barre shouted back. "Somebody will collect you shortly before nine. I'm going off duty now. Best of luck."

"Thank you," she replied.

She walked over to Treghan, and shook him by the shoulder. He sat up, and looked around, disoriented, then looked at her.

"What is it? Where are we? Oh, right."

He stood, and looked at her, smiling as they walked to her area.

"We finally made it, didn't we?" Treghan asked.

"Yes, we did."

He looked at her bunk, a light scorching on the stone around it, the edges of the woollen blankets showing some faint singes.

"How did you sleep?" he asked.

"What? Oh, fine," she replied, then followed his gaze, and saw the burns for the first time. "Oh, wow, I don't even remember having any dreams, let alone one with flames in it. Was that really me?"

"It must have been," Treghan said. "But it wasn't too bad I guess."

"I guess not," Corilai replied. "Lets get washed up and into our new clothes, then we can have a look around in the daylight, before our assessment."

"OK then."

Taking their clothes, they went to the wash rooms, and got ready. In a short time, they were both refreshed. Together, they left the barracks and stood in the early morning sunshine, looking around at the many stone buildings.

"Where should we go?" Treghan asked.

"Do you think you could find that mess hall again? I'd kill for some breakfast right now," Corilai said.

"No, I wouldn't know where to start, but I'm sure we can find somebody who might know where it is."

Setting out across the courtyard, Treghan picked a building, one sitting between the four houses and the large, central building. He walked towards it, and Corilai followed.

"Just make sure you remember which way we came," Corilai said. "We have to get back to our barracks in time."

"It'll be fine," Treghan said. "Don't worry about it."

As they walked, they passed some of the residents of the academy. They all smiled, nodded or said a quick greeting, then continued on their way. Treghan continued towards the building he had selected, not knowing what it actually was. As they reached it, a woman was leaving. She stopped, looked the pair over, and smiled.

"You two look lost," the woman said. "Can I help you?"

"Yes, please," Corilai said sweetly. "We were looking for the mess hall. We have our assessment this morning, but I wanted to get something to eat first."

"I can take you there," the lady said, offering a smile as she began to walk back towards the main building. "I have a little time to spare right now, before my students arrive for their morning lessons. My name is Loka, and I'm one of the trainers here. You'll probably be seeing a lot of me. And don't worry about paying for the breakfast, its on me today."

"Thank you so much!" Corilai said. "Everybody here is so kind."

"We all know what it's like to grow up with the fire as our companion. We've all had our run ins with bigots and the paranoid before we came here, so we know what it feels like when you first arrive. Most of us come here scared, and feeling very alone."

"I don't feel alone," Treghan said, trying to sound tough, but then he blushed, which ruined the performance. "I have Corilai, we're never alone any more."

"Now that's sweet," Loka said, then laughed, causing him to blush even more. "Corilai, that's your name? It's pretty. Corilai, this boy is a keeper."

"I don't know what that means," Corilai said.

"Just keep your eyes on him, the girls around here are going to like him a lot."

"It's not," Corilai stammered. "We're close, but it's not..."

Loka laughed at her discomfort, and tousled her dark hair, before turning and touching Treghan's cheek gently.

"You two really are so sweet. I look forward to teaching you both."

Loka led them in the front of the main building, along a corridor which wound around its perimeter, then out into a courtyard at the back. She crossed the courtyard and entered a building on the other side. They followed, and found themselves in the same mess hall that Symin had taken them to when they arrived.

They walked over to the serving counter, where the same lady was working as had been there the night before.

"Welcome back, you two," she said. "I hope you had a restful night."

"Jarls, please put their breakfast on my account," Loka said. "Can you two find your way back from here?"

"Yes, thank you so much!" Corilai said.

"We'll be fine now, Thank you." Treghan said.

Loka smiled, tousled both their hair, and left.

"What's with all that hair tousling lately?" Treghan moaned.

"It's your own fault," Corilai said, laughing at him. "If you didn't have such white, soft looking locks, nobody would be tempted to touch them!"

"She did it to you, too," he complained.

Jarls laughed, then served up two plates of bacon, eggs, mashed potato and more of the delicious orange drink, placing it all on a carry tray.

"Enjoy your breakfast you two, and good luck today. I hope you do well."

"Thank you," they replied in unison, then took their food to a nearby table and sat to eat it.

As they were finishing, Symin walked in. He saw them, and approached, smiling and waving a greeting.

"I'm glad to see you two found the mess hall OK. It would have been sad if you got to the assessment without food in your bellies."

"Yes, and it's such great food, too!" Treghan enthused.

"Are you going to have breakfast?" Corilai asked.

"No, I already ate, but I wanted to check on you two, and since this was closer to my quarters than your barracks, I thought I'd stop here first, in case you found your way here for breakfast. I figured Barre would have woken you both early."

"Yes," Corilai said. "We met Loka, and she showed us the way here."

"And she paid for our food!" Treghan said through a mouth full of potato.

"Treghan, don't talk with food in your mouth," Corilai snapped.

Treghan looked at his plate, chastised, then cheered right up again when he saw some bacon still there. With a grin, he ate it, then leaned back in his seat, satisfied.

"I'll be going now, but I'll be sure to be there for your assessment. Just make sure you're back at the barracks by about half past eight, because the bursar will collect you from there."

"Yes, Sir," they both replied.

Symin left, and they sat there, finishing their drinks. After a short wait, Treghan stood, and Corilai followed as he led the way out of the mess hall. Crossing the courtyard, he led the way back through the main building, then across to their barracks.

"I wonder what time it is?" Corilai asked.

"I'm not sure," Treghan replied. "But we probably still have a while to wait."

"Well, let's just wait here," she said. "We can explore some more later. I'd hate for us to miss out because we got lost and weren't around when the bursar came to collect us."

"OK then," Treghan said, walking inside and sitting on a chair near the door.

Corilai walked down the long barracks, through the communal hall, to the end near the wash rooms.

"There are some books here," she called, standing before a low shelf unit, which had a handful of well worn leather bound tomes resting on top of it. "Can you read?"

"Yes, a little," Treghan said, following her. "Not that my parents cared about school, but I have learned some. I used to read in my room when I was trying to stay out of trouble."

"Good," Corilai said. "I think that we'll be reading a lot from now on."

She picked up two of the books, and walked back to where Treghan was still sitting.

"Here," she said, passing him one of the two books. "This should pass the time well enough."

"OK then," he replied.

They read in silence, both trying to make sense of the theories they were reading. The books were both the same, and bore the title “Fundamentals of Flame,” on the cover in shiny red print. They were still reading some time later, when there was a knock at the door.

“Coming,” Treghan called, and they returned the books to the shelf, then opened the door.

A heavy set man with a long brown beard smiled at them as they walked outside.

“I'm the Bursar on duty,” he said. “My name is Trest, it is good to meet you both, Treghan, and Corilai. Am I saying that right?”

“Yes, Sir,” they both replied.

“Good, follow me. Oh, and good luck to you both.”

“Sir, what will we have to do?” Treghan asked.

“Sorry, Son,” Trest replied. “It's good that you're keen, but I can't divulge any details of the assessment at this time. But you'll be finding out soon enough. Don't worry, you'll both do just fine, I'm sure of it.”

They walked behind the main building, past the mess hall, and beyond a series of small apartment blocks, before arriving in a large, walled arena. Trest led them into the arena, and out onto the grounds at its centre. Stepped high along the walls around them were enough to seats for many thousands of spectators. A handful of people sat together at one end. Among them, Treghan thought he saw Symin.

“I will leave you here,” Trest said.

One of the people in the group stood, and walked down to the arena floor, waving at them to approach. Treghan and Corilai walked across the floor till they stood before him.

“I am Chancellor Howe,” he said. “I am pleased that you both made it here safely. I will be conducting your assessment today, as this is a single event. Usually, our dedicated assessment staff would be running things, but they have completed the assessments already and are busy getting the new students assigned to classes and the like. You will enter the stands with me, Corilai, while Treghan completes the first test.”

“Yes, Sir,” she said, following him into the stands, while Treghan walked back out onto the sand.

“Treghan,” shouted Howe, once he was back with the group and Treghan had returned to the centre of the arena. “You will now produce a flame, as strong as you can.”

“Yes, Sir!” Treghan shouted.

Treghan closed his eyes for a moment, to calm himself, then held his hands out in front of himself, palm facing upward. He concentrated, and focussed his energy.

Pushing with all his might, Treghan tried to make the energy flow from his hands, and set a spark. The white sparks danced between his hands for a moment, and he thought he was done. Then, as the first burst of sparks died out, Treghan redoubled his efforts. A tall white flame lept forth, reaching around a foot into the air, tall and proud, that single flame shone with brilliance that surprised him.

"Keep it burning!" Howe shouted.

The flame lowered a little, but Treghan continued pushing all his efforts and energy into it. After several seconds, it was reduced to half the initial height, but it continued to shine bright and strong. It was a greater flame than he had ever managed on his own before, and although it was small, Treghan was proud of his efforts.

"That's good, Treghan," Howe shouted. "Keep it as long as you can."

Treghan fought to feed the flame, but he was feeling drained, and his will was wavering fast. He managed to keep the flame burning for a full minute, before it suddenly died, leaving nothing but the familiar sparks. Treghan fell to his knees, spent, his breath coming in gasps as he struggled to stop himself from collapsing.

"Good work, Son," Howe shouted.

Treghan smiled, and after a moment, regained his composure and stood.

"Thank you, Sir," he said.

"Come into the stands, and we will see what your friend can do," Howe instructed, then turned to his companions. "What do you think?"

"It is strong, for a new white with no training," a red haired lady replied. "But definitely still only new first year in level. He will require a lot of fundamentals training before he can start following the scouts or the enforcers on ranger missions."

"That's true," Symin said. "But it is true of most new recruits. He has the control, not the power, where normally it is the other way around."

"This is the nature of the white flame," Howe said. "The reverse is true of the demon flame, which is why the peasants call it that."

"The black flame is indeed unwieldy at times," another man agreed.

"Corilai," Howe said. "Please make your way to the centre of the arena. When your strength test is complete, we will move immediately into a control test."

"Yes, Sir," she replied, then stood and walked down to the floor of the arena, passing Treghan as he made his way into the stands. "That was amazing, Treghan!"

"Thanks, Corilai," he replied.

Corilai had just reached the centre of the arena, and turned to face them, when she heard the call.

"Begin!"

Like Treghan had done, she closed her eyes for a moment, then held her hands out in front of her. She focussed her energy, then pushed a jet black plume of fire into the sky. She held it like that for a moment.

"That's not all you've got," Howe shouted. "I want you to push as hard as you can. Let the fire really burst forth. Don't worry, we'll all be safe. We won't let anything bad happen."

Still remembering the events of her village, and the smelter, Corilai was nervous and hesitated.

"Hurry, child," Howe shouted.

Corilai nodded, swallowed her fears, and pushed with all her might. The energy coursed through her like gushing rapids in a flooded river. The tall black flames doubled their girth, then tripled. The flames crept up her arms, and soon her entire body was emitting the deathly black heat of the demon flame.

"Keep pushing it," Howe shouted as the fire grew ever greater.

"Arrrrr!" Corilai screamed, as she felt it run further and further beyond her control.

The intense heat was filling her body with adrenalin, and the flames fed on her fear, to burst outwards in wave after wave of intense darkness. As the heat grew, so did the darkness, until it was engulfing over half of the arena floor.

"OK, That's enough," Howe shouted.

"Aaaahhh!" she screamed in reply.

The flames pulsed, and grew again. Howe turned to Treghan.

"Son, we start a mixed flame control test now. You know what you have to do. Get in there. I want to see how you handle a situation like this with my own eyes."

"Yes, Sir," Treghan said, and ran to the arena floor.

The heat from her flames was intense, but so was his determination. He pushed through, the black fire searing his lungs as he rushed to her side, and thrust his hand into hers. He felt the rawness of her energy, powerful and enormous, and for a brief moment, his scream echoed hers. But then, he calmed himself, focussed his energy, and drew on her seemingly unlimited supply.

An immense white flame lept from the centre of the arena floor, Treghan at its heart. The dark flames subsided, and formed into an enormous plume, spiralling high into the clouds, her body its source. Treghan concentrated, and matched her black flame with a white one of his own, and held it there, towering over the stadium.

The twin spires of flame shot skyward, visible from all of Emberdale. Treghan held her hand, squeezing it in gentle encouragement, until she recovered her full control. He looked at her face, watching her eyes as they cleared, and she smiled. Still he held her hand, and they held their flames.

"Hold on to it as long as you can," Howe shouted to them from the stands.

"Yes, Sir," they shouted in unison.

Together, they looked up, staring into a sky both darkened and lightened by their opposing flames, and watched as the twin fires danced into the low clouds, rolling down from the mountains. For twelve minutes, the pillars of fire towered over the city, until finally Corilai began to waver.

"I Can't keep it up any more," she said.

"OK then," Treghan replied, releasing her hand.

Instantly his white fire died out completely. A few seconds later, the black flames were also gone, and the two young flame wielders stood there, embarrassed as the group in the stands applauded their efforts. They cheered as Howe descended to the arena floor, to approach them, the rest of the group slowly following.

"My Friends," he shouted. "Please join me in welcoming our two newest members of the Academy. Treghan And Corilai, the demon and the angel flames, both destined, I am certain, for great deeds among the ranks of the finest rangers this academy will ever produce."

Chapter 15 – Settling In

"Listen, and listen carefully," shouted the Master at Arms. "I want you to think before you answer. This one question may have a devastating impact on your future here, or it could save you, opening a new life to you. Why did you join the bandits?"

"Because," Fletcher replied. "If I did not cooperate, they were going to kill my mother."

"I see," the man said. "And where is your mother now?"

"I do not know. They were keeping her chained up in the basement of the tavern in Judd. After the scouts took me, I do not know what will have become of her."

"What of your father?"

"The bandits beat him senseless when he tried to save her. That was when they demanded he sell me to them, in order to win her back."

"So he sold you to them? They did not release your mother?"

"No," Fletcher replied. "He demanded it, but they beat him again, and said that they would do the same to her, if I ever refused to do as I was told, and that if I ever betrayed them, they would kill her, then they would hunt him down, and kill him as well."

"I see," the Master at Arms said.

He walked to the doorway of his office, where the two guards who had escorted Fletcher from the cells waited, and stared out into the parade grounds while he considered the situation. Finally, he turned to face Fletcher again.

"So what you are telling me," the man said. "Is that you have experienced some rather extraordinary circumstances, which resulted in you being indentured into service to the bandits against your will."

"I... I," Fletcher stammered. "I guess so..."

"Do not be so nervous, boy," the Master at Arms said. "Fear not. I believe you have strong grounds for clemency. I will present this finding to the Chancellor, and he will return with a decision on your possible recruitment into the academy as a student."

"Is that really possible?" Fletcher asked.

"Yes, it is," the man said. "You would, of course, be considered on parole for at least the first six months, which would limit your movements beyond the gates, but you would be free to move around the Academy grounds. Also, you would be permitted to attend first year classes as a student in preparation for entering the ranks of the rangers on completion of your studies. Would this be acceptable to you?"

"Ye, Yes Sir, it would most definitely be acceptable."

"Good. The guards will return you to your cell, until such time as Chancellor Howe has made his decision on the matter. I wish you the best of luck, boy."

"Thank you," Fletcher said, standing and walking to the door.

The two guards led him back to his cell, in the basement of the main building, where they left him to contemplate his future.

"I must thank Treghan, if I ever see him," Fletcher said. "That scout had already rejected my application, and then Treghan says a handful of words, and not only am I saved from arrest and prison, but I am probably accepted into the academy, which was always my dream. I treated him so poorly when we were still at home, and now, I owe him my life. I guess he was the better brother after all."

* * *

"Welcome," shouted Symin, as he stood before a throng of students and teachers in the first year barracks on the lower floor of one of the four student residences. "To Plains House. Treghan and Corilai, as our newest members, we all welcome you to our ranks, and we hope you will remain dedicated and loyal members of our family for the remainder of your days."

The crowd of students and teachers behind him cheered heartily in reply, as Treghan and Corilai stood there, stunned at the welcome. Ribbons and shiny decorations were hung from the rafters, and a long table stood at the end of the barracks, piled high with food. The bunks and other furniture had all been pushed to the end of the long hall for the celebration.

"I know this wasn't just for us, but it kind of feels that way, doesn't it?" Corilai said.

"After Symin's speech? It sure does," Treghan replied. "Though apparently this party was already scheduled, to welcome all the first years and celebrate the start of the academic year. Anyway, let's put our stuff away and get stuck into that food!"

"Good idea," Corilai replied.

Before they could move, Loka pushed her way past Symin, and grabbed Corilai in a warm hug, before turning and doing the same to Treghan.

"I'm so happy you two sweethearts are going to be in Plains House! We're the best house, but don't tell the teachers from the other houses I said that!"

"We won't, but isn't it wonderful?" Corilai said. "We already have so many new friends, just waiting to meet us! Loka, Symin, you two especially, have already done so much to welcome us, I just can't believe it!"

"From now on, that's Sir to you," Symin said, smiling broadly. "And Loka will be referred to as Teacher. At least, when there is anybody other than us in the room. We must keep to protocol. In private, say what you like, provided the person you are speaking to doesn't mind."

"Yes, Sir," Corilai said.

Treghan, having escaped to the food table, was happily piling pieces of fried chicken onto a plate. A tall, blonde girl appeared beside him, and introduced herself.

"Hi," she said. "My name's Marni. I'm a green flame, and a first year. It's wonderful to meet you."

"Thank you," Treghan said. "I'm Treghan, a white flame. I'm glad to meet you too. Isn't this place amazing?"

"Yes, it is. I've been here about six weeks now, in the candidates' barracks up until last week. So I've already had a good chance to learn my way around. If you need any help finding stuff, let me know, OK?"

Smiling broadly, Marni waved cheerily and disappeared back into the crowd. As she left, Corilai came over to stand beside him, and began serving herself some food. Loka leaned close, draping her arm over Corilai's shoulder.

"Did you see that?" Loka said. "Don't say I didn't warn you. Keep a close eye on that boy, if you don't want to lose him."

"What? Why would I..." Corilai stammered, blushing. "It's not like... I mean, Treghan and I are close, we wouldn't do anything without... I mean, I trust him, OK?"

Loka was laughing hysterically, as Symin approached.

"Are you teasing the poor child, Loka?" he chided.

"Oh," Loka whined. "I was only joking. I didn't mean anything by it. All in fun, you know. Still friends, right, Corilai?"

"Yes, Teacher," Corilai said as Treghan slipped a small cup of pudding onto her plate.

"You gotta try that, Corilai. It's amazing!" Treghan said.

"Really? Thanks Treghan!" Corilai said, then turned back to Loka. "You see? There's nothing to worry about. As long as there's food around, he will never have eyes for any girls!"

Symin and Loka both burst into laughter at that, before a group of giggling senior students came rushing past the table, to sweep the two grown ups away in a flurry of questions. Corilai turned back to Treghan, and smiled.

"Let's find somewhere to sit, so we can eat this stuff in peace," she said.

"Sure thing, Corilai," he replied.

* * *

Fletcher stood nervously, in the centre of the arena, as the chancellor and the others talked about his results. The test had seemed simple enough, but Fletcher was nervous, none the less.

"Boy," one of the men shouted, who Fletcher recognised as the scout who had rejected his application. "I visited you at your home, and I rejected your application. Do you understand why I did that?"

"Because of my lack of maturity, and my spoiled attitude, Sir!" Fletcher shouted.

"Very good. And how are those things now, boy?"

"I hope they are improved, Sir, however I would not have the impertinence to assess myself. I was wrong before, I dare say I would be wrong now."

"Excellent answer. Fletcher, you have my blessing as a scout."

"Wonderful," Howe said, standing to lead the group down to the arena. "In that case, we will not hesitate, young man, in welcoming you into the ranks of our first year students. You will join Hills House, and train to the best of your ability. You remain on parole for six months, and can not leave the academy grounds under any circumstances, if you are not accompanied by at least two members of staff. Is this acceptable?"

"Yes, Sir!" Fletcher replied with a grin from ear to ear, rushing forward in his eagerness to shake the Chancellor's hand, in thanks for this second chance he had never dreamed possible.

"You might not see him for a while," Symin said. "Is there any message you would have us take to your brother in Plains House?"

"Yes, Sir," Fletcher replied without hesitation. "Please, can you tell him I am sorry for the past, and will do what I can to make amends, and tell him thank you, for helping me to change my life and enter the academy. Oh, and one more thing, tell him, I hope to tell him face to face, the answer to his question. One day soon, I will tell him why I was with those men."

"It will be done, boy. Now, you will be escorted to your barracks. I wish you luck."

* * *

Symin stopped by Plains House the next morning, to deliver the message, and see how Treghan and Corilai were settling in. The barracks did not look like it had held a party the night before, however the first years were milling around in a tired daze. Symin knew at a glance that the party had run late, and the seniors had made the youngsters clean up before letting them rest.

The first floor rooms were laid out the same as the candidates' barracks had been. Seats lined the walls, a row down either side of the long room, boys on one side, girls on the other, each assigned the chair which mimicked the place in the sleeping chambers where their bunk was. Several strides separated them, and a raised platform at one end was manned by a house supervisor, a member of staff who was tasked with the job of ensuring that no shenanigans took place in the night.

Treghan and Corilai's seats were opposite each other, and nearest the door.

Symin found them, standing together at Corilai's seat, talking as the other students milled around minding their own business.

"I see you are settling in well," Symin said with a smile.

"Yes, thank you, Sir," Treghan replied.

"I bring you news, and a message," Symin said. "You brother has been granted clemency, and allowed to enrol in the academy, on parole for the first six months. He will enter Hills House, and commence his first year classes this semester."

"That's good news. But what was the message?" Treghan asked.

"Your brother says to tell you, he is sorry, for everything in the past, and he will do what he can to make amends."

"The best amends he could make," Treghan said. "Would be to not waste this opportunity."

"Well said," Symin said, smiling. "He also asked that I pass on his thanks, to you, for making his admission to the academy possible, and promises that one day, soon, he will tell you in person why he was with those men. Given that promise, I won't tell you what I know."

"Thank you, Symin," Treghan said.

"I have a favour to ask you, Symin," Corilai said, interrupting the moment.

"What is it, Corilai?"

"There's a black flame wielder who works here, at the academy. I met her sister, a lady named Uma, who helped me out a lot. I promised that in return, I would speak to this lady who has the black flames, but I don't remember her name."

"Well, I can tell you there are four people who wield the black flame working on staff at the academy. Two, you can discount immediately, as they are men. How old is this lady?"

"I don't know," Corilai replied, "But her sister, who I met, was young, but not overly young. She had two children, both under ten years old."

"Well then, that settles it. One of the lady wielders is in her sixties, and the other is much younger. I would suggest you go and see her now, before the second years start their classes for the day. I can take you, if you like?"

"Yes, please, that would be wonderful."

Symin nodded, and stood, then led the way as they left Plains House. Walking to the end of the houses, he approached a building between them and the main academy building.

"We came to this building the other day. We didn't go inside, but I remember it," Treghan said.

Symin nodded, and smiled enigmatically. He opened the door, and entered, leading them through the corridors, past classrooms and offices, and up a flight of narrow stairs. At the top, he walked along, past two classrooms, and knocked on a door.

"This office belongs to the woman you are looking for," Symin said, then nodded, and left.

"Sorry, I'll be right there," somebody called from inside, opening the door just as Symin reached the stairs. "How can I help you?"

Corilai and Treghan both stared in surprise, and heard Symin chuckle as he walked down the stairs.

"Loka," Corilai said. "It's you! I was expecting somebody else."

"No need to sound so disappointed, girl," Loka said, feigning indignation. "You're not disappointed to see me, are you Treghan?"

"Not at all, Teacher," he said, smiling.

"Ha!" Loka laughed. "You know how to please a lady. Now then, what was it you wanted? I'm sorry, but I am preparing for my second year class."

"Oh, that. I promised Uma I would come and see you."

Loka's jaw dropped, and tears began forming in her eyes as she stared at the girl.

"What did you say?" Loka asked, her voice suddenly softer.

"I made a promise, to your sister. She helped me, when I was running from the villagers who were looking for me. She saved me, and I said I would come and speak to you, as my thanks for her doing what she did for me."

"My god," Loka said. "Come inside, both of you. I would like to not be seen crying in the halls. I've not heard anybody say her name in so many years. Please, you must tell me everything. Is she alright? Did she marry? Does she have children?"

Loka ushered them inside while she was speaking, and closed the door. She leaned on the back of the door, and pointed at two chairs, indicating they should sit down.

"Well, she told me she missed you, and longed to see you again one day," Corilai said.

"And I her," Loka said. "Was she well?"

"She was, she has a husband, who she trusts, but the rest of them were suspicious, so she urged me not to enter her village. She has two wonderful children, who found me first. They went and fetched her. But her life is, overall, a happy one."

"I am glad to hear that. I have long worried that she may have suffered a similar fate to mine. I had sent her letters, but she has not replied."

"She told me she received them, I do not know why she would not have replied. She said those letters were a treasure to her, and she longed to speak to you again some day."

"So she was never chased away for her flames?"

"No, she has flames, but she has spent her life suppressing them, because she feared them, after what happened to you."

"That would make sense, I guess," Loka said. "Thank you, Corilai, for bringing this news to me. My heart is eased by it. I would like to talk of this more with you, but not right now. I should try to compose myself before my classes, which start in a little while. Thank you, from the bottom of my heart."

She stepped away from the door, then opened it to wave the two young students out. As the door closed, Loka collapsed to the floor, hugging her knees and letting her tears flow freely, finally letting out the tensions she had held back her entire life since leaving the home of her childhood, so many years ago.

Chapter 16 – Equipment

The supply officers stood behind a table at the end of the first year barracks of Plains House. On the table, were placed enormous piles of clothing, blankets, and other equipment. They called the new students up, one at a time, and spent around fifteen minutes with each.

The students were instructed to sit on their chairs and remain quiet, while they waited for their turn, and once finished, were instructed to change into their new uniforms, including cloaks and gloves, and then return to their seat, to wait for the rest to be finished.

It seemed to be taking forever, but finally, Treghan heard his name called, and walked forward to the table. One of the Supply officers came around the table, and looked him up and down, then pulled out a tape measure, and measured his shoulders, his waist, and his height. They then handed him two new tunic tops, two pairs of trousers, belts, and two vests. All were coloured grey in the style of a first year, and matched the cloak, which they added to the pile in his arms.

"Flame colour?" the supply officer asked.

"White," Treghan replied.

"Oh, So you're the one," the supply officer answered with a smile, and picked up three pairs of gloves from a pile on the table.

"Try on the right glove of each pair, and we'll see which is the best fit," he said.

Treghan stood there, confused as he tried to juggle the clothing in his arms so he could get a glove on his right hand.

"Let me help you with that," the officer said, taking Treghan's hand. "That one's a bit big."

The officer took the glove off, and tried the second, then the third.

"That one feels about right," he said. "OK, let me check that size."

The officer removed the glove, and looked at a label stitched into the cuff, then stepped over to the table, and rummaged through a pile of gloves till he found the ones he was looking for. Returning to Treghan, he placed them on the pile.

"Magnesium gloves. Look after them, and whatever you do don't loose them. Replacements are expensive."

"Thank you," Treghan said.

He carried the pile to his chair, and dropped them there, before pulling out one set of clothing, the gloves, and the cloak, then walking to the wash rooms to change.

While he was walking through the hall, he heard Corilai's name called. He did not turn to watch as she took her turn, walking straight to the wash room, and joining the line of students waiting to go in. Only then did he turn to watch as Corilai collected her things.

She walked up to the table, and was given her two uniforms, her cloak, and her gloves, imbued with onyx. When she turned to walk away, the officer stopped her.

"You're a black flame. There's something else you need. Put those down, then come straight back, before you go to get changed."

"Yes, Sir," she said.

Treghan watched, curious, as Corilai dropped her things on her chair, then returned to the table. The supply officer's voice sounded louder, and Treghan wondered if it was for the benefit of all the students, or just his imagination.

"Take these, and do not lose them," the officer said. "This is a full set of bed linen, sheets, pillow case, and blankets, all imbued with onyx, like your gloves. Only black flames receive these, and should they need replacement, you will be required to pay for them."

"Thank you, Sir," she said. "But why?"

"Black flames, especially inexperienced ones, have a risk that they may flame against their will while sleeping. You are aware of this I am sure."

"Yes, Sir, I am aware," she said softly.

"These items are to address that problem. It is common among all black flames, so you need not feel ashamed. The onyx bed clothes have the same effect as the gloves, suppressing your flames so they are controlled, to stop you from burning the barracks in your sleep."

The officer's voice then grew louder, so nobody in the room, or the wash rooms, could mistake his words.

"This is for the safety of all students, but especially your own. If any student tampers with these onyx imbued items, they will be expelled without appeal."

"Thank you, Sir," Corilai said, carrying the bed clothes to her chair, and placing them there, before collecting her new uniform, cloak and gloves, and walking to the line at the wash rooms.

As she got there, Treghan turned to her, smiling.

"I never knew those things existed," he said. "Isn't it amazing? They'll mean you can relax about sleeping, and not worry about your flames at night any more."

"Yes, it will be wonderful to sleep without doubt or worry."

As she spoke, the door opened in front of Treghan, and he walked inside. She waited until a short time later, the other wash room opened, and Marni came out, looking splendid in her grey uniform. Marni flashed her a grin, then walked away. Corilai entered the wash room, and closed the door behind her.

"I hope I look that nice in this get up," Corilai said as she stripped, then ran some water in the basin.

Quickly, she washed herself, then pulled on her new clothes. First, the trousers and top, followed by the belt, and the cloak. Then, she picked up the gloves, darker than the rest because of the onyx, and admired them.

Slipping on first one, then the other, Corilai held her hands out in front of herself, and for the first time realised that not only did the gloves help the wearer, they also helped those around them to identify their flame colour at a glance. Treghan's had been much lighter in colour, with their magnesium, and the others had all varied slightly in hue according to the wielder's flames.

Finished, Corilai looked at herself in the steel mirror, and decided she did, in fact look even better than Marni! With a bounce in her step and boosted confidence, she was satisfied. Picking up her old clothes, Corilai left the wash room with a beaming smile. She found Treghan outside, waiting for her.

"You look amazing," he said, looking smart in his own uniform, the white tinted gloves setting it off with his clean, shoulder length white hair matching it as he pushed a stray lock away from his eyes.

"Thank you," she said, her cheeks glowing red. "You look pretty amazing yourself."

Grabbing her hand, Treghan led her through the barracks, an act not missed by any of the other students. As they passed Marni, Treghan flashed her a smile, but she turned her eyes away, looking disappointed. Corilai, on seeing that look, felt a twang of smug pride.

Then, she felt guilty for it. She promised herself to be friends with Marni. She seemed nice enough. Soon, they reached her chair, and Treghan released her hand, then leaned in close.

"I know what Loka was saying," Treghan said. "I know how she teased you about me. But don't worry, I'd never do anything to hurt you. Now, I'd better get back to my seat. Talk to you soon."

"OK, thanks," she said, still blushing, then watched as he crossed the room to his own chair, picked up his things and sat down, then flashed her a big grin.

Corilai smiled in reply, then sat on her chair, moving her things to the floor, to wait as the last few students received their gear and then changed.

"Now, your old gear," a supply officer said. "The applicants colours. We will come around and collect it. You are not to wear those again. If you have spare sets, please take them out and hand those in as well."

They quickly visited each student, two officers walking down either side of the room, and collected all the applicant uniforms, then returned to the table. They began packing the things that were left, and the old uniforms, into wooden crates, which were carried outside and placed on a cart. Once they had cleared everything away, one of the supply officers returned to the table, and stood there until he had silence.

"With that distribution complete, you are now officially all fully enrolled as first year students. On behalf of the supply team, I would like to offer our warmest welcome to you all. Should you ever need repairs or replacements for any of your gear, please find us at our office and warehouse, beside the arena where your assessments were conducted. We wish you all the very best of luck in your studies. Students, dismissed!"

A cheer rang out from the first years, who then all stood and began mingling. Corilai stood, smiled at Treghan and rushed to Marni's bunk. The tall girl turned and looked at her, then tentatively returned the smile.

"Hi, you're Marni aren't you?" Corilai said, offering her hand. "I'm Corilai, and I do hope we can be friends. Treghan and I are going to have a look around, if you'd like to come with us."

Marni hesitated a moment, then took the hand, shaking it vigorously.

"I hope so too, but I don't know, you two might want to explore without me."

"Nonsense," Treghan said, stepping up beside Corilai. "Besides, I have a brother who has just entered Hills house, and I wouldn't know where to go to look for him. Your help would be awesome. I'm sure you'd like him, and I think he probably needs a few new friends."

"He'll find plenty of those in Hills house," Marni said, then smiled. "But OK then, I'll come along. Let's all be friends from now on."

Together, the three of them, resplendent in their new uniforms, walked together out of the building, and Marni led them to hills house, at the opposite end of the four barracks. When they got there, the cart from supplies was parked outside, and the supplies officers were busy unloading crates in preparation. One of them saw the trio, and approached.

"I'm sorry," the officer said. "Hills house are just about to receive their equipment. If you were hoping to visit somebody, please come back in a couple of hours, at least, and you can see them then."

"Yes Sir," Treghan said, disappointed. "Oh well, in the mean time, can you show us around a bit, Marni? Since you've been at the academy for a while already?"

"Sure thing, Treghan," Marni said with a smile. "What have you seen so far?"

"We've been to the candidates' barracks, Plains House, Loka's, um, the teaching building next to the houses, the arena, and the mess hall," Corilai said.

"OK then, so I can still show you the chancellery, the sporting amenities and recreation section, the gardens, the research buildings, and the ranger's section, which has its own recreation, residential, and research buildings, as well as offices for the various arms of the ranger organisation."

"Sounds like plenty to pass some time," Treghan said.

"And if it isn't," Marni said. "We can always take a look around the city later."

"It sounds like Ranger Academy is enormous," Corilai said.

"It is, it's way bigger than anything back home," Marni said. "I grew up in Oaklands, and we had nothing to compare. The biggest thing was our regular school, and you'd fit that into the chancellery!"

"I was in Judd, and the whole town would fit in the chancellery," Treghan quipped.

They all laughed, as Marni led them away from the houses, taking them around the perimeter of the academy.

"These are the teaching buildings, first year in this closest building, and some in the second, then second and third year in the second building, and the third building, which is the one I guess you have been to. Each building has twenty classrooms, ten on each floor, and offices for the teaching staff."

"There must be a lot of students here," Treghan said.

"Apparently there used to be more," Marni said. "But the last couple of years the scouts have been recruiting less people. I don't know why. There are rumours that somebody else is stealing recruits, but I don't know why."

"Yuri," Corilai said. "He's a bandit from Grey, who is trying to build a rebellion. His people have been kidnapping flame wielders before the scouts can get near them."

"How do you know about that?" Marni said, her eyes wide. "All that kind of information is being classified and kept from the applicants and students."

"We were taken by them," Treghan said. "We trashed their place and escaped, and were on the run when the scouts found us."

"What?" Marni squealed, impressed. "No wonder you were rushed through the admissions process late, instead of waiting for next semester! I bet they had you make all kinds of reports, and they probably don't want you telling anybody about it either."

"I hadn't thought of that," Treghan said. "We told everything to Symin, and Barache, and I assume they will report it on. But we haven't had to make any other reports. I think they wanted to focus on getting us both enrolled before thinking about anything else."

"That makes sense," Marni said. "Classes start next week, they couldn't afford to wait. But your information is probably important, so they'll be calling on you to give your reports directly at some point."

"I guess so," Corilai said. "But we told Symin everything already, so I don't know how that will help."

"It would just be a matter of following protocols," Marni said.

By this time, they had passed the teaching buildings, and reached another line of similar structures behind them, as they followed the long curved wall of the academy.

"These are the research buildings. They contain all kinds of labs where they study the different types of flames and what they can do. You know that some flame wielders can have special abilities because of their colour, right?"

"Yeah, I couldn't tell you what, but I had figured that much."

"Well, this is where they study the flames, to find new ways to use those abilities, and enhance them."

They continued around the wall, and found themselves entering a lush, ornately landscaped garden. There were many private, secluded spots and open areas for picnics or other meetings, and a winding trail through them all. Tall oaks and other hard wood trees dominated the landscape, but the low shrubs screened most of the gardens from prying eyes. It would be possible to find a secluded spot for study, or anything else, with no fear of interruptions.

Soon, the gardens gave way to sporting fields, with goals and nets erected for several team sports, and buildings containing other recreational facilities. A complex of swimming pools dominated the space on the opposite end of the area, overlooked by the arena, and on the far side of that, an immense building which housed the warehouse, and the supply personnel who ran it.

Beyond that, sat the first of several large stone buildings, as they completed the circuit around the perimeter of the academy.

"These are the buildings for the various departments of the flame rangers. This closest one is for the Scouts. Offices on the lower level, and residences on the second and third. That would be where your friend Symin lives."

They passed the buildings, and Marni pointed to the second and third in turn.

"The second one is the Enforcers, who conduct criminal investigations once the scouts bring them the information that warrants such action. Normally they make arrests as well, but sometimes the scouts do that, if they catch somebody in the act."

"Symin's men arrested the bandits we were fighting when they found us," Corilai said.

"Yes, if they feel there is a strong case against you, the scouts won't muck around and let you escape. Their primary roles are reconnaissance and recruitment, but they are permitted to step beyond that and do the job of the enforcers if necessary."

"What are the other groups?" Treghan asked.

"The research corps, in the third building, who are mostly academics, and include the trainers and teachers from the academy. The fourth building is the archivists, who maintain the libraries and also include the people working as scholars of history, geography, literature and the like."

After that, was a large open space, which wrapped around the candidates' barracks, to meet the parade grounds which occupied the large area between the main academy building, the gates, and the houses. Along side that space, beside the main building, sat the chancellery. Marni led them across the open area, and between those two imposing buildings.

"The main building houses the student services and administration staff, as well as the actual archives, and the library. The chancellery has some other auxiliary staff and of course the academy's governing body."

Passing out the other side of the lane between the buildings, they found still more. The building on their right contained the mess hall, where they had already been, and on the left was another ancient looking stone building.

"This is the student support building. It includes a small hospital, a handful of shops for purchasing books and other supplies, a stable at the rear, and other facilities for the use of all students and staff of the academy."

"And that's everything?" Treghan asked.

"Pretty much so, yes," Marni replied. "There are a few things here and there we'll discover over time, but that's the general tour. The walk took us about an hour, did you want to go into the city for a while or try to see your brother now?"

"We can go past Hills House on our way to the gates, and see if he's finished yet," Treghan said. "And if not, by all means, I'd love to have a bit of a look around the city."

Chapter 17 – City and Reunions

The trio returned to Hills House, however the supply officers were still far from finished there, so Fletcher could not leave, and they were not allowed in. Instead, they decided they would go and explore the city, as they had already discussed.

"Have you spent much time in the City, Marni?" Corilai asked.

"Not a lot of time," Marni replied. "But I know a few places. It's a nice city, much bigger than Oaklands, but just as pretty."

"Judd was never pretty," Treghan said. "At least, not to me."

"Remember Grey?" Corilai said. "It was a horrible looking place. All dirty, and always covered in smog, and it smelled bad."

"I remember," Treghan said. "I hated that place."

"You've been to Grey?" Marni said. "I've only heard stories. Nothing good though. The stories of Emberdale I heard, they made it sound amazing."

"Have you heard anything about the other cities?" Treghan asked.

"Well, not much really. I mean, I know that there's Leusbay in the north, but nothing about it. Then there's Windwall in the highlands to the north west, which is known as the city of ice, and of course south west of Grey there's the desert city, Horde, where they mine for diamonds and opals. But the only one I ever wanted to see, was Emberdale."

"It was the same for me," Corilai said. "I heard nice things about Oaklands, but it was just a town. The stories made the city sound more exciting. Of course, there are dozens of villages and I never wanted to see them either, because they're all the same. But some of the bigger towns like Oaklands might be nice to see one day."

"If you join the Scouts, you'll probably see them," Marni said.

They reached the gates, and the guards smiled and waved them through. Before them, a long avenue, lined with tall oaks, ran from the academy gates down to the city's commercial centre. Wide streets, lined with beautiful houses, each with its own small garden out front, stretched away on both sides, spaced regularly along the avenue.

"Come on," Marni said. "I know a great little bakery, let's go buy something nice."

"We don't have any money yet," Treghan said. "We just got here, remember?"

"Well, I've not been using the small allowance Ranger Academy gave me, apart from food in the mess hall, so I have a little extra saved. It's my treat," Marni said.

Walking proudly in their uniforms, hoods draped down their backs, the ranger emblem shiny and new on the cloaks, the three young students made their way along the avenue, admiring the houses on the way, until finally they entered a large plaza. All manner of stalls were spread about, as well as a stage with plays being performed, and a variety of other street performers, playing music or performing sleight of hand, all to the thrills of a respectable crowd of onlookers.

The thriving market was shaded by more of the mighty oaks that the city seemed dominated by, and there was a merry atmosphere everywhere.

"It could not possibly be any more different to Grey," Corilai said, smiling as she watched a man juggling a random assortment of objects.

"This way," Marni said, running off to the far side of the plaza.

Treghan and Corilai followed her, catching up as she entered a small hut on the edge of the plaza. They followed her inside, and immediately their noses were bombarded with a cacophony of delicious smells.

"It smells so good!" Corilai whispered.

Marni was beaming at them as she watched the delight on their faces. She ushered them over to the counter, and began rummaging in her pockets, finally pulling out a handful of coins.

"What would you like?" Marni asked.

"I honestly have no idea," Corilai said.

"I don't think there's much in here I've ever tasted," Treghan said. "So I'll trust you to choose."

"OK then," Marni said, handing a selection of the coins to the plump man behind the counter. "Can I get three of the strawberry pastries please? The ones with the cinnamon powder on top?"

"Of course you can," the man said, smiling as he fetched her order, and placed the three pastries into a small paper bag. "Would there be anything else today?"

"No thank you," Marni said. "These will be enough for now."

She happily collected the bag from the baker, and paid for them, then smiled as she led them back outside.

"Let's go to the park, and sit by the pond. It's so pretty there. It's the perfect place to eat our pastries."

"Sure thing," Treghan said.

Corilai smiled, and they followed as Marni led the way through the streets. Soon Treghan and Corilai were both lost, but they continued to admire the place as they walked. After a short time, they entered a pretty little park, with a fountain and a pond at its heart.

Marni led them to the fountain, and found a long bench seat, sitting at one end. Corilai and Treghan joined her, Corilai in the middle. Marni opened the bag, and handed a pastry to each of her friends, then took a huge bite out of her own. Corilai and Treghan followed suit, and both went wide eyed as they tasted the pastries for the first time.

"This is incredible!" Treghan said.

"I think I'll be spending a lot of money in that bakery," Corilai said.

Marni laughed between mouthfuls, and they sat there in silence for some time, enjoying the pastries, and then simply enjoying the fresh air, the pond, and watching the birds which frolicked in the water. Finally Corilai spoke.

"We should probably head back now. Thank you so much for showing us around, Marni."

"And for the pastries!" Treghan said with enthusiasm.

"It was my pleasure," Marni said. "I have a feeling us three are going to be great friends from now on."

“I'm glad,” Corilai said.

“Me too,” Treghan added. “And I just know that Fletcher will fit in, if we can ever see him!”

“I hope so,” Marni said. “It would be so sad for twins to be forever apart.”

“Well, we are twins, but in recent years, we've not been on the best of terms a lot of the time.”

“Do you think that will change?” Corilai asked. “I mean, now that you're both at the academy, aren't things different to how they were?”

“I hope so,” Treghan said. “I really do.”

* * *

Walking through the gates into Ranger Academy, Treghan walked straight towards Hills House, intent on speaking to Fletcher. The two girls followed without question, and shortly they found themselves in front of the house doors, which were closed.

The supply officer's cart was gone, and they could hear voices inside. Treghan stepped forward, raised a hand to knock, and stopped, his clenched fist hanging in the air, his indecision palpable.

“We don't have to do this now,” Corilai said. “If you don't want to.”

“No,” Treghan replied. “I want to. It's just, I'm not sure what I should say.”

“Then don't say anything,” Corilai said. “Wait and see if he says something first, and if he doesn't, just ask how he's settling in. Things will work out from there.”

“OK then,” Treghan said. “I hope you're right.”

Swinging his fist hard, he knocked twice against the door. After a short wait, the door opened, and a tall, older boy, one of the senior students, stood there, looking them over.

“You three aren't from Hills House,” he said. “What do you want?”

“His brother is in Hills House,” Marni said confidently. “And they haven't seen each other for a while.”

The boy looked them all up and down for a moment, thinking.

“OK,” he said, making his decision. “Is he a first year?”

“Yes,” Treghan said. “His name is Fletcher.”

“OK,” the boy said. “Wait here, I'll get him for you. You won't be able to hear each other talk in here right now. We're in the middle of a Hills House welcoming ritual. It gets a bit loud. Don't keep him too long, we have to keep to schedule.”

“Yes, Sir,” Treghan said.

“Don't call me Sir,” the boy said. “I'm not a teacher. Call me Senior, if you must call me something. Now wait here.”

The boy closed the door, and they heard him shouting Fletcher's name over the noise inside. After a brief pause, the door opened, and Fletcher tumbled out, as though he was pushed, the door slamming closed behind him. The two brothers looked at each other for a long, awkward moment. Finally, Treghan plucked up his courage to speak.

"I'm glad they let you in," he said.

"I am too," Fletcher replied. "I have you to thank for that. So thanks."

"Don't mention it," Treghan said. "I hope we can get along while we're here."

"I'd like that. I know I was a bit of a bastard to you at home. I promise, that's all over."

"I'm glad. But I have to know," Treghan said. "And I'm sorry for rushing into it, but please, why were you..."

"With the bandits?" Fletcher interrupted. "They have our mother. And they beat father senseless for even asking to see her. They told me if I didn't do exactly what they asked, they would do the same to her."

"That's horrible!" Marni exclaimed, eyes wide.

"That's not the worst of it. They said if I ever betrayed them, they'd kill her. So being here, I hope they get the story I was arrested, like the others."

"Enough of them saw you in chains," Corilai said. "Including that boss man you were with, and he escaped. I'm sure your mother will be fine."

"Even so, I hope to rescue her, one day. But I can't leave the academy for the next six months, at least not without at least two rangers. Conditions of my release."

"Don't worry," Treghan said. "We'll make them pay. And we'll rescue our mother. Both of us. When the time is right. If I were in your position, nothing would have changed."

"Thank you, Treghan," Fletcher said, then looked at Marni with a smile. "Now aren't you going to introduce me to your friends?"

"Of Course," Treghan said, grabbing Corilai's hand. "This is Corilai, we've been travelling together for a while. You kind of met her of course, but you weren't talking to us on the way here. And this is Marni, our new friend, who we met here. You two would get along, I think."

"Great to meet you," Fletcher said, shaking both girls' hands, but giving Marni a warm smile as he did so, gazing at her a fraction too long.

Before it got too awkward, the door was flung open, and the senior boy stood there.

"OK junior, you're up. Get back inside. You can see your friends another time."

"Yes, Senior," Fletcher said, then looked back at Marni. "Thanks for coming by. I hope to see you all soon. Good luck with classes!"

Fletcher ducked into the door, and it slammed closed behind him. Treghan stood there for a long while, staring at the wood. Corilai placed a hand on his shoulder, then looked at Marni.

"What do you think, Marni?" Corilai asked.

"Oh, he's cute," Marni replied. "And it's sweet of him to make amends with Treghan."

"I think you two will be good friends," Corilai said.

"I think all four of us will be great friends," Marni replied.

*　　*　　*

Entering Plains House, they immediately bumped into Loka, who was standing just inside the door.

"There you are!" Loka said. "Where the hell have you three been? Wait, never mind that. I need to ask something of you, and you can say no."

"What is it? Corilai asked.

"We have six days before you start classes. How long do you think it will take to get to Uma's and back, on horseback?"

"Oh, I, um, I don't know," Corilai said. "I've never done it on horse back. But I was hiking for three days to get to the bend in the road. That was across country, not on roads, and then you have the rest of the way as well."

"I think we can make it," Treghan said. "But why would you need us?"

"I left that place in the same way Corilai left her home. I may not be welcomed back. I'd rather go stop outside of town, and find her children, then I can send them into the village to collect her. But only Corilai has ever seen them, out of everybody here."

"I see," Corilai said. "But you've been gone years, why the sudden urgency?"

"I," Loka said, then paused, looking at the ground. "I never really believed that she wanted to see me, or that anybody from that life really cared enough to miss me. But what you told me, that proves I was wrong."

"OK, but why now? Why not wait until a break in classes a few months from now?"

"In three days, it will be Uma's birthday. You kept saying how much she helped you, and how you wanted to repay her, but that all she wanted was for you to talk to me?"

"Well, yes..."

"Can you think of any greater gift than a reunion on her birthday?"

"Let's do it!" Marni shouted.

"Well, OK, I guess," Corilai said. "As long as it's OK with the Academy."

"It's fine, don't worry. I have it all sorted. I figured you lot would want to come, so I got clearance from Chancellor Howe. His words were, if it's what you need to do to get your focus on teaching, go for it, and it would be good for those two to see that you can travel around without being on the run all the time."

"OK then, Let's go!" Treghan said.

"We will leave in the morning, before light," Loka said. "I'll come by to wake you all. Get to sleep early, if you can. I've told your house supervisor that you are leaving on a special mission in the morning, so you won't be expected to participate in late night activities."

'Yes, Teacher," Corilai said.

* * *

Next morning, it was still dark when Loka woke them. Quickly, the three first year students got ready, and quietly crept out of the house, mindful not to wake their fellow students.

Outside, four horses waited, already saddled and ready to go. Each had a pack full of provisions for the journey.

"We ride for as long as we can, and break as little as we have to, so we can get back in time." Loka said.

"That's fine," Corilai said, stifling a yawn.

As they left the city, they saw a long line of men on foot trudging in the gates, shackled, and being led into the city courthouse.

"Who are they?" Marni asked, eyes wide.

"They're the men from Judd," Loka replied. "A lot of them were local men, some were imported from Grey, but they were the bandit cell that operated out of the tavern there. They were the ones attacking Corilai and Treghan when they were rescued."

"Wow," Treghan said. "It took them a long time to get here."

"Yes, well, you rode," Loka said. "And the Academy has fast horses, well trained to go long periods without rest. These men are on foot, and in chains. It would take them much longer. Which is why I was confident we could do this, when Corilai said she walked over rough country."

"What's going to happen to them?" Treghan asked. "I mean, Judd must be a ghost town at the moment, with so many men gone."

"Don't worry," Loka replied. "Most of them will probably be released, once they have been interrogated and tried. I think you will find a good many of them whose stories are similar to your brother's. Once they've been assessed as not a threat to the peace of Judd, they will likely be released. But they will know what awaits them if they rejoin Yuri's men."

"You know about Yuri?" Corilai said.

"Yes, I have been fully briefed on the matter. That's another reason why we must go to Uma's now. We need eyes and ears in as many parts of the southern districts as we can get. If Yuri is building an empire, he will be trying to infiltrate all the towns and villages between us."

"And you would use her eyes?" Treghan asked.

"Yes, we would. If she has no horse, we will leave her one of ours. As a gift from her dear sister, of course, but should things there get out of hand, she will run for Emberdale. At least, that is my hope."

Leaving the city, they rode without incident, camping beside the road, until on the third day, they were approaching a small village, near the sea, coming from inland by a well travelled track.

"We need to find the children," Loka said.

"We should skirt around the village, and go down to the beach," Corilai said. "They were playing down there when I met them."

"OK," Loka said, and led the way slowly into the trees.

They passed close to the village, but had no idea which of the homes belonged to Uma and her family. They paused behind a particular house, its stone foundations scarred by ancient flames. The building appeared abandoned, and stood separated from the rest of the village by tilled fields. Loka stared at it for a long moment.

"What is it?" Treghan asked.

"This was my childhood home. I haven't seen it since they chased me away. They must have repaired it, but it looks like nobody lives there any more. I guess my parents must have either died or moved away."

After a moment of silence, Loka began riding again, leading them towards the sound of the ocean. Shortly, other sounds began to reach them. Children, laughing and screaming at play. Shortly, the four riders left the trees, entering the grassy dunes above the sand. Sunlight streamed down on them, and they paused, waiting for their eyes to adjust, their hoods hiding their faces from the worst of the glare.

On the sand, a group of children ran around, playing some kind of game of tag. One by one, the children saw the four rangers, and stopped to stare.

"You there," Loka shouted. "May we speak with you?"

The children ran up the dunes, excited at the site of rangers, which they had only heard of in stories, and soon were all crowding around the horses.

"Please, step back from the horses," Loka said. "They are well trained, but I would rather not risk any accidents."

Suddenly quiet, the children backed away slowly. Corilai looked at them, and finally spotted two familiar faces at the back of the group. She reached up a hand, and pulled the cape back from her face.

"You two, at the back," she said.

"It's You!" The little girl squealed. "It's great to see you!"

"Thank you," Corilai said, giggling at the girl's enthusiasm. "But this is important, can you fetch your mother for us?"

"I can try, but she might not want to leave the house right now," the child said. "You see, it's her birthday, and the grown ups are having a party for her. We have to go back there soon ourselves."

"We know it's her birthday, we have a special gift for her, but you mustn't let her know who we are. I want to surprise her, and she might figure it out if you tell her. Can you just tell here there is a surprise for her on the dunes?"

"OK then, but if she won't come, what then?"

"Then come and fetch us," Loka said.

The two children ran off towards the village, leaving their friends to sit on the dune, staring at the strange visitors. The rangers stayed on their horses, for fear of any possible hostile welcome. They had no idea if Yuri's group already held this village in its sway.

After several minutes, they heard voices.

"I'm sure it's nothing to worry about, dear," Uma's voice said.

"That's her," Corilai whispered.

"Honey, I know, and I'm sure there's nothing to be concerned about, but the children were so secretive, I just want to be sure you're safe, especially today. Besides, if they concocted some great surprise, I would like to see it."

As he spoke, the pair came through the trees and into site of the rangers. They stopped there, and stared. Uma's husband moved in front of her, protectively.

"Who are you?" he shouted.

Corilai turned to face them, and Uma gasped.

"Wait a moment," Uma said. "I know you! Corilai, isn't it?"

"Yes," Corilai replied. "You helped me out, and I am here to return the favour."

"It's OK dear, they're friends," Uma said, stepping around her husband, grabbing his hand as she did so, squeezing it reassuringly, then approaching the horses.

As she approached, Loka dismounted, then removed her hood.

"Uma?" she said, tears forming in her eyes. "Uma? Is it really you?"

Uma gasped, and fell to her knees. She stared in disbelief at the ranger who stood before her.

"Loka!"

Uma's husband gasped, and rushed to his wife's side.

"You're my wife's sister?" he said. "She has spoken of you every day of our marriage. And you're here, for her?"

"That's right, Sir," Loka said. "I was not sure how I would be greeted in the village. I'm sorry for the secrecy."

"I understand," he said. "Your last time here was unpleasant for everybody. Please, come back to the house. You'll all be welcomed. Rangers are needed now, more than ever. The bandits grow strong in the south, and we're glad for your protection."

Chapter 18 – Bandits Return

After a long afternoon of catching up and celebrating Uma's birthday, the four rangers left the village, Corilai and Treghan sharing a horse. They left the other with Uma, ostensibly as a birthday gift from her loving sister, but primarily as a means of running to Emberdale for help, should the bandits make trouble in the village.

Uma, her husband and children, and several other villagers waved them away cheerfully, shouting that they should visit again, soon.

Riding out along the trail towards the highway, they picked their way slowly, careful for holes or anything that might trip the horses in the dusk.

"We should have stayed overnight," Marni complained.

"We can't afford to waste time," Loka said. "We need to get back to the academy as quickly as we can. You need to be prepared for your classes. We can still ride for a few hours. The moon light will be good tonight."

As they rode, the shadows long and the trees concealing the sky, the darkness was almost at a point where they would be forced to stop for the night, as they heard the sounds of many riders, slowly passing on the highway.

Loka signalled they should stop, then led the others into the trees and forward, until they were watching out onto the highway, the moonlight shining down from a clear deep blue sky, the last rays of daylight casting a subtle tint to the impending blackness of the night sky.

There, in the moonlight, several men milled around as they set up camp.

"Hurry up," shouted their leader.

"That's Yuri!" Treghan whispered, shocked the bandit leader would be there.

"Why would he be so far from the city?" Loka asked.

The men were obviously planning to stay the night on the road, not beside it as was the usual custom. Further, they had carts loaded with building supplies. Two of the men were pulling immense beams of oak from the carts, and laying it out on the ground, as if to create the pattern for their planned construction. Loka shook her head, dismayed.

"This can only mean one thing," she said. "They are planning to blockade the road while they're travelling. They have decided to stop operating in secret. How brazen are they going to be?"

"Shouldn't we get out of here?" Marni said. "If they catch us here, they'll follow the trail back to Uma's village, and that could be bad for them."

"You're right," Loka said. "We'll have to go back towards the village, then cut through the forest until we reach the highway further north. We have to report this immediately."

As quietly as they could, the four rangers moved back to the track, then rode towards the village. Once they were a reasonable distance away from the highway, they turned into the trees and headed north. After several hundred meters, they cut back towards the highway, then rode north from there, hopeful they had avoided being seen by Yuri and his men.

"What do we do now?" Marni shouted as they rode.

"You three go back to the Academy and start your classes. The rest, you leave up to the scouts and the enforcers," Loka replied.

They rode long into the night, before finally setting up camp. They shared the watch, and continued long before sunrise the next morning. Riding in this fashion, they reached Emberdale on the evening of the fifth day, at around midnight.

Barre was on duty, and he ordered the gates open as soon as he realised who it was.

"Welcome home," he said as they dismounted, all four of them clearly exhausted. "Why are you arriving so late in the evening? Wouldn't it have been better to camp and finish your journey tomorrow?"

"Things are changing in the south, and time is of the essence. We must report to the Chancellor immediately. I will go there myself. The children need not be concerned. Please see them to their house, and explain the late arrival to their supervisor. I will await you outside the chancellery."

"Yes, Teacher," Barre said. "Come, students. I will see you to your house."

As he led the youngsters away, Loka strode with purpose across the parade grounds. Soon, she was standing at the door to the chancellery, which was locked for the night. She pounded her fist on the door, and shortly, a night watchman slid open a small panel, to stare out into the night.

"What is it?" the man hissed.

"It's Loka, returning from the south. I bring urgent intelligence and I must give my report to the Chancellor."

"Can't it wait till the morning?" the man groaned.

"Perhaps it could, but I believe the Chancellor will wish to send word sooner rather than later to his man in the field. The bandits are becoming more brazen, and have blockaded the road not far from Barache. I believe Barache may be in danger, if the bandits are acting to expand their territory."

"Indeed, that is urgent. I will wake the Chancellor. You wait there."

As she waited, Barre arrived. Soon, the door was opened a crack, and the watchman ushered Loka inside, while Barre waited in the night. The Chancellor arrived at his office just as they reached it, and he waved them inside. Closing the door behind him, Howe turned to stare disapprovingly at Loka.

"Why is it I am awakened at this ungodly hour?" he said with a scowl.

"The bandits from Grey are making their move," Loka said.

"How so?" Howe demanded.

"They are erecting blockades on the highway, not far from Barache."

"That is of concern," Howe said. "I will send a pigeon to Barache immediately, and ask him to report on this. If it appears he is in danger, I will recall him to the academy."

"Very good, Sir," Loka said.

"However," Howe continued. "Should he assure me of his safety, I will retain him there for as long as possible. We need as many eyes in the field as we can get. On that matter, how was your journey, Teacher?"

"It was productive, Chancellor," Loka replied. "We have the eyes of the village of Scholl. And the blockade is on the highway near them, so we will have a second source of information on that location. Should Yuri's activities in the region escalate, they will send word."

"Good," Chancellor Howe said. "There is another location we must watch closely. I will send an enforcer to Judd."

"To Judd?" Loka asked. "Why, Sir? The bandit cell there has been decimated."

"That is exactly why," Howe replied. "There is a power vacuum there now, and I am concerned it will create a greater problem for us down the track. Judd is strategically positioned. If we find ourselves at war, that village could well decide our fate."

"So you are sending an enforcer, to observe?"

"Yes. And to placate others who are concerned. The people of Oaklands sent an envoy while you were gone, to enquire about the men who were arrested in Judd, and whether the events there might spark an attempt by Yuri to move on Oaklands."

"Has it escalated that fast?" Loka asked, surprised.

"The escalation is of our own doing. We have struck fear into the bandits, and Yuri wants that fear squashed. So he has accelerated his plans. Your blockade is the proof of that."

"But we only knew of his existence recently. How could he expand so fast?"

"The bandits of Grey have been building their influence for a long time," Howe explained. "And it seems the recent take over of the city was in name only. That is how they did it without raising any suspicion of conflict in the region. They have been controlling the government there for a long time. And now, they are in open control, and seeking to build an empire."

"How do we know so much?"

"Byron has returned. He did not find safe port in Grey. Yuri has a large force."

"But we took so many men from Judd," Loka said.

"Exactly," Howe said. "That would have angered Yuri a great deal. But even so, that was a small cell, in a remote location. He has a city as big as Emberdale, with a long history of being disenfranchised."

"Even so," Loka said. "Would the civilian population fight in his revolution?"

"Grey has always had a powerful criminal element and a stark contrast between rich and poor. Yuri is no fool, he has used that to his advantage, and recruited many hundreds of men, from both sides of that divide in wealth. He has appealed to their own vested interests, no doubt using any means necessary. Blackmail or threats to family are both common in his recruitment, we know this from those Symin arrested."

"If they are that great a force, can we still fight them?" Loka asked.

"We must, for the sake of the people, and for the sake of Cinder. Our nation must prevail against this new evil."

"Of course, Sir," Loka said. "But do we have the troops required?"

"The senior students can support the rangers. It is something that every student agrees to do if necessary, from the moment they enrol, is it not?"

"Yes, Sir."

"On that note, how were the three first years? Was there any problem on your journey?"

"No Sir," Loka said. "They all conducted themselves well. They were tactful and took great care in their presentation of the rangers. They will all become mighty warriors for our cause one day."

"There was no sign of a battle for control?"

"No Sir," she said. "Corilai is coping wonderfully. The onyx has done its task, and while there was no need for any of them to flame on the journey, there was also no need for any of them to be supported in controlling their flames. All three colours remained quiet and controlled throughout the duration of the trip."

"Wonderful. That is just the news I was hoping for. I can rest easy then, knowing that we will not be having any episodes like we have had in the past, with new students possessed of the black flame."

"Yes, Sir," Loka said, hiding her chagrin at the comment, and remembering well some of the things that happened when she was a new student, with no control and the onyx blankets not yet in use.

"Now then, if you will excuse me, Teacher, I must send my message to Barache immediately. You are dismissed."

"Yes, Sir," Loka said as she stood and turned to leave.

The watchman followed her from the room and escorted her out to the parade grounds. As she walked away from the chancellery, the watchman returned to the building, closing and locking the door as he entered. Barre joined her as she crossed towards the houses, planning to pass them and continue to her own accommodation.

"Is everything alright, Teacher?" he asked.

"Yes," she replied. "Thank you. It's just, I have a lot to think about. I have met with family for the first time since I came here."

"That's good news," Barre said.

"Yes, but my parents were not there," she said. "And I still don't know where they've gone. I dared not ask, not this time. But one day, I will return and make those enquiries. It is good though, to have my sister back in my life."

"It is always good to be reunited with those we have lost."

"It is," she said, waving him away. "Thank you Barre, for your concern. But I'm exhausted. I will be returning to my quarters now. Good night."

"Good night, Teacher," he said and left her to make her way alone.

* * *

Yuri left the barricade, now a sturdy barrier across the highway, taking three men and riding north. Beza rode beside him, still a trusted ally and a mostly competent lieutenant. The dozen men he left at the blockade would serve well to hold at bay any prying northerners. His men had erected a large camp behind the blockade, several tents for sleeping quarters, and a stabling area for horses.

"Sir," Beza said. "I appreciate your willingness to participate in this mission yourself, but why? Wouldn't it be better to keep you safe? We are nothing without our leader."

"Exactly right," Yuri snarled. "But I have learned from that mistake. If I want something done right, I need to do it myself. There is incompetence everywhere, and my army would falter if I did not squash it. The more I lead by this example, the more the incompetent rabble will improve. One day, I may be able to rest in Grey, but today is not that day."

"But surely, Sir, this mission could have been trusted to another?"

"Trusted to another?" Yuri snapped. "You mean like we trusted Judd to that fool Harv? Or like I trusted the delivery of those two kids to the docks to somebody I thought capable of such a simple task? Need I remind you who that was?"

"No, Sir," Beza replied, looking down, suitably chastised.

They rode in silence for several minutes, before Beza spoke again.

"Sir, if I may ask, why are we going to Judd?" he asked. "I mean, we have the blockade, it seems a good location, within reach of Grey, and securing our territories, but we already lost Judd, do we need to extend our reach so thinly?"

"We are going to Judd precisely because we lost it. We will retake what was ours, as an example to those who would defy us."

"I see, but sir, do we have the resources?"

"We will soon," Yuri said in a firm, confident voice. "Those men who were arrested, many are returning to Judd already. I'm confident they will not all be placed in the cells of Emberdale. The rangers couldn't pin them with certainty of criminal acts. Being on a horse in the forest, last I checked, was not a crime. No matter who you're with."

"Yes, Sir," Beza said. "But will those men return to us? Or will that arrest scare them into subservience to the rangers' law?"

"What's more terrifying? The man who burns your neighbours house? Or the man who sits in judgement from a thousand strides away?"

"You would take that step?"

"I would raze Judd to the ground, then rebuild it and charge the bastards rent, if that was what it took. Make no mistake, Beza. Judd is critical to my plans. It rests at the heart of all routes for trade and information, between the north, the south, and the west. Nothing passes to the cities, that does not first pass through Judd."

"Then shouldn't we be taking more men? We are only four of us here now. What if the rangers are there?"

"We are going to observe, for now," Yuri explained. "If need be, we will come in force later on. But I will select a handful from Judd, and question them carefully. If I can set up a new cell, to replace that which was led by Harv, then that will be the easy path for us."

"What if the villagers refuse to cooperate?" Beza asked.

"Well then," Yuri said. "Should it prove more difficult, I will choose my time, and do it right. We will take Judd, completely and without mercy, when it is the time to do so."

"When will that be?" Beza asked.

"Within days of their refusal. The time it takes for me to bring a hundred men from Grey will decide the time that Judd falls to our will."

Chapter 19 – Lessons Learned

Barache lurked in the trees, and watched as the men milled around behind their blockade. He counted twenty three of them now. Their camp was growing, and it was clear they had set themselves up for an extended stay. Carts and horses were in plentiful supply, and large stacks of wooden crates dominated the far side of their compound, along side an open sided marquee with long tables for meals.

"I must report this to the Chancellor," Barache thought as he turned and vanished through the trees again.

As soon as he arrived at his house, Barache gathered all his ranger gear and anything else that might link him to the academy, and went into his garden. Digging up the strong box, he deposited it all in there, and buried it again.

"Can't be too careful, not with those idiots running around the place," he muttered as he went inside, and wrote out a lengthy message, strapped it to the pigeon's leg, and set the bird loose.

Around fifteen minutes later, there was a pounding on the door to the cottage. Collecting his cane, he pretended to be lame, and hobbled to the door.

"Just a minute," he said in a croaky voice.

Opening the door, he saw two young bandits standing there. He looked them up and down, then took a shuffling step closer, to see them better. Squinting, he peered into their faces.

"I'm sorry Gentlemen, do I know you?" he croaked. "It's just with my old eyes, and my failing memory, I can never tell any more."

"No, old man," one of the two said. "We're just looking around the area. We have a new outpost nearby, and we need places to store our horses and feed, and to station a handful of our men. And we need any new recruits we can find. Do you live here alone?"

"Yes, it's only me here these days. You're free to look around, if you don't believe me, Just one old fool in a cottage, that's all you'll find here."

"Good," the other man said, then raised a fist and struck Barache, sending him to the floor. "In that case, there's nobody to protect you. We'll be taking this place off your hands, so you'd best clear out. Our boss needs a proper house, not some scabby tent, for when he's passing through to inspect the men."

"But where will I go?" Barache croaked, struggling to his knees. "I've always lived here, and my family are all gone. Where's an old man to go?"

"We don't care," the man shouted, kicking Barache in the ribs, to send him sprawling again. "We'll be going back to our outpost, and returning with more men, and supplies. If you're still here when we return, you're dead, got it you old fool?"

Barache did not reply, he just sat there as the bandits spun on their heels and left. As soon as the pair were out of sight, Barache ran to his garden, dug up his strong box, and removed everything. Rushing into the house, he changed into his ranger gear, and stuffed as much of value as he could into a large, heavy backpack. He then took his barrel of lantern oil, and spread it over everything in the house, then over the gardens as well.

With tears in his eyes, and knowing he could not fight off Yuri's men alone, he fetched his remaining two pigeons. Writing a brief note to the Chancellor, he attached it to one of the bird's legs, explaining that his house was burned and he was returning to Emberdale. He then wrote a second identical note, and strapped it to the other birds leg, before releasing them both.

Barache stood before the cottage, looking at it for several minutes, before he decided he was ready. Raising his arms before him, he unleashed an intense, yellow inferno, setting the cottage and gardens ablaze in an instant. By the time those bastards returned, there would be nothing but a ruin for their boss.

"If he likes to sleep in ashes, more power to him," Barache muttered, watching long enough to ensure the fire would finish its task, before setting off on the long walk north.

*   *   *

"Welcome, Plains House first years, to your first class," Loka said, smiling. "I am Loka, and you will be seeing a lot of me in the next few weeks as I run your house's home class each morning."

She paused, and walked across the classroom, stopping in front of Corilai. Smiling, she returned to the front centre of the room, and looked over all the students.

"After that, you will see me a lot next year, but also occasionally in your first year classes. I am a black flame wielder, and I will be teaching control techniques. As you have a black flame wielder in your class, this is more important than usual, as you are all no doubt aware."

She walked to the lectern, which stood to one side of the front of the room, and stood behind it, facing the class. They sat in rows, watching her attentively. She eyed them critically, then raised to her full height, held out her arms, and created a black flame.

"Should any of you seek to break the rules, or misbehave in any way, and this includes anything at all that can be seen as bullying of your fellow students,"

The flame reached out, like a probing finger, and flicked past each student in the front row, as if inspecting them.

"You should know, I am also a ranking member of the Enforcers, so your punishment shall be swift and merciless. However, should you follow my directions, and adhere to the rules of this academy, what you learn in this classroom will serve you well for the rest of your days, and you will find your time here not only passing quickly, but also passing with many great memories and good times while you learn to control your gifts."

She stepped down from behind the lectern, suddenly seeming less stern again.

"Are we all clear on that?"

"Yes, Teacher," the students said.

"Good," Loka said, walking through the students, counting heads as she made her way to the back of the room. "Once my time with you is done in about eight weeks, another member of the teaching staff will take over your home room duties and this time will be spent on matters related more directly with your needs as students of the school."

She returned to the front of the room, speaking as she walked.

"However, in this early stage of your studies, the Academy feels it is important to ensure that all of you have fundamental control over your flames before focussing on any other aspect of your study."

She took a chair from behind the lectern, placed it centre front of the classroom, and stood behind it.

"Now then, for lesson one. I need a volunteer. Somebody a little scary. Who's up for it?"

All the students sat, looking around at one another, murmuring. They were all too timid to go first. Finally, Corilai stood.

"I can take a hint, Lo, I mean, Teacher."

"Excellent. Come forward, and introduce yourself to the class, though I am sure most of them already know who you are."

Corilai walked to the front of the classroom, and stood beside the chair.

"My name is Corilai, and a lot of you have probably already heard something about me, rumours being what they are," she said.

"Please, Corilai," Loka said. "Take a seat."

Corilai sat in the seat, then looked up at Loka.

"Please, tell them about your flames," Loka said.

"I have the black flames," she said as some of the students who did not know her gasped. "Some call them the demon flames."

"And how did you come to be here?" Loka asked.

"Um, after my flames started a fire while I was sleeping, the villagers chased me away, and I was running from them when I met Treghan," she said.

"Who is Treghan?" Loka interrupted. "For the sake of those in the class who do not know."

"He's sitting over there," Corilai said, pointing at him. "He's a white flame, and together, we were kidnapped by bandits and taken to Grey City."

There were more gasps from the students who had not heard the story. Loka put her hand on Corilai's shoulder, and leaned closer to her.

"And tell us, what happened there?"

"I set my flames lose, and lost control. I destroyed the bandits equipment, so they got angry and were going to sell us as slaves. That was when we escaped."

"And then you ran, and eventually were picked up by the scouts, am I right?"

"Yes, Teacher, and they brought us here."

"So, your flames, are the demon flames. Like my own."

Loka moved away from Corilai, approaching the rest of the class, who somehow seemed further away than before. Turning to face Corilai, she smiled wickedly.

"I want you to release your flames. All of them," Loka said.

"What? In here?" Corilai shouted. "But Lo, I mean, Teacher, it's too dangerous!"

"Just trust me," Loka said as Corilai began to release her flames. "Remember students, and this is the first thing you should always remember. All flames have one essential requirement."

Corilai's flames grew rapidly, soon engulfing her immediate area, and shortly reaching a size where the heat from the fire was felt even at the back of the classroom. Loka released her own flames, shaping them into a dome, covering Corilai.

"All flames require a steady supply of oxygen from the air around you. Starve a flame of oxygen, and it will die out."

Corilai's flames had already filled the space inside the dome, and she could be heard screaming as she lost control. The dome of fire pulsed, like a living thing, almost as though the living flames inside were pushing at it, trying to find a weakness, to escape through.

Loka's flames danced like lizards on hot rocks, skipping around the dome, making a show of the apparent struggle. But Loka's composure belied that struggle. She remained in complete control.

Soon, Corilai had stopped screaming from inside the dome. Loka stood, and dropped the flames. As the dome was lowered, there was no flame left inside, and Corilai was slumped in her chair.

"Corilai," Loka said. "Wake up, dear. You weren't without breathable air long enough to be concerned. Only a few seconds at worst."

Corilai opened her eyes, and looked through hazy vision, feeling like she had not slept.

"Loka, what happened?" she asked.

Loka ignored the use of her name.

"I starved your flames of oxygen, and they died. As you become better at controlling your flames, you will all be able to do the same thing. This is the kind of ability I am responsible for teaching. Pay attention, and you will be skilled combatants with your flames."

* * *

Soon, all the first year students settled into their routine, with classes in a variety of fields, spread across the week. Their control and power was improving for all the students. The complimentary control techniques which were added in because of Corilai and Treghan's example, while difficult for some students, were found to quickly improve the students' individual control to the pleasure of the teachers and students alike.

It also saw the student's bonds growing tighter, as they came together as a group in support of one another. By the end of the first week, Corilai, Treghan and Marni had already settled into a regular routine as an obvious trio, their friendship already solid. At the end of the Friday lessons, they were all walking back to Plains House together.

"I..." Marni said, then paused. "I mean we haven't seen Fletcher for ages. Let's see if we can drag him away from Hills house for a while."

"OK," Corilai said. "Perhaps we can take him to the pools for a swim?"

"I don't know if that's a good idea," Treghan said. "Neither of us ever really learned to swim."

"Then why not try to learn?" Marni said. "I bet Corilai could teach you both, her village was much closer to the ocean than yours. I learned in the rivers near Oaklands."

"But do we have to be learning? We've been in classes all week. Let's just go for fun. I'm sure Fletcher will be OK with that. But do you have something to wear?"

"Oh, good question. I do, but Corilai probably doesn't..."

Corilai was blushing deep scarlet as she realised what she had suggested, given that she had no swimming clothes. She looked from Treghan to Marni, and back again, her eyes fearful.

"I guess that's out of the question then," Corilai said finally.

"Not necessarily," Marni said. "We can go into town, and buy you something. Treghan and Fletcher could probably do with something too. I know boys wear their shorts, but then they have to put their clothes back on over wet shorts, which is a bad idea with your uniform, believe me."

"We could do that," Treghan said. "But Fletcher can't come into town."

"Then we can go to town first," Marni argued. "And buy him some while we're there. He'd be the same size as you, Treghan. We all got our first allowance yesterday, so we should have enough money."

"I don't know about that," Corilai said. "Half of ours went paying for all our food we've eaten in the last week."

"We might still have enough," Marni said. "I can give you some of mine if you need it."

"OK," Treghan said. "Let's go then. We have about three and a half hours of sunlight left, so we should be able to go shopping and still get some time at the pools."

"They have flames lighting the pools, so we can stay there a little after dark," Marni said.

"Really?" Corilai asked.

"Yes, they do," Marni said. "But we should hurry anyway. Before Fletcher gets dragged off to some Hills House party or something."

Dropping their study notes and textbooks from the day at Plains House, the three walked through the gate and down the long avenue to the market area. Shopping around, they soon found a stall with plain brown swimming trunks for the boys, and a modest, one piece swimming costume for Corilai.

"You can have them for half price today," the man at the stall said. "Because you're all first year students, and I know that at this stage you probably don't have a lot to spend. When my brother went to the academy, it took him months to get the hang of managing the allowance."

"Thank you so much, Sir." Corilai said.

"Yes, Thank you," Treghan said as they pooled their money together and counted out the required amount.

Turning to leave the market, they saw a familiar but bedraggled face, as a tired looking old man rushed towards the avenue, headed for the Academy. Treghan rushed after him.

"Barache!" Treghan shouted, and the old man stopped in his tracks. "Barache! Do you remember me?"

"Of course, young man," Barache said. "Treghan isn't it? And your friend Corilai? Oh! And you have a new friend. Well, it's wonderful to see you both, and great to meet you, young lady, but I must speak to the Chancellor as soon as possible."

"Wait, Barache, what happened to you?" Corilai said, concern in her voice.

Looking at her, he relented, and waved for them to walk with him. As they left the plaza and began walking along the avenue, away from the crowds, he began to explain.

"Yuri's men returned. They blockaded the road near my home, and then came to my house, looking to take it. I was only one man, against all of them, so I left. They said they wanted the house for their boss, that Yuri bastard, so I burnt it to the ground before they could come back to claim it. So here I am, after that long walk, in need of a feed and a bath, and hopefully a warm bed at the Academy."

"I'm sorry, Barache," Treghan said. "You had such a nice home."

"It's OK, I'll get it rebuilt, once these bastard bandits from Grey are all taken care of. But for now, I'll be returning to the Academy. I don't know what job they'll give me, but I know they'll let me stay. I'm a ranger, after all."

"Just a moment," Corilai said. "Barache, you said they blockaded the road near your house?"

"Yes."

"How far from your house was the blockade?"

"About half a day's walk. Why do you ask?"

"Because we saw them setting up a blockade, and if they're searching the countryside, on your side of the road, then they're probably doing similar things on the other side of the road."

"Of course, Child," Barache said. "What are you thinking about?"

"I Hope Uma and her children are safe."

Chapter 20 – Crisis in Scholl

Uma wondered about the smoke in the air as she rode through the trees west of Scholl. Reaching a small brook, she dismounted, and allowed the horse to drink. Kneeling by the water's edge, she scooped a handful up, and splashed the cool liquid on her face. Then, leaning down, she scooped more, and drank.

It was then she noticed the reflection in the water, skipping on the edge of perception like that lost dream in the morning. She looked up, and into the eyes of torment.

It was a young man, probably in his late teens, in the clothes of a peasant farmer's lad. Blue and piercing, his eyes were deep and cold, framed in blood. He stood there, on the other side of the shallow water, his front propped up against a tree. Three long arrows protruded from his back and shoulder, a dark stain running down his shirt from the wounds. Shaking, he stared at her, his cheek against the bark, his breath sharp and gasping.

"I came," he rasped, blood bubbling from his mouth as he forced himself to speak. "From Dent. Please, I..."

The boy paused, struggling to stay upright, even with the help of the tree. He coughed, a ragged, terrifying sound, the bark splattered red from his efforts.

"Need to," he stammered. "Go Scholl. Warning."

On her feet in an instant, Uma strode across the brook, and to the boy's side. Carefully, she took a knife from her belt and used it to shorten the arrows. Then, lifting him from beneath his arms, she half dragged him back to the horse, his efforts to walk essentially no help to her at all.

Worried she may be hurting him even more, she struggled to help him onto the horse, then took the bridle in her hand and began to walk back the way she had come. Glancing back, she saw the lad close his eyes. She hoped he would live long enough to explain what had happened in Dent.

She walked as quickly as she could, without causing the boy to fall. Eventually, after an hour of fretful hiking, she walked into the centre of the village, and the people crowded around.

Uma looked at the boy, scared for a moment that he had died on the way, but his eyes fluttered open and he gasped as she began to help him down. Her husband and two other men rushed to help, and shortly they had him on the ground, holding him in a seated position.

The boy coughed, and a spray of blood flew over his legs, staining the ground. Uma knelt before him, gently lifting his chin.

"Please, tell us what happened."

"Dent," he said, coughing and pausing to struggle for breath, the blood pooling in his lungs spelling imminent end to his words. "Is gone."

The villagers gasped and murmured to each other, speculating on his meaning.

"Everybody, quiet, please," Uma demanded, then urged the boy to continue.

"Bandits from Grey," he rasped. "They took women and children, told..."

He coughed again, taking longer this time to recover. His sentences were fragmented, like he was saving his words, knowing the number before death claimed him was finite.

"Told men if not cooperate, families, tortured, or worse. Some men fought, bandits killed. Men surrendered, bandits put those with the women. Men ran, shot dead, arrows. Burnt village. Mother begged, warn Scholl. I ran."

He slumped, vomited blood, then coughed again. He was now sitting in a pool of his own blood and filth. He looked into Uma's eyes, pleading for release.

"Please," he gasped. "Run. They come you next. I want, you live."

She caressed his bloodied cheek, noticing the head wound which had framed his delicate features with blood had already clotted. The boy had been stumbling through the trees a long while, before she found him. She smiled, though her tears showed a less cheerful face.

"It's OK now. Your warning will do its job well, and the people of Scholl will be OK. What is your name? That we can honour your sacrifice, when this is all over."

"Hes," he said. "Hestor Luchis."

Closing his eyes in a squint of pain, the boy coughed a final time, looked at Uma, gave a weak smile of thanks, then slumped as he went to his final rest. The men lowered his body to the ground, his eyes finally at peace.

Uma lept to her feet, and looked around at the stunned villagers.

"You heard the boy. Gather whatever you can carry. We leave immediately."

"I ain't going nowhere, Uma," one of the men said.

"Me neither," another said, and the rest cheered.

"But you will all be killed," Uma pleaded.

"No, we won't," Uma's husband said. "But we needn't all stay. Ten men will suffice, just to give them a fright, show them they can't just do as they please. But the rest of you, you all have to run, run as fast as you can. Get to Emberdale. We know the rangers will respond, but they can't if they don't know what has happened here. When you're free and clear, and you know the bandits aren't following you, Uma can ride ahead for help. Don't worry, the ranger's will not willingly allow us all to die."

The men drew straws to decide who would stay and defend their homes, while the rest fled to safety with the women and children. Uma was heartbroken to see her husband lead the fighters, but knew she could never persuade him to run. She looked at the women and the children, frightened and uncertain. She had to rally them to a purpose, before they fell apart.

"We run," Uma shouted. "We head for the beach, and we walk on the water's edge. The waves will clear our tracks. We take the rocks up the headland, and down to the next beach, where we do the same. If we go through the trees, they'll track us easily. But if the bandits arrive, we get out of sight as quickly as we can. If that means back into the trees, then so be it. Now quickly, everybody! Gather only what you can carry. We leave in twenty minutes."

*   *   *

The long line of women and children slowly climbed the rise at the end of the next bay along, having long ago passed the one near Scholl. On the horse, Uma reached the top first, and checked for trouble ahead, before turning and watching as the others slowly made the rocky ascent to the headland. The waves gradually eroded their passage, and she was thankful.

The few men who had come along, including boys whose parents forbade them to stay, or the elderly who were too frail to help in a pitched battle, did the best they could to help the children, some of whom were too small to climb the rocks unassisted.

As the last of the line reached the rocks, their feet wet from a sweeping flow of salty water, Uma thought for a heart stopping moment she saw a wispy thread of smoke begin to rise from the direction of Scholl.

She watched the horizon, not sure if she was imagining things, but then a great plume rushed into the sky, and dark smoke told of the burning of their homes. With tears in her eyes, Uma raised her arms high, then lowered them in a dramatic motion, to point to the trees.

"Into the trees!" she shouted.

In moments, the entire line was gone, hidden in the foliage nearest their rocky climb. The journey would be slower now, but they could not afford to be seen. The villagers continued to climb the headland, within the safety of the trees, while Uma stood just inside the line of vegetation, intently watching the headland in the distance, where they had crossed so many hours earlier.

The smoke grew thicker, and filled the sky over Scholl, but Uma blocked her fears from her mind, instead focussing on the task at hand. She must see these people to safety. Every one of them. Once she was sure they were not being followed, then she could think about their loss.

Suddenly, two men on horses appeared on the far away headland, gesturing at each other in animated debate. After several minutes, the two men turned and moved away, soon out of sight as they descended the far side of the headland. Uma breathed a sigh of relief, but continued watching, as slowly the woods around her filled with her friends.

"OK, keep moving," Uma ordered. "I will ride back to the village and take a look. I'll be as quick as I can."

Making her way downhill, on horse back, and not over rocks and sand, she made far quicker time. It worried her, because she soon realised that this meant the bandits could catch them quickly if they suspected where they had gone. With that in mind, Uma made her way inland a little, until she found one of the many hunters trails.

She would leave a less obvious track for anybody to pursue back towards the villagers if she used a worn trail like this. Riding at speed, she made rapid progress, and in barely a few hours had reached the edges of Scholl. Smoke hung in the air, a shroud over the desolation.

She waited there, listening for any sounds from the wreckage of her home. There was nothing but the crackle of the flames. No sounds of any people. No voices, no movement. Just an eerie silence overshadowed by the snapping sounds of burning wood.

Pulling herself together, she rode into the centre of the village. The stench hit her hard, and she wondered what could have made it smell so bad. Then, the horse recoiled, nearly tossing her to the ground. There, in front of her, she saw them. Three charred, unrecognisable bodies. And suddenly she knew exactly what that smell was. Carefully guiding her horse around the three unfortunates, Uma searched the village, but found no others.

There was a lot of disturbed soil at the edge of the village, and track marks that ran off towards Dent. Briefly, Uma wondered who the three dead were, but she pushed it aside. She had no way to know, other than to be captured herself, and that was out of the question. The three lifeless men would want her to return to their loved ones, to lead them to safety.

Weeping as she rode, Uma left that terrible place, and rushed along the hunter's trails as the evening fell on the weary forest. It was late in the evening as she rode down the far side of that second headland, and across a grassy valley. There were less trees here for cover, and soon she could see the dim light of a camp fire up ahead.

While she cursed them for risking discovery, she thanked them for guiding her home. Slowing, Uma composed herself before she reached the camp, and gave the people her report of the fate of their village, and the sad news of three dead men.

It was a long, mournful night for the people of Scholl, nobody sure if their loved one was among the dead. Uma watched as her people fretted, and felt a rage growing inside her. She looked at the horse, and was formulating a plan when an old lady came to sit beside her.

"Uma" the woman said.

"What is it, Hulnes?" Uma replied, looking at the woman's tired eyes.

"Uma, we can run as far as we like, but we lack the supplies to live long on the land. We can hunt, and we can gather, but that would slow us down, and how long would it be before we were rounded up like cattle, to be carried off to the bandits' city and forced into slavery?"

"You're right, of course," Uma said. "But what can we do?"

"You have to take that horse," Hulnes said. "You ride it better than any here. You take it and you ride as fast as you can. You go ahead to Emberdale, tell them what has happened, and beg them to help us. It's our only hope. The rangers would never allow this horror to stand."

"But, my children," Uma protested. "I can't leave them."

"Then take them both with you. The horse is strong, and they are small. Please, go, with all our blessings. We know you go to fetch our saviours, and not to run away. The entire village will be praying for your safe return."

"OK," Uma said. "I will go, at first light. Inform the others that you will continue to head north, for as long as it takes. The rangers will find you."

"Good," Hulnes said. "It is settled."

* * *

As the sun rose over the ocean, the villagers waved as a single horse trotted north. On its back, Uma's children watched as their friends disappeared from view. They clung to their mother, one in front of her and one behind, holding her clothes with a grim determination as they were jostled by the horses movements, its rippling muscles offering no comfort to the youngsters. Riding as they were, their mother's urgency only added to the fear of the past day's trauma which was etched forever into their young minds.

By late afternoon, they had already reached the bend in the highway, as it swept down from the hills, and Uma for the first time felt as though they might have a chance. Coming to a stop, she encouraged the children to let go of her, and helped them to climb down from the horse.

Dismounting, Uma fetched bread and water from the saddle bags, and shared it with her children. The sun beat its warmth into their souls as they fed on the meagre meal, and Uma felt a surge of confidence in the knowledge that soon they would be eating a real meal with her sister and their other new friends, who soon would rescue the villagers from their flight.

After watering the horse, and not wishing to waste any more time, she climbed back onto the animal's sturdy back. She then helped her son up behind her, and her daughter in front. They rode as fast as the horse could manage, using the smooth road north to their advantage, in spite of the risk of discovery. Uma knew the bandits would be less likely to pounce so close to Emberdale.

Long into the night, they rode, the moon swinging across the sky like a lantern of hope, beckoning them onwards. The hours wore on, and the horse began to show signs of exhaustion, but with a heavy heart and feeling guilty for pushing the poor animal, Uma pressed on into the night. As the small hours of morning greeted them, she could see a large shape in the distance, silhouetted in the moonlight.

"Emberdale," She said, kicking the horse's rib in a desperate bid to get there sooner.

The horse slowed, and she leaned around her daughter to stroke its neck, trying to encourage the animal to keep moving, but it was no good. The horse slowed, and soon merely stumbled along, trying to please its master in spite of knowing it had run out of energy to go on.

Uma woke her sleeping children, and helped them off the horse's back, before dismounting herself. Walking to the front of the animal, she took its head in her hands and touched her forehead to it, then stroked the beast's lathered neck.

"I'm sorry," Uma said. "It was cruel to push you so hard. But do you see that city up ahead? That's your home, isn't it?"

As if in response, the horse offered a snort, then shook its head.

"If we can walk there, you can rest, but I promise we won't ride on your back any more tonight."

She turned to her sleepy children, and embraced them both in turn.

"You are both so brave," she said. "Please stay brave just a little longer. We have to walk from here. We can not be so cruel as to make this proud beast carry us any further tonight."

For another two hours, they walked, until the walls of Emberdale towered above them. A sceptical guard looked down from above, inspecting the tiny group.

"Is it just you three?" he shouted down, "and the horse?"

"Yes, Sir," Uma replied.

"Where are you headed?"

"To the Ranger Academy," Uma said.

"Fine, I will open the gate, but you must go straight there. No loitering in the streets at this hour, you hear me?"

"Yes, Sir," Uma replied, and the gates creaked open just enough to allow them inside.

Once inside the gate, she asked the men who were closing it behind them for directions, which they gave in swift, cursory detail. Following their directions, Uma led the horse and her children through the streets of Emberdale, and so found herself before another, smaller gate. She pounded her fist upon it, and a man looked down from above.

"Who is it?" he shouted. "The academy is closed for the evening."

"Please, Sir, we need help," Uma said. "My sister is here, Loka, can I just see her?"

"I will not wake a teacher for some random stranger claiming to be a relative! Now go. If you must see her, return in the morning."

"Please, we have nowhere else to go," Uma pleaded.

"What's going on here?" boomed a voice from behind her.

Uma turned to look at an attractive man, in full ranger uniform, with an equally attractive, and very well dressed woman on his arm.

"Ranger Symin," the guard said. "Sir, this woman claims to be a sister of Loka, and demands entry. Obviously I told her to return in daylight hours."

"Stupid man! If she says she is a sister of Loka, then for the sake of all people, let her in you damn fool! A relative of one ranger is a relative of all rangers. If there's anybody giving you trouble for it later, send them to me."

"Yes, Sir," the guard said, and the gate opened.

Symin stepped forward and led them all inside, then took the horse from Uma. A man was rushing across the grounds towards them, and Symin walked to meet him.

"Barre," Symin said. "Take this horse to the stables, and see to it the poor creature is fed, watered, and allowed to rest. I will be taking these visitors immediately to visit Chancellor Howe on an urgent matter. My dear friend will have to accompany us, before I escort her to her residence."

Chapter 21 – Mercy and War

The Chancellor stood on a dais at the edge of the parade grounds. Uma and her children stood behind him, lending a human face to his story.

"It is clear," he said to the assembled crowd. "That we, as the peacekeepers of this nation, the law enforcers and governors of the people, have been too remote in our dealing with the business of governing."

He leaned on the lectern, casting his gaze over the crowd in an exaggerated, sweeping movement.

"All of us here, have become complacent, and it is understandable that some of the people of Cinder have taken it on themselves to stage an attempted take over of control."

He paused, and looked at Uma, who clung to Loka behind him. Facing the crowd again, he continued.

"The towns all pay their taxes to keep the academy and to fund the activities of the rangers. However, we have sought to be invisible, so as not to oppress them. We were wrong. In striving to appear peaceful and benevolent, we have instead appeared weak, and idle. There are those in this world who would use that perception, twist it, and manipulate it, to claim a right to rebel."

He turned, picked up Uma's son, and held him high, so all the crowded rangers could see him, holding him there as he spoke.

"These are our people, and it is our sworn duty to protect them," Howe paused, returning the child to his mother. "So when the bandits from Grey attack the villages to our south, as they have done, killing those who refuse to join their ranks, and abducting the wives and children to use as hostages to ensure loyalty of the men they conscript, it is our honour bound duty to act with swift and deliberate justice."

He paused as the crowd stared. Loka stepped forward, seeing that he was tired from a long sleepless night, and overseeing the preparations for today.

"Sir, may I?" she said.

Chancellor Howe nodded, and stepped back from the lectern.

"These people are our charges, and our responsibility is to keep them safe. We can not simply charge in like brainless warriors, and slaughter the bandits. A large majority of those men are fighting under duress, in fear of harm coming to their loved ones should they not cooperate. A more delicate and considered approach is needed."

She paused, considering her next words.

"However," she said. "We have a much more immediate duty to perform. It is a rescue mission, not a war we must embark on, both in the short term, and in terms of the overall war we find ourselves on the brink of. First, we have the women, the children, and the elderly of Scholl, travelling on foot, without provisions, with no shelter, and no food, running to us, to seek our aid, while the bandits destroy their village and kill their men."

There were murmurs in the crowd, so she waited for them to be quiet.

"Aside from that immediate concern, we must conduct a much greater mission, to send forces to Grey sufficient to depose the self appointed bandit rulers, and free the many hostages who are being kept there. Once those hostages are free, the majority of the conscripted men will surrender immediately."

Three men entered through the gates of the academy, and one shouted from the back of the crowd.

"We come from the merchants guild of Emberdale, to see if we can help."

"Indeed," Loka shouted back. "The refugees we must rescue will be exhausted, hungry, and many will likely be unable to walk to the city. We would gratefully accept any assistance you can provide, be it food, water, or carts for them to ride in back to Emberdale."

"The merchants guild will donate as much as is needed. For if we fail to help those in need, who will come for us when the tables are turned?"

"Thank you," Loka replied. "Gather your carts and donations, and meet us at the southern gate of the city in three hours. We will leave from there on this urgent mission at that time."

"It is agreed. May your mission be a success," the merchant said, before leading his companions out of the gates.

"OK," Loka said. "I hand this back to Chancellor Howe, to instruct you of the arrangements."

Chancellor Howe stepped up to the lectern, nodding his thanks to her before speaking.

"The scouts, under the leadership of the capable ranger Symin, will coordinate this mission. There are two separate groups who will depart from Emberdale today. Symin will issue the commands to you individually. The nature of the mission dictates secrecy if we are to be successful."

Symin stepped up to the dais, and nodded his acceptance of the role as the Chancellor continued.

"Please obey his command as if it were my own. Some students will be required, for reasons of intelligence they hold, to work with the scouts. Their safety will be paramount, and I sincerely hope that you all work together to ensure that every person here, student, or ranger, returns safely at the conclusion of their mission. Rangers, I give you your commander."

Symin stepped up to the lectern and looked out over the crowd. He smiled, then bowed slightly.

"I look forward to a victorious mission working with you all. I have your individual assignments on a table beside the dais, and you will each take your orders, read them, then destroy them. You will find a number on your orders, to tell you which mission you are participating in. Those numbered one, will make your way immediately to the southern city gate. Those rangers will seek the refugees, and return them to Emberdale, after which you will continue on your mission. Those numbered two, will assemble in the candidates' barracks for a full briefing. Loka will be leading mission one in her capacity as a commander of the enforcers, and I will be leading mission two. Students are to return to their houses until they are given further instructions. That is all."

He stepped away from the lectern, and made his way to the table, where Loka and Uma were already distributing assignments. Joining them, he assisted in ensuring the correct assignments were distributed. They read names from lists and handed an identical sheet to each ranger according to the number of the list.

Before long, the parade grounds began to empty as the rangers made their way to their assigned starting points, and the students returned to their houses. When the last of the assignments had been given, Symin stood, nodded to Loka and Uma, then left, walking directly towards the candidates' barracks. Standing, Loka embraced her sister.

"Don't worry, Uma, we'll bring them home, all of them."

"I know you will, Loka. Thank you."

"I have instructed the bursars and the chancellery that I wish you and your children to use my accommodation while I'm gone. I may be a while, but don't worry. Just stay safe. We'll be back before you know it."

"I hope so," Uma replied.

The sisters embraced, and Loka left, walking with purposeful strides across the parade grounds. Making her way to the stables, she fetched her horse, and checked its saddle and packs. To her surprise, the packs were already filled, stocked with her spare riding cloak, and the standard ranger's supplies. There was a note from Symin, wishing her well on her mission, and promising his group would fulfil their goals, and soon they could all put this trouble behind them. She smiled.

"Symin," she said. "You big fool. Ever since first year, you always worried about me. You're the best brother I never had."

Mounting up, she rode out of the stables and headed for the academy gates. Riding down into the city, she sensed a buzz in the air, people running about with a frantic purpose she was not accustomed to seeing. Then, as she turned into the long street which led down to the southern gate, she saw why. Merchants were rushing back and forth, stacking goods onto carts near the gates, going back to their stores for more, and then returning. An incredible display of generosity. She smiled.

"This was why I fell in love with Emberdale," Loka said.

"It is wonderful, Isn't it, Madam ranger?" said a woman, standing on the roadside. "All this, for those poor people, whom none of us have ever seen. I hope you can rescue them all. And don't worry about housing them, the merchants guild are arranging billets already, so you just get them home safely, you hear me?"

"Yes, Ma'am!" Loka said, smiling broadly at the woman before riding on towards the gate.

Reaching the gate, she watched with pride as her fellow rangers worked tirelessly to help the merchants organise the enormous donations. Twenty four carts were lined up in a convoy, each with horses to pull it. Four of the carts were now piled high with bedrolls, blankets, clothing and food. One had several sturdy barrels of water.

The merchant who had spoken at the parade grounds approached her.

"Madam ranger," he said with a smile. "As you can see, the Emberdale Merchant's Guild has come through with a sizable donation. In return, I ask only that you bring our new friends home safely."

"Rest assured, that we will. And we all thank you from the bottom of our hearts for all you have done."

"As soon as you are ready to leave, please go, with our blessings. We have plenty of billets on offer, I hope we have enough."

"We also have the use of the candidates' barracks at the academy, if necessary. We can house a hundred individuals there, temporarily at least."

"That's good," the man said. "But you lot just focus on protecting the innocent, and bringing down the bastards responsible. Let us look after the refugees, once you get them here, we'll make sure they're all safe, fed, and housed until they can return home again."

"We will. This situation can not stand. The rangers will return peace to our nation, and we will ensure this does not happen again."

"Thank you, Madam ranger," the man said, before turning and rushing to help another man carrying a large bundle.

Riding to the head of the line, Loka began making preparations to leave.

* * *

Symin stood before a small army, crammed into the candidates' barracks. Many stood on the furniture, in order to make room for everybody to fit in.

"Rangers, you are all here because you are each selected, by myself and the Chancellor, to participate in the most important part of our plan. We will march west from Emberdale, past Silverton, through the Sanctuary Hills, until we reach the highway south of Norton's Pass."

The rangers murmured their consternation at such a plan.

"Why west? Aren't the bandits to the south?" one ranger shouted.

"Yes," Symin replied. "They are to the south, but they will be watching that way closely. We know they have an interest in Judd, and they will likely already be making their way towards establishing a base of operations there. We know they had one previously, which we broke up. However, many of those men we could not hold, and many of those men had relatives kept hostage in Grey, so will have rejoined the bandits by now."

"So why not just take them on? A frontal assault. We'd take them in no time," the same man asked.

"We are not about to murder innocent men, those conscripted through threats to their loved ones are not the enemy, though they oppose us. We must take down those who are holding the hostages, and end their tyranny of terror over the people of Cinder."

"How is going west going to help us do that?" the man shouted.

"Wait, Grent," the man beside him said. "I think I see it. We're going to out flank them, aren't we, Sir?"

"Yes, we are," Symin said, smiling. "We know the bandits have been unable to take Oaklands, and that the town guards there are determined to keep the bandits out of their home. Oaklands is safe territory for rangers, and it will stay that way. We travel south, from near Yakk's Valley, to Oaklands. We will be leaving a small number of you there, as a gesture of good will, to help defend the town. In return, their trackers will run information back through Silverton, to Emberdale, to aid in our efforts to crush Yuri and his men."

"What do we do after Oaklands?" Grent asked.

"We continue south," Symin said. "We bypass Judd altogether, travel on the top of the Lizard's Spine. We establish a small base in the abandoned ruins known as the Temple of Vera, which is situated on the top of the Lizard's Spine cliffs. From there, we will be able to watch over a large area to the south of Judd."

"So we're splitting our forces twice?" Grent asked.

"Yes, but still the largest portion of our group will continue south from there. We will still be a formidable force in the hundreds. We will take an inland route, following the edge of the mountains, and the glaciers, until we reach the mining districts to the west of Grey. From there, we march on our target. We must take out the bandits who remain in their home base, end their rule over that city, and free all the hostages who have been taken there."

"It's a big mission for such a force," Grent said. "However, if you think a few rangers can do it, then I'm in. Who's with me?"

A roar erupted, deafening in the barracks, as the rangers agreed.

"Then we are all in agreement," Symin shouted over the noise. "We embark today on the greatest rescue mission in our history, and once we are done, we will ride north from Grey, and take the hostages home. As soon as the conscripts see that we have saved their families, I believe the majority of them will turn on the bandits, or at the very least lay down their arms against us. At that point, victory will be ours. The troops led by Loka will be holding the attention of the bandits while we conduct our mission, but we must still take great care to ensure that we are not discovered prematurely."

He paused, looking around the room at the crowded rangers. Symin raised his arms high above his head, and smiled.

"Are you all with me?"

"Yes, Sir!" the rangers roared in unison.

"Then we ride! To the stables, organise your affairs, and then we head for the western gates, and on to our destiny."

* * *

Hulnes huffed, her breath ragged as she clung to the arm of her daughter, struggling to keep herself upright as the younger woman encouraged her to walk.

"You must leave me here," Hulnes insisted. "I'm too old for this. I'm going to get you all captured by the bandits. Or worse."

"Don't be foolish, Mother," the young woman said, wondering what could be worse than the bandits. "We're not going to leave anybody behind. We made that mistake once already. We won't do it again."

Hulnes looked at her daughter, tears welling in her eyes as she remembered that her daughter had no idea if her husband was among the dead.

"Rulka," Hulnes said. "Please, I want you to get to safety. If that means you leave me here, then so be it."

"No, Mother, I won't!"

"We really don't have a choice any more," Hulnes said. "We're almost at the highway now. If you find the rangers, tell them where I am. They'll find me."

"Mother, we're not leaving you behind. I'll carry you myself, if I must."

The lead walkers had crested a rise, and before them stretched a long valley, in which the highway curved from the west, to the north.

"It's the road!" one of them shouted.

"See, dear?" Hulnes said. "They'll find me soon enough. But you must go on ahead. I want you to reach safety, before it's too late."

"No, I won't go without you, and that's that!" Rulka said, as they caught up with the lead walkers, who were paused on the rise, surveying the land before them.

"Riders to the north!" one woman shouted, taking out a spyglass and peering through it. "Rangers. It's rangers! And lots of them! Coming south from Emberdale!"

"You see that, Mother?" Rulka said. "I'm not leaving you behind, because help is almost here."

Chapter 22 – Underway

Symin stepped through the door into Plains House. He walked straight over to where Treghan and Corilai were sitting, watched by all eyes in the room. Everybody there had suspected this might happen, since that unusual assembly two hours earlier.

"You two," he said in a voice of authority. "You are both to accompany me. You will take part in our mission to rescue the hostages of Grey."

"Yes, Sir," they both said in unison.

"You will be given horses. Collect your possessions and meet us at the west gate in fifteen minutes."

"Sir," Treghan asked. "Will Fletcher be permitted to come with us?"

"No," Symin replied. "That boy is still on parole. We can not yet trust him to be completely on our side were the bandits to take him, but aside from that, we can not trust the bandits not to execute him as a deserter should we be overcome in battle."

"I see," Treghan said. "We will be at the gate, Sir."

Symin left, and Treghan turned to face Marni.

"Please, keep an eye on my brother while we're gone," he said.

"I will," Marni replied.

Treghan and Corilai were packed and ready, waiting at the west gate well before the allotted time. While they waited, rangers were arriving on horseback. Several gave them questioning looks, but none approached. Finally, Symin arrived, riding his stallion, and leading two young mares.

"Treghan," Symin said. "Take these horses. You two will keep as close to me as possible at all times, unless I direct you otherwise. Do you understand?"

"Yes, Sir," Treghan replied, taking the horses, handing a bridle to Corilai, and fixing his pack to the saddle of his horse.

Once they were both mounted, Symin raised an arm high in the air, and issued his command.

"We ride for Silverton."

"Yes, Sir!" the rangers called out in unison, and the ponderous gates opened, the hills spreading into the distance before them.

* * *

Loka rode at the head of the column, which stretched out behind her like a snake. The hours passed slowly, but she decided it was best to make haste slowly. Tired horses could not pull carts full of tired refugees. So they rode at a sensible pace, while lookouts watched both sides of the road and the distance before them, for any signs of the people of Scholl.

Far ahead, a lone figure stepped into the road, and waved their arms high. Loka pulled a spy glass from her pack and looked through it. It was a young woman, long brown hair unkempt and her clothes dirty.

"Wayland, Perry, ride on ahead, start them preparing to meet us," Loka shouted.

Two riders rushed ahead, and soon met the young woman, who guided them off the road. Loka continued at the same pace, leading her people, as one by one, the frightened villagers began to emerge from the trees.

"I'm glad they thought to hide themselves, just in case," Loka said.

Soon, the column began to arrive, and Loka dismounted. She saw Wayland and Perry, still in the cover of the trees, and walked over to them.

"Wayland, Perry," she said. "I want you to get all the refugees assigned to carts, and then begin distributing food and water as soon as possible. They will all be hungry, and no doubt exhausted. The sooner they are feeling refreshed, and safe, the sooner you can lead them back to Emberdale."

"Yes, Ranger," Wayland said. "What if we don't have enough room on the carts?"

"Obviously the fittest can walk, but I leave that to you to sort out. Perhaps some can ride on horses with the rangers."

"And what will you do, Ranger?" Perry asked.

"I will be taking my troops, and continuing towards Judd. We have a further mission to complete. Don't worry, a third of the rangers will remain with the column, to guard the refugees. They will make it safely to Emberdale."

She turned, and returned to her horse. Riding back along the column, she began directing them to pull along side one another, ensuring they all crowded into the small area beside the road.

"Tara!" she called.

A young ranger rushed towards her, leaving a frail woman she had been tending to on a cart, along with a second, younger woman who Loka guessed might have been the woman's daughter.

"You called, Ranger?" Tara said, her voice husky and soft.

"Yes, you will come with me, as my lieutenant. Wayland is taking charge of the column."

"Yes, Sir!" Tara said.

"Tara, it will take too long for me to select all the rangers to come with us on my own. Can I trust you to choose one hundred? I will take the rest. Once you have your hundred, move south down the road, just far enough to be separate from the column, but not far enough to frighten the villagers, that we might be abandoning them."

"Yes, Sir," Tara said. "How many will stay?"

"Enough to protect them. We will take two thirds, one third will remain. One hundred rangers to protect the villagers is more than enough, and they will oversea the situation in Emberdale until we return, unless we have need of them."

"Might we have need of reinforcements?" Tara asked.

"I don't know. If Symin is successful, I hope we will not. Our job is only to stall the enemy long enough for their servitude to end."

"What does that mean?" Tara asked, not knowing the full details of the plan her superiors had devised.

"Never mind, but know this: what we do today, could change our world tomorrow. So take care, and follow your orders."

"Yes, Sir!"

Tara, true to her word, followed her orders, and soon was making her way south with one hundred rangers behind her. Loka smiled, Watching them go, as a similar crowd grew behind her.

"She has chosen well," Loka mused. "Not all the strongest, but a good mix of experience and a few of the younger ones who will benefit from the experience. I am pleased she has not taken any too weak for field duty, and yet has not left the column without strength in its guard. Tara will make a good lieutenant."

She led her hundred, to merge with Tara's, then turned and rode back to the column. The remaining one hundred rangers were spread among the carts, and the villagers seemed not to have noticed their reduced numbers.

"People of Scholl," Loka called out. "I am Loka, commander of the forces which have come to meet you. My subordinates, Wayland and Perry, have been dealing with you during this process, and will now lead this column to Emberdale, where safe lodgings will be provided. Do not fear. I leave you with one hundred rangers, for your protection. No bandit will harm you now. And I take my remaining forces to investigate the deeds of those men, that we may expedite your safe return once the bandit organisation is defeated. Go with the guidance of the flame. May your nights be well lit, and the darkness held at bay."

The villagers cheered, and Loka turned away, to return to her forces, waiting behind her. As the column began its slow journey back to Emberdale, Loka led her small army south, before turning west. She led her troops along the highway as it wove between the Devil's Teeth to the south, and the Grey Wolf Mountains to the north.

"This is where those two were abducted. We must not allow ourselves to be complacent," she said, before shouting to her troops. "Look sharp, and do not allow your guard to falter. The enemy could well be watching us already. We must be prepared for conflict at any turn, we are not safe. This is not a sunny afternoon picnic with our sweethearts, this is war, and we are starting it. Do not falter in your resolve, or your commitment. We will prevail!"

The troops, many of whom knew her not only as their commander, but as their teacher in past years, cheered with enthusiastic voices as they rode towards an unknown destiny.

* * *

Barache rode behind Treghan and Corilai, seated high in his saddle, his back straight and proud. Symin looked back, over his shoulder at the old man.

"Barache, I do wish you would reconsider," he said. "This journey will be tough, and your greatest fighting days are past. You could have stayed behind, and played chess with the Chancellor."

"Impudence!" Barache scoffed. "Young man, I am as fit as I've ever been!"

"Perhaps you are," Symin said. "But we must consider our best use of all personnel."

"In which case, I am right where I need to be. You have these two youngsters along, because they have seen Yuri, they know his face, and they know his operations in Grey. Am I correct?"

"Yes, Sir," Symin said.

"Then you also need me. Remember, I have faced down these ruffians already. They threatened my life, and my home. My home is burnt, rather than give over ranger territory to them. I must make them pay for my sacrifice. And nobody knows the woods around my home better than I do. I will get you past their little outpost, and they will never see us coming when we return from Grey to defeat them."

"All fair points, Sir," Symin said. "But seriously, how is your health? Are you up for this task? It will not be easy."

"Spare your concern," Barache said. "Though I appreciate you worrying about my welfare, it is not necessary. I made my way to Emberdale, without injury or capture, after giving those bastards a bloodied nose for their troubles. I can take care of myself, and I can protect a few of my comrades while I am at it. And besides, I am needed in Grey, when this is all over. The chancellor has further plans for after the conclusion of this little conflict."

"I had suspected as much," Symin replied. "And I must say, it is probably far beyond the time to do it. We have been too invisible as a governing force in Cinder these past few decades."

"You were aware?" Barache asked, his eyebrow raised.

"I had my suspicions," Symin said. "I have long discussed the possible needs with the Chancellor. I am glad he has seen sense at last."

"Beware your own impudence, boy," Barache snarled. "The Chancellor has had good reason for operating as he did."

"No offence is intended, of course," Symin said. "I am aware that Cinder has lived in unprecedented peace since he rose to lead us, but all such things are temporary. It was only a matter of time before somebody tried to take control for themselves, and this is the context in which he and I have discussed the need for a more visible presence, among other things."

"What other things?" Barache demanded.

"Surely you have noticed our declining numbers?" Symin said. "Though, living as you have done, in the field for so long, perhaps not. Our recruiting drives have been less successful in recent years, and the decline is growing more rapid. This year's student intake was the lowest in our recorded history. We can't continue like this, without losing our ability to effectively enforce the laws of Cinder, or distribute proper justice when necessary. Our powerful old guard is getting too old to continue, and we have not enough strength as yet in the next generations. A presence in every town will help us to find those we need to fill our ranks."

"Sir!" Treghan shouted. "You don't mean, rangers working from offices in the towns? Like in the old days?"

"Yes, Treghan, but more than that. There will be an appointed administrator in each town as well. They will oversea the autonomous governance of the town, and should anything occur that may threaten the peace, such as this rebel uprising in Grey, they will be tasked with ending it and replacing the corrupted local government. Am I right, Barache?"

"As always, Son" Barache said. "You are perceptive and yes, you are right. But this does not go beyond us. My mission must not be revealed."

As they crested a hill, the town of Silverton came into view. Symin raised his arm, and signalled for them to stop.

"Rangers," he shouted. "Silverton is a friendly town, and they are often visited by our people, for peaceful purposes. However, we can not have them panicked by such an army descending upon them. I will ride on ahead, and inform them of our arrival. Meanwhile, you will all take up station in the fields to the south of the town. We will not be here long, simply long enough to water our horses and take refreshments. Then, we continue to the west. I hope to be well into the Sanctuary Hills before midnight, and then we camp. Without carts, we have the advantage of speed, let us not waste it."

"Yes, Sir!" the rangers replied, their voices booming on the late afternoon air.

Symin turned his horse to face the town, and rode away. Not having been instructed otherwise, Treghan and Corilai followed, as did Barache. The remainder of the men made their way towards the fields, as Symin had ordered.

Entering the town, Treghan and Corilai were fascinated. The architecture was more ornate than they had seen in their own villages, though not as grand as they had seen in Emberdale.

"You two, don't stare," Symin rebuked. "It's rude, and we must be good to these people."

As he spoke, two men approached.

"Good rangers," one of them said. "To what do we owe this visit?"

"Sir, we merely pass through, however we wish to water our horses and refresh our people. We have a large force waiting in the fields south of the town. We will of course pay your people handsomely for the water and food we use, and of course the grass the horses eat while we are stopped here. We will be gone by evening."

"Very well," the second man replied. "You are indeed welcome, as all rangers are welcome in Silverton. The young ones will gladly carry water and refreshments to your people, and we will send our bill to the Academy on your departure."

"You are too kind, good sir," Barache said.

The second man looked at Barache through narrowed eyes, before bursting into a broad grin.

"Well, I'll be damned!" he exclaimed. "It couldn't be! Barache? You sly old dog, where have you been hiding all these years?"

Barache leaned forward, trying to recognise the man.

"My word, the years have not been kind to you, or perhaps to my memory," Barache said. "Wait, I do know you. Lailon Hart! It's been decades! So this is where you've been hiding since you left the academy."

"Indeed, I am co mayor of the proud township of Silverton. And clearly you never left the Academy, but why have I never seen you? In all these years, I have visited Emberdale many times, but never run into your craggy old face!"

"Craggy? Why you! If you must know, I was living far from here, on a long term assignment. Which is why your particular brand of sleaze was unable to corrupt me whenever you were in the city!"

"Sleaze?" the first man shouted. "How dare you insult the mayor!"

"Calm yourself, Jodahn," Lailon said. "Barache and I are old friends, and we have always insulted each other. It's a little game we play affectionately with each other. Barache, old friend, it is good to see you."

"And you too, Lailon. I must say, the simple life seems to agree with you."

"And with you, but come now, let's go into the tavern, and catch up while your people do their thing."

"A grand idea," Barache said. "Symin, you will not have need of me for the next little while?"

"Go, old man. I will send for you before we depart."

"Thank you, boy."

"Isn't it strange," Corilai whispered. "All these rangers have such different pasts, and you never know who might know who."

"Well," Treghan replied. "They did come to the academy from all over Emberdale, and we have no idea which towns or villages they all came from, so it should be no surprise to run into old friends in strange places."

"Enough gossiping, you two," Symin said. "Head to the field, to meet the others. I will be along shortly, and the townspeople will be along also, with refreshments. Quickly now."

"Yes, Sir," the pair said in unison, riding off towards the fields.

Chapter 23 – Oaklands

The next day, Symin led his army out of the hills, and into the blustery heights. They would meet the highway south of Yakk's Valley, and ride on towards Oaklands.

"Fasten your cloaks," Symin said to the two young rangers behind him. "The winds howl down the mountains from Windwall and Norton's Pass. They carry the cold down from the snowy peaks, and it will freeze your blood if you aren't prepared."

As if his words carried the weather to them, an icy wind whipped at their clothes, its freezing intensity numbing their faces. The highway loomed ahead, and the wind was visible in the scattering dust and snow, which fell in sparse flurries, ahead of the storm clouds which obscured the mountains in the distance, and blocked out the dawn sun.

As they turned onto the highway, the conditions worsened, and soon they could not see the long column of rangers behind them. Symin lit a guiding flame from his right hand, and they pressed on, the bright yellow light shining like the morning sun.

Soon the storm worsened, and an icy sleet pelted their backs, the wind swirling the tiny particles of ice before them in a dizzying dance. With the reduced visibility, they slowed to a crawl, and even then nearly ran into a heavy cart, which sat across the road, blocking their passage. The enormous vehicle was stacked high with crates.

Symin led the youngsters around to the far side, where they would be sheltered from the driving wind for a moment.

"Who goes there?" a man shouted.

"We are rangers, from Emberdale, travelling to Oaklands," Symin replied as they rode into the lee of the massive cart.

His light shone upon a pitiful sight. Six people, huddled together, their several oxen lay nearby, clearly exhausted. The people shook with the cold, their thick furs soaked through. The man who had spoken stood, and moved towards them.

"Please, Sir ranger," the man pleaded. "We have no fire. The storm hit too quickly for us this time, and we were unable to get a fire started before everything was too wet. Can you help us?"

Looking around, Symin noticed a pair of crates, smashed on the ground near the cart. He dismounted, and walked to them. Gathering the splinters, he approached the huddled traders, and dropped the wood in a pile. Kneeling before the pile of wood, he held a hand before him. Symin focused his energy and lit a bright yellow flame, holding it on the wood until it began to burn on its own.

Standing, he beckoned to the people, who immediately crowded around the small fire.

"You'll need more wood," Symin said, as he turned away.

The rangers had began to crowd around the fringes of the sheltered space, and the man turned to Symin, wide eyed.

"This is not a few rangers, this is an army! What has happened, Sir?"

"It is nothing you need fear. Focus your energies on surviving this storm, then make your way to town as quickly as you can."

"But Sir, please, we would rest more easily if we knew our friends and family were safe. There has not been a force this large in these parts for a generation or more. Tell us, what has happened, that the flame rangers of Cinder move in such force?"

"Good sir," Symin replied. "We travel south, to investigate stories of uprising and barbarism. Bandits are reportedly sacking villages as they travel. As soon as you can move, I suggest you take your people, and make haste to a walled town, whichever is closer in the direction you are travelling, and await news. Do not speak of us, but await word from Emberdale. We will be placing rangers in all towns, for your protection, when this is concluded."

"So the rangers will return to the way of the old days, when we could see your presence, and trust in your protection. This is good news, in spite of the cause. Thank you, Sir ranger. We have travelled from Oaklands, and happily report the town remains secure and safe. We were headed for Windwall, but will stop in Yakks Valley, as you suggest. It is not as secure as Oaklands, but it is safe, and sheltered."

"You would welcome rangers in your towns?" Treghan asked.

"Young one, you would not remember anything other than how it has been in recent years, but there was a time that every town and village had a ranger outpost, and they ruled, in some cases, with an iron fist. But even then, it was better. You had somebody you could go to, if you had trouble. Now, many towns have taken the law into their own hands, but in some places, criminals run roughshod over the merchants and traders. We travel the land, and we can attest to the dangers which have been growing this past ten years. A stronger, visible presence from the rangers will be welcomed by many."

"But not all," Corilai said.

"Indeed, young lady," the man replied. "It is as you say, but those who do not welcome it, will come to accept it. And the ones who don't accept it, those are the reason it is necessary."

"It is as you say," Symin said. "Would you have further need of our assistance?"

"No, Sir ranger," the man said. "We are grateful, but now we have fire, we will be fine. We can keep the fire fed. It will dry our clothes and warm our skin. And once the storm is gone, we will be ready to continue our journey. Go with our thanks, and when you arrive in Oaklands..."

The old trader pulled a small card from his cloak, and handed it to Symin.

"Hand this to the mayor, and tell him we are safe. The wait for news when storms come is sometimes difficult for those who wait for our return."

"It will be done. Farewell," Symin replied, taking the card and walking back to his horse.

Climbing into the saddle, Symin turned and rode back into the wind and snow, the two youngsters following. Almost immediately, they lost sight of the traders, just as they had lost sight of the army behind them. But Symin's flame guided them, as they made slow progress south.

An hour later, the winds were subsiding as they descended from the edge of the highlands, and made their way through the foothills to the north of Oaklands. By the time they reached the walls of the town, the clouds were a dark scar behind them, stretching low across the horizon of a clear blue sky.

The gates opened as they approached, and the rangers entered. The army from Emberdale soon crowded into the town as they made their way to the central square. Once there, they were greeted by a well dressed grey haired man with a tidy short beard.

"Welcome, rangers," the man said. "I am Bray Forgart, Mayor of Oaklands."

"Thank you," Symin said. "I lead these forces south, to investigate the activity of the bandits from the steel city. I shall leave a small contingent here, as per your request, made recently to the Chancellor."

"That is welcome news," Bray said. "For now, your people have had a difficult ride through that storm, rest here a while before you continue."

Symin dismounted, and approached the mayor. Retrieving the trader's card, he handed it to the mayor.

"We encountered this group in the storm. They asked me to relay the message that they are safe."

"Thank you," the mayor said. "If you are happy to look after yourselves for now, I will visit the families and let them know the good news. I am sure they will be relieved."

"Of course, I have a visit I would like to make myself. My people will be happy to spend some time relaxing before we move out. We will likely do so at first light."

"Very good. I will have the town guard assist you in finding adequate accommodation. The town square would be too crowded for all of you."

"Thank you," Symin said, then turned to Treghan and Corilai. "You two, dismount and come with me."

"Where are we going?" Corilai asked.

"I need to visit my family, and I would prefer you two are not left unattended at this time."

He led them out of the square and towards the southern side of town. They soon found themselves walking through one of the poorer areas, the small homes still more substantial than anything Treghan had seen in Judd.

Nestled against the town wall, there sat a larger house, wooden fences surrounding a modest yard, the protective stone towering above. One of the many stairways that ascended the wall ran behind the house, accessed from the lane beside the yard. Symin walked to the house, and opened the door.

As he stepped inside, Treghan and Corilai heard a commotion, and paused, unsure if they should follow. Then a rotund woman rushed out, and hustled them inside, grinning broadly and screaming a torrent of words they were not able to catch.

"Mother," Symin shouted. "Slow down, the children aren't use to your way of greeting."

She stopped, looked at him, an expression of shock on her face, then her grin returned.

"Of course, Symin, you're right," she said. "Welcome, children, to our home. I'm sure Symin has told you nothing about us. My name is Garuda, I'm Symin's mother. We run a small bakery from the side of the house, which is why we can afford a bigger place than most of the neighbours."

"My name's Treghan, and this is Corilai," Treghan announced as Corilai offered a curtsey.

"My word, such polite youngsters. What on earth are you doing with my spoiled brat of a son?"

"Enough, Mother," Symin said. "We just stopped by for a quick hello. We'll be scouting ahead this afternoon. If possible, we'd like to stay the night here, and we head south in the morning."

"That would be wonderful!" she exclaimed. "But first, why don't you go upstairs to your old balcony? There is somebody there who will want to see you."

"He's here?"

"He was this morning, along with his mate and their three chicks. I swear, that creature is psychic. It's like he knew you were coming."

Symin took off up the stairs, leaving Treghan and Corilai bemused.

"Go on then," Garuda said. "Follow him, but be quiet and move slowly. They're shy around strangers, at first."

Not sure what awaited them, Treghan and Corilai followed Symin, and found him as he strapped a gauntlet to his arm and stepped through a doorway onto a small balcony, making a strange cooing noise. Turning, he stepped back into the room, a large falcon on his arm. He looked at the pair, and smiled.

"I raised this fellow from the egg. His name is Hunter. Ever since I left for Emberdale, and was unable to take him, he always comes to see me if I'm in town. Today, he has some little friends."

As Symin spoke, a second falcon poked its head around the door frame. The female. She looked left, then right, then disappeared for a second. Then, she trotted in, three chicks behind her, so young that they were probably only newly fledged.

"They seem so tame!" Corilai whispered, kneeling on the floor to get a closer look at the babies.

"Squaark!" said the female, warning her not to get too close.

"He is, more than her," Symin said, laughing. "It's just the trust they have because I raised him."

Walking to a chair, Symin sat, holding the arm with Hunter perched on it up before his face.

"You have made yourself some beautiful children this year," Symin said.

Hunter chirped softly, then preened himself as his mate fluttered to land on the arm of the chair. One by one, the three young ones fluttered up beside their mother, as she pecked at Symin's glove.

"This is a side of you I'd never have suspected," Corilai whispered in awe.

"It's nothing, really," Symin said. "All rangers have a life before they were rangers, but being a ranger becomes your life. So you will always be surprised when something from a ranger's past presents itself."

Symin stood, and faced the door. All the birds watched him intently. He raised his arm and smiled.

"Off you go for now, Hunter. We have some scouting to do."

The falcon leaped from his arm, and flew out the door. The others followed, and the three rangers were left alone.

"Come, we should head out. I want to see what kind of bandit presence there is on the south spine road."

"South spine road?" Treghan asked.

"Yes. It is the inland route from here to the temple, which you have already been to. It travels the top of the Lizard Spine cliffs, from the temple south, which you already travelled, but if you had gone north west from the temple, instead of down the spine towards Judd, you would had taken that road all the way to Oaklands."

"I see," Corilai said. "And you want us to see if it's safe?"

"Not safe, but clear. I'd prefer if the bandits were not aware of an army passing by. If we can ensure a clear road, then we can give them as little warning as possible before we hit Grey. Now, follow me, and stay close."

"Yes, Sir," they both said.

Symin led them downstairs, then outside. Walking around to the side of the yard, he led them to the base of the stairs. Shortly, they arrived atop the wall, and the fields outside the town stretched to the edges of a dark forest to the south. The road they would take was a visible scar across the grassy fields, which disappeared into the canopy of the trees.

He led them along the wall until they reached stairs which descended inside the wall, to emerge through a gatehouse where the road passed through a sturdy gate which stood open. Stepping through, they made their way out onto the road, watched by a handful of the town guards who stood on the outside, watching for the approach of travellers, or bandits.

The afternoon sun beat down on them, baking a warmth into their bones which the earlier storms had not prepared them for. A bird cried overhead, and the three rangers looked up. Hunter circled them, high above, moving with them as they crossed the fields.

Soon, they entered the trees, and continued walking. Symin set a fast pace, and the two youngsters found themselves hard pushed sometimes to keep up.

"Sir, please, why are we moving so fast?" Treghan said.

"This is not fast. As scouts, we have to travel quickly, and silently. If this is too much, perhaps you need to consider your options."

"It's OK, Sir," Corilai said. "We're just not used to it yet, that's all."

"I guess you're both still young," Symin said. "But remember, you must consider this entire journey advanced training. Don't ever think it's too hard, your job is to make it not hard. The only way for that to happen, is if you both knuckle down and push as hard as you can, until it becomes second nature to you."

"Yes, Sir," Treghan said, sounding short of breath.

Just when the hike was getting long, Symin surprised the youngsters by breaking into a run.

"You have to keep up," he called out to them.

With a collective sigh, Treghan and Corilai both ran after him, pushing themselves well beyond their normal endurance levels. Symin stopped, and waited for them on a rise.

As they approached, they heard a noise from the undergrowth. A strangled, anguished cry, like the yelping of an injured dog. Not stopping, Corilai disappeared as she ran after the sound. Treghan and Symin rushed after her.

Breaking through into a narrow animal trail, Corilai saw the source of the sounds. A bobcat was dragging a struggling bundle of fur away, presumably as its next meal.

"No! Stop right there!" she shouted, and the bobcat paused, looking at her, a low growl erupting from its throat, as the tiny wolf cub it was dragging off whined and thrashed.

Corilai stepped slowly towards the tableau, raising a hand in front of her, grim determination in her eyes.

"I will not let you harm that innocent baby," she snarled, as black flames raced from her finger tips, to blast the bobcat in the head and neck, causing it to scream and drop its prey.

Turning, the bobcat vanished into the forest, leaving its meal. The wolf cub whimpered as Corilai approached. It was tiny. She guessed it had likely left the den for the first time in the last day or so. Turning, it looked up at her as she bravely reached out to touch the animal's side. There was blood in the fur, but the wound was not fatal.

"It's OK, young one," she said. "You'll be OK now. Can you find your mother?"

Not understanding a word of it, the cub nevertheless seemed to understand she was not a danger. Turning its head, the cub sniffed her hand, then licked it, before staggering to its feet and running off into the undergrowth.

"Why did you do that?" Symin said. "We aren't here to stop cats from eating."

"I'm sorry, sir," she said. "I just, I don't know, I felt sorry for the little guy."

"Be that as it may," Symin said. "We must ignore the things which distract us from our task. Do you understand?"

"Yes, Sir."

Symin led them back to the road, and they continued on their way. Within the hour, they found themselves standing at the edge of a clearing, atop a hill. Walking out, Symin led them to the peak and they stared out over the sea of treetops. In the distance, they could see the temple of Vera, where Treghan and Corilai had slept so long ago.

"I hadn't dreamed it was this close to Oaklands when we were here before," Treghan said.

"It's further than it looks," Symin said. "But still, this is far enough. We can bring the troops here without worry, and camp on this hill while we scout ahead. That would mean we could be back here, and preparing to lead the army on to the temple by noon. I don't know how many bandits might be in the woods beyond there, but at least we will have avoided detection this far."

Symin turned, and led the way back to Oaklands. There was no further incident along the way, and as the night settled over the walled town, the gates were secured and the rangers settled in for the evening.

Garuda spent the evening fawning over Corilai and Treghan, and they enjoyed their time in her home. She served a delicious stew, fresh bread drizzled with melted butter, and even let them try a small cup of dry ale,

By the time they slept, both Treghan and Corilai were well fed and happy. Symin, catching their happiness, was relaxed, Hunter on his arm as he talked to his mother and father long into the night.

Chapter 24 – Enemy Territory

Loka stood atop the rise, looking down at Judd. There were far more people there than she remembered, and they were hard at work. One man in particular seemed to be barking out orders, as he moved among them.

Enormous amounts of timber lay in piles to the south, and the men were using the lumber to construct walls, effectively blockading the road to the south, and barricading the village of Judd against attack.

"We're too late," Loka said as Tara came up beside her. "I had hoped we could reach Judd before them, and hold it against the bandits."

"Didn't the intelligence say the bandits had already held Judd?" Tara asked.

"Yes, but that was the group Symin arrested. A lot of them will be returning, but I hadn't expected these numbers. Yuri must have sent a lot of recruits north."

"Shall we attack?" Tara asked.

"No," Loka said, then paused, considering the situation. "We must stop any further advance, and it would be nice to secure the safety of any remaining villages, as well as the road to Oaklands, but it is too risky now, because anything like that would mean trying to get past Judd, and that would likely turn into a full blown war."

"So we might have to fight anyway?" Tara said.

"No, we won't fight, not unless it is absolutely necessary. Remember, most of these men are conscripts. They only follow Yuri for the sake of their wives and children."

"But what if we have no choice?" Tara insisted.

"We will always have a choice. We have the power. Our fire should be their saviour, not their doom."

"So what are your orders?" Tara asked.

"Collect the rangers, establish our camp on this rise. I want them to see us, but not fear us. We will set up our camp, and make it clear we are not leaving. In fact, I have a devious idea..."

Loka trailed off, and then remained silent for several seconds. Finally, Tara had to ask.

"What is it?"

"What is what?" Loka demanded.

"Your devious idea," Tara explained.

"Oh, that," Loka replied. "We will sneak down there after dark, and steal some wood. We'll build our own barricade, right here on the rise, where they will see it continuously, a reminder that we could squash them at any moment."

"That's mean," Tara said. "I like it. But how long do you plan on staying here?"

"As long as we need to. As long as it takes for Symin to enact his part of the plan."

*　　　*　　　*

Symin led his army through the gates of Oaklands at dawn. Staying behind, a small contingent of twenty rangers waved from the top of the wall. Stretching far into the distance as they filed three abreast into the trees, it was an impressive show of force.

The people of Oaklands gathered alongside the road near the gates, cheering as they passed. Many had offered beds for the visiting rangers over night, and those men and women had enjoyed hearty meals with their hosts, with promises to return another day.

"It's good, to feel so welcomed," Symin said. "Oaklands remains a good friend to rangers."

"Why is that?" Treghan asked.

"Because the rangers have helped them in the past. There was a situation, much like the one we face in Grey today, many decades ago, but the people of Oaklands resisted, and many were killed or tortured by the despotic governor. Then the rangers stepped in, and freed the people. It is something that Oaklands has made a solemn vow to remember."

They continued on, and as the sun climbed higher into the morning sky, they rode into the clearing on the hill. Symin arranged for the rangers to set up camp there, while he led the way, on foot, towards the temple. Treghan and Corilai followed along, and they made good time.

After two hours running, they came to rest on the outskirts of the abandoned remains of the temple complex.

"I hadn't realised this was such a big place," Corilai said. "I thought it was just the main temple building on the cliff."

"No, there was a sizable settlement which supported the temple, hundreds of years ago, before the fall."

"What does that mean?" Treghan asked.

"Of course," Symin said. "Most people in the villages wouldn't remember their history. You'll learn all about it in class though. Many hundreds of years ago, something happened, which ended the nation we were a part of and forever cut us off from the rest of the continent. That event, which is shrouded in mystery, is what caused Cinder to come into being as a nation. It was after that the rangers were formed, and Emberdale was established as our capital."

"What was the event?" Corilai asked.

"We don't know a lot about it," Symin said. "But it is why our landscape is struck by glaciers, and deserts, and all the other terrains, in such close proximity to one another."

"What could possibly do that?" Treghan asked.

"I don't know," Symin admitted. "But one day, we will find out. There are rumours the borders of the old nation were far greater than those of Cinder today. But without being able to journey beyond our borders, we can't find out. The mountains are treacherous to the west, in the north they meet the oceans which are treacherous to the east, and the desert to the south can not be safely crossed. One day, maybe an expedition can go beyond those boundaries, and return with news of the outside world, but in the past few centuries, that has never occurred."

"Is there nothing we can do to find out more?"

"There is, and I intend to do it one day," Symin said. "I will visit Horde, the city in the desert, south west of Grey. From there, I will investigate the desert, and what lies beyond it. If I can ever convince the Chancellor to allow such an expedition."

"Would it be dangerous?" Corilai asked.

"Incredibly," Symin said.

Quietly, they picked their way through the ruins, heading towards the main building, and the cliff face. Symin held up his hand, signalling for them to stop, as he picked his way ahead. As he rounded a stone wall, Corilai walked away from Treghan, skirting the edge of the ruins.

Suddenly, there was a shout, and the sounds of swords clanging on stone, as Symin beat a hasty retreat, expertly dodging the attacks as three bandits pursued him. Once they were in the open, the bandits separated, spreading out to hamper any further escape routes.

One of the three was then immediately in front of Corilai, who was caught by surprise. He swung his ham sized fist at her, knocking the girl to the ground, just as Symin reached Treghan. Symin glanced around, and realised he could not reach her in time, as the bandit raised his sword high, intent on dispatching his prey.

"Corilai! Flame him!" Treghan shouted.

Corilai, groggy after striking her head on the ground, flailed her arms And let out a weak black flame. The bandit laughed.

A growl, deep and ferocious, was followed by a brown and grey blur, rushing from the trees. The bandit's laughter stopped as the blur struck his chest, sending him to the ground, the sword clattering away harmlessly.

Standing over the man, the enormous timber wolf snarled, and snapped at his face, while Corilai clambered to her feet. She retrieved the sword, and tossed it away, to clatter harmlessly across the rocks, out of reach of the bandit, then faced the wolf.

"You're that pup's mother, aren't you?" Corilai said.

The wolf looked at her for a moment, then snapped at the bandit once more, before loping off into the trees. Seeing his chance, the bandit began to stand, turning as he did so, as if to run.

"Don't even think it, you bastard." Corilai snarled, casting dense black fire around them both. "You're mine, so get back on the ground, where you belong."

"You, you control the wolves?" the bandit stammered. "And the demon flame as well?"

"I said on the ground!" She shouted, her flames roaring hotter and higher.

"Yes Ma'am!" the bandit squealed, dropping to all fours.

"Symin," Corilai shouted. "Do we have rope?"

"Yes," he replied. "Just give me a minute to subdue this last idiot."

Corilai lowered her flames, and she could see Treghan sitting atop one of the bandits, who was unconscious, as Symin wrestled the third along side him, binding his arms behind his back.

"You, get up," Corilai demanded. "Over there with your friends."

The bandit did not resist, and staggered towards Symin, who quickly grabbed him, and bound him to his friends.

"We'll have to leave them behind, and then have them taken back to Oaklands once the rest of the rangers are here," Symin said.

"Yes, Sir, but how do we stop them running?" Treghan asked.

"I'll just tie them to this rock," Symin said, indicating a hole through an enormous boulder. "If they can move that, then they are probably not worth our trouble."

Once the three men were secured, Symin led the way, and they arrived back at the camp on the hill near noon, just as predicted. Given they had left Oaklands with the earliest appearance of the sun, that meant that even with the forward scouting, they were making good time.

On horses, they returned to the temple complex in a very short while, compared to their earlier run on foot. As they set up camp, Symin stood looking at the three bandits, who remained bound to the rock.

"What should we do with them, Sir?" a ranger asked.

"Trida," Symin replied. "Select two of our fellow rangers to help you, and take these three back to Oaklands. We can't risk releasing them, they have seen too much already, but we can't be wasting our efforts watching over them either."

"Yes, Sir," Trida said. "What shall we tell them in Oaklands?"

"Ask that they put them in the prison at Oaklands, and tell our people there to ensure they come to no harm. We do not know yet where their loyalty lies, and I would rather have them abandon Yuri, if they are conscripts. Once that is done, return here. I will take the bulk of the rangers on towards Grey, but you will remain here, along with a handful of others, to watch over the area."

"Yes, Sir."

"Barache!" Symin called.

"Yes, Ranger?" Barache replied, rushing over.

"From here on out, you're our guide. Nobody knows the forest to the south better than you. I will have you lead the army from here, by my side."

"Of course, Ranger," Barache said. "I just wonder if they are using my clearing, after I torched the house?"

"We have no way of knowing, without going there. But I dare say they will not have spread themselves so thin, not after you denied them the benefits of accommodation."

"I hope you're right," Barache said. "But when we get close to that place, we should send a scout forward to check it out."

"Agreed," Symin said. "We should move out as soon as possible. I'll assign ten rangers to stay behind, including the three who have gone back to Oaklands. Start the preparations to move out."

"Yes, Ranger," Barache said.

* * *

Loka stood on a platform behind the ramshackle barricade the rangers had thrown together over night. They had stolen an enormous percentage of the wood the bandits had gathered and cut, ready for their own fortifications.

Now, as she watched, a small band were sneaking along the edges of the tree line to the south of the road, intent on a large pile of as yet unused wood Loka's troops had stacked in front of their barricade.

She smiled, amused that they seemed to think they were cleverly avoiding detection. Teasing, she waited. As they came within a few paces of the place where the wood was piled, one of them struck out into the open, while the others stayed behind.

Loka waited, and waited, as the man circled the pile, looking for guards and finding none. Then he reached out to grasp one of the planks. Loka's grin widened, as she sent a large, black fireball towards the man. He braced himself and lifted the plank, just as the fireball hit him, singing his cloak.

The man screamed and ran back to his companions.

"Where did that come from?" the man screamed.

Before his companions could respond, Tara and three others, standing a short distance from Loka, released fireballs in their direction. Red, yellow and green, the flames burst around the bandits, in a fiery splash of colour. The bandits scattered, running back towards Judd.

The rangers laughed, knowing the flames they had sent were more for show than harm, but the bandits, terrified, did not look back.

"Tara," Loka called, waiting as the girl came closer. "Take those three, and begin inspections on the barricade. It's a rough structure, thrown together overnight in the most rudimentary of fashion. I don't want any dangerous parts left as they are. Reinforce, prop up, whatever it takes. This barricade is more than a silly joke played at the bandits' expense. I want it safe and solid. We can keep the bandits from taking any wood back, but we shouldn't rest on that. We must spend whatever time is necessary now, to make this thing stay standing."

"Yes, Ranger," Tara said as she walked away, leading her three companions out in front of the barricade.

"I hope we don't have to stay here too long," Loka murmured, turning to look back at the camp, stretching away down the sides of the road towards the ocean. "I've never seen a military camp this large, in all my time with the rangers. I hope the Chancellor knows what he's doing."

* * *

Yuri stood in the entry to his offices in Gray, in conversation with Beza. They had returned from the north two days earlier, and Yuri was disappointed with the state of his headquarters.

"The smelter is operational," Beza said. "As of this morning."

"Finally!" Yuri spat. "Those two brats, if I ever catch them, they'll pay for what they did. Any news on who helped them escape?"

"No, Sir. They left no tracks," Beza said. "At least, nothing we can follow now."

"Never mind," Yuri said. "Whoever it was, they're probably on the front lines by now. Let the rangers kill them."

"Are you sure that's wise, Sir?" Beza said.

"Your skills are better employed on things other than wild goose chases," Yuri replied. "Anyway, there will be a daily messenger from the north shortly. You should be present for their report."

"Yes Sir," Beza said.

Yuri and Beza walked into the office, and sat down, remaining quiet for some time. When there was a knock at the door, Beza stood to answer, but Yuri waved to him to sit back down.

"Enter," Yuri shouted.

A sweaty, tired looking man entered, closing the door behind him.

"What is your report?" Yuri demanded.

"The rangers," the man said, pausing for breath. "Have made their move."

Yuri jumped to his feet, stepping towards the man in his excitement. Intimidated, the messenger stepped back.

"Well, quickly man, what have they done?" Yuri demanded.

"The rangers," the man said. "Have set up camp on the highway, between Judd and the sea. They stole..."

The man paused, and reconsidered his words. It would not do to anger Yuri, so he edited his report accordingly.

"They have erected a barricade across the highway, and camp behind it, firing their flames at any of us who approach."

"How many of them?" Yuri asked.

"A small army. I would say around two hundred. Our scouts have reported sightings of a smaller force returning to Emberdale, leading refugees from the south."

"So some of the villagers did escape after all," Yuri spat. "Just can't find good generals these days. Oh well, it doesn't matter. Go on."

"Well Sir, the men in Judd are acquiescent, and cooperative. There is no dissension. Your forces grow daily. However, we can not continue north. We are effectively pinned from the north, with the mountains north of Judd, the rangers to the east, and Oaklands, the walled town to the west. We need to take down either the town or the army."

"We will not be taking the town. Oaklands has a strong militia, and by now will have called on the rangers for help. They will be a hard target, effectively defended. The army, on the other hand, is looking west. They will not defend from the east."

"Yes, they are sir. What are your orders?"

"We will gather our remaining forces, and set sail. We will take the ships along the coast, and launch an assault on the ranger army from the beach. They'll never see it coming, and we can weaken them considerably, allowing the main forces in Judd and in the fort to the south of there to over run the remains. That should send a potent message to Emberdale. Then we expand north, blockade the highway near Emberdale. We'll take those bastards down. All of Cinder will fall, once we take Emberdale."

"You are indeed ambitious, Sir," Beza said.

"It takes a man of ambition to rule a nation such as this, and for too long Emberdale has squandered its power. We will rule from Grey, a much more fitting capital, a steel city from which to subdue the nation with an iron fist."

Chapter 25 – Imminent War

Barache raised his hand high, signalling for them all to stop. He turned to face Symin, and nodded.

"You two," Symin said to Treghan and Corilai. "Wait here. Barache and I will ride ahead, and see what there is at his home."

"Yes, Sir," they said.

Barache led the way, and the pair rode ahead of the army, until they found themselves on the edge of a familiar clearing. Three men were there, dismantling a tent.

"When are we running the next training here?" one of the men asked.

"Three days from now, we'll bring the next group," another replied.

"Why so long?" the first man said. "And why not leave the tents?"

"Because we have other things to do. The rangers are camped outside Judd, we have more important things to do than coddling the new guys."

"Besides," the third man said. "We're all sick of having to hike in here all the time, and now Yuri has returned to Grey, who needs it? The new men can get trained in the fight, whenever that comes."

"But why not leave the tents and stuff?"

"What if there're rangers around? They'll torch our gear. We can't have that."

"You really think they're around?"

"They might be. Not in any large numbers, but it only takes one. Remember that old bastard torched the house, and he was only one."

"Where do you suppose he went?" the first man said.

"We don't know. He could be here now. Who knows?"

"You trying to scare me?"

"Shut up, you two!" the third man shouted, clearly agitated as he retrieved a cart from the trees. "We have to get back to the main camp. So get a move on. Leave the wooden posts and hurdles, just take the tents. If we need to fashion new props we can. Plenty of trees around."

"Yes Sir," the other two said.

Barache was anxiously watching, keen to fight, but Symin held a steadying hand on the older man's shoulder. After a while, the three men left, taking the cart loaded with tents and equipment, but leaving a lot of training obstacles and other equipment which had clearly been manufactured on site.

"Symin, we have to burn it all," Barache said. "You heard them. They fear the old guy in the woods. We should put them on edge by feeding that fear. Plus, when our army has passed by, torching the ground will conceal our tracks."

"Good thinking," Symin said. So we return to the troops, and lead them through. You stay and finish up, then catch up as we march to Grey."

"Agreed, Ranger."

*　　　*　　　*

Yuri stood on the dock, watching over operations as his men loaded the fleet of six ships. They packed enough supplies for their journey, as well as supplies for the men in Judd, then boarded. The ships rode low in the water, treacherously so if they were not sticking close to the coast.

"Only a handful of men in Grey?" Beza asked. "Is that enough?"

"They will be more than enough to defend our operations against the rabble of the city. We know where the rangers are. There will be no significant assault on the city."

"I hope you're right," Beza said. "We might have rule over the city, but we don't have the hearts of the people. They see all the hostages coming back to work here, and they fear their own fate."

"But none of the people of Grey will oppose us. They've seen what we do to dissidents. They have enough brains to value their lives. And their children's lives."

"Yes, Sir," Beza said.

As the last of the ships embarked on their journey, neither man knew the gravity of their mistake. A trail of smoke rising from the distant horizon sparked curiosity but nothing more. Surely no major force could pass their men undetected.

*　　　*　　　*

Smoke rising from the forest alerted the bandits at the fort on the road to the trouble on the training grounds.

"Damn it," the leader of the three who had just returned shouted. "Yuri will have my head! Come on, you two, we ride for the clearing now. As fast as we can go."

Without delay, the three took horses and rushed into the trees, following the now well worn trail to the place where Barache's house had once stood. As they reached the clearing, they saw that the ground was scorched, and there stood the old man, deliberately and systematically torching anything that had survived.

"Hey!" shouted the lead bandit. "You'll pay for this."

"For what?" Barache said. "I have every right to maintain my own land any way I see fit."

"This ain't your land no more!" the bandit replied, drawing his sword and advancing on Barache.

"Well it's sure as hell not yours!" Barache snarled, firing a powerful blast of flame into the man, who backed away.

The man's two companions circled around, intent on flanking the lone flame wielder. Barache was having none of that. Fire erupted in great plumes, striking each of the three men full on, as Barache walked backwards, away from them. As they screamed and retreated, furiously trying to pat out the flames that clung to their clothes, Barache made good his escape to the west.

Circling around, he retrieved his horse, then fled again to the west, before picking a careful path over rocks and through a stream, to circle back to meet Symin and the rest of the rangers.

“How did it go?” Symin asked.

“I had some guests. But they weren’t terribly polite, so I had to flame them. They'll be fine, but they'll fear the old man in the woods a bit more now.”

Symin laughed, slapping the older man on the back in congratulations.

“Will they suspect we are anything more than that sly old bastard?”

“No,” Barache said. “I was careful to obscure your tracks for a good distance both north and south of the clearing.”

“Excellent,” Symin said. “Treghan!”

“Yes, Sir?” Treghan answered.

“You two travelled from grey to the clearing, without being caught. What path did you take?”

“Well, we skirted the edge of the glacier until we hit a stream, then we went inland a bit, and down to the clearing from the hills.”

“Fine, we already crossed a stream, so we head west till we hit the Glacier, and we strike Grey from the west.”

“If I may make a suggestion?” Barache said.

“Of course, Sir,” Symin said.

“The city will likely be defending the northern gates, and possibly the western, however on horse back we can reach well into the mining district and approach from the south, along the desert road. I suggest we make our way as far as we can before midnight, then rest, and attack the southern gates at dawn.”

“Agreed,” Symin said. “I like how you think, old man.”

According to plan, the army of rangers followed the glacier far to the south, and into the night. Finally, having long passed the western road into Grey, they continued through the mining districts until they met a highway, beyond which stretched a wide flat plain of sand and grasses.

“The Desert of Souls,” Symin whispered. “It's not far from here. Where the sand lightens, and the grasses stop. Nothing lives there. The sulphurous soil is dead, and to cross it is certain death to the unprepared. To think the people of Horde manage to live on its edge.”

The rangers soon caught up, crowded around the road.

“We camp here,” Symin shouted. “Camp light. No tents. We ride on Grey and attack at dawn, so get what sleep you can, and make sure you can be on the move as quickly as possible.”

“Yes, Sir,” came the loud reply of hundreds of men and women.

*　　　*　　　*

Loka watched from the barricade. Judd was quiet, the Bandits seemed unconcerned with their presence. They ignored the rangers on the hill, going about their business as though there was no enemy, no threat.

“I'm worried,” Loka said.

“Why?” Tara replied.

“Because the enemy is not.”

She thought about it for a moment, then walked to the edge of the platform and climbed down. Tara followed, and they walked through the gate of the barricade and out onto the road.

"It's their attitude," Loka said. "It's not the attitude of a group in fear of the enemy. They know they will win this."

They walked towards Judd, and there was no evident change in the enemy lines. Their sturdy wooden wall remained closed, the guards along its top were unconcerned.

"These bandits think they have us right where they want us," Loka said, turning and walking back to the rangers' barricade.

They walked in silence until they were back in the camp, the gates closed behind them. Loka stood, staring towards the sea.

"Why do you think they believe that, Sir?" Tara asked.

"Give me a moment," Loka said, thinking as she walked to the east.

The ocean in the distance disappeared behind the next rise as she walked, then a while later it reappeared as she reached the top. The road continued to the east, up and down hills, until the trees, the beach and the ocean beyond replaced it.

Angry clouds dominated the horizon, and she saw a small fishing boat from Emberdale, fighting against the winds as it made its way back to port.

"Those two," Loka said. "Treghan and Corilai."

"What about them?" Tara asked.

"They were abducted near here, before they went to Grey."

"So?"

"They were abducted, and taken by ship. From the beach."

"What's your point?"

"My point is, the bandits of Grey have ships, and they are known to travel along the coast, as far as the bay in front of us. The bandits in Judd aren't concerned now, because they know they have reinforcements coming. Further, they think their reinforcements from Grey will take us by surprise. Tara, set a watch on the southern headland of the bay, leave them with a fast horse. We will not be taken from behind."

"Yes, Ranger."

"One other thing, Tara," Loka said. "The reinforcements will be coming from Grey. Chances are, they will be loyal to Yuri. They're not conscripts from the villages. We may need to fight them with our all. We must prepare the rangers for that possibility."

"Yes, Ranger."

* * *

The orange light of a glorious sunrise reflected across the sand, bright in their eyes as Symin led the rangers towards Grey. Treghan and Corilai, riding behind him, gazed around in wonder at the vast open spaces.

In the distance, the walls of Grey cast long shadows, reaching out like an immense, grasping hand, beckoning. The sun, rising slightly north of them, in the east, peered over the corner of the city, menacing in its intense light.

"Corilai," Treghan asked. "Are you scared?"

"No..." she said slowly. "I think we're safe. We have this army with us. And Symin will keep us safe."

"I guess you're right," Treghan said. "But I am. What if something goes wrong? We barely got out of here last time."

"But last time, we were alone."

The horses trotted on towards the city, their hooves clopping on the hard stone road. The pace was rapid, but steady, conserving energy so the animals would carry them through the battle, and on into the rest of the war.

The city gates loomed before them, as they rode in the shadow of the wall, and they sat open, welcoming. No guard rushed to meet them, but a bell tolled as they charged in.

"This is too easy," Symin said. "It's like there is no enemy to meet us. Treghan, Corilai, lead us to Yuri."

They rushed through the empty city streets, the people closing their shutters, hiding from the invading forces. Reaching the central plaza, Treghan and Corilai turned left, and towards the enormous complex where Yuri's men had taken them before.

Ahead, in front of the gates to the complex, twenty men stood, their steel armour glowing with the reflected orange light of the early morning sun. Their swords were raised, and they were clearly prepared to defend the gate to the death.

Treghan reached a hand to Corilai, who grasped it as they slowed to a gentle stop, their horses turning until they were touching noses, forming a V, like a wedge ready to drive through the armed bandits. Giving Corilai's hand a gentle squeeze, Treghan raised his other hand, and shot forward an intense white flame, as Corilai did the same, her flame dark and terrifying.

One of the bandits, with a long green plume in his hat, stepped forward, and the flames rushed to meet him. As the flames, both white and dark, surged around him, he screamed, and frantically tried to remove his steel armour as it heated, burning his skin.

"Oh no!" Corilai screamed, and her flames stopped, her arm lowered as she stared in horror at what they had done.

Treghan gasped, and dropped his hand, jerking on the reins such that his horse started to back up. The man writhed on the ground, still fumbling with his armour, as the heat slowly dissipated.

"Get back," Symin ordered, firing his powerful yellow flames into the remaining bandits.

Barache moved in front of them, along side Symin, shielding the youngsters from the carnage as the front riding rangers joined them. Soon there was no resistance left and the gates of the complex were reduced to ashes.

Symin directed ten rangers to deal with the wounded bandits, and soon they had been locked in the small area to the side of the gates where the carts had been kept.

"Treghan, Corilai, with me, now," Symin yelled as he dismounted. "I need to know where Yuri is."

"Yes Sir," Treghan replied as Symin rushed into the main entry.

They ran along the corridors of the building as the youngsters tried to remember their way around the building. There was sparse resistance, until suddenly an intimidating man blocked their view. Symin raised his hand to flame him.

"Wait!" Corilai screamed. "It's Beza. He's a friend."

"Corilai?" The man said. "So you got to the academy after all. I'm glad. But why are you here?"

"They bring an army, to take down Yuri. Whose side are you on?" Barache demanded, as he caught up, huffing.

"Yuri has run roughshod over the people of Grey for too long. I have worked to stay his trusted man hoping to find a way to depose him, but that has not happened. If you bring an army, and can guarantee safety for the families of my men, then Yuri will be handed to you."

"Most definitely," Barache said. "Lead us to him, and you will be spared."

Beza turned and ran deeper into the building, taking a flight of stares and then turning back towards the front of the complex. Soon, they arrived at a sturdy, double door, its ancient mahogany carved with glorious patterns, reminiscent of coals in a fire.

"Yuri is in there," Beza said, as five more rangers caught up.

Barache and Symin both placed their hands on the door, and in an instant it was smouldering splinters as it exploded into the room.

"What the hell is the meaning of this?" Yuri shouted from inside, drawing his sword to advance on the invaders. "You two! What is the meaning of this? You trashed my smelter, and now this? You'll pay!"

"Halt!" Symin shouted, his booming voice echoing through the chamber. "The only one who will pay today, is you, Yuri, bandit king."

"Just try it!" Yuri shouted, lunging at Symin, his wicked blade poised to run the ranger through.

At the last moment, Symin's hand flashed before him, grasped the sword, and shattered the blade. Intense heat filled the room for a moment, as the sword's fragments lay on the floor, molten, slowly cooling into shining beads.

As Yuri stared at the floor, Barache stepped behind him, grabbed his arms and bound him tightly.

"Yuri," Barache said. "I place you under arrest in the name of the Chancellor. I, Barache, am hereby appointed governor of this city, and the rangers will be replacing your current militia in ruling over the people. May this act bring peace and prosperity to Cinder. And may you pay dearly for your crimes."

Barache shoved Yuri, and two of the rangers grabbed him, dragging him from the room. As they passed the door, Yuri saw Beza, and stopped, wrestling against his bonds.

"You!" Yuri snarled. "It was you, all along. You traitorous worm. When I'm free, I'll kill you myself. And all your family."

Beza returned the man's scowl, then punched his face, leaving a red welt, blood trickling from his mouth.

"You will never know freedom again, scoundrel."

"One question," Symin asked. "Why was there so little resistance here?"

"We sent the majority of our men north," Beza said. "By ship. They will outflank the rangers near Judd. Three hundred and then some men, prepared for war."

"Then we can not delay. Barache, I must leave as soon as possible. Will you be alright to tidy things up here?"

"It will be fine. Go, rescue Loka. And take Yuri in chains, as an example to his men."

Chapter 26 – Freeing the Slaves

"I have records of all the hostage and slave placements," Beza said. "I will gladly provide them, and assist in their liberation."

"How can we trust you?" Symin demanded.

"We can trust him, Symin," Treghan said. "Without him, Corilai and I would have never escaped, and would have wound up in who knows what condition at the docks."

"The docks?"

"That's where Yuri wanted to sell us," Corilai explained.

"OK then. We have enough rangers, we can split into groups, and each take a different section of the city."

He began to leave the room, signalling for Beza to follow. Barache raised a hand, beckoning them to stop.

"I know it sounds barbaric," Barache said. "But we need to send a strong signal to the people of Grey that Yuri is no longer in charge here. I want him in chains, to be paraded to the docks and back."

The old man's stern expression told them all he was deadly serious. After a long pause, Symin turned away and continued out of the room.

"Do whatever you must do, to show that rangers are in control here," Symin said. "Treghan, Corilai, assist Barache in his task. I am sure Yuri would love to see you two as his captors."

"Yes sir!" Treghan said, while Corilai simply nodded, looking at the floor.

"Yuri's going to be mad," she said.

"All the better," Barache replied. "A blithering fool like him will scream and rage and carry on with impotent aggression. And none of it will help him escape justice. It will make a better show for the people. Those who support him will think twice, those who despise him will rejoice all the more fervently."

"Well, to keep him secure, they have caged carts they used for the hostages coming from the north."

"Then we start by finding them."

"Yes, Sir," Treghan said, leading them from the room.

Treghan felt a flush of pride at his sudden authority as he led the rangers through Yuri's compound. He hoped he could remember the way out to the courtyard. As they made their way down to the ground floor, then to the front of the building, Treghan breathed a sigh of relief that he was not going to look like a fool.

In the courtyard, nearly a hundred rangers were waiting, the rest scattered throughout the city. Barache beckoned four of them over, muttered something to them, and they rushed into the building. He then strode to the storage area, where the carts stood, three with sturdy steel cages on them. Ten angry men sat in there, scowling in impotent fury.

"Perfect," Barache said, turning to call out to the nearest rangers. "Place these men in irons, then secure them in one of the caged carts. I want the cart ready to roll in ten minutes."

On closer inspection, two of the carts had irons permanently fastened to the cages, and the men were soon placed inside, where they thrashed and screamed against their captors. As the cart was pulled into the courtyard, the four who had ventured inside returned, dragging a writhing, incoherent monster of thrashing arms and screamed obscenities. It was Yuri.

"Chain him to the roof of that cage," Barache ordered. "I want the people to have no doubt as to who is so confined. And chain him well. I would have no escape at the docks."

Barache then moved among the rangers, selecting one after another, until fifty were grouped around the cart.

"The rest of you, find Symin and take your orders. He is coordinating the liberation of all those who are held here against their will. Treghan and Corilai, you are on the cart with me."

"Yes, Sir!" the rangers shouted.

Shortly, the gates were opened, and the cart, surrounded by rangers on horseback, moved through the city. Its captives shouted, while the apparent captors, two young rangers atop the cage, tormented them with the discipline of black and white flames.

Treghan and Corilai stood, hands held between them, directing fire at any bandit, Yuri included, who became too violent or aggressive towards them, or the crowded escort. Soon, as Barache rang a bell loudly, which was fastened to the front of the cart, the people began to emerge from the buildings, to gawk at the spectacle.

As the parade reached the main street which ran down towards the docks, the crowds of onlookers had grown such that it slowed them considerably, even as the crowds parted to let the rangers through.

"What is this?" one of the men shouted. "I am Targa, the former head of the guard, and as such I demand you explain."

The rest of the onlookers, emboldened by the question, began shouting their own demands. Barache stood on the driver's bench, and raised his arms for silence. He removed his cloak, and held it high, the ranger's symbol on the back clear for all to see, as he turned, to afford the sight to all in the crowd, before placing it back on his shoulders.

"The man you see atop this cage," Barache shouted. "Is a criminal. This man has caused endless pain to the people of Cinder, and is henceforth deposed from his stolen throne."

There was silence, then, slowly, some of the people began to cheer. Barache waited as the sound grew to a roar, then raised his arm for silence. They quieted down a little faster than they had cheered.

"All false taxes and threats made by his administration are henceforth ended. I, Barache of Emberdale, am appointed by Chancellor Howe as the new governor of this fair City. I shall, for now, take up office and home in the tyrant Yuri's former estate, however will move out of that place when more suitable arrangements can be made. That building will become once again available for the use of the people, along with any other ill gotten assets of the tyrant Yuri."

"How do we know you're any better than him?" a woman shouted, as

Yuri shouted abuse and threats at Barache.

Corilai and Treghan both struck the tyrant with bursts of intense flame, which heated the cage and brought screams from the men below them.

"Don't question him, woman!" a man said. "See that? Two kids can bring down Yuri, and you challenge a man of his stature and experience?"

The crowd pushed back, away from the cart, as if fearing they would be next.

"We will never rule with fear, as this man has done," Barache proclaimed. "Please, I ask the good people of Grey to work with us, and help bring back the steel city of old, where people lived in freedom and prosperity, with no need for slavery or poverty."

"If that is indeed your goal," Targa shouted, loud enough for all the crowd to hear. "Then I will support you. It is time for our city to be fair again. We will work with you to restore her beauty. And those who fight against us shall be dealt with swiftly, and with justice."

"If that is the case," Barache said. "Will you, Targa, accept your commission once again, as the head of the guard? You will be working along side the rangers of Grey, a new garrison to be stationed in this city, to prevent a recurrence of Yuri's tyranny."

"I would be honoured, Sir ranger," Targa said, bowing low before the new governor as the people applauded. "What of the men who followed Yuri?"

"Any who are still at large, must be delivered to me. They will face trial, and be punished for their crimes. Anybody who brings them in, will be rewarded with one month of guard's salary for each man who is found guilty."

"So the people will do your dirty work?" Targa said. "I believe that is fair. The people allowed it to reach this sad state of affairs, it is only right they help to end it."

"Then we shall return to my offices. See to it the city knows what has occurred today. I would see this transition run fast and smooth. But there is one more thing I must tell you."

Barache paused, looking long at the crowd, turning to pass his eyes over every man, woman and child.

"Rangers will be amongst you today, seeking those imprisoned or enslaved by Yuri and his criminal gang. Please, I ask the people of Grey to cooperate in this matter. I must warn that resistance in this task of freeing those so unjustly incarcerated will be considered actions of the criminal gang, and thus be dealt with swiftly, and not in a way that guarantees future trial of those offending."

Leaving the threat hanging in the air, Barache turned the cart, and the rangers began their return trip to the new Governor's offices.

* * *

Barache watched as a long column of more than five hundred freed hostages moved slowly through the northern gates of Grey. Fifty rangers stayed behind, to work as his new guard, the rangers of Grey.

Many rode on carts, some shared horses with rangers, some rode alone, and a few of the young and healthy chose to walk. It would be a slow trip north, but along the way many would leave the column, to return to their homes.

As they reached the bandit outposts, they would attempt to convince the men to leave the ranks of Yuri's men, to rejoin their now freed loved ones. Any who refused, would be dealt with in whatever way was required.

"I hope there isn't too much fighting," Corilai said.

"There'll be some," Treghan said. "Remember, a lot of the men are conscripts, but there are a few loyal to Yuri, who lead the bandit army in his name."

"But we have him. Might that not be enough to sway them into surrendering?"

"We can hope," Treghan said, glancing at the cage, in which the deposed tyrant fumed. "And we'd best hope nobody tries to rescue him, before he faces the grand trial in Emberdale."

"Enough dallying, you two," Symin barked. "I need every ranger's eyes sharp. We have no idea who may be out here. As long as the bandits are still working to the north, every one of these civilians is in danger."

"Yes, Sir!" they both replied.

A woman among the hostages pushed her way through the crowd, making her way closer to the cart. As Treghan pushed his hood back, she shouted.

"Treghan! It's really you. I'm so glad you're OK."

"Mother?"

"Yes, Son," She said, then paused, looking at the ground. "I'm sorry. For everything."

"It's OK, Mother."

"No, It's not," she protested. "If I can ever make it up to you..."

"Forget it, Mother."

"What about the others?"

"Fletcher's at the Academy. I've no idea about Father."

"I will find him," she said. "But please, when you can, come home and visit. Both of you."

"We will. I'll tell Fletcher you are safe, and send him your love."

"Thank you, Son," she said, as Treghan pulled up his hood and turned away.

As they rounded a shallow bend in the road near sunset on the first day, they encountered the first small outpost Yuri's men had established. Two men advanced on them, swords drawn. Several more hung back, glancing at each other as the rangers approached.

"What's the meaning of this?" One of the men shouted.

"Yuri is deposed, and we take him to face trial in Emberdale for his treasonous deeds," Symin replied. "His little empire is no more. You are now all free men."

A rousing cheer erupted from the men behind. The two in front braced themselves and the second shouted at the men.

"Stand your ground. Any of you run, I'll kill you myself, in great Yuri's name!"

Symin laughed, then fired a yellow ball of flames at the man, startling him.

"Idiots! Can't you see? Yuri is deposed, his hostages freed. You have nothing to hold over those men now. They're free. It's your choice, do you challenge us, in Yuri's name? Or do you join them in freedom from his tyranny?"

"Never!" the first man screamed, lunging at Symin with his sword. "Yuri will rise again, and we will be there, to support the great Yuri's return!"

"No, you won't," said one of the men from behind him, as he hurled a wooden spear at the man, striking his leg. As the man went down, the conscripts advanced.

"You tormented us, beat us, and denied us our proper meals and rest. You shouted your vile hatred continuously, and now, now you will pay with your lives!"

The six men set on the two in a vicious display of vengeance. As the two bandits lay bleeding, the conscripts stood back, suddenly calm in the realisation of the horrible thing they had done in their rage.

The palpable silence stretched on as the shock of the sudden change in the situation sank in. After a while, one of the conscripts looked up at Symin, fear in his eyes.

"Sir ranger," he said. "I, we're sorry. Please, we only wanted to go home."

"That was murder," Symin shouted.

As he finished, a woman climbed from one of the carts, and ran towards him.

"Brun, my darling husband!" she shouted, throwing herself around him, looking back over her shoulders.

"Ranger, if you must punish him, you must burn me first. Let these men go. They have only done what those two deserved."

"What they deserved?" Symin yelled. "What they deserved was a fair trial, the same as any other man in their situation."

"Trial?" she snorted, her derision plain. "That pair made plain their intent to fight. If my husband and his fellows had not acted, you would have been forced to do the job in their stead."

"Madam," Symin said, pausing for a long while before he continued. "You may be right. How far is your home?"

"We came from the village of Friss, on the seaside. It is almost directly east from here, perhaps a day's march."

"Then you will be free to go, but I advise you camp here with us for tonight. We will continue north at first light. You may journey east at that time."

"Thank you, Ranger," she said.

"I will send some of my people with you, if you wish," Symin said.

"No, we will fight for our homes if need be," Brun said, straightening his shoulders. "It is up to us to finish this task, now you have shown us the way."

"As you wish," Symin answered. "But are you sure Friss is not occupied?"

"I'm sure," Brun said. "Yuri has concentrated his men in the north, at two locations. Some a day north of here, on the road, but most of them in the village of Judd. We will not find effective resistance in reclaiming our homes."

"That's good, but if Friss is on the shore, please take care. Yuri's men travel by ship along the coast. If they see you at Friss, they may choose to deviate from their mission and investigate. They left Grey before we arrived, and are unaware of their leader's demise."

"If that happens, let them come. We will sink them before they can reach land."

* * *

At daybreak, the rangers continued north, while a small number of civilians departed to the east, heading home. The journey was eerily quiet, but they made good time. With the departure of the villagers from Friss, the young civilians who elected to walk for much of the first day were able to fit onto horses or carts.

As promised, however, near sunset on that second day, they arrived at a second, larger outpost. This time, a great number more men stood defiant, in support of Yuri.

Even so, behind them, many more men, conscripts seeing their loved ones now free of the tyrant, mutinied against their leaders, and a pitched battle commenced. The men fought fiercely against their captors, and the rangers stepped in to try to encourage a swift end, hoping for a surrender which did not come.

Symin rushed into the battle, demanding they stop. Many conscripts obeyed, only to be attacked anew by Yuri's faithful followers. Forced to defend themselves, the conscripts fought back, and soon, the battle was over.

As several bandits lay dying on the road, and several more lay wounded, the dust cleared on a sad liberation.

"I guess it can't be helped," Symin murmured. "If these men are so intent on fighting for their leader, we can't hold their former prisoners responsible for causing deaths in the act of defending themselves."

The wounded men had their wounds treated, then were placed in irons in the cage with Yuri. Symin directed the rangers to bury the dead beside the road, and they then moved a short distance to the north before setting up camp for the night.

"I just hope we aren't too late," he mused.

"What do you mean, Sir?" Treghan asked.

"It will take four, perhaps five days for those ships to reach Loka. They left Grey a day before we arrived. We were there a full day before we departed, and have travelled two days now. Loka will be fighting a pitched battle on two fronts by morning. If she can't hold her own until we arrive, there might be severe casualties. We have perhaps a day and a half of travel ahead, and we can't go with no rest, or else we risk arriving as a weakened force. Even without Yuri in charge, the bandits are a dangerous enemy, as long as they have those conscripts in thrall."

Chapter 27 – Twelve Hour War

Loka stood staring towards the sea. She had ordered her rangers to build a second barricade, a short distance behind the first, and now stood atop it, waiting. Twenty riders waited for her orders on the other side.

Finally, a flair lit up the dawn sky over the bay. She was right. As quickly as was safe, Loka climbed down from the barricade, and mounted her horse, riding out through the barricade.

"With me!" she shouted, and the twenty riders followed, down towards the sea.

"What will we do, Sir?" one of the rangers asked.

"We have to hold the enemy at bay as long as we can. We're going to set fire to the forest at the beach, then retreat. Once we get back to the barricade, we launch an assault on Judd. We burn their barricades. We want the fires burning on both sides as long as possible."

"But what will that achieve?"

"It will keep them busy. Hopefully until the reinforcements arrive."

"Why do we need reinforcements?" the man persisted.

Loka looked at him, and realised he was not aware of the entire plan. She shook her head.

"Just trust me on this," she replied. "The majority of the men in Judd are not there out of loyalty. They are there against their own wishes. We can not cause any more harm to the innocent citizens of Cinder."

"But I don't understand."

"Have faith, ranger. We will prevail, and so will Cinder. If we lead an assault on Yuri's conscripts, we would win the battle. But Cinder could fall."

The man fell silent, and they rode at speed to the bend in the highway. Loka turned to face all her people.

"Give me a wild fire, like they have never seen before!" she ordered.

Flames erupted all along the tree line, and in response, more flames burst skyward near the head land, expanding towards them. Loka smiled, and rode towards the coming fires. Soon, Tara emerged from the trees.

"Tara," Loka said. "Good work. You join us. We return to the barricade shortly. The fire will burn as long as needed, and the bandits from Grey will not pass without first tackling it."

As the last of the tree line nearest the road was well ablaze, Loka lead her rangers back to the west, and to the coming battle. The diversion away from the barricades had been several hours, but Loka had faith in her people. There would have been no unauthorised assault on Judd, and any surprise attack would have been rebuffed without casualty.

As they approached, she could hear the sounds of a skirmish, and rushed to the other side of the camp. Rangers lined the barricade, shooting flames out at the enemy.

"What's going on?" Loka demanded as she climbed onto the barricade to see for herself.

A group of a dozen bandits were in the road, behind an upturned cart. One of them had a bow, and at any break in the flames, would stick his head up, take aim, and fire an arrow. So far, he had failed to hit anyone, and his arrows littered the ground in front of the barricade.

"We just duck out of sight if we see him jump out," one of the rangers explained.

"I've seen enough of this," Loka said. "Nobody is to hide on the next attempt. When I give the word, you all stop shooting."

She watched, and waited, choosing her moment, as she prepared herself. Carefully, Loka was considering distance, wind, and other factors. Finally, she shouted.

"Now!"

As one, the rangers stopped. As Loka expected, the man with the bow emerged and began to take aim, his crude wooden bow already armed. Loka raised her right arm, and fired. A menacing black flame raced out across the battle field, to strike the bow, intense heat and darkness enveloping the man.

In seconds, the bow was gone, nothing more than ash, and the bowman, screaming, was running towards Judd. After a brief pause, his comrades followed.

"Let them run," Loka said as she turned away from the scene. "We will assault Judd on the hour. Await your orders."

"Yes, Sir," the rangers on the barricade replied.

Loka went to her tent, to freshen up after her long ride. The rangers had done well so far, but she knew the worst was still to come. As she dried her face, she heard a sound at the entry to her tent. She turned, to see Tara, waiting patiently.

"What is it?" Loka asked.

"Sir," Tara said. "Some of the rangers are nervous. We've never seen battle before. Cinder has been at peace for decades. Even domestic disturbances have been minor as long as most of us have lived. Do you think this is going to end well?"

Loka smiled, and walked over to her, resting her hand on the younger woman's shoulder.

"Do not fear, Tara. We have considered this. We do not intend to enter a full scale assault on Judd unless absolutely forced to do so. When Symin returns, things will change. You'll see."

"But why? Why do we have to do this?" Tara asked.

"Because if we don't our country is doomed. Yuri and his like will never give in if they think there's nobody willing to stand against them. So we must, for the sake of our people, our families, our children's future, stand against tyranny wherever it raises its head."

"Then why not crush the bandits in Judd before this? Why wait until they have reinforcements from the sea?"

"Because the men in Judd are not the true enemy. Most of them are conscripts, only working for the guaranteed safety of their families, just like we are. Those from the sea, many will be loyal to Yuri. They will be the true enemy."

"But how can Symin change that?"

"Have faith in the Chancellor's plan, Tara," Loka said, walking past her and into the sunlight. “You and those who lit the fires to the east, can rest for now. I will take some of those who waited here for the assault. We will only be lighting more fires, for now. The real battle is still many hours away.”

“Yes, Sir,” Tara said as Loka walked away.

Gathering two groups of twenty rangers, Loka gave her instructions.

“Group one, you take the left side of the road, wait until you are within a hundred paces of their barricade, then start torching the trees, the grass, anything flammable. This is their warning to get away from the barricade. Group two, you're with me, on the right. We do the same. As we reach the barricade, we set it ablaze, then retreat along the road. There will be archers, so be extremely careful. If necessary, we light it up from a distance and get back here. I want no casualties, understand?”

“Yes, Sir!” the rangers shouted.

Leading her team, Loka ran along the tree line, keeping one eye always on the barricade ahead. She glanced at the other team, and noted they were keeping close formation, not venturing out into the open any more than necessary.

“Good,” she said, taking a moment to look back at her own team, to ensure they were doing the same.

Facing back towards Judd, she ran on, until finally they were within a hundred paces of the barricade. Glancing across at the other team, she noted they had commenced flaming of the trees. Raising her hand, she did the same, bursting her black fire into the foliage as she ran.

Wordlessly, her team followed her example, and soon a rainbow of coloured flames were tearing into the landscape, igniting a wildfire to compete with the one they had previously set near the beach. She began to hear shouts from the barricade in front.

Loka glanced behind just in time to see a young ranger step into the open. It was not far, or for long, but it was enough of both. She heard the arrow as it passed, and saw it spear through the ranger's shoulder.

“Keep to the trees!” she shouted as she turned and rushed to the wounded man's side. “You, and you!”

Loka beckoned at two of the passing rangers, and they quickly came to her assistance.

“Take this man and head back to camp. Quickly now, and try not to get shot yourselves.”

As they rushed back the way they had come, keeping as close to the burning trees as they could, Loka turned and ran towards the barricade again. Her people were already reaching it, and hitting it with all the flames they could muster.

Loka looked up, and saw that the bandits had archers, atop the barricade, who were gathering in the centre, where the flames had not reached. They were already taking aim.

“No you don't!” Loka screamed, as the first few arrows flew.

She raised her hands and fired an intense, uncontrolled burst of the demon flames directly at them, and as it hit, the archers scattered. Confused, they did not reappear as she hit the barricade again and again. Soon, the entire barricade was ablaze, and she rushed to assist her people.

Three of Loka's team were down, arrows protruding from painful wounds. She assessed them quickly, and assigned others to assist them back to the camp.

“Thankfully, none are fatal, but this is still not good,” she said as she rushed to the other team.

Only two of them were down, but one was serious. The arrow had pierced her abdomen, and there was a lot of blood confusing the issue. The ranger's comrades were milling around her, clearly confused.

“This was too much,” Loka said, then shouted as she approached. “Quickly, cauterise the wound, and carry her to the camp. The barricade is burning. That should keep them busy for a while.”

It seemed like forever, that hike back to the rangers' camp, and all manner of thoughts competed for space in Loka's mind. Had she rushed in too soon? Had she failed them in their training? Had she been too eager to spare the enemy, and now, would some of her own trusting followers die because of her arrogance in thinking the rangers were invincible?

She shook her head, determined to focus on the task at hand as she watched for pursuit or archers from the barricade. Walking backwards, she fired the occasional bolt of blackness at the enemy, but deep down, she knew that she was only fighting shadows now. The bandits were busy inside the village, defending against the roaring fires she had set.

After an eternity, she was finally back within their own camp. She directed the wounded to the infirmary, glad they had the foresight to set it up days earlier, and called for Tara to assist. Tara, Loka remembered, was one of the most promising students before she graduated, in the area of field medicine. They had never had to use it like this, but she was confident Tara would handle it. Then, exhausted, she retired to her tent.

“Please hurry, Symin,” Loka said. “I bought us some time, but I don't know if it's going to be enough.”

Still fully clothed, Loka laid her head down on her pillow, and was asleep. This might be her only chance for rest before the battle was over.

*　　　*　　　*

Loka woke suddenly. The light was fading outside, and Tara was shaking her.

“What is it?” Loka said.

“The fires by the beach are going out.”

“Damn it. How long was I out?”

“Nearly five hours. The village Barricade is rubble, but still smouldering. The trees are still burning to the southern side. The men in the village are preparing for an assault.”

“How is their morale?”

“Its patchy. It seems Yuri's men are having some difficulty motivating the conscripts. They did do something you should know about, either to motivate the conscripts, or to scare us.”

"What was it?"

"They dumped a body on the road." Tara said, pausing for a moment. "A ranger."

"A Ranger?" Loka said, shock in her voice. "I see. It must be the enforcer Chancellor Howe sent to Judd. He was dead?"

"Yes, and clearly tortured."

Loka looked at her hands, then faced Judd, grim determination in her eyes.

"They will pay for this, in good time," she said, then turned back to face the east, her face composed. "Any sign of the reinforcements from the south?"

"Theirs or ours?"

"Both."

"We haven't seen either, but theirs can't be far away now. As for ours, we have seen no sign as yet."

"Dammit," Loka murmured. "I hoped he'd be here by now."

She stood, brushed herself off, straightened her clothes, then walked out of the tent. Tara followed, looking anxiously around as they walked through the camp.

"Sir," Tara said.

"What is it?"

"Will we survive?"

"Of course we will. Symin will be along any time now. We just have to keep them at bay."

"Yes, Sir."

"Tara, I have a task for you," Loka said. "Wait, have you rested recently? Or have you been treating the wounded all this time?"

"I came to you as soon as I was finished with them, Sir."

"Right, Well, I want you to pass on the order to as many as you can find, then go to your tent. You need rest as much as anybody else."

"What is your order, Sir?"

"I want every able ranger on the barricade, nothing gets through. Both directions. I'll start getting them up on the eastern side, you get them up on the west."

"Yes, Sir."

* * *

Smoke still billowed in the east, but the fires near Judd had finally been extinguished. A furious band of men snapped their orders at the rest, and their barked demands found their way in whispers to the rangers atop their barricade.

Loka watched, concerned, and wondered where Symin was, daring to hope he might come in time.

"How long can we hold out?" she murmured.

Then, she saw something, and her worry grew. The bandits were dragging barrels of oil out, and wrapping the heads of arrows in cloth. Loka had burned the bandits' barricade. They were planning to return the favour.

"Tara!" Loka shouted.

A few minutes later, Tara appeared, having run from her tent.

"What is it?" Tara said, looking tired.

"I'm sorry," Loka said. "I forgot you were resting."

"Never mind that, what's the problem?" Tara said, seeing the concern in her leader's eyes.

"They're going to hit us with flaming arrows. We have to keep this barricade standing as long as possible. We can't afford a skirmish on the ground, and if we lose it, that's what we'll have."

"So we need to put out their fires before that happens," Tara said. "But we won't have enough water."

"Water won't help us with this. They're soaking cloth in oil. Sure the water will stop the wood and cloth burning, but my worry is the oil."

"There might be another way," Tara said.

Loka looked at her, narrowed her eyes and shook her head.

"I'm sorry, Tara, I don't know where you're going with this."

"Think back to the second year classes at the academy. One of the things we spent weeks on was extinguishing. Sure, water is vital, but sometimes you have to do other things, like smother with a blanket."

"Do we have blankets that are large enough to reach down the wall?"

"No, Sir," Tara said. "But that was only one of the methods. What about fighting fire with fire? We have plenty of rangers."

"What are you getting at?" Loka said, then her eyes widened. "You think we can smother the fires with our own flames? It's a theory. Yes, it has worked against ranger's flames, and in other experiments, but can we make it work for something like this? It can stop a demon flame, but can it stop oil?"

"Do we have a choice?"

"You're right. You go that way, I'll go the other, tell the rangers what to do. I just hope this works. Even if it only slows them down, that might be enough."

"Yes, Sir," Tara said.

Loka rushed along the wall, shouting the orders. "The bandits are going to use flaming arrows to burn the barricade. I want you to hit every arrow with a fireball, as hot as you can make it without igniting the wall yourself, and smother their flames. As much as possible, you need to suck the air from their arrows, so the fires can't take our barricade down. When you extinguish your fireball, their flames will go with it. Timing is the key."

She reached the end of the barricade, and worried that the bandits might come from the trees. She looked down towards Judd, and saw the burnt areas, where she had led the rangers in destroying the forest. And along side the village, the farmers' fields lay. If they planned to attack from the trees, they had to cross that open space first, and surely one of the watching rangers would have given the alarm.

She looked to the east, and noticed the smoke was weakened, the inferno clearly stopped.

"They're coming," she said, thinking of the men from Grey, who would be like a surging wave up the road from the sea. "Tara sighted six ships. At fifty soldiers per ship, that's three hundred men."

As she considered that worrying news, a shout erupted behind her. She turned her gaze back to the village of Judd, in time to see the first volley of flaming arrows and the running men as they advanced on the barricade.

Chapter 28 – Reinforcements

"Keep them back!" Loka shouted, as the men ran towards them. "Anybody gets within fifty paces of the wall, you light them up. But I want no casualties, unless they make it absolutely necessary."

Beneath her, a flaming arrow struck the barricade, the oil soaked cloth splatting against the wood. With no hesitation, Loka reached a hand over the edge, and fired a large black fireball at the arrow. As her flames engulfed it, they obscured the fire with their darkness. She held them there, watching, for several seconds, as the oxygen in the air around the oil was sucked out by the demon flame. Then, she let it go. The cloth smouldered, but the fire was gone.

All along the barricade, the rangers followed Loka's example, and one by one the arrows which struck the wall were extinguished.

"It might just be enough," Loka said. "I thought the heated oil would reignite when it was hit by air, but I guess there's something cooling in the smothering properties of our flames. They aren't regular fire after all."

The first wave of conscripts reached the fifty pace line, and the rangers let loose with a rainbow of fire. The flames burst into the men, and they scattered, confused and frightened. The first wave surged back towards Judd. Yuri's men met them with swords raised, and demanded they attack again.

"Cowards, all of you!" the man leading the bandits shouted, his voice loud enough to carry to the barricade. "How many of you were injured by their little fireworks?"

The conscripts looked around at each other. All were accounted for.

"Nobody was even injured!" the leader shouted. "Why are you letting those cowards scare you away, while they hide in their camp? Charge the rangers, kill them all!"

Still, the conscripts hesitated.

"Cowards!" the leader shouted. "Watch, they will not harm you. These charlatans can't harm a man."

He pushed past the conscripts and strode towards the barricade.

"Enough of this," Loka shouted, and raised her hands. "Do not come closer."

"Your flames are nothing to real men!" the bandit leader replied. "You can't harm us. They dance among us and burn nobody."

"Do not test me," Loka snarled.

The man grinned, his face etched with twisted, wicked intent, and strode towards the wall.

"I will burn you, if you do not stop," Loka shouted.

Still the man came on, while his men watched the display in awe.

"You will not be a martyr. You will be an example, you fool!" Loka shouted, as she fired a massive burst of the demon flame at the man. With grim determination, she held the flame, as it surged around him.

"You can end this, by leaving now," she shouted.

"I will not be intimidated!" he replied.

Loka focussed her energy, and the flames intensified. Shortly, his hair ignited, as did his cloak, adding an orange hue to the fire as it consumed them. Loka released her flames, and the darkness around him dissipated. But his own flames remained, as he dropped to the ground, his screams piercing.

"Collect your general," Loka shouted. "You may yet save him, but heed this warning, all of you. We will not be taken lightly."

Three men rushed forward, carrying buckets, and doused the fire, then dragged the man, who was still screaming, back to the village. The conscripts backed away, as Yuri's bandits hesitated. Shortly, the next volley of arrows struck the barricade.

"Keep stopping those arrows," Loka ordered. "I need some air."

Climbing down from the barricade, Loka walked through the camp, towards the east. Her mind raced with the ramifications of what had happened. Would they all be murderers by the end of this? Tara approached.

"Are you OK?" Tara asked.

"Yes, I'm fine," Loka said. "I had to light one up."

"That bandit?"

"Yes."

"His own fault. You tried to warn the big idiot."

"I did. But it doesn't make it easier."

"Nothing ever will, but we will all have to face that by the end of today. Even if Symin gets here in time. Those reinforcements from Grey will not be swayed easily."

"I know. But still, I hope it ends quickly. I would prefer not to have too much blood on our hands."

"It's already on theirs," Tara quipped. "I wouldn't lose sleep over it."

"I guess you're right. Let's check the eastern barricade."

"OK."

Together, they walked to the wall, and climbed to the top. The rangers lining it watched intently to the east, where the smoke from the fires was all but gone. A dark wave could be seen in the distance, swallowing the road as it advanced. Six specks sat on the distant horizon, the ships which had brought Yuri's army from Grey.

"How long before they reach us?" Tara asked.

Loka raised her eye glass and peered into the distance. She could almost make out the faces of the men, running towards them. All were in the uniform of Yuri's private army, all marched with steadfast determination. There would be no turning of this army with the faces of their loved ones.

"We have maybe two hours, before they arrive. They made good time, in spite of the fires."

"How many?"

"At least three hundred. I guess fifty per ship was an accurate assumption. And they don't look like conscripts. These will not be an easy foe, like the men in Judd."

"I wouldn't call the men in Judd an easy foe," Tara said.

"Then you can expect a hard battle before this day is over."

"We should have sunk them before they landed," Tara moaned.

"How were we going to do that?" Loka said. "Their ships would have been far from land, when that strategy might have helped, and they would likely have doused our flames quickly and landed anyway, to find us exhausted by our efforts."

"And now, they find us under siege, half our army already exhausted from the fight to the west, when they come at us from the east."

"But they come at us already having sailed, fought back the fires, then marched all day to meet our defences. They will not hit us hard immediately. They will camp, just as we did."

"But we'll still be fighting the others, in Judd. When do we rest?"

"Don't be so worried," Loka said. "Symin will be here before our barricade falls. I have faith in him."

"I hope you're right," Tara said.

Together, they returned to the western barricade.

Already, the wall was covered in scorch marks, and in some places, smoke rose from smouldering timbers. The plan was only working as well as the skill of the rangers on the wall, and they had not been called on to do this before.

"We must hold this barricade firm for as long as possible!" Loka shouted. "Hit those arrows faster. I need three volunteers, to run water from the kitchen. Use it sparingly, but use it. If we're all dead, we can't drink it anyway. I want those areas where the wood is burning put out before it becomes a problem."

Four rangers volunteered and ran for water, while the rest continued their defence against the arrows. Loka walked along the wall, and tapped one in four of the rangers as she went. Reaching the far end, she turned and called out to them.

"Those who I have just tapped, you are to stop being concerned about the arrows, and target the archers themselves. Slow down their assault in any way necessary. We must defend this camp for as long as it takes. And we are now beyond the point where we can afford to play nice."

"Yes, Sir!" the rangers replied.

Loka watched as several colours of flame began to erupt among the enemy, as the rangers targeted them directly. Several bows were incinerated, and the men who wielded them fled the front lines in terror, some of them with their clothes alight. Others rushed to their aid, quickly dousing the flames, while Yuri's men snarled in distaste for their cowardice.

More men were pushed forward, to take the place of those who had been hit, but it had slowed the attack. Loka smiled. Perhaps they could do this after all. Then, with a sinking terror in her heart, she watched as six of the bandits dragged a lumbering device from the village.

"What is that thing?" Tara whispered.

"A trebuchet," Loka replied, awe in her voice as she took in the sight of the immense siege engine. "I wonder when they built that?"

"Who cares when they built it, what do we do about it?" Tara asked.

"We have to destroy it. Before they can kill us all."

"That thing will take a lot of flames to burn," Tara said. "What do you supposed they will throw at us?"

"We'll know soon enough," Loka replied. "But I think I know, and it has me worried."

As the immense device came to a stop behind the archers, two men hoisted a huge barrel of oil onto its cradle, and one hefted a small axe, splitting the lid as a third man approached with a lit torch.

"Clear the wall!" Loka shouted. "For the sake of Cinder, everybody clear this barricade now!"

In a mad rush, the rangers jumped, climbed, and ran from the barricade. Just as the last were clear, there was a shudder through the barricade, as the oil barrel struck it, and its contents splashed along the ramparts, then burst into roaring fire.

"There's no way we can stop that," Tara said.

"Don't be afraid! Strip the section of barricade to either side! Knock it down and get that wood away from the fire!"

Loka rushed back to the barricade, not looking to see if the others were following her orders. The barrel had ignited a five meter length of the barricade. Several meters still stood clear on either side. They would not for long. Frantically, she began smashing away at the first section to the right of the flames. Several others joined her, and in a few short minutes, they had pulled away a meter of the barricade, stopping the flames from spreading. The same was done on the other side.

"Sir," Tara said. "This leaves our defences open at the centre."

"Then we defend from the centre. To the last man. I want rangers stationed on both sides, and the rest of you, target that trebuchet! I want it destroyed. Now!"

"Yes, Sir!" her rangers shouted, and it was done.

A barrage of flame, in all colours was fired at the trebuchet. Then they were joined by half of the rangers from the eastern barricade, and in moments, there was so much fire around the device, that it was no longer visible. The bandits scattered, and the arrows stopped.

The intensity of the heat from the burning barricade could not stop them, as the rangers made their way in front of it, intent on standing their ground. Backed by fire, their cloaks billowing in the breeze, their faces firm and resolute, and the fire dancing from their hands, the rangers lined up, dozens upon dozens.

For the first time the conscripts of Judd got a true picture of the enemy. And they ran. In their hundreds, the men of Judd, Yuri's faithful and the conscripts alike, retreated into the village while their toys of war burned.

"This buys us some time," Loka said. "But not much. We will have a harder fight in the east very soon, and now our rear is open and vulnerable. I hope Symin arrives soon."

In answer to her words, a horn blasted its call from the east. Loka shuddered.

"I hoped they would give us more time."

Running, Tara behind her, Loka made her way to the eastern barricade, and climbed to the top. Two hills away, the army was marching. They were so close, and they seemed still so fresh. The horn blew again, and a cheer could be heard in response from Judd.

"Great," Loka said. "Just when we got them running, these bastards give them the will to keep fighting. That's the last thing we needed. Tara, stay here, lead them well. Do not attack too soon."

Loka climbed down and ran back to the burning rubble of the western barricade, around it and out into the field. In moments, she met the line of rangers who stood there, flaming with all their might at the enemy.

Reinvigorated, Yuri's men in Judd were pushing the conscripts ahead, out into the battle fields around the smouldering trebuchet.

"At least that thing's ruined," Loka said. "Remember, we don't want to kill unnecessarily, but if they will not be dissuaded, we have no choice. Oh, Symin, where the hell are you?"

The bandits in Judd moved forward, joining the line of conscripts, and began to pass out bows. But the rangers were not having that. As each bow changed hands, it was struck by fire. Frustrated, three bandits drew their swords, and charged.

Instantly, those three men were ablaze. Then they were screaming. They fled, through the lines of conscripts, to be met with water from the men behind.

"Enough! We charge as one," the bandit commander shouted. "Any man who fails to run, will feel my sword!"

"That man burns first!" Loka shouted, pointing to the commander as he screamed and charged, his men prodding the conscripts forward. As one, the enemy advanced, and as one, the rangers fired, igniting the commander with a fury to compete with that which struck the trebuchet earlier.

The commander's men still pushed, and the conscripts trampled his body as they continued to advance.

"Steady!" Loka shouted. "Wait until we have no other choice. The conscripts are not the enemy."

The rangers watched, as the bandits came closer. Then, as they were about to reach the fifty pace mark, another horn blew, this time from the road to the south.

"Rangers approach!" came a shout from the barricade.

The horn blew again, and the sound of shouting came with it. Hundreds of voices. Men, women and children yelled to their loved ones. They begged them to stop fighting. Then, emerging into the open space around Judd, came the horses, and the carts. Hundreds of people. Rangers in front, and civilians behind. Symin stood tall in the stirrups, atop his horse and bellowed to the men of Judd.

"Conscripts, those of you forced to fight for Yuri, be aware! Your loved ones are free, and Yuri is fallen. Rangers now rule in Grey, and Yuri is our prisoner. You are all free men once more!"

The conscripts halted, and milled about for a moment, trying to decide what to do. Then, some of the civilians pushed their way through the rangers, to see the men, calling out as they did so.

"The rangers speak true!" a woman shouted. "We are all free, please, put down your weapons and come home!"

“Martha?” one of the conscripts said. “Is it really you?”

“Yes, Dari, my love. We're free now. And Yuri will go on trial in Emberdale for his crimes. We can finally go home together.”

The conscripts had heard enough. As one, they turned on their captors, and swarmed around them, shouting and swinging their fists, until some took swords from Yuri's men. In short order, the crowd dispersed, and the blood of the bandits stained the fields. They then turned to Symin's men, and ran, dropping their weapons as they did so. The civilians surged forward, to meet them.

The reunions were short lived, before another horn sounded, and the sky to the east was lit by a burst of fire. The reinforcements had arrived.

Chapter 29 – Final Battle

"Charge!" Symin shouted, and kicked his heels into the horse's flank. Like a surging wave, he led his men to the fray, charging through the crumbled western barricade in moments, and bringing a cheer from Loka's people in the camp, particularly those who were fighting to hold the eastern wall.

Three hundred armed men were charging the camp from the east, and the rangers were firing all they could at the invaders, but it was not enough. Symin led his men around the barricade, half following him and the rest riding in force around the opposite end.

Meanwhile Loka led her people atop the wall. Some ran through the gates, firing on the enemy from in front of the barricade. With the numbers on the barricade almost doubled, as those who had fought in the west joined the eastern defenders, the road to the east was alive with flames.

The bandits from Grey were too late in seeing their predicament, and soon found themselves surrounded. They had been buoyed by the knowledge that Loka had only a couple of hundred rangers at her disposal, according to the intelligence they had been given before leaving the steel city.

Now, they saw at least that many on and below the wall before them, and that again on horses rushing to their flanks. The riders joined the efforts, casting their flames upon the bandit army, and soon the men at the fringes were ablaze and screaming.

"Push forward! Victory awaits us if we stand firm!" Shouted a commander, from the centre of the field.

Loka's black fire answered him, and he shouted no more orders, his face ablaze, his screams a strangled, choking sound as he fell to the ground. Those nearest him beat at the flames with their cloaks, trying to save him.

In response to the fall of their leader, the bandits surged forward, soon dangerously close to the rangers on the ground, their angry swords glinting with the reflected flames.

"Behind the wall!" Loka shouted, and the rangers on the ground rushed to fall in, as those on top of the barricade fired on any bandit who came too close to the retreating fighters.

Several rangers struggled to push the gates closed, in order to stop the advance, but they were too slow. As the wave of bodies slammed into the barricade, it shook, and they pressed against each other to make it through the gates, all while multicoloured fire rained down from above.

"Damn it!" Loka shouted, then looked in surprise and awe as another force charged in from the west.

Waving swords stolen from the supplies of the bandits in Judd, the conscripts charged the gates from the inside. They soon pushed the bandits back, and the gate was closed. Several bandits lay dead by the conscripts' swords, but in a minor miracle, no conscript had fallen.

Now trapped as the riders closed in behind them, the bandits began to fall. In terror, they crushed in to the centre, so they no longer had room to swing their weapons, or fight their captors. As the bodies around them burned, they begin to throw their swords to the ground.

"Hold your fire!" Loka shouted. "We are rangers, not murderers. These men are beaten. Fetch water, save those you can from the fire. I want every bandit in chains. Do not allow them to escape."

In quick response to her orders, a large number of rangers left the wall, along with the conscripts, to fetch what they needed. With over a hundred on the barricade, there was no chance the bandits would take the opportunity to renew the attack. The riders all sat motionless, holding flames in their hands, a menacing display of power which no bandit would ever forget.

Soon, the conscripts had reached the carts of Symin's forces, and informed Treghan and Corilai of the situation. Leading a line of carts, they made their way to the camp, and then through the barricade, to parade Yuri before his defeated men, before joining Symin near the wall at the northern end.

Several rangers joined them, and began loading the unwounded men onto the carts, securing them with chains, while others sought to treat the burns of the wounded. Once the carts were full, bandits crammed in like sardines in a jar, twenty riders accompanied them as they moved away from the barricade, where they would wait for the rest, before their journey to Emberdale.

Still fully two hundred bandits remained, and Symin ensured they were bound or chained securely. Once done, they were forced to march, a long line of broken men, going to face justice for their master's crimes. The wounded were loaded onto a final cart, taken from Judd, and would be properly cared for throughout the journey.

The conscripts, reunited with their loved ones, trickled away, to return to their homes, as the rangers departed for the city. A dozen rangers remained in Judd, to establish a permanent presence, as per the Chancellor's plan. None of the conscripts returning there voiced any disagreement. Those rangers would be responsible for the burial of the dead and the removal of the wreckage.

*　　　*　　　*

"The rangers return!" bellowed the city guard, as the gates of Emberdale swung open.

Riding at the head of the column, Loka, Symin, Treghan and Corilai all were awestruck by the cheers of the crowd. It was truly a hero's welcome. Yuri, still chained atop the leading cage, screamed in impotent rage. Among the crowd, several refugees began shouting abuse and throwing whatever was close to hand at the former despot. Nobody moved to stop them.

Travelling through the city, the entire column entered the grounds of the academy, where the prisoners would be held until trial. For the sake of official appearances, the city guard joined the procession, and remained as guards inside the academy, while the rangers were permitted to return to their quarters for a well deserved rest.

One of those men, named Grindle, seemed unusually determined to take a post guarding Yuri. Nobody in the guard questioned his motivation, and he was permitted, with the aid of a second guard, to take first watch over the tyrant from Grey.

The sun would soon set, and the guards were due to change for the night, but under the circumstances, that would not happen. Grindle approached his companion.

“Jodal,” he said. “A strong brew would be good. May I go and fetch one? I'll bring one for you as well.”

“Good idea,” Jodal replied. “He won't be going anywhere. Not as long as I have anything to say about it.”

Grindle left, and returned a short time later with two steaming cups. He handed one to Jodal, and sipped his own, smiling.

“It's a good, warming brew,” he said.

Nodding his thanks, Jodal held the cup to his lips, and sipped. He smiled, then drank a long draft from the cup. As the warming fluid ran down his throat, Jodal smiled. Then, he felt something strange, and an intense pain shot through his abdomen. He looked at Grindle, who stood there, laughing at his discomfort.

“What have you done?” Jodal demanded, as the poison took effect and he tumbled to the ground.

In seconds, Jodal was silent, and Grindle went to work, rummaging through his companion's clothes, and taking the keys to the cell.

“Quickly, take his clothes,” Grindle said as he released the prisoner.

With the traitor's help, Yuri squeezed into the guards clothes, several sizes too small for his large frame.

“It'll have to do. Quickly, lead me out of here,” Yuri ordered.

Careful to avoid any confrontation, Grindle and Yuri made their way out of the academy, and as the gates closed behind them, a commotion erupted in the academy.

“They found the body,” Grindle said. “Run, Sir!”

*　　*　　*

Hulnes stood atop the gates to Emberdale, looking south, along the road they had travelled in their rush to escape Yuri's men. Her daughter stood beside her, watching as well.

“Rulka,” Hulnes said. “We can go home soon. Yuri has been captured, his bandits hold no more sway over the land.”

“Yes, Mother.”

“Rulka, when I asked you to leave me behind, you know why I did that?”

“Yes, Mother.”

“It was because I have led a good life. I would see my grandchildren given the chance to do the same. As long as that man was out there, this was the only safe place, where I could know that you would be safe, and them as well.”

“I know mother, but it's over now. Wait here, I'll fetch us some tea.”

Hulnes watched as her daughter walked to the stairs, which led down to the street below. The guards were all up in the academy, watching over the prisoners, including that man. Hulnes shook her head sadly. She would never forget that man's face. She smiled, remembering his expression as she had struck him with a tomato, as they took him through the streets.

"He deserved worse than a tomato," she murmured, turning and crossing the walkway, to look down into the city.

The shadows cast by the orange sunset stretched long through the city streets, giving an eerie beauty to the quiet places and the bustling thoroughfares alike.

"Still, I'd do it all again, for the future of my grandchildren," she said to herself.

Faintly carried on the wind, a shout reached her from somewhere in the city.

"It's him! Don't let him escape!"

Shocked, Hulnes scoured the streets, her vision not great, but good enough. Then she saw what she most feared. Two men were running for the city gates. One was a city guard, the other, dressed in the uniform, clearly was not. The uniform was ill fitting, the man's ponderous gut swinging as he ran. She watched his face for a while, to be sure. It was him.

"I will not allow this," she said. "My grand children deserve a future where they can live in peace. They deserve a world not ruled by the tyranny of a criminal like you."

As she spoke, Hulnes climbed over the parapet, to stand precariously on a tiny ledge on the other side, barely as wide as her heels. She stood there, her hands grasping the parapet, and waited.

"I die happy, knowing I can grant my descendants a guarantee that you will not haunt their future with your vile hatred."

She leaned forward, her arms stretched out behind her, as the two men came closer. Her stomach turned as she glanced down, realising how high from the ground she was. The rooves of the nearby buildings seemed further away than she had realised, and the cobblestones beckoned her from the distance. Hulnes wept, as she swallowed her pride and met her resolve.

"For their future," she said. "I will gladly surrender my own."

Timing it perfectly, Hulnes waited until the last moment, as the two men approached the gate. Finally, eyes closed, she released her grip on the parapet, and plummeted to the ground. Just as Rulka reached the top of the stairs, two cups in her hands.

"Mother! No!" Rulka screamed, throwing the cups aside as she ran to where Hulnes had just been.

Leaning over the parapet, the tears streaming from her eyes, Rulka looked down, to see her mother, spread eagled on the cobble stones, a heavyset man beneath her. The man's head hung at an odd angle, his neck clearly snapped. Neither of them moved as their blood mingled on the stones. His sword had cut them both as they collided.

"Mother!" Rulka screamed, running for the stairs.

The second man, spooked by the incident was running, but a quick thinking guard, rushing from a nearby home, raised a bow and fired, bringing him down. Rulka reached the bodies just as the crowd started to arrive, and lifted her mother's lifeless head in her arms.

"Oh, Mother, why? Why?" Rulka moaned as she wept, until a city guard draped his cloak over her shoulders, and encouraged her to stand, before escorting the distraught woman away.

"Your mother is a hero, and will be honoured by the city as such," the man said, but she was not hearing a word, stricken as she was by grief.

*　　　*　　　*

The bandits were all put to trial, and many were sent home, while many others were sentenced to prison, depending on their own cases. In recognition of this, Fletcher's case was reviewed, and all the youngsters were delighted to hear his parole was ended early. Fletcher was finally free to go wherever he wished.

According to the plan, each town and city had a permanent ranger presence established, and soon it was normal to see the rangers in all corners of Cinder, as it had been in the old days.

The students spent more time travelling, as well, to see how things operated in those places. Chancellor Howe insisted this become an important part of the curriculum, and so it was that four young students rode into Silverton on a fine, warm evening three months after the battle of Judd.

"Treghan," Corilai said. "Shall we rest here tonight?"

"Yes," Marni said. "Please? I'm tired, and we can bill our accommodation to the academy."

"Well," Treghan said. "What do you think, Fletcher?"

"I'm with the girls," Fletcher said. "It's already dark. Why struggle without light to set up camp, when we can find a warm bed for less effort?"

"Agreed then," Treghan said. "We'll find the local tavern, and stay the night. It would be better if the academy had it's refurbishment of the old post here finished, but they haven't yet. The local rangers are being billeted with the townspeople."

Finding the tavern at the centre of town, Treghan dismounted, and led his friends inside. Selecting a table, they sat down as a smiling innkeeper rushed over to greet them.

"Four fine young academy students, to what do I owe this pleasure?"

"We're travelling, and seek rooms for the night," Treghan said.

"Of course! I'm more than happy to provide whatever you need. I will bill it to the academy, of course. May I have your name?"

"I am Treghan," Treghan said.

"Of course you are. Now I will have some food brought, as we get your rooms prepared. Only the best for academy folk in Silverton! But may I enquire, where you travel to?"

"You may," Treghan said, smiling. "We're on our way to Windwall, to see how the rangers there are integrating with the people of the city, and see what is different about the way they live in the mountains."

"A worthy endeavour!" the innkeeper said. "It's good for young ones like you to experience all the varied ways of the world. It will be an educational experience for you, I'm sure. But if I may offer some advice?"

"Of course," Treghan said.

"On your way, I would strongly recommend you travel north from here, and then west to Norton's Pass. The way through Yakks Valley is treacherous at this time of year. Especially for youngsters like yourselves."

"Thank you, Sir," Treghan said. "We will do that. I appreciate your wisdom."

"It's no trouble. And when you reach Windwall, tell Symin I await his next visit. I still owe him for his victory in our last game of cards."

"I'll do that. But how did you know Symin was there?"

"Rangers are not the mystery they were, and it's better for Cinder this way. You're good people, and the rest of us need to see that for ourselves. Symin is a good representative, for those of us with drinks and women to share!"

"I might have known," Corilai said. "Symin always seems to have a pretty woman in tow, when he's not working."

"Please, young lady," the innkeeper said. "Do not judge that man harshly. He is kind to the girls, and he does nothing untoward. A bit of gentle company, while he enjoys a meal or a few drinks, it's not something to be concerned about. You will not find an innkeeper in Cinder that would not trust his daughter to that man."

"Strangely," Marni said. "I believe you. I have heard that Symin has befriended dozens of ladies in Emberdale, and many at the same time. If he were romantically involved with any of them, I expect there would have been trouble by now."

"You don't suppose he's interested in other men?" Corilai said, with a gasp.

"No way," Fletcher said. "He just loves somebody who he thinks he can't be with, for professional reasons."

"What are you talking about?" Treghan demanded.

The innkeeper laughed, slapping his fist on the table.

"Youngsters can be so perceptive!" he said, his belly shaking with his mirth as he chuckled. "But fear not, The object of his affection returns it in spades, they simply aren't aware of it yet. Give them time. This trip he's on to Windwall might be all they need to see it. You have to admit, they make a fantastic couple."

"Wait," Corilai said, thinking about it. "Who else is in Windwall? Oh no, You don't mean? I mean, we were going there for field study, so our teacher is there. It couldn't be..."

"Symin," Treghan interrupted. "And Loka?"

The innkeeper left the table, laughing raucously, still talking.

"You kids crack me up. It's as if you couldn't see it, when it was right in front of you the entire time. Or were you too busy worrying about each other? You lot are just as obvious as they are!"

"You, Sir," Corilai said to the Innkeeper. "Are a very dangerous man."

"But of course!" he said, returning, leaning in close to whisper, so only they could hear. "I work for the Chancellor, always have done. So I know an awful lot about the rangers. I can tell you this much, if you are spending time in Windwall, you will all return much wiser, and far more powerful. I wish you all the best of luck."

Book Two
Ice Rangers

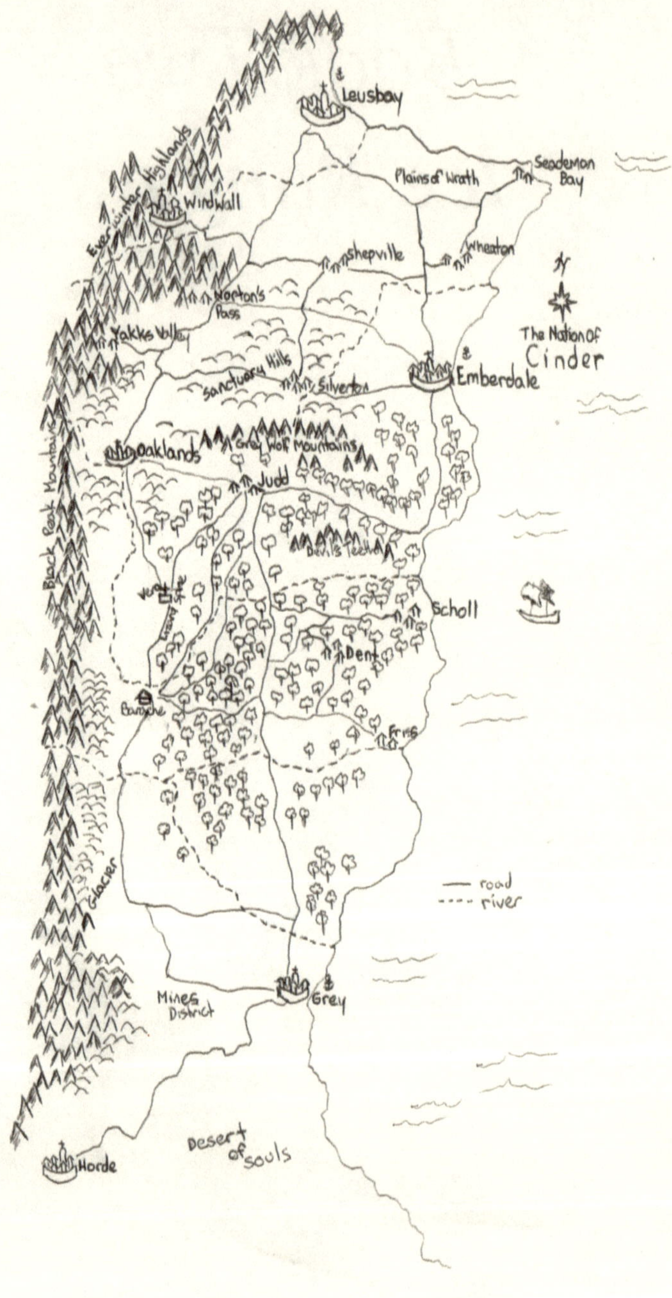

Leusbay
Seademon Bay
Plains of Wrath
Everwinter Highlands
WindWall
Shepville
Wheaton
Norton's Pass
Yakks Valley
The Nation Of Cinder
Sanctuary Hills
Silverton
Emberdale
Oaklands
Grey Wolf Mountains
Judd
Black Peak Mountains
Devil's Teeth
Scholl
Dent
Glacier
— road
---- river
Mines District
Grey
Desert of souls
Horde

Chapter 1 – Hills of Innocence

Four young riders left Silverton on a warm, sunny morning, heading north. The students were on their way to the mountain city of Windwall, to study under their old friend Symin, as he undertook field work in the area.

Loka, another of their teachers, who was also an accomplished member of the enforcers, the police arm of the rangers, was also in Windwall. Nobody had told the four students what was happening in that city to warrant the scout and the enforcer spending a prolonged time there, but all assumed it was safe.

"After all," Treghan told the others in the tavern the night before. "The Ranger Academy wouldn't knowingly send students into danger would they?"

Corilai looked at him, like he was an idiot.

"What just happened?" she snapped. "It only ended three months ago."

"What?" Treghan replied, then thought about it for a moment. "Oh..."

"Exactly," Corilai said. "We were never far from danger all throughout that campaign against Yuri, and you forgot already? We could have died! Dozens of times."

"I guess you're right," Treghan murmured, as Marni and Fletcher both laughed at his discomfort.

"Well, they would never risk us," Marni said with a wicked grin and a sparkle in her eyes. "Fletcher and I had to stay back in the academy, remember? And you two missed all those classes. Maybe we're the important ones."

"Hey!" Treghan said. "We were needed on the mission, that's all."

"Or maybe," Fletcher said, with a wink at Marni. "They thought to themselves, hmmm, a demon flame and a white flame, both a little dangerous. Perhaps if the enemy deal with these two, we won't have to worry about training them."

"That's unfair!" Corilai complained. "Symin would never have let the enemy touch us."

"Oh, sure, he says that now," Fletcher said, not willing to stop teasing.

The four had retired for the evening still friends, though this morning they rode in silence as they left the town behind. The sun was shining, the air was crisp, and a gentle, icy breeze blew down from the mountains.

Corilai and Treghan rode in front, while Marni and Fletcher followed, and they made steady progress as the rolling hills passed them by.

"Sanctuary Hills," Corilai said. "Remember last time, Treghan?"

"Yeah, but we went directly west that time," he replied. "And it was less peaceful, with Symin's army behind us."

"It's not fair," Fletcher said. "You two got to see everything, while we were stuck in classes."

"But you learned a lot about your flames while we were gone," Corilai replied. "We'll all be second year soon, but Treghan and I had to catch up on our classes. You didn't."

"That's true," Fletcher said. "I'm way better than I was. Stronger, and more in control. So is Marni. She's even better than I am. She even started learning her colour's secondary ability."

"Really?" Treghan said. "That's amazing! I thought most students only got that far later in their second or third year."

"Not that it makes much difference to you," Marni said. "Whites only have their control as their secondary ability. It's not really fair that you start with yours from the beginning."

"True, but whites can't flame at all to start with, remember?"

"You're right," Marni said. "I think I prefer it the normal way."

As they came over a low rise, a group stood in the road before them. Three boys, and a young girl, all around ten years of age. The girl was on the ground, her basket overturned, loaves spilled on the road as the boys stood over her.

"Stop taking your food out to that freak, and we'll stop taking it from you," one of the boys snarled.

"Hey!" Corilai shouted. "What's going on here?"

"Nothing, Miss," the boy said. "Not that it's any of your business. Tell the lady, Ivy. Tell her we were only playing."

"I," the little girl said. "I'm fine, they were only playing."

"Well it's no game I like to see played," Treghan snapped. "You three, clear out, if you know what's good for you. And we'll be watching. If I hear of you lot harassing kids again, you'll all burn."

"Ha! You don't scare me, Mister," the boy said.

"Arrie, be careful, look at their cloaks. They're rangers, those four," one of the others said.

"What are you babbling about, Jinno?" Arrie snapped, then looked at the four riders again, before gasping. "You're rangers? From Emberdale?"

"That's right," Marni said. "And little Ivy here is under our protection. If you know what's good for you, you'll clear off and never bother her again."

To punctuate the threat, Marni let loose a long, bright, green flame from her hands, flicking its heat across the boy's face. She then waved the tendril across the grass beside the road. Fed by her flame, the grass sprang tall and dense, blocking escape as the other two turned to run.

"You won't be running off into the hills," Marni said in a sweet voice. "You three are going to march straight back to town, and tell your parents exactly what you've done. If you don't, just think of the trouble when we tell them later."

"Ye... yes Ma'am Ranger Sir," Arrie stammered, as he and his two companions nervously passed the four riders and ran off towards Silverton.

Fletcher dismounted, and approached the girl, helping her to restock her basket.

"Tell us what that was about, Ivy," he said in a soft voice.

"I was taking this stuff to my aunty. She lives in the hills, and is old, so she can't make it to town to get it herself sometimes. Those boys say she's a witch. But she's not. She just burns things sometimes. That's why she chose to live in the wilderness."

"Is she a flame wielder?" Fletcher asked.

"I don't know what that means. But she has these shadow like flames when she's mad."

"A demon flame, like you, Corilai," Treghan said.

"So you take her food? From the town?" Corilai asked.

"Well, yes, but I don't come from the town. I live with my aunty now, and I go into town early to get things she needs."

"We can escort you home, if you like. Want to ride with me?" Corilai said.

"I'd love it!" Ivy squealed.

Fletcher helped the child onto Corilai's horse, and secured the basket to the saddle, before mounting his own horse. As they began riding, Treghan moved his horse closer.

"You said you live there now, so you moved from somewhere else?"

"My mum and dad live on a farm outside of Windwall. They sent me here to live with my aunty after my big brother was kidnapped."

"Kidnapped?" Marni said, shocked.

"Yeah. A few kids have gone missing in the mountains and everybody thought they just got lost, but when my brother was taken, people saw the horses riding away, and they said they thought there was a scuffle, because he resisted. So people are scared to let children go anywhere in the mountains now."

"That must be why Loka and Symin went there," Treghan said. "I thought it would be something like bandits, but abductions would explain it."

"We need to turn away from the road along here, on the trail to the left," Ivy said.

They followed the child's directions, and soon arrived at a small farm house, where they dismounted, allowing the horses to nibble grass as they approached the building.

"Your horses won't run away?" Ivy said.

"No, they're well trained. They'll wait for us," Corilai said.

Grey haired and stern of expression, a woman came out of the house to meet them. She looked them over, then beckoned to the child. Ivy ran to the woman.

"What's gong on, Ivy?" the woman asked.

"These people saved me from those boys I told you about."

"Well, they'd best come inside for some tea, as a thank you."

The woman turned, and walked inside. After a brief hesitation, the four students followed her and found themselves standing in a simple, but homely room. The woman beckoned for them to sit at a long, wooden table.

"The tea won't be long," she said, fussing over a wood stove and scooping leaves into a large pot. "So tell me, where are you four youngsters headed?"

"We have to visit Windwall. It's part of our training. Our teachers are there already."

"Rangers are in Windwall?" the woman asked.

"Remember, Aunty?" Ivy said. "I told you the merchants were talking about the rangers going to all the towns now, and that there will be less bad people because of it."

"Good," the woman said. "Maybe they'll do something at last, about all this foolishness in the mountains."

"What foolishness?" Treghan asked.

"Why, the abductions of course. Some mountain fool is building himself a little orphan army in the mountains. Nothing good will come of it."

She tutted to herself as she poured the tea into large mugs, and placed them on the table in front of the youngsters. She then took a seat opposite them, and drank a long gulp from her own cup.

"Come now, don't let it go cold. And besides, that's enough talk of those mountain folk. You four are from the academy. Is old man Howe still in charge?"

"Yes," Corilai said.

"Good. He has it in him to go a while longer I'd guess. He always was a stubborn old man. But better than that cranky oaf he replaced."

"Cranky oaf?" Fletcher asked.

"Oh, he'd be long dead by now. But when I was a little girl, old man Garack ran that place, and he was a mean old fool. He hated the black flame, and refused them admission. Otherwise, well, my life may have been different."

"I'm a black flame too," Corilai said. "The way the villagers treated me, I was glad the academy was so welcoming. Without it, I don't know where I would have ended up."

"You are?" the woman said, tears welling in her eyes. "I'm so glad. It's good to know that girls like I was can have a better life."

"It's still hard in the villages, where they're superstitious. But if you can make it to the academy, life gets better."

"I'm pleased for you, dear. And you obviously have wonderful control. You'd be about sixteen or seventeen years old? By the time I was your age, I'd already burned down three homes by accident."

"They helped me a lot with that," Corilai said.

"And what about you other three? What flames do you have?"

"I'm red," Fletcher said. "And Marni is green."

"And I'm white," Treghan finished.

"A black and a white?" their host said, an eyebrow raised. "The demon flame and the angel flame, together. What a wonderful omen for the world. I hope you can bring peace to all the people you visit, by your good example of opposites getting along."

"They don't just get along," Marni said, bursting with pride for her friends. "They make each other way more powerful."

"Really? That's good to hear. I am sure you four can bring about whatever changes you desire in this world."

She downed the last of her tea, then stood.

"Thank you again for helping my niece. But if you will excuse me, I have to tend to the garden. I wish you all safe travels."

They all stood, and prepared to leave, thanking the old lady as she left the house. Ivy grabbed hold of Treghan's sleeve as he headed for the door.

"Please," Ivy said. "If you can get outside of Windwall, can you find my big brother? Please, I want to know he's safe."

"We'll do what we can," Treghan said. "I'm sure he's glad you're safe here, with your aunty."

Ivy nodded, and followed them outside, where she watched as they mounted their horses and rode away, the little girl waving them farewell.

As they reached the road, they met a ranger. Throwing back her hood, Tara greeted them with a smile.

"I'm headed to Norton's Pass, but I heard you were going this way. I thought we could travel together for a while."

"We don't need a chaperone," Fletcher said.

"Maybe not," Tara replied. "But you're still young, what? Sixteen now? Adult company might still be useful. Besides, I outrank you all, and I'm coming along, so put up with it. I'll stay out of your way, it's your journey, your choices, but if you need a hand, you know who to ask."

They continued north late into the afternoon, until they arrived at a highway. Running from Emberdale in the south east, eventually it led all the way west to Norton's Pass, south east of Windwall.

They followed the highway west until nightfall, and they set up camp beside the road. In the dim light of the moon, with the help of the fire, Treghan sat and consulted his maps.

"What are you doing?" Corilai asked, sitting beside him.

"That innkeeper in Silverton told us to go north and then turn west, to avoid the worst of the weather. But do you remember if he said to go through Norton's Pass?"

"I think he did. Why?"

"Because I'm thinking if we leave the highway, and go directly north from where we are, we should be able to reach Shepville by tomorrow afternoon, then go west from there. That would mean we go west almost directly to Windwall, whereas if we go via Norton's Pass, we then turn north, for some distance through the mountains before we turn west for Windwall."

"He must have sent us that way for a reason," Corilai said. "And besides that, look at your map. It's nice open highway, all the way to Windwall, if we go the way he said. You're suggesting we leave the road altogether, for half a day. But you're measuring that half day based on what we already travelled."

"So?"

"So use your head. If we travel off road, it will have to take longer, and who knows what the terrain might be like. I say we stick to the highways."

"I guess you're right," Treghan said. "But look, there's a road, just like the one we took north from Silverton. And I'd like to see the north sometime."

"Treghan is right," Tara said, sitting beside them. "It's your journey, I'm just tagging along, but taking the Shepville route gives you another night in a proper bed, it's the only way you can avoid sleeping rough. Unless you divert yourselves south to Norton's Pass and add another day to your trip."

"OK, so we can go to Shepville, but it's straight to Windwall from there," Corilai said.

“Fair enough,” Treghan replied. “Besides, there’ll be other times we can see those northern towns and villages. If I had my way, we'd see them all right now.”

“And then get expelled for not arriving in Windwall as ordered. That would go well, don't you think?”

“You're right, as usual,” Treghan said, folding his map. “But I would love to see Leusbay one day.”

“One city at a time, Treghan. We're rangers now. Or will be one day at least, when we graduate. Then we can see all the cities of Cinder.”

“If you're there with me, that sounds amazing,” Treghan said.

“Stop flirting, you two!” Fletcher called out from across the fire. “We have to eat before we sleep. Come on, it’s Treghan's turn to cook.”

Grumbling at the interruption, Treghan went to his horse and retrieved one of the saddle bags, in which there were dried meats and root vegetables. Adding water from his canteen to a pot, he cooked the vegetables and warmed the meat, before serving up a small portion to each of them.

As they ate, the ever present icy breeze from the mountains chilled their backs, as they faced the fire.

“If it's this cold here,” Fletcher said. “How will it be in the mountains?”

“Let's try not to stay outside there,” Marni said. “At least until we can get some warmer clothes from the city.”

“I thought we had warm clothes,” Treghan said.

“Not warm enough, is my bet,” Fletcher said. “But the clothes in Windwall will be better made for the conditions than anything we could buy in Emberdale.”

“Whatever the case,” Treghan said. “I vote we try to get there without having to sleep in the snow.”

Chapter 2 – Ice Roads

A chill wind, blowing a light sleet across the plains, cut through the cloaks of the four students from Ranger Academy. Tara followed a short distance behind the group, and showed none of their discomfort. Pushing through the unbearable cold as the sun hid behind the highlands, they approached Shepville from the south. The young ones hoped to stay in the town and then follow the road west at dawn, towards the distant mountains.

"It's unusual for the snow to blow this far into the plains," Marni said. "But I guess winter brings it down from the mountains."

"Doesn't mean we have to like it," Fletcher said. "Let's get into town quickly, and find a warm fire."

"Agreed," Treghan said, and willed his legs to move faster, leading his weary horse to trudge through the crunching layer of icy snow which covered the road.

Before them, the small town of Shepville stood shrouded in the driving sleet, a signal fire shining through the weather in defiance. Smaller than Silverton, the town was barely larger than Judd Village, where Treghan had grown up, and it lacked the protection of a town wall.

Instead, a set of small wooden barriers erected to the west of the town did their best to stop the worst of the winds from freezing the inhabitants. The task was not easily met by the small defence, and the wind still tousled their robes as the four youngsters walked into the central square, where a guard stood watch over the fire at its centre.

"Welcome, travellers!" the guard shouted over the wind. "If you seek the inn, it sits behind me, across the square. Best you get out of the wind, though this fire is warm. You'll be warmer still in a comfortable bed, and Shiro the innkeeper will gladly provide you a hot meal for a reasonable price."

"Thank you, Sir!" Treghan shouted in reply, and they made their way to the building and let themselves in.

The light was dim, but tolerable inside the inn, and a buxom woman beckoned them over to the bar. Her warm smile, framed in curled blonde hair, was a welcoming sight.

"Four young rangers, students I'd guess, choosing a poor night indeed for travel," she said. "I am glad you made it to our Inn. My name is Gaera, and my Husband is Shiro. Do you require separate rooms? Or will you accept a dorm with six beds? You may have others bunking with you, depending who the storm blows in this evening."

"The dorm will be fine," Corilai said. "Thank you, Gaera. There's a fifth ranger right behind us, who will be joining our group for the evening. I am Corilai, and these are Treghan, Fletcher and Marni. You guess right, we are students, on our way to Windwall, for the purpose of study under our masters who are there as we speak. This is our between semester field study, not classes."

"It is wonderful, that you get to see the world, but be careful in Windwall," Gaera said. "I hear rumours which concern me about that place."

"What kind of rumours?" Marni asked as Tara entered.

"I hear the highlands are a dangerous place for young ones like yourselves, with many strange disappearances and kidnappings, and that band of thieves in the mountains. Windwall is safer than the hamlets and farms, but do not leave your backs unguarded."

"Thank you for the warning," Treghan said.

"I'm sorry," Gaera said, "I don't mean to be chillier than the winds outside. Come, I will show you to your room, and you can stow your belongings. Come back out here when you're done, and we will see to some warm food for you. If you have horses, I'll send Shiro to put them in the stable, where they will be warm."

"Thank you," Treghan said, and the four of them followed her to their accommodation. "Our horses are out the front."

Soon, they were back at the bar, their bags stowed safely in the dorm, the door locked for security. A man entered from the back of the bar, and approached them.

"I am Shiro," he said. "Your horses are warm and fed, and will be safe in the stables. It is an honour to house such fine animals. The academy is fortunate indeed. When you leave, you can find them through the door at the bar, through the corridor."

"Thank you," Corilai said. "But right now, I smell something delicious."

"That would be the stew, which I keep filled in a cauldron in the kitchen at this time of year. It means we can have warm food immediately for any travellers who come in during the colder times. We serve it with bread. Only a few coins each, and you'll be warmer than a pup in a whelping box."

"That sounds great," Treghan said, fishing in his pockets for his coin purse and passing it to Shiro. "We'll all have some then."

Shiro took several small coins and passed the coin purse back with a smile, then wandered out to the kitchen.

"That was very trusting, Treghan," Fletcher said.

"He has no reason to steal from us," Treghan replied. "And he knows we have the backing of Ranger Academy. He wouldn't try anything."

"Even so," Tara said. "You should be careful not to flash your money around. Not all towns are as friendly to rangers as this one."

Soon, Shiro returned, carrying a tray laden with five large bowls, filled to the brim with a thick, steaming stew. Large chunks of root vegetables and meat crowded for space in the bowls, and a fat slice of bread sat beside each.

"Follow me," Shiro said, leading them to a corner table, where he placed the tray. "It's always better to eat at a table than sitting up at the bar. Call myself or Gaera if you need anything."

"Thank you," Corilai said. "We will."

Shiro left them to eat their meal, returning to the kitchen as Gaera put four steaming cups of tea on the table and then went to join him. They ate quietly for a minute, before Corilai spoke.

"That's another warning, and more stories of kidnappings and other things in the mountains."

"I guess we know why Symin and Loka are really there now," Treghan replied. "What do you think, Tara?"

"I can't speak of their activities in Windwall, but while it is safe down here, you should take care in the mountains," Tara said.

"They must be investigating things," Marni said. "I hope the fact we're being sent there means they have it under control."

"It probably means they needed bait," Fletcher said. "I mean, how best to catch a kidnapper than with the kind of people they're kidnapping?"

"That's a worrying thought," Corilai said. "But I'm sure they wouldn't do something like that. Not without telling us first."

"I'm sure they don't think there's any risk to us going there," Treghan said. "Or else they would have sent us somewhere else. Rangers are being posted all over Cinder now."

"And besides," Marni said. "We don't even know the kidnappers are targeting anybody in particular. They're not Yuri."

"We'll find out soon enough" Corilai replied, as Shiro rushed to the table.

"I'm sorry," Shiro said. "But somebody has taken one of your horses."

"Wait here," Tara said, running with Shiro to the stables.

She mounted her horse, and rushed into the night. She followed the fresh tracks, and soon saw a youth on the stolen horse. The young man was kicking the animal's sides hard, frantically trying to urge it to gallop. The horse was ignoring his demands. Effortlessly catching up, Tara rode alongside, and pulled the man from the saddle.

"Without ranger commands, that horse will never do what you say." Tara said. "Now get out of here, and never touch ranger property again."

"Ye… Yes Ma'am," the youth stammered, running away.

Tara rode back to the tavern, leading the stolen horse. Once both horses were safely in the stables, she returned to the four students.

"This is why you sometimes need an adult around. But I'm sure you'll be fine now."

The five finished their meals, and talked for another hour before heading to their beds. They rose at first light and made their way to the stables, almost getting away before Gaera found them, and insisted they have breakfast.

Gaera ushered them back into the dining room, where she had already set a table with a large pot of tea and four plates, piled with bacon, eggs and toast.

"Don't worry, it's on the house," Gaera explained. "I can't let four youngsters like you head out on that road with empty bellies. And the ranger, of course."

Expressing their thanks, all five dug into the food, and soon sat back, sipping their tea as their breakfast settled. Shiro approached, sitting at the end of the table.

"You four are headed to Windwall?" he said.

"That's right," Treghan replied. "And Tara to Norton's Pass."

"Please, be careful. You should know the storms in the mountains that reach us here, like they did last night, usually hang around that city for days after. They have chains along the trails, so travellers in blizzards can follow them, but even so, one missed step and you're a corpse in a gully. I'd hate to hear that had happened to one of you."

"Thank you," Corilai said. "We'll be careful."

"Good. And I'm sure you can all look after yourselves, being with Ranger Academy and all, but watch your backs. Young people are disappearing. Especially those children who are about the age their flames are coming in, so younger than you four. I'm not saying the kidnappers are taking flame wielders, but you lot aren't that far from the age they seem to prefer. So look out for each other, and don't go wandering about alone."

"Thanks for the information, and the warning," Treghan said. "We'll be careful. We'll be staying with our teachers in Windwall at the new ranger outpost, so hopefully it will be safe there."

"That's good," Shiro said, standing to leave. "I've saddled your horses, so they're ready when you are, but please, stay as long as you wish."

Finishing their tea, they stood, and Treghan led the way to the stable, where they found their horses, looking refreshed, and prepared as promised.

Gaera had attached a bag, with a farewell note, containing a loaf of bread and a lump of butter in waxed paper, to the saddle of Treghan's horse. Each saddle had a filled water bag, with something added for flavour.

"They thought of everything," Marni said as she grimaced at the flavour. "They've put a bit of alcohol in the water to stop it freezing, and a bit of lime to improve the taste. But don't drink too much at once. It won't be enough alcohol to make you drunk, but you should conserve your water any way."

"With these conditions," Tara said. "I'm sorry, but I have to leave you. I must get to Norton's Pass tonight, and then back to Emberdale. Please, travel safe and take care. Remember your training. You are rangers."

"We will," Corilai said. "See you when we get back to Emberdale."

Mounting his horse, Treghan made his way out of the stables, and into the still morning. Tara had already disappeared into the distance, her tracks clear. Thick white snow blanketed the fields and the surrounding hills, the road disappearing into the morning fog as the sun peered over the eastern horizon. A simple wooden fence alongside the road was the only indication of where they should go.

"This is way more snow than they would usually get this far from the highlands," Marni said as she looked around.

Moving slowly at first, they rode out of Shepville, heading west towards the mountains. The trip was uneventful apart from the cold. As the sun shone through a break in the growing clouds at noon, Treghan stopped and dismounted, fetching the bread from the bag on his saddle.

"We should eat now, while we still can," he said. "We'll be hitting some rough weather this afternoon, if Shiro's warning is anything to go by."

Treghan unwrapped the butter and they scraped their bread across it. They ate the simple lunch without speaking. Soon, the sun was concealed by clouds, and the wind was beginning to pick up, occasionally blowing flurries of snow across their feet. Corilai mounted her horse as the others finished, looking with a worried expression towards the west.

"If there's another storm picking up," she said. "I'd like to reach those guide chains before it gets too bad. The more chance we have of reaching

Windwall tonight, the happier I'll be."

"Agreed," Treghan said. "But if it gets too bad, There is probably a house or a tavern where we meet the highway, if we have to stop there tonight, that's what we'll do."

"I don't know about that," Marni said. "I think we're too far to the north. I think there is such a place at Norton's Pass, but that's going out of our way."

They continued on, the journey becoming slower as the wind grew worse and it began to snow. The road was hard to follow, and more than once the horses stumbled on the unstable ground. By mid afternoon, it was impossible to see more than a horse length in front of them as they trudged ever so slowly onwards.

Finally, they reached an obvious meeting of roads, with a weathered signpost indicating they should turn south for Norton's Pass, or north for Windwall and Leusbay. Treghan dismounted, and trudged into the whiteness, invisible as soon as he was a few steps away.

Shortly, he returned, his white flame guiding him, as he followed his own almost obliterated tracks in the snow.

"There's a shelter, on the other side of the highway," he shouted over the wind. "It's just a big lean to, but it should fit us and the horses, and we can rest there for the night."

"It's still early," Fletcher said, as the wind scooped a flurry of snow into his face. "But I guess it can't be helped. It's better to stop in a shelter, than to die on the road."

Treghan led the way, and soon they were all under the shelter, open to the road but shielded from the worst of the wind as it drove down from the north west. They tied the horses to a rail at the southern end, where a trough had been placed for feed and water.

"Whoever built this shelter must know the area pretty well," Marni said. "We should light a fire in front of it, but where can we get dry wood?"

"There's a pile of wood behind the shelter," Treghan said. "And we can dry it, that's not a problem. I think the merchants have these shelters all along the highway. It wouldn't be unusual for them to need shelter in a storm."

"That's right," Corilai said. "We met some before, with Symin. They're resourceful people. They might even have left some supplies around here."

Corilai began scratching at the ground with her feet, as Treghan and Fletcher fetched fire wood, moving the thin layer of snow which had drifted into the shelter, until her boot scraped wood.

"Marni, give me a hand," Corilai said, as she knelt down and fumbled with a board.

Together, the girls scraped soil and snow away from the wood, until they had exposed a panel about the size of a large chest. Grasping one edge, they lifted, and after a moment of stubborn resistance, the panel lifted, exposing a wooden lined hole in the ground beneath it. Inside were sacks of preserved meat, root vegetables, and skins filled with water and alcohol, as well as a single large cooking pot, with several small bowls inside it.

"I guess we eat tonight," Marni shouted, jumping up in her excitement, to hit her head on the roof of the shelter.

"But not too much, only enough to survive," Corilai said. "The Merchants rely on these stores during emergencies, and there are a lot of mouths to feed in those caravans. They wouldn't mind us using them, but they might get annoyed if we leave them short."

"Fair enough," Marni said. "But I'm not going to lose sleep over not starving to death in a blizzard."

Taking out the pot, and four bowls, the girls fetched a selection of the meat and vegetables, and one of the water skins. By the time the boys had a roaring fire going for warmth, there was enough food in the pot with water added to make a hearty stew, which cooked slowly on the edge of the fire as the snow piled up even deeper on the road outside.

"We might want to bring enough wood inside to last the night," Marni said. "And once the food is gone, we should melt some snow in the pot. Even if we're not thirsty, the horses are."

"Speaking of the horses," Fletcher said. "Treghan, can you help me? I think I saw a couple of hey bales behind the wood, mostly buried in snow. We should give them one. They'll be starved, the poor things."

Without a word, Treghan stood and followed Fletcher back into the snow. By the time they returned, dragging a large bale of hay between them, the stew was ready, and Corilai was serving it into the bowls.

Lifting the bale, the boys tossed it into the trough, and tore at it in an effort to make it easier for the horses to eat, before returning to the warmth of the fire and accepting their food from the girls.

Settling in, they found the shelter far more comfortable, granting a place out of the storm, than its simple structure would have otherwise suggested. Once they had eaten, and the horses had water, they erected a second fire closer to the animals, to warm the southern end of the lean to.

As they grew tired, Treghan agreed to take first watch, to ensure the fires remained burning, while the others climbed into their bedrolls. Soon they slept soundly as the winds roared through the trees behind the shelter.

Chapter 3 – Mountain Way

As day broke, the winds slowed, and the snow fell gently upon a crisp white landscape. Marni tossed the last of the wood on the fires, and then filled the pot with water, to make tea. While it slowly came to a boil, she woke her friends, and they carefully packed their bedding and prepared their packs.

Finding some leaves in the merchants' stores, Marni brewed a warming tea and served it in the bowls. She then put some of the root vegetables in the pot to cook as a simple breakfast. Corilai helped her to put out first the fire near the horses, and then the one they had been cooking on, and they ate the vegetables while they carefully returned everything to the store.

When they were done eating, they used snow to quickly wash out the bowls and pot, placed them in the store and closed it, thankful for the merchants and their preparedness.

"We should get a move on," Treghan said as he led his horse out of the shelter. "Thanks for making the tea, Marni."

"No problem," she replied, leading her horse out after him as Corilai and Fletcher did the same.

Mounting up, they began the northern part of their journey into the mountains. They rode slowly, careful in the frigid terrain, but less than two hours later, found themselves at an intersection. A massive stone wall jutted out of the snow, with an arrow painted high on its surface, along side a single word.

"Windwall," Treghan read aloud, turning his horse and following a path between trees which moved in a north westerly direction.

They travelled uphill, passing several hazardous ravines, any one of which could have killed them if they attempted the same route at night. Before the second hour of the climb had passed, the road turned and travelled directly west, up and down the rises, but tending higher as they journeyed into the mountains.

They travelled around the sides of the steep cliffs, and crossed many long wooden and stone bridges between them, when the treacherous terrain grew too dangerous for the path to continue skirting the dangerous heights. At one point, the clouds parted, and they could see beyond the side of the mountain they were on, far into the north east, as Cinder's northern districts spread out before them.

"That's Leusbay," Corilai said, pointing at the northern city, a speck in the distance.

The road veered north, and a little way along from them, it crossed a river, which they could hear cascading in a torrent of rapids and falls, as it made its way inexorably to the plains below. The horizon was obscured by ferocious clouds, far out to sea beyond Leusbay, and arcing to land, meeting the point where the mountains met the sea and marked the deadly boundary of Cinder. The waves beneath those distant clouds writhed and foamed, forever halting attempts by the wooden ships of Cinder to sail beyond them, just as the depths of the forbidding mountains hampered travellers from journeying further west.

"Cinder seems so small, from up here." Marni said. "But it would take us many days to reach that ocean."

"Yes, it would, and we should keep moving," Treghan said. "Or else it might still take us many days to reach Windwall, if those storms return."

Wordlessly, they continued their journey, taking care as they travelled through the mountains. Soon, as if Treghan's words had been prophetic, the storm clouds began to close in, and the winds became fierce. The snow, thick on the ground, began to stir as the wind picked it up, and flurries blasted the youngsters' faces as they battled to continue.

Just as the conditions seemed set to worsen, a post appeared on the trail, with a chain attached. It hung for several paces, until it met a second post, and so on. It guided them still further west, and higher, leaving them no doubt that they had truly entered the Everwinter Highlands. Soon they would arrive at the walls of the city.

That is, if they could even see Windwall in the worsening conditions. Soon, the chain was no longer visible from on their horses, and Treghan started a bright white flame to try to penetrate the storm. Even that proved fruitless, so he stopped, climbed down and grasped the chain with one hand as he led his horse.

Treghan pushed a guiding white flame from the hand which held the chain, and the others followed. The snow grew deep in some places, and then, suddenly, the chain dropped within a heavy drift and was swallowed. Treghan stopped, and looked ahead, trying to see where it re-emerged.

"Wait here," he shouted over the wind. "I'm going to walk ahead a bit, see if I can pick up the road again."

He left his horse with the others, and focussed his energy to create a larger flame, in the hope it might afford better vision. As he did so, the wind slowed, and the snow eased. Still, he kept his flame going as he made his way slowly across the soft snow.

Already a dozen horse lengths across the drift, and unable to see an end, Treghan stopped. Only then did he here it, a voice, high pitched, and soft, carried on the breeze.

"Hey! Is there somebody out there? Please, we need help."

Treghan looked around, wondering who it was, and then, as the wind stopped, he saw a wheel. Some distance from the road, it poked up through the snow drift, and nearby, the corner of a carriage, with a tiny human arm protruding from it, waving frantically. Treghan grabbed at the wheel, and found it was only half of one, then continued towards the carriage.

"We're here," Treghan shouted. "Hold on, We're coming to help."

Turning, with the conditions eased, he could see his friends and the horses a short distance away. He waved for them to come, and then struck out across the snow, towards the carriage.

"Please, help us!"

"It's OK," Treghan said as he reached the carriage and began digging the snow away. "I'm here now."

Looking in through the broken corner of a window on the carriage, he could see a small girl, who beamed a broad smile in her relief.

"I knew it!" she squealed. "I thought I saw a light, that was why I started calling out. Mummy, Daddy! We're saved!"

The child's parents only replied in muffled noises. They must be trapped back there, Treghan thought as his friends arrived. Together, they started digging, much quicker with the four of them. Treghan suddenly realised, if there was a carriage...

"Hey, where are your horses?" he asked.

"We had two," the child replied. "But when the carriage started to go over, Daddy cut them loose and they ran off. He says if the carriage pulled them with it, they'd break their legs and have to be killed. So he let them go. They'll still be attached to each other, so he says they won't have gone far."

"We'll try to find them, after we get you out of there."

"How many horses do you have?" a man said from in the carriage.

"Four," Treghan said.

"Good. I have ropes in here. Do you think they can pull us out?"

"I think so. If we can get the front of the carriage uncovered, but the snow's soft, so the cart might bog down again."

"It's worth a try," the man said. "Bogged is better than buried, after all. I have a shovel here, if that'll help."

"It will," Treghan said, as he cleared another section of the window, and found a latch.

Twisting the latch, he wiggled the frame until it reluctantly opened, pushing more snow away, to give them a small access. The man inside passed a shovel out, and Treghan went to work, digging faster than before.

"Why don't we just melt the snow?" Fletcher asked.

"Don't be silly," Treghan snapped as he continued digging. "We don't want to drown them!"

Thankfully, the soft snow was not hard to move, and soon they had exposed the front of the carriage.

Meanwhile, the man had tied four improvised harnesses, and the girls accepted them, and put them on the horses. Then, he passed lengths of rope and they attached the horses to the front of the carriage, and began to slowly and carefully pull.

It stubbornly refused to budge, so Treghan picked up the shovel and began digging along the side. Suddenly it lurched, then slowly began to pull free of the drift. The wheel on one side was badly damaged, its remains matching the half wheel Treghan had first seen. However, the cart had long skis attached to the underside, so Treghan looked at the other wheel, and observed that it was held in place by a single large pin.

Using the shovel, he struck the pin several times before it came out of its socket. With a great deal of effort, Treghan was able to remove the wheel, which he left in the snow as he jumped clear. The carriage rolled upright onto its skis as the horses pulled, and soon it was lurching across the ground, an enormous hole in the snow drift where it had been.

The man opened a door in the side of the carriage, and came out, beaming an enormous smile as he grabbed Treghan in a bear hug.

"Thank you so much, rangers!" he shouted. "Wait a moment. You're too young to be rangers."

"Yes, we're students," Corilai said. "From Ranger Academy."

"That explains it then!" he replied. "They must have some good teachers, if the students are this competent."

"If you're heading to Windwall," Corilai said. "You can decide that for yourself. We're on our way to meet them."

"I have heard the rangers are spreading out into Cinder again. It's a good thing, and will make us all safer. Especially in the mountains, with so much talk of kidnappings and theft."

"Anyway," Marni said. "I'm Marni, this is Corilai, and the boys are Treghan, and Fletcher."

"Oh, of course, sorry," the man said as a woman climbed out of the carriage, carrying the child. "My name is Brun, my wife is Fari, and my daughter, who is seven years old, is Jiddi. We work a quarry in the foothills. We spend winter in Windwall, but we ran late this year."

"It's nice to meet you all, and I'm so glad you aren't hurt," Corilai said.

"We're fine," Fari said. "Though our horses..."

"Don't worry, they're smart animals," Brun said. "They'll have found shelter nearby. Now the weather is picking up, they'll come back. Still attached with the yolk from the carriage, they won't have gone far. I'll find them."

Brun struck out into the snow, to look for his horses, while his wife and daughter began collecting the broken bits of wheel and putting them in the carriage. Treghan helped them man handle the unbroken wheel in as well, and as they finished, they heard a shout from Brun. He walked from across the road, leading two enormous draft horses, which seemed miraculously unharmed, though very clearly spooked.

"They were in the shelter of a boulder down the side of the hill a bit from the road," Brun explained as he approached. "They'll take a bit to calm down, but we should be fine now. There's enough snow for the carriage to slide on without wheels all the way to Windwall now. We normally would have removed the wheels anyway about now, so you kids can head off to town. Thanks again for all your help."

"OK then, bye!" Marni said with a smile and a wave as she climbed on her horse.

"We might see you around Windwall," Fletcher said. "See you!"

"Good luck," Treghan said.

"Travel safely," Corilai said, waving as she mounted her horse and the four of them made their way to where the chain rose out of the snow, indicating the road continuing west into the highlands.

"It was lucky we came by," Fletcher said after some time. "They might not have been able to get out without help, and the next snow fall would have buried them until spring."

"That's a morbid thought," Corilai replied. "But I'm glad we were able to help. And that carriage was great, with those skis on the bottom."

"Built for the trip, I'd say," Marni said. "Obviously they know the journey well. And now, they'll get to take it again next year."

A light snow began to fall, gentle compared to what they had already seen. A strong breeze blew the worst of the clouds away, so they could see a good distance ahead in spite of the conditions. The snow was sparse across the slanted road. A steep escarpment allowed the snow to blow off and down into a menacing ravine.

They reached the end of the narrow escarpment and rode onto a long stone bridge. It crossed a ravine, which wrapped around the escarpment like a coiled snake, ready to strike and drag careless travellers to their deaths. While they crossed, they heard a voice, carried on the wind from the far side.

"Ahoy there!" Symin called. "I had hoped you four had the sense not to travel this way in the night. I'm glad to see my confidence was well founded."

"It's Symin!" Corilai squealed. "We must be almost there."

"You have an hour to ride," Symin said as he rode out to meet them. "I came to find you, because that storm was perhaps the worst I've seen. I was worried you might have fallen prey to it in the mountains. There are places the snow can drift over the guide chains, and then travellers get lost in the blizzard."

"We found a family in exactly that situation," Treghan said. "Their carriage was tipped over off the side of the road, because the guide chains had been buried in an enormous snow drift."

"Were you able to help them?" Symin asked.

"Yes, we dug them out and pulled the carriage free. The wheels were no good, but the carriage had skis on the bottom, so they pulled the wheels off, found their horses, and will be on there way to Windwall now. Nobody was even hurt."

"That's good news," Symin said as he turned to lead them west. "It's not unusual for the nomadic families who winter in Windwall to suffer great losses if they wait too late into the season."

"Are there a lot of them?" Marni asked.

"Indeed, there are many thousands, who work the warmer months in the hills to the east, or even throughout the Everwinter Highlands, in mines or quarries or even a handful of farms which grow things that thrive in the cold, or run yaks for their wool. When winter arrives, it becomes impossible to survive long in their caravans and hovels, so they flood into the city and wait for spring. Most of them make enough money in the warmer months to keep themselves in the city, but sometimes the poor turn to crime, which we will likely be called on to help the city guards tackle."

"I don't think that family will turn to crime," Corilai said. "That carriage seemed pretty nice."

"The ones with caravans to live in tend to stay in a designated area near the northern wall, and form their own community. They bring a lot of business to the city merchants as well. Often they have a plot they own and use every year."

"It sounds like a very different place from Emberdale," Treghan said.

"It is," Symin said. "But the people are just as generous. Remember how Emberdale welcomed the Scholl refugees? It would be the same in Windwall, as shown by how they treat the nomad families."

"Good to know," Treghan said. "But Symin, there's something worrying me. We've heard a lot of rumours about kidnappings and people disappearing in the highlands. Do you know anything about that?"

"It's one of the reasons I'm here, apart from helping establish the Ranger Academy outpost. But we can discuss it later."

"That's why you rode out isn't it?" Marni said.

"It's one reason, yes," he replied. "It wouldn't be a good look if rangers were taken, when the people see us as the ones who are going to fix the problem. If we become victims, we lose our legitimacy, which is only slim up here to start with. But we can discuss these things in a warm room later. Let us hurry, before the weather changes again."

They rode in silence for another hour, before the immense walls of Windwall rose before them, and they passed through the gates of the mountain city, stunned by both its size, and its crowds. People surged around them as they rushed to do their business in the brief spell of calm after the storm. Thousands of residents, both permanent and temporary, moving with purpose, courtesy, and speed as they did all those things they had not been able to do for the last few days while the city waited out the early winter storm.

"Does the storm hit hard inside the walls?" Corilai asked.

"Not like outside," Symin replied. "The walls cut the wind, but the snow falls were heavy and the cold was bitter. Most people stayed inside, warmed by their fires, rather than venture outside unless they absolutely had to."

Chapter 4 – Windwall

The towering wall of stone merged into the rock of the mountains as it curved away into the distance. The young rangers stared along the wall as they paused inside Windwall, stunned by its size.

"How did they do this?" Treghan asked.

"They spent decades building it," Symin replied. "With insufficient flat space, the city's architects built across the gaps between several smaller peaks, and quarried others inside the perimeter for the stone they needed to build the walls and pave the streets. The dirt and gravel left over they used to fill the ravines that remained inside the walls."

"Where the walls cross the ravines, they're enormous!" Marni said.

"Yes, they are," Symin said. "The city covers an area at least as large as Emberdale, and it is over some terribly difficult terrain. Considering that, this city is a great wonder."

"It certainly is," Marni said. "What a spectacular feat of human effort. I mean, it must have been incredibly heavy work."

"As I said," Symin replied. "They spent decades building it. Many hundreds of men died in the building of Windwall."

"Where do we go now?" Fletcher asked. "I'd kill for a warm fire. All that snow, the damp has even crept through my skin. I swear there's moss on my bones."

"Quit your grumbling, Fletcher," Treghan rebuked. "It's not that cold. A bit wet, but not so bad as all that. I mean, we had shelter through the worst of it."

"We'll head straight for the outpost," Symin said. "We'll get you settled in. You can look around the city later."

"How big is it?" Marni asked. "The outpost."

"You'll see soon enough," Symin said. "Big enough, for a local campus."

They rode through the frigid city streets, until Symin turned left and led them towards the wall. Finally he stopped before a large manor, three stories high, and half the size of a small city block.

"This would house at least fifty rangers!" Corilai said. "And in comfort."

"We have the building behind as well," Symin replied. "We hope to establish a regional campus of Ranger Academy, not simply an outpost."

"Why?" Treghan said.

"One of the best ways to be welcomed and accepted by the locals, is to become locals ourselves," Symin replied.

"You mean adapt to their way of life?" Marni asked.

"No, I mean make ourselves a part of the city, in spite of our differences. Become a new and integral part of Windwall society. Introduce them to our ways in a manner that broadens our understanding of each other. We have many rangers from Windwall, and some have already volunteered to return here, once the campus is established."

"Are we really that different?" Corilai asked.

"Not as different as we may at first appear," Symin said. "The people of Windwall are good people. And they share the values of all the citizens of Cinder. Some of the local traditions and customs will strike you as odd, to say the least. At heart, they are not greatly different from the things you would find in Emberdale, or

Leusbay, or Oaklands."

"All terribly interesting, but I'm frozen!" Fletcher grumbled. "Can we please just get inside already?"

"Of course," Symin replied. "The stables are around the back. We'll leave the horses there, then get inside."

They followed him around to the back of the building into a small stable yard. Before long they sat in a small dining hall, before a roaring fire, to Fletcher's delight. A dozen or more other rangers sat in small groups around the dining hall. Loka came in, her smile as warm as her words.

"Welcome, you four," Loka said, moving beside Symin and stealing a glance at his face. "I'm so glad to see you all made it here without trouble."

"Wet and cold," Fletcher said. "But perfectly safe. It was really not a bad journey."

"That's good. But I had no doubt you four were able to look after yourselves. Even with that storm."

Behind Loka, a familiar woman entered, carrying a tray, with bowls of warming stew for the youngsters.

"Jarls? Why are you here?" Marni said.

"I grew up in Windwall. So when they said they were opening a campus here, I asked to transfer here, to run the kitchens and be closer to my family."

"I thought the food in Emberdale had changed recently," Treghan said. "I figured you were on holiday or something. They'll be missing your skills in the academy mess!"

"Perhaps, but they have a few skilled cooks there. And is nice to see my family more."

"I'm sure it is," Fletcher said, smiling as he accepted a bowl and began eating. "How big is this campus of yours anyway?"

"We have the two buildings," Loka said. "This one, and the one behind it, about the same size. Both have three levels above ground, and a basement. We hope that one day we will start running classes here, for potential initiates. We will of course provide security, policing and investigative services to the city. But anything you think of which might help us to be accepted by the people of Windwall, would be appreciated."

"I'd like to look around," Treghan said. "Get a feel for the place."

"Perhaps later. I suggest an early night would benefit you all," Symin said. "After all, it will be your first warm beds in several days."

* * *

Treghan lay awake in his bunk, Fletcher across the room. The new campus was going to require a significant amount of renovation before they had enough room for separate dorms for each house. A chill wind whistled in the shutters, but the snow had stayed away for the evening. A small fire burned in a hearth by the door, keeping the frozen mountain winter at bay.

"You know," Fletcher said. "It feels like forever since we shared a room."

"This one's nicer," Treghan replied. "Can't sleep?"

"No. Hey Treghan, I'm sorry. I know when we last shared a room, you got the poor end of the deal."

"We're past that now, Fletcher," Treghan said. "Want to go look around?"

"Sure."

They got out of bed, and changed into their day clothes. The full uniform of the Ranger Academy student differed from a ranger only in colour. Even the gloves were the same. Everybody in the city would know exactly who they were, but warmth was better than anonymity. The clothes were dry and warm, thanks to the fire.

"Where shall we go?" Fletcher asked as Treghan opened the door. "Let's just look around the City a little. Just the nearest neighbourhood for now."

"OK."

Together, the boys walked along the corridor, towards a flight of stairs that led down to the ground floor. Along the way, they passed the girls room, and the door flew open as they approached. The girls stood there, and all four were silent for a moment.

"Where are you two going?" Corilai demanded. "You know we're supposed to be sleeping."

"We were going to have a look around the city," Treghan said. "And I think you girls were going to do the same."

"We were not!" Marni protested.

"Then why are you both fully dressed?" Fletcher said.

"OK, we were," Corilai said, looking at her gloves. "Just going to step outside for a moment, to have a look around. It's such a quiet night and all..."

"Then we're all agreed," Treghan said. "We're going to take a look around the City. But we have to be quiet. If Loka or Symin catch us, there'll be trouble."

Making their way downstairs, they passed through the dining hall, into the foyer, and finally out into the street. The wind hit them immediately, and they raised their hoods against it. Picking a direction, Treghan led the way from the building.

It was not snowing, but the cold was still penetrating. The old snow was banked high against the buildings, and a mean slush filled the streets where it had been crossed by many thousands of feet and cart wheels. Thick clouds obscured the stars, and the moon was only intermittently visible, its wan light doing little to lift the oppressive mood of winter.

Soon, they reached the end of the block, and Treghan turned to follow a narrow street between buildings, deeper into the City, away from the outer wall. The buildings, close together, blocked out much of the light from the city lamps, which did not continue into the narrow lanes.

Treghan lit a small white flame from his fingers, as a guiding light. Eventually, they reached an intersection, where a wider street crossed the one they were on. Treghan turned left, and they continued, as he put out his flame. The city lanterns cast a soft light on the icy stone of the city, orange and mild.

In the distance, they heard shouting, and the slamming of doors. Thinking little of it, they continued as the noise subsided, the night returning to its peaceful cold. The city streets were uniform in their stone, and dull in the evening light. The brisk air bit their lungs, and the mist gave the scene a mysteriousness which struck them silent.

They reached another intersection, and crossed it, to continue in the same direction. The same stone, the same style of square buildings. Nothing like the colourful gardens and architecture of Emberdale.

"I suppose it might be nicer in the day time, when the people are out and the shops are open," Corilai said.

Nobody responded, and they continued, till the next intersection, which was haphazard, compared to the previous grid like pattern. Five streets branched out from the same point, three smaller lanes and two wide streets, the wide streets meeting the one they had come along, like a letter Y, and the smaller lanes running out between them, like points in a star.

Treghan selected a lane, and started along it, lighting his white flame again as he walked. The lane turned slightly, then turned back, as it meandered through a densely packed residential area. As they wandered, they saw something unexpected.

On the front step of one of the houses, a small child sat. The house was dark, the inhabitants clearly retired for the evening. The child held his knees to his chest, shivering in the cold, wearing only a night shirt.

"You poor child!" Corilai said, approaching the boy. "Are you OK?"

"I'm fine," the boy said. "Go away."

"But you're frozen!" Corilai persisted. "Why are you out in the cold?"

"I'm being punished. I deserve it, so you just go on, get out of here. My father will be angry if he hears us talking."

"Punished? By being put out in the street?" Marni said. "That's barbaric!"

"It's how it is in Windwall," the boy said. "I won't freeze. I never have before."

"When will they let you inside?" Fletcher asked.

"After sunrise."

"Then you will surely freeze."

"No," the boy said. "You see, the lady over the lane had her son stolen a while back. She's kind, because she misses him. When it gets a bit later, and everybody is asleep, she'll come and get me. She'll boot me out again before sunrise, so my father doesn't know. But I shouldn't tell you this. What if you tell him?"

As he spoke, a young couple came along the lane, stopping before him.

"I see our Thom is out again. You been misbehaving, boy?"

"I took an extra lolly from the jar this afternoon."

"Well, you should have known how your father would respond to that," the lady said. "Did you get dinner?"

"No," the boy said, miserably.

"Here, take this then," the man said, pulling a small package from his coat, steam erupting from it as the boy opened it. "It's just a few left over chips from the tavern. I was taking them for the dogs, but you need them more."

"Thank you," the boy said. "Thank you so much."

"Don't mention it, Thom. Be good now, you hear?" the man said as the couple left.

"You see? I won't freeze. The punishments here are harsh, but the people are kind. Now you should go. The lady over the way has lit her lantern in the parlour, so she'll be out to fetch me soon. I'm one of the lucky ones. A lot of us kids don't have hot chips from the tavern, or ladies over the lane. But if she thinks I'm getting help, she won't bother again."

"You're sure you'll be OK?"

"I will. But thanks for stopping. And please, don't ignore any others you see. They might not be as lucky as I am. In Windwall, we stop and help, if it's safe to do so."

"OK, be safe, Thom," Treghan said, as he walked away.

The others followed, a fog rolling along the lane as the temperature dropped further. The lane turned and they lost site of the boy, as a gentle snow began to fall.

"We should get back," Marni said. "This snow might settle in and we don't want our clothes to be wet in the morning."

"OK," Treghan said. "When we reach the next intersection, we'll head back towards the campus."

A long time later, they finally found their way back to the campus, let themselves in, and made their way back to their rooms.

"I don't think we were missed," Corilai said as they stood outside the girl's room.

"Even so, we should be careful not to make any noise," Fletcher said. "Goodnight, girls."

"Goodnight," Corilai and Marni said.

Treghan and Fletcher walked away, as the girls door closed, and soon were back in their warm room, changing into their night clothes. As they climbed into their beds, the door opened and Symin stepped in.

"Care to tell me where you lot have been?" Symin said.

"We just went for a walk." Treghan said, realising that it was pointless to lie.

"And what did you learn?" Symin said.

"That in Windwall, the punishments are brutal, but the people are kind."

"Well then, it wasn't all bad I guess. Get some sleep. Loka and I will have a brutal punishment for you all tomorrow."

*　　　*　　　*

The four students found Symin and Loka waiting for them in the dining hall the next morning. Symin waved for them to sit down as Jarls brought in steaming bowls of hot porridge, sweetened with honey.

"So, you four had a bit of an adventure last night. What did you learn about Windwall?"

"It's not as pretty as Emberdale," Marni said. "And it's ridiculously cold."

"I mean other than the aesthetics," Symin growled.

"Well, the punishments for children who misbehave are barbaric," Corilai said. "I mean, in those conditions, to kick your child out into the streets for the night is just too cruel."

"But it is how they do things here," Symin said. "And it has been for generations. The citizens of Windwall see nothing wrong with it. Why do you think you can judge them?"

"I can't. Not really," Corilai said. "And besides, there's another side to it."

"What would that be?" Loka asked.

"The people of Windwall have all shared that experience," Treghan said. "So when they see a child in the street, they're kind to them. They bring them hot food, or offer them a warm place to sleep."

"Is that true of all of the children?" Loka asked.

"No," Fletcher said. "But it happens often enough, to show them they must be kind to others, without judging them."

"Very good," Symin said. "Why?"

"Because somebody will be kind to them in return."

"And this makes them particularly vulnerable," Loka said. "We have suspected this to be part of the peculiar situation in this region."

"I don't understand," Marni said.

"Think about it," Symin said. "Young people, children, going missing. Being kidnapped. From a town where they are punished cruelly and taught to accept the charity of strangers when stuck out in the cold."

"You think this is a factor?" Corilai said.

"We know it is," Loka said. "We didn't know until recently how pervasive this form of punishment was in the city's culture, but it is. On any given night, there could be fifty or a hundred children out on the streets. Easy pickings for somebody with food and a warm bed."

"So the kidnappers are taking advantage of the local custom. But why?" Treghan asked. "What do they want with all those children?"

"We don't know that yet," Symin said. "But we know they're responsible for the increased theft and other crime. And we know the children are leaving the city."

"Is there nothing we can do?" Marni asked.

"I have an idea," Loka said. "And that brings us to your punishment."

Chapter 5 – Hostel Nights

Loka led the four students out the back and to the second building. It was in far worse condition than the first one. Along the ground floor, almost all the windows and shutters were smashed, allowing the snow and wind to howl through them. Loka took out a key and used it to unlock a sturdy wooden door, then led them into a small foyer.

"Was it worth locking the door?" Fletcher said.

"Perhaps not," Loka replied. "But we will secure the building soon enough. Or rather, you will."

"What?" Corilai said. "We wouldn't know the first thing about fixing those windows."

"Then I hope you can learn fast. Don't worry, there will be a builder along tomorrow to show you what to do. Today's job is much colder, and wetter."

Loka opened a door and waved them through, into a long hallway, lined on one side with the smashed windows. Snow, slush, and mud filled the room, piled deep along the back wall after years of winters finding their way inside the neglected old building.

"Today, you four are going to clean this place," Loka told them.

"Should be easy enough," Fletcher said, sparking a fire in his hand. "This should melt away in a few minutes."

"Not so fast, hot shot," Loka snapped. "You are forbidden to use your flames in this task. If you melt the snow and ice in here, you'll only flood the basement, and good luck getting the water out of there, because that will be your job for as long as it takes. Up and down the stairs, with goblets to carry the water."

"Goblets?" Corilai squealed.

"Yes, goblets. If you think I would reward you with buckets to do the job after cheating on this one, you don't know me very well."

"That's cold," Marni said.

"Not half as cold as you'll be when you're finished," Loka said. "But get to work, and it will be done soon. Here's Symin now."

Symin dragged a small hand trolley in the door, piled high with shovels, buckets and other tools for the work.

"Loka has explained your duties?" he asked, casting a glance and a smile in the enforcer's direction.

"Yes, Sir," Treghan said.

"Good. There is a lot to be done. Once you get the place cleaned, and the windows and shutters are installed, there is still a lot to be done to this area. The quicker you work, the quicker we can proceed with the plans for this building."

"Plans for this building?" Marni asked.

"Yes," Symin replied. "Well, for this small part of it anyway. Now, I suggest you all get started. The sooner you have the snow and ice all removed, the sooner you can set a fire to warm the place up."

Turning, Symin left, and Loka followed, rushing to his side. The four youngsters looked around at the mess of mud and snow. One by one they picked up shovels and started digging.

"Where do we put this stuff?"Treghan asked.

"Out the windows?" Fletcher replied.

"No," Treghan said. "It would make too much mess in the street between the ranger buildings. Symin would yell at us. Besides, we'll need that area clear when we do the windows and shutters."

"Wait, I know," Marni said, and went to the trolley, Carefully removing all the tools, and stacking them near the door. "We can load the stuff on this, and take it out the back. I'm sure there's somewhere we can dump it without causing any trouble."

"Great thinking, Marni," Treghan said.

Working together, they began shovelling the snow onto the trolley, and soon it was piled high, with no room for any more. Treghan grabbed the handle, and dragged it from the room. Leaving the building, he walked along, past the windows, and turned the corner. Following the wall, he soon turned again, and dragged the trolley along the back of the building.

The City wall towered over him on the other side of a long ditch. There were places the ditch was filled with snow, and places where its side had collapsed, leaving a deep chasm reaching into the lane.

"That will do nicely," Treghan said as he reached one of the collapsed places.

Tipping the trolley over, Treghan dumped the mess of slush and snow into the hole, then returned to the front of the building. Entering the room, he found the others with several loaded buckets, ready to dump onto the trolley. He picked up a shovel and began digging. Soon the trolley was full again.

"I'll take it this time," Fletcher said. "Where did you dump it?"

"Around the back of the building. You'll see where I put it. There's a collapsing edge on the ditch which runs along the city wall."

"OK, I'll be right back," Fletcher said, dragging the trolley from the room as the girls put down their shovels for a rest.

"Shouldn't we fill the buckets while he's gone?" Treghan asked.

"Nuh," Marni said. "We'll see him coming past the windows, and we can do it then. Just use the buckets to scoop it up, and they'll all be full in no time."

"Did you do that when I went?"

"We," Corilai said slowly. "May have."

The day went slowly, as they continued in this manner, but by noon the room was beginning to look like it had a real stone floor. Jarls came then, pulling a trolley, with four large mugs of steaming tea, and four bowls of her wonderful stew.

"Come now, you four youngsters must take a break," she said as she entered the room. "It looks like you're all doing a marvellous job. It's a big area, should be more than enough."

"More than enough for what?" Corilai asked.

"Oh, they didn't tell you?" Jarls said. "Well, we're going to divide this area into a dormitory, with a hallway opposite the windows. So there'll be a new wooden wall built across the centre, and a long wall parallel to the inside wall, to make the hallway, which will wrap around to enclose the door. Then we put a door from the hallway into each of the two rooms, and that makes a boys and girls dormitory."

"What about the fire place?" Marni asked.

"We'll put one in at either end, so each dormitory has heating."

"So who will these rooms be for?" Treghan asked. "Are we getting a bunch of students coming? I thought there was enough room in our dorms for now."

"There is," Jarls said. "These dorms aren't for rangers, or students. They're for the local kids, who are put out on the streets at night. It's part of Symin's plan to stop the kidnappings."

"I see," Corilai said. "If the kids know they can always find a warm place to sleep, they won't be as easily led astray by whoever it is that's kidnapping them."

"Exactly. Anyway, I've told you enough. I'll be going now. Just make sure you get as much done before dinner time as you can."

With that, Jarls left, and the four youngsters spent the next several hours cleaning the room, until they were all done. Symin came by at mid afternoon, and left them a pile of tarpaulins to cover the windows, so any storms in the night wouldn't undo their hard work.

After dinner, the four were exhausted from their labours, and took to their beds early, sleeping late the next morning. By the time they arrived at the work site, the builders had already installed a third of the windows, and they did not require much help.

So the four students ran jobs as the builders asked, fetching tools or materials and holding things steady while they were secured, but did not need to do any heavy work like the day before.

By lunch time, the new dorms were secured against the weather, and the builders had begun erecting the walls inside. Local craftsmen began arriving with furniture, including ten sets of bunks, a table for each dorm, and chairs. Working around the builders, the students placed them in the dorms, stacked as much out of the way as they could, and by dinner time, the frames for the walls were erected.

Next morning, the builders returned and fitted wooden panels to the frames, and soon completed the wall, before painting them in a crisp white. Doors were installed, and a stone mason began working on the two chimneys and fireplaces.

"This must be costing a lot," Treghan said as they sat at dinner that day.

"If it works, it's worthwhile," Symin replied. "And if it doesn't, it still gives us a good head start on the remodelling of the second building. In the morning, you four can set out the furniture and go into town for bedding. Once that's done, the masons should be just about ready to trial a test fire in the two fireplaces. Then you can go out in the evening and let the children in the streets know there is somewhere safe to sleep."

"But wouldn't the chimneys need longer for the mortar to set?" Fletcher asked.

"Yes, so tomorrow night the fires won't be burning in a full heat, but a bed with blankets must be better than a kerbside without," Symin replied.

* * *

As promised, the rooms were completed before the next evening. The one closest to the entry for the girls, the other one for the boys, and a small reception area fitted with a large, reclining chair, a small desk, and a book shelf stacked with Ranger Academy texts. Four small chairs lined the wall away from the door to the outside.

Treghan stood with Corilai in the foyer area, near the desk while Fletcher and Marni were lighting the fires. The sun had set, and the clouds were rolling in. It was going to be a cold night. Jarls entered, and placed a large iron pot on a trolley in the corner. Steam and wonderful smells poured from it when she lifted the lid and stirred the contents.

"The young ones might be hungry when they come in," Jarls explained. "So I made a pot of stew. They can eat whatever they need, before they go into the rooms."

"Good idea," Corilai said, as Fletcher and Marni entered.

"Something smells amazing!" Fletcher said.

"Jarls made a stew for the kids," Corilai explained.

"Can I have some?" Fletcher asked.

"No, I have something in the main building cooking for you kids. But this is for the poor wee ones in the streets. And it's probably about time for you to do your first run through the city to find them."

"Yes Ma'am!" Marni said, and walked to the door.

Reluctant to leave the warmth, and the possibility of food, the others followed, drawing their hoods up over their heads, and soon the four were walking through the city streets. They reached an intersection and paused.

"We should split up," Treghan said. "It'll be quicker that way."

"Good idea," Marni said. "Fletcher and I will go this way, you two go the other way."

They split up, Treghan and Corilai heading north from the intersection, to turn at the wall and follow the next road back to the centre, where they once again saw Fletcher and Marni.

"Did you find anybody?" Fletcher asked.

"Nobody," Treghan replied.

"We found one, but they refused to listen." Marni said. "So sad they'd rather be obstinate than warm and fed."

"We can only try," Corilai said. "If they won't listen or accept our help, we can't force them."

"True. Well, we should continue down the next lane," Treghan said. "Maybe this time."

Corilai followed him as he walked away, and soon they saw a young girl, sitting on the step of a darkened house, crying.

"Are you OK?" Corilai asked.

The girl looked at them suspiciously, then shook her head, and stood, dusting her jacket of imaginary snow in a show of indifference.

"I'm fine," she said. "Leave me alone."

"You don't look fine," Corilai said softly. "Please, we can help."

"As if you two would help, you're not even from here. You rangers think you can waltz in here and everybody will love you?"

"We're not rangers, yet," Corilai said, lowering her hood.

"What?" the girl said. "But you're not much older than me! Who are you kids?"

"We're students," Corilai said, sitting on the step, the girl hesitating a moment before sitting beside her. "From Ranger Academy, in Emberdale. We're staying at the new ranger campus here in Windwall for a while. And we're not kids."

"So why are you walking around the streets at night?"

"Looking for kids like you," Treghan said.

"No, you're not creepy or anything," the girl snapped.

"He didn't mean to be creepy," Corilai said. "But we found out how a lot of kids are punished by being put out of the house at night. And we know about how there are young people and kids being kidnapped."

"Yeah, what about it?" the girl asked.

"Well," Corilai said. "We've had them build a girls dormitory and a boys dormitory in one of the buildings at the ranger campus, with fires, warm beds, and food available."

"So?"

"So, if a kid is kicked out into the streets at night, and doesn't feel like freezing their toes off in the cold, they're all welcome to go to the campus, to the second building, the one behind, near the wall, and go in there, from the lane between the buildings. There will be a warm bed in a comfortable dorm room, and food to fill your belly."

"Right, and what will it cost us?"

"Nothing. It is only to make you safe, because we don't want any more kids getting kidnapped."

"Well," The girl said. "I might go have a look, but I'm not saying I'll stay there or anything."

"That's fine," Corilai said. "My name is Corilai. Tell them I sent you."

"Fine. But what about the morning? If my father finds me missing at sunrise, he'll get angry."

"Oh, there'll be a wake up call before sunrise, don't worry."

"Fine, I'll think about it."

"You do that," Treghan said as he walked away. "Perhaps we'll see you later then."

Corilai stood and followed him. As they reached the next intersection and looked back, the girl was already gone. They found two more children, a boy and a girl, before meeting Fletcher and Marni at the city gate.

"How did you go?" Fletcher asked.

"Three kids. I don't know if they'll go," Treghan said.

"We found three as well. I thought there'd be more," Marni said.

"There might be more," Corilai said. "Some will already be in their usual hiding places, some will have just hidden from us, and some might not be kicked out yet. It's a start, and if they tell others, this thing might really start to help."

"I'm sick of the cold. Let's go back," Fletcher said, shivering as he walked.

Walking directly, it took a lot less time for them to reach the campus, and they walked around the back to find Jarls standing in the doorway of the new dormitory. She smiled as they approached and waved them in.

"Four so far," she said. "It's a start."

Three of the children were sitting in the foyer eating stew, while the fourth had apparently already gone to bed. Symin entered soon after, and said something to Jarls, who left the building.

"How did it go?" Symin asked.

"I hoped there'd be more here, but it's a good start," Marni said.

"It will be better soon," Symin said. "I saw a couple more walking this way."

As he spoke, two more children entered. One was the girl Corilai had sat with, and the other was a girl none of them had spoken to.

"Is it OK that I brought my friend?" the girl asked.

"That's fine, help yourself to some stew," Symin replied, then turned to face the students. "And you four should get over to the main building. Jarls has your evening meals prepared, and will be needing to come back over here as soon as you're all done."

"Yes, Sir," Treghan said, and the four of them left.

"I'm going to sleep well tonight," Marni said. "The last few days have been hard work."

"But so worth it," Corilai replied.

Shortly they were in the main building mess hall, enjoying a hot meal and warming drinks before the roaring fire. Loka had the fires stoked in their rooms, and when they retired, it was to sleep deeply as their tired bodies relaxed into the warmth of their blankets.

Chapter 6 – Visitors

By the end of the week, the dormitory was full, and they were tasked with extending it into a second room behind the first one, doubling capacity. It was an easier job, the second room not having the broken windows letting the elements inside.

As word spread among the youth of Windwall, the beds were filled and the stew was eaten, all by grateful children who were happy to help tidy up before leaving in the morning. Treghan and Corilai were with Jarls, one even in the third week, when there was a knock on the door.

"Oh," said a woman in the doorway. "Sorry to disturb you, your teachers said it was OK if we came to say hello."

Treghan looked at the woman, trying to place her face, but then Ivy pushed passed her and ran to embrace Corilai.

"It's good to see you, but why are you here?" Corilai said. "I thought you wanted to keep Ivy away from Windwall."

"We had a family emergency," Ivy's aunty said. "This dear child's grandfather is unwell, and we fear not long for this world. We decided it was important for the child to say her goodbyes, and for us to be here to help with the relevant arrangements when the time comes. Never fear, Ivy will not be venturing outside the city walls."

"But I can visit here, can't I?" Ivy pleaded.

"If nobody minds, I don't either," the child's aunt said. "But mind, I don't want you wandering around after dark."

"I won't, I promise," Ivy said, then turned to Treghan. "Have you found my brother yet?"

"I'm sorry, Ivy, we haven't found anybody yet. But we'll try, I promise."

"Well OK then. As long as you promise," Ivy said. "But if I hang around here, I can always help out. Maybe I can help you find my big brother!"

"Was he taken, child?" Jarls asked.

"Those rotten kidnappers took him from our house in the mountains. That's why I live with my aunty now."

"That must be terribly hard on you," Jarls said, shaking her head sadly.

"Those horrible evil kidnappers!" Ivy spat. "I hate them so much! I wish they were dead and gone, instead of my brother being missing."

"Now child, we mustn't hate, it's not good."

"But I do hate them!" Ivy shouted, stamping her foot. "I hate them so much! They took my brother. I can't forgive them for that."

"Sometimes, we have to try," Treghan said. "I hated my father for the longest time. I even hated my brother for siding with him. But then I realised my brother wasn't really bad, and my father wasn't really evil. He's just a drunk fool. I pity him, more than anything now."

"That's very wise, Treghan," Jarls said.

"Well those kidnappers are evil," Ivy spat, starting to cry. "Plain and simple. I can't pity them. They don't deserve it. I hate them, and I always will."

"Now child," Jarls said. "Dry those tears. The rangers are going to save your brother, and punish the kidnappers. But it doesn't make you feel good, hating them, does it?"

"Well, I guess not..."

"That's right. You see, evil people aren't always evil because they want to be. I mean, if you had an illness that made you do horrible things, would you rather be hated, or pitied?"

"Well, I don't want to be hated..." Ivy said slowly.

"Then don't hate others. Pity them," Jarls said. "Pity is the greatest weapon against evil. Pity them for they will never know the happiness of giving, or of loving unconditionally, because everything in their lives is done with conditions, and nothing in their lives is done in pursuit of the true joy which comes with belonging in a happy community where you can enjoy the act of kindness towards another person."

"But how does pity help?" Ivy said.

"Well," Jarls continued. "The evil among us see being pitied as a sign of weakness, and they hate the weak with a vitriol unmatched in their filthy little worlds. Pity them, and make them weak, and the only one being hated will be themselves, but not by you. And when they believe themselves weak, they become weak, and then are open to change, because nobody wants to be weak. Emotions are as powerful as the greatest of swords. Do you understand, child?"

"I..." Ivy said slowly. "I don't think so. But if you say hate is bad and it is better to feel sorry for them, I think I get it. OK, I'll try from now on. But I can't make any promises not to hate them!"

Jarls laughed, then tousled the child's hair. "As long as you give it some thought, and try, that's the best promise any of us can make. Now, you must both be chilled from that wind outside. Let me get you some nice hot stew."

"Well, we shouldn't impose," Ivy's aunty said.

"Nonsense," Corilai said. "Besides, Jarls here makes the best stew in Windwall!"

"Well in that case," Ivy's aunty said, but Ivy had already answered for them, fetching two clean bowls from the shelf in the cart with the stew on top. "I guess we can sit and enjoy some more talking with you all."

* * *

Later, the four students waved a cheerful goodbye as Ivy and her Aunty left. Together, the four students returned to the main building, where they found Loka and Symin in the mess hall, talking to a stranger. The man was wearing a cloak like a ranger, but without the emblem of the academy, and he wore chain mail beneath it.

"Oh, there you are," Symin said. "This man is Broll, chief of the city guard. He is here with some important information."

"You mean we have a lead on the missing children?" Corilai asked.

"Loka and I have a lead, you four don't," Symin replied. "Remember, you're here to study, and to learn, but not to participate in the investigation. It's too dangerous."

"But Symin," Fletcher pouted. "Surely we can be useful."

"Indeed you can be," Symin said. "And with your work getting the emergency accommodation set up to reduce the temptation of children to follow along when a stranger offers them a place to stay, you have contributed to helping stem the tide of abductions in the city. But for now, you are all to stay here in Windwall. Loka and I will be gone a few days."

"Where are you going?" Corilai asked.

"We have information," Symin said. "A group of young people recently visited Leusbay, in the north. When they left, they took a cart loaded with stolen supplies, and headed into the mountains, instead of along the highway."

"You think they were the kidnapped children?" Marni asked.

"Some of them," Loka said. "But you need not concern yourselves. This is something for the rangers to investigate. You students need to stay here in the campus, and obey Jarls."

"Yes Ma'am," Treghan replied, looking at his friends. "But when will you be back?"

"A few days, maybe a week, possibly even two. We won't spend long there. Just long enough to ask a few questions."

"There's more information," Fletcher said. "Isn't there?"

"Very perceptive," Broll said, his tone gruff. "But as your teacher has told you, you need not concern yourself about it. And you rangers need not concern yourselves over the safety of your young charges. This campus will be watched and they will be under our protection until you return."

"Thank you, Broll," Symin replied. "Now, if you will excuse us, we have preparations to make."

"Of course," Broll said. "Good evening, Ranger."

As the guard left, Symin and Loka walked to their rooms, leaving the four students to gossip for a long time, until Jarls walked in and offered them tea.

"Have you heard?" Corilai asked.

"Yes," Jarls said. "Your teachers are going to be away for a while. But we have much to do here. I'll be needing all your best behaviour, and help with that dormitory while they are away. Luckily nine more academy staff are arriving in two days. But until then, you four are it."

"Nine?" Marni asked. "And what about the other rangers who are here?"

"They have their own duties to attend to. As for the newcomers, there is one permanent receptionist, to field enquiries from the citizens, two to help in the kitchens, and the rest as general support staff around the campus. And about time too. It's been quite exhausting until now."

"But that means..." Corilai said.

"Yes, child," Jarls finished the girl's thought. "As of now, this outpost is an official, fully functioning campus of Ranger Academy. By this time next year, there will be classes operating for the local children, in history, philosophy, mathematics and social sciences."

"So a regular school? That's a little unusual," Marni said.

"Yes," Jarls replied. "But that will gain us greater acceptance in the city than simply opening a school for flame wielders. Though that part of the operation will come soon enough."

Jarls left them to their continued gossip, disappearing into the kitchens. She had an enormous pot continuously boiling in there, to provide a non stop supply of stew for the dormitory children. After a while, they heard her shouting for them to come.

Running into the kitchens, they found her there, with the cart from the dormitory foyer. A fresh pot of the stew steamed on top of it, and a pile of dirty bowls and spoons rested in the sink.

"I need you four to clean those dishes, and then take them, with the trolley, back out to the Dormitory. Hurry now, I'll be going out there immediately, in case we have any early arrivals tonight."

"Yes, Ma'am," the four students said in unison.

Corilai and Treghan both rushed to the sink, Marni and Fletcher following behind. In short order, they got the work done, and pushed the trolley outside, taking extra care not to spill the precious stew. As they arrived at the dormitory, the sun was setting behind the mountains, and a steady wind was already bringing a chill to the night air.

Three children of the city were already in the foyer, talking to Jarls, as they pushed the cart to its usual position.

"It seems word is getting around," Jarls told them. "These three are here for food, as they have been forbidden to eat at home tonight after an embarrassing mishap with their mothers needlework. However, they will not be staying the night. Their mother is fearful of the kidnappers, so allowed them to stay out long enough to find something small to eat after her husband issued the punishment. They are even offering to pay."

"You aren't going to take money are you?" Marni asked, shocked.

"Of course not, dear!" Jarls said. "But it is charming that they wanted to help out. The Ranger Academy is happy to pay the costs for this though. The people of Windwall pay taxes like everybody else. I think they deserve something in return."

"We'll gladly pay, though," one of the children said. "Our mother gave us a little money to buy food. We just have heard that your stew is wonderful, and decided to try it for ourselves."

"Save that money and use it for something nice another day," Jarls said, smiling at the boy. "The stew is free, for everybody, if you stay the night or not."

"Thank you so much, Ma'am!" the boy said with delight.

The three children ate their stew, then hurried away, hugging Jarls in their thanks before they left. Shortly after, the first child staying the night arrived, and then another. This would turn out to be the busiest night yet, and also one of the coldest.

So it went for the next several days, and much to the students' chagrin, even after the new staff arrived, they found themselves kept more than busy, helping Jarls.

* * *

"They've had a bit of rain here." Symin said, looking at the sodden fields and slushy roads as they approached the gates of Leusbay.

"There hasn't been a dry field since we left the mountains," Loka replied, riding close beside him, hanging on his words. "So I'm not surprised. There's even a house in that third field with water over the floorboards."

"It must have been their end of that big storm in Windwall," Symin said, stealing a glance at his companion.

They continued riding, a comfortable, familiar silence falling between them. They soon reached the city gate, where the guard eyed them with a mix of curiosity and suspicion.

"Who goes there?" the man called from on top of the gate.

"We are rangers, and have journeyed from Windwall to enquire regarding a matter of relevance to our current investigation," Symin said.

"Wait there," the guard shouted. "I'll send for the local ranger to verify your story."

They waited for many minutes, until a man pushed through the gate, his hood drawn up and his expression harried.

"Who is it?" the man moaned. "Oh, it's you two. I'm sorry about the sour welcome. Leusbay is still not as welcoming for rangers as I'd like."

"Do you need some help in the city?" Symin asked. "I'm sure we can get the Chancellor to send you some extra staff."

"It might not be a bad idea, but first, why are you here?"

"We heard of a story about a group of youngsters making off with a cart load of stolen goods."

"Yes, they headed west, across the fields and into the rain."

"You didn't pursue them further?" Symin said, scowling at the man.

"Well, no. We had other pressing issues."

"Pressing issues?" Symin snapped. "Our duty as rangers is to protect the people, and that includes protecting them from thieves and bandits. A group, young or old, who come out of the mountains and rob the people is a group we have a duty to stop, but you let them get away, then you stand there and tell me rangers aren't liked here. Well it's no wonder. I will report this to the chancellor. You'll get your help. Perhaps a new supervisor to make sure you do your work."

"But Sir," the man argued. "You have to understand, we couldn't just run off into the hills, the city guard would have called us deserters."

"And when you returned with the stolen goods, they would have welcomed you as heroes," Symin said. "You can't pick and choose your missions here. This posting is one mission, including all the things this city throws your way. You will never win them over with your half on duty approach. Now, fetch your horse, and lead the way."

"The way where?" the man gasped.

"Into the mountains of course! You're going to show us where they went!"

"Yes, Sir," the ranger moaned.

"Weren't you a little hard on him?" Loka said, resting a hand on Symin's arm as the man disappeared through the gate.

"Not at all," Symin said. "We have a duty, and he knows it well. If he has come to this place thinking he can slack off and not be seen, we have to change things. The chancellor will replace him as supervisor of the outpost here, and then we can hopefully see some of the good results we have in Windwall duplicated here."

"But they might not be as receptive here. Remember the rangers have had no regional outposts in a generation. It's going to take time for some of those without bandit problems to accept it."

"Any time is too long," Symin said. "We're doing things that make us members of their community, and a desired addition. Clearly that's not happening here, or else they would have chased down that cart. The laziness of these rangers has added to our own work, and possibly cost us a speedy resolution of our case. Imagine if those children were already caught, safe in the holding cells of a ranger outpost?"

"Yes, but they weren't, and now you're punishing a man for it, but is it really so bad that he doesn't think like you?"

"Thinking like me has nothing to do with it. He must think like a ranger. We have our missions, and failure to perform those missions is dereliction of duty, and punishable by demotion."

"So you are going to demote him?"

"Not I, but I will report to the Chancellor, and he will act in the best interests of Ranger Academy and of our people. Understand, Loka, the next ranger to come here will have a harder time because of this man's laziness. And that could be us."

"Yes, Symin."

The gate opened, and the ranger returned, riding a bedraggled mare. Striking out across the sodden fields, he waved for them to follow. His countenance was bereft, as he led the way towards the straggling tree line at the base of the foot hills.

A miserable, drizzling rain began to fall, making his pathetic visage seem even worse to Symin and Loka as they followed, but neither mentioned it. Symin silently made a mental note to include this in his report. The man was clearly struggling with his post, so extra support was critical if they were not to lose access to Leusbay forever.

Chapter 7 – Chasing Ivy

Ivy became a regular visitor to the dormitory, though she never stayed over night, as her aunty was staunchly opposed to the practice of making children sleep in the streets as punishment.

Treghan was pushing the cart with a fresh pot of stew for the morning when the girl's Aunty rushed towards him with a stricken expression.

"Have you seen Ivy?" she called out.

"Not since yesterday afternoon," Treghan replied.

"I'm worried," she said. "I woke up this morning, and she was gone!"

"Is that that little girl I see here sometimes?" said a boy, walking out of the dormitory, stretching as he yawned. "I thought I saw her with two teenagers, walking towards the western side of the city. I didn't think anything of it."

"When?" Treghan demanded.

"Last night, when I was on my way here, about midnight."

"Oh no, please, no!" the woman wailed.

"Don't worry, we'll find her." Treghan said, pushing the cart into the foyer area, where Jarls waited with Corilai and Marni. "We're going out, Corilai, come with me. Ivy's missing. Marni, run and get Fletcher. We'll go to the western gate, and find out if anybody saw her last night."

Treghan rushed out into the morning chill, heading directly for the western gates of Windwall. He did not pause as he strode with purpose through the city, Corilai rushing to catch him. After a long march, they arrived at the western gates, still closed against the night.

"What are you looking for, ranger?" a man shouted from the gate house.

"We are looking for a child, she was seen heading this way around midnight."

"We get that a lot around here. Nobody passed through this gate though, and we certainly didn't see anybody try. If you think the child was taken like the others, they will have found some other way to sneak her out of the city."

"Damn it," Treghan said. "We'll ask the residents nearby, they might have seen something."

Three carriages rumbled by as they turned to walk away from the gate. Treghan ignored them as the man in the gate house called out his greetings to them and began the slow process of opening the huge access to the mountains beyond the city.

They soon began to encounter the citizens of Windwall, and asked those who would stop, but nobody had seen or heard anything. Dejected, they stopped at a small bake house, and stepped inside to buy something to eat.

"You look harried, young rangers," the baker said as they entered. "What would be the problem on this fine morning?"

"We're looking for somebody," Corilai said. "A small child. She was seen with two teenagers heading towards the western gate about midnight, but nobody here saw a thing."

"I did," the baker said. "As I was opening the back of the shop to get the fires going. I have to start baking before three in the morning, so I tend to sleep in the afternoon and get in here around one or two in the morning, so I can work through until my wife comes in to take over the shop around mid morning."

"What did you see?" Treghan asked.

"Well, there was a carriage parked in the lane behind the shop, you see. Two others down near the corner, none of them were familiar to me, so I was paying attention, when I saw three figures, two taller, probably your teenagers, and one small, like a child, climbing into the back of the carriage. They were fairly dragging the little one, but she was not complaining, so I figured they were together willingly. As soon as they were in the back, a young man climbed out and up front, whipped the reins, and the carriage left."

"Can you show us where they were?" Corilai asked. "There might be tracks we can follow."

"Of course, come through," the baker said. "My son was taken a month ago. If I can help you catch the bastards doing this, I'll do anything it takes."

The baker led them through his kitchen, and out into the lane. No fresh snow had fallen over night, and clear tracks could be seen of the carriage, leading away to the west.

"Thank you, sir, we should keep moving, if we're going to catch them," Treghan said.

"Wait, you came in for a bite to eat, did you not?" the baker asked. "I'll grab you both a pie each, and be right back. My treat."

"Thank you, Sir," They both said.

The baker rushed into his store, and returned a moment later with two steaming meat filled pies, handing them to the young rangers with a smile.

"Enjoy them, and I hope you find the poor child. If I can be of any help to the rangers, let me know."

He did not wait for a reply, rushing back inside as they looked at the warm food. Treghan walked west, following the tracks in the snow, enjoying the delicious pie as he went. Corilai followed. As the lane reached an intersection, they could see where the other two carts had been, but with their tracks, on the busier thoroughfare, were dozens of others, making it hard to follow the ones they wanted.

"There you are!" Fletcher shouted from a short distance away, as he and Marni rushed to meet them. "Did you find anything?"

"She was loaded into a carriage in this lane," Corilai said. "Which left heading this way when the baker was arriving to work this morning. There were two other carriages."

"Well, the gate was closed all night, and nobody left the city that way," Marni said.

"We know, we spoke to the guards first. Wait a minute," Treghan said. "After we spoke to the guard, we passed three carriages, heading for the gate. What if that was them? They must have stayed in the city till morning, so they could leave without suspicion!"

"If that's true, we don't have any time to waste," Corilai said. "We have to go after them!"

"But we should get the horses, we can't catch them on foot," Marni said.

"There's no time!" Treghan shouted. "I know, you two, get the horses, and bring them to the gate, we'll start following, on foot. We'll make sure the gate keeper knows which way we went. You two catch up. That way, we won't lose the tracks."

"OK," Marni said, grabbing Fletcher's hand as she ran back the way they had come.

Treghan struck out, grim determination on his face, towards the western gate.

* * *

Jarls passed the stables, and heard noises of scuffling hooves inside. Leaving her soup cart outside, she slipped in, to find Fletcher and Marni, with four horses saddled up, leading them out the back.

"What's going on here?" Jarls demanded.

"Damn it!" Fletcher cursed.

"Ivy's been taken," Marni said. "The kidnappers just left through the western gate. Treghan and Corilai are after them on foot, we're taking the horses so we can catch them."

"You know Symin forbade you to leave the city," Jarls said. "It was fine for you to search the city, but..."

"I know, but this is urgent," Fletcher said. "If we don't catch them now, we might never be able to."

"Fine," Jarls said. "But you four are to come home immediately if it gets dangerous. Do not stay out over night, and do not try to pick a fight with those kidnappers. Just see where they go, and then you'll have some information for Symin."

"Yes, Jarls," Fletcher said.

Rushing to catch their friends, Marni and Fletcher mounted up and led the spare horses to the western gate. The guard waved at them as they passed, and shouted out. The pair came to a halt, outside the gate, and turned to face the guard, who ran over to them.

"You friends headed north along the wall," the guard said. "Then followed the western road into the highlands. You should catch them up fast enough on those horses. But don't stay out too late, there may be another blizzard on the way."

"Thank you," Marni said. "We'll be careful."

As the guard returned to the gates, Marni and Fletcher struck out in the direction he told them, and soon saw the place where the cart tracks, and two sets of foot prints, turned to follow a road west. They set out after them, and found themselves crossing a sturdy stone bridge to the side of another mountain, where the road skirted around and continued down the other side.

As they began the descent, they saw their friends, and soon caught up to them. Corilai and Treghan both mounted up, and the four continued. They rode at a faster pace, following the tracks of the carts as they crossed an abutment and rose again as they climbed around the next peak.

A frozen wind picked up, and as they rose on the back side of the mountain, they saw an enormous suspension bridge across a vast chasm between it and the next.

"How did they build that?" Corilai whispered in awe, as she looked at the towering stone pillars which held the thick steel cables.

The immense steel lines spanned the gap, holding a sturdy wooden span aloft as it swayed slowly in the wind which whistled in icy tones through the tight ropes which ran from the cable to the deck.

A small sign at the entry to the bridge read "Naga's Bridge. Proceed with caution. High winds and sudden gusts at the centre."

A long way ahead, beyond the bridge and passing to the left, then around and through two large protrusions, the road continued. There, just passing out of sight, were the carts.

"We have no time to waste," Fletcher said, and spurred his horse into action.

The others followed, at a more sedate pace as Fletcher's horse galloped onto the bridge. Barely a third of the way across, the horse's hooves slipped on ice, which clung to the deck of the bridge, as a heavy gust tossed the structure sideways.

Flailing impotently, the horse went down, throwing fletcher from its back. He hit the deck hard, his left ankle folding painfully as he did so, before a second gust tossed the bridge again, and he slid, helpless, to the edge.

"Fletcher!" Treghan shouted, spurring his horse on, in spite of the danger.

Fletcher slid to the edge, and did not stop as his body flew out over the open chasm. He looked at his brother briefly, as if to shout something, then dropped out of sight. Screaming incoherently, Treghan dismounted and rushed to the place he had last seen his twin. As he reached the edge, he saw from the corner of his eye the two shapes as his and fletcher's horses, both spooked by a third gust, bolted back the way they had come.

Fearing the worst, Treghan lay flat on the deck, and inched his way over the edge, to peer down into what he thought would be the bottomless white of a snow blown chasm. Instead, he saw a flailing Fletcher. A long, scooped net which ran along the underside of the bridge had saved him from death, but only just. Fletcher was hung by the elbow, his arm hooked through the edge of the netting, as he was tossed about in the heavy wind.

"Fletcher!" Treghan shouted.

"Treghan!" Fletcher shouted back. "That hurt, damn it!"

"Anything broken?" Treghan shouted.

"My ankle feels like it has a red hot poker through it, but the rest of me is fine. Any chance I can get a little help? I'm not sure I have the strength to pull myself up right now."

"Hold on, I'm coming to get you," Treghan said, as he grasped the nearest of the bridge's support ropes, and slowly swung himself around, and over the edge.

"Treghan!" Corilai shouted from somewhere behind him. "No! It's too dangerous! We'll find another way!"

She was too late to stop him. With grim determination, Treghan lowered himself until he felt his feet touch something. Looking down, he saw it was a sturdy rope at the edge of the net, opposite from where Fletcher dangled like a decoration. Looking to his left and right, Treghan immediately saw his mistake.

The net rose to meet the bridge every dozen paces, but he had swung down at the mid point, where it was hanging at its lowest. If he let go now, he'd be just as likely to fall to his death as fall backwards into the net.

"Corilai!" he shouted. "Quick, help me up!"

The two girls grasped a wrist each, Corilai held his left in both her hands as tight as she could, and Marni held his right. Together, the girls pulled and soon lifted him back onto the deck of the bridge.

"Remind me to think about things before I do them in future," he said as he stood.

"You pair of idiots have almost gotten yourselves killed," Corilai said, then laughed. “But the look on your face was priceless.”

Ignoring her tease, Treghan walked the few paces to where the net met the deck, and climbed down onto it. The gaps in the mesh were the size of his hands, so he knew he could never fall through it. However, when he looked down into the abyss, Treghan found little comfort in that fact as his stomach lurched and the net fluttered in the wind.

Forcing his eyes up, he gazed across what felt like acres of open air, into the face of his twin. Fletcher was looking tired, dangling there, clinging with both arms now as the wind buffeted his precariously hanging body.

“Hurry, Treghan,” Fletcher mouthed at him, though the wind stole the words.

“Hurry, Treghan!” Corilai's voice sounded oh so distant as it met his ears. “Look at the sky! The wind's getting worse, I think there's a storm about to hit!”

“Oh, that's just perfect,” Treghan muttered as the daylight faltered considerably.

Hand over hand, he made his way across the net, thanking whoever had thought to install the safety measure, but cursing them at the same time every moment that his feet caught in the mesh as he struggled to clamber across it.

“I can't hold on much longer,” Fletcher shouted.

Treghan clambered faster, the net shaking with his efforts, making the thing seem even less secure than it did with the wind. Finally, he was within reach of his twin, but things were going from bad to worse.

With the weight of the two youngsters in the same place on the loose net, it sagged dangerously low. Instead of a safe basket, it was a down hill slope, and they were at the bottom of it.

“Treghan, Hurry! I can't pull myself up,” Fletcher moaned.

Treghan carefully threaded his feet into the mesh, securing himself in case of the worst. He reached out, and down into the open air, to grasp Fletcher's collar. Pulling, he lifted his brother, the net swinging dangerously because of the motion. For a moment, Treghan thought he was upside down, and felt his stomach begging to release its contents, but then, by a miracle, he was back on top of the net, with his brother by his side.

“We're not out of this yet,” Fletcher said. “Look!”

Treghan followed his brother's pointed hand, to stare wide eyed under the bridge, along the chasm. There, in the distance, was exactly what they least wanted to see. A whirling, icy vortex at the front edge of the coming blizzard.

“Where did that come from?” Treghan shouted, as he scrambled across the net, Fletcher pulling himself hand over hand behind him.

As they moved away from the edge, the net returned to its safer seeming basket shape, but now the climb was even harder. The looser feeling mesh provided less purchase to push against, and every inch was gained with only herculean effort.

“Treghan, Hurry!” Corilai screamed from above, as the last two horses clattered along the bridge and away, spooked by the threatening storm.

After an eternity, Treghan reached the point where the net met the deck, and reached his hand up, to be grasped by Corilai, who helped him onto the bridge. Right behind him, Fletcher reached a hand up, and both girls hauled him up. He sat on the bridge, breathing hard and wincing as he inspected his ankle.

The skin was blue and black and brown, bruised and swollen as the foot below it hung askew. Fletcher looked up at his friends, and smiled, though his eyes spoke of intense pain.

"I'm sorry everyone," he said. "I can't walk on this."

"Don't worry," Treghan said as he knelt beside the wounded boy, taking his arm around his neck to lift him. "We'll get you home."

As they turned around, the blizzard struck, and they were tossed against the ropes. This time, nobody landed in the net, but the situation was no less terrifying. Still clinging to his twin, Treghan reached out a hand to Corilai, but she batted it away, and shouted something at him. He couldn't hear her over the sound of the wind in his ears, and she vanished behind a wall of snow and ice. Then Marni was there.

"Don't worry," Marni shouted. "She says she's got this, I hope she's right."

Suddenly, all was still, and there was blackness. Corilai appeared before him, smiling, though she had the grimace of enormous effort.

"Hurry," she snarled. "We have to get off this bridge."

Together, Treghan and Marni half carried Fletcher as they walked, the deck of the bridge lurching back and forth beneath their feet, as Corilai followed, her face a picture of intense concentration. All around them, blackness swirled, but there was no wind, no cold, just the roaring sound of the flames which surrounded them all in a cocoon of stillness while the world beyond it was plunged into the chaos of ice and snow.

"How is she doing that?" Treghan whispered, awed by his friend's actions.

"It's the black flame's secondary ability!" Marni said. "I never thought it could be used like this. They create a vortex of flame, which swallows all light. Nothing can break through it. Not wind, not light, not heat, nothing. They use it for camouflage normally. But to pass through a blizzard? That girlfriend of yours is a genius!"

"But when did she learn it?" Treghan asked.

"I don't know," Marni replied. "I mean, we've both been trying to learn our secondaries. You saw mine a few weeks ago remember? I knew she knew what hers was, I didn't know she had mastered it!"

"I haven't mastered anything, this is just a fluke!" Corilai shouted. "I don't know how long I can keep it up, so shut up and walk!"

"Running on adrenalin?" Treghan said as he quickened his pace. "Got it! We have to move."

Step by step, with the deck beneath them pitching and twisting against the force of the blizzard, they crossed over. A scorch mark was left on the wooden planks from the black flames as they travelled. Finally, after an eternity, they reached the rocky surface of the road, and ran face first into the cliff face of the next mountain.

"Damn it!" Treghan shouted. "We went the wrong way!"

"Well we're not going back!" Marni scolded him. "Just keep moving, we have to find shelter."

They made their way along the road, using the cliff face as a guide to avoid falling down the mountain, until a sudden gap opened up, and they found themselves in the shelter of a small overhang. A cave opened out at the back, and they entered it with a sense of relief as Corilai dropped her vortex.

"Thank the flames for that," Corilai murmured as she collapsed to the floor. "I'm exhausted."

"Corilai!" Treghan shouted, dropping his hold on Fletcher and running to her side.

She was shivering, and clung to him as he removed his cloak and wrapped it around her, over the top of her own.

"You saved us, Corilai," Treghan said. "But you have to rest now. Don't worry, I'm not going anywhere."

Chapter 8 – Ice Mountains

Symin looked ahead into the mountains, where a worn trail, hardly anything like the roads and highways around Windwall, meandered into the highlands.

"They went this way?" Symin said.

"Yes, into the mountains," the Leusbay ranger said.

"And this road leads south west?"

"Yes. There are a number of hamlets, quarries, farms, that sort of thing, and they tend to trade to both Leusbay and Windwall."

"And you let them go at this point?" Symin pressed

"The storm was coming in. We determined it not safe to follow."

"But clearly the thieves determined it safe to proceed."

Symin spurred his horse forward, and began picking his way along the muddy trail. Loka followed, with their guide from Leusbay behind. A slushy muck greeted them as they descended a trough, trickling run off from the mountains forming a corrugated muddy bed. The horses struggled to pass as the sticky sludge gripped their hooves.

Pushing on, Symin's horse climbed the other side and continued, rounding a bend to find an immense snow drift blocking the road. Symin dismounted, and approached it with care, looking all along it for any signs their quarry had failed to pass.

"Damn it," Symin said. "They must have passed here before the worst of it came down."

"Yes, the snow had not yet started here," the Leusbay ranger said. "But we could see it over the highlands."

"So it was not yet dangerous to proceed," Symin snapped. "You could have followed them further, and provided us with better information."

"But, these mountains, they're unpredictable!"

"I know exactly what these mountains are. Your lazy attitude may have cost us our investigation. I've seen enough, we will be returning to Windwall. The less time I have to look at your pitiful face, the better."

Nobody spoke as they rode back to Leusbay, and when the man entered the gates, Symin followed, but left him to return to the ranger outpost alone. Instead, Symin led Loka to a nearby tavern, dismounted, and strode inside.

"What are we doing here?" Loka whispered, grasping his arm as the locals eyed them with growing suspicion.

"We have to stay the night, and I won't be going to that outpost with its unearned luxury. The sooner that man is removed and some hard workers sent to replace him, the better off we'll be. Look around you."

Loka did as he said, and was shocked by the animosity she felt from the men and women in the tavern. The scowls on their faces, the tense grip on their eating utensils or drinks, the anger in their eyes. None of them spoke. There was no noise, in the obviously rowdy venue. She shivered as Symin approached the bar, speaking loud enough to be heard by all in the room.

"I would like to book two rooms for the night," he said. "One for myself, and one for my companion. I will be paying up front, of course."

The barman approached, his movements slow as he looked around the room.

"What are you doing here ranger?" he snarled. "Don't you know you have accommodation for free in that damned palace your man has stolen from us?"

"Exactly why I refuse to go there." Symin snarled back. "That man will be replaced shortly, by my authority. I will be sending word to the Chancellor of this."

"What do you mean?" the barman said.

"I have seen the actions of that man," Symin said. "And the lack of any service to your city and its people which he seems to think acceptable, and for which he has exacted his luxury. I spit in his face by refusing his ill gotten hospitality, and request humbly that you permit us to stay here, before we return to Windwall in the morning."

"My cousin is in Windwall," the barman said, loud enough for the patrons to hear. "He has told me of the rangers there, the good work they are trying to achieve, for the benefit of the city. For the benefit of the people. He has told me how you are searching for their lost children, and how you are rumoured to be providing food and rooms to those left on the streets at night. Is all this true?"

"It is. We work hard alongside the people of Windwall, for their benefit alone."

"Then, on my cousin's report, I will offer you your two rooms. But only if you promise to arrange for the rangers here to be removed, in preference for those of your own kind."

"That's fine. It will be done."

"Then I will show you to your rooms. Maurice, tend to their horses, and see to it no harm comes to them or the possessions of these two. And if anybody," the barman said as he looked around at the patrons. "Has a problem with that, they can speak to me about it, before they leave."

The evening passed without incident, Symin and Loka enjoying a hearty meal of roast pig, root vegetables and steaming hot tea. It took a while, but some of the patrons in the tavern even began to warm to them a little, and engaged them in some conversation.

"So why are the rangers entering into all the towns again?" a man asked.

"Yes," a woman interrupted. "We've been at peace here for generations, with little crime. The city guards do a good job. Some of us feel punished for no reason."

As carefully as he could, Symin explained the situation that had arisen in Gray, and why the Chancellor had taken the difficult decision to establish outposts in all major towns and cities, and what it was they were hoping to achieve. He explained in detail, and a handful of the patrons stayed to listen.

"Well, the men you sent here have failed in your vision. They're greedy, ignorant layabouts," a man growled.

"They will be removed shortly," Symin assured him. "What we are trying to achieve is for the benefit of all the people of Cinder, to help keep our nation at peace with itself. These men have failed in that duty, so will be punished."

The man grunted in approval, and offered Symin his hand.

"I hope that you are true to your word, ranger," the man said, shaking Symin's hand slowly.

Symin and Loka both slept well. When they left at sunrise, there was no challenge, and only a little of the previous tension remained. They rode for Windwall, Symin brooding as Loka followed, staring at his back with concern. There was no doubt in either of their minds that their task in finding the children was to be harder now than they had hoped, thanks to the loss of time on this fool's errand.

*   *   *

The four students remained in the cave, as the blizzard coated everything outside in white. In the overhang, slowly being enclosed in snow, there was a pile of wood and debris. Broken cart wheels, branches of trees, twigs, and other burnable refuse. It was clearly stacked there for a purpose.

"This cave is probably a regular refuge for travellers on the road who get caught out by the storms," Marni mused as she piled some of the wood near the cave opening, hoping the smoke would be drawn outside as she lit it with her green flame.

Treghan mumbled something in agreement as he watched Corilai's sleeping form, the concern in his posture clear. She slept fitfully, mumbling in her sleep about flames, wind and dragons, and Treghan wondered what it was she was seeing. He held her close, uncaring if she should release her demon flames in her sleep, only caring that she was alive, and they were safe.

Fletcher sat up against the wall, his ankle splinted with one of the spokes of a cartwheel they had found in the pile of wood. His foot, ankle and lower leg had become swollen and purple before they had made it to safety, and now it throbbed with intense pain as he watched Marni working.

"I'll help you," he said, making to get up, his visible agony no deterrent.

"No you won't!" Marni snapped, rushing over and pushing him back down. "You're badly injured. Let me do this. Treghan and Corilai aren't going to be much help either, so stop worrying. Just sit there, and wait while I figure out how we're going to survive the night."

Before long, Treghan slept, still clutching his friend. Fletcher dozed off soon after, leaving Marni to tend the fire and watch over her friends, wondering how they had come to be in this situation.

"Symin's going to yell at us," she moaned.

Taking a pouch from her pocket, she rummaged through it, sifting through seeds until she found the one she wanted.

Reaching into the overhang outside the cave, she scooped some dirty snow in her hand, and placed it on the ground near the wall of the cave, watching as it slowly melted due to the heat of the fire. Then, she carefully placed the seed in the soil, and held her hand over it. She focused her energy, drawing on the power of her green flame, pushing its life into the tiny plant as it sprouted.

Ethereal green flames surged around the plant, and it grew, soon standing a full foot above the cave floor, tendrils reaching to find support for the vine, and she stopped. The plant sat there, testament to her green flame's secondary power, tiny buds forming in several places. Pushing a little more flame into the plant, she made the flowers open, then touched them against each other, carefully pollinating them, as her tutors in Emberdale had taught her.

Satisfied, Marni fetched more snow, melted it into the soil, and pushed a last burst of her life giving green flame into the plant, watching in amazement as the fruits formed where the flowers had been. She stood back, bathing the fruit in her green light, ripening them until she was satisfied. A dozen ripe, bright red tomatoes hung from the vine, inviting her to taste, and her hunger got the better of her.

Plucking one of the fruits from the vine, Marni bit into it without hesitation. She knew there would be no parasites, no worms or anything like that in the fruit, because her flame only helped the growth of the plant, not the animals which might infest it.

The tomato was large, the size of a good apple, and it was satisfying. She sat beside the plant, her back to the wall, and looked at her friends. They all slept, while she ate her tomato, regretting that she had not grown it sooner. She wondered if she should wake them to eat, but they all looked so peaceful, and she felt her own sleepiness trying to take her.

"I wonder when the boys will find their colours' secondary abilities?" she mumbled. "Of course, whites don't have any, that we know of. Theirs is just the filtering aspect of the white flame, which isn't really secondary at all. But Fletcher should have his soon, if he's been doing his study and practising like Corilai and I."

Marni yawned, and watched as Treghan stirred, then woke, looking at her. He smiled, then looked down at Corilai, cradled against his side. He gently moved her hair away from her face, then looked back at Marni.

"How long was I out?" he asked.

"Not terribly long," Marni said, as she plucked a tomato and tossed it to him. "I grew these to eat. We need to keep our strength up. Corilai will need food when she wakes up as well. There's plenty on the vine."

"Thanks," Treghan replied, catching the fruit with his left hand, while still holding Corilai with his right arm. "You look exhausted. I can keep watch while you sleep, if you like."

"That would be wonderful," Marni said, stretching and yawning as she stood.

Marni walked to where Fletcher was slumped, snoring lightly. She quickly inspected his splint, then lay down beside him, close enough to be there when he woke, but not so close as to touch. Soon, her soft breathing joined his light snoring as she slept.

Treghan stared into the blustery night beyond the fire, slowly eating the tomato Marni had grown.

*   *   *

The storm lashed Windwall as ferociously as the last one had done, but thankfully of shorter duration. Jarls had fretted through it, worrying for the youngsters who had gone off chasing that poor child into the mountains.

"What will Symin say when he returns?" she moaned.

"He'll be upset, but don't worry, those kids will be safe," said the young ranger working beside her in the kitchens.

"Why are you so sure, Kala?" Jarls asked.

"I remember them from the rebellion in Grey. They led Symin's army to the villainous Yuri, having already escaped his clutches once. Those youngsters are as experienced and adept in the field as any ranger, even though they're still students. They're not children, not really..."

"I guess you're right," Jarls said. "I just worry about them. They still have the impulsiveness of youth to get them into trouble."

"Just have faith in them. If they don't return, Symin will find them, and then, he'll be angry with them, only so long as is needed, because he cares deeply for all his charges, students or subordinates alike."

"You're right, of course," Jarls replied. "I'm glad to have such a level headed assistant. It's needed here in Windwall."

"I'm sure you'd cope wonderfully without a girl like me around," the young ranger said. "Look what you all managed before the rest of us arrived."

"We didn't do a lot," Jarls said. "But thank you anyway. We did try to lay the ground work for a strong ranger presence in the highlands."

"You did that marvellously," Kala said. "With the girls out spreading good will in the city, and the boys off talking to the guards, you've got us already doing what will work in this place. I still find it strange how they define the people by their gender, but you've worked with that to start changing their minds for the better. Imagine if I'd been here instead of you. I might not have seen that the guards would not accept a female ranger at first, and it could have been bad."

"It would have been fine in the end," Jarls said.

"But this way it's easier. You've worked with them, in their own world, and can start to change things from there. I hear some sad stories about some of the other towns. Windwall is already a success story. Nobody else has locals sleeping in ranger run facilities, willingly accepting ranger food, none of that."

"The dormitory and free meals were the work of those children," Jarls said with a smile.

"You see?" Kala replied. "I told you, they are among the most competent of rangers already. They make a difference everywhere they go. Wherever they are, those four will weather the storm and return. Why, I wouldn't put it past them to actually find the missing children while they were at it. Now wouldn't that upset Symin? Those kids stealing his thunder like that!"

"Ha!" Jarls shouted, her laughter echoing from the stone walls. "I dare say that would rather put a spur in his side. I'd love to see those fireworks, it would be like a stage drama brought to life."

Kala smiled, returning to the root vegetables she was cutting up. They fell to silence again, working on preparing the stew for the next day, Jarls' mind at ease and the world in order. The older woman hummed a lively tune as she worked, and soon the work would be done.

"I do wonder what Symin will find in Leusbay," Jarls mused.

"Probably not much. I think the thieves will have left little trail, and the rangers in Leusbay will not have gained the trust you enjoy here."

"You're probably right," Jarls said. "Though I wish you weren't."

Chapter 9 – Taken!

Treghan woke to find Corilai awake, and staring at him. The wind howled across the cave mouth, and the fire had declined to hot coals. Marni and Fletcher slept soundly, but the temperature in the cave had dropped considerably.

"How long have you been awake?" Treghan asked, chagrined he had fallen asleep on watch.

"Only a little while. I think the cold woke me," she replied.

"I'll get some more wood," he said, finding his left arm had gone to sleep beneath her.

"Wait," she said, blushing. "Just stay here a minute more. I'm comfortable."

"OK then," he stammered, blushing even darker than she had.

"I'm hungry," she said.

"There's a tomato plant over there," Treghan replied. "Marni made it. There were several good fruits on the vine. You can eat one of those."

"Good idea, I'll get one in a moment," she said, glancing over at their sleeping friends. "I'll have to thank her when she's awake. I had no idea her secondary ability had come so far."

"She said the same thing about you," Treghan said. "That was incredible, what you did."

"Thank you," Corilai replied. "Honestly, I didn't think I could do that, until I tried. I don't know if I could do it again, I feel so exhausted from it."

"You'll get your energy back soon enough."

Extracting herself from his embrace, Corilai stood, and walked to the tomatoes, taking one from the vine and biting into it. Her eyes grew wide and she ate the rest with more eagerness than Treghan expected.

"These are amazing," she said. "Marni really is incredible."

"She's not the only one," Treghan said, standing and walking to the cave mouth. "I feel like a nobody, with my white flame and no secondary."

Corilai turned to correct him, but he was gone. A few moments later, he rushed back into the cave, covered in snow, his arms loaded with wood from the pile in the overhang. He carried it to the fire, and dropped it onto the coals. Corilai walked to his side, and they watched as the damp wood smoked and smouldered for a while, before the smaller pieces caught and began to burn properly.

Taking another tomato each, they sat down together in front of the fire. The pair passed the next hour in silence, until Marni woke and joined them.

"How much longer do you think the storm will last? Marni asked.

"Could be an hour, or a day, it's hard to tell," Treghan replied. "You can barely tell it's morning, there's so little sunlight getting through."

"You think it's morning?" Marni asked.

"Yeah, early morning. Probably an hour after sunrise."

"Long night," Corilai said.

"You slept through most of it," Marni said. "Fletcher kept waking up and moaning with pain. I tried to help him as best as I could, but there's not a lot I can do for him."

"You did enough," Fletcher moaned from where he lay on the ground. "Though a miracle healing herb would have been better."

“So what do we do now?” Marni asked.

“We wait,” Treghan replied. “Not a lot else we can do, but if you can grow us some more food, it would be great.”

“I'll see what I can do,” Marni said, rummaging through her pouch for some seeds.

Following much the same procedure she had used to grow the tomatoes, Marni grew another plant, this time with long tuber shaped fruits.

“These are chocos,” She said. “Easy to grow, and you can cook them in the coals without having to wrap them, then break them open and eat the insides. They don't have a lot of flavour, but they’re nutritious and warming.”

“We used them at home to fill out pies when we didn't have enough of whatever fruit we needed, because it doesn't drown the taste of the good stuff,” Corilai said. “They'll do, though I wish we could make them taste better.”

After a short wait, Marni picked four of the green fruits and handed them to Corilai, who nestled them in coals at the edge of the fire.

“How long do we wait?” Treghan asked.

“Not long. Ten minutes or so should do it,” Corilai said.

They waited in silence, until Marni reached a gloved hand into the coals and plucked out a choco. Using a rock, she split it open and tried some of the flesh from inside.

“They're ready,” she said, taking a second one and walking to Fletcher.

Taking one each, Treghan and Corilai split them open and began to eat, grimacing at the bland taste.

“They'd be better with some butter, or maybe mixed in with the tomato,” Treghan said.

“At least it's food,” Corilai replied. “Thanks, Marni. You're amazing.”

Treghan began drawing in the dust, and initiated a game of noughts and crosses on the ground, then looked at Corilai, an eyebrow raised in invitation. She complied, and won the first game.

“I guess this will kill a bit of time,” she said, and drew a fresh grid in the dirt.

Though they soon tired of the game, they passed the next few hours in relative calm as the storm raged outside.

*   *   *

Symin and Loka shared a small sofa in front of a roaring fire, in a tiny cabin beside the highway. It was one of the many merchant safe places, and had been left well stocked with supplies and firewood. Outside, heavy rain and lightning pelted the windows and made further travel unnecessarily uncomfortable.

“There's probably a blizzard in the highlands,” Symin said.

“But everybody will be safe in Windwall,” Loka replied, leaning against him.

“I would certainly hope so.”

He stood, walked to a door, and opened it, looking into a small stable where the horses nibbled lazily at hay.

“At least we’re warm, dry, and the horses are fed,” he said. “I'll see what I can find for us to eat.”

Opening a small cupboard, he found a pot, a skin of water, and a variety of root vegetables.

"This will have to do," he said, putting water in the pot, and throwing in four potatoes, two sweet potatoes, and two carrots.

Picking up a small steel rack, Symin carried the pot to the fire, placed the rack over it, and carefully rested the pot on top. After making sure it was secure, he returned to his seat, and sat staring at the flames as the water slowly came to the boil.

"How long do you think this one will last?" Loka asked.

"The storm?" he replied, looking at her. "Probably another day of this, then we're a day away from Windwall."

"That's what I figured," Loka said. "I hope those stolen children are as warm and dry as we are, wherever they are."

"If not, somebody will pay for their discomfort when I find them," Symin snarled, staring at the flames again.

Loka smiled as she looked at him, as comfortable in his presence and as sure of his words as she ever had been.

"Thank you," she said with soft affection.

"For what?"

"Just for being you. I'm glad to know you, and to work with you. I feel safe near you."

"I feel safe near you as well," Symin said, somewhat awkwardly, as he stood and leaned over the pot, before sitting down again. "We should head into the mountains as soon as possible, try to find some leads on the location of the kidnappers. We've been delayed too long already."

"Agreed," Loka said. "Have you thought about what you will assign those four to do?"

"I won't be taking them into the highlands, if that's what you're asking. It's too dangerous for them. They don't have the experience to work in such conditions."

"So we leave them in Windwall. I'll talk to Jarls about what they can do while we're gone. Once we're back in Windwall of course. They're probably bored out of their minds by now."

"They probably are," Symin said. "But they have to learn that being a ranger is not about having fun all the time."

* * *

Around midday, the wind died down and the clouds began to clear. The students watched nervously for a while from the safety of the cave, until they were sure the worst of the storm was over. Eventually, Marni was the one who ventured out of the cave, and then out of the overhang, onto the snow covered road.

Watching from inside the cave, Treghan could see the sun bath her in its warmth as she twirled on the spot, then let out a joyous shout.

"It's beautiful!" Marni shouted. "Not a cloud in the sky! I can't believe it passed so quickly. We can go home now."

As Marni jumped around, Treghan stood to go outside, Corilai grabbing his hand.

"Wait," Corilai said. "I'm worried. I have a bad feeling about this."

"It's fine," he said, looking away for a split moment as Marni screamed.

He looked back at the girl, and she held her arms over her face as wave after wave of sleet, like walls of ice, blasted at her, until she fell to the ground. There was still no sign of bad weather remaining, and they could see that in spite of the icy blast, the sun had continued to shine.

"Marni," Corilai shouted. "Are you alright?"

Marni was climbing to her knees, and looked up to answer. She never got the chance. As she opened her mouth to speak, a rider on a horse rushed by, dropping a sack over her head, followed by a second rider who scooped her up, before turning and riding back the way they had come, into the highlands. Marni's muffled scream echoed through the mountains as they rushed through the deep snow.

"Wait and look after Fletcher!" Treghan shouted, running from the cave. "I'm going to save her, don't worry!"

"Treghan, wait!" Corilai screamed, but he was already gone, and would not change his mind.

Leaving the overhang, Treghan looked and saw why Marni had been so excited. The day was sunny and clear, and there was nothing that could explain the sleet which hit her. The horses tracks were clear on the trail, and he ran, as fast as he could trudge through the freshly laid snow, following the tracks as they passed between two enormous obelisks.

He was looking down, and did not see the attack until it was too late. He was already out of sight of the cave, when the flat of a shovel caught him in the gut and he went down. As he knelt up, a foot caught his chin, and that was the last thing he saw as he slumped to the ground, his consciousness fading fast in the bitter cold snow.

* * *

"Treghan!" Corilai shouted, but to no avail.

She watched along the road, but though she could still see his tracks, she couldn't see him, or Marni, or the strangers on horseback. Growing anxious, she looked back at the cave, where Fletcher sat, unable to follow.

"I'm just going to check along the road a little way," she shouted, before striking off in the same direction her friends had gone.

She made her way carefully through the snow, until she reached the two obelisks, and stepped between them. The road stretched ahead a little way before again disappearing around a bend, but before that, there was a lot of disturbance in the snow. She rushed to it, and she could see where Treghan's footprints stopped, right before a large impression in the snow. A divot the size of a body.

"Treghan!" She screamed, and only the silent mountains answered back, echoing her voice on the wind.

Aside from the divot, there was a mess of tracks, including several horses, and at least two carts, all heading off into the mountains. Clearly, she decided, Treghan had met with foul play. It would be foolish to go after them alone.

"We have to find Symin," she said. "He'll know what to do."

Tearing herself away from the pursuit her heart demanded, she made her way back to the cave, where Fletcher looked at her, his face stricken with worry.

"They're both gone," she said in answer to his unspoken question. "We have to get back to Windwall, and find help."

"But I can't walk!" he said.

"You're going to have to. Hop if you must, but we're going. We have to get Symin back here before the track goes cold."

"Of course, you're right," Fletcher said. "Why don't you go? Just leave me here."

"I can't," she shouted. "Treghan asked me to look after you, so that's what I'm going to do. It's not that far to the city, but with your foot like that, it's going to take at least the rest of the day. Come on, you can lean on me."

"You're not going to take no for an answer, are you?"

"Like hell I will!" she shouted. "Get up! We have to move quickly. We can't afford to let them get too far ahead before we can come back with help."

"Fine, I'll come with you. Here, help me up."

She grabbed his arm and hauled him to his feet. He winced with pain, but stifled the scream that tried to follow. As he leaned heavily on her arm, they shuffled out of the cave, and made their way back towards Windwall.

"And if you fall off the damn bridge again," she said. "I'm leaving you hanging in that blasted net."

"Understood," Fletcher mumbled.

*　　　　*　　　　*

Symin paced in the sitting room of the Ranger outpost in Windwall. They arrived home on dusk, to find the four students missing, and immediately demanded information. Jarls had told him about the girl, Ivy, and how the four had run off to find her, but that was before the blizzard hit, and none of them had been seen since.

"What were those brats thinking?" he shouted. "After everything we do to keep them safe, they turn around and do this?"

"Calm down," Loka said. "I'm sure they're fine."

"I bet they are, too, those brats. I'll have them shipped off back to Emberdale with a failing grade for this!"

"And what if they found something for the investigation?"

"Well," he said, stopping. "They would too, those brats. Always getting into things. Never far from trouble those four!"

"Just wait and see what they have to say for themselves then," Jarls said.

"Them?" Symin snapped. "What about you? You let them go in the first place!"

"Could you have stopped them?" Jarls shot back.

"Probably not," Symin admitted as he sat. "Get me a fresh horse, and a supply of torches. I'll go after them immediately."

"Yes, Sir," Said a young ranger by the door, who rushed out of the room.

"Now?" Loka said. "In the dark?"

"I'd rather that than risk another storm before we can go to find them."

"You won't be swayed on this, will you?" Loka said with a sigh.

"No."

"Then I'm coming with you. I'll catch that ranger, have him get two horses."

"I can't sway you from that either, can I?" he said.

"No. Where you go, I go."

"Fine, we leave as soon as the horses are ready."

Chapter 10 – First Return

The walk was slow, with Fletcher barely able to make it across the bridge, which swayed in the breeze as they hobbled across. Corilai found herself dragging him and holding him upright more and more as the extent of his pain became clear.

"You're going to have to leave me," Fletcher insisted.

"No!" she shouted. "I said I'd look after you and that's what I'll do, but we can't waste time sitting around back there in the cave. We need to get help to Treghan and Marni as soon as we can!"

"That's right, so if you leave me behind, then you can run ahead. It will be so much quicker."

"But I can't just leave you behind."

"You might have to. I see clouds forming on the horizon again."

She looked at the clouds he was talking about, thick and fluffy, low in the sky over the end of the canyon. She re-doubled her efforts, dragging the boy with her as she tried to rush across the bridge. She ignored his howls of pain until finally, after what seemed an eternity, she dropped him on the solid ground where the road led towards the city, and the bridge swayed behind them.

"Five minutes, then we get going again," she said. "Even if I did leave you here, there's no shelter. You'd die if another blizzard came through. And we don't have time to take you back to the cave."

"Then you should have listened to me before!"

"And left you in the cave, unable to collect wood for the fire? Unable to move around to feed yourself? If another blizzard hit, the fire would go out and you'd freeze to death! Treghan would never forgive me."

"So it's only for Treghan, huh?" he moaned. "I see how it is."

"Don't you dare give me that!" she shouted. "Aren't you the least bit worried about Marni? Those men could be doing anything to her!"

"Of course I am! But I'm damn useless like this. That's why I wanted you to leave me behind, so my Marni could get help faster! But no, you wouldn't listen!"

"Your Marni?" Corilai teased.

Fletcher blushed as red as the tomatoes they had eaten from Marni's vine, and looked at the ground, the wind gone from his anger. He shook his head, then winced in pain as he tried to stand.

"Come on, we have to get moving. For Marni, and for Treghan. Just please, don't you dare tell her I said that."

"I'll think about it," Corilai said.

They moved in silence for a long time, as the daylight slowly faded, and they found themselves wandering in the dark.

"You should light a flame to guide us," Fletcher said.

"That's going to work well, isn't it?" Corilai said. "My flames are black, you idiot. Why don't you do it?"

"Because it hurts, but maybe it will take my mind off my foot if I focus on my flame."

Fletcher lifted his free hand out in front of them, and kindled a small red flame. It flickered in the breeze, but lit a short distance with flickering, dancing shadows.

"The darkness might have been less creepy," Corilai said.

"Well at least we won't fall off a cliff," Fletcher replied.

They continued, pushing on as they descended into the bottom of the same trough where Fletcher and Marni had caught up to Corilai and Treghan when they left the city. Then they had to climb the other side, and the going was even slower as the steep incline took its toll.

It was full night now, and the clouds from the horizon had moved over head, to obscure the stars and block out all moon light.

"We're not going to make it, are we?" Fletcher moaned.

"We'll live through this," Corilai snapped. "I've lived through worse."

"No, I mean, we aren't going to make it back to Windwall tonight. We need to find shelter."

"You're probably right," Corilai said. "I'm still so exhausted from yesterday, that whole thing with the flame bubble took it out of me. I don't think I could flame still if our lives depended on it."

Adding insult to injury, the wind grew brisk, and a light snow began to fall. The snow already on the ground was picked up by the breeze to form eddies of frozen nightmares, ghosts of the cold returning from the blizzard of the previous night, to haunt them with their threat of exposure.

"We need that shelter, Corilai," Fletcher demanded.

"I know! But where?"

"I don't know. Just keep going. We have to find something."

They pushed on, and after a long painful climb reached the top of the rise, the trough behind them menacing now as the wind whistled through it. Dragging their way through a building drift of snow on the road, they worked their way around a bluff, sticking close to the wall on the high side.

Just when Corilai was ready to give up hope, they rounded a bend and were hit full in the face by a wall of sleet.

"Damn it!" she screamed, pushing on.

Corilai dropped her grip on Fletcher as the wind nearly knocked her over. She caught the cliff face beside her, and held on, looking around for his flame. It flickered, dim in the night, nearly obscured by the swirling snow.

She left the safety of the wall and struck out three paces till she reached him, and struggled to lift him as he held her arms in a vice like, grip, his gaze frozen in fear. Slowly, she dragged him to the wall, then continued to pick her way along it.

"We're going to make it. We'll be fine, trust me," she huffed.

Fletcher seemed to wake from a trance, and began to try harder, heaving himself through the snow in spite of the pain. Then, a small miracle happened. Corilai reached for the wall and found nothing there. She waved her arm back and found the wall split, a small alcove rend into the rock face, and she hurled herself into it, dragging Fletcher behind her.

Turning, Corilai planted her back against the rocky rear of the tiny space, and watched as the wind and snow whistled past, their little shelter spared from the worst of it. Then she thought she heard something else. The wind subsided for a moment, and she was sure. Horses approaching, at least two of them. Who would be out in this wicked weather?

She panicked, and drew on all her strength, to construct a camouflaging flame over the alcove. The noise and wind stopped, only muffled sounds from outside the cocoon of flame reaching their ears.

"I don't know how long I can hold this up," Corilai said. "But if that's the kidnappers, or bandits, we're done for if I lose it."

Fletcher did not reply, and they huddled there in fear as the muffled sounds drew closer.

"Why can we hear them now?" Fletcher whispered.

"I don't know, I guess my flames are too weak now to block everything out."

The horses came close, then stopped as a muffled voice called out.

"Wait, there's a flame here!"

Corilai panicked, holding her breath as she reached her hand out towards the flame wall, as if trying to hold it up. Just then, a hand broke through it, wreathed in shadows, and snatched her wrist, before jerking back, to drag the screaming girl out of her safety.

She screamed like her life was over, as the flame wall dissolved to expose Fletcher, huddled in the alcove. In a last ditch effort to survive, Corilai lashed out, swinging her fists at her would be captor while she screamed incoherently.

Her captor simply pinned her arms to her side, and enclosed her in a warm, gentle yet powerful embrace. It was only then that Corilai recognised the voice.

"It's OK child, I have you now. It's going to be alright."

"Loka!" Corilai whispered, then surrendered, collapsing into the woman's arms as she let the exhaustion she had been fighting flood over her.

Corilai could barely watch as Symin lifted Fletcher, and placed him on his horse, before climbing up behind the boy. Then she felt herself lifted, Loka tossing her like a rag doll into the same position on her own mount, before climbing up behind her. Corilai relaxed, slumping back against the woman as she held her close with one arm, the other reaching around to grasp the reigns of the horse as they galloped back towards the city.

*　　　*　　　*

Treghan stirred, groggy as he came to. He tried to reach a hand to brush hair from his eyes, only to find his hands bound with sturdy rope to the railing on the side of a cart as it jostled its way along a track in the highlands.

A canvass cover flapped in the wind, and a cold unlike anything he had felt before seeped into his bones. He groaned as he looked around.

"Treghan?" he heard Marni's whispered voice. "Thank the flames! They kicked you so hard, I was worried about you."

"Where are we?" Treghan asked softly, whincing as pain shot through his abdomen and chest, presumably where they had kicked him.

"On a cart somewhere in the highlands. I don't know more than that."

"Whose cart?"

"I don't know. But they had a bunch of kids with them, helping them to tie ropes, that sort of thing. But the thugs who beat you up were adults, or at least older teenagers. Probably between eighteen and twenty five, four men."

"So do you think these are the kidnappers?" Treghan asked.

"I think so."

"Where do you think they're taking us?"

"Probably back where they take all the kids and young people. We're basically still kids ourselves, even if we are in ranger uniform, and likely as old as some of the kidnappers, so they might have thought we'd be useful."

"Or a threat to be disposed of..." Treghan quipped.

"I don't think so. They could have easily disposed of us while you were unconscious. Dumped our bodies in a snow drift. Nobody would ever find us. No, I think they wanted us for some reason."

"Any ideas why?"

"No..."

Treghan looked at the ropes, binding his hands. Strong, but organic, a fibre, made from a plant. It should burn easily. He focussed his energy, and created the sparks. But nothing else happened. The sparks danced between his fingers, taunting him with the memory of what it felt like to be the useless twin so long ago.

"Damn it," Treghan muttered. "I'd forgotten how pathetic those damn sparks were."

"Yeah, that's all we'll be doing for a while," Marni said.

"What do you mean?" Treghan replied.

In answer, Marni started a spark, green, incandescent, and tiny, dancing between her fingers, mimicking the level of spark Treghan had spent so long stuck with.

"They forced us to inhale the smoke from some herb which they burnt," she told him. "Ever since, I've been unable to do anything more than this. It's silenced my flame. I don't like it. It feels like they tore away my oldest friend, without even letting me say goodbye."

"Bastards. Don't they know how hard we worked for our flames?"

"They don't care how their actions effect us. They're only thinking of themselves. If we burn the ropes and escape, we're a threat."

"Yeah, that makes sense."

Treghan leaned forward, and began chewing at the ropes.

"No, don't do that," Marni said.

"Why not?"

"Think about it. It's windy and cold out there, and we have no idea where we are. Why not ride it out, when they get where ever it is we're going, then we can escape, get an idea for how they're base is set up, how many of them there are, and take valuable intelligence back to Symin."

"You're right," Treghan muttered. "But I hate being trussed up like this."

"It's only for a little while," Marni assured him. "Think about how long it took them to take Ivy and come back for us. We have to be close to their headquarters by now."

"No question," Treghan said. "You're the brains in this outfit today. OK, I'll wait. Who knows, we can probably even find Ivy."

Marni smiled at the compliment, but said no more as the cart stopped. They waited several minutes as they heard the sound of the children working outside, men's voices barking orders about moving things off the road, before the cart began moving again.

"Must have been a land slide or a fallen tree or something," Marni said. "There were at least three others while you were unconscious."

"They must have the routine pretty well practised by now," Treghan said.

"They'd have been dealing with these situations for months already."

"Yeah, I think so," Marni replied. "But I think some of the kids are on their first trip with them, by the way they talk. I'm pretty sure they didn't take the kids all the way to the city, because if they did that, they'd just go home. I also heard the men threaten a couple of them that if they didn't do what they were told, their siblings or parents would be hurt for it."

"Bastards. Not that again," Treghan growled.

"What do you mean?"

"Remember Yuri and his conscripts? He forced them to tow the line by threatening their families, but at least they were adults. These bastards are playing the same game, but this time it's innocent children, with no way of defending themselves, or their families. It's a monstrous thing to do, and I won't stand for it."

"You won't stand at all at the moment, tied up like that," Marni quipped. "Just calm down, bide your time. We'll figure things out like always. Don't worry. We should try to learn as much as we can about them."

"You're right."

The cart stopped again, and again the children worked for a while clearing something from the trail, before they started again.

"Must have been quite a storm through here," Marni said. "The stops are getting more frequent."

"It makes me wonder what kind of settlement they have. Most of the farm and quarry homes are abandoned through winter because they can't hold out against the cold."

"I'm guessing underground," Marni said. "There are clearly a lot of them, with the number of kidnapped children from Windwall. "They must have somewhere large and easy to warm. Cabins or even stone buildings would be hard pressed to provide enough room and still be manageable. There just isn't that much firewood up here."

"They could be burning coal for heat."

"Which points to there being a mine, so I still say they're underground."

"I guess we'll know soon enough," Treghan replied.

The wind outside the cart seemed to ease off, and they stopped. After a moment, the canvas was pulled aside and two of the young men climbed in and untied them from the cart. Their captors dragged them from the cart and wrestled them both the face it. They bound their hands again, and joined them with a rope, before leading them away, pulling the rope like a leash on an animal.

"I was right," Marni whispered. "We're underground."

"Yeah, looks like a converted mine," Treghan said as he looked around. They were in a relatively large chamber, sturdy wooden beams acting as columns to support the ceiling. Three carts could fit across the space, he guessed, and six along it, before it narrowed into three passages which disappeared into the mountain's rocky heart.

They were led down the middle of the three passages, one of the men carrying a torch. They walked for a long time, descending deep into the old mine. Finally, they were shoved into a small cell, which was locked behind them.

"Stay put," one of the men snarled. "If you try anything, you'll pay. We'll be back for the girl in a while."

"I don't like the sound of that," Marni said as the men walked away, leaving them in the darkness.

Chapter 11 – The Hunt Begins

Corilai wept openly as Loka led her to her room, and put the exhausted girl to bed. They had been through so much in such a short time, and now, they had lost Treghan and Marni. Treghan, that brave idiot. What was he thinking?

"Are you going to be OK, Corilai?" Loka asked softly, an unusual tenderness in her eyes.

"I... I guess so."

"Did you want to talk about it?"

"No," Corilai said, then paused. "It's just..."

"Yes?"

"That big idiot had to run after her."

"Who?"

"Treghan," Corilai said. "Marni was taken, and he didn't think twice. He just ran after her."

"Did he say anything?"

"He asked me to look after Fletcher."

"Why?"

"Fletcher was already hurt. And I had no energy, I was exhausted from the cocoon."

"The cocoon?" Loka asked. "What's that?"

"Oh, you know the camouflage thing for black flames?" Corilai said. "I made a big one, to keep the blizzard out so we could keep moving and find shelter."

"You made a flame orb?" Loka asked, her eyebrows raised. "Big enough to enclose four people?"

"Yes," Corilai replied. "It stopped the wind, and the snow, and we were able to keep moving."

"I'm impressed. Most people think it's only good for camouflage. When did you learn it could also block out wind, and be used for cover in a storm?"

"When I did it," Corilai murmured.

"That was very brave," Loka said. "Not many people would have thought of that, let alone tried. And fewer still could have succeeded."

"Can anybody do it?"

"No," Loka said, shaking her head. "It's a factor of the black flame, one element of its secondary ability. To have achieved it so soon, you must be working very hard on your lessons."

"Marni and I have been practising together a lot, at least, in Emberdale we were, after classes most days. She's amazing."

"Marni is a green flame, right?"

"Yes," Corilai replied. "She's already carrying a seed pouch. She grew us food out of nothing, well, out of her seeds, while we were trapped in that cave by the blizzard."

"That's also impressive. The green flames are beautiful, but many don't achieve their secondary ability with any great skill."

"That's true of all colours, isn't it?"

"Yes," Loka said. "Except the whites. The only known secondary for them is their purifying filter, the very thing which makes them seem weak, and manifests itself in their initial flame. As far as we know, Treghan will never achieve any other ability from his flame."

"I feel sad for him," Corilai said, crying. "And now, he's gone. I should have stopped him, and now I might have lost him forever!"

"No, don't be silly, dear," Loka said. "Symin will get him back, and Marni. And then, he'll find all the other lost children as well. Just wait and see."

"I hope so. I'm so worried about him!"

"I know, Corilai, but please, have faith in your teachers. We aren't just teachers, after all."

"I hope Fletcher's OK, I promised Treghan I'd look after him."

"And you did that job wonderfully. He'd have perished out there alone, you did the right thing bringing him along. And then you sheltered him with your flame. You make a wonderful protector."

Corilai blushed, looking out the window from her bed.

"But I failed to protect the others."

"That's not true. You protected them just fine. You shielded them from the blizzard, and got them to safety. You can't help what happened afterwards. What did happen, anyway?"

"Oh, that, well, after the weather cleared, Marni went outside, and shouted about how wonderful it was. Then out of nowhere, she was hit by a blast of sleet, even though there was no storm, no clouds or anything, and then two men on horses rushed in and snatched her. Treghan chased them, and when I went to see where he had gone, I saw his footprints end at a mark in the snow where he fell, and the tracks of carts leading away."

"So it was an organised group, abducting two powerful rangers. You can't blame yourself for that. Now, get some sleep, I'll speak with Symin, and we'll decide what to do next. Don't worry, soon your friends will be home and safe."

"I hope so," Corilai murmured as Loka left the room.

* * *

Symin led several rangers on horseback out of Windwall, following the same road they had travelled when they found Corilai and Fletcher the night before. Soon, they passed that place, and continued, until they found the bridge, swaying gently in a soft breeze.

"Those children were caught on this bridge by a sudden blizzard," Loka said, worry in her eyes. "Be careful, Symin. We can't afford to lose you."

"There will not be another now. There was a small storm last night, but look at the sky. We will be fine."

"Even so, we should hurry."

"Agreed."

Together the rangers struck out across the bridge, and crossed to the other side without incident, before making their way in single file along the road on the other side. Soon, they passed the cave, which Symin recognised from the description given to him by Fletcher.

They continued along, and passed between the great twin obelisks. Then Symin called the party to a halt. He dismounted, and walked forward, hoping to find something, anything, to indicate the events of the previous day.

"This would be where Corilai thought Treghan had been captured," Loka said, walking beside him.

"Yes, but the storm last night has obliterated the tracks in the snow. We should keep moving."

They climbed back on their horses, and rode on into the highlands. The hours passed slowly as they took their time to inspect every possible sign of their quarry. Occasionally, they found a disturbed patch of ground, or a snapped twig, but never any definite cart or horse tracks. The storm, while brief, had done a thorough job of concealing their quarry's passage.

"Symin, we're not going to catch them now, are we?" Loka said.

"No," he replied. "I hoped there would be something, but if we're caught out here now, we're done for. We should return to Windwall, and prepare for a longer march."

"Yes, Sir," Loka said, turning her horse. "We'll need a caravan of carriages, equipped with skis for the snow. I will begin the arrangements as soon as we get back."

*   *   *

Four men charged into the cell, two rushing directly to Treghan, to hold him as he struggled. They lit the strange herb again, forcing him to inhale its sweet smelling smoke. Meanwhile, the other two grabbed Marni, and dragged her out of the cage while she screamed in protest.

Once she was gone, one of the pair holding Treghan struck his jaw, hard enough to knock him to the floor. They turned and left, locking the cell and following their companions.

Treghan sat on the floor, his head spinning a little as he looked around, confused and wondering what he could do now. He stood, his legs shaky as he walked to the bars, and looked out into the gloom. A single torch burned in a sconce opposite his cell, casting a wan light only a few meters into the darkness.

A soft shuffling noise reached him from the darkness, and Treghan peered into it, trying to see what was there. His eyes could not penetrate the gloom, so he raised his hand up, between the bars, and focused his energy.

As the feeble white sparks danced between his fingers, and the white flame refused to rise from within him, Treghan remembered the strange, sweet smelling smoke.

"Damn it," he muttered, then tried again.

Once again, the feeble sparks were all he could muster, casting no light. The sparks danced at his finger tips, mocking him, and he felt his anger and frustration rising. Then he heard a gasp, and the shuffle of feet on the floor, creeping towards him.

Slowly, the light revealed a shuffling, scared looking child, a boy, who looked about eight years old.

"Hello," Treghan said. "I'm Treghan."

The boy did not answer, but came a little closer, and raised his hands, to show a tiny, white spark between his fingers.

"You have white sparks?" Treghan said, amazed. "But you're so young! The sparks shouldn't have come yet. They don't turn up until puberty!"

"It's the smoke," the boy said.

"The smoke?"

"Yes, it awakens the ice spirits."

"What are you talking about?" Treghan said.

"The ice spirits. The older boys can do amazing things. They make ice walls, create blizzards, like you saw when they took your girlfriend."

"But the smoke, it quelled my flames. I don't understand. What are you talking about?"

"When your friend was taken, you remember? The sun was shining, and then there was that sleet? The ice on the wind? That was them. They wield ice, just like you rangers wield fire. But only those with the white sparks can do it. The rest are just servants, but Dreighton makes the white sparks into his officers, once they learn to ice."

"Do you have some with other coloured sparks?" Treghan asked.

"I've heard rumours, but they aren't useful to us. They don't seem able to do anything with their sparks, so they just work. The kids who cleared the landslides when we brought you back, they were the ones without the white sparks. They were the ones doing the hard work. The ice officers are our superiors, and they work for Dreighton. He pays them with comfortable quarters, but we all eat the same here."

"What do you eat?"

"Not enough," the boy moaned. "I wish there were a way home for them all, but there isn't. We're all here now, and Dreighton will never let us go."

"Who's Dreighton?" Treghan asked.

"He's the leader. There were four families here, and he rose to lead them, when his eldest son learned to ice. He took control, and started looking for more who could ice. He says he'll build an empire, and rule the world with their blizzards."

"Why did they take Marni?"

"Dreighton's son needs a powerful wife, and she's a ranger, like you. The guards said he was going to take her."

"Do you know how to ice?" Treghan asked.

"Only a little. I just concentrate, and picture the air freezing and swirling in my mind. It's hard to explain, but that's how it works."

"A lot like the flames. OK kid, I'm going to learn to ice, and fast. I already know how, it's just like the flames. And just like Marni's trees. Ice must be the secondary ability of the white flame. Thank you, now I know it's there, I'll learn it."

"If you want to use it to save your friend, you'd better learn it fast."

"How fast?"

"Today. Nobody has ever done that."

"Nobody was me, or I would guess had ranger training as a powerful white flame."

The boy's eyes grew wide.

"You're a white flame?"

"Yes. All with the white spark are. Didn't you know?"

"No," the boy gasped.

"Does Dreighton know?"

"I don't think so. Nobody does. Nobody here has flame, I think they'd use it if they did."

"All those with sparks are flames, and all children with flames can apply to the academy. Students are fed well, housed well, and paid an allowance. Much better than being stuck in a hole in the ground and fed slop."

"Could you get me into the academy one day?"

"I think so. You can spark already. You'll be a powerful white flame one day, just like me."

"I'll help you then, but you have to take me with you when you leave."

"Deal. Can you find the keys and get me out of here?"

"I'll be back soon. You teach yourself to ice while I'm gone."

Treghan smiled as the boy ran into the darkness. He looked at his fingers, pushed the sparks between them, then grasped the steel bars. Closing his eyes, he focused his energy, but instead of conjuring flames, he focussed on cold, icy power. He imagined his hands wielding a charge of frozen air which would form into a mighty blizzard.

Opening his eyes again, Treghan looked at the bars, and smiled. A smoky layer of frosty condensation coated them.

"Finally," he said with satisfaction. "I can be like the others. I have something to learn, a new power."

* * *

Marni struggled against her captors, but it was to no avail. They were strong men, and held her tightly as they dragged her through the twisting passages of the old mine. Shielding her hand inside her cloak, she watched it as she tried to flame. Nothing but those green sparks. Cursing under her breath, she imagined how worthless Treghan must have felt when he could only spark while his brother awed the villagers, and for the first time she felt true understanding.

"Where are you taking me?" she demanded.

"You'll be meeting with Dreighton. He'll decide your fate."

The walk was long, and they never left the mines. Finally, they arrived at a pair of sturdy wooden doors, which opened to reveal an enormous vaulted chamber. At the far end, on a raised dais, a large, black bearded man sat.

"Bring her closer," he shouted.

The men dragged Marni across the chamber, and she felt many eyes watching them. Dozens of torches filled the vaulted ceilings with smoke and cast their harsh orange light on her. The men shoved her forward, and pushed her to her knees before the man.

"Who are you?" she demanded.

"I am Dreighton, I rule here, and you are now to be my subject."

"As if," she spat. "I'd never bow to a criminal like you."

"Oh, this one has spunk. She might suffice after all."

"Suffice for what?" she spat.

"My son needs a strong hand, by his side. You will make a grand wife, once we tame you."

"Only one man can claim me as his wife," she shouted, straightening her shoulders. "And he is a greater man then you could ever be. If your son is twice the man you are, he will never be the man for me!"

"That boy who was with you? He'll die in that cell, if you wish to challenge me."

"Ha!" Marni laughed, hoping to build a bluff they could not ignore. "Not him. That boy is feeble, no threat to anybody."

She rose to her feet, and slowly straightened her cloak. Pushing the hood down to her shoulders, Marni released her long hair, to flow down her back, concealing the ranger emblem.

"My Fletcher will rip the head from your shoulders without ever raising his hands to your throat. That's the power you face. That's the power you anger."

"You jest! No person could do such a thing," one of the men snarled, stepping up beside Dreighton. "We will tame you, then we will kill him, when he comes for you."

"So you are the son?" Marni sneered. "As feeble as the old man then. Wait, no, feebler. I reject you."

She turned her back on the pair, with an audible humph of exasperation. She used the ploy to survey the room, spying two dozen others, mostly children, beside the four men who had brought her in. A few around her own age, all looked thin, malnourished. She turned back to face them again.

"Your people are weak," she snarled. "They look barely fed, yet you think I could be tamed and forced to live here? Your house is a house of cards, and it will fall soon enough. Your delusions, while grandiose, are as feeble as your minds."

"Your bravado is misplaced. We are not your enemy. There will be no escape. The sooner you welcome us as your new family, the happier your life will be."

"I will never welcome scum like you. And as soon as I find out what you did to our flames, I will have my revenge. You have doused my fire, but she will return, and when she does, I will burn you where you sit."

"What are you rambling about, girl?" Dreighton snarled.

"You burned that herb, and made us inhale that smoke."

"It awakens the ice, it causes the white sparks to form in those so disposed, and allows them to ice. All those who come here are treated with the same methods. Some of them learn to ice, the others become our workers."

"Then what about this?" she shouted, and held her hands out before her. "I am a powerful green flame, from the ranger academy in Emberdale. But you smoked me with your herbs, and now, my flames are quiet. What did you do?"

As she spoke, she focused her energy, and launched bright green sparks between her hands, and that was all. No flames burst forth.

"What is this? Green sparks? It's like the ice wielders, only green!" the man beside Dreighton said. "Father, what is the meaning of this?"

"She is unique, after all," Dreighton said. "Return her to her cell. If she is a flame ranger as she claims, and her cloak implies she is, we may have use of her regardless of her boasts."

"No!" Marni shouted. "You will tell me the truth!"

"I feel it is you with a truth to tell," Dreighton said softly. "We use the herbs to awaken the ice, that is all. Your green flames are a fire and fire can always be snuffed out by a blizzard. That is all there is to it. You are in company which is stronger than you. All four officers who escort you wield ice. Try anything, and I will not blame them for your demise. You will welcome us in time, and join my son by my side. If not, you can die in that cell, with your feeble friend."

Chapter 12 – Dreighton's Mine

Treghan practised, and slowly felt the frost on the bars grow into ice, then continue on into greater depth. Turning, he face the area behind him, away from the bars, and performed the same thing, opening his eyes to see a swirling vortex of ice and wind before him.

It was small, and not powerful, but it was a mighty storm in his eyes, when his flames had deserted him. Eyes open, he looked at his hands, and focused his energy. The sparks were brighter, and larger than before.

"Maybe that smoke is wearing off," he muttered. "or maybe the ice is helping me break free of it."

He focused his energy again, and this time he managed a tiny white flame, like the flame of a candle. Smiling, he returned to the bars, and used the flame to melt the ice away. As he worked, the flame grew, and soon was like it had been when first he attained it, before he had practised enough to work properly without borrowing energy from Corilai.

Satisfied, Treghan walked back to the wall opposite the bars and sat down, to rest for a brief while and wait for the child to return. Then, he would decide on his next move.

Shortly after he sat down, he heard the sound of several feet coming toward him. He looked up and watched as the four men led Marni back to the cell, opened the gate, and pushed her inside.

"Stay there, you can be feeble together for a while," one of the men snarled, as he locked the cell, then turned to leave, the others following as he strode off into the dim passage.

When they were out of sight, she walked to Treghan, and sat beside him.

"Well, that was fun," she mumbled. "These guys are pathetic. And they think I'll marry one of them."

"Idiots. Did you learn anything?"

"Yes, they're not that strong. The people are mostly just kids, and they are way underfed. The idiot in charge is called Dreighton. One of those megalomaniacs who thinks they can rule the world, but can't even feed their own people."

"Great. Those are the dangerous, delusional ones," Treghan said. "What about that smoke? You find out anything?"

"They don't seem to know what it does to flames. They kept rambling about it awakening the ice."

"That makes sense," Treghan said.

"Why? What do you mean?"

"I learned something as well, he said, raising his hands and conjuring a blast of icy sleet, then blasting it away with a strong white flame."

"What the..." Marni squealed, jumping to her feet. "How did you do that?"

"It's my secondary ability," Treghan said, with a shrug. "By using it, I cleared the fog from the smoke, and my flames are returning."

"But how? White's don't have a secondary! Not that we've ever heard of. Everybody knows that."

"Everybody was wrong," Treghan said. "I spoke to a child, must have been about eight, and he already had white sparks. He said the smoke did that, that it awakens the ice, and they know who can ice because they have the white sparks. It's not much to put two and two together and figure it out."

"Not for a ranger at least," Marni replied. "But these people know nothing about flames or rangers."

"We should keep it that way," Treghan said. "Hey, have you tried using your secondary since we were captured?"

"No, I just assumed with my flames gone..."

"Then stop assuming. I think the smoke pushes the secondary out by suppressing the flame, in which case..."

"In which case," she said, standing and growing excited. "My secondary should be stronger now!"

"What's a secondary?" said a small voice.

Marni jumped, and span around to see the child outside the cell.

"Did you get the key?" Treghan asked.

"I'm sorry, I couldn't get it. But what's a secondary?"

Treghan stood and walked over to the bars.

"Don't worry. A secondary is something all flame rangers can learn, and it's different for each colour of flame. The ice is the secondary for white flames. It's normally something you only learn after years of wielding flames. But with the ice, it's different, if you use the smoke."

"I see. So that means, you have a different skill?" the child gasped, staring at Marni in awe.

"Yes, and if the smoke has made it stronger, while it suppressed my green flames, I should have us out of here in a moment. Treghan, can you make us some water, using your ice ability?"

"You learned to ice? Already?" the boy gasped.

"Of course, I said I would, didn't I?"

"But how? Who are you people?"

"We're flame rangers," Marni said. "We're stronger than these mine dwelling fools could ever imagine. Once Treghan knew what the ice was, that it was his secondary, well, he's already had the training to master it, once he knew it existed. Of course he would learn it in mere hours. Now, stand back, I have to break these bars down."

Marni pulled out her seed bag, and rummaged until she found a proud acorn. Half burying it in the dust at the floor, near the gate, she looked up at Treghan.

"I've never grown one of these before, but if the smoke has enhanced my secondary, it might do the job. Give me some water, please."

Treghan formed a swirling cloud of ice in the air, and she held her hands beneath it. He slowed it down then stopped, the moisture in the air dropping to the ground, a small amount landing in her upturned hands.

"Thank you," Marni said, turning and drizzling the water over the acorn. "Now, stand back, child."

Marni focused her energy on the seed, and at first nothing happened. After several seconds, it cracked, and a sprout began to grow.

"Treghan, give it some light, please."

Treghan stood beside her and kindled a proud white flame. The child gasped, and the light fell upon the seed, bathing it in the warmth of life. The sprout grew fast, and soon climbed tall against the bars, and broadened. Roots snaked out into the rocky ground, and across the floor, ripping through the stone as the tree grew. Soon they spread wide and bent the bars outward. The tree's limbs reached the low ceiling and grew along it.

"Marni," Treghan said. "You're incredible!"

As the tree grew broader, the roots ran along the floor, uprooting the bars. The branches thrust along the ceiling, ripping bars down as the lock popped open, unable to resist the broadening trunk of the mighty oak tree, impossibly grown in the belly of the mountain. Soon, the bars began to fall, as they were ripped away. Once the gap opened enough to allow them to squeeze through, Marni stopped, and turned to smile at Treghan.

"That felt amazing!" she said. "I never knew my secondary could feel so powerful!"

"Can you flame now?" Treghan asked.

She held her hands out, and a tall green flame lept out of her palms, casting its light all around them.

"Good," Treghan said. "Let's get out of here. You coming, kid?"

"Yes Sir!" the child said, as he backed away to let them through and into the passage. "But we should run. That thing made a lot of noise as the bars broke. Follow me, we'll go to the junior barracks, they won't look for you there."

* * *

Symin looked over his troops, arrayed outside the gates of Windwall, ready to depart. Fifty rangers had arrived from Emberdale that morning, and now stood before him, Loka by his side, waiting for the command to move out.

"Men," he shouted. "We go out today, to face children. They are not to come to harm. If any attempt to fight, you are to subdue them peacefully, to be returned to their families."

The citizens of Windwall, standing atop the walls, nodded their approval. Symin cast his gaze over his people before continuing.

"Any adults you encounter, are to be considered the enemy. They are the criminal we truly face, the kidnappers responsible for this mission. You are to treat them as such, and face them with the full force of justice. No mercy is needed in facing such cowards as these men and women who would steal children from their beds."

Some of the citizens cheered at his words, but Symin ignored them as he went on.

"We know little of their power. We have intelligence that hints at an ability unlike anything we know, but no hint that they have flames with which to fight us. Take care, we do not know yet how many or how strong we will face. But we know we have an advantage. You are all strong men and women with great discipline and ability. Draw on all of that this day, as we go to rescue the children of Windwall!"

The rangers cheered, and the citizens joined them, the thunderous roar of the crowd echoing back from the mountains. Loka stepped forward, and waited for silence.

"These criminals have taken two of our own. If we find their base, we must search it thoroughly, and be sure to return them home. If we do not, we must continue to search for them until we do. Should we find anybody who has escaped the criminals, we must return with them to Windwall that they may be given whatever help they require, but then depart immediately to continue the mission. We will all be living in the frozen highlands from this moment until the mission is at an end. Are we clear?"

"Yes, Ranger!" the rangers shouted in unison.

"Rangers," Symin shouted. "Move out!"

The long column of rangers on horseback and carts full of supplies was an impressive sight as it moved away from the city, and into the highlands. Soon, it was no longer visible from the city walls, and Symin saw the clouds forming low over the highlands. Still, he pushed on.

"We will camp if we must, but we go on as long as we can," he said. "Loka, do we have anybody familiar with this road?"

"No, Sir," she replied. "It is a road used only by the local miners and farmers. There is little out this side of the city and no reason for anybody other than those who live and work in this direction to ever use the road."

"Then we follow the road as far as it will take us. Be mindful for any sign of a trail leading away from the highway. Chances are they are not on this road, but rather somewhere more hidden, that they can hide from our view for so long."

As they crossed the immense wooden decked bridge, a stiff wind began to blow, and still Symin urged them forward. They continued beyond the cave where the students had sought shelter, and on past the twin obelisks, but then, the weather snapped, and the wind became a driving sleet.

The drop to one side was treacherous, and the visibility almost completely gone, when finally Symin barked an order to camp. The wagons and carts were pulled into a circle at a wider point on the road, and tents strung between them. A fire was lit at the centre, to warm the tents against the icy winds.

Tarpaulins were pegged around the outside of the circle, covering the carts and wagons. They dropped to the ground where they were pegged with sturdy steel spikes to block the wind. In quick order, the well trained group had themselves set up, and crowded into the shelter, to ride out the storm.

"I hope we can travel further than that between camps," Symin moaned as he surveyed his people.

"We just got unlucky," Loka replied, touching his arm encouragingly. "We'll get further into the highlands tomorrow. The weather here is probably worse with the wind being driven along that canyon at the bridge. With luck, the road will be more sheltered as we go deeper into the highlands."

"We can't know that. The highlands are not well travelled, and not well known, except by those who live in them."

"The locals always know best," Loka said. "But rangers are resourceful. We'll tackle this mission like we always do. Quickly and professionally. Have faith in your people."

* * *

"Will there be anybody in your junior barracks now?" Treghan asked as the boy led them deep into the mines.

"No, they should all be out working by now. Might be a new one or two, but we can get them to keep quiet."

"What's your name, child?" Marni asked.

"I'm Lonay."

"Well, it's good to meet you, Lonay. I am Marni, and this is Treghan."

"How long have you been here, Lonay?" Treghan asked.

"I've always been here. My father is one of the four fathers of the families who have always worked these mines."

"So why are you helping us?"

"Everybody's hungry here. If I can go to the academy one day, and eat better food, then I'll make a better life there."

"Is that why you're free to wander around the mines?" Marni asked. "Because you're one of the original family members?"

"Yes. The others can't ever walk around unsupervised like I do. Not until they get older and the fathers trust them."

"I see," Treghan said. "They really are prisoners."

"I guess," Lonay said. "Quiet, we're almost there."

"How old are you?" Marni asked.

"I'm ten," Lonay said. "I know I look younger. I've never had good food like you, so I didn't grow well. But quiet!"

They stopped in the darkness, before an intersection in the passage. Light shone into the intersection from both directions.

"The guards sometimes hang around to the right, the barracks is to the left," Lonay whispered. "Wait here."

Lonay walked ahead and disappeared around the corner to the right. Shortly they heard muffled voices, but couldn't make out what was said. After a short while, Lonay returned.

"They're gone now," Lonay said.

"What did you tell them?"

"I said my father was looking for somebody, but I didn't know who it was. They rushed off to join the search. Those older boys will do anything to earn the favour of the fathers. I guess when they get closer to twenty, they start to think they should be men or something."

Lonay led the way to the intersection, then left, and into the junior barracks. Bunks were packed together tight into the small room, four high and end to end in three rows twelve deep. They were smaller than a bed should be, but allowed for many children to be housed in the tiny space.

The air was stale and smelled like soiled sheets. A shaft in the ceiling ran to the surface, a dim pinprick of light showing just how deep into the mountain they were. Water dripped down to form a puddle in the centre of the floor. At the far end of the room, a child cried, her sobs soft and miserable.

"Who's there?" Marni said softly. "It's alright, we won't hurt you. We're friends. We're here to help you."

"Marni?" the child said. "Marni? It is you!"

The little girl ran to her, and grabbed her, burying her face in Marni's cloak.

Instinctively, Marni embraced the frightened child, looking down as the child turned her face upwards. Marni gasped.

"Ivy! I never dreamed we'd find you so soon. It's OK, we'll get you out of here."

"But my brother! We have to save him before we go. I already found him, but the guards caught me. They hit me so hard! But my brother is working in the mines, because they said he was no good for anything else."

"We'll save him and all the others," Treghan said. "But first, we need to get ourselves, and you, to safety. We should return with the rangers. Symin will know how to handle this."

Chapter 13 – First Break Out

The shouts of furious men echoed deep into the mines, along with the stomping noise of many running feet. The tree had been discovered, already. Treghan looked at the others.

"OK, We can't get out now. We need a better place to hide."

"If we can get deeper," Lonay said. "There's a reservoir. It's just a natural cave, so there are lots of deep alcoves. You could freeze over the end of one, since you can ice now."

"Can we get there without running into any of the guards?" Marni asked.

"I think so. Follow me."

Lonay led them out of the barracks and into the mine's twisting passages. They soon were lost, but Lonay continued on, confident and unfaltering in his direction.

"How did you learn your way around this place?" Ivy whispered.

"I've always lived here. It's the only place I know, so I know it better than anybody."

Soon, they found themselves in an area where no torches lit the way, so Treghan lit his white flame, strong again now, and they continued. Echoing from the walls, they still heard the sound of the guards searching for them.

They almost did not notice when the sounds faded away. Then they were surrounded. Suddenly torches were lit and a group of six men had them trapped.

"Lonay! You led us to a trap!" Ivy screamed.

"You've betrayed your father for the last time, Lonay!" one of the men growled, swinging a ham sized fist at the boy.

Treghan deftly stepped between them, deflecting the blow before firing a short bolt of white fire into the man's chest. His tunic smouldered for a moment as he stepped back, dazed.

Not intimidated, two others lunged at Treghan, and his white flames met them. Strong, and tall, wrapping their heads in thirsty heat. The two men screamed and ran, their hair smouldering from the attack. The others broke ranks to follow, but not before one of them turned to shout.

"We'll be back, and you'll all be dead. I don't care who thinks she'd make a good wife, or whose son he is, we'll kill you all!"

"Well that decides it, I can't stay here now," Lonay moaned. "Follow me."

They ventured through the mines for a long time, until they finally entered a chamber where ice caked the walls and the sound of dripping water was never ending.

"If you block up an alcove here, we can hide there as long as we need to, at least, until they stop looking so hard."

"Yeah, and freeze to death!" Ivy quipped.

"We'll hide here till morning, but then we have to find a way out." Treghan insisted. "I know it's a risk, but we'll find a way."

He walked into a nearby alcove, with ice on its walls, and played a white flame over the frozen rock, melting the ice.

"Get in here," he demanded, and the others did as he said.

Treghan then used the water he had melted to form the basis of his wall, and slowly built up a barrier of solid ice over the opening of the alcove.

"How did you do that?" Marni whispered in awe.

"It's nothing special, just more of that same ice wielding stuff I showed you before. I figured if I had water as a base instead of the vapour in the air, it would form ice faster."

"It's amazing that you learned that so fast," Lonay said. "But our ice wielders can do that in a second or two, so you're still no match for them."

"I'd better keep practising, then," Treghan replied. "What do they use that for, if they're so good at it?"

"They conceal the roads leading to the mine, and all the entrances. No ranger or city guard snooping around will ever find this place."

* * *

The rangers followed Symin as he led the way along the treacherous mountain road, winding further into the highlands. They found several smaller tracks leading into the wilderness, and each time they sent a scout party along to investigate. So far, they had found nothing but ice drifts, cliffs, and the occasional desperate wild animal.

The road was getting worse as they made their way deeper into the forbidding highlands. The sparse population of the region, which was by now safely nestled inside Windwall until spring, had not grown larger for obvious reasons. In the several hundred year history of Cinder, nobody had ever crossed the highlands to see what lay on the other side.

The stone road was now giving way to mud, and slushy, dirty snow drifts as the westward journey reached the furthest limits of known habitation. They rumbled into a clearing where the road seemed to end, surrounded by huts and backing onto a quarry, cut from a mountain side.

Symin stopped, and turned his horse to face the rangers, as they filed into the area.

"We camp here," Symin ordered. "And begin more detailed searches back along the trail, as well as in the surrounding wilderness."

The carts were pulled into a circle again, and the same method they had used previously employed to provide a shelter from the wind and snow. Symin instructed the rangers to set the camp adjacent to one of the huts, which was clearly a well constructed stable, so the horses could be placed there, saving some room in the shelter for them to spread themselves out more than they usually could.

Symin walked around the perimeter, observing the drift of snow flowing through the quarry, and the worsening condition of the road they had travelled in on. He stopped, watching as the evening set in. Loka found him there, and brought him out of his reverie by placing a hand on his shoulder.

"Sir, we should retire to the camp."

"Of course, Loka," he replied, placing his hand over hers.

"Sir, what were you thinking about?"

"That road. If it gets much worse, we may not be able to get the carts out of here."

"There's plenty of rock, we could fix it," she said, not entirely serious.

"That's a good idea," Symin said, seizing on the thought.

"No," Loka said. "Sir, we don't have time to build roads."

"No, I don't suppose we do," he replied. "But there will be many barrow loads of loose rocks, gravel and shattered off cuts from the quarry. We should spread them across the road, it will make the road more passable than the mud which is there now."

"Yes, Sir."

* * *

Nearly ten hours had passed when Treghan stepped up to the icy barrier, rested his hand on its chilly surface, and willed it to dissolve. Not looking back, he led the way into the darkness, listening for any sound of nearby guards, before lighting a small white flame to guide them.

"Are you sure we should go so soon?" Marni whispered.

"We have to get out of here," Treghan replied. "And we can't stay down here in the dark going hungry, or we'll never get out."

They slowly made their way through the mine, Lonay leading the way. Soon the group passed the first of the torches lighting the mines, indicating a more used area. Twice, they heard people nearby and hid themselves in the darkness as guards and children passed by.

"How much further?" Marni whispered.

"Not far now," Lonay said. "We've got about another fifteen minutes before we reach one of the less used exits from the mine. It will be sealed with ice, but Treghan can take care of that."

They continued, avoiding other people until they turned into a well lit passageway. It ran at a steep incline, straight to an ice cap at the surface, dim light seeping through the frozen barrier from outside.

"We have to get through that before we're seen," Treghan said. "But it's lit up like a festival in the city. Run! The longer we take, the more chance of getting caught."

Together, they ran as fast as they could. Ivy soon lagged behind, her young legs not up to the pace, so Marni scooped her up as Treghan hung back, watching the passage behind them. It looked like they could make it, as they finally reached the last sprint before the blocked exit.

"Hey! What are you doing there?" came a bellowed voice, followed by several sets of footsteps echoing up the passage.

"Treghan, quickly!" Lonay said.

Treghan lit a white flame, and hit the ice with all he had. At first, nothing happened, but then Marni threw her own, green flame at the barrier, and together their flames were enough. The ice cracked, then exploded outwards, as the flames burst through in a searing, steaming blast of heat.

"Run!" Treghan shouted, pushing Marni and Ivy through the opening, then watching as Lonay followed them.

Turning, Treghan hurled white fire down the passage. A ferocious blast of icy wind, sleet worse than he had experienced anywhere in the highlands, smacked Treghan in the face, stunning him for just an instant, before he followed his friends into the open.

They found themselves on a tiny, winding track in the mountains, a steep drop to one side, and foreboding cliffs on the other. Treghan looked back into the passage as a second icy blast struck him.

"Run!" Treghan yelled, waving his hands in the air to form a shield of ice as a third blast buffeted his improvised barrier.

Abandoning the shield, he ran after his friends, who were already making their way along the trail. He glanced back, and saw four young men, guards from the mines, approaching at a speed he did not dare copy on the treacherous path.

Lonay was leading the way, Marni behind him, carrying Ivy, and Treghan realised they were too slow to escape. Facing the enemy, he hit them with a mighty blast of fire. When it cleared, a shield of ice stood on the trail, and the four men were safe behind it. Then that shield seemed to be obliterated from behind, to form a driving barrage of icy shards.

Treghan barely erected his own shield in time to deflect the frozen assault, and breath a heavy sigh of relief when none broke through. Leaving the barrier in place, he turned and strode towards his friends, hoping to reach them before building a new barrier.

Treghan heard an enormous crack, as something hit his ice barrier, then felt intense pain, glancing to his right to see a long, deadly spear of ice pierce his shoulder. He screamed, as the momentum of the weapon carried him from the path, and into the ravine below.

"Treghan!" Marni screamed, before his head struck the snow bank, and he rolled, the spear snapping and his blood pouring from the wound.

Treghan soon felt consciousness leaving him, and briefly wondered if he would die here? Would his friends from Emberdale ever find Marni, before the unthinkable happened to her as well? He stared death in the face as the darkness took him, muttering to himself and the snow.

"This is not the end. This can't be."

* * *

The rangers had packed dozens of barrow loads of gravel into the mud, and now the road was more forgiving than it had been, but still they questioned the activity.

"Why are we wasting time? I thought we were here to find the kidnapped children," a young ranger moaned.

"Ranger!" Symin snapped, "How will we make hundreds of children travel along this mud, if we find them today?"

"I... I mean,"

"Exactly. We have a great task before us, and the more of this work we do, the more the residents of the highlands will appreciate our efforts when they return in the spring. But in the mean time, we have a duty to make sure our charges experience as little hardship as possible, once we find them. If they have to put up with trudging through that muck, or sitting in bogged carts while they slowly freeze to death, we will have failed utterly in our sworn duty as protectors of all the citizens of Cinder."

"They live out here already, Sir," the ranger said. "Can we really make any difference?"

"We have to try. We have to show them that the people of Windwall want them to come home, and that the rangers will look after them. We have no idea what they face daily with their kidnappers, but we have to be sure they can see that our efforts are not a half hearted attempt. That we are determined to see them returned to their families, and to safety. I want every person who might see us here, to believe we are here for the long haul, and will not give in until all the children have been saved."

* * *

Treghan felt the ground moving beneath him, and struggled to open his eyes. He could see feet, clothed in fur lined boots, trudging in the snow beside him. Then, as his addled brain began to process things, he realised he was strapped to a wooden sled, being pulled by three young highlanders.

Two others walked either side of the sled. Treghan glanced at his shoulder, and saw that it was bandaged, then laid his head back down, and let the darkness of unconsciousness take him again.

Some time later, Treghan awoke again, and felt the warmth of a fire at his side. He opened his eyes, and saw he was now on an animal skin rug, before a stone hearth in a sturdy wooden cabin. He moaned, and tried to sit up, causing intense pain to shoot through his wounded shoulder.

"Hush, young one," said a kindly voice.

Treghan turned his head, searching for the owner of the voice, and finally saw the woman, a comely lass in her twenties. She approached him with a bowl of warm tea, made from a grass of the mountains. Its unforgettable aroma was still new to Treghan, but he recognised it immediately as something he had smelled often during his time in Windwall.

Kneeling beside him, the woman held the bowl to his lips, and Treghan drank without question. The warmth was good as it flowed through him, and he smiled his thanks to his benefactor.

"Where am I?" he asked.

"Hush, young one. You were gravely wounded by the men of the mines. This village is called Bhenar. You must rest now. There will be time for questions later."

"Who are you?"

"My name is Rona. I am the medicine woman and leader of this village. And you, you are a ranger, though a very young one. There is a mighty story in you."

"A story?" Treghan said. "Well, I guess I've seen some things, but I'm nobody special."

"Ha!" Rona laughed. "The greatest of men are nobody before they are great. But I sense there is greatness already within you, young one. Otherwise, you would not be already garbed as a ranger and alone, wounded, so deep in the highlands of my people."

"You live here, all year around?"

"Of course. Nobody who is truly of the highlands leaves the highlands when the winter comes. We survive in comfort, but there are those who abuse the kindness of mother mountain, like Dreighton in his mine. We trade with Windwall, and hear stories of the rest of Cinder. But we rarely travel outside of the mountains."

"I did not know there were villages here."

"There are villages everywhere, young one." Rona said.

"Have you ever been to the other side of the highlands? Are there villages there? Outside of Cinder?"

"I told you, we rarely leave the highlands. But I know of nobody who has gone to the western side. I do not believe it is possible for our people. However, if there is land beyond the frozen wastes, then there will be villages there as well."

"Frozen wastes?"

"The western most boundary of the highlands is the frozen wastes. A mighty plateau of snow and ice, with constant, never ending wind, blizzards the like of which no man of Cinder could survive."

"Is that why nobody ever crossed the highlands and returned?"

"Yes, just as there is the sulphurous desert to the south, and the turbulent maelstroms of the ocean to the east, which curve with the land to the north to meet the edge of the highlands, there is the Frozen Waste to the west, and between those barriers, Cinder remains forever apart from the world. But you, a ranger, would know this already."

"Yes, though I had only considered the highlands the barrier, not a single part of them."

"That would make sense, for people who have never ventured here. Most of cinder would not know of us, just as there are men on the islands of the east who know more of the maelstroms than any other in Cinder. And of course, the people of Horde would know more of the Desert of Souls than anybody else in Cinder. Indeed, it is said those who know that desert, know the truth, and are the only citizens with the answers to everything about Cinder."

"Are their villages in the Desert of Souls then?"

"I do not believe so," Rona replied. "I believe the city of Horde is the only surviving settlement in that part of the world. But I hear tales that once, there was a greater city than any in Cinder. And it holds the key to our history, and the mystery of all life on this land. The desert holds its secrets close, so all we have are stories. The stories told around camp fires, or by grandmothers to children at bedtime. But even they tell us more than we know."

"What do you know of Dreighton?" Treghan asked.

"I know that he is evil. That he is stealing children from all over these highlands. I know that our own sons and daughters were taken by his men, and that one day, I will have my revenge."

Chapter 14 – Highlanders

Marni stood before Dreighton, head bowed slightly, her hood drawn over her head, obscuring her eyes. Ivy clutched to her ranger's cloak on the left, and to her right, bloodied and bruised, stood Lonay, shaking uncontrollably after the beating he had received from the guards for his betrayal.

A heavy steel shackle, clasped to her ankle, was chained to the floor of the chamber. The same was true of both children.

"I'm not a monster, you know," Dreighton said.

"My experience has shown me, if a person has to tell me that, it's a lie," Marni snarled. "Look at this boy, he's like that because of you. Only a monstrous coward would sanction such a thing."

"Be reasonable, young lady," Dreighton said. "I can not control the minds of my men."

"But you can punish their deeds. If you ignore them, you condone them. You are a monster by proxy of your men, even if you are too cowardly to hit the boy yourself."

"Enough!" Dreighton snarled, standing and marching to face her.

With a single, brisk movement, he snatched the hood back, to reveal her face. The enormous, blackening bruise around her right eye spoke of the moment she had intervened with Dreighton's men, in trying to save Lonay from his punishment. Dreighton whirled on his heels to face the three guards.

"Who has dared lay their hand on my son's future bride?" he yelled.

One of the guards stepped forward, his hands raised. Dreighton, in a whirlwind of fury, struck the man and set him sprawling on the ground, before laying his boot into the man's gut. Satisfied, Dreighton returned to face Marni.

"You see?" he whispered. "I will punish my men for abuse. But abuse and punishment are not the same thing. I'm not a monster, but a leader must choose his path with care."

"A great leader will not condone the beating of a child," Marni said, her voice steady and calm. "Not for punishment, or abuse. There is no line between the two. Only a coward would mince his words to wriggle away from his responsibility. You are, and always will be, a monster."

"Enough!" Dreighton shouted. "Your boyfriend is gone, dead in that ravine. You will never escape again. You will come to call us family in time. And then, you will I believe still make a fine wife for my son, and a fine mother for my grandchildren. Your skills will benefit our dynasty."

"It will never happen!" Marni shouted.

"It will," Dreighton said. "But first, I would know how you wove your evil spell, that you could create a mighty tree in the dark of your cell. You will speak, witch!"

"I already told you. If you're too stupid to figure it out, then why don't you go drown in that damned reservoir we pissed in?" Marni snarled, hoping the lie was enough to rile him even more. "You hide here underground, like an animal, and think you have power? I've seen power, and it isn't here."

"You will do as you are told, insolent girl!"

"No, I will do as I see is right," she replied. "And you will never prevail. Rangers are strong, our skills are varied, and you can never prepare yourself for the assault which is coming. Your days in these mountains are numbered, Dreighton the mole."

"Silence!" he shouted. "Guards! I will take my meal now. She is to go hungry, along with those two. The females will remain here, so I can keep an eye on her. Only when she shares her secrets, is she to be fed."

* * *

"How is it you know so much about the world?" Treghan asked. "Given you don't leave the highlands."

"I trade stories with the merchant caravans. They will return in the spring, and the recent events of the outside world will be told."

"I see. But I can tell you some things, if you would like."

"Agreed," Rona said. "Your stories will be your payment for your accommodation, and your food, and your healing. You had best be sure they are good stories."

"I think they will be. A lot has happened in the last year, and I was there for some big events."

"That is promising. And you, you have the outlook of a ranger. It will differ greatly from the perspective of the merchants. They will likely tell me the same stories, however their view will differ, so the value of your opinion is great."

"Why do you value the stories so much?"

"Knowledge is power. The power to avoid calamity, when it has struck others. The power to learn from the mistakes of the world, and to know when to hide away, and when to reach out. If we know of the world, we can be prepared for whatever it may send to bother us in our mountain homes."

"What would you like to hear?" Treghan asked.

"Begin at the beginning," Rona said.

"I lived in the village of Judd, with my brother, and my parents. He was a flame wielder, but I was unable to match his skill..."

Treghan went on, speaking for hours, and she listened, as he told her of his flight from Judd, how he met Corilai, and they in turn were taken by Yuri's men. At each new place, she stopped him, and asked him about it. The smells, the scenery, the types of trees, what the weather was like. She drew from him details he barely realised he had, and after what felt like an eternity, as he told her of the escape from Grey, when he and Corilai had ridden the horses out of the city and headed north, she stopped him.

"It is time for the evening meal, and the tradition here is that I give a sermon to the people. I will give them a taste of your story, in a sermon about leaders, and talk of this man Yuri, and the danger he brings."

"But Yuri is gone now," Treghan said.

"You misunderstand. The danger is in falling prey to his greed, his lust for power. Thank you, you have given me a new story. Now come."

As he stood, Rona fetched a warm fur and placed it around his shoulders.

"Your ranger garb is not sufficient to warm your wound, and the winter is cold in these highlands. Follow me."

She led him out of the house, and he turned to look at it, larger than he had expected. Three chimneys puffed smoke from warming fires in different rooms of the sturdy stone dwelling.

They walked through streets of a large settlement, Treghan guessed twice the size of the village of Judd, where he grew up. All the buildings, made from carved stone, stood strong and proud against the icy winds, their steep rooftops shunning the snow, as it piled on the ground beside them.

The front entrances were on the flat end of the building, so the snow was not deposited over the doors, but it piled high between the homes, as the steep sloped rooftops caused it to cascade into the lanes and alleys where it would remain until the villagers either dug it out, or spring thawed it.

"Will that snow be a problem in spring?" Treghan asked.

"No, these are called the Everwinter Highlands for a reason. The snow will not melt as fast as it would elsewhere. But it will fall less, what does melt will run through drainage we have prepared behind the homes, and in that time we will clear out the rest, ready for the next cold season."

As they crossed to the opposite end of the village, a communal long house came into view. Treghan could see many people walking to it and entering.

"What is that place?" he asked.

"It's the village hall," Rona said. "We have daily meals there. We also hold any important meetings, weddings, funerals, all those sorts of things there. Everybody in the village is expected to attend, unless they are bedridden with illness or injury. It helps keep the village together, because we can see each other, and know if somebody is having troubles, so we can help each other out in the hard times. Better to be together, than live by each others sides and be forever alone."

"That makes sense," Treghan said. "I suppose living somewhere as hostile as this, it means if somebody doesn't show up, you can go to their house and find out what has happened to them."

"It is true. There are stories of other places. Other villages. Where the dead are not discovered till the spring, trapped in their houses, when they could have lived another season if only they had been found sooner."

"What about those others? The bedridden ones?" Treghan asked.

"It is another of my duties. After the sermon and the meal, I must carry their meals to them, and check on their well being. Often, they have family who would take a meal to them, but sometimes a family feels pride which hinders them admitting that the welfare of a person is poor. So I am required by the law of this village to attend to them all, daily."

As they spoke, they had reached the village hall, and she led him inside. Long tables ran the length of the building on either side, and a short table sat on a platform at the far end. Rona led him there, and indicated he should take the seat to the left. A young woman and an elderly man sat at the far end, and Rona sat beside Treghan.

Teenagers began to bring out plates of food, and every villager had the same meal placed before them. They were quick about their task, and then brought out large pitchers of herb flavoured water, which were placed along the tables. A small wooden cup was placed in front of each seat, before the teenagers found their places along the tables, and sat.

Rona stood, and raised a hand high.

"In thanks to the mountains which keep us, I bid you eat, before the chill steals the warmth from your food."

She sat, as the villagers ate, and looked at Treghan.

"Eat, young ranger. When the food is gone, I will give the sermon, it keeps the villagers still while the food settles, and after that, they are free to raise any questions or complaints they have about events in the village."

The hall was quiet for some time, aside from occasional whispered words among the villagers. When the majority had finished their meals, and were talking softly amongst themselves while drinking the flavoured water, Rona stood.

"Friends, we have with us a guest, whom some have already seen. A young ranger, who was found wounded in the snow, as a consequence of crossing paths with Dreighton's men."

Several villagers booed the name of the ruler of the mines. Rona ignored them, and continued.

"This young man, scarcely old enough to avoid the serving tasks in this place, has already seen more of the world than most outsiders even see in their lifetimes. He has a great many stories to tell, and a great many more still to live."

All eyes were on her, no sound apart from the occasional sipping of the water.

"From some of what he has told me already, I bring you today's sermon, for it is one which is always important, in all times and all places."

She paused long enough to take a drink of water, then continued.

"We are lucky indeed, here in this village. We are all equal, we all are heard, seen and supported as members of one community. There are no elite here. But we need not look far to find places where this is not the case. We all know of the men in the mines, who have spent these past many months abducting children from all over the highlands. We know they work under one man, a tyrant named Dreighton."

The villagers booed the name again, louder this time.

"But today I will speak of a different tyrant. One whose name was Yuri, and who this young man had a hand in deposing, bringing liberty to the city of Grey, which sits on the coast far to the south and east of here. Yuri was a man who rose to power through violence. He sought to use his might to rule over an entire city, in order that he become wealthy and powerful, to the detriment of his people. And he managed to do exactly that, for a long time."

Rona took another drink, looking at Treghan as she did so.

"But Yuri's greed was still not satisfied. He sought to expand his dominion to the surrounding areas, and hoped eventually to rule over all of Cinder. Perhaps he may have succeeded, if he had not bitten off more than he could chew, when he abducted this young man, and his friend."

Some of the younger villagers gasped, immediately realising the similarities to Dreighton.

"You see, Yuri was hunting for those with the ability to wield flames, as the rangers do. But he did not want rangers. Instead he wanted those who were not yet recruited to the law keepers of our world. He wanted to capture and enslave those who did not have powerful connections, who would be indebted to him for the protection of their loved ones."

She paused again, and Treghan sensed it was as much for effect as to catch her breath. All the villagers were listening intently to her words as she spoke in a voice which led the listener in ways Treghan had never witnessed. This woman had power, and it was more than just the words.

"Yuri placed threats over the families of the young flame wielders, but when some of those he took had no love for their homes, but similarly had no love for enslavement, finally a weakness in his plot was revealed. When those young people returned to face him, they brought with them an army of rangers, all highly trained and skilled flame wielders, and Yuri fell. Not because they attacked him directly, but because they quickly won the hearts and minds of his people, by seeking to free his slaves, and to rescue his prisoners."

Another pause, and this time she smiled. Slowly, Rona looked around the room, allowing her eyes to fall on every man, woman and child in the room.

"They were a community, connected and strong, even while they were oppressed. The people of Grey never lost sight of who they were, and when the moment came, rose in defiance of the tyrant Yuri. He was brought down by the rangers, but it was the community, the people, who allowed that to happen. In our little world, we have Dreighton, and he has many of our children, but in time, we too shall rise, and take back that which was stolen from us, and Dreighton will fall. He is a little man. A small tyrant in a hole in the ground. If the people of Grey could see the end of Yuri, who had ambitions to enslave all of Cinder, then so we, too, can see the end of Dreighton!"

The villagers cheered as Rona smiled, and sat. Treghan looked at her.

"Rona," he whispered. "I never told you about how Yuri was overthrown."

"No, but that part of the story I have already heard," Rona explained. "From the merchants. They told me your story, from a different perspective, Treghan the white flame. I wish I could have seen the moment you rode atop that cage, with the tyrant in chains. It must have been an awesome sight."

* * *

Marni sat on the cold, stone floor of Dreighton's audience chamber, Ivy curled up against her side. The child shook occasionally with fear as the men of the mines barked out their raucous laughter at each other's crude humour.

"Marni," Ivy said. "I need to use the bathroom."

"OK," Marni said, standing and facing the men. "The child needs to use the bathroom. Please allow me to take her."

"The child can do it here!" Dreighton shouted. "Guards, give them a bowl."

"How barbaric!" Marni said. "Fine, but can you give me some water?"

Dreighton nodded, and one of the guards took a jug and placed it by the bowl. Marni took out her seed pouch, and searched through it, picking out a particular, small seed and lining dozens of them from the wall out, then turning at a right angle, and back, leaving a gap before reaching the wall again.

"What the hell are you doing?" Dreighton demanded, but Marni ignored him.

She fetched the water, and sprinkled it along the floor, soaking the seeds along the line and around, until she had applied a small amount to every one of them. Then, she focussed her energy, and cast her flame along the line of seeds, willing them to grow. Nothing happened at first, then the first sprout began to form, and soon, the line was green, and rising. She kept going as Dreighton's men rushed to stop her, fearing another tree and an escape.

"Wait! Leave her be," Dreighton cautioned, walking towards her himself.

As they watched, a green tendril, barely visible, lept between the sprouts as she focused her energy and encouraged them to grow. Then, they seemed to falter for a moment. Marni added more water, and redoubled her efforts, and the reeds grew tall, until their stems thickened, and soon a living bamboo screen stood there. Several feet tall, and thick with leaves, the stems pressed tightly together, the screen was like a living wall.

"There you go ivy, now you can go to the bathroom in there. Take the bowl."

Ivy did as she was told, the long chain from the shackle on the child's foot pulled tight as Ivy tried to get as far inside the screen as possible.

"Simply incredible," Dreighton said, striding to Marni, and grasping her chin.

He turned her face one way, then the other, as if inspecting a prize fruit at market.

"Who could have guessed such miraculous power resided in something so plain. Never the less, I am sure you will scrub up nicely for my son."

Chapter 15 – Alliances

Corilai rode beside Fletcher, their horses fresh and the youngsters well rested. Fletcher's injury had already recovered well, though he was still limping, and on the medic's orders still carried crutches for use once he was dismounted.

Loka led the way, as the chill winds dared them to continue. Symin had sent for them, but they had no idea why. As they crossed the bridge, where Fletcher had acquired his injury, the pair exchanged a glance, and he shuddered, remembering how close he had come to death.

They passed the cave, where they had sheltered, and then the pillars, beyond which Treghan and Marni had disappeared. There was no evidence of the struggle which had taken place there. It was as though the mountains were telling them to forget their friends had ever been here. Just let them go, and Corilai shuddered in response.

"Do you think we'll ever find them?" she asked.

"Don't worry," Fletcher replied. "My brother is a tough nut. He'll be fine, and I know I can trust him not to let anything happen to Marni. Because he knows I'll knock him senseless if he does."

"You love her," Corilai said. "I know, you don't have to hide it. I think she feels the same way. I hope she's OK."

"I know she is. She has a level head, and a cool temper. Treghan is the one to worry about."

"No, Treghan will be fine," Corilai replied.

"Then why are we both so worried?"

"Because your friends are in danger," Loka shouted back at them. "Hurry, the winds are changing. We have to get beyond the next peak, and then it's a hard ride all the way to camp. Symin is expecting us, and we don't want to keep him waiting."

*　　　*　　　*

Dreighton surprised Marni by allowing the screen to remain. It became their private space for the bathroom, but away from the pot, against the wall, both girls felt it a safe place when it came time to sleep.

"This is a reminder that power lies in the simple things," Dreighton had explained. "My men need to be reminded not to underestimate the power in their charges, and to squash it when it becomes rebellious."

Now, Marni looked around. Dreighton had gone somewhere, and only two guards remained at the only exit from the chamber. They watched her with suspicion, and were unmistakeably alert.

They were also much larger and stronger than she was, and Marni bemoaned the fact. She had hoped she would find her chance to escape, but this was not the moment to risk the life of young Ivy in an ill fated enterprise. She sighed, and sat with her back to the screen. Ivy joined her a moment later as a child entered the chamber, looking nervous. The child, a young boy, approached the two girls, carrying a basin the same as the one behind the screen.

"Lord Dreighton has instructed me to clean your basin," the boy said. "I'll change it for you."

"What is your name, child?" Marni asked.

"I'm Hudson," he said, walking behind the screen.

"Have you always lived here?" Ivy asked.

"No," he said from behind the screen. "I was taken from a highlander village not far from here. All because my cousin had those damn sparks Dreighton is so obsessed with."

"You don't have them?" Marni asked.

"No. They even did that smoking thing with me, but still I had nothing. So I'm worthless in his eyes. Still, they never let anybody go home, so I'm stuck here, just like my brother and sister. My brother works in the mines. My sister though..."

"Are there many like you?" Marni asked.

"Yeah, most of us don't have the sparks, and become the workers," Hudson explained. "Slaves more like. You can't become a guard, or an officer, unless you're one of the four families, or you have the sparks and learn to ice. The rest of us, well, we'd escape if we could, but nobody ever has."

"Treghan did!" Ivy said, a little too loud. "I mean, he's not here any more, and he was, and that's why we're here instead of the barracks."

"Really?" Hudson asked. "You think he escaped?"

"I know he did," Marni said. "And I know he'll be back for me. Hopefully with a bunch of our friends."

"Will they take us all with them?" Hudson asked, barely daring to whisper the thought.

"I'm sure they will. We've been looking for you all for a long time. The rangers are here to rescue every kidnapped child, and return them home. But Dreighton doesn't know that, and even if he did, he doesn't stand a chance against the might of Emberdale."

"You think so?" Hudson said, as he re-emerged, carrying the stinking basin out in front of himself, arms stretched to distance himself from the smell.

"I know it," Marni said with an expression of grim determination. "I'm a ranger myself, and I have seen how weak Dreighton really is. The rangers will destroy him soon. And when they come, there will be nothing to stop them from taking you all home. Dreighton will never bother anybody again."

"I hope so," Hudson said. "But he caught you, and chained you to the floor."

"And I destroyed the last cell he put me in by growing an oak tree in minutes, in the dark, on the stone floor. I grew this screen for privacy in minutes in front of everybody, you can ask them if you doubt it. Trust me, if I wanted out, I'd be gone. But the more I know about you children, the more the rangers can save."

"I hope your rangers come soon," the boy said as he walked toward the guards. "See you soon."

* * *

Treghan awoke and felt the dull ache in his shoulder, already familiar, and already fading. Rona's treatments were clearly working, and much faster than he had expected. Climbing from the bed before the fire, he found his shirt, and his ranger cloak, and pulled them on, before stepping out into the brisk dawn air.

Already, highlanders were up and going about their business, and many nodded greetings to him as he walked through the village, towards the hall. Days had passed, and he felt an urgent need to move on to the next part of his journey, to go and find the rangers, and bring them back so they could help him rescue Marni and the others.

"Treghan!" Rona called from behind him.

He turned to face her, and felt immediately chastised when he saw her expression.

"What are you doing walking around like that?" she rebuked him. "You need the extra warmth of fur over that shoulder! Your ranger cloak isn't made for this place. Come, follow me."

"Yes ma'am," he said as she led the way back to her house.

*　　　*　　　*

Corilai looked around the camp, amazed at how much they had done in such a short time. She saw several rangers pushing barrows of gravel out to the road, where they had already improved hundreds of meters of what had been nothing but sticky mud.

The group dismounted, a ranger taking the horses from them, and Loka led them through the camp to a small command tent. Symin greeted them with a curt nod as they entered.

"You requested we come, Sir?" Corilai asked.

"Yes, I have a plan, but you can refuse if you wish."

"What is it?"

"We have yet to find the enemy, but when we do, I want to send you two in first, as new hostages, to find out as much as you can before the rangers assault the place. That way, we can focus our attack on those doing the kidnapping, and avoid harming the children."

"Sir," Fletcher said. "With all due respect, I think that's a bad idea. I think my brother and Marni have already been in there long enough to find out all you need to know. We should rescue them, and then find out what they know."

"A good point," Symin replied. "But we still need to get in there and find them. How do you intend to do that?"

'I don't know..."

"Exactly. Now, we have rangers scouring the highlands for any sign of the foe, and when they find them, you will have to decide if you will participate in the plan or not."

"I already decided," Corilai said. "I'll do it, for Treghan, and so will Fletcher, or else."

"Good. Now follow Loka to your tents, and get some rest. This mountain weather takes it out of you, and I want you ready to go as soon as we have a destination. You'll be accompanied to the place by a group of us, but you go in alone."

"Yes, Ranger."

Loka led them out of the command tent, and past the circle of carts, out into the basin of the quarry, where dozens of small tents had been erected, sheltered from the wind by boulders and gravel piled in a long levy. Approaching one tent, she waved fletcher inside, then ushered Corilai to the next.

Stepping inside, Corilai found the tent equipped with a bed of furs and wool blankets, and little else. Climbing between the blankets, she was surprised to find herself sleepy almost immediately. She had not realised how tired she was, and it seemed an instant later when, after she had slept for several hours, Loka opened the flap and shook her foot to wake her.

"Come, Symin is calling for you," Loka said, before going to Fletcher's tent to wake him.

Corilai straightened herself up, and stepped out into the brisk air. A bright moon cast its light on the quarry, and it made for an eerie sense of cold in the surprisingly still air. She followed Loka and Fletcher as they made their way back to the command tent. They walked inside, and Symin nodded. There were several others crammed into the small space, but Loka pushed through, and grasped Corilai's hand, dragging her to the front, so she was closest to Symin.

"Our scouts have located a highlander village some distance from here, in which they believe they saw somebody in a ranger cloak. We are leaving immediately. It will be morning by the time we arrive, and I would like to use the day productively. Are you still committed to the plan, Corilai? Fletcher?"

"Yes, Ranger," they both replied.

"OK," Symin said. "We take horses as far as we can, but be warned. The track is rough. We leave in five minutes. You can eat rations as you ride."

Corilai followed the others from the tent and to the stabling area, where she found her horse, already saddled up and ready to go. She climbed into the saddle and began to ride out to where she could see the others gathering.

"We're going deep into the highlands, away from the highway," Symin said. "However, there are roads. Merchants visit these highlands, and it is quite possible they visit our target as well. If you see a better path, speak up. The scouts were hiking back in the dark, so may have missed a better path. Move out!"

Symin led the way, and Loka ushered Fletcher and Corilai up behind him, so the four formed the lead group, as twenty rangers filed out two abreast behind them. The going was slow, and the trail was rough, but the morning passed without incident as they crossed many miles of white, rocky highland.

"How can people live up here?" Fletcher said as he shivered in his cloak.

"The same way they live anywhere," Loka said. "The best that they can manage."

"Still, given the choice..." he moaned.

"It is not a choice for some people," Loka replied. "Some people are intimately connected to the land their family has claimed. Moving away is no more likely than finding a way to live without breathing for them. It can be a good thing."

Little more was said as they continued to ride, but as the sun light began to lighten the horizon, Symin raised an arm, signalling them to stop. He then splayed his fingers, before closing his fist and slowly lowering his arm, the signal for silence.

He turned, looking at Corilai and Fletcher, before dismounting, and signalling them to follow. He led the way as they approached the top of a deep, steep edged ravine. A road wound its way along the bottom.

When they reached the edge, Symin crouched low, and made his way along it, before lying flat and crawling the rest of the way. The ravine opened out into a wide valley, which sheltered a large settlement. Many stone buildings filled the valley, and they could see dozens of people walking about their business in the dawn air.

"There," Loka said, pointing at two figures walking across an open area below them, headed roughly towards them. "Is that Treghan?"

"It is," Fletcher said.

Beside Treghan, walked a tall young woman, perhaps in her twenties. Corilai narrowed her eyes. The pair seemed very familiar as they entered a house.

"She's beautiful!" Fletcher said, sounding breathless in his efforts to keep quiet.

That was enough, Corilai lept up without thinking, and dove over the edge, half sliding and half running as she plummeted down the slope, ignoring the loudly whispered shouts of her friends to stop.

Striking the floor of the valley, behind the houses, Corilai found her feet sinking deep in snow. Nevertheless, she hurried on, dragging herself forward until she was between two buildings. Glancing behind her, she saw Fletcher clumsily and slowly making his way down the slope, Symin and Loka still peering over the edge at the top.

Reaching the front of the buildings, Corilai peered out, to check the coast was clear. When she was sure it was safe, she rushed out of the cover between houses, and straight to the door she had seen Treghan enter.

Not pausing to consider her next move, she burst inside, and blinked as her eyes adjusted to the fire light. Looking around, finally she saw him. He sat, facing away from her. He had no shirt on, and sat there naked from the waist up. The woman stood behind him, her left hand on his should, as she did something with her other hand which Corilai couldn't see. Something to him. To his naked body! She was touching him! Corilai was enraged.

"Just what the hell is going on here?" Corilai screamed, throwing caution to the wind in her jealous outburst.

The woman turned her head and smiled, calm and slow, before waving her hand towards a table near the wall opposite.

"Shut up and fetch me those bandages," the woman said. "The boy's wounds aren't going to dress themselves."

Corilai, instantly deflated, blushed bright red in embarrassment at her misunderstanding of the situation, and rushed to do as she was told. Collecting the bandages, she rushed to the woman's side, and saw the wound for the first time. Corilai gasped, raising a hand to her mouth in shock at the sight of the wound, where something had ruptured Treghan's body.

"Treghan!" she whispered. "What happened to you?"

"Hush," the woman ordered. "You can talk later. Right now, if you make him talk, he'll move and the dressing will have to be done again."

"I'm sorry," Corilai said.

"It's OK," the woman replied, indicating the end of the bandage on Treghan's shoulder. "Hold that, Corilai. I'm Rona by the way."

"How do you know my name? Did Treghan tell you?"

"We did speak of you, Corilai of the demon flame."

"Treghan! Did you call me that?" Corilai shouted, angry at the name.

"No, he never called you that," Rona said. "However, the stories from the merchants I heard about you two did use that name. If it upsets you, I will remove it from my story telling in future."

"No," Corilai said. "It's OK, its true I guess. It just upsets me if he says it. Our flames are more than a stupid name to us, so he should know better. If it's the stories the merchant's are telling, I'll never stop it now."

"Yes, once a story is told," Rona said. "And is spread across the continent, that's a genie you can never force back into the bottle."

Just then, Fletcher entered, more cautiously than Corilai had done. He paused as his eyes adjusted, then looked around the room, seeing Treghan, Corilai and Rona standing together. Then he grew panicked.

"Treghan! Where's Marni?"

"She's not here, I'm sorry. I think they caught her again, after I fell."

"You were supposed to protect her!" Fletcher shouted, striding across the room, anger in his eyes.

"Your brother did indeed protect her," Rona snapped, silencing him with the rebuke. "How else do you think he got a spear through his body? Your friend might have died if Treghan had not put his life on the line. In fact, he's very lucky. Anybody who was there most likely believes him dead right now. His sacrifice probably saved their lives as Dreighton's men would not happily kill more than they had to when they escaped."

"Who's Dreighton?" Corilai asked.

"He's a monstrous villain," Rona said. "He lives in the mines and makes a sport of stealing children from the highlanders."

"Then you're victims of the kidnappers as well?" Fletcher asked.

"Indeed. Many of our young ones are in the hands of the miners. We would dearly like to find the strength to take them back, but we are a small village."

"Do you know where they are? And how to get in?" Corilai asked, getting excited.

"But of course," Rona replied. "We scout their boundaries daily. That's how we found Treghan."

"Then perhaps we should work together," Corilai said. "The rangers have the strength, but lack the knowledge. You have the knowledge, but lack the strength. Together, we can end Dreighton's tyranny and return your children."

"That would be agreeable," Rona said. "Are your leaders nearby? We should hold a meeting and make a plan."

"I'll go get them," Corilai said, running from the house.

She ran out into the open space before the house, and looked up at the edge of the incline, where she could just make out Loka and Symin, still watching, and several others along the edge, such that an idle passer would not notice them, but a trained ranger who knew they were there, could see them easily. Raising her arms high over her head, Corilai waved them repeatedly, before dropping her thumb and pinky finger on each hand and waving the other three fingers in a signal of safety, telling her friends to come to the village.

Chapter 16 – Plans and Pain

"So what you're telling us," Symin said. "Is that Marni is still in the mines, and there are men who can wield ice."

"Yes, but there's more," Treghan said. "They use a smoking herb which silences your flames altogether. They didn't know it had that effect, until it happened to us."

"If they didn't know, then why did they use it?" Loka asked.

"Because, in their words, it awakens the ice," Treghan said.

"I don't get it." Corilai said.

"They're taking a lot of children, but they're looking for kids with white sparks in particular. When kids with the sparks are exposed to the smoke, they develop the ability to wield ice. Kids who are too young to spark, will have their sparks appear. I don't know if it has an impact on their abilities later on."

"You mean only dormant white flames can do it?" Fletcher asked.

"Well, only white flames can ice, yes," Treghan replied. "It's their secondary ability."

Nobody said anything for a moment, until the implication sank in.

"So, you have a new secondary skill?" Fletcher asked.

In answer, Treghan raised a hand before his brother's face, and hit him with a small blast of frozen sleet. Fletcher screamed and jumped back, startled by the icy attack.

"Yes, that's right," Treghan said. "But there is another implication to all this."

"Marni," Symin said. "I see. What happened to her?"

"Wait, what do you see?" Fletcher demanded.

"Think about it," Symin replied. "The smoke awakened Treghan's secondary ability..."

"But Marni already had hers," Fletcher said.

"Yes, she did," Treghan replied. "And now, her secondary power is significantly more powerful than it was a week ago. She grew an oak tree from a seed, in a cave, on a stone floor, without light. A tree big enough to destroy the cell they had us in."

"So if we get in there, and they hit us with that smoke, we'll be even stronger!" Fletcher said.

"No," Treghan said, shaking his head. "The smoke does a number on you for a while. It stops your flames completely for hours, and leaves you slow and groggy as well. If you use your secondary, the flames come back quicker, but you're still groggy and slow. We can't risk being hit with it."

"But a lot of rangers don't have a strong secondary. It's a great opportunity!" Fletcher exclaimed.

"No," Loka said. "It's a shortcut. You know what I've told you in class about them."

"I know," Fletcher said. "No shortcut is helpful in the end, because with a shortcut, you miss half the journey, and it's the journey that makes you strong, not the destination."

"That's right," Loka said. "I'm glad to hear you paid attention. I wonder sometimes."

"Of course we do!" Fletcher said, indignant. "Anyway, when do we leave to save Marni?"

"We have some things to do first," Symin said. "You young ones can come with me back to Windwall. I have to send a report to the Chancellor, and check in on things there. I will also order some reinforcements. We need all the rangers we can summon before we march on Dreighton."

"You will have the highlanders also," Rona said. "With you at our side, we will march as deep as we must into that man's mines."

"Thank you, friend," Symin said. "We will end this tyrant's hold on the mountains once and for all."

* * *

A young man walked up to Marni, and stood over her, looking down as she sat, her back to the privacy screen. She looked up at him, unperturbed, and recognised him as the man who had been pointed out to her as Dreighton's son. The man Dreighton wanted to force her to marry.

He continued to stare for some time, before he turned away, and stood there, his back to her as he spoke.

"I guess you will do, but don't expect any affection from me. You're just a womb to me, and it's only for the advancement of our family dynasty."

"You think I want any affection from you? And if you lay a finger on me, you're going to lose it. The same goes for any other part of your body which comes too close."

"Marni, isn't it?" he said, turning to face her again. "You'll soon realise there's no point to your ignorant defiance. Nobody leaves this place."

"Treghan did," she snapped.

"Your boyfriend's dead."

"He wasn't my boyfriend," she replied. "And if you think a ranger would die out there, your stupider than I thought."

"If he wasn't your boyfriend, why are you resisting so much? What have the rangers ever done for you?"

"They've done everything. I was recruited young, like most students of Emberdale, but it was my choice. I wasn't abducted by some highlander with delusions of grandeur. The rangers take us in, feed us, house us, clothe us, and train us."

"We do all those things here," he said.

"Ha!" she barked. "You can barely feed yourselves, and you damn near starve these poor children you stole. This isn't a life, you should let them go and give up. Your dynasty is a failure and you haven't even begun to stink yet."

"You think we don't stink?" he said. "Then there is hope."

"No, there is no hope for you. By stink, I meant you aren't a corpse. Soon enough, you will be."

He ignored the attack, and knelt on the floor in front of her.

"Let me reintroduce myself," he said. "My name is Kurn. I am the son of Dreighton, and soon enough I will rule over this place. If you choose to spurn me, then you spurn the opportunity to rule by my side."

"Rule over a hole in the ground?" she snapped. "I'd rather die. As a ranger, I have access to an entire world. Wonders your feeble mind can't imagine are mine to command. And you think for one second I would agree to give up all that, to sit in a hole and watch kidnapped children slowly starve? Idiot."

"Your mind will change, you'll see," Kurn said as he stood, facing Dreighton as the older man entered the room.

"Son," Dreighton said. "Can you still enter Windwall at will?"

"Of course," Kurn said.

"Good. This girl says the rangers will come, so we need reinforcements. Or shields, to be more accurate. Take ten men, and enter the city. Round up as many children as you can. I don't care if they have sparks or not, or if they're too young. They're going to be our insurance. If these rangers think they can intimidate us, we'll show them who they're up against. I want you back by morning. Take the carts, pack them full of those whining brats."

"Yes, Father," Kurn said.

"And you think you're husband material?" Marni shouted. "You're as bad as your pathetic father!"

Kurn struck her, the punch to her jaw sending her sprawling.

"You watch your mouth, filthy whore!" Kurn snarled.

"Fine, hit me all you like, it just means you'll be the first to die," she shouted. "After you bring back even more children, to starve in your filthy hole in the ground."

"Oh, nobody is going to starve, little girl," Dreighton sneered. "Not unless you want them to. You're going to grow enough food for all of them, or else you'll be beaten within an inch of your life, along with your little friends there."

"Yet you still claim you aren't a monster," Marni snapped.

"Of course I'm not," Dreighton replied in a calm tone. "I have found a way to provide food for my charges. That makes me a great ruler. If you fail to provide, it is you who is the monster, not me."

* * *

Treghan, Corilai, Fletcher and Rona followed Symin as he returned to Windwall. Loka had stayed behind at the camp, making preparations to move half of the rangers there into the village. It was noon as they approached the gates, which stood open as the sun bathed the mountains in a rare moment of warmth.

They entered the city, and made their way to the ranger's buildings, all of them looking forward to a bath and a warm room. As they approached, a man ran out to meet them, breathless, and clearly upset.

"Please, you have to help me," the man said as he looked them over, their faces revealed as the sunlight warranted putting their hoods back. "Wait, I know you, Treghan, you saved my family in the snow before. It's me, Brun. Remember?"

"Of course," Treghan said. "I remember, your cart had gone off the road in the storm. How is your wife? And your child?"

"That's exactly why I'm here," he said. "Somebody took Jiddi. They stole her from her bed this morning, and several others. There are parents out all over the city, looking for lost children."

"I'll get her back, I swear," Treghan said.

"But how can you say that?" Fari said, rushing to her husband's side. "You rangers have been promising the world, but you still have no answers and our children are still disappearing."

"I've been there, seen where the children are being held, seen the defences of the kidnappers, witnessed their scheming and their evil first hand. Don't worry, we're here to call Emberdale for more men, to help us tackle the bastards who are doing this. But even without their help, I'll rescue Jiddi myself, on my honour," Treghan said.

"Thank you, son," Brun said. "But don't go getting yourself killed. I can see you are already wounded under that cloak."

"How can you tell?" Treghan asked.

"I've been on the road in these mountains long enough to know when a person is favouring an arm, or a leg. If you are injured, wait for your help from Emberdale, but please, promise you will find her and return her to us, safe and sound."

"I promise," Symin said. "We will return all the stolen children of Windwall, and the highlands."

Treghan followed as Symin spurred his horse and moved around the distraught parents, before making his way to the building. Treghan looked back briefly at Brun and Fari, offered a weak smile, then focused on the building in front of him as they went around the back to the stables.

Once the horses were stabled, they made their way to the common lounge, where they sat, weary from their travels and the days out in the cold, as Symin beckoned for a messenger. Shortly, a young man entered the room, and Symin handed him a note he had already prepared.

"Please, be as quick as you can. Do not stop for anything, time is of the essence. Give this message to the Chancellor. And beg him to hurry. We need as many rangers as can be spared, and we need them yesterday. Understood?"

"Yes, Ranger," the young man said, and rushed from the room.

* * *

Loka looked back along the column, remembering the last time she had led an army across Cinder. This time, it was much smaller, and a far shorter distance. But somehow, it seemed harder.

The road was little more than a goat track, the winter had left it a frozen wasteland of ice and mud. They had resorted to leading their horses, instead of riding, simply because it was too hard to see where it was safe to step from a mounted position.

The day was leaving them behind. Already low in the sky, the sun was casting long shadows across the highlands, and Loka worried they would lose light long before they reached the village.

Briefly, she wondered how Symin and the others had gone on their trip back to Windwall, but she pushed the thought of calamity from her mind.

"That road is as safe as they come in these parts," she mumbled. "It would be best I focus my worry on the men behind me. This way is treacherous, and we must reach the village before the next storm. Today's clear skies have to be an omen, but of what? I don't like it."

"Ma'am," said a young ranger, from behind her. "Excuse my impertinence, but you were speaking quite audibly. Don't you worry about us, we are all of the same mind. We are strong, and we will not succumb to the mountains."

"Thank you, Ranger," Loka said. "We must hurry. Keep up."

She pushed on, walking faster, urging her horse to do the same, as she made her way through the growing twilight. Finally, as the last of the sun's rays had abandoned them, she saw the light of a camp fire flickering in the night. They had made their way down into the ravine along the narrow road, instead of taking their horses dangerously down the incline behind the village they had run down earlier.

Now, as the ravine opened up and the village spread out before them, they could see an enormous fire burning in the central plaza, welcoming them to its warmth and its guiding light.

* * *

Seven carts clattered through the main entrance of Dreighton's mine, and rumbled to a stop. The drivers climbed down, and threw back the canopies, to drag their charges out. Roped together, the children were marched into the mines without any instruction.

Terrified, the children obeyed submissively, and were soon dragged one at a time past Dreighton, in the audience chamber, where he assigned each to a dormitory based on his first impressions of their strength.

Every now and then, Dreighton barked out the order "Shield," and instead of going to work in the mines, those children were dragged away to be shackled to the walls of the mine at key points where any invader was likely to pass.

He planned to station his ice wielders behind them, such that they could attack, but the rangers could not risk retaliation for fear of harming the children.

"You really are monsters," Marni moaned as the last of the children was ushered away. "The rangers will see to it you all pay."

"Your rangers are fools," Dreighton said. "They hid away in Emberdale for generations. You think they have a chance here, on our soil? We know this place, they can't possibly find their way far enough into this mine to make a difference."

"You still don't get it, do you?" Marni quipped. "It's not just flames. Your ice wielders are nothing more than white flames with no flaming ability. The rangers have many dozens of white flames. And they're properly trained to use their skills with the flame. A disciplined force with superior weaponry to what your pathetic men have. Every ranger has a secondary skill, which is considered a vital part of the learning progress of a ranger. They strive to master those additional skills, and many are incredibly powerful. Far more so than I am with my seeds. And you still have no clue about those abilities. How can you be prepared to defend this place when you can't even predict what they will be using against you?"

"Silence!" Dreighton barked. "You insolent wench. How dare you? My men are more than capable of repelling your rangers, and they will do so."

"Father," Kurn said. "Perhaps she is right. Is it not wise to know all we can about our foe? Shouldn't we question this girl further? How can we defend against them if we have no idea what they can do?"

"Oh, so you're siding with the girl now?" Dreighton yelled. "Well, if that's how it is, you can be shackled along with her! Guards!"

"I don't think so, old man," Kurn snarled as he raised a hand towards his father, palm flat as the air before it began to swirl. "Guards, you know what to do."

Three guards rushed to position themselves around Dreighton, and each raised a hand as Kurn had done.

"What is this?" Dreighton shouted. "Mutiny? From my own son? I'll have your head for this!"

Dreighton rushed towards Kurn, but was met with a forceful blast of ice and snow, which knocked him back as the walls of ice began to grow from the floor.

"Kurn you traitorous boy! Stop this immediately, and I might let you live!"

Still the walls grew, reaching the roof of the cavernous chamber, where they began to thicken. Dreighton's voice grew softer as the ice obscured the sound, but still he continued to rage in his frozen prison.

"It's the girl, isn't it?" Dreighton said. "What has that whore said to you?"

"I'm so sick of being called a whore!" Marni shouted.

"He doesn't mean you," Kurn said, before shouting at the ice wall. "She has done nothing to provoke this. It all rests on you. Oh, don't you worry, father, the plan will continue. But you are not fit to lead it. You can't even ice like us, and you think to rule us? But no, I will lead and the plan will go on. It is too late to change it now, however it will be under my guidance, not yours. And I will bring her here, to be my bride. That village is too small for her ambition. And this one?"

He rushed to Marni, grasping her hair and dragging her to her feet.

"This ranger bitch will still serve our dynasty, and she will serve it well, but never as my bride. Her wonderful blood will spread deeper through our four families than that, under my rule."

Marni spat in his face, and Kurn dropped her.

"You're as bad as your father, you idiot. You think any girl would willingly marry you knowing what you are planning to do to me?"

"Of course she will," Kurn spat. "She's more twisted than I, and ambitious to boot. And with me in charge around here, she'll be quick to finally accept my proposal."

"How is this girl twisted?"

"Never you mind," he snapped. "But she is already the most powerful person in that village of hers, and she is only twenty four years of age. And she has a beauty unrivalled in the highlands. I will make her mine. This should make you happy. It means you're free to shack up with that boyfriend of yours, if he lives, once he's recaptured."

"He's not my..."

"Shut up!" Kurn snapped. "Just know this, if he tries to stop you from fulfilling your duties in bringing your blood to the dynasty, I'll spear him myself. And this time, I'll have better aim."

"Ha!" she shot back at him. "I bet you couldn't kill him if your life depended on it. And I'd wager this girl of yours is no more infatuated with you than I am. What girl in charge of a village would be interested in a rotten whelp like you?"

"Rona would!" he shouted. "She will learn to love me, like I love her!"

"Rona huh?" Marni said. "So she does have a name. Don't worry, if she has a peaceful village, which survives out there, and she doesn't have to hide in a hole in the ground like you lot, then you'll never be a match for her."

Kurn struck her again, and stalked from the room, shouting as he went.

"I will silence that tongue of yours, as soon as I bring her home to rule beside me. Guards! With me."

Dreighton's maniacal laughter could be heard from behind the ice as the men left, and then he began striking the ice wall with his fists.

"What is it, deposed monster?" Marni snarled.

"You did well, getting rid of him like that. You know how to pull his strings. I bet you were doing the same to me, earlier. But now, thanks to you, I can do what I must do, and my wicked son isn't here to stop me."

Dreighton knelt on the ground, rummaging in his pockets, and produced something. He was working at the base of the wall for some time, and Marni could not see what he had there.

"What are you doing?" she asked.

"My idiot son thought he had me," Dreighton said. "But I was prepared. I expected this day would come. I have here a small charge of explosive, the same stuff we use to bust through the toughest of rock when we expand the mine. Best cover your face, whore."

Marni grabbed Ivy, and clutched her close, holding the girls face to her chest as she turned away from the ice wall. The blast shook the cavernous chamber, dust and gravel showering from the ceiling as the ice wall collapsed.

"Guards!" Dreighton bellowed in rage as he strode through the rubble. "Guards, Seniors, ice men, come to me! We go to battle, and my son will pay for his treacherous mutiny!"

Chapter 17 – Ice and Death

Kurn strode through the main entry and approached the ice barrier.

"Halt!" shouted the guards posted there. "What is your business outside?"

"Stand down!" Kurn shouted back. "My father is no longer in charge here, and as the ruler of this place, I call the shots. You will stand down and let me pass."

"Kurn," one of the guards protested. "Protocol still demands we ask your destination. Should we need to send help, they would need to know where to go."

"How dare you!" Kurn shouted. "Are you saying your great leader is weak, that he might need your help?"

With that, Kurn raised a hand and blasted the wall with an immense spear of ice. As he stepped through the gap he had created, he turned to the guards.

"Fix that, immediately!"

He smiled as he walked in the brisk mountain air, a wicked grimace which his companions knew meant he was scheming something. The four men were high on adrenalin, knowing they were now the most powerful group in the entire mines. Kurn laughed to himself as he corrected his thought; "No, in the highlands!"

He turned, and took them along a winding, narrow track, cutting away from the well used road. He knew he might have gotten to his destination faster if he had used one of the side exits from the mine complex, but this way, he was able to demonstrate that he was the new ruler much faster than sneaking around where nobody could see.

"My idiot father will see how a real man leads!" he snarled beneath his breath.

"Kurn, you will lead us all to greatness, and we three remain loyal to the end," one of his companions said.

"I know," Kurn replied. "If you weren't I would have already disposed of you all."

"We're getting the girl?" one of the men asked.

"Of course," Kurn replied.

"What if she refuses to come?" the man continued.

"Don't be an idiot, man!" Kurn shouted, turning to strike the man. "Why are you here, if there was any doubt that she'd resist?"

"Yes, Sir. I see Sir."

Kurn looked ahead along the trail, ignoring his men as he fumed. Finally, he spoke again.

"Clearly, if I attend the village alone, she will never believe I have taken control. I have to have an entourage of capable guards, to demonstrate to her that I am in fact the new ruler of Dreighton's mines."

"Of course, Sir. But if she still refuses, how are we to force her?"

"You drag her, carry her, whatever it takes man!" Kurn shouted. "There's three of you, and one of her, and she is not the trained warrior you are!"

The words had the desired effect, as the guards heard themselves complimented as trained warriors. They took pride in their skills, and were faithful to their leader. And now, they would help him secure his bride.

"Sir, I would wish you a smooth and pleasant marriage," one of the three said.

"I thank you. But now, quiet, we are approaching the other road."

*　　　　*　　　　*

Dreighton gathered a dozen of his most trusted allies, and armed them to the teeth. Among them were the other three fathers of the four families in the mine, and several of their brothers. Older than the younger, ambitious upstarts, they did not have the ice ability. They had long since become too old for the smoke to have an effect when it was discovered by Dreighton's wife. He considered that discovery as they walked.

She had found it accidentally when she burned the herb as incense, in an effort to clear the smell of soiled clothing from their home, and the young boy Kurn had inhaled the smoke. They had since awakened many more ice wielders, but Kurn remained the most powerful.

"We must take care. These young men will not surrender, and they are our four most powerful with the ice," Dreighton grumbled.

"We must take them down - whatever the cost," one of the others said. "I know for a fact they left through the main entry."

"I know, Warreigh," Dreighton said. "If my son must pay with his life, so be it. I have been ready for that possibility since the first day he iced. We will take the side exit, cut him off before he can reach the wench's village."

"One of them is my son also," Warreigh said. "I can not admit to being so prepared. However, for the good of the four families, and the future of the dynasty, what must be done shall be done. But let us not be hasty."

"Kurn has betrayed us all," Dreighton snarled. "I will not show him any undue mercy, and if your sons get in my way, they will fall with him."

"But Dreighton, we must approach this situation with cool heads, and reason," one of the others said.

"Of course you'd say that, Taro," Dreighton replied. "But if we do not strike this group hard, fast, and without mercy, how long is it before we have another mutiny on our hands, from somebody else?"

"I understand," Taro said as they approached one of the side exits from the mine, the one closest to the road leading to Rona's village. "But if we are too harsh, we will only sow dissent amongst those who remain."

"That is a risk we must be willing to take," Dreighton said without emotion. "We all know the goal, we all know the outcome we strive for. Allowing these upstarts to try to steal from us the reward for our decades of work, that would be to put everything in jeopardy."

"Understood, Sir," Warreigh said as they broke into the open air and began to jog. "We must cut them off before they reach the village. Otherwise, we risk the villagers coming for some justice of their own, when we're already preparing for the rangers."

*　　　　*　　　　*

Rona walked among the rangers in the courtyard beside the outpost in Windwall. Some cast her curious glances, which she ignored. Beside her, Symin walked, with Treghan and Corilai, talking in soft tones about the coming attack on the mines. Four city guards stood on the edge of the crowd, chatting idly with a young ranger, oblivious to the highlander's presence.

"You have sentries placed on the known exits?" Symin asked.

"Always, but our numbers have been too few for this to be much help. It only allows us a few moments to hide our children, and our valuables, should a raiding party head our way."

"Do you think Dreighton has any idea we're there?"

"Probably, though any link between us and your people would have eluded him so far. There have not been any spies from the mines these past few days."

Just then, a young highlander ran into the courtyard, and rushed to speak with Rona. He whispered a brief message, before she dismissed him with a wave, and he wandered away. She stopped walking, and turned to face Symin directly.

"Two groups have left the mines. The four senior ice wielders, Dreighton's son among them, from the main entrance and heading toward the village. A second group has left from a side entrance, with Dreighton himself leading the charge."

"We should scout ahead, and see what is going on."

"I will join you, as a guide," Rona said. "He is a misguided fool, that son of Dreighton, but I do not believe him to be inherently evil. We were once friends, and I would see him forget his father's ways one day. Hopefully, I can reason with him before he attacks my people."

"I'll get the horses," Treghan said.

"Yes, but once we reach the quarry," Rona commanded. "We must travel on foot to meet them, if they have not already attacked. If they have, I trust your people will ably defend my home. But on the hunt for the enemy, horses will be too obvious. We must not be seen until we are ready for them."

"Agreed," Symin said. "Treghan, Corilai, Fletcher, you may come if you wish, but know this will be a dangerous mission."

"I'm coming," Treghan said.

"Me too," Corilai answered.

"You couldn't keep me away," Fletcher said. "Until Marni is safe, I'm taking every opportunity to face those bastards."

"Good," Symin said. "Tara!"

Loka's lieutenant rushed to his side at his call, her youth evident in her smile, but her grim experience etched into her eyes.

"Yes, Ranger?" Tara said.

"Assemble the troops, all of them, and follow us. We leave immediately, but we five will be riding at speed, to get there as soon as possible. You are to lead the rangers to the quarry at the end of the road, and from there, you will be directed to Rona's village of Bhenar. You are to be ready for battle as soon as possible. I will see you there soon, once we have investigated matters of concern in the highlands."

"Yes, Sir!" Tara said, offering a salute before spinning on her heel, to bark orders at nearby rangers.

"That girl is going to replace me, one day," Symin said with a smile. "Now, we ride, and if you fall behind, I will not be waiting for you. To the stables with you!"

"Yes, Sir!" the three youngsters said in unison, as they ran to find their horses.

* * *

Kurn wore a grin fuelled by his wicked intent, as he rushed through the trees, his three compatriots close on his heels. He stopped, and raised a hand, signalling them to stop.

"We should take care," Kurn said. "Rona's villagers will have sentries along the trails, she's smart like that. The intersection is just ahead. We should check it out carefully before we continue."

"They'll be your villagers soon enough," one of the men said.

"That they will, Girfyn," Kurn said. "Please, scout ahead for me, we will follow your signal."

"Yes, Sir," Girfyn said, and stealthily walked ahead.

With absolute quiet, Kurn and the others followed, several paces behind. Girfyn raised a hand as he reached the intersection, signalling they should stop, before he slowly made his way out of the trees, onto the larger road which would lead them to the village.

Girfyn knelt on the ground, inspecting the dirt for any signs of traffic. He looked up towards Kurn, who signalled with his hands.

"Any signs of people?"

"Nothing recent" Girfyn signalled back.

Girfyn stood and looked up and down the road, then into the trees opposite. He stared into the shadows for a long moment, before he slowly raised one hand, and waved a slight motion forward, indicating that the others should join him.

Kurn stepped out of the cover and into the road, as a chill wind blew from the north. The snow capped pines shivered, as if they felt the cold, and the rustling sound sent a shiver down his spine, as though a bad omen had come, and his fate had been sealed.

In a sudden, unexplained panic, Girfyn turned, poised to run, opening his mouth as if to shout a warning, but the words were never to be heard, as a silent arrow pierced his skull.

The steel head of the projectile erupted from Girfyn's face, high on the bridge of his nose, and the man's blood sprayed into Kurn's eyes. Kurn frantically brushed his face with his hands, screaming, as Girfyn's lifeless body crashed into him, knocking him to the ground. Realising the danger, Kurn struggled to push the body of his friend from on top of him as he rolled onto his hands and knees, desperate to make his escape from the unseen attackers.

He looked up, into the eyes of his other two companions, as they fell before him. One was speared through the chest, the other clutched at a sword which protruded from his shoulder, skewering him from behind.

"Who are you?" Kurn screamed. "Why are you doing this?"

As he tried to stand, he felt a boot in the centre of his back, pushing him down. Unable to resist the strength of that kick, Kurn fell flat, his face mashed into the dirt, before the same boot kicked him in the side, sending sparks of pain from his kidneys as he rolled onto his back and looked up.

Gazing back at him, fiery rage burning in them like the inferno of hell, were the eyes of his father, who held a sword high, ready to strike.

"Father!" Kurn cried out. "Please, don't do this!"

"You insolent little snot!" Dreighton barked. "You try to destroy everything I have built, and now you beg for mercy?"

"But Father," Kurn said. "I only sought to make your wishes come true! We will rule this country one day, thanks to your plan."

"But never with you as our leader," Dreighton shouted, as he plunged the sword into his son's chest. "You thought to overthrow me, and would have brought everything to an end with your silly infatuation for that woman. You never had the right stuff to lead our people. You are an embarrassment. I won't make the same mistakes I did with you when that little ranger bitch of yours bears me a new son."

Kurn watched his father's eyes, as the older man twisted the blade, their gaze locked together as the young man's vision began to fade.

"Father... Only wanted... Proud," Kurn mumbled as the last of his energy faded and his life came to a premature end.

* * *

Dreighton did not move for several minutes, as he stared into his lifeless son's eyes. Finally, as his companions dragged the bodies of the other three fallen young men to the side of the road, he sighed, and stood.

"Now, we have to start again," Dreighton said. "But we should have enough young people who can learn to ice, and this time, we won't let them think they can take control. My son, you will be remembered. For your legacy, our dynasty will only be stronger, as we will learn from today's events, and nobody shall ever take such foolish action against me again."

Walking slowly, Dreighton left, heading back towards the mines. His companions carefully placed Kurn's body with the others, before following, none of them speaking as a foul mood engulfed the men.

* * *

Rona led the way as they ran through the alpine forest. The rocks and snow broke through the vegetation like rugged reminders of the savage heart of the mountains. The village was not far away, and as they reached the start of the trail through the ravine, there was an eerie peacefulness about the scene.

"I doesn't look like they came here," Rona said.

"I hear only the usual sounds of men at camp," Symin said. "And I see no unusual smoke or other signs of battle. Perhaps it was a false alarm?"

"No, something has happened, but it did not involve my people," Rona replied. "Come, we must follow the road back to the mines."

"Yes," Symin said, as they reluctantly left the warmth of the fire in the village, and headed into the cold night.

Symin lit a yellow flame and set it out before them, to light the way. They ran for what felt an eternity to his steadily tiring bones, but in fact must have been less than a half hour, when suddenly his flames lit upon a gruesome sight.

Blood was smeared across the road, trails of crimson death where the four bodies in the ditch at the road side had been dragged away from the site of their deaths. They stopped, and Rona slowly approached.

"Oh no," she murmured, as she began to walk faster towards the bodies. "No, it can't be."

Kneeling beside them, she turned over the one on top, then stifled a gasp as his lifeless eyes bore through her soul. Unashamed, Rona let loose her tears for her childhood friend.

"My dear Kurn," she mumbled, almost incoherently at first. "How sad that it has come to this. I know you harboured feelings I could never return, but for those to have twisted you such that your actions led you to this end..."

Carefully, she closed his eyes as she lowered her head in silent prayer. Then, she stood, looking at his lifeless form.

"Travel safe to the land of the dead, my dear friend. I will miss you, as I have done these past few years. But your father shall come to justice, and whoever did this to you will join him in his fate. I swear it. Blood should never be spilled in the thirst for power, I know you felt that as much as I did in our youth. That yours is the blood spilled is such terrible irony, and though we have been enemies in recent times, I will still avenge you, that your spirit may find closure."

Rona turned to face the rangers, the tears continuing to stain her cheeks as she addressed them.

"Please, my friends, return to the village, and bring me a cart, that we can take these boys home and give them proper burial. I will wait by their sides, to guide their spirits home to our ancestors, as is our custom in the highlands."

Chapter 18 – Fear and Loss

Marni sat with her back to the screen as the young boy sat inside, ostensibly cleaning, but instead talking to her and ivy in whispers.

"My brother will come with us if you can escape," he said.

"It is not yet the right time," Marni replied. "I have to know which villain rules this place first. Kurn has gone, and so has Dreighton. I fear only one will return."

"Which one?" the boy asked.

"I do not know. Both are as twisted as each other, but I feel Dreighton is more predictable. Kurn, therefore, is the more dangerous enemy."

"So you think Dreighton is finished?"

"No, Dreighton is cunning, and has years of experience silencing his enemies. Kurn is a hot headed young man and is brash and foolish. He will be killed by his father, I fear."

"You are brave, to speak with such disrespect for our leaders," the boy said.

"They are not and never will be my leaders, remember that," Marni snarled.

They fell quiet as a commotion erupted in the passage outside the chamber. Dreighton stormed in, as his guards waited by the doorway, and rushed towards Marni and Ivy. He stood, towering over her, then reached a hand down to grasp her hair and drag her to her feet.

Dreighton's foul breath assaulted Marni's nostrils, and she turned her face away.

"Look at me, you bitch!" he snarled as he slapped her face. "Yes, you will do for me after all. Once I silence that tongue of yours and break your spirit, you will bear me a son, to replace the one who has left us."

She looked into his cold eyes.

"You murdered him," she said in a simple, monotone voice.

"He betrayed us all," Dreighton snarled.

"So you murdered your own son, in cold blood, for the sake of your own lust for power."

"He was no more a son of mine than you, from the moment he sought to overthrow me."

"So you killed him. You went out, with cold intent, and you murdered your own son. Your boy, who you raised to lead, tried to do what you wanted for him to do one day, and because it was not on your timetable, you killed him. And you still think you are not a monster?"

"Shut up, ranger whore. You'll learn to hold your mouth closed, and you will bear me a son to replace the one you corrupted with your wiles."

Dreighton dragged her closer, smelling her hair, then licking her neck. Marni shuddered, and began to fear she could not hold him back. Still holding her hair in his right hand, his left hand snaked its way inside her cloak, slithering around her like a tentacled demon, seeking to devour her soul.

"Understand, woman, you are mine now," he snarled.

"What fabric is your shirt made with?" she asked.

He leaned away from her, though he still held her tightly, taken aback by the seemingly random question.

"It is a fibre woven from the blades of mountain grasses. Though such knowledge will not help you, except if you are asking of your other wifely duties."

"Wifely duties?" she snarled. "No, I am a demon come to end you. I am your nemesis. And you will fall at my hands long before I bear you a child."

Marni focused her energy, and flamed strong and green, engulfing her body such that the lecher's hands were singed. Startled, he released his hold on her, and stepped back, but it was too late. The green flames engulfed his clothing, and faded, swirling, missing the intense heat which would burn him. He smiled, and stepped towards her again, reaching out to grab her.

"So, your flames are weak after all, they don't burn me at all!"

"Those are not my burning flames. If I wished to use those against you, you would already be dead on the floor, and I would be long gone. But I do not work like that. Another unknown monster would rise to replace you. I kept you alive this long for exactly that reason. You are mine, Dreighton mine holder, not the other way around."

"What are you talking about, wench?" he shouted, his rage growing.

"Now grow, mountain grasses, return to the life which was stolen from you!"

Dreighton's shirt, engulfed in the swirling, pale green flames, began to writhe. Then, as he struggled against it, trying to remove it, it burst into life, fresh grasses sprouting and growing around him, reaching for light, they swirled around his face, sending roots deeper into his clothing, and across his skin, seeking any source of moisture and food they could find.

Any opening, any crack to burrow into, and in his panic, he began to sweat, and the grasses rejoiced, drinking his salty fear as they grew, and soon he could not be seen, as the tower of grasses stood there, where his screams could be heard as his arms were pinned, his wrestling attempts to disrobe a losing battle. Marni turned away, and looked at the shackles on her foot and Ivy's.

She slipped a seed in between steel and skin, and burst them free with a sprouting shaft of wood, snapping the locks like twigs, then thrust her arm through the screen to grab the boy, pulling him through as she incinerated a section of the reeds with her green flames.

Dragging the two children by the hands, she ran from the chamber, blasting the two guards outside the doorway with hot flames and not looking back as she led the youngsters deep into the darkness of the mines.

"Did you kill him?" Ivy said.

"No, those guards will save him before the grasses do any lasting harm to his body."

"Why didn't they run in and stop you?"

"I didn't want them to," Marni said. "So I stopped the sound of his screaming using my flames over the door."

"You're getting to be one scary lady, Marni," Ivy said. "And how can flames stop sound anyway?"

"Sound is waves in the air. Match the wave just right, and you can bounce the sound back so nobody outside the flames can hear it."

"When did you learn that?" the boy asked, awe in his voice.

"Just now," Marni replied. "Ever since that smoking thing you miners did, my secondary powers have been growing ridiculously fast, and I keep discovering new tricks."

"Ivy's right," the boy said. "You are one scary old lady. I hope I don't make an enemy of you."

"Call me old again, and you will, boy," Marni snarled. "Now, lead us to a good hiding place. We have some things to do before we leave this horrible place."

"What did you do to his clothes?" Ivy asked.

"The same thing I do with the seeds. I understand it now. There is genetic material in everything plants create. Seeds, fibres, all of it. It's not the seeds I awaken, its the living or once living materials. That DNA never leaves the fibre, and if I awaken it with my power, it will grow, the same way the seed does."

"What's DNA?" the boy asked.

"It's a theory, based on ancient texts. I learned a little about it in my classes at the academy, but we don't have the technology to study it as more than an idea in Cinder. Apparently, once upon a time, mankind had all manner of amazing technology, and some of that ancient knowledge is still talked about in the texts. DNA is the stuff that makes you how you are. If your DNA were different, you might be a tiger instead of a person."

"I don't think I want a tiger's DNA," the boy said. "It sounds like that ancient knowledge is pretty scary, too."

"No, it is useful, which is why we study it. Even Yuri, the tyrant of Grey, used the ancient texts. That's how he was able to build those turbine things and create the lightning power to fire his furnace without coal. But there aren't a lot of them around, so we guard them well in the library at the academy."

"It sounds like your history class is more fun than the ones here," the boy mumbled.

"Does your DNA make you flame?" Ivy asked.

"I don't know. The flames are not mentioned in any of the ancient texts. I think there is something else causing them. Something which we have, but the ancients did not. But quiet, we have to keep moving, and we can't be discovered. Dreighton is going to want to kill us now."

* * *

Rona sat in the back of the cart, holding the hand of her childhood friend. Treghan and Corilai sat on the back of the driver's bench, watching her, while Fletcher and Symin rode up front. Nobody spoke as the cart trundled its way through the ravine, heading for the village as steam rose from the nostrils of the two draft horses.

As they approached the village, Tara and Loka stood there, waiting for them to arrive. Tara had led the troops into the village shortly before the cart's return, but they were still fired up and ready for the assault, in spite of their dash from the city.

The horses on the other hand, were heavily lathered and crowded in their corral eating hay and lazily drinking from the trough. Tara approached the cart, and swung herself up beside Symin.

"Sir, the rangers are ready for an immediate assault," she said.

"No," Symin replied. "We have a change of plan. These four men were our enemy, but they were once the friends of this village. These men were children when last these people spoke to them, and in recent times have been powerful enemies. But that does not mean we can deny them the respect of a solemn memorial. Tara, I give you the reins, I must speak with Loka. Follow any directions Rona may have in the treatment of these bodies. When the memorial is over and the burial is done, then we will consider our next move."

"But shouldn't their own people have done this?"

"Their own people have abandoned their bodies in the cold wilderness, knowingly leaving them to the wolves. When your own people disrespect your life by neglecting you in death, it behoves the more reasonable of this world to step in, that you may find peace. We owe it to them, in the hopes that should a similar fate befall us, somebody would take similar mercy on our own poor souls."

"Yes, Sir," Tara said as she took the reins and Symin climbed down from the cart.

Tara drove the cart according to Rona's directions, behind the village hall to an open field, dotted with marking stones. She came to a stop in the centre of the field and climbed down, walking around to the back where she helped Rona down.

With the help of the young rangers, they unloaded the four bodies. A young girl came into the field, carrying a bundle of fabric.

"Oh good," Rona said. "Bring those shrouds over here."

Carefully, they placed each of the bodies on a shroud, as three young men arrived with shovels and began to dig. Treghan grabbed a spare shovel from the cart and helped. The soft top soil was easy to dig with the holes crumbly around the edges. It was nevertheless hard work, as the ground beneath was frozen.

While the boys were digging, Corilai helped as Rona and the girl anointed the bodies with oil and herbs, as they wrapped them in the shrouds. They finished their work long before the boys, and watched in solemn silence as the graves were dug.

Treghan took his lead from the other boys in how deep to dig, stopping when they did to stand in the pit he had dug, the length of a man and about three quarters as deep. Careful not to collapse the side of the hole, he climbed out, then helped one of the others as they carried a body to the fresh grave.

Soon the four bodies were all interred, and the four boys began to fill the graves as Rona stood before them, head bowed in whispered prayers. Tara, watching from the cart, climbed down and walked to stand beside her, sensing the sadness of the woman and seeking to provide silent support.

As the last of the soil was packed down, Rona smiled weakly at Tara, before grasping the young woman's arm for support as the tears spilled anew for her lost friend.

"Please, I would ride the cart back to my cottage. I do not feel I could walk there right now."

"Of course," Tara replied, leading Rona to the cart.

The young ones began to walk towards the village hall, their grim task complete.

* * *

Hudson led the way through the mines, his knowledge of the passageways as complete as Marni could have hoped. They walked for nearly an hour, through the twisting passages, before he stopped, and carefully edged closer to an intersection. Light glowed softly from the side passage, and he peered around the corner as Marni joined him.

Two young men were stationed at a door, looking bored. Hudson looked at Marni, and smiled.

"Wait here, I think you need to see this," the boy said, before walking out into the open and approaching the guards. "I need to check their bedpans."

"Go ahead," one of the guards said, lazily opening the door and letting the boy through.

Hudson walked in, and Marni heard the sound of bedpans clanging before there was a loud crash, and Hudson shouted something she could not quite understand. With a sudden bluster of activity, a whirling tornado of crazed flesh burst from the room, smacked one guard to the ground, and ran out of reach of the other, before pausing.

It was a boy, perhaps fourteen years of age, but his face was twisted, contorted with fluctuating emotions as his eyes darted around, seeking something. His movements, erratic and unpredictable, were nevertheless powerful. His fist caught the second guard as he reached to grab the boy, sending the man to the ground in a clattering mess of sword and armour.

"Where," the boy screamed. "Where is it?"

He looked around, and his eyes fell on Marni. He took several steps towards her, then stopped, his eyes widening as he stared at her ranger's cloak. Even as dirty as it was, it was still an impressive garment.

"Ranger," the boy screamed. "I would have been one too. But they took it. They stole it from me! My yellow friend is gone forever, and the silence sickens me!"

The boy span on his heel, and ran, passing the two guards who were getting to their feet, and bolting away, down the passage, away from Marni. Hudson appeared then in the doorway, rubbing his head.

"I'm sorry," Hudson said. "I didn't think he was awake."

"Never mind that," one of the guards spat. "Just tend to the others, we'll take care of that one."

"Yes, Sir," Hudson replied

The two men ran after the escaped boy, until they disappeared from sight. Hudson frantically waved at Marni and Ivy to join him in the room.

Marni ran into the room, Ivy on her heels, and turned to close the door as Hudson followed them inside. She looked around the room. It was a long wide barracks, bunks lining the walls and running down the centre of the room two abreast. She counted at least a hundred beds, and most of them were occupied by thrashing, screaming children.

Marni walked past the first few bunks, her hand raised to her face in shock as she gazed in pity on the poor children.

"What happened to them?" Marni whispered.

"This is the truth of what the smoke does," Hudson said.

"I don't understand," Marni replied. "What do you mean?"

Hudson walked to a girl. She twisted and snarled, chained to her bed, the shackles rubbing her wrists and ankles raw as she thrashed about, trying to escape.

"Hush, Kres," Hudson whispered as he took her hand in his own, looking back at Marni. "This is my older sister, Kres. She was exposed to the smoke, the same as you were. But there were no special powers for her, none of those, what did you call them? Secondary abilities? Not for her. All the smoke brought her was madness."

"By the flame, how horrible!" Marni swore. "How many have this reaction?"

"More than half. It's a gamble on our lives, when Dreighton's men use the smoke to make us ice."

Marni walked slowly to the bedside, the girl's eyes burrowing through to her soul as they twitched. Her thrashing had eased since her brother took her hand.

"It's OK," Marni said. "I'm not going to hurt you, I'm a student from Ranger Academy. I was given the smoke, like you, but I was lucky."

"Lucky?" Kres whispered. "Yes. Lucky. I was not. They took it from me, before I knew I had it, and now I am alone."

"What did they take?" Marni asked, fearing she had already figured out the answer, remembering what the other boy screamed in the hall.

"My other self, the second spirit, the voice I could never quite hear in my head, the thing that meant I was never alone. You have yours still. I envy you. Mine, mine is silent, and the quiet darkness consumes me. I miss it, and I never even got to know it."

"Your second self?" Marni asked.

"What does it mean?" Ivy asked, tugging on Marni's cloak.

"Outside," Marni said. "In Cinder, some people speak of a second spirit. They say the flames inhabit you like a possessing ghost, that the flame is a spirit which accompanies you in life. It's just old wives' tales, but if there is some truth in it, perhaps… I know I would hate life if I lost mine."

"Hate life," Kres whispered. "Yes, I hate life. I want it back. My flames are gone, but yours are bright, and powerful. I want that power which they stole from me. I want it back."

The girl's eyes grew wide and she looked at Marni.

"The academy can help. They have to help. Nobody knows the flames better than they do. They can bring it back to me! Please, just tell me you can try?"

"Don't worry, the rangers are coming to this place, to save everyone. I will make sure you are not left behind, and that the academy does whatever it can to help you."

Chapter 19 – Resistance

Marni looked around the infirmary, and noticed an enormous wooden closet at the far end. She walked to it, an idea slowly forming in her mind. Reaching the closet, she opened the door, and looked at the sturdy oak panel in the back.

"Is there anything behind this closet?" she asked.

"Uh, rock?" Hudson asked, in a tone that hinted she was simple.

"I mean, any passages or rooms back there?"

"Oh, I don't think so," Hudson replied.

"Good," Marni said, reaching a hand to press her palm flat on the back panel of the closet. "I'm going to make us a little hide out. We can run a resistance from there, against Dreighton and his cronies. Does anybody come to this infirmary?"

"No, only me and the other kids who look after them," Hudson said. "The guards usually don't even look in here."

"Good," Marni said, as a soft green flame began to lick around the panel.

Focusing her energy, Marni willed the oak panel to spawn new life, casting roots into the rock wall beyond the closet. The roots spread, grew, and thickened, in huge numbers, crushing the stone of the mountain and splitting it with the power of nature. She felt the roots burst into a cavity, and set them around its walls. The roots filled the space, about the size of a small room, and pressed into its sides. They consumed the minerals within the rock, to fuel their rapid growth. Thinking for a moment, Marni sent a root upwards, seeking daylight.

After a while, it burst free of the mountain, to explode into life, leaves and branches forming on the mountain side, where Marni would never see them. She stopped the tree outside, and focused on enlarging the roots. Dust fell from the ceiling in the infirmary as the rocky structure of the mine was shaken by the cracking stone.

Then, those leaves and branches outside burst into flame, green and fierce. Soon they were consumed, and the fire followed the question roots down, following the living wood and incinerating it as it went, the smoke billowing from the new crack in the side of the mountain.

Finally, the fire reached the clustered, massive clump of roots which had splintered and consumed the rocky mountain's insides, and those roots burst into an inferno, sending flames racing back to the surface, and smoke in a plume reaching far into the sky.

As the last of the roots were burnt, the panel of the closet began to smoulder, and Marni removed her hand, before striking it with her foot, sending splinters into the smoky darkness beyond. Just then, a boy could be heard screaming outside.

"The guards must be bringing him back," Hudson said, dragging Ivy into the closet and closing the door.

They listened as the guards entered the infirmary, strapped the boy to his bed, then left, closing the door behind them. Softly, Marni lit a green flame, and its light fell upon a cavity large enough to house several people, rugged stone and dirt in irregular shapes forming the walls and ceiling.

"Is it going to be stable?" Ivy asked.

"Not yet," Marni said. "Wait here."

Marni stepped into the strangely shaped space, and reached into her cloak, removing her seed pouch. Carefully, using a flame to see, she sorted through the seeds, and took out a selection of the larger ones. Placing them evenly around the edge of the cavity, she started them growing, but she realised she was missing something.

"Fetch me some water," she said.

Hudson went into the infirmary and returned with a large pitcher of water, and handed it to Marni. She smiled, and carefully dribbled a small amount on each seed.

"I think I can work without it if I need to, but the water will help, and the seeds will sprout quicker."

She then gave each seed a little of her flame, and willed them to grow. Each seed, one at a time, began to sprout and grow. Shortly, saplings were climbing up the walls, growing faster as they matured, until fifteen skinny trees reached the ceiling, where they began to spread their questing branches.

Marni smiled, and pushed more of her flame into the trees, and their stems became trunks, and broadened, soon sufficient between them to hold the weight of the mountain, should it start to cave in. Still, she continued, moving from tree to tree, giving each her flame, until each tree had a sturdy, mature trunk. They reached all the way to the ceiling, holding the weight of the world at bay. It took many hours from the moment they had entered the closet, but finally, Marni was satisfied.

Carefully, she used her flame to prune the excess growth, trimming a bit here, a bit there, until the trees did not protrude at all into the cavity, aside from that necessary to support the roof. Finally satisfied, she turned to face the others, who stood open mouthed in the closet, watching in stunned silence.

"Fetch us some lamps," Marni said, too exhausted to make flames. "I don't want to be using my flames for lighting all the time. The smoke should find its way out the chimney my roots made."

"Yes, Ma'am!" Hudson said, rushing out into the infirmary.

"That was amazing," Ivy whispered.

"That's just the beginning," Marni said with a smile. "We got lucky. There was a cavity here. Without that, this might have taken me several days. Now we have a base to work from. And now I know it works, we can start making some changes around here."

"What sort of changes?" Ivy asked.

"The kind that will drive Dreighton's men insane," Marni said. "Imagine if that passage you always use is suddenly gone? And what if suddenly a new, strange one appears? I'll be much quicker as I learn more and get practice."

"That would be funny, but why would you do that?" Ivy asked.

"Because when the rangers arrive, what is the biggest advantage Dreighton's men will have over them?"

"Oh, I think I get it, They know their way around, but you're going to make all their maps useless by changing the passages!"

"Exactly. And if we can manage it, I'll send a correct map with our modifications outside, to the rangers, before they attack."

Hudson returned, carrying three lanterns, which he placed around the floor. He then sat on the lip of the closet, where the panel had been broken away.

"What now, Marni?" Hudson asked.

"Do you know of Lonay?" Marni asked, sitting with her back to the wall.

"Yes, he's one of the sons of the four families, but he got in some sort of trouble recently. They have him locked in his room."

"Good, I want you to get him, and bring him here."

"Yes Ma'am!" Hudson said enthusiastically, running from the room. "I'll be back soon!"

"And what about us?" Ivy asked.

"Just rest for a while," Marni said. "We've been unable to sleep properly for days, chained up in that audience chamber. Try to sleep, if you can."

"Yes, Marni," Ivy said, finding a corner and sitting down, with her back to the wall. "It's awful dirty."

"Get a blanket from the closet, and lie on that," Marni said.

"Of course!" Ivy said, doing as she was told.

Marni watched the child for several minutes, until she was sure the little one was asleep, before she stood and made her way into the infirmary, wanting to see what else she could learn about the victims of the smoke.

* * *

"When will we attack?" Tara asked. "I mean, we came here with a real sense of urgency, and now, now we're just sitting around."

"Be patient," Loka replied, picking up a small rock and tossing it across the cobble stones. "Symin was impatient, but he has realised we can not simply rush into this. We know they have some sort of smoke, and it knocked Treghan's flame out of commission for a while."

"But in the end he got a new ability!"

"Treghan did, yes," Loka said. "But if we're hit by it, we'll be vulnerable for a critical period. What if it can do even worse things?"

"Even so, we have the highlanders, and they know about how to get inside the mines."

"Yes, the highlanders have knowledge of the entries to the mines," Loka said. "However, they can't guide us through them any more than you can."

"Oh," Tara said. "I guess that is a problem."

"Yes, it is. Once we enter the mines we will be stumbling in the dark against a foe who is on home ground, and knows every twist and turn the same way we know Emberdale. We must be slow and careful. We have to plan meticulously, so that we can face any eventuality. Even the children themselves may oppose us."

"Why would they do that?"

"Why wouldn't they? Some of them may have joined up willingly. It may be that Dreighton provides for them better than their parents did, or it may be that they fear the repercussions for brothers and sisters also in Dreighton's sway."

"I guess, but even so..." Tara said.

"We can't forget that these children could become our enemy," Loka said. "And we must be ready to face the prospect of them attacking us, and having to defend ourselves. Obviously, we want to avoid harming the children we are here to save, but if we must defend ourselves, that may be something which is beyond our control."

"That's terribly unsettling," Tara moaned.

Loka walked across the courtyard, until she reached the central fire. Tara followed, to stand beside her commander.

"Of course, our enemy is ruthless," Loka said.

"How so?" Tara asked.

"One of those four young men who was killed was Dreighton's own son. We can only assume it was a killing either ordered or perpetrated by Dreighton himself. In that case, we know he is a truly evil man. He is dangerous, and nobody in his company is safe. If a man can murder his own son, or order it done by another, then there is no knowing what other evil he is capable of."

"I see what you mean," Tara said softly, as Rona joined them by the fire.

"I heard what you said. If Dreighton did kill his own son, I will have his head for it. But even if it was not him, he is responsible, of that I have no doubt. I hope he faces stiff justice for his crimes, and the sooner the better."

"Rona," Loka said. "Do you have the mine entrances on a map?"

"Yes, but not all of them are accessible at this time of year."

"What about inside?"

"None from this village have seen beyond the primary entrance hall. Even when we were at peace, the miners would not allow any outsider beyond that, claiming safety concerns."

"Well, they let hundreds of outsiders past there now," Tara said.

"They do not consider the kidnapped children outsiders," Rona said. "They consider them recruits, I have no doubt of that. Whatever they are doing inside that mountain, the amount of child labour they have at their disposal now is formidable."

"Anyway, fetch your maps," Loka said. "I will find Symin, and meet you in the village hall. We need to start planning for the assault."

"Agreed," Rona said.

*   *   *

Dreighton sat in his audience chamber and fumed. He had woken from nightmares of being eaten alive by trees three times the previous night, and he knew exactly who was to blame.

"That damned little ranger bitch," he muttered, for the twelfth time that morning. "I'll kill her myself."

"So you keep saying," Warreigh said. "But we aren't doing anything to catch her."

"She's not going anywhere. She can't sneak past the guards at the exits from the mine, and I can afford to let the little witch think she's won for a while. It will make it all the better when I break her."

"Your rage has passed, at least," Warreigh said.

"What the hell does that mean?" Dreighton shouted.

"You know how you get when somebody pushes your buttons," Warreigh said. "You've been like that since we were kids, remember?"

"You're right of course," Dreighton said. "And that's another good reason to let the bitch wander about in the dark for a while. If she was here, that snarky cow would be saying everything she could to push my buttons. She drives me insane."

"Is that why you were going to force her on Kurn?"

"Ha!" Dreighton shouted. "Would have served that bastard brat right. But in the end, I guess that wasn't to be."

"No," Warreigh agreed. "So what about those rangers that witch said were coming?"

"No sign of them near the mines. We should send a party out to check the road to Windwall. If they have moved any numbers along there in recent days, it will be plain to see. We have no reason to think they know where we are, of course, so her idle threats are likely just that."

"I hope you're right." Warreigh said. "What if they find those villagers? Do you think they might join forces?"

"Let them. The villagers will only bring the rangers to our door. They can't help them beyond that. And if they try to get inside, we have the upper hand. This place is a rabbit warren. No ranger would find their way out without having to fight every last one of us."

"That's true," Warreigh said. "We really don't have much to fear, do we?"

"No. Nothing at all, so letting that wench stumble around in the darkness, thinking she's making a difference, just makes her breaking so much more delicious."

"I'll send a scouting party to look over the road anyway," Warreigh said. "And they can take a peak at the villages as well. If the rangers are camping with anybody we need to know, if for no other reason than to be ready when they come."

"Wise words," Dreighton said. "Do it. And when you're done, come back here, and bring the other two fathers with you. We need to talk over a few things."

*   *   *

Hudson ran through the tunnels as fast as he could. He knew exactly where he was headed. Lonay had asked him to keep an eye on Marni for him. Hudson didn't like the four families much, but he trusted Lonay for some reason. He knew Lonay was in trouble with the families, and it had something to do with the rangers, so if Marni wanted to see him, Hudson would make it happen.

It hadn't taken much to be assigned to clean the prisoner's basin, and it had paid off, big time. Hudson grinned. Soon he would be free.

"What are you smiling about, boy?" shouted a guard, stepping in front of him to block his path.

"Oh, nothing," Hudson said, looking at his feet.

"It's never nothing," The guard said, slapping Hudson hard enough that he stumbled.

Hudson looked up, wondering who it was, and recognised Fero, Kurn's younger brother, Dreighton's second son. An ice wielder.

"Nothing important," Hudson said.

"I'll decide if it's important, now spit it out. Why were you smiling just now?"

"It's just," Hudson said, faking embarrassment. "A girl said she likes me."

"Who?" Fero demanded.

"I don't know her name. She came into the mines a couple of weeks ago, from the city."

"Really?" Fero snarled. "Well, forget it. You don't get to indulge in women.

That's the private entertainment of the guards and the officers. Scrubs like you aren't permitted such things."

"Yes, Sir," Hudson mumbled.

"What was that? I didn't hear you!"

"I said yes, Sir!" Hudson said, louder this time.

"Good. Now get out of here."

"Yes, Sir," Hudson said, scurrying around the guard and running as fast as his legs would take him.

Hudson rushed as fast as he could towards the area where Lonay was being held. He knew there was an air shaft from a back passage, which carried sound into Lonay's room, so he made his way there. Climbing until he could get his chin on the lip of the tiny shaft, Hudson whispered loudly into it.

"Lonay! It's me, Hudson."

He waited several long seconds before he heard the reply.

"About damn time," Lonay said. "Where have you been? The guards are a bit on edge, what's happened?"

"Kurn's dead."

"Kurn?" Lonay replied, shock in his voice. "How?"

"Dreighton killed him, because he tried to take over."

"He always was an idiot," Lonay replied. "What about Ivy and Marni?"

"Dreighton tried to take Marni on, and she gave him what for. They're both safe now, and in hiding. She's asked me to take you to her."

"Good," Lonay said. "Wait there. If Kurn's dead, none of the sons of the families are safe."

Hudson listened as Lonay made loud, groaning, wailing noises, and he heard the lock to his room click and the guards walk in. Lonay then grunted, and there was a thudding noise.

"What the hell is going on?" one of the guards shouted. "Quick, get him up off the floor, I'll fetch a medic."

Heavy footsteps echoed down the air shaft, as one of the two guards left. Then Lonay screamed, and there was a second, much louder thud. After some rustling, Hudson was amazed to hear Lonay's voice.

"I'll be right there."

Hudson climbed down from the wall, and waited in the dark for several minutes, until Lonay appeared in front of him.

"What happened?" Hudson asked.

"Oh, I faked a seizure, and after the one guard went for help, while pretending to have another one, I grabbed a torch and clubbed the other guard with it. Right on the head. He went down like a sack of potatoes."

"That was pretty damn risky!" Hudson said.

"I know, but it worked. Now, take me to Marni."

Chapter 20 – Making Trouble

Finding the infirmary unguarded, Hudson led Lonay into the closet, watching his face, and knowing the reaction was going to be good.

"What in the Caves of Bex!" Lonay swore, the old miner's curse sounding strange in his young voice. "How is this even possible?"

"Marni's pretty amazing now, isn't she?" Hudson enthused.

"I'll say," Lonay replied. "Are those walls made of trees?"

"Yes, Lonay," Marni said, approaching and resting a hand on his shoulder. "I created this place for us to stay safe and hidden, while we make merry mischief for the four families. Are you in?"

"Of course!" Lonay said. "What do you need?"

"I need a map, because we," she paused waving a hand to indicate herself and the three children. "are going to change things up a bit."

"Change things, how?" Lonay asked.

"Oh, perhaps collapse a passage here, create a new one there, so much so that none of the miners will know which way is up any more."

"I love it!" Lonay squealed, then tapped his own forehead. "Get me something to draw with, and I'll get you a map. I've got this whole place up here, in my head."

"Hudson," Marni said.

"Yes, Ma'am," Hudson said with a grin as he ran from the room, returning a short time later with several sheets of parchment and a pencil. "I gave these to my sister a while back, took them from the stores. Here, you can have them all."

"You never cease to amaze me, Hudson," Marni said. "Lonay, I want you to draw as complete a map as you can on one of these sheets. Then, we are going to make our planned alterations on it."

"Yes Marni!" Lonay said, sitting on the floor near one of the lanterns and getting to work.

"Hudson," Marni said. "You should probably leave for now."

"What? Why?" he demanded.

"Because they don't actually know you're working with us. We need you, on the outside of our group, to bring us new recruits, and information."

"Like a spy?" Hudson whispered.

"Yes, like a spy. You think you can handle it?"

"Hell yes!" Hudson replied, rushing from the room, only to return a moment later and carefully close the door. "We got a problem, the guards are back. How am I going to get past them?"

"Oh, I should have foreseen this," Marni moaned. "We need another exit. Lonay! How's that map? Give me the area around us now."

"Just a minute, Marni," Lonay said, moving to a different part of the sheet and drawing in a rush.

"Here," he said after a minute, rushing to show her the paper. "This is your little room here, with the infirmary outside, and the passage running past. There is another passage, passing us over here, down the side. You could bust into that, it's not used much."

"Thank you, Lonay, but we still need to secure it somehow."

"Oh, right. Hey, I know, how far can you tunnel?"

"As far as I need to," Marni replied.

"Good," Lonay said, taking the pencil and adding to the drawing. "See, that passage runs down here, to a storage area. There would be several cabinets in there, you could punch your way in, and cover the opening with a cabinet, just like the closet in the infirmary. I'm sure there will be one of the cabinets not being used."

"OK, stand back," Marni said, pulling out a seed. "I'm going to be a bit more careful this time, and go slower through the rock."

"Good idea," Lonay said. "When digging the mines, we sometimes come across cavities in the mountain, like sealed up caves, and if you charge in there too fast, sometimes they collapse."

"Something is going to collapse if we keep doing this anyway," Marni said. "It's what roots do, after all. They break things apart and push their way through, but all that moving rock has to go somewhere. This will probably start to cause cave ins about the place."

"Well, there's not much else but that passage near here, so we should be OK," Lonay said.

"Good," Marni said, pushing her seed into the wall and focussing her energy.

In the same way she carved the room, she started her root driven tunnel, moving into the wall and then turning, to follow the lines on the map, running parallel to the passageway. For hours on end she worked, pushing roots through the stubborn rock. Marni felt the mountain's reluctant submission with every crack of stone. About halfway down, she stopped when there was an almighty thunderous crashing noise.

"I'd better stop for the moment," Marni said, worried.

"I'll go check it out," Hudson said, running from the room.

Passing through the infirmary, Hudson found the guards had left their post. Ducking into the passage, he ran towards the source of the sound, and soon saw the guards, along with several others, frantically digging at a cave in along the passage. There were cracks in the walls, but no sign of Marni's roots.

"What happened here?" Hudson said.

"Just a cave in, unusual for sure, but not unheard of. Go to Dreighton and tell him we need the masons to come and reinforce this ceiling, so it doesn't happen again."

"Yes, Sir," Hudson said, and ran back the way he had come. Ducking through the infirmary, he stuck his head into the hide out.

"The passage collapsed. They asked me to tell Dreighton, so I'd better go, but there was no sign of your roots so you should be right to do your thing," Hudson said, before running from the room.

"OK then," Marni said. "I'll burn the roots from this end, so I can direct the smoke up the chimney. Stand back."

As she had done before, Marni burned away her wooden minions, leaving a crumbling cavity. She took out some seeds, and grew twisting, strangling vines along the tunnel to form a woven, wicker like tube down which they could travel.

She stepped inside, and walked slowly along it, trying to remain quiet. After some distance, she reached a point where the vines converged to a point where she could not continue, and she stopped, listening.

Somewhere, not far away, on the other side of the rocky wall, she could hear the voices of the men working to clear the cave in. She returned to her friends in the hide out, and sat on the lip of the opening to the tunnel.

"I guess that's as much as we can do for now. Lonay, can you please finish the maps?"

"Yes Ma'am," Lonay said. "If only there was some way you could know where the cavities were. Then you could use them, by carefully cutting your way in and then reinforcing the roof, and that means you're not going to cause collapses nearby like that did."

"If only," Marni said. "We had a yellow flame with us."

"Why?" Lonay asked.

"They're amazing at sniffing things out. They can sense all kinds of things. It's why the scouts recruit so many of them. I bet a good yellow flame would be able to find the cavities without a problem."

"Can we find a yellow flame?" Ivy asked.

"I bet there was at least a couple in the infirmary," Marni said. "It's a shame they can't use their abilities any more."

"But the children who didn't go crazy, have any of them shown coloured flames?" Ivy asked.

"Not that I know of, besides rumours," Lonay replied. "But Dreighton, I mean, the families, they weren't looking for flames, only for ice. I guess it's possible, given what happened to you and Treghan, that there might be a yellow flame among the children in the mines."

"Right, so that will be Hudson's next mission," Marni said. "Finding us a yellow flame."

* * *

Loka watched for several minutes, not sure what she was seeing. She stood in the road, at the centre of a short stone bridge, and she stared into the sky. Somewhere in the distance, a large amount of smoke was being created.

"There couldn't be any wildfires, so what is that?"

"It's near the mines," Rona said, standing beside her. "I wonder what it means? It's not the time of year for wildfires, and the camp fires of Dreighton's men could never create that much smoke."

"We should send somebody to take a look," Loka said.

"I'll find out if any of the village scouts are up there," Rona replied. "We should get back now anyway, and we should delay our assault while we investigate. It would not pay us at all well, if we were caught up in a wildfire started by Dreighton's men."

"Agreed," Loka said, turning and walking away.

"Wait," Rona said. "I have been wanting to ask you..."

she paused, considering her words, and the silence grew into a lengthy pause as the woman's words did not come. Loka stood there, arms folded, and finally broke the silence.

"Well? What is it?"

"Symin. Are you and he..." Rona asked.

Loka blushed, deep scarlet beneath her dark locks.

"No, I mean, I don't know. We've been close a long time."

"You love him," Rona said simply.

"Yes, but sometimes I think he doesn't even see me as a woman."

"Oh, he does. I've seen how he looks at you," Rona replied.

"I don't know..."

"It's OK. I'm sorry, I should not have asked," Rona said. "But I get it now. He's yours. I'll keep my hands off, don't worry."

* * *

Warreigh watched from one of his many lookout points as the ranger and the highlander walked from the bridge. Clearly, they were already working together. There was no indication of the strength of the ranger presence, but any presence was something he should report to Dreighton immediately.

The fact the two woman were obviously scouting together told him they had already joined forces, which made the situation far more urgent than Dreighton had implied.

Once the pair on the distant bridge were out of site, Warreigh stood, and began his walk back to the nearest mine entrance. Once there, he walked with a hurried pace directly to Dreighton's audience chamber, where he found the leader of the four families in conversation with a young guard.

As Warreigh approached, the guard left with a curt nod, and Dreighton beckoned him closer.

"That little ranger bitch is still hiding," Dreighton said. "But no matter. One of the less used passages in the western quarter of the mines has collapsed. I have instructed the guard to send masons to fix it, once the rubble is cleared away."

"It's unusual to have a cave in in the old passages," Warreigh said.

"Yes, but not unheard of. I don't have any reason to believe it is the result of foul play. The walls were cracked, in the same way we have seen in the past with natural events."

"We should be careful just the same," Warreigh replied. "I bring you news, and you won't like a word of it."

"Spit it out," Dreighton said, with a dismissive wave of his hand.

"The rangers are already working with the highland villagers. I do not know their numbers, but I saw a ranger scouting with that woman who wielded such power over your son."

"I see," Dreighton said, as he began to pace. "We may be running out of time then. I expect they will launch an assault some time soon. But first, take as many men as you need, and gather every scrap of that smoke herb from this mountain you can find. I want all of it in this room before morning."

"I'll head out immediately," Warreigh said, as he left the room.

* * *

Marni stood at the end of her tunnel, thinking. She desperately wanted to continue, hating the idea that she was idle, standing still while the rest of the world rushed towards the final confrontation between Dreighton and the rangers.

She also could not risk another uncontrolled cave in. Those had to be deliberate, and to her own directions. Drawing four of her dwindling, precious seeds from the pouch, Marni poked each into the end wall, around the edge, and dabbed each seed carefully with a small amount of water from the pitcher she had with her.

Then, focussing her energy, she pushed roots deep into the wall, pushing between soil and rock alike. Long, thin, wispy tendrils of potential thrusting deep into the mountain's heart.

"I can't go big and ridiculous, but perhaps if I take a gentler approach," Marni mumbled.

As those roots pushed further in, she began to expand them, closing the gaps between the four hungry plants, and then pushing inwards. She took extreme care to push inwards, and never outwards, so they crushed the rock in the space which would become her passage, reducing it to a fine powder under the pressure. Almost as an after thought, she directed the roots to seal the end of the passage, and then continued expanding them.

There were many loud sounds of cracking stone, and clouds of dust began to puff out from the wall, until she felt certain no larger chunks of stone remained. Carefully, Marni willed a second layer of roots to grow outside the first, this time remaining thin, wispy tendrils only strong enough to hold the mountain at bay while she cleared the passage.

She then burned away the thicker, crushing roots, severing them from the still living outer plants with surgical precision. She covered her mouth and nose against the smoke which soon filled the passage, but did not stop until the dirt left from her actions slumped with a loud whoosh, flowing like fine sand, to reveal a half filled cavity lined with living roots.

"Wow," Lonay whispered, before blowing a long, low whistle to express his awe and admiration. "That was incredible, but what'll we do with the dirt?"

"For now, we pile it under the beds in the infirmary. Make sure all the bed sheets are hanging down to hide it."

"Yes, Ma'am!" Lonay replied, rushing out of the passageway, to return after a short time carrying two bedpans from the infirmary. "These will do to shovel it out."

"That's going to take an age," Marni moaned. "We need more recruits."

"Don't worry, I have a feeling Hudson will come through for us on that score. For now, focus on getting this passage to the storeroom, let us locals handle the other stuff."

"Thank you, Lonay," Marni said as Ivy entered the passage.

"Marni, you've worked out something new, haven't you?"

"Yes, Ivy."

"Good, we need to keep going. By the way, the guards have left their post, so Hudson might come back soon."

"Good, Let's hope he brings friends."

*　　　*　　　*

Hudson burst into the barracks without waiting to see if there was anybody around, and startled a group of seven children to one side, where he could see a range of strange, coloured lights, before they all stopped whatever they were doing and stood, looking at him with a challenge which dared him to tell the guards.

"What's going on?" Hudson asked.

"Nothing," a girl spat, about twelve years old.

"If it's nothing, why are you hiding it?" Hudson said. "Don't worry, I won't dob you in. On one condition."

"What's that?" the girl demanded.

"You keep anything you see me doing that looks suspicious a secret as well."

"We weren't doing anything suspicious!"

"Really?" Hudson said as he sidled closer to the group. "Then what were those lights?"

"Nothing," the girl spat.

"I don't think they were nothing. You lot have coloured sparks, don't you?"

"How could you know that?" she asked.

"I spend a bit of time with the ranger."

"What ranger?" the girl asked.

"Wait, I know who he means," a boy around the same age as the girl said. "There was a ranger being held captive by Dreighton. I hear she escaped recently."

"Can't be a good ranger if Dreighton caught her," the girl said.

"Wrong," Hudson said, indignant. "She was only there because she was studying him, to know how he thinks, so they can take him down. As soon as he wasn't useful, she escaped just like that, and I know it was impressive, because I was there when she did it. Dreighton was never any match for her power."

"So where is she now?"

"I can't tell you that."

"Then what use are you to us?" the boy said.

"Now now, Jaer," the girl said. "That doesn't mean the boy doesn't know."

"You're right, Yera," Jaer replied. "So what use are you to us?"

"I can tell you what those sparks are, and why you only have them since you were smoked when they brought you here."

"Really?" We just think of them as something cool which we shouldn't tell Dreighton and his men about."

"They're flames," Hudson announced, proud of his superior knowledge. "Like the rangers use."

"But why?" Jacr asked.

"The smoke wakes them up. Dreighton thought the smoke only woke up ice, but Marni says it wakes up all flames, and their secondary abilities. I think that's what she called them anyway."

"I don't get it," Jaer said.

"It means Dreighton accidentally made you all into flame wielders, because he didn't know that ice was just a secondary ability for white flames, so you guys could never ice because you have other colours."

"And that's why we have to work in the mines and stuff, instead of being guards?" Jaer asked.

"All because Dreighton is an idiot who never knew what he was doing," Yera said.

"Exactly," Hudson replied. "What you really need, is access to a ranger who can teach you to use your new powers."

"But how will we ever get that?" Jaer said. "We can't leave the mines."

"You don't have to. Marni needs recruits to help her. She's going to run a resistance to weaken Dreighton's position, before the rangers attack the mines."

"The rangers will attack?" Jaer said.

"Of course, they're here to rescue all the kids Dreighton took."

"Some of them will fight for the mines," Yera said. "The ones who can ice, who earned privileged positions."

"That's their choice. The rangers have made a promise to save the rest of us. Anybody who faces them as an enemy will have to deal with the consequences. But enough of that, are you with me?"

"Take us to Marni," Yera said.

Chapter 21 – Training

Marni led Ivy out of the passage, and sat on a chair they had taken from the infirmary, in the first room she created.

"Ivy, can you get me some water?"

"Of course," Ivy said, worry in her eyes as she looked at Marni's exhausted face. "You should take it easy, I know you need sleep, and all this work with the plants must be hard."

"It is," Marni said. "Thank you Ivy, but don't worry. I'll be fine. I have to be. Until we take down Dreighton."

Ivy ran into the passage, and found the pitcher where Marni had left it, passing Lonay on the way, as he carried two bed pans of dirt out to the infirmary.

"We'll have help soon, Lonay," Ivy said, trying to be cheerful.

"You're pretty encouraging," Lonay said. "Thanks."

The little girl smiled, and continued about her business, returning to Marni, and handing her the water.

"Thanks," Marni said, taking a long drink of the water, before handing it back with a sigh. "You have a drink too, you must be thirsty."

"But I haven't been working, not like you."

"But you're a child, and children need to drink. Go on, take as much as you need."

Ivy nodded, and drank from the pitcher, as Hudson burst in.

"Thankfully the guards are gone for the moment. I brought friends."

Seven children filed in behind him, ranging in age from around nine to thirteen, Marni decided as she looked them over.

"Excellent. See Lonay. He'll direct you on what we need done."

"Wait a minute," Yera said. "Hudson here tells us you can teach us about our flames."

"You're all flame wielders?" Marni asked.

"We all have sparks, since they smoked us. Dreighton doesn't know, and we don't want him to."

"I see, well, I will see what I can do for you, but first, we have things we need done, and fast. Please, help Lonay, and later, I'll help you all grow those sparks into something useful."

"Deal," Yera said. "But remember, you promised. If you forget, I'll be real angry."

"I won't forget, don't worry, but please, Lonay can explain what we need. And why," Marni said, pausing as she thought for a moment. "Wait, have any of you got yellow sparks?"

"I do," Yera said.

"Good, you're with me, now. I need a yellow flame, and I don't have time to wait for the rangers to get here. I hope you can learn fast. What's your name?"

"I sure can!" Yera said, suddenly excited. "My name is Yera."

"Good. Now, sit on the floor over here, out of the way of the others, they'll be carrying a lot of heavy dirt around, so we have to keep out of the way."

"Yes, ma'am," Yera said.

"Please, say yes, Ranger," Marni said. "That's how rangers address their superior officers and teachers. You should do the same, because I'm your teacher here."

"And you're kind of like our commander now too," Yera said.

"I am?"

"Yes, Ranger."

Marni smiled, and leaned forward, to look into the girl's eyes. Marni tilted her head a little, nodded, then sat up straight again.

"You have resolve in your eyes. That's good, but you also need calm, and focus. Close your eyes."

Yera did as she was told, and slowed her breathing, visibly growing calm as she waited for Marni's next instruction. Marni smiled.

"You are going to be a good student," Marni said. "Now, you are a yellow flame, a type highly sought after by the ranger scouts. Do you know why?"

"No, Ranger," Yera said.

"It's because the yellow flame can sense things. They can reach out, with their minds. Symin tells me he feels a tendril of his flame going out, looking for things. They can seek out hidden objects and people. They can find their way around without a map, even in the dark, all using the secondary power of the yellow flame. This is why we need you."

"So I can spy?"

"Well, not exactly, but you'll get it soon enough." Marni replied. "For now, don't think about that, just focus on what we're doing together."

"Yes, Ranger," Yera said. "But if that's all secondary ability, I can't do that can I? I mean, I figured you'd have to be a good flame wielder to do that stuff. I'm only a sparker now."

"But you spark because Dreighton's men exposed you to the smoke of that mountain herb which awakens the secondary ability in flame wielders. It also, as it turns out, prematurely awakens your flames in their primary state as well, if you didn't have them awake yet."

"So you think, I'll already have that spy ability?"

"I do," Marni said, nodding. "And to make it come out, we just have to turn that spark into a little flame, so it can join you in the world for the first time. Then, your secondary ability should come to you as well."

"How do you know?" Yera asked.

"I don't, but I'm hopeful. You'll be the first person to have experienced it like this. But based on what I've seen with my own power, and that of my friend Treghan, as well as the people here who can ice without even realising they have a white flame, I believe this will work."

"Then I believe too," Yera said, smiling as she nodded. "I trust you, Ranger."

"Good," Marni said. "Now, close your eyes again. I want you to focus on your breathing. Concentrate on it until it's all you're aware of, but at the same time, I want you to try to ignore it, like it's only the background to your world."

"That doesn't make sense," Yera moaned.

"Of course not," Marni said with a chuckle. "It's all about the contradictions. Your breathing is there, always, but you usually ignore it. I want you to became aware of only it, and then push it away, so you ignore it again, and then, then you'll be thinking truly of nothing. You'll be alone in your mind, in your space. And calm."

"Is this how you learned?"

"My first teacher, before I went to the academy, used this method to teach me to flame, yes. Now, quiet, and concentrate. I want you say my name when you think you're ready."

"How will I know?"

"Trust me, you will know."

Marni watched the child, as she slowed her breathing, and it became deeper, then relaxed, and settled into a gentle rhythm. Over many long minutes, the child struggled. Marni watched as her face contorted with effort at first, then suddenly, like everything fell into place, Yera gasped, let out a long breath, and fell into a truly meditative state of relaxation and calm.

As the child's breathing slowed, and her face became a picture of blissful peace. Marni thought she saw the corners of Yera's mouth curl up in a slight, subconscious smile. Suddenly, the child's lips parted, and her voice was barely audible.

"Marni," Yera whispered.

"What do you see, Child?"

"Yellow. Like a fog of fire, but it's warm, and gentle, and it caresses my soul. It feels like love, like my mother's hugs, and like my happiest days, all at once."

"That's your flame. Your closest and dearest friend. Say hi to your friend, Yera."

"Hi," the girl whispered.

"What happened?" Marni asked.

"I think it said hi back to me."

"Did you hear the words, or something else?"

"No, I didn't hear it. I kind of felt it. And the yellow flashed brighter, and happier, and danced about for a second, then settled down again."

"That's how it was for me, too, that first time. Remember, whenever you're sad, or lonely, or in trouble, you can do this, and feel the warmth of your flame, and be reminded that it wants to protect you, to hold you, and to be near you at all times."

"What is my flame?" Yera asked.

"I don't know," Marni said, taken aback by the question. "Some people say it's a spirit that shares your body, matched to your soul, but nobody really knows what they are, just that they exist, as a part of every wielder in Cinder."

"I see," Yera said. "I wonder if it has a name?"

"Perhaps you can ask it, one day," Marni said, chuckling at the child's innocent curiosity. "But for now, I want you to say thank you to your flame, and then open your eyes."

"Thank you, flame," Yera whispered then opened her eyes, looking up at Marni, that same serene peacefulness still washing over her.

"Now hold out your hands," Marni said. "And make your spark between them."

Yera raised her hands, and squinted with effort, to be rewarded with a blinding flash of light, which startled her, causing her to break her concentration and drop her hands.

"Carefully, and slowly," Marni said.

"Yes, Ranger," Yera replied.

Slowly, the child raised her hands again, took a deep breath, and focused her mind on the task at hand, willing her energies to burst forth, begging her flame for help. First one, then a second bright yellow spark lept from her left hand to her right, then back again, and then, almost without warning, a bright, strong flame burst into life, surging in the air between the child's hands, small and insistent.

It burned with a fervour, and an insatiable lust for life, and in response, Yera beamed the brightest smile she had ever experienced in her short life. Marni met the child's eyes, and beamed a smile to match.

"You see?" Marni said, "You're a flame wielder now."

The reverie was broken by excited cheers from the others, who had stopped working to watch what they were doing.

"Hey!" Lonay shouted, before lowering his voice. "You lot trying to get us all caught? Keep it down!"

"Yes, Sir, Lonay, Sir," the children said, chastised by the boy's rebuke.

Marni ignored them, keeping all her attention on Yera. The child squinted, exerting more effort, but the flame faltered, and faded out. The others had returned to their tasks, and Yera did not even notice them. She was crestfallen it had gone out.

"That was very impressive," Marni said. "Don't try to make it any bigger than that, it will take a while for your flame to grow. But now, we need to focus on your secondary. You remember that feeling, that warmth where you saw the yellow? I want you to go back to that."

"Yes, Ranger," Yera said, closing her eyes, and quickly returning to her relaxed state, her breathing slow. "Marni."

"Good, you're there now?"

"Yes."

"Excellent. Now, reach out, beyond yourself, into the world around you. I'm hoping it works for yellows like it does for me."

"I can see things," Yera exclaimed. "I see you, wow, you're so bright! Your flame is enormous! So much power, Marni, you're awesome!"

"Ignore me," Marni said. "Look for softer things. Subtle things."

"I see a shape around us. Is that the walls?"

"Yes, You should be able to sense the rocks around us, and the plants, and the people."

"Yes, I see it now. And there, I see your passage, and behind me, there is the infirmary. It's like a big gap in the rock, carved out of the living earth. I see all the children in there. They look dark, like flames which have gone out."

"Very good, I'm frankly amazed you can tell that much already."

Yera's face scrunched, as she recoiled from the infirmary, and focused instead on the other children.

"I can see my friends, they look different, but each one of them, I can see their flame, the blues, the green, the orange and the red, all of their colours, I can see them."

"Excellent," Marni said. "That's how the scouts find new flame wielders to recruit. They travel around the country, and look at people like you are looking at all of us now. But ignore them. You said you saw the infirmary. I want you to look in the other direction, through the wall behind me. I want you to reach out, and see if you can find any other spaces like that."

"There are lots and lots of them," Yera said, almost immediately. "Some huge, some tiny, but only three close by."

"Good," Marni said. "Focus on those three, make it clear in your mind, and memorise where they are in relation to us, and the passage. I want you to figure out exactly how far they are, and memorise it. When you're done, say my name."

Yera sat like that for half a minute, before smiling.

"Marni," she said.

"Open your eyes," Marni said. "Lonay! Bring me the map!"

Lonay dropped the two bedpans of dirt he was carrying, and rushed to comply, soon following Marni's waved direction and placing the map on the floor between Yera and the ranger.

"Can you see those three spaces on the map?" Marni asked.

"Yes, one of them, this one," Yera said, pointing to the storage room they had been tunnelling towards. "But there's another one, closer to us, which isn't on there. A pretty big one."

"Lonay, a pencil," Marni said. "Yera, I want you to draw it in for me."

Yera nodded, accepted the pencil from Lonay, and carefully drew a large, oddly shaped cavern on a vacant part of the map, about thirty paces to the left of the end of the passage so far.

"So it's right behind me," Marni whispered.

"And a little bit higher than us," Yera said. "I think there's water in it, but not a lot, like a pool in the middle, which drains away over here."

Yera drew a wiggly line, away from them on the map, to indicate the underground stream. She continued, drawing a splash, and a wiggle, to indicate where the water fell into the cavern from the ceiling, having flowed down from the mountain side above.

"If you cut into it from this side, where the passage is, you shouldn't get any of the water in here."

"That's amazing, Yera," Marni said, smiling at the girl. "Thank you. Not only have you given us a larger area to use, you've given us a water supply, and a place to lay all the dirt without arousing suspicion from the guards. We can level out the floor of the cave, to make a flat surface to walk on, using all the dirt from our tunnelling."

"Thank you, Marni, You're such an amazing teacher. I don't think any other person in this place could have done that for me. I said you were our commander, well, you're my commander forever now."

"One more thing," Marni said. "Who has a green spark? I'd like to give them this same lesson. Then they can help by lending me their flame to help with the tunnelling."

"Grelis does," Yera said. "He's in the passage, I'll fetch him."

"Please do," Marni said. "I'll teach him what we need immediately."

Chapter 22 – Renovations

Marni led the way to the end of the passage, clambering over the mounds of dirt that still remained there. Once she reached the end, she looked at the map, and then at Yera, who pointed at the wall. Grelis stood beside Marni, ready to follow her lead.

Marni smiled, thankful she had left a living root structure there, so she didn't need to use more of her dwindling supply of seeds. Reaching out her hands, Marni placed them on the root covered wall, and focused her energy. Grelis did the same, and Marni placed one hand on his, drawing on his flame and directing it as well as her own.

A green misty glow swirled around the roots, and she pushed them outward, and away from herself. Using the same technique as last time, Marni crushed the mountain rock into dirt. This time she did not cap the end, instead pushing onwards deeper into the wall until she felt the roots burst free into open space.

As the rocks became dust, and she once again sent a second layer of roots and incinerated the first, the dirt fell to reveal a long shaft through which a chilly wind blew.

"Quickly, we need to clear this away and get some light on things," Marni said.

The children all began shovelling at the dirt, pushing more of it back into the existing passage, before Hudson waved frantically at them to stop. Clambering to the top of the dirt in the new passage, where a gap had opened as it fell away to take up the space left open by the incinerated roots, he began digging his way into the dirt, climbing through.

"Follow me, we can take the dirt out the other end, instead of moving it twice."

The other children, in single file, climbed up into the new passage, and followed as he made his way along.

"Be careful!" Marni said. "We don't want anybody getting buried alive."

"Don't worry," Hudson replied. "I'm sure your roots will protect us."

Not wanting to take any chances, Marni strengthened the outer shell of living roots as the children made their way across to the newly opened cavern. By her side, Yera and Grelis both bristled with excitement.

"You can go too," Marni said. "Your yellow flame can give them light,"

"Yes, Ranger!" Yera squealed and scrambled after the others, Grelis right behind her.

After a few minutes, Marni could hear them chattering on the other side, but it didn't seem much digging was happening.

"Hey you lot," Marni called. "If you think I'm crawling through dirt, you're mistaken. Hurry it up and get that stuff moving!"

"Yes, Ma'am!" Hudson called out.

"Hudson," Marni replied. "You should get back here, and go find us some more recruits. You think you can do that?"

"Yes!" Hudson said. "My brother and his friends, I think they'll come. That'll give us a bit of help digging."

"Good, go now, and be quick about it."

Lonay clambered back out of the passage behind Hudson and stood looking at her for a moment. Marni stared back at him, wondering what was up, an eyebrow raised.

"Marni," Lonay said. "Why don't you just use the roots to push most of the dirt out the other end? It's safe to do it now, and that will be so much quicker. Even if Hudson brings twenty kids back, this will take us days to dig out!"

"Good thinking, Lonay," Marni said. "It will take more of my energy, but it'll be worth it to get in there."

"Guys get back!" Lonay called out as Marni knelt down and touched the roots at the floor.

Concentrating, she grew new shoots upwards, then broadened them to largely fill the space, before shoving a massive clump of new growth into the dirt which filled the new passage.

As the roots pushed, the dirt flooded out into the newly opened cavern, as the children squealed and jumped to avoid being buried. Then, as the passage was mostly clear, Marni flashed an intense burst of green flames, hotter than ever before, and incinerated the new roots in a flash. Their ashes fell to the ground to leave a wide open passage leading to the new cavern, where Yera held a steady, small yellow flame aloft.

Marni walked carefully to join the children, then raised a bright green flame of her own, casting an eerie glow across the cavern. She looked around, awed at the size of the space. It had as much usable floor space, once they levelled it, as two of the infirmary plus their existing hideout, and then the lake, which dominated the space.

The sound of water trickling in from the mountain side, and then out again echoed throughout the space, but not so loud as to be irritating. Marni took a pan from nearby where a child had dropped it, and began using it to shovel the dirt out and fill the holes in the floor.

"This is incredible," Marni said. "This will be a much better place for us to work out of."

"Marni," Yera said. "You should go continue the passage, we can do this stuff."

"You're right, of course," Marni said. "The sooner we have that new entrance, the better. I have another idea, once this space is prepared, I want to collapse the infirmary, so we need to move all of the victims in here. I'm sure the rangers will have some idea how to treat them, and I know with my plants we can feed them, probably better than they get now."

"Yes, Ranger," Yera said. "We can do the moving. You focus on our new tunnels and entrances."

Marni nodded, and took one last look around the room, before leaving again, Grelis following her. Lonay entered as she left, carrying lanterns to light the cavern. Marni smiled her thanks to him, and went to work, extending the tunnel to the storage room where they would place their new access to the rest of the mines.

Marni had learned from what happened when she made the tunnel into the cavern. Carefully she made her roots push the bulk of the dirt back into the passage once she reached the storage room. It largely filled the space, but still allowed them to get through. The children immediately began carting the dirt away, to continue the task of levelling the floor in the cavern.

Placing an opening into the store room, Marni took a disused cabinet and moved it a few paces to cover the opening, before smashing out it's rear wall, so it acted as both door and disguise. She then returned to the cavern, and found Lonay.

"We need to post a sentry at the new entry, to shout warning if we're discovered," Marni told him, then looked around and found Yera. "Yera, I need you to go and find Hudson. Tell him we have a new entry, and not to use the infirmary any more. Once everybody from the infirmary has been moved, along with anything we can use in there, I'm going to cause it, and the passage outside it, to collapse."

"Yes, Ranger," Yera said, rushing from the cavern to complete the task.

Marni looked around, and saw the children had already mostly levelled out an area immediate to the entry. But the dirt was still an enormous pile, and then there was the stuff in the passage. It all needed to be moved before her plan for the infirmary could take place.

Smiling encouragement for the children, Marni began moving the dirt herself, the hard manual labour feeling somehow refreshing after using so much of her flame energy on the tunnels.

* * *

Loka, Symin and Rona listened as the highland scout explained what he had seen.

"The smoke came from within the mountain," the man explained. "I was nearby when I heard a cracking sound, then a tree sprouted like a weed from the ground, grew tall, and then was snuffed out in a burst of green flame. It was like nothing I've ever seen! What kind of demon is at work here?"

"No demon," Loka replied. "That would be the work of a green flame wielder. Marni, our student who is still inside the mines, is a green flame wielder. Her secondary ability was not anything close to that capacity when I last saw her, but I have seen the impact of the smoking herb the miners used on Treghan, so I am willing to believe it was her doing. Which means she has escaped from Dreighton, but remains inside for some reason. Thank you, this is good news."

"How do you know she has escaped from him?" Rona asked.

"Because no ranger would reveal their secrets to the enemy under duress."

"She's not a ranger, you said she was a student."

"Perhaps," Symin said. "But between her and her friends, they have seen more action than most experienced rangers. I have faith in Marni to do what has to be done in a professional and skilled manner. But this does mean we must find a way in there. She is going to need our help."

"But why would she do that? Grow a tree to snuff it out?" Rona asked.

"If she is growing and burning vegetation underground, she would need a chimney to release the smoke," Symin said.

"Why would she do that?"

"Tunnelling," Symin said. "I have seen a green flame use roots before. The smoke has to go somewhere, and if she is doing that, it would be taking away the one advantage Dreighton's men have. If she changes the layout of the mines, they're going to be as lost as we are."

"But your student will not be lost, or whoever she works with," Rona said. "I hope you're right, because that makes your student a clever one, and her work could save us a lot of trouble during the assault."

"I don't doubt it," Symin said. "We should ensure our lookouts are stationed at all the known exits. But expect a new one some time soon. If she can get out to us, then we get Treghan and the others in first, to work with her. They make a strong team, and will know what to do to prepare for the assault."

"That, and the children inside will be more inclined to trust and follow rangers closer to their own age," Loka added. "But will it be safe?"

"If Marni can do what we think she has, then the four of them will endure and come out of it victorious," Symin said.

* * *

"Yera," Marni called, as she looked at the map. "You said the water was coming from outside. Can you show me on this map the exterior of the mountain?"

"Yes, Ranger," Yera said, rushing over and sitting to draw on the map. "It's a long way from here at this level, but the water flows from a crack not far above the ceiling and to the west."

"We need a way up there then," Marni said. "If I grow a tree, we can reach the ceiling, but if we dig a tunnel from there, how long would it have to be?"

Yera closed her eyes, and concentrated. Soon, she opened them again and began scribbling on the map. She drew a series of lines, and Marni was confused, until she figured out what the girl was doing.

"Contour lines," Marni said.

"Yes," Yera said. "So you can see what I do. If you plant your tree close to the western wall, to the right of the point the water is coming in, that's the shortest distance. You will need a steep incline, but you can reach the outside in a few dozen paces."

"Excellent," Marni said. "Good work. Come with me, you're going to help me place the tree, so it reaches the right point."

Together, they walked across the bumpy floor and around the lake, until they reached the point Yera had indicated on the map. Retrieving her seed pouch, Marni retrieved an acorn.

"This is my only remaining large seed. Let's hope this works."

Pushing the seed into the ground, Marni went to the lake and scooped up some water in her hands. Returning, she applied the water to the seed, and fed it some of her soft green flame energy. It soon sprouted roots into the floor of the cavern, and then began to grown upwards. Marni carefully guided the tree to grow at an angle, to make it easy to climb, and it twisted and turned as it rose to the ceiling high above.

"Wow," Yera whispered in awe as the tree grew. "That's incredible."

Soon, it had reached high up the wall, near the ceiling, but Marni did not stop there. She caused it to grow along the wall, and broadened the branches to form a kind of landing. Only when she was satisfied with the stability and strength of the tree, did she stop. Yera following behind, Marni climbed the tree, until she stood on the landing.

Grelis joined them, ready to lend her his flame. Looking at the map, Marni walked along until she was standing close to the ideal point they had marked. She then began pushing seeds into the wall and ceiling, and started them growing, drawing on Grelis's flames as well as her own.

Looking down, Marni saw the children had gathered below to watch, awestruck by the power that had allowed her to create a mighty tree out of nowhere.

"Stand back, on the other side of the cavern!" Marni said. "When this tunnel lets go, all the dirt's going to pour out into the cavern, and I want you all as far away as possible."

The children did as she told them, and Marni returned her attention to the task at hand. As the roots grew through the rock and soil on the mountain side, she carefully stepped to one side, then started her second layer, before expanding the first, to squeeze the heart out of the stone.

As it burst into dust, it flowed like a great geyser of earth, to poor in what seemed an endless stream for several minutes, and pile on the cavern floor below. The last of the dirt was followed by tumbling snow and ice, with a slushy, muddy trickle. Finally all was still except the icy breeze which flowed into the cavern, refreshing the stale air.

The children cheered, as the bright mid day sunlight shone at the end of the new passage, and Marni stepped in to venture outside, silhouetted in the daylight and revelling in her success.

"Yera," Marni said. "Do you know the mountains at all well?"

"No, But Jaer was from a highlander village, he knows them as well as anybody."

"Jaer!" Marni called. "I need you to go and find the rangers. They will be in the mountains somewhere, probably looking for us."

"Yes, Ranger!" Jaer replied as he climbed up to meet her. "I'll go to my village. If there's anybody wandering about, our villagers will know about it, and Rona will know what to do."

"Excellent. Do you have time to get there before dark, or is it better to wait until tomorrow?"

"I have plenty of time, but you don't, so I'll go right away."

"Do you need to take any supplies?"

"No, I won't be that long, and I can come back after anyhow. I want to help more."

"OK then, and if you come back, then you can be seen in the mines if necessary, to hide the fact you can escape whenever you like. Plus, I will want to take the rangers a new map soon, so be sure to let them know to wait a little longer if they have a big attack planned. But if they want to send help, we'll take all we can get."

"Yes, Ma'am, I'll see you soon," Jaer said, smiling and waving to the others, before he ran up the passage and out into the daylight.

Chapter 23 – Reunion

Hudson sat in the barracks, tired and alone, waiting for his brother to return from a shift in the deep mines, working to extract metal ore for the enrichment of the four families.

Clayton was Hudson's older brother, and stronger, but had shown no sparks or ice or anything after the smoking. So Dreighton had seen his strength and put him to work in the mines, along with many other young men who had been abducted.

Hudson was concerned he would get found by a guard and punished for being in the worker's barracks instead of his own, but he had to take the risk.

After what felt like an eternity, he heard a group coming along the passage, approaching the barracks. Hudson stood, and moved to stand by the door, out of sight from the passage, and waited as the boys filed in, exhausted and beaten down by the cruel whips of the guards who had driven them to work long past what their bodies could handle.

Once they were in, and Hudson was sure there was no guard, he made himself known.

"You poor guys, you look exhausted," Hudson said.

"Hudson!" Clayton exclaimed. "What are you doing here?"

"Just checking on my big bro," Hudson said. "And his friends, of course."

"You'll only make more trouble for yourself, idiot," Clayton said.

"I'd rather be making trouble for Dreighton," Hudson quipped. "Wouldn't you?"

"Of course we would, isn't that right guys?"

"Yeah!" the others all said.

"But we can't," Clayton said. "You know as well as we do, we're all trapped here, and none of us can fight our way past those guards and the officers who ice."

"What if I told you we could?" Hudson said. "What if I said there was already an easy way out of here, but an even better way to make Dreighton's life a misery?"

The boys crowded around as Clayton towered over him, almost menacing.

"Spill it, bro," Clayton demanded. "And if you're messing with me, I swear, you'll be feeling the bruises for a year!"

"So, had you heard about the ranger?"

"What ranger? You mean that broad the four families had cooped up somewhere? Apparently she had Kurn killed for some reason."

"Rumours never do the truth justice," Hudson said. "Her name's Marni, and she already gave Dreighton what for. She's incredibly powerful, more so than any feeble ice wielder, and she's running a resistance right here in the mines. She digs out tunnels with her powers in minutes. She already has a way out, and has sent for the rangers. But we need your help, to hurt Dreighton and mess up his plans."

"I'm in," Clayton said. "What about you guys?"

"If it means I can get some of that beer the guards have been hoarding, I'm in," one of the older boys said, drawing laughter from the others, before a third boy stepped forward, knelt before Hudson, and placed his hand on the boy's shoulder.

"I'm Hikharn, the de-facto leader among us, and if I say we're in, we're all in. But you have to level with me, right now, before I put our lives on the line. Are you speaking truth? Are you seriously telling us this ranger girl is going to bring down the four families and get everybody out of the mines?"

"I am," Hudson said firmly, with a sturdy nod of his head.

"Then I say we let this kid take us wherever we're needed," Hikharn said.

* * *

Jaer rushed into the village, as dusk took hold and the evening meal was being prepared. He was stunned to see so many rangers, four at least he guessed for every villager. He saw a village scout nearby and ran up to them, soon recognising it as Kreig, a friend of his father.

"Kreig," Jaer said. "It's me, Jaer, I've escaped the mines, and I have to speak with Rona right away."

"Jaer!" Kreig shouted, breaking into a broad grin. "It's a miracle! I swear I thought you lost for good. You run ahead, Rona is with the ranger leaders in the village hall. I'll find your parents and tell them you're safe."

"Yes, Sir," Jaer said, returning the smile as he rushed to find Rona, feeling overjoyed to be home after so many months a prisoner.

Bursting into the village hall, he forgot his manners, shouting out his news in a disorganised and nonsensical ramble, interrupting the meeting which was in progress.

"Young man," Symin shouted, standing to rebuke the boy. "This meeting is vital, and not to be disturbed! Out, you can return in an hour."

"No, Wait!" Rona shouted, overriding Symin. "This is Jaer, a village boy, who was taken by Dreighton's men several months ago. How are you here?"

Symin stared at the boy, as did the others. Village elders and rangers, all of them looked at him in amazement as he pulled himself together and spoke, coherently this time.

"It was thanks to Marni, she sent me to find the rangers, so I came here."

"Tell us what you know," Rona said.

"Marni was held by Dreighton, who planned for her to be married to his son, but when Kurn tried to take control, then ran away to capture you, Rona, Dreighton and his men followed, and killed Kurn and his friends. Dreighton then decided he would have Marni himself, but she fought him off, and is now running a resistance in the mines, building new tunnels and destroying old ones, to mess things up so they don't have the advantage when the rangers attack."

"I knew it!" Symin barked, slapping his hand on the table. "Those students never cease to amaze me!"

"But she needs help. She controls a new entry to the mines, and she wants people in there to help her recruit the workers and free the children, but also to help with clearing rubble from the new passages and stuff, while she rearranges the mines. She plans to send out a map so the rangers know where they're going while Dreighton and his men don't."

"Well, if she controls a new entry, that may be enough. So help she will have," Symin said, standing to shout. "Treghan! Corilai! Fletcher!"

The three youngsters ran in from outside, wondering what was up.

"You three, are to go with this boy to help Marni in the mines. I will accompany you as far as her new entrance, so we know where it is, and I will station a squad outside, so you can get messages to us quickly. I will send five rangers along as well, but this is Marni's game, they will follow her orders."

"Sir!" Loka said, standing. "Having rangers follow a student? This is unheard of! They'll never agree."

"They agree, or they go home. I'll see to that."

"Yes, Ranger," Loka said. "Then send Tara, as the leader of the group, she can take her cues from Marni, and I can trust her to do it. The other rangers will follow her without question."

"Agreed," Symin said, then faced Jaer. "Boy, get yourself a good feed and a good night's rest. At first light, you lead us to Marni."

"Yes Sir!" Jaer said as he turned to leave.

"Treghan, Corilai, Fletcher," Symin said. "You three stick close to that boy. Do not let him far from your sight. You have to be ready to go at first light also. Bring him here, where we will meet you after briefing everybody involved. See you then."

*　　　*　　　*

Marni watched in wonder as Clayton and his friends dug with ferocious speed. They soon had all the dirt removed from the passages and the floor of the cavern, at least an enormous section of it, levelled out. They arrived in the early morning, after a gruelling night shift, yet they launched immediately to work.

Showing incredible stamina, born from the adrenalin of seeing an unguarded exit and a friendly leader, they continued even though they were visibly exhausted from their recent labour in the mines.

"Please, you must rest!" Marni pleaded, but they smiled at her, and kept on working.

After they were satisfied with the floor, they then began carting the children from the infirmary. Not even taking them from their beds, a boy at either end, they carried them without removing them from their rest and began lining them all up at one end of the cavern.

The remaining furniture from the infirmary, they brought as well. It was smashed to build a fire, to fight back the cold now blowing in from outside. As they were half completed with moving the children from the infirmary, Hikharn dragged in a pair of guards, who had entered the infirmary to investigate the noise.

Both guards were badly bruised from the ensuing scuffle, but now were bound tight, and Hikharn dragged them to the edge of the lake, near the base of the tree, where he tossed them, before going to find a stake and some rope to attach the pair to. Once he was done, he faced Marni, and bowed his head.

"I'm sorry, Ranger, we could not risk them informing Dreighton of our whereabouts. But now they are sure to be missed."

"Do not fear," Marni said. "Just complete the emptying of the infirmary, and I will bring the roof down on that place, and the passage beyond it. Dreighton and his men will think these two dead in the cave in, along with the children."

"Yes, Ma'am," Hikharn said.

Marni stood and watched, as so many young people worked together at her command. For the first time she realised the strength of Yera's words, a few short days ago.

"I really am their commander," She whispered.

"Marni!" Shouted a familiar voice.

Turning and looking up, Marni was stunned to see Symin, standing on the tree landing, surveying her handy work. She blushed, sure it was insufficient in the ranger's eyes. Then she saw Treghan and Corilai, entering behind him, and finally, Fletcher emerged, walking slower, his injury from the bridge obviously still paining him, or perhaps paining him anew after the long walk here from wherever the rangers were camped.

He beamed her a smile, and Marni felt tears welling in her eyes as she rushed to climb up and meet them. She headed directly for Fletcher, wrapping him in a warm embrace before turning to greet the rest of them.

"I'm so glad! I thought I may never see you all again. And Treghan! I feared you dead!"

"I nearly was," Treghan replied. "But thanks to the highlanders I was saved. Now I'm as good as new."

"How's your icing ability?" Marni asked.

"Good enough," he said, turning to erect an icy wall over the end of the passage. "How about I put a few of these halfway across the passage, like teeth from either side, to stop the wind roaring down here and freezing you all?"

"Please do," Marni said as he took the icy wall down again.

A second group walked down the passage from outside. At the front of them was Jaer.

"Jaer, thank you," Marni said. "You've done very well."

"Anything for my commander," Jaer said, drawing quizzical looks from the others.

"I can't stay," Symin said. "However, I congratulate you on your work so far. I will await your new map, once your modifications are complete. I wish you good luck. We will be stationing a group here with you, led by Tara, who will report to you directly. I will send a squad to stand guard outside, as we are doing at the other known entries to the mines. As soon as you're ready, we will attack."

"Symin," Marni said. "Thank you for coming. But before the attack, may I ask of you two things?"

"What is it, Marni?"

"Firstly, has Treghan told you of the smoke?"

"Yes, it is a fascinating thing."

"And it is a dangerous thing also. We have a good many children here, who had a poor reaction to the smoke. They number more than half those who had any reaction to it at all."

"What happened to them?"

"They have gone mad," Marni said. "They scream of the loss, the separation, from that which has been stolen from them. I believe they have lost their innate flaming ability, before it could awaken."

"That's horrible," Symin said.

"Which is why I ask you, can you find out if there is anything we can do for them? I have taken them into my care, as Dreighton's men were not looking after them. They were the last to be fed, and left to rot in their own filth."

"Of course, we'll look into it. What of the other thing?"

"I would like to try to get as many children out of the mines as I can, before the attack, so they are not hurt in the fighting."

"Of course, we will work with you on that. When you're ready to start the evacuation, let the rangers outside know. If at all possible, we will take them to the village before the attack commences."

With a wave to the others, Symin left, and Tara stepped up to face Marni.

"Marni, we are here to help, and will complete whatever tasks you require."

"Thank you," Marni said. "For now, please help the boys moving the children from the infirmary. We intend to collapse that room, and the neighbouring passage, as soon as it is empty."

"Yes, Ranger," Tara said, offering a salute, before leading her five companions down into the cavern.

"Marni," Fletcher said. "Did you grow this tree? And make these tunnels? All with your secondary ability?"

"Yes, I did," she replied.

"And Corilai does her camouflage thing, and Treghan has his ice now, so I'm the only one left without a powerful secondary."

"Yours will come soon enough, my dearest Fletcher," Marni said. "I'm sure of it. Now, come with me, we have work to do."

"Well, I brought you these, anyway," Fletcher said, handing Marni a pouch filled with a fresh supply of seeds.

The young green flame smiled and embraced him, as she took the pouch, touched by his thoughtfulness.

Marni led her friends down into the cavern, and soon they stood at the entry to the infirmary, inside the closet. Tara and her rangers were carrying the last two beds out of the room, and the boys were quickly rounding up the last of the furniture.

As they all left, Marni smiled, entered the room, and placed some seeds in several cracks along the walls. Ushering the others back into the hideout, she sent forth her energy, and awakened the seeds, sending their questing roots up into the stone above, to seek moisture and in so doing, crack the mountain rock, as she had already done so many times.

In a short time, there was a rumbling as the ceiling began to protest, and then, all at once, it came down. The collapse blasted air, dust and rubble into the hideout, with sufficient force that Marni was thrown backwards, to be caught by Fletcher, who was standing a short distance behind her.

"Thanks, Fletcher," she said with a smile, before approaching the old opening where the infirmary used to be.

Now, a towering wall of rubble blocked her way, and the rumbling continued as the passage on the far side of the infirmary also gave way, the rumbled roar of the mountain's anger echoing deep into the mines.

*　　　*　　　*

Tara looked over the maps with Marni while they planned. She thought for a long while, before drawing a similar map in the dirt.

"You see how they have the mines arranged? There are main shafts, smaller alleys, and crossways. If we collapse the right ones, we can force them to retreat how we want."

"And how is that?" Marni said.

“We hunt with rangers from here, where we are, and these other three entrances, we have a squad already placed deeper down, where the mines proper are being worked, and they push up, while the rest push in from the sides. Then, we round them up at the main entrance, where there’s a large open area. Of course we have a large force outside to trap them in that area.”

“Right, so there are two problems,” Marni said. “We have to collapse, at my count, twelve crossways and a couple of passages, all in quick succession. Also, we have to tunnel down into the mine proper, so we can smuggle a squad in there.”

They both looked at the map for a long while. There was some distance between them and the area in question on the map, but it was on roughly the same level. Then Marni saw the answer, as Lonay sat beside her.

“The passage to the old storage area, where we have our new entry to the hideout from the mines, it runs the full length of the complex, but only intersects three times with the rest of the map. Once near the infirmary, which is already gone, once at this point half way, where it has stairs leading to the higher levels, and once close to the other end, where a cross way joins it to the central complex where Dreighton and his officers all hang out.”

“So, you’re saying we knock out those other access points, then tunnel a new one to the mine proper from the other end?”

“It’s an option,” Marni said. “Though I’d rather be able to access that central complex area as well.”

“Then we make a new access. We drop the roof along the side passage from beyond the stairs, then take a left hand turn and dig down from there. That will put us into this room. What’s that?”

“That’s the kitchens,” Lonay said. “It’s a good entry point though, and they won’t expect it. So if you collapse the passage like you said, and the other cross way leading into where the families are, you can control all movement from there back, which means we’re even more secure here.”

“Good, then I think that’s what we do first,” Tara said. “We collapse those two points, then secure our two new passages to move our troops in and push them up towards the main entrance.”

“Then that’s what we do,” Marni said, nodding. “And after that, we send our people through the new access points to do the rest.”

Chapter 24 – Preparations

Marni watched thankfully as the two guards were taken away by the rangers. It was too much of a risk keeping them there, if they would be going out into the mines. She couldn't rest easy knowing those two young men might threaten the well being of the children who worked so hard for freedom.

She climbed down from the tree landing, and made her way across the cavern, to where Treghan and Corilai were kneeling by the bed of one of the children from the infirmary. The boy on the bed was calm, but his eyes were darting around. He was young, perhaps only nine or ten years of age.

"I can't believe they'd do this to a child," Corilai said.

"It's horrific, and they don't care at all, so long as they get a few strong ones to fight for them."

"Surely the ones fighting don't really support them? They were kidnapped after all," Treghan said.

"Not all of them, there are the four families, which as far as I can ascertain, are quite large, and they are all here united under one ambition. As well as that, the ones with the ice power, they know nothing about their flames, and just believe Dreighton has given them a miraculous new ability. They swear their allegiance to the one they think has helped them, and ignore the plight of their fellow kidnapped."

"Surely some will see reason," Corilai said.

"Maybe they will, but I'll not be counting on that. I expect a tough fight ahead, even after we get most of the children out."

"Do you think there's anything we can do for these ones?" Treghan asked.

"I hope so," Marni said. "I know if you get them calm, they're much better. Maybe there's something the rangers have which can calm them long enough that they recover."

"That would be good news," Corilai said. "I hope they can all recover."

"Can you two come with me?" Marni said. "We have some work to do."

She led her friends out of the cavern and around to the mine entry in the storage area. Along the way, Tara and her five rangers met them, and followed. Marni waved away Hikharn and his friends, and with a smile they returned to the cavern.

Walking out of the storage room, they began walking along the passage, a formidable group of rangers in the heart of Dreighton's mines. Tara looked about, anxious, on her first foray into the mines. She kept her voice low as she spoke to Marni.

"If we're seen now, the operation will be over unless we capture and subdue the enemy, before the alarm is raised."

"I Know, and even so, I feel we should split up," Marni replied. "You take your rangers to the second intersection, and do whatever it takes to cave it in. We'll go up the stairs at the first intersection, and bring down that passage, then prepare the area for the new tunnel into the kitchens. I'll dig that one later, when they stop looking around the cave in. Once we've blocked it off, we'll continue to the end and start working on the passage into the mines proper. We'll meet you there."

"OK, it will be done as you say," Tara said.

As they arrived at the first intersection, three guards appeared, and yelled. Thinking fast, Treghan erected a solid ice wall, stopping them from returning up the stairs. The three guards looked them over, and panic lit their eyes. As one, the guards turned and ran, headed for the second intersection.

Tara and her rangers ran after them, moving at an astonishing pace. Marni and the others were still standing there, as Tara pulled out a pouch, tossed a spray of seeds, and hit it with a tendril of green.

"What?" Marni exclaimed with a gasp. "She's a green flame like me? How did I never realise that before? I should have noticed her gloves!"

As Tara's flame awakened the seeds, strong tendrils of creeping vine shot forth, to entangle the feet of the fleeing guards. The vines continued, snarling their legs and arms, and holding them tight.

"Marni!" Tara called. "We need them taken back and handed over to the rangers outside."

"Send one of your group to the cavern," Marni ordered. "They are to find Hikharn, and have him come with as many of his boys as he can muster, to take them away and deliver them into the care of the rangers stationed outside. Once Hikharn has them in custody, the rest of us proceed exactly as planned."

"Yes, Ranger," Tara said.

"Can you use your seed to bring down the roof?" Marni asked.

"I've never tried, and most of my training has been in combat techniques, but I am sure I can give it a good shot," Tara replied. "If there's any trouble, between us, we'll get the job done, mark my words."

"Good," Marni said. "Treghan, please remove your ice barrier. I don't want anything to arouse the suspicions of anybody else coming this way. If they find us here, I want the element of surprise."

"Yes, Marni," Treghan said, rushing back to his barrier, and taking it down with a single flash of white.

"You, please, you know your mission," Marni said to one of the other rangers, who nodded and ran back towards the cavern.

They waited in silence, nerves on edge, the three guards gagged with vine, until after what felt like an eternity, Hikharn and seven others arrived with the returning ranger. Tearing at the vines, the boys separated the three guards, while leaving them well bound. They carried them away, soon disappearing in the darkness of the passage.

"OK, we know our mission, and we rendezvous at the end for the new tunnel into the mines proper," Marni said, turning and walking up the stairs, her three friends following.

"Yes, Ranger," Tara said, leading the five rangers with her to the second intersection.

Reaching the top of the stairs, Marni moved along the passage a small distance, and beckoned the others to join her.

"We must be quick. Corilai, please erect a camouflage, I know you can, after how you were in the blizzard that time."

"Yes, Marni," Corilai said, concentrating and building a swirling maelstrom of darkness around them.

"Treghan, I want you to build me the strongest ice wall you can manage, to stop the cave in from blowing out and hitting us. Do you think you can manage that?"

"Yes Marni," Treghan said.

"What do I do?" Fletcher mumbled.

"Just hold me up from behind," Marni replied. I'm exhausted after days of this, and I need your support right now."

"Of course," Fletcher said, rushing to her aide.

Marni began placing seeds, until she was satisfied, and nodded at Treghan, who immediately erected a thick, sturdy wall of ice. Marni focused her energy and fed her tendrils of green flames into the seeds.

*   *   *

Tara led her rangers into the intersection, and rounded the corner, straight into the light of a torch. It was held by a young boy, who promptly turned and ran. Tara set out after him, but soon realised it was all for nought, as the boy could be heard screaming.

"The rangers are here!" the boy shouted, his voice echoing through the mines.

"Dammit," Tara cursed. "Well, we still have to do this. We're not letting some brat ruin it all for us."

She rushed deeper into the cross way, and planted a line of seeds, sprinkling more and more as she ran back to her companions. Then, she sent her green flames dancing along the passage.

"We're running out of time fast," Tara cursed.

*   *   *

Dreighton sat in his audience chamber, fuming. One cave in was bad enough, but now a second, terrible one, had crushed the infirmary, not far from that first one which they had to clear a few days ago.

"We have to keep it secret," Dreighton said. "Too many of the brats we have here had siblings in that infirmary. And besides, we lost two good men as well. We need all the guards we can muster, with the rangers skulking around outside."

"The rangers are no threat to us yet," Warreigh said, drawing agreeing murmurs from the other two men in the room, Taro and Pilt, the heads of the other two families.

"Well," Dreighton snarled, turning on them. "If they're no threat to us, why do I still feel concern? Think about it, one bratty girl, and how much damage has she done? Was she responsible for the cave ins? Or is that just coincidence?"

"We have no reason to believe the girl could be capable of such power," Taro said.

"I hope you are right," Warreigh said. "but I fear Dreighton's concerns are well founded on his experience with the girl."

"Ha!" Pilt spat. "So the girl spurned his advances. That hardly makes her super human."

"Maybe not," Warreigh said. "But the brat is still lose. I say it's high time we take her down."

"Agreed." Dreighton said. "It's time we remove her from the equation."

Just at that moment, they heard a voice, echoing from somewhere nearby.

"The rangers are here!" came a boy's high pitched scream.

"Damn it!" Dreighton snarled, slowly dragging himself to his feet. "Get ready for the fight of your lives."

"They can't do too much," Warreigh said, also rising.

Just then, an almighty roar assailed their ears, as the crashing thunder of multiple cave ins shook the heart of the mountain, and rattled Dreighton's steely resolve.

"Damn those ranger bastards!" Dreighton shouted. "They must be doing this!"

He rushed to the corner where Warreigh's men had piled several months supply of the smoking herb.

"Close those doors," Dreighton demanded as he struck a flint. "If those rangers want a fight, we'll give them one!"

"Dreighton, what are you doing?" Warreigh asked.

"I'll take Kurn's power!" Dreighton shouted, smashing a lantern on the floor to spread its oil over the plants, encouraging them to burn. "If this stuff did that much for him, it had damned well better do the same for us! Imagine it, we four, supreme lords of the mountain, fighting back a hoard of ranger scum, all thanks to this ridiculous plant. Shut those damn doors!"

As Warreigh and Taro closed the doors and fitted a sturdy bar across them to seal them in, Dreighton struck flame to the enormous pile of herbs, the flames burning bright and ferocious across the spilled oil, and igniting the herb with vigour.

Soon, the room began to fill with the acrid, dangerous smoke which had sent half the children who reacted to it insane. One by one, the four men succumbed, and soon the four lay there, unconscious, as the effects of the large quantities of mind altering smoke slowly flowed into their blood.

* * *

As the roof came down, Marni grabbed Fletcher's hand and dragged him down the stairs, with Treghan following. Once in the main passage, they looked back, and watched as the ice wall cracked, and then shattered under the pressure of the rock from above and behind it. The rubble spilled outwards, some tumbling down the stairs.

"I may have gotten a bit carried away," Marni said, gasping for air as Fletcher held her with concern in his eyes. "We can't stop now, come on."

Together, they ran along the corridor, and as they approached the second intersection, they heard an immense rumbling. As the four youngsters reached and passed it, Tara and her five rangers ran out to meet them, turning and joining them as they continued down the passage, a cloud of dust and debris bursting out of the cross way behind them while the ceiling, for nearly a hundred paces into the now blocked cross tunnel, met the floor with a cataclysmic roar.

Reaching the end, Marni pulled out her map, and looked at it for a long moment. Then she looked up at the wall and squinted.

"Tara, I might need your help now," Marni said. "I'm so tired."

"No problem," Tara replied, pulling out her seed pouch, and placing seeds in the wall to one side, while Marni did the other.

They then held hands, and both concentrated. The seeds sprouted, and pushed their way into the rock, and after a long journey, burst free into a cave at the heart of the mine.

"We should push with the roots from this end," Marni said. "But only once we crush the rock into dust."

"Understood," Tara said.

Together, the two green flame wielders sealed the wall in front of them with roots, and expanded the walls of their new passage inwards. Then, both exerting their full focus, they pushed, and the roots surged through the mountain, shoving an enormous plume of dirt into the mine on the other side.

"I hope there was nobody there," Marni said as they burned the roots.

Shortly, as the smoke and dust cleared, they began to make their way through the new tunnel, to emerge into a scene of bedlam. Two teams of miners, the older, stronger children Dreighton had drafted to do the hard, physical labour, were in a pitched battle with five guards, who were striking them with ice and swords.

Not waiting for introductions, the rangers rushed in, overwhelming the guards with their superior numbers, in a swift flanking movement. It was over quickly, Tara's vines tangling the guards and binding them.

"Thank you for coming!" one of the boys said, approaching them. "I am Jistun, and these are my boys. I take it you're here to take down the four families?"

"Yes," Marni said.

"Then we're all with you. What do you need?"

"Go back the way we came," Marni said. "Take those men with you, there will be rangers who can take them into custody. We prefer that than allowing them a chance to escape and raise the alarm."

"About that," Tara said. "We were seen by a boy, who ran off shouting into the central complex."

"Then we must act fast. You boys, go now, but first, tell me," Marni said. "Are there other teams down here working?"

"Yes, four other teams. There were eight guards. You buried three guards with the rubble, they were of the four families. Then five more subdued in the fight. The last one's still around, and he's a bastard, so be careful. Each team is down one of these main shafts."

"Thank you, Jistun," Marni said. "Tara, your team can take two shafts. We'll split up, Corilai and Treghan down the third shaft, and Fletcher and I will take the fourth."

"Yes, Ranger," they all said.

"But where are we going?" Jistun asked.

"Follow the passage to its end. There is a secret entry to our hideout in the storage room you will find at the end of the tunnel. There should be a sentry there, they can guide you out of the mines."

"Yes, Ma'am!" Jistun replied with a clumsy salute, before rallying his boys to haul the five bound guards out of the area.

Splitting up, the rangers set about finding the rest of the slave boys. Marni ran to the fourth shaft, Fletcher at her side.

"Are you sure you're OK?" Fletcher asked. "You look so exhausted."

"I'll be fine, we have to finish this."

"OK then."

Holding hands, they walked down the long shaft, Fletcher lighting the way with a small red flame. After several hundred paces, they finally arrived near the end of the shaft, where ten boys were swinging axes at the walls to break away the ore from the heart of the mountain.

"Boys!" Marni called out. "You are freed from Dreighton's rule. Please, go to the end of the shaft, and find the new passage we have made, and follow it to your freedom."

Nine of the boys run up the shaft, cheering. The tenth loitered behind.

"Did you hear us?" Fletcher said, brightening his flame as Marni approached the boy.

In a sudden, rapid movement, the lad spun around, and then they saw his face, and realised their mistake. This was no boy. This was that final guard, and he lunged towards Marni, who was too tired to respond quickly enough to escape.

The guard dragged her back against him, clutching her tight, and raised a wicked, jagged blade to her throat.

"Stop right there, filthy ranger!" the guard shouted. "Or the girl dies."

"You bastard," Fletcher snarled. "Let her go."

"No, here's what's going to happen," the man said in a lilting, sing song voice. "You are going to raise your hands, and stand back, against the wall, while we pass. If you try anything, this blade will liberate her head from her body, before it kills you. If you behave, I'll release her once I reach the end of the shaft. How alive she will be, I couldn't rightly say. But you will be."

"Her life is worth more than mine," Fletcher said, his rage building. "How dare you try such a foolish ploy. Your life is the one to end today, not mine, and certainly not hers!"

The red flame flashed, and then shot out from Fletcher's hands like a spear, a long, solid, glowing red lance of fire, hard as steel and swirling like a maelstrom of lava, it pierced the man's shoulder, then retracted as he dropped the knife, screaming.

"Bastard!" Fletcher shouted, as the lance flashed, then struck again, bringing a second scream and the smell of cauterised flesh as it burned the man from the inside.

Panicked, the man released Marni, and she rushed to stand behind Fletcher. The lance retracted, then the flame manifested as a mighty, broad, two handed sword, hard and glowing with the menace of Fletcher's rage. He swung the sword, and it carved a chunk of the wall away, to crash to the ground. Fletcher grinned, a wicked grimace of anger as he approached the wounded man, who cowered against the end of the shaft like a frightened animal.

"You see what power you thought to face?" Fletcher snarled as he raised the fiery sword for the final blow. "You won't face it again!"

"Fletcher no!" Marni screamed, causing Fletcher to halt his action, though he never let his eyes move away from his target. "He's not worth killing. Please, for me, spare this monstrous person, so you don't become him."

As her words struck him, Fletcher stepped backwards, away from the man, lowering his sword. He watched as vines rushed past his feet, to bind the wounded guard in a cocoon so tight, even unwounded, he would never escape.

"Now, drag that bastard out of here," Marni commanded with venom as she slumped to the floor.

Fletcher used his flame to trim the vines, leaving enough to use as a rope to drag the man. He began pulling him along the shaft, pausing to offer a hand to Marni. She gratefully took it and leaned on Fletcher's shoulder as they slowly made their way out.

"Fletcher," she said softly, with pride in her voice. "That's one hell of a secondary,"

"Yeah," he replied, smiling. "It really is."

Chapter 25 – Rescue

Tara and the others were waiting for them as Marni and Fletcher returned. They looked them over for a moment, before rushing to help. Treghan and Corilai took the man from them, and continued to drag him away as Fletcher paused and Marni looked around.

"Tara," Marni said. "You told me somebody already raised the alarm?"

"Yes," the ranger replied.

"Then we can wait no more. We'll take this bastard back to the cavern, and notify Symin we intend to begin the assault as soon as he can get his men in here. We'll have to rescue the children as we go. I don't have the energy to open another access point, and we probably don't need it anyway. Just save the kids, and round up the four families, and their sympathisers. Push them out, towards the main entry, as we planned."

"Yes, Ranger," Tara replied. "Please, get some rest, even if it's only brief. We need you at your best. And don't worry, we'll dig out the buried guards. If they survived, we'll have them looked after. The boys were insistent those three were of the four families, no parent in Windwall is going to hate us."

"Thank you, Tara," Marni said.

"Now go," Tara said, waving Marni away. "My people and I will hold this area, now we have it cleared out. I will collapse the secondary access points, and focus on the main shaft up to the next complex. Tell Symin, and adjust the map."

"I will, and please, be safe," Marni replied.

"We will see you soon, Commander," Tara said.

Marni blushed at the enormous compliment. She continued to lean on Fletcher's arm as they made their way back towards the hide out, following their friends.

* * *

Only a few hours later, Symin, Loka, Rona, and Marni stood on the tree landing, while a hundred rangers and highlander warriors crowded into the cavern below, barely fitting into the space along with the freed children.

"Rangers, and Highlanders," Symin said. "We fight together. Know that we push from the depths of the mines, while our remaining forces push in from all known entries. The main entry is left untouched, but guarded, and we will push them to it. Along the way, any children we find are to be escorted back here, to this cavern. Marni has provided us a map, and we have drawn up twenty copies, which have been distributed to your officers, so if you get lost, find an officer. But if you stick with the group, you'll be fine."

"My people!" Rona said. "We fight with the rangers, our friends, for the safety of our children, and the end of a tyrant. For too long, this man, Dreighton, and his cronies, have held sway in these our mighty highlands. Today, that sway comes to an end, and with the help of our friends, we will usher in a new age for the people of the mountains."

"Rangers," Marni shouted. "Highlanders, go!"

With a cheer, the combatants surged out of the cavern, along the tunnels and into the mines.

"Shall we?" Symin asked.

"We shall," Rona replied.

"Let's do this," Loka said, and Marni smiled, pleased to finally see an end to all her hard work.

Together the four of them climbed down into the cavern where they were met by Fletcher, Corilai and Treghan, and they joined the end of the long line of warriors heading into the mines. Once they reached the cavernous mine proper, where the fighters had paused to wait, Tara approached.

"I kept them here for now, but we march on your orders," she said to Marni.

"I'm so tired," Marni said. "And there is much experience to be used here now. I officially hand the operation to Symin, may your flames burn true."

"Thank you, Commander," Tara said, with a smile and a nod to Marni, before turning to Symin.

"Ranger, we await your orders."

"Begin the operation," Symin said.

With a nod, Tara ran back to her group, at the single entry to the rest of the mines, and began shouting her orders, and waving people through to commence the assault.

"Marni," Symin said. "Perhaps you and your friends should hang back,"

"Yes Sir," Marni replied. "We can help guide the children out of here, once the rangers and the highlanders are all inside. There will be many still to save."

"That is good thinking," Symin said. "As we clear areas of the enemy, you are to lead them through to locate and rescue all the children. But take care, and we will see you soon."

"Yes, Ranger," Marni replied.

As the fighters surged into the mines, Marni began to wonder if their plan were flawed. Then, as prisoners began to emerge from behind the battle lines, she understood. Not all the enemy were in places they could flee from. Those who were cornered when the rangers found them, would fight and die, or be captured. And those could not be logically sent anywhere but back, to where they waited to send the innocent to freedom.

Realising the problem, Symin returned, with a group of ten Rangers, to help control the prisoners. Treghan erected a wall of ice over one of the shafts, and they began placing the prisoners in there, resealing with each new addition.

Then, the first child prisoner arrived, and Marni questioned everything she had thought about this enemy.

"I'm a son of Dreighton!" the little boy squealed. "Take your hands off me!"

"You will submit to the law of this country," the ranger dragging the boy said. "That means, you cooperate, or you face prison."

"Ranger!" Marni shouted. "This is a child! What are you doing?"

"This child tried to kill our people, with this," the ranger said, tossing a savage short curved blade to the ground as the boy fumed.

"I'm not a child!" the boy snapped. "I'm nearly ten years old, and one day, this whole place will be mine to rule!"

"Not on my watch," Marni said. "You will not come to harm in ranger custody, but if I let you go, I have no doubt, with your sense of entitlement and your false air of superiority, you would bring harm to others."

"I'm one of the four families!" the boy screamed. "You can't do this to me!"

"It will be done, and you will soon realise it is for the best," Marni snapped. "Put him with the other prisoners. I will discuss his fate with Rona, once this is over."

As the sounds of battle echoed to them, the wounded began to appear as well. First, a ranger with a gaping wound in his shoulder, where an ice wielder had speared him, then the ice wielder who had done it, covered in burns and screaming in agony. He was just a teenager.

Marni watched as Treghan used his white flame to melt the seal on the shaft, to admit three more prisoners, and then used his ice to seal it up again.

"This is a messy business," Marni murmured. "That children are fighting in such a place, speaks only of evil. But is it theirs, or ours?"

"It's not your evil, ranger," the ice wielder said. "It was ours. I fell for the promise of power, but the man who burned me, with his white flames, he was just like me. I see that now. Your friend over there, he ices like me, but he flames in white, like the man who defeated me. How is that so? Was Dreighton that badly informed that he didn't know what he was doing to us?"

"You figured it out," Marni said, kneeling beside the young man. "Just from seeing Treghan seal the prisoners?"

"No, I suspected already, but I was giddy with the power Dreighton had given me, I was too foolish to realise it was not the ice talking to me."

The young man looked down at his hands, and sparked a simple, white spark. He looked at Marni, and smiled.

"Please, I have to try."

"Go ahead," Marni replied.

He looked back at his hand, and squinted, straining in his concentration, until finally, a tiny white flame appeared for just a moment, and he slumped back, exhausted.

"Then it is true. The ice is just a white flame's ability. I wasn't hearing my ice, being kept company by it, it was my flame all along, and I wasn't listening. Dreighton never gave me the flame, never even knew about it. He only used us for his own ends, and didn't care what he was giving us, or denying us. A lot of the kids had coloured sparks. Could they have had flames too?"

"Every one of them," Marni said. "You have wisdom, for a young man."

"Will they be able to join the rangers one day?"

"Perhaps."

"Will I?"

"I don't know," she said, standing.

"Wait," he said. "I have to know. Will your officers forgive us? Will they let us come to learn under you, to be better people? Now that Dreighton's rule is ended?"

"That depends on you, and how you go in your trial, the same as every criminal in Cinder. But sadly, it also depends on the others, the poor, mad ones, those little ones your smoke did such harm to."

"Oh, I'm doomed then. They're all dead, after the cave in. Dreighton tried to keep it quiet, but the rumours spread fast in the mines."

"No, they're alive. I don't know if they'll recover though, and what you did to them, was rip their flames away. The rangers will not easily forgive such a thing."

"I see," the boy said. "Then I will face my trial, and accept my punishment, but I thank you, for showing me the truth of my ice and my flame."

Marni stood, and walked away, visibly shaken. Fletcher, who stood nearby, listening, followed.

"Marni," he said. "I'm proud of you. I couldn't have done that. I couldn't have spoken to that boy, and given him that comfort. My rage would have never let me."

"That will change, Fletcher, don't worry. As you grow, and learn, you'll see, but for now, your flame is strong and bright and impulsive, and ruled by your emotion. You see that right? Why you needed that moment, for your secondary to come out? Now it's out, you can tame it, and I'll be right beside you the whole time."

A sudden flood of children ran into the area, shouting in excitement as they looked around, marvelling at the rangers in their midst. Loka entered with them, and rushed to Marni and Fletcher.

"This is most of them, I think," Loka said. "We found three groups holed up in their barracks, with guards stationed outside."

"Thank you," Marni said. "At least somebody here cared for them enough to put them out of harm's way during the attack. I'm thankful for that. I'll lead them out. Children! Follow me."

Marni led the children out, Fletcher by her side. She was anxious to be somewhere, anywhere, away from all the pain and anguish she sensed in that room. Somewhere she could get her thoughts in order, and calm down. Back to her safe space, the refuge she had built, which now would be a refuge for all the innocent ones, until the war was over.

* * *

Dreighton stirred first, and clambered to his feet, looking around the smoke filled room. He twitched, and laughed, then held up his hands before him. He concentrated on his fingers, and they sat there, doing nothing. He laughed again.

Warreigh stirred, and stood, and looked around, disoriented. Dreighton watched as the other man stumbled, then caught himself, shook his head, and smiled.

"Did it work, old friend?" Warreigh asked.

"Nothing magic over here," Dreighton shouted. "But I feel strong, Ha! And I feel the gods in me! I am a god! I see it now! I can't have the ice, or the flame, or whatever that bitch had, because that would be unfair! Because I'm already a god! Why else would the world give me the mountains to rule?"

"And I stand beside you, your sword as always!" Warreigh replied, quick to realise the situation.

"Good!" Dreighton barked, striding towards the remaining two men, and kicking Taro in the gut. "Wake up, you old fool!"

"What?" Taro grumbled as he slowly climbed to his feet. "What are you shouting about, you mad idiot?"

"Yes," Pilt said, standing, the last of them to wake. "You mad old goat, what the hell did you do to us? We're going to be attacked, so you knock us all out? Are you stupid?"

"Silence!" Dreighton screamed, his voice cracking as he strode to Pilt, swinging his massive fist at the man's head. "I will not hear such insolence from you! I am a god, did you not hear me?"

Dreighton's fist struck Pilt's head, and the man flew sideways, his head flopping limp, his neck snapped in that one colossal impact. Dreighton laughed again, finding humour in the man's death.

"You see? Only a god could have this strength!"

"Dreighton, what did you do? Settle down man!" Taro shouted as he rushed to check on his friend.

"I am not a man!" Dreighton bellowed. "I am a god! Kneel before me Taro!"

"You're no god, you're a mad man!" Taro shot back.

"With my strength, you call me your god," Dreighton snarled, as he approached the man. "Or you die."

Taro flinched under the gaze of Dreighton's cold, red eyes, but he stood his ground.

"You are a mad man, and you have doomed us all," Taro said calmly.

"No," Dreighton replied, equally calm. "I have only doomed you."

Dreighton's hand shot upwards and forward, catching the man's chin in his palm, and snapping his head backwards, breaking his neck in that single motion. As Taro's body crumpled to the floor, Dreighton spun to face Warreigh.

"What of you?"

"I am your sword, as always," Warreigh replied.

"Of course you are, you said that already, didn't you?" Dreighton said, smiling. "Open that door for me, sword!"

* * *

The rangers crushed into the main entry, forcing the guards, the ice wielders, and the many remaining members of the four families, to push back, towards the opening to the outside. Then a second line of rangers, fresh and ready, and champing for a crack at the enemy, moved in to seal the only escape route.

In the front of the push, Tara pulled out her seed pouch, and called to the assembled enemy.

"You are all now prisoners of the rangers of Emberdale. You will be sorted, and processed, and will face trial for your involvement in this place, and the crimes committed in the name of your leader, Dreighton."

She cast a line of seeds, walking the perimeter of the crowd.

"Green flames, assist!" Tara shouted, and several rangers pushed out of the crowd to help her, spreading seeds of their own.

Then, a green glow spread across the floor, as the rangers applied their skill, focusing the power of their green flame, and a cage of thick vines sprung into the air, up and over, to form a dome over the prisoners.

"You will stay there, until we're ready to deal with you," Tara shouted, before pushing through the rangers, intent on finding her way back to Loka and Symin.

It took her some time, but eventually she reached the rear of the surging army, and she commanded three rangers to follow her.

"We must conduct a sweep, to be sure there is nobody left to be captured, or needing to be saved. Symin and Loka are already working on it, we will join them, and assist."

"Yes, Ranger!" the three said.

Chapter 26 – Dreighton

Dreighton and Warreigh burst out of the audience chamber and into darkness. They could still hear the echoes of battle, but somebody had smashed the lanterns.

"I guess we missed something," Warreigh said.

"That we did," Dreighton snarled. "You go that way, I'll go this way. You find anybody not from the four families, you kill them."

"Yes, Sir," Warreigh said.

"Wait," Dreighton said. "Those two did not have faith in our allegiance, their families are no longer with us. Anybody not of my blood, or yours, kill them."

"Yes, Sir," Warreigh said. "Good hunting, Sir."

"And to you," Dreighton said, laughing like a merry child as he ran off down the corridor.

Warreigh shuddered, and made haste, hoping to put as much space between himself and the mad man as possible. He ran as fast as he could, figuring he would make haste to the main exit of the mines, and from there, disappear into the highlands. Hopefully the rangers would take care of Dreighton, before that mad fool came after him.

"You there!" shouted a woman's voice.

Warreigh stopped, and looked ahead, into the darkness. A blackness swirled there, menacing and hot. This was no ordinary woman.

* * *

Loka marched along the passages of the mines, dark and deserted, seeking any stragglers that had not met with either salvation or judgement. Her black flame swirled around her, a maelstrom of intent, and a protective cloak of fire. Her power was intense, and she had not had opportunity to wield it like this in some time.

Just like those young ones, she had felt her power growing, and her skill improving, ever since the battle of Judd, which seemed an eternity ago now. Loka smiled, as she sensed a body in the darkness, running towards her.

He was not even trying to hide. But he was not a child. And he was not a ranger. That made him an enemy.

"You there!" she shouted, as she continued her slow advance.

The man stopped in his tracks, and stared at her for a long moment, before glancing back the way he had come. He seemed to be considering something.

"You are trying to decide what you fear more, aren't you?" Loka said. "What lies behind you, that has you so spooked? Is it Symin?"

"Who?"

"Well, never mind. You will be fighting me, now. You will likely never see that other horror you flee from ever again."

"Good enough," the man said, drawing a savage, serrated edged sword, and swinging it from hand to hand with expert precision. "I am Warreigh, head of the second family, descendant of Bex himself, who first tamed these mountains five centuries ago. I am the sword which will cut you down, ranger."

"Well spoken," Loka replied. "But I am Loka, master of the demon flame, enforcer of Emberdale, and a fighting power unmatched in all of Cinder. You will burn at my hand. Your blade shall melt and fade away, and your reign over the sword will come to an abrupt end in this passage. Come."

Warreigh snarled, and ran, sword raised. Loka countered immediately, lashing out at him with a hot, black whip of fire. It cracked across his face, and he screamed, jumping back.

"I see," he said, stooping down and scraping up a hand full of dirt from the floor. "This is how it's going to be, is it?"

With expert aim, Warreigh threw the dirt into Loka's face, the dirt flying straight into her eyes.

"Dammit!" she shouted, dropping her flames and throwing her hands over her face, too late.

She brushed the dirt away and looked up, just as his sword came crashing down at her head. With skilled movements, Loka dodged to the side, and the sword tore at her cloak, before crashing into the floor. With a well placed boot, Loka hit his side, and sent the man rolling into the wall, as she raised her fiery maelstrom again, and struck him, three quick lashes across his back, while she circled around and backed away.

Warreigh screamed at the searing heat as his coat and shirt smouldered, the flames scorching and blistering his skin underneath, gaping holes in the fabric exposing the wicked wounds to the air.

"I'll kill you for that, witch!" he snarled as he climbed to his feet.

Sword levelled, he lunged at her, hoping to run her through. Loka stepped aside again, holding her cloak open so the sword slid inside, then wrapping the cloak over the blade, and twirling away from the man, in an effort to disarm him. As he came close due to the movement, she planted her knee firmly in his abdomen, and while he crumpled slightly, he never released the blade, and its serrations tore at the cloak.

"Arrr!" he yelled as he heaved backwards on his sword, and ripped it loose, leaving her cloak in tatters.

"Damn you," Loka snarled, raising her hand to send a swirling ball of darkness at his face.

Warreigh ducked, and planted his fist in her abdomen, causing her to back up and buckle from the blow, before he span, and landed a swift kick to her shoulder, sending her over onto her side. As Loka scrambled to collect herself, Warreigh raised his sword for a savage blow.

"Loka!" Tara screamed, her vines already shooting forward to stop Warreigh's swing.

"Don't interfere!" Loka shouted, rolling aside as the sword struck the floor.

Tara's vines fell away at Loka's command, and the young ranger stepped back from the fight.

Warreigh's sword bit into the floor, and he strained to remove it, but he was too slow. Loka's fist, encased in demon flames, struck the side of his head with a force which sent him sprawling, his sword left behind. Loka grasped the hilt, and snatched it up. Her flames engulfed the sword.

Holding the weapon at arms length, Loka pointed it towards her enemy, as it began to drip, molten steel pooling in the cracks of the floor as her fire demonstrated its superiority over the work of Warreigh's blacksmith.

"You are beaten," Loka said. "Tara, bind him."

"Yes, Ranger."

* * *

Symin rushed through the corridors, away from a dead end where there had been what he surmised was a kitchen. There had been a sealed door, and he was heading towards it, in the conviction that his final quarry lay there. Suddenly, he heard giggling, like that of a little girl, only it was in the voice of a grown man, deep and menacing.

He stopped and listened, and waited. Soon, he heard the shuffling, erratic movement of the man's feet, coming towards him in the darkness. Symin lit his yellow flame, bright as day, illuminating the tunnel for a long distance.

There, a short distance away, the man stopped, taken aback by the sudden light, and the man holding a yellow flame before him.

"Who are you?" Dreighton demanded.

"I am Symin, scout commander, I am a ranger of Emberdale. Who are you?"

"I am your new god. Will you bow to me, or die?"

"You are not my god. I will not bow. I ask you again, foolish man, who are you?"

"I am Dreighton, and I rule over this place, and you are my prey. I will end you now."

"You will not. If you do not surrender, I will be forced to subdue you. I can not promise you your life in that instance," Symin said.

"And I would never grant you yours," Dreighton replied, dancing in close and swinging a fist at Symin.

Symin dodged, and hit the man with a burst of yellow flame, hot and searing. Dreighton ignored it, and continued swinging. The second punch landed on its mark. But Symin's jaw, moving away already, did not snap backwards as Dreighton had intended. Symin span as the force of the blow sent him away, but he did not fall.

Planting his feet and crouching down, Symin raised both hands and thrust them upwards and into Dreighton's ponderous gut, bursting his hottest fire into the man. Screaming, as the flames took hold of his shirt, Dreighton backed away, enraged, tearing the fabric away.

"I'll squash you like an insect, you meddling ranger!" Dreighton shouted, charging forward again, his fists swinging. Symin dodged again, once, twice, and a third time, before swinging his right fist, encased in fire, at the berserker's head.

He felt the impact, he saw the flames engulf that savage maw, and he felt the crack of bone, but Dreighton was not even slowed by the punch. He seemed without pain, without shock, as he swung on, his rage unstoppable by the yellow flames of a scout.

Symin realised he was in a bind, but he fought on. He dodged one, then another swing from the brute. Then a third swing from the berserker narrowly grazed the ranger as he stepped back the other way. Still trying to keep his footing, Symin swung another fist, and struck with yet more fire, but the man was not feeling it. While not impervious, and clearly taking injuries, the powerful miner fought on like a lumbering juggernaut, unhindered by pain.

Dreighton hit Symin's chest with a sturdy jab, and the ranger flew backwards, landing upright but unable to stop his momentum. Symin tumbled backwards, and fell to the ground, as Dreighton rushed forward, intent on the kill.

Symin struggled to his hands and knees, and as the tyrant reached him, Symin darted away and around, sticking a well placed kick into the side of Dreighton's knee as he passed. The heavy man fell, crashing to the ground with a roar born of rage, not pain.

Symin reached his feet and faced the beastly man, as Dreighton lumbered his way back up. Cumbersome and slow in righting himself, his torn clothing revealed mounds of muscle slowly turning to flab with age and idleness.

"Clearly you feed yourself better than you feed your charges," Symin snarled. "I will end you now, you wicked, greedy old fool."

"Raaarrr!" Dreighton snarled, surging forward again.

Symin raised both hands, and fired a ball of hot yellow flame at the man, but it burst around him and had no effect. Symin shot another, massive fireball, the heat intense as he strove to put all he had into the flames. He dodged to the side as Dreighton passed, the flame's heat barely affecting his power, in spite of the heavy smell of burning meat which filled the air. The miner's shirt was gone, replaced by blistering skin and terrible burns.

"You can never defeat me, ranger!" Dreighton growled as he turned, and prepared for another charge. "As soon as I get my hands on your puny neck, it will snap just like all the others."

"And soon, you will succumb to your burns, as your flesh falls away from your bones," Symin snarled. "I will not lose to you."

"You will lose," Dreighton said. "But first you will suffer. I had intended to simply snap your neck and kill you, but now... now I want to break all your bones, and make you scream for mercy. You will beg for death, before I am finished with you, you filthy ranger."

Dreighton advanced, slower this time, swinging his fists at Symin, and Symin dodged again. The first swing met nothing but air, as Symin stepped aside. The second brushed the rangers side as he twisted to change direction. Still pushing, Dreighton grinned, and laughed.

"Got you!" he yelled, as Symin, still moving to the side, had not regained his footing after the move to dodge the second punch, and Dreighton, seeing this, swung at the ranger's arm, landing a powerful blow just below the shoulder.

Symin screamed as the bone shattered. He reached his other arm up to aim a bolt of flame at Dreighton's face, but he was too slow. Dreighton caught the arm and hurled Symin from his feet, tossing the ranger like a rag doll down the passage.

Landing on the broken arm, Symin struggled to right himself. As he scrambled on the ground, trying to get back to his feet, Symin was well aware of the approach of his enemy.

Dreighton kicked out, and stomped his foot down on Symin's right ankle, eliciting an agonised scream from the ranger, as more bones splintered. The brute kicked the ranger in the side, sending him sprawling even further into the darkened passage, the yellow flames now extinguished by his pain.

Symin barely heard the rapid footprints of a new combatant as Dreighton loomed over him, reaching to grab him by the collar and drag him up into the air. Dreighton seemed oblivious to the approaching company, and Symin was in no mood to mention it.

Hauled up into the air by his shirt, his legs dangled uselessly above the ground. The enormous man lifted him high, intent on choosing the next bone to break. Symin dared a glance over the tyrant's shoulder and, just in time, he saw it.

Twisting his head to the side, Symin dodged as a spear pierced the berserker's head from behind. It erupted from his right eye socket, to continue with the force of the thrust, narrowly passing Symin's ear.

"This is for your son, you bastard!" Rona screamed, as she dealt the final blow to the man who had brought so much harm to so many.

Dreighton dropped the ranger, and in his final seconds, tried to turn to face his killer, but the long spear, too long to fit across the narrow corridor, prevented him from doing so, as it protruded from his broken skull. The life flooding out of him, Dreighton fell to his knees, then toppled to the side, as dead as the stones which caught him.

"Symin!" Rona shouted, scrambling over the huge corpse, to reach the ranger, who sat up, and propped himself against the wall. "Can you walk?"

"I don't think so. Do you mind?"

"Not at all, my friend," She said, lifting him up and offering her shoulder as support. They walked in the darkness, him in too much pain to flame, and her unable, and slowly made their way back to where they knew their friends would be waiting.

Chapter 27 – Endings

The village was swollen with people, as the rangers and the highlanders took all the freed children and the prisoners back there, from the mines. Symin sent to Windwall, requesting all the carriages which could be made available to help transport everyone back.

The next day, after spending a night packed like sardines into every building in the village, everybody was relieved when a long line of carts and caravans began to arrive. The people of Windwall, so grateful to the rangers for rescuing their young ones, had travelled the perilous road over night, to reach the village as soon as they could the next day.

The open carts of the city guard were used to transport the prisoners, in chains, to be placed before a judge in the city at the earliest opportunity. Everybody agreed these people should face trial on a case by case basis, according to what their involvement had been.

Many children among the captured were immediately released, when it was found they had been forced to work for the guards, or the four families, and as such were caught up in the final battle.

But the difficult cases were the guards, and the ice wielders, many kidnapping victims themselves, forced to fight for the tyrant Dreighton. Some of them felt a debt to the man for granting them power, which they were only now discovering was power they could have likely gained without his intervention.

Brun, head of the guard, his deputy, and the mayor of Windwall had all come with the caravan, and now sat on stools outside the village hall, talking with Symin and Rona.

"We have many children in need of ongoing treatment," Symin said. "We need to arrange a place for them to receive the care that is required, preferably in the city."

"That can be arranged," the mayor said.

"The children of the four families," Rona said. "I would ask they be placed in the care of my people."

"Agreed," Symin said. "We also have a large number of children who have had their latent flame wielding abilities prematurely and artificially awakened. We would like to be able to provide training for them also."

"What are you asking for?"

"We would expand our current outpost, to build a full campus of Ranger Academy in Windwall, in order to provide proper training and education for all the children who have been impacted by this crisis. Our hope is that with time, those in the infirmary will recover such that the building used for that purpose, can instead become one part of that academy."

"Of course, Windwall and its people will cooperate in any way necessary," the mayor said. "However, in the trial process, I ask that I sit with your people, so a local representative is present for all proceedings, to ensure justice is fair, and the trust is kept between us."

"Understood," Symin said.

"Further, for the interests of justice, I request that those convicted of participating with the enemy as ice wielders or guards after being abducted by that enemy, be put to work both building the infirmary for the injured, and in looking after those children, until such time as all the children have recovered, and that only at that time, may they seek admission to your academy."

"I think we can all agree to that," Symin said.

"And if that is all you have to tell me, I have work in the city, and preparations to make. What say we load up all these people and begin the journey home?"

"Yes, Mayor," Symin said, shaking the man's hand with a warm smile.

"Before you go anywhere, Symin," Rona said. "You must allow me to check your wounds. You clearly can't walk and you have an arm out of commission as well, so you won't be riding a horse."

"Of course, but first, have you seen Loka?"

"She is at the stables."

"Good, can you help me to her?"

"Of course."

Rona offered her shoulder, and Symin gratefully accepted it.

"You saved my life, my friend, I will not soon forget it." he said.

"It was nothing you would not have done had the situation been reversed."

"Perhaps, but still, this experience has shown me something important."

"What's that?"

"Life can end in a moment, so I must ensure no regrets, were that to occur."

"Hence you must speak with Loka," Rona said. "I understand. I've seen how she looks at you, and you at her."

Symin blushed, and said no more, as they ambulated slowly towards the stables. With no more talking, it felt a little awkward, but all that fell away when they rounded the wall at the end of the stables, and he saw her, standing there. He hair was glistening in the mountain sun, her brand new cloak shining with a fresh dusting of snow from her morning walk.

"Thank you, Rona," Symin said. "I'll be fine from here."

Rona nodded and left them, as Loka watched him lean against the wall for a moment, before grasping his crutch, and clumsily walking towards her.

"Symin," she said.

"Hush, Loka," Symin said. "I have to speak with you. This is important, and it's private."

"Yes, Ranger?"

"No, no formality now, please Loka, my friend, my oldest friend, I must tell you..."

"I know, Symin," she said, with a sigh, as she stepped towards him, holding her open arms for him to collapse into.

They held each other like that, for a long while.

"I almost died," Symin said.

"I know, my love," Loka replied.

"I couldn't live with myself, knowing how close I was to death, if I came that close again without speaking to you, about us."

"It's OK, Symin,"

"No. It would have been a great regret for me, and I fear for you, had I died. Loka, we have spent so many years watching over one another, but never saying the words, so here it is. I love you. Not as a friend, not as a mere lover, not as a colleague. I love you as my companion, now and for the rest of my life. I would have you know this, before I die."

"Oh Symin," she whispered with a sigh. "I love you the same way. There is no other man could hold my heart as you do. You have been my mentor, my pupil, my guide, and my guardian. You have been like my brother, and my father, and my son, all in one uncompromising, and undying truth. So now, I ask you this one thing. Be my all, for the rest of my days, that neither of us need regret it when we die?"

"Of course I will be, as you are for me too."

They said no more words, standing there in each other's arms as the snow began to fall anew outside. Then, a cough from the doorway brought them back to reality.

"It's time to load up," Treghan said.

They looked at him, standing there with a grin from ear to ear, Corilai by his side, blushing redder than Fletcher's flames. Her grin matched Treghan's, and they knew, these two had heard everything.

"I'm so happy for you both," Corilai said. "It's about time!"

"Nobody says a word," Symin said. "We'll tell the others when we're ready.

"Of course, Ranger," Corilai replied.

*   *   *

The people of Windwall lined the streets and the walls as the long caravan entered the city. There was cheering, music, and streamers. The caravan made its way to the courtyard of the ranger outpost, where people began to climb down. Parents cheered as their children ran to them, with tears of joy at their longed for reunion.

Some parents watched as their older children were led down in chains, to speak with them, before going off to the guard house to face trial as accessories to Dreighton's tyranny. These brought tears of a more mixed variety, but even so, their children were returned to the city, alive, as promised.

Then many other parents were led, in a sombre mood, to greet the carriages of the injured. Those who had lost parts of themselves to the smoke. Those who would be spending time in the new ranger hospital for treatment. For them the tears were also mixed, but for different reasons.

All of those parents, however, felt gratitude to the rangers. When the request was made for help in preparing the infirmary and the new academy, many would go on to donate a lot of their own time and resources to the project, finally welcoming the rangers to their city with open arms.

Temporarily, the infirmary was set up in the existing dorm, but it was terribly crowded, and not sufficient. Jarls took on the task of running the facility, demonstrating her wisdom and knowledge as she led the team of rangers assigned to nurse the ill children back to health.

With the number of people helping growing daily, the new, wooden building for the infirmary was erected within a mere five weeks, and the children were moved in without delay, as soon as they were able. It was a simple facility, but Jarls made the most of it, indulging her charges with the best of food and only the most loving and tender of care.

The parents and other relatives were allowed to visit, but only under strict controls, to ensure the children were not upset by undue stimulation while they recovered. So it was, that one day, six weeks after the opening of the new infirmary, Hudson sat on the steps of the building, and waited while one of the nurses fetched his sister.

By this time, the new campus of the academy was already in full operation, and many of his close friends, made under the command of Marni when they were working as a resistance force in the mines, were attending classes there. Hudson himself had been attending, but as he did not have flames, many of the lessons were not suitable for him, which he did not mind as it gave him extra time to spend with his sister. She had been showing steady progress, and he was hopeful she would be able to go home soon.

Hudson was roused from his thoughts by the nurse, who opened the door and beckoned him into the waiting room. Kres stood there, hands clasped before her, her eyes focused on the floor.

"I think she's ready to go for a walk outside, today," the nurse said with a kind smile.

"Are you feeling that much better, Kres?" he asked.

"Yes, I think I can stand seeing the city again now," the girl replied. "I may even be able to come home in a few weeks, though the thought of it makes me rather nervous."

"That's wonderful!" Hudson said. "Come, I'll take you to the bakery. We'll buy some sweet breads, and go and eat them in the park, OK?"

"I think I'd like that," Kres said.

Taking her hand, Hudson led his sister out of the infirmary and down into the city. Eventually, they found their way to the bakery and went inside. Paying the last of his allowance to the baker, Hudson bought them a raspberry sweet bread and a bottle of juice each. He led her back into the street, where they nearly ran into a passing group of rangers.

"Oh, I'm sorry," Hudson said, as one of the four turned to face him.

"Hudson!" Marni said with a warm smile. "And Kres, isn't it?"

"Yes, How have you been Marni?' Hudson asked. "I've missed seeing you guys around."

"We've been well. We returned to Emberdale for classes, but we wanted to come back and see how everybody here was doing, so when Symin said he had to come here for the week, we decided to tag along. Kres, it's wonderful to see you up and about."

Kres shied away, blushing and looking down as she clung to her brother, hiding behind him.

"It's OK, Kres," Hudson told her. "You've met Marni before. She help us a lot, in the mines. She was the first one to take pity on you in the infirmary, remember?"

"Mar… ni?" Kres said. "Yes, I think I remember. I felt safe with Marni."

"Yes, that's right, and you should feel safe with her friends too, because they're our friends as well."

"If you say so," Kres said. "Will they come to the park with us?"

"If you would like us to, we will join you in the park," Marni said.

"Yes, I think I would like that, I feel safer with you here."

Together, they walked to the park and found a pair of benches, facing each other, in the shade of a towering fir tree. Treghan rushed ahead, and used his power to clear the powdered snow from the seats, and they all sat down, while Hudson and Kres ate their sweet breads. The four young rangers talked softly among themselves as they waited, and finally Kres jumped up and clapped her hands, before shyly sitting again, and looking around the group.

"Hudson, I had something I wanted to show you, and I want to tell Marni about it as well."

"What is it?" Hudson asked.

"Remember, I had lost something? Something important?"

"You mean..." Marni said.

"Yes, in the mines, I told you..."

"Yes, we all remember," Hudson said.

"Well, it started talking to me again. I think it's coming back."

"Wait, talking?" Marni said. "You mean, you can feel it again?"

"Look," Kres said, holding out her hand and smiling.

Her eyes twinkled and she looked at the space between her fingers. As they all followed her gaze, they saw it. Undeniably and unbelievably, it was there. Tiny, but very bright. A dancing, golden spark.

Book Three
Sand Rangers

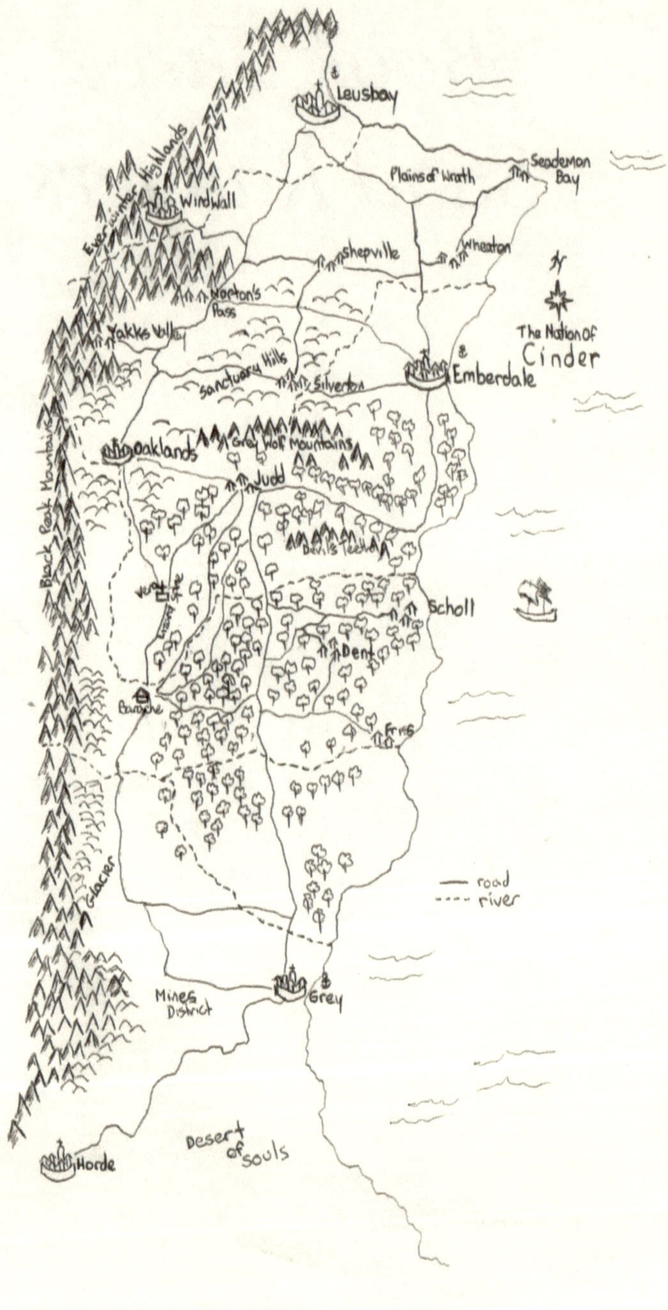
Leusbay
Seademon Bay
Plains of Wrath
Everwinter Highlands
Windwall
Shepville
Wheaton
Norton's Pass
Yakks Valley
The Nation Of Cinder
Emberdale
Sanctuary Hills
Silverton
Oaklands
Grey Wolf Mountains
Judd
Black Peak Mountains
Devil's Teeth
Scholl
Dent
Fris
Glacier
road
river
Mines District
Grey
Desert of souls
Horde

Chapter 1 – Southern Rumours

Hyren was excited as he rushed through the streets of Horde. Today was to be his initiation. At fourteen, his sparks finally came in, so his father took him to a secret back room at the nearby tailor's, and had his cloaks fitted. Now, scarlet and new, the silken garment rested safely concealed in the satchel Hyren carried from a strap over his shoulder.

His feet slid in the sand as he rushed across a vacant plot of land between the tavern and the armoury. The sun beat down on his face as he glanced up into the cloudless southern sky.

"You must never reveal this robe," Hyren remembered his father telling him. "And you must never reveal your flame. If the rangers come, you are talentless. But best to hide if they do. They have ways of sniffing us out. But for these seven hundred years, the order has remained hidden, buried in the sands of Horde, just as our ancestral home rests beneath the sands of the Desert of Souls."

Hyren had so many questions! He always knew his father would sneak out and go somewhere, that there were secret meetings and strange visitors in the night. But it was only now, when he was about to be initiated into the Order of the Essence, that he was even aware of its existence.

What were they, really? Hyren's father said they were keepers of the truth, and concealers of the flame. Whatever that meant. He also said the order was the thing that would keep and protect him, once he was initiated, for the rest of his life.

He would not need to work in the conventional sense, besides as a cover for his involvement. People, Hyren's father had told him, would ask questions if a well fed man sat idle. But that was irrelevant. He was finally going to learn about his father, what he was really doing when he crept out of the house at night!

There was an entire world, previously hidden from him, and Hyren was going to enter that world, and make it his own. As he rushed along the street, head down, he almost didn't see them until it was too late. Hyren glanced up just in time to see the two rangers walking towards him.

"What are they doing here?" he muttered, and ran down an alley to avoid the men.

*　　　*　　　*

Pirette and Gurrei walked together through the streets of Horde. The weather was hot, but they kept their full ranger uniform on, with the hoods down, and sweated in the intense heat of the southern city.

The locals looked at them with bemused expressions, many wondering about the foolish northerners, who must be terribly uncomfortable in all that excess clothing. Not for the first time, Pirette considered abandoning protocol to cool off.

Most of the locals ignored them, treating them no differently to any other stranger. The occasional person, however, looked at them with distrust and even malice in their eyes.

Stepping around a bend, they saw a young lad, carrying a satchel. The boy was looking down, and heading right for them. The rangers stopped, and watched the boy.

The boy stopped, looked up, and saw them. The boy was startled, having come close to running into the pair. Without a word, the boy dashed away down an alley. He seemed genuinely concerned with getting away. The rangers followed, Gurrei casting his yellow flame after the boy.

"He's a flame," Gurrei said. "Let's see where he goes."

The pair stopped, and found a quiet alcove where they sat. Gurrei continued the pursuit with his flame. The boy darted from lane to lane, following a twisting and convoluted path. Gurrei kept pace, and did not lose him. Then, a dark wall appeared in his mind's vision, and the boy stepped through it.

He vanished.

"What?" Gurrei said.

"What is it?" Pirette asked.

"The boy vanished."

"Impossible. You must have just lost him."

"No, I was right there, on his flame, and it just vanished. Snuffed out."

"You mean he's dead?"

"No, I don't think so. It's just like his flame went quiet, like it's behind a shield of some kind."

"Do you remember where it was?"

"Of course."

"We should walk there, see it with our eyes," Pirette suggested, throwing a flurry of sand high into the air with his orange flame's secondary ability in exasperation.

"Agreed," Gurrei said, standing and walking back into the lane.

The two rangers walked slowly and purposefully, following the same route taken by the boy a few moments earlier. Finally, they came to a square. On the far side, the walls of an ancient building stood, unmarked and mysterious.

"Do you know that building, Gurrei?" Pirette asked.

"No, I haven't been to this part of the city before. Any idea what it is?"

"Well, it's ancient, and it has no markings at all. If there's some kind of business there, it's only known to those inside."

"Perhaps a temple?" Gurrei said.

"Perhaps, but a temple to what religion?"

Pirette strode out into the square, and an unease came over him. He walked back to his colleague.

"Something feels… not quite right about this place."

"Let me see," Gurrei said, casting his yellow flame out. "It's black, like nothing. It's like somebody ripped that building from reality."

"Do you think the boy went in there?" Pirette asked.

"I know he did."

"We should ask the locals," Pirette said, waving at a small boy running nearby. "Hey, boy, what is that place?"

"That's the church of the essence. Nobody goes there besides the monks."

"What do they do?" Pirette asked.

The boy shrugged, and ran away.

"I guess it's a temple, but for what purpose or who it's devoted to is anybody's guess," Gurrei said.

"No, it's the temple of the essence, whatever that means. Shall we see if we can enter?"

"Not now, this place is creeping me out. I'm not setting foot in that place without as much knowledge of it as this city can give us."

The two rangers turned and wandered away, careful to make a note of the location of the temple. Returning to their small outpost, a tiny shop front between a bakery and a blacksmith, Gurrei and Pirette nodded greetings to Hillis, their receptionist, and walked through to the back common room.

They removed their cloaks and threw themselves into a pair of armchairs as a young ranger brought them tall jugs of water. They smiled their thanks and each took a long draft of the cooling liquid.

"I'll be reporting that odd building to Emberdale," Pirette said.

"Of course," Gurrei said. "Be sure to include the information about the disappearing boy. Be certain to explain that this boy entered the darkened temple and that was when I lost him. I've noticed an unusual lack of visible flames here, and this was not the first time one has slipped away from me."

"Really? Why haven't you mentioned this before?"

"I didn't want to report it because they might question my abilities. But now, well, tell them this is a repeated occurrence and the number of flames we can sense is low. There might be a greater mystery here, and it may require more hands and an experienced mind to solve."

"Agreed," Pirette said, standing to leave. "I'll file my report and have the bird take it immediately. I am sure we will have an interesting response from the Chancellor."

* * *

In the temple, Hyren found a small alcove, lined with shoes and jackets. Stepping into the alcove, he changed his clothes, donning the beautiful red cloak of the initiate.

Slipping out of his sandals, he stepped back into the main foyer, and looked around. The temple was eerily quiet, but he knew to expect that. They'd all be downstairs, waiting for him in the basement for the ceremony.

A single flame, green and bright, was burning in a sconce at the top of the stairs, which stood at the rear of the foyer. Hyren looked around, and for the first time noticed an old man by the door. He watched the boy with a quiet deliberation.

"I," Hyren said, to be interrupted by a waved hand.

"Do not speak, young one. I stand guard lest the commoners or worse, those rangers who followed you, try to enter during the ceremony. You had best hurry lad. Your ceremony is about to start."

With a nod, Hyren turned away from the old man and rushed to the stairs, which he descended carefully, hitching his long robe so as not to trip. Reaching the bottom, he found himself at an intersection. A corridor ran across the base of the stairs.

The passage to the right was darker than a moonless night. To the left, a second flame lit the way. Hyren followed the passage to a sturdy wooden door, with elaborate steel trim.

Raising his fist, Hyren paused a moment, then knocked. Three taps, as his father had told him. He waited for a long time, until the door creaked open and a hooded figure gestured for him to enter. Hyren found himself walking into a pit. He was surrounded by dozens of hooded figures, each shrouded in flame.

All different colours were there, some flames of red and orange, violet, blue and green, and even the dreaded black and the mysterious white. All colours of wielder were present, and they stood hooded and hidden, humming a single, monotonal sound in unison as Hyren walked to the centre of the pit.

Drawing his hood over his head, Hyren raised his hands, and added his voice to the others, before launching his orange flame to the ceiling. A gong sounded, and they all stopped, as flames burst into being in lanterns around the room. The men and women of the order of the essence removed their hoods and approached him, hands out to congratulate the boy on his initiation.

*　　　*　　　*

Treghan smiled as he sat in the back of the class room in Emberdale. He watched as the students performed their end of year demonstrations for the class "secondary application." It was a slow process, and there was great variety in skill shown. They only had to show the secondary was present, not that it was in any way strong or useful.

Seated beside him were two third year students, wielders of the white flame, who had volunteered to take the second year class after the discovery of the ice secondary of white flames. Prior to this, the white flames had been exempt from the class.

Now, all colours were required to attend, but those already beyond the second year were offered the option to return and complete the training on a voluntary basis. Nobody knew how difficult the ice secondary would prove over time for students to attain.

At the front of the class, an orange flame was twirling dirt into complex structures, the flames surging in a dust storm then settling to reveal intricate sculptures of far away buildings, or people. Treghan joined in when the class applauded, but he wasn't paying attention.

Soon enough it would be their turn. The white flames would have to stand there and demonstrate their ability. Treghan was nervous, but not for himself. The ice had not come easy for the third years, and one in particular, Ferron, had barely managed a foggy cloud of moisture before now.

"You go first," Ferron said.

"No," Treghan said. "I don't want to make anybody more nervous by blowing up a storm. Just do your thing, but do it on the windows. The glass will chill, and then the condensation formed will freeze up into a frost. That way you can pass, even at your current level."

"That's a great idea!" Ferron replied. "Thanks, Treghan. How did you think of that?"

"When I first discovered my ice, I did that on steel bars. I was desperate, but it was what I needed to spur me on."

"You had that smoke treatment from the miners though," Ferron said.

"And I was desperate to get out of there. But I had been attending the classes with my brother, so I had some secondary training already even though they thought there was no secondary for whites. You have the training now, so you'll be just fine."

"Besides," Kyru, the other student said. "We're third year already, and only here voluntarily. They can't stop us graduating, or hold us back to repeat a year. Even if you fail this class, it's fine, not like the second years or those coming up from first year will have. For them, they have to pass or else."

"You're right," Ferron said. "Say, Kyru, have you thought about what you want to try for after graduation?"

"I'm going to the support staff. Too much danger out there for a white who can't fight."

"Whites can fight," Treghan said. "I can tell you that!"

"I'm not like you Treghan," Kyru said. "I came here from Silverton, where my family are well off, and I have never seen danger. I've never been desperate. My flame doesn't burn with resolve like yours. I sometimes wish… Never mind. I just don't have your strength. My flame is lazy I guess."

"Don't be such a wet blanket," Ferron said. "You'll never grow without pushing yourself, isn't that right, Treghan?"

"I guess so," Treghan replied. "But if support is what you feel suits you, go for it. I bet you'll become a great administrator or something. Hey, maybe you could even go for Chancellor one day!"

"What are you doing, Treghan?" Ferron asked. "Schools out next week."

"Well, obviously I'll be back for third year, but I put my name down for the field study again."

"Why?" Kyru spat. "You damn near died last time, in the mountains."

"But I got so much stronger because of it," Treghan replied, absent mindedly rubbing his shoulder, where the ice spear of the miners had pierced his body. "I want to try to be the best ranger I can be, and these field study trips are amazing. You get to see so much of Cinder, you'll never get that in support."

"Whites!" the teacher shouted from the front of the classroom. "Since you lot want to talk through the demonstrations, you go next. Get up here, all three of you."

Chapter 2 – Calling

Symin tossed and turned, his mind struggling to make sense of what he was seeing in his dreams, as bursts of soft yellow light fluctuated around him. In his mind, he watched a young man at the controls of some kind of machine he could not recognise.

"Sena, can you please check the container?" the young man said. "Let me know when it's secure, and I'll start the next round."

"Yes," Symin heard a feminine voice reply.

He felt himself walk out of the room, and through a sturdy steel door into a small chamber. At the centre was a pedestal with an elaborate and confusingly familiar piece of equipment on it. Tubes and pipes and gauges covered the thing, which was roughly twice the size of a horse's head.

Symin watched as feminine hands manipulated the tubes and set clamps in place, before disappearing from his field of vision.

"All set," the female voice said. "Leaving the chamber now."

* * *

Symin sat at the table, his breakfast going cold, his countenance moody. Idly, he stirred his eggs with a fork, mumbling to himself

"What does it mean?"

"What does what mean?" Loka said, sitting beside him.

"The dreams. I'm having these, recurring dreams about these people I've never met. There's all this strange technology in their world, and I just can't make sense of it."

"That explains your mumbling last night. It wasn't making much sense, and you got pretty loud at one point."

Loka stood, picking up his mug, which sat empty beside his plate.

"I'll get you another drink. You have to eat that, or you'll be useless for the graduation ceremony. Those third years are relying on you not to screw this up."

"And those second years have all applied for the field work. You know who I mean," he said.

"I know. We'll take them with us, of course."

"You're coming?"

"What did you think I'd do?" Loka snapped. "Sit here in Emberdale and wait while you wander about without me?"

"Well, no, but… I'm not sure what I'm going to be doing. This time there isn't any big emergency or mysterious kidnappings to investigate."

"That reminds me," she said. "You have a meeting with the Chancellor right after the ceremony. Don't forget."

"I won't," Symin replied.

"Good, now finish your breakfast," Loka said, standing to leave. "I have some student meetings this morning, to help them plan for next year. I'll see you at the ceremony."

He watched as she left the mess hall, passing several rangers at the door, then looked back at his food. He waved his right hand over the eggs, and released a soft, questing tendril of flame. The yellow light skipped and danced away from the plate, and around the table.

"Just what is it you're trying to tell me?" he mumbled.

* * *

Hyren smiled, gleeful that he had been admitted into the order, though he still knew nothing about it. His father walked beside him, leading him with a hand at the small of his back, to where three old men sat in ornate chairs on a raised dais.

"Ignitors," his father said, bowing. "I introduce Hyren, newest member of the order, and wielder of the orange flame of the earth."

"Welcome Hyren," one of the three men said. "I am Rogan, first ignitor of the Order of the Essence. I am sure you have many questions."

"I do, Sir," Hyren replied.

"You will stay here in the temple for the next month, and each day we will teach you our history, and our purpose. Also, you will be trained to know your flame."

"Is that like ranger training?" he asked.

"Foolish boy!" another of the men shouted, standing in his anger. "The rangers know nothing of what they wield! To them a flame is a tool, a device. Your flame is your companion, not to be disrespected by forcing it to work for you, producing secondary powers for your own glory. Your flame lives within you, but it is not simply a part of you. You must respect it, hear its wishes, and treat it as your brother. This is why rangers are not welcome here."

"Be calm, brother Malthus," Rogan said. "The child is merely ignorant. As are the rules of our order, he has clearly been told nothing before today. Until now, the rangers will have been all he knew of the flame."

"You're right, of course," Malthus said, sitting. "But you must never compare us with those heathen rangers. We are the true guardians of the flame, now and always."

"Ye… Yes, Sir" Hyren stammered.

"We shall start by explaining who we are." Rogan said. "Krytus, will you do the honours?"

"Of course," the third ignitor replied, before leaning forward and looking long and hard into Hyren's eyes. "I believe you are ready to begin learning the truth of your world. We, are the Order of the Essence. We guard the flames of this world, and the essence which was the cause of their creation. The essence was a tool, a fuel for a powerful technology, used by the ancients, our ancestors. You are descended from them, and they were mighty indeed."

"Where were they from?" Hyren asked.

"They were from this region of the world, when Cinder did not yet exist. The world was shaped differently then. The desert of souls was a verdant forest, and at its heart, the city stood, which was our ancestors capital. Fertile fields provided more food than we could eat, and we traded all across the world, and we became wealthy."

"So where did they go?"

"I will get to that soon enough, child," Krytus said. "They developed knowledge unmatched in other nations, and we grew powerful. The emissaries of the ancients spread around the world, and brought back new technologies, and new ideas. Those which were good, we incorporated into our own and became greater still."

"So there were other countries?"

"There were many. Hundreds, some suggest. All unique, some powerful, some feeble, some prosperous, some whose citizens starved in the streets. Never did they find another nation where the essence was used. Never did they share the knowledge of that power, though the ancients brought back much knowledge from the world."

"What was the essence like?"

"It is a liquid, green and luminescent. We still hold large supplies of the essence, though without a store of the technology, it has only limited applications today."

"And what happened to the ancients?"

"They sacrificed themselves, and created Cinder, to give mankind a safe haven when the outside world was destroyed by war."

"They created Cinder?" Hyren said. "What does that mean?"

"We do not know precisely, but they were powerful. I believe it means they created the situation which would forever isolate Cinder from outside hostilities. I believe that they somehow created the mountains and the maelstroms, and in so doing sacrificed themselves, their forest and their home to create the third boundary, the desert of souls. This fearsome power may have saved the people who would become the nation of Cinder, but it doomed the ancients. Their power was soon forgotten, by all but the order. We were entrusted with their secrets."

* * *

Symin stood to the side of the parade grounds, smiling as the last of the third year students accepted their cloaks, the colours denoting the posting they had accepted. Only a handful were the plain grey with no emblem, a gift to the few each year who graduated with ambitions outside of the Ranger organisations.

These leaving graduates would usually be from merchant families who need all the hands they can get, or wealthy families in the cities who considered themselves nobility, above the work of the rangers. They would return home better people than they were and with a better understanding of the world than their families who demand they not take a ranger post.

As the leaving graduates filed down the centre lane and waited by the front gates, Chancellor Howe stood at the dais, and raised his arms.

"I hereby declare this year's finishing students officially graduated from the academy, and welcome you into the wider family of rangers. Those prodigal children who leave us today, all know you have a home here with us, or in any other ranger facility, for the rest of your days."

He smiled, lowered his left hand, and scratched his beard. The anticipation of the students was palpable as the Chancellor milked the pause for as long as he could keep a straight face. Finally, with a laugh, he looked to the sky, and released a towering pillar of blue flame from his right hand.

In response, a roaring cheer erupted from the crowd, as each and every graduate raised their right hand, and poured their flames into the sky. All colours mingling, the fire burned with an intense heat in the air above the academy, as bells rang out around the city, signifying the completion of another year.

After a moment, the teachers and staff of the academy joined them. The flames towered for several seconds, before an enormous roar sounded with the smothering of the flames by a massive black gust from the dais, where Loka and five other black flame wielders had appeared. Suddenly stilled, the air crackled in the aftermath, and the cheering grew louder still as families rushed in to find their young graduates.

Symin's grin was broad, as he reminisced about the day he and Loka had stood side by side on the parade ground to graduate. He made his way to the dais, where his lover stood talking animatedly with the Chancellor. Climbing the stairs to the side, he approached them as the Chancellor turned to face him.

"I guess that's another year over. Are you all prepared to go out and find our next year's recruits?"

"Yes, Sir," Symin said. "This graduating year was a strong one, but next year will be interesting."

"Yes, it will be. This year and next are both smaller cohorts, due to the problems we had with those incidents to the south and in the mountains, but the year following is back to the strength of numbers we once had, and I fear we may be struggling to find jobs for them all before long."

"All the more reason to be thankful for Windwall," Symin replied. "As the second campus becomes fully operational, it will absorb large numbers of graduates. I believe we need to look further afield though, and decide on a location for the third campus before too long."

"True," Howe said. "But we could not yet staff it with experienced hands. Before my time is up, it will be done."

"Where would such a facility be placed?" Loka asked. "Surely not Leusbay? It's too close to Windwall, and still not as friendly to us as some of the other places."

"That is true," Howe said. "Although Leusbay tolerates our presence and works well with us for the benefit of Cinder these days. But its wielders can readily travel to Windwall. I feel it important to open a third academy to the south, perhaps in Grey, or..."

The Chancellor paused, thinking as he turned to lead them down from the dais, towards the mingling families and graduates.

"... Horde, which reminds me. Symin, we must discuss your field trip, I think it is time for you to go there. But first, we must speak to the parents, and congratulate these new rangers."

* * *

"That will be us, next year," Corilai said, watching from the window, her elbows propped on the sill.

Treghan stood behind her, the house a bustling hive of activity as they prepared for the after graduation party. Barre entered, and posted a notice on the board near the door, then left. Curious, Treghan walked to the board and looked at it.

"It's the field work assignments," Treghan said. "They must have had a lot of applicants this year. There are six in our group."

"Who did we get?" Corilai asked.

"We're with Symin and Loka again. I guess they trust us and know our strengths and weaknesses. You, me, Fletcher and Marni, as well as Yera and Jaer."

"Yera and Jaer?" Corilai asked. "They're very young."

"Yeah, but they have been training. From what I hear, they worked very hard this year. The Windwall academy had to start all those kids years before normal on preliminary classes, but they will be attending the actual first year courses eventually. I bet they'll be good too, given the head start they'll have."

"At least there's no big emergency this year, we'll just be following Symin on the recruitment drive. I guess that's why they're with us and not on an enforcer field trip."

"Just so long as we're not stuck baby sitting the whole time," Treghan grumbled.

"That'll be Marni," Corilai said, with a laugh. "It's thanks to her they're in the academy after all."

"That's a bit mean, isn't it?"

"Not at all," she said with a wicked grin, before changing the subject. "Where do you think we'll be going?"

"Probably everywhere. All the villages."

"That's what I was worried about. I'm not ready to go home yet. I don't know if I can face them."

"Of course you can. You're a ranger now, and greater than they ever gave you credit for."

"Thanks Treghan," she said, embracing him, her chin propped against his arm. "It will be easier if you're there."

Chapter 3 – Reasons

"As you are well aware," Howe said. "We have historically only received a small number of recruits from Horde."

"That's true," Symin replied, seated opposite the chancellor in his office.

"I would like to know why."

"Well, we generally don't find flame wielders in that area, so naturally..."

"I know that," Howe replied. "But why is that? Do you believe, as was the conventional thought until recently, that there are simply less flame wielders born into the desert city?"

"That's the natural conclusion..."

"But it is not the right conclusion," Howe said with an air of certainty.

Symin looked at the Chancellor for a long moment, not sure what to make of the sudden proclamation. Finally, his curiosity won out.

"Sir, do you have evidence of this claim?"

Howe looked at Symin for a moment, then stood, walking to the window.

"Rangers have been dispatched to all the cities and towns of Ember, including Horde," he said. "However, in no other city or town have the rangers reported sightings, and pursuits, of emerging flames where the flame simply vanished."

"What do you mean?" Symin asked.

"I mean, the rangers are following a flame, and it disappears. What is more, there are buildings in horde into which we now believe those flames are taken, or go voluntarily, with unusual properties."

"What kind of properties?" Symin asked, believing he knew the answer.

"The yellow flame wielder's secondary ability can not penetrate the walls and sense anything inside. Our rangers on site describe the sense in their reports as a hole in the world."

"So you believe," Symin said, jumping several steps into the Chancellor's explanation. "That there exists in Horde a group or groups with knowledge and awareness of the flames, who are concealing themselves by way of some hitherto unseen technology, and that the flames in the area are recruited and trained by that group?"

"I do. Consider it a rival academy. Not villainous or else we would have encountered it before now. But the reports I have received refer to it as 'the Order of the Essence.' You are to investigate this order, to determine their goals. Ascertain if they are a threat, or an asset, to the nation of Cinder."

"Yes, Sir," Symin said. "And while we are on the topic of Horde..."

"Yes, I believe this is likely connected to your long desired investigation, so while you are there, provided it does not draw resources or efforts away from this primary investigation, by all means conduct your private study of the area. I will be interested to see what it is you discover."

"Yes, Sir," Symin said. "I will begin my preparations."

"Ranger," Howe said, in a formal tone. "Please do not rush into this. I ask that you conduct at least one sweep for recruitment purposes as usual, while you make your way south. We can not miss an intake because of this matter. It carries no such urgency."

"Yes, Sir," Symin replied.

*   *   *

"Ignitor Krytus," Hyren said. "You say the ancestors sacrificed themselves to create Cinder. What does that mean?"

"It means they brought about the downfall of their own world, so that this one could be born, and protected."

"Why? And how?"

"That is too many questions for you to learn the answer to today, young one. In time, all the answers will come to you."

"So what do we do?" Hyren asked.

"You, young one, must learn and grow, as we all strive to do each and every day of our lives, until the first flame returns."

"The first flame?"

"Yes, boy. Every thing that exists has a first one. The first flame was Sena, and it was through her that the order was formed. We await her promised return, when the order will turn a new leaf and embark on it's next chapter. Until then we study, we learn, and we wait."

"Through her? What do you mean? Are some flames female? Do they have to make new flames like people make babies?"

"So many questions," Krytus said, laughing before he continued. "These, too will be answered in time. Suffice it to say, at this point, all you need remember is that flames are flames, they are our companions, and our leaders, and our followers. They are a part of us, as much as the air we breath becomes one with our bodies and gives us life. Now go and celebrate; this is your initiation day. Your lessons will begin tomorrow."

*   *   *

"Maalo," the now familiar female voice said in Symin's dream. "Maalo, my brother, I am coming home, soon."

Symin fought with his fear to understand this dream. There was nothing around him but green and yellow mist. Occasional flashes of other colour flitted into his perception. Again, the same voice spoke those same words. The colours shifted. And as they parted, he saw a window into another world, an opening which revealed to him the room he had seen before.

"Maalo," she said. "It will not be long now."

"What won't be long?" Symin tried to shout, but he did not hear his own words.

"Do not wrestle with the words in here," the voice said. "Yours is a voice not meant for this world. Just as mine will not sound as it should in yours. One day soon, you will understand."

"Am I going to die?" Symin thought.

The voice laughed, a tripping, giddy sound of merry amusement. Symin thought it rude to be mocked so.

"You are going to live," she said, the lilting of the laughter still in her voice. "Indeed, you will live as you have not lived before. We all shall, now that the time is almost upon us."

"What time?"

"The time we have all longed for, these past seven centuries, while Cinder rested in hiding from the world."

"I do not understand," Symin thought.

"You do not need to, not yet. You have much work to do. Has your Chancellor not given you his orders?"

"Yes,"

"Follow them, and in time you will see. We will meet properly for the first time, my companion."

Symin awoke with a start, sitting bolt upright in bed, cold sweat dripping from him as though he had showered not five minutes ago. He looked around, checking Loka, who slept beside him. He saw his arms and hands were slightly aglow with yellow light, and the fibres of his bedsheets lightly singed.

"What's going on?" he muttered, as he climbed from the bed and went to the bathroom.

* * *

Corilai and Marni stood at the southern gate to the academy, watching and waiting for what seemed like an eternity. Finally, a long column of riders came into view.

Thirty horses, trotting with the proud gait of academy mounts, their riders all wearing the familiar cloaks of the rangers, made their way through Emberdale. Several were in the colours of students, with the stylised crenelations of Windwall Academy added to the ranger logo on their backs.

"There they are!" Marni shouted, raising her arms high to wave.

Two of the students returned her wave, and were immediately chastised by a ranger near them in the column. Corilai giggled.

"Don't go getting them in trouble," Corilai said.

"They'll be fine," Marni said.

Marni did not wave again, but both girls smiled as the column passed. They followed alongside when the pair reached them.

"You may as well wait at the candidate barracks, that's where these young ones will be staying," a ranger said, with stern disapproval.

"OK, settle down, Ranger," said the one riding beside him from beneath her hood, her voice as familiar as any of their teachers.

"Jarls!" Marni exclaimed. "You came back?"

"Just for a visit, young Marni."

"Wait, this is Marni?" the other ranger said. "The tree demon of the mines?"

"Watch your tongue!" Jarls snapped. "And yes, it is. If these two wish to speak with their friends, they may do so. Or would you fight me on this, Ranger?"

"It is fine, I guess..." The other one said.

"Yera, Jaer, it's good to see you!" Marni said, now that permission had been granted.

"It is wonderful to see you, Commander," Yera replied, causing Marni to blush. "Hudson, Kres and the others all said hello, and apologised they couldn't make it."

"They have things they have to do, just like we do," Marni replied. "I'm glad to see you both."

"And you'll be seeing us both a lot!" Jaer said. "We got ourselves assigned to Symin's group, for the field trip. It's going to be such fun!"

"Those trips aren't for fun, Jaer," Corilai scolded. "You know how much danger we faced in the last one, and you never saw it, but the one before that was even worse. People died."

"I know, I was there. But learning about flames and helping people out, you can't say you don't enjoy it," he said.

"Perhaps, but we're careful how we say it," Marni replied.

"That is wise," Jarls said. "You should listen to this one, Jaer and Yera."

"Oh, we will. She's our commander, after all!" Yera said. "So who else will be with us?"

"Symin will lead," Corilai said. "Loka will probably be along for the trip, and of course Treghan, Fletcher, and us."

"Where will we go?" Yera asked. "I've never been this far from the mountains! It's already amazing."

"I think it will just be a recruitment drive this time. Nothing exciting like bringing down a tyrant or fighting a war."

"It's not fair!" Jaer said. Why did you get all the exciting stuff?"

"Just lucky, I guess," Marni snarled sardonically, causing Jarls to laugh. "You young ones should stop wishing for trouble, you might get more than you can handle one day."

* * *

Gurrei and Pirette rushed together through the late evening stillness, a sulphurous tang in the air. They had been searching the area around the temple, trying to find a way they could get inside without being discovered.

The pair were determined to solve the riddle before the academy sent somebody else to do it for them. A large group of locals had seen them, and believing them burglars, rushed to attack with swords, shovels, pitchforks, whatever weapons they could find.

The cloaks inside out so the ranger emblem was obscured, they had run from the scene, but now they feared somebody had known who they were, all along. As they rounded the last corner before the ranger outpost, they stopped and watched helpless as the building was engulfed in fire.

They could see several cloaked figures rushing to the well and back, tossing ineffectual amounts of water on the fire. One of the three saw them, and rushed towards the pair.

"I don't know what happened," the young receptionist said. "Just suddenly the entire place was on fire. We got all three of us out, but the horses, we couldn't save the horses, and Law was in the basement when it happened. None of us have seen him."

"Right," Pirette said, rushing towards the building, dropping his cloak as he ran and raising his hands out to the side.

Around the orange flame wielder, a swirling maelstrom of dust began to grow, and slowly he descended into the ground. As the sand was blasted away from him, Pirette began to approach the burning building until his head disappeared below street level. Soon, the trench he was digging with his secondary earth moving ability dug into the ground and formed a tunnel, and he burrowed his way forward with grim determination.

Soon, he passed beneath the walls of the outpost, as the fire raged above him, and he continued on, compacting the walls of his tunnel as he went, determined to reach his lost colleague before it was too late.

As he began to tire, Pirette finally reached the sturdy stone wall which surrounded the basement, and began striking the stones with hurled bolts of sand and debris. The booming sounds of the impacts reverberated through the tunnel, and boomed out into the still night air.

At long last, the first of the stones gave way, and Pirette pushed and shoved his way inside. He found flames licking across the beams of the basement's low ceiling, and a black flaming orb, small and dense, in the corner; Law's attempt to wait out the emergency in his private cocoon.

Law, being young, was not yet well practised in his abilities, and Pirette could see that the maelstrom of black flame was fluctuating and inconsistent. He wouldn't have held out much longer. Pirette rushed over, and waited for a weak moment in the orb, before thrusting his arm inside. Screaming as the black flames burnt his skin, he grabbed the hair of the man inside, and pulled.

Almost instantly, the orb vanished, and Law began to scream incoherently. Pirette could see the panic in the young man's eyes, and realised the poor fellow was already exhausted from his efforts and was not seeing the man who tried to save him, trapped as he was in his fear.

"I'm sorry," Pirette shouted, as he struck the man's jaw, hoping he was not doing any lasting damage as Law fell, stunned enough that Pirette could pick him up by the shoulders, and drag him to the tunnel.

As he reached the escape route, the door to the basement fell in, sending a flood of smouldering embers into the small space. The mix of air and fire caused a rushing inferno to finish the fire's work on the supporting beams.

Just in time, Pirette caused the end of the tunnel to collapse, and darkness surrounded him as he made his way to the mouth of his tunnel, dragging the other man. Flickering light from outside guided him and he finally emerged from the ground. Law began to scream as Pirette fell to his knees, his adrenalin spent.

Chapter 4 – Old Demons

"I was hoping to see Leusbay," Fletcher complained.

They were assembling at the southern gate of Emberdale, travelling light, for the first leg of the annual recruitment ride. They each sat astride their horse, with a single saddle bag behind them and small pack over their shoulders.

Treghan, Corilai, Marni and Fletcher were joined by Yera and Jaer from Windwall, as well as Loka, Tara, and Symin, who would lead them. A gentle breeze ruffled their ranger cloaks, hoods lowered, the emblem on their backs shining in the dawn light.

"We're heading south for a reason," Symin said. "And I am aware some of you may be uncomfortable about visiting some of the villages, but this is something you will have to just get over, if you are to succeed as rangers. Sentimental demons are not something we have the luxury of holding onto in this job."

"Why are we going south?" Corilai asked.

"Because we have been ordered to travel to Horde, and investigate some curious phenomena there, which may be part of the reason Horde has traditionally not yielded many recruits to the ranger academy."

"I didn't know that," Treghan said. "Why not?"

"That's what we hope to find out. While we're there, I have a personal investigation I will be conducting at the same time. Chancellor Howe seems to feel these two matters are related."

"So you finally get your journey into the desert?" Loka asked.

"Yes. If any of you are concerned for the safety of such a journey, you can back out now and no judgement will be made."

"Are you crazy? Corilai said. "As if we'd miss this! Just think. Horde and The Desert of Souls. It's worth it."

"I'm ready to face them anyway," Treghan said. "My demons, that is. And it's worth it to see Horde. I hear all sorts of stories about that city, I want to see it with my own eyes."

"I go where my commander goes!" Yera said, crossing her arms and fixing her stare on Marni.

"I'm not missing it for anything," Marni said, smiling at the young ones.

"Then I'm going too," Jaer said.

"OK then," Symin replied, turning to look at Loka and Tara. "I am guessing I can count on you both?"

"You're not going anywhere without me," Loka said.

"And I will always do my duty, as a ranger," Tara said.

"There is one more to reply," Symin said, looking at Fletcher.

"Well, I go where Marni goes. Somebody has to fight beside her, and it should be me."

"Well said, young ranger." Symin replied. "If that's all anybody needs to say, we ride. Keep close and do not stray from the road. First recruitment is Judd. We camp as needed, on the road."

* * *

"Malthus, you damnable fool!" Krytus bellowed. "We know well your detestation of the rangers, but this has gone a step too far. Somebody could have been killed."

"And so what if they were?" Malthus spat. "These rangers are not welcome in our city. They should back out of Horde. They have no business here."

"Malthus," Rogan said, his voice soft, his level tone speaking of greater anger than an outsider would realise. "Your actions this day have placed the Order in great peril."

"Lies!" Malthus shouted. "You sympathise with those vermin!"

"I sympathise only with our people," Rogan replied. "Horde is an ancient city, and we exist to protect it. But if we bring an unwanted war upon it, we have not only failed it, we have betrayed it. That betrayal hangs on your hands alone."

"There will be no war," Malthus replied, sounding nervous.

"There will not be, if we do not act as enemies of the nation of Cinder. Remember, Malthus, we are a part of that nation, and the rangers are its government and its military. They are the police and the protectors. If they are threatened, they will strike hard and with swift retribution."

"What evidence is there of that?" Malthus replied. "Old man Howe has kept them hidden away for a generation!"

"Hidden no more, or did you already forget whose house you foolishly burned?" Krytus snapped. "We have heard the story of Grey. That city was quickly subdued, in spite of the best efforts of its little dictator. And the merchants tell the story as though the heroes who ended his rule were mere children, students of the academy. You'd do well not to anger such a foe as that."

"Well, nobody was killed. And we took their horses before the fire burned the stables. I acted for the good of the order."

"Perhaps your flame's voice is not clear in your mind," Krytus said softly. "But this situation is precarious. We must act only with great care from now on."

"I will be more circumspect," Malthus promised. "But I act in nothing more than a desire for the protection of the flame, the essence, and the order."

"We know this, Malthus," Rogan said. "But your flame is volatile. Most so of the three we hold, which have led the order much of this past seven centuries. Heed our warning, and do not give in to rage again."

Rogan stood, and walked to the door, opening it to stand silhouetted in the light of torches from the main temple hall outside the small triumvirate chamber. He watched through the doorway as a group of the order's officers rushed among a class of recent initiates in a fast paced training game, smoulder, in which the teachers stalked the students, engulfing them in a smothering fire. The last student holding a flame would win the match.

"The order will not fail," Rogan said. "And our resolve will not falter.

But we must never forget our duty to the city which has sheltered us."

*   *   *

Treghan halted his horse as they entered Judd, their hoods drawn. It was late afternoon, and the long shadows of the trees hung along the road. He sat, watching in silence as a woman outside a nearby house stretched cloth on a frame. A shingle hung over the door of the house advertised her as a seamstress.

"Who is that?" Marni whispered to Corilai, noticing that Treghan had stopped.

"I think it's his mother," Corilai replied. "Symin, we should wait."

Symin looked back, and nodded, turning his horse to face them and closing the small distance to Treghan.

"Treghan, we will wait. Do what you must do."

"Yes, ranger," Treghan said, dismounting.

Fletcher did the same, and rushed to his brother's side as he strode towards the house. The woman looked up, and narrowed her eyes. Shaking her head, she managed a weak smile.

"Rangers, for what do I owe this honour?" she said, her tone one of weariness and exasperation.

"We will only take a moment of your time," Treghan said, lowering his hood as he reached her.

Her hand rushed to her face, covering her mouth as she gasped. She then reached forward to touch his face as Fletcher lowered his hood. She faced her other son, and smiled, before looking back to Treghan, tears in her eyes.

"My two boys, here together. What a blessing! Please, come inside, I'll make some tea."

"I," Treghan began. "I'm sorry, Mother. We can't stay. Please tell me, are you well?"

"Well enough. I suppose. I make us a small living, mending clothing and making new things for the villagers when needed."

"Where's father?" Fletcher asked.

"He's at the tavern," she said, lowering her eyes. "He spends most days down there, I'm afraid."

"He no longer works the fields?" Treghan asked.

"He hasn't worked since we returned from that place," she said. "Would you go and speak with him? I think it might help."

"Well no, we shouldn't," Fletcher said, glancing at his brother in concern. "We shouldn't bother him."

"No, Fletcher," Treghan said. "It's alright. If it might help, we should go. I would like to see him."

"Please do," she said, before rushing to embrace Treghan, and then after a long moment, releasing him to hold Fletcher. "He may still be conscious, they normally carry him home about dusk."

Treghan walked away, towards the tavern, Fletcher following. Corilai dismounted and ran to Treghan. She slipped her hand into his without speaking, as the others rode slowly behind. Their horses followed, long years of training at work.

Villagers and the men returning from the fields watched, as the rangers made their way towards the centre of Judd. The smith waved from his anvil without looking up, and the village seemed somehow more alive than Treghan recalled.

Finally, Treghan paused in front of the tavern, and took a deep breath. He stepped through the doorway, still holding Corilai's hand, and she and Fletcher followed him inside. The others dismounted and tied the horses before following.

Treghan stood in the dimly lit room and looked around. A man stood behind the bar, cleaning the counter with a rag. He looked up and stared at Treghan for a long moment, before nodding and pointing to a booth at the far end of the room.

Treghan approached the booth, and saw his father for the first time since running from his house. The man was haggard, his hair a dishevelled grey mess, his hands dirty, but not from working. He clutched the empty tankard before him, his hands shaking, sticky patches on the table testament to his jitters.

"I thought," Treghan whispered to Corilai as they stood, beside and behind this wreck of a man. "I thought I'd be angry, but I'm not. I'm only sad. Sad for him."

"You should sit down," she replied.

"Please, sit with me."

Treghan walked around the end of the table and slid into the booth, opposite his father. Corilai slipped in beside him. Fletcher hesitated, then sat beside Corilai as the others approached, stopping to wait a few steps away.

The man looked up, his head bobbing like a cork in a barrel, as he turned his head from one son to the other.

"Are… Are you rea… really there? Or is it the dreams again?" he stammered.

"We're here, Father," Treghan replied. "How have you been?"

"Ha! You can see very well how I have been," he spat. "Not fairing even a fraction as well as you two. Why did you come here? Is it to mock your old fool of a father?"

"No, Father," Treghan said. "I just…"

"It's good to see you, Father," Fletcher said.

"It is good to see you too," he said. "Both of you. And your pretty little friend."

"This is Corilai," Treghan said, wrapping an arm around her protectively.

"Good for you, son," he said. "I never really called you son, did I?"

The old man looked down at the table, and tears escaped the confines of his dry, weathered eyes.

"I'm sorry, son. I was never much of a father to you. And Fletcher, I sold you out. I was a monster to you both, in the end."

"You did what you knew," Treghan said.

"What I knew?" he replied. "Son, I knew better. But that never changed me. I deserve to be the failure I am."

"And what about mother?" Treghan said.

"Your mother?" he said, his eyes lightening as he looked up. "She's the world. And she holds it all together. She's a saint, that woman, to have stood by me, even now."

"You earned her love, somehow, Father," Treghan said. "One day, you must have done something to earn her loyalty. I have to believe that."

"I'm not that man any more, Son."

"We have all changed, Father. It doesn't mean it's the end. We can change again."

"I know we change, but it's too late for me. But look at you two, huh? My sons, the rangers. You know, you make me immensely proud, both of you do. Your mother too. You know she supports us now? She's a tough one alright. I don't know how I deserve to call myself your family. So proud. So proud."

As his words faded, his head dropped, until he snapped back up, as though waking. He looked across the table at the three of them, his eyes settling on Treghan.

"I'm so sorry, son," he said. "I always wanted my boys to be better than I was. And when Fletcher started to send out red fire, I was so proud of him, and I couldn't understand why my other son couldn't do it too. I didn't know anything about flames. I thought they were all equal. I wanted you to be more than I was..."

The grey haired old man released his grip on the tankard, and held his hand up, flat, his palm to the ceiling. He stared at his hand, and squinted, seeming to exert some effort. He looked up and met Treghan's eyes.

"There was a white flamed fellow, came here last spring. I asked him about you. He explained how the white works. You were already so much better than me, and I treated you like a worthless fool. I was the fool. I was always the fool. And I never could do anything more than this."

The old man looked back to his hand, and they all followed his gaze, to see a feeble, tiny blue spark skipping across his palm. The spark died, and he dropped his hand to the table, breathing heavily from his exertion.

"I'm sorry son, you're better than I could dream of being."

"That's enough," Treghan said, standing. "Enough of the self pity, Father. You say we make you proud. But it's time for a new change. One for you this time. Mother is waiting. She's always waiting. How much longer?"

Treghan looked at his father, who raised his eyes to meet his son's. Following Treghan's lead, Corilai and Fletcher stood, and made their way out of the booth.

"It's time to stop letting us make you proud, Father," Treghan said. "It's time to go out there and make yourself proud. Make mother proud. Make this a better life, for her, and for you. The past is over. She deserves a future. No more being sorry, it isn't necessary. We're our own men now, and nobody but ourselves answers for our lives. History is done with, time to move on. Oh, and Father..."

Treghan paused, as the old grey haired man looked at him. The young man slowly backed away from the table, Corilai taking his arm and staring at his face.

"... It's OK. I forgive you."

Treghan turned away and strode from the tavern, pulling his hood up to hide his tears as the grey haired old man stared after him, audibly weeping in cathartic release.

Chapter 5 – Hunter

Having scouted Judd, the rangers returned to the tavern and ordered rooms for the night. Treghan was pleased to note his father was gone, as they were lead to their rooms.

"I thought you'd find more candidates for the academy," Yera said.

"No, it is usually a bit slow in the villages," Symin said. "There are not that many people, and if they can at all stop us taking the young ones to the city, they will, as they need all the help they can get in the fields. Getting one recruit from Judd is as much as we could expect."

"Will he be good enough?" Treghan asked.

"Perhaps, but if he fails the entry examination, he will be returned home. He will not be simply discarded, there will be another year. If he grows and becomes stronger, he can try again."

"So what do we do with him?" Corilai asked. "Do we take him back to Emberdale?"

"No," Symin said. "We go to Oaklands tomorrow. We will leave him with the outpost there."

They soon settled into their accommodation, and the night passed without incident. As they left the town, several of the townsfolk came out to wave them farewell. At the front of the crowd, Treghan saw both his parents, smiling, though his father squinted against the sun.

He appeared sober, if hungover. Treghan saw that his mother was holding her husband, supporting his weight by one arm, but he was trying to stand on his own just the same. Her lips moved, and she mouthed the simple words.

"Thank you, son."

They rode into the morning air, brisk and fresh, and Treghan felt a weight had finally been lifted. Corilai was watching him, a smile on her lips, as she rode beside him. Fletcher and Marni followed, Yera and Jaer behind them. The young recruit sat in front of Yera on her horse, his farmer's clothes a stark contrast to the ranger's cloaks and other expensive gear they all wore.

His eyes darted around, observing all around him, as he whispered questions to Yera.

"So are you a ranger too?"

"No, I'm a student."

"What about him?" he said, pointing at Jaer.

"No, Jaer is a student as well, in my year."

"Is that why your cloaks have a different symbol? Are the others all rangers?"

"No, we have the symbol of the Windwall campus of Ranger Academy. They wear the symbol of Emberdale."

"Windwall has its own academy?"

"Yes, since last year."

"Wow, why did that happen?"

"That's too big a story to tell you now. But hey, don't tell anybody I told you. They made it happen," Yera said, pointing at the older students.

"Really? So they're rangers then?"

"No," Yera said. "They're students, but ahead of us. They start the third year classes soon. And they have already done a lot of field work for the rangers. Haven't you heard the stories about Yuri?"

"Yuri the tyrant? Yeah, he was taken down by a couple of kids," the boy said, then his eyes grew wide. "Wait, you don't mean… Is she Corilai the demon flame?"

"Yes," Yera said, laughing at the boy. "But don't ever let her hear you calling her that. She might burn you to a crisp."

"Oh, yes ma'am!" the boy whispered.

They rode on through the morning, stopping at any house or hamlet they happened to come across, but never for long. At around midday, Symin called them to a halt at the top of a rise.

"We camp here for the night," he said. "I will be riding alone into the hills, and shall return this evening. Do not move from this spot."

"What are you doing?" Fletcher asked.

"I will be scouting some of the farms and other places in the hills, and I will be faster on my own. And the boy is not likely to cope with travelling much further today. Your friends from Windwall are looking a bit worn out as well, remember it is warm today, and they're not used to this low altitude weather."

"Thank you, Sir," Yera said. "A break would be a nice thing right about now."

"Treghan, Corilai, Fletcher and Marni, you are to watch over the young ones, and ensure they are safe. Any trouble, tell Loka or Tara immediately. I will return."

Spurring his horse into a trot, Symin disappeared into the trees. Dismounting, the others set up camp, and Loka pulled out a small package. It contained a selection of printed cards, and she sat on the ground, beckoning the students to sit with her.

"What's that?" Marni asked.

"A set of flame wielder exercises. We're not going to just sit here. I want you all working on improving your abilities at every opportunity."

Loka passed a card to each of them, except the new boy.

"What was your name again?" she asked him.

"Nie," the boy said.

"OK, Nie," Loka continued. "You will not be doing one of those exercises, but you are to watch closely everything they do. In these exercises, all the basics are covered, and by watching them, you will begin to understand what you will be learning in your practical classes once you are admitted to the academy."

They worked on their exercises throughout the afternoon, the many colours of their flames casting their light deep into the trees beside the road. Around dusk they stopped and lit a fire for cooking, though the weather was fine so it was not needed for warmth.

As the water was coming to a boil for some tea, Symin returned carrying several fish in a wet sack.

"One of the homesteaders in the foothills of the Grey Wolf mountains gave me these. Cook those, and save our supplies for later."

"Yes, Sir," Corilai said, handing Treghan a knife so he could prepare them.

With the food cooked and the sun set, they climbed into their bed rolls and slept. Symin woke them before dawn, and they continued on their way. They rode faster this time, stopping less frequently. Finally, in the afternoon, they entered the town of Oaklands.

Their first stop was the outpost, where Nie was handed to the local rangers to be taken care of until he could be escorted to Emberdale. After stabling all the horses, Yera and Jaer both stayed there while Fletcher and Marni went into the town together. Loka sat in the lounge of the outpost and seemed determined to stay put, but Symin looked at her, pleading.

"Tara can stay here," he said. "but I was hoping you'd come to visit my family."

"Can we come as well?" Corilai asked. "I'd love to see Hunter, and your wonderful mother again."

"I guess that's fine," Symin said, with a sigh.

Together, the four of them left the outpost and made their way to Symin's family home, nestled against the town wall. As they arrived, his mother came out to meet them, smiling as she embraced her son, then turned to face Loka.

"And I see you finally deigned to bring your love home. I guess this means he got over himself finally?" she said as she grabbed Loka in an embrace even warmer than the one she had given her son.

Releasing the startled ranger, the woman then turned to look at Treghan and Corilai.

"My have you two youngens grown up! Well, that's enough standing around outside. Quickly now, into the house. I'll put on some tea."

As they made their way inside, Symin pulled his mother aside.

"Is Hunter home?"

"Oh, son, I'm sorry," she said, looking down. "His mate arrived this morning, but Hunter, he hasn't been around for weeks now."

"Oh no!" Corilai said, overhearing. "You don't suppose something has happened to him, do you?"

"A bird has a limited life span," Symin said. "For a falcon, Hunter is getting quite old. Certainly older than much of his species. He's nearly fifteen years old now."

"We should look for him," Corilai said.

"There's probably nothing we can do for him," Symin said.

"We can bring him home," Corilai demanded.

"Wait here," Symin said, going upstairs.

Corilai followed, in spite of his instructions. Treghan tagged along as well, and they entered the room with the balcony. The female bird was there. She squawked, then hopped onto the balcony railing.

"What is it, girl?" Symin said, approaching her.

The bird squawked again, louder this time, and launched into the air. Circling, she returned, called to them, and flew out once more.

"I think she wants us to follow her," Corilai said.

"Yes, I think so," Symin agreed, running from the room. "Come on."

They headed out of the house, ignoring the questions of the others as they rushed out the door. Symin lead the way around to the side and along to the gate in the wall. Rushing into the fields, they looked up. She saw them and swooped down low, before flying off into the sky again. Symin rushed after her, Corilai and Treghan close behind.

"Should we get our horses?" Treghan shouted.

"No point," Symin replied. "She wouldn't be leading us that far."

As if she heard his words, the female falcon dropped out of the sky into the trees. They rushed into the forest, following the sound of her repeated calls, until they stood at the foot of a tall tree. Looking up, she could be seen, silhouetted against the sky, dancing back and forth. Symin grabbed a low branch and swung into the tree with an agility which surprised the others.

Soon, with the female screaming abuse at him, Symin lifted the nest, and began to climb down, carefully balancing the large bundle of sticks and leaves on one arm as he climbed to the ground. The female followed.

As he stood on the ground, the others looked into the nest, to see three chicks, not yet able to fly and Hunter, their father, crouched over them. One of Hunter's wings was snapped backwards, blood dried in his feathers.

"What have you been doing, you silly boy?" Symin said, brushing the falcon's face with a finger.

Hunter reached around and nipped at him, softly grabbing the finger in his beak. The female flapped about on the low branches, making an enormous racket.

"It's OK, I'll take them home," Symin said as he started walking back to town. "He can get properly looked after there. Mother will heal his wing up good as new."

The female flew after them, swooping and circling their heads as she kept a close eye on her babies. Walking through the trees, they didn't see it until it was too late. A large wolf blocked their way, snarling.

"Wait, I know you," Corilai said, stepping towards the animal.

"Corilai, no," Symin ordered.

"It's OK," Corilai said. "I know this wolf. Remember? She saved me at Vera."

"Are you sure?" Symin said, still nervous about the animal being so close to Hunter.

"I'm positive," Corilai said, kneeling before the wolf and lighting a small black flame, then putting it out again. "You remember me, girl? You helped me before, after I helped your baby."

The wolf growled, then turned its head, looking behind herself into the trees. She snarled, and a second shape sauntered out. It was a second wolf, younger, lean and male. He nuzzled the older wolf, and she let him for a moment, before pushing him away, towards Corilai. She snarled again, and he looked between her and the human, kneeling on the ground.

"Is this your baby? The same one?" Corilai whispered. "He's grown so beautiful. So proud."

A low growl came from the female, and the male lay down, still looking at Corilai. The female tapped the male's rump with a paw and snarled again. The male rolled over, submissive, never taking his eyes from Corilai. Nervously, she reached her hand to the wolf and he licked it. Braver now, Corilai moved closer, and ruffled the fur on the young male's neck.

"We have to hurry, Corilai," Symin said. Both wolves looked at him, growling.

"It's OK," Corilai said, regaining their attention. "Thank you for bringing him to see me, but we have to go now."

Corilai stood, and the female sauntered off. The male followed, hesitating. The female turned on him, swiping her powerful front paws at him, snarling, such that he backed away and let her go. The young male looked up at Corilai and whimpered, sidling up to her until his flank brushed her hip. Without thinking, she brushed the fur on his back with her hand, and it seemed that something had been decided between them.

"This is not a normal encounter," Treghan said. "Wolves don't hand their young to a human, ever."

"She recognised the one who saved him. I guess she has taught the lad all she can, and wanted to find him a new teacher," Symin said.

"What do I call you?" Corilai asked.

In response the wolf uttered a plaintive cry.

"Arool"

"Ok then," Corilai said with a laugh. "Arool it is. Come."

She led the way, walking through the forest towards the fields around Oaklands, Arool staying by her side. Symin followed, keeping a wary distance while carrying Hunter and the chicks. Hunter's mate circled warily over head, never far, but obviously nervous of the wolf. Treghan remained near Symin, unsure how the wolf would respond to him being close to its human.

Crossing the fields, a handful of farmers working late stopped to watch the strange group. They stayed back, obviously unsure of Arool. Finally, as they approached the gates, a guard stepped forward to confront Corilai.

"Symin's birds are fine, but that thing can't come in," the guard said.

"Then I'll stay out here, with him," Corilai replied.

"No," Symin said. "You have to come into the town. The wolf will just have to wait out here."

"I haven't trained him yet! He might just run off and get in trouble!"

"Exactly why he has to stay outside," Symin said. "But you have to enter the town, so I will hear no more argument."

Corilai led Arool away from the gate, and knelt down. The wolf laid there, watching her. She stood, still looking at him. The head of the guard had arrived and watched, along with the others.

"You wait here," she instructed, and walked back towards the gate.

The young wolf, not understanding human commands, followed her. It seemed determined not to let her out of its sight. She stopped, and tried to shoe him away, but Arool merely backed up, then as soon as she walked towards the gate, was at her side again.

"This isn't going to work," she said.

The head of the guard, watching, was impressed.

"He's clearly not going to leave your side. If you are in the room with him, and you have the doors and windows locked, he can stay, but it is at your risk. And three guards will accompany you in town."

Chapter 6 – Temple of Vera

Townspeople watched them as they made their way through town the next morning. Arool still walked beside Corilai, but seemed not to mind the others being close.

"How do you think he will go with the horses?" Treghan asked.

"He'll be fine," Corilai said. "He thinks I'm his leader, so I'll just tell him off if he tries anything."

The three guards walking behind them were nervous, in spite of the creature seeming tame around the girl. Finally, they reached the outpost where Tara and the others waited, the horses ready. They stared in shock at the new addition.

"What's going on here?" Tara said.

"This is Arool. He's coming with us. Apparently," Symin said.

"Coming with Corilai, more precisely," Treghan explained. "She saved him from a bob cat when he was a pup."

"That explains nothing!" Tara snapped. "Why have we got a wolf? That thing might be dangerous."

"He'll be fine. I'll stake my graduation on it," Corilai said, reaching a hand to ruffle the animal's fur.

"Don't go making foolish bets," Loka said. "Don't be surprised if he wanders off and we never see him again. And if he hurts any of our group, or our horses, you know he will have to be taken care of."

"He won't! I promise!"

"How can you know that?" Tara asked. "Wild animals don't just attach themselves to people."

"I just know it," Corilai snapped. "I feel it like I feel my flame. Now can we get out of here? Before somebody decides to chase Arool out of town?"

"Where to now, Symin?" Fletcher asked, trying to change the subject.

"The temple of Vera. We have a ranger settlement there now, rebuilding the ruins. From there, I will visit the nearby villages and bring back any recruits. You will all wait there and help the rangers with their work."

"When do we go to Dent?" Corilai asked.

"You don't," Symin snapped. "I'll cover the villages in that area while you are in Vera."

"But my family. I'd like to know what became of them, what with the Yuri episode and all that."

"You're not ready to face them," Symin said softly. "Are you?"

"I don't know," Corilai replied. "But I'll have Arool, and I can go anywhere if Treghan is with me."

"Is it that important to you?" Symin asked.

"Yes, I feel it's more than time to make my peace. If I'm going to be a ranger, I have to face my demons."

"OK, you will wait at Vera, until I have done the rest of my rounds. I will come for you, and we stop by Dent before going south."

"Thank you, Symin."

They mounted their horses, and Arool looked up at Corilai, his head tilted. She looked down at him, and nodded slowly.

"You walk there," Corilai said. "Mind you don't get stepped on."

The animal just continued to look up at her, though he slowly straightened his head. After a long pause, she began riding and he followed beside her. The others rode as well, all of them stealing occasional glances at the wolf, nervous of the wild creature in their midst.

The rangers rode throughout the morning and continued without stopping until mid afternoon, when Symin called them to a halt.

"I know it's early, but we camp here tonight and continue in the morning. Tara, you are to ride on ahead and meet the rangers at Vera. Warn them we are coming, and that we bring," he paused, looking at Arool before he continued. "An unusual guest. Have them ensure a pen for the animal beside Corilai's tent."

"Yes, Sir," Tara said, as she turned and rode away.

Throughout the day Arool had not left Corilai's side, apart from a couple of times when he whined at her, and she told him he could go. At those times he ran into the trees, but a few minutes later he would return to her side. Now, as she dismounted, he sat watching her as she worked with the others to set up camp.

Once she had the horses settled and her bedroll laid out before the fire, Arool whined.

"It's OK, I'm fine here. You can go if you want," Corilai said.

As if he understood her words, the wolf left, running into the trees. This time, he did not return after a short time like before, and she began to worry that he may have wandered off. She looked around and couldn't see anything to indicate where he was, so she stood and began walking around the edge of the camp.

"Forget it, Corilai," Loka said. "If he wants to come back, he will. Please help me prepare some vegetables for our evening meal."

As they were finishing the preparation of the handful of root vegetables from Loka's saddle bag, Arool returned. With an air of pride, he trotted through the camp to stand before Corilai, three small adult rabbits clutched by their legs, hanging from his jaw. Lowering his head, he placed them on the ground at her feet.

"Are they for us?" Corilai said, rubbing the wolf's fur. "Thank you Arool! Here, you keep one."

She knelt down and picked up one of the rabbits and handed it to the wolf, who took it and wandered to her bedroll, flopping down beside it and starting to eat. Corilai looked at Loka, who wordlessly handed her a sharp knife and pointed at the bodies.

"Oh," Corilai said. "I hadn't thought of that."

Picking up the rabbits, Corilai stood and walked to the edge of the camp. She stood there, considering how she might complete her gruesome task. Symin walked over to her.

"Have you ever butchered an animal before?" he asked.

"No," she replied.

"I'll show you. You might need to do it one day, if you're ever stranded in the wilderness."

"Thank you," Corilai said as he took the knife and one of the rabbits from her.

Symin knelt on the ground, and placed the animal down, then slit an incision on the back of its neck. Corilai was stunned at how easily he peeled the skin off, his hands moving quickly as he stripped it away. Flipping the animal over, Symin cut an incision in the belly and cut out the organs, leaving a wet, slippery carcass ready for the pot.

"Did you get all that?" Symin asked, handing her the knife.

"I don't know, I'll try."

With a grimace of distaste for the task, Corilai attempted to copy Symin's actions, but found where he made the skin slide off like a glove, she couldn't seem to do anything remotely as swift.

"Twist your hand, like this, and poke your fingers beneath, to push it into a pocket to hold," Symin said, grabbing her hands and moving them.

To her amazement, the skin began to peel away in her hands. Then she saw the fresh meat beneath, and felt the sticky blood on her hands, and her stomach lurched. Gagging, Corilai dropped the animal and rushed to a nearby tree, leaning on it as she wretched.

"Don't worry, that's a natural reaction the first time," Symin said. "I'll finish cutting these up to go in the pot with the vegetables you already prepared. They'll make a great stew. Clean yourself up, and go relax with some of your field exercises."

Corilai did as he suggested. She sat on her bedroll, Arool by her side, and ran through a series of small flame exercises. The wolf watched, head tilted in fascination, as the dark flames skipped in the air above her hands.

Treghan joined her and after a short time he took her hand and did some fusion exercises, spires of white and black flames mingling in the air above their heads. After they had been doing their exercises for a couple of hours, they realised the others were doing theirs also. Loka called out to them.

"Food's ready, you lot!"

The sun was nestled on the horizon, the trees shading them from the last of its warmth, as they sat around the fire to eat their fresh rabbit and vegetable stew. Loka retrieved bread from her saddle bag and passed it around, each of them tearing off a chunk before passing it on.

Arool was asleep in front of the fire, beside Corilai. As they finished their food and retired for the evening, he stirred and wandered to the edge of the camp, where he sat staring into the darkness. The humans took turns on watch, but the wolf never left his post, guarding them from the creatures of the forest.

* * *

As dawn broke, the group was already riding, closing the distance between them and The Temple of Vera rapidly. As the shadows of the trees slowly grew shorter, the temple complex came into view. Things had changed a lot since that first time Corilai and Treghan had stayed there, and then subsequently passed through with the rangers.

Much rebuilding had already taken place, and the primary temple building was complete. The roof was replaced, sturdy wooden shutters over the windows, and mighty doors on the side and front entrances.

Scattered around the complex, other smaller buildings had sprung up, the base of their walls in older stone than the building above. The remains of the stone wall along the cliff's edge had been removed, the stone recycled for some of the building work.

Now, the wall removed, they were treated to an unspoiled view to the distant horizon. Tiny in the vastness of view afforded by their height, the trees and beaches gave way to ocean, before the ocean met the sky in a great, curved line. The maelstroms beyond it gave rise to a permanent blanket of storms, barely visible in the distant sky.

Tara rushed out to meet them as they entered the cleared area around Vera from the north west. Behind her, several senior rangers followed, their eyes immediately fixed on Arool as the group made their way through the strewn rubble of the ancient ruin.

"I'm glad you made it," Tara said. "How was the evening?"

"Uneventful," Loka said. "The wolf stood guard all night, after it provided us with a catch of fresh meat."

"Unbelievable," Tara exclaimed. "I still don't understand how that animal came to be with us. But if he continues to prove himself useful, so be it."

"Waidon is commander here, is she not?" Symin asked.

"Yes, I am, Ranger," one of those behind Tara said, stepping out from behind her. "Cara Waidon at your service."

Cara lowered her hood, allowing her striking orange hair to cascade over her shoulders with a simple flick of her wrist to free it from the cloak. She reached a hand to shake Symin's, and he complied.

"Your reputation precedes you, Ranger Waidon," Symin said with a smile. "You are working wonders with this outpost, if the building works already completed are any indication."

"Thank you, Sir," Cara said. "My people are hard working and efficient, more than any commander could hope for. I consider this post an honour and a privilege. Particularly for a Captain of the Archivists. Field work is rare for us."

"But your reputation would have you proficient in all settings and circumstances," Loka said. "And who better to ensure nothing of historical value is lost or damaged?"

"Yes, and my people keep a keen eye on the region, in case of trouble."

"Has there been any?" Symin asked.

"We have dealt with some stragglers who remained from the bandits who terrorised the area in Yuri's name."

"I had thought such men rounded up long ago," Symin said, raising an eyebrow in surprise.

"Not all. There are many places for desperate people to hide in these woods, and the mountains west of here. My people have ensured no such trouble makers can bring harm to the villagers in the valley below us."

"What kinds of places?" Marni asked, drawing shocked looks from the rangers of Vera at the impertinence of a mere student addressing their leader.

"Young lady," Cara said. "There are many places. Ancient caves, abandoned mines, former settlements from past centuries long since abandoned due to the harsh winters in the mountains, or other natural phenomena. And who would you be?"

"My name is Marni. I am a student of the academy, and we are accompanying Symin's group as field experience during the study break."

"I see," Cara said. "Most unusual that a student would mention their teacher's name so casually, but I will let it pass, since your name has preceded you to our ears, just as mine had reached his. Your efforts last year in the Everwinter Highlands speak of great things in your future."

"Thank you, Ranger," Marni said, blushing as she looked at the ground.

"Hold your head high, girl," Cara said. "You are all rangers now, with the adventures you have already seen. I am assuming these other older students are your companions, Treghan the white, Corilai the demon, and Fletcher the red. You are all welcome. But be aware, those younger students are your responsibility while you are here. Keep them out of mischief."

"Thank you, Ma'am," the students all said, snapping to attention.

"We will keep them under close supervision," Corilai said, winking at Yera and Jaer.

"See that you do. One more thing, Corilai," Cara said. "You have a special companion with you. He is entirely your responsibility. Should he do anything out of line, you will be held responsible. Should he harm another ranger, expect yourself punished. You must keep him in sight and under your direct control at all times. Am I clear?"

"Ye… Yes, Ranger," Corilai stammered.

"Good. I have arranged student accommodation in the small hut on the northern end of the cliff face. There is a small stable attached, which the wolf can sleep in. You are to secure him in the stable unless you are accompanying him. If he must go outside the complex, you are not to accompany him, but you must stay on watch until the animal returns, that you may regain control the moment he is back at Vera. Understood?"

"Yes, Ranger," Corilai replied.

"Also," Cara said. "I will have two rangers stationed watch at your end of the complex. They are to take whatever actions are necessary to subdue the creature should trouble arise. Am I quite clear?"

"Perfectly," Corilai said.

Chapter 7 – Dent

Vera was a bustling outpost, and Cara worked hard to ensure nobody had idle moments. There was rebuilding to do, patrols to run, and plenty of other duties. When the students rose in the morning, things were already busy.

They were sent to patrol the road to Oaklands as their morning duty along with two senior rangers, both of whom were unsure of Arool at first, but soon came to accept that he was just another element of this strange team.

Symin had long since headed east, taking Loka and three other rangers with him. They visited the villages and hamlets in the area, as well as those further afield towards the coast. By the end of the first day, the first recruit had already arrived, travelling the road from the south.

Unusually, he was unaccompanied, but the farm lad explained he travelled that road alone when going to Oaklands to sell his family's produce. His family had moved into the area after the incident with Yuri when he had been taken to work in the smelters for his flaming ability.

Completing a patrol of the outpost perimeter, Treghan and Corilai wandered over to see what the fuss was about. They saw the new boy in conversation with Cara. Treghan and Corilai looked at the boy, trying to place his face. Finally they both recognised him as one of the night shift children who had mocked them when they were tested by Yuri.

"It seems you're doing well since your time in Grey," Treghan said, offering his hand to shake.

"You are too," the boy replied, taking the offered hand with a smile. "I remember you making a mockery of Yuri in that smelter, it was one of the best laughs we had. Clearly you were mocking him deliberately, since you wear the uniform of a ranger now."

"What's this?" Cara asked, looking at Treghan. "You know this boy?"

"He was one of those conscripted by Yuri to work in his smelters in Grey. We met briefly when Corilai and I set about trashing the place."

"There's more of a story in that, but for now, you two will take him to the bursar in the main temple and have him assigned to quarters. Then you are free to do as you please for the evening. But mind you inform the lad of the rules of this place, and strictly adhere to them yourselves."

"Yes, Ranger," Treghan said.

"One other thing," Cara said. "I have reports of the conduct of your unusual companion from the rangers you patrolled the road with earlier. It seems the creature is quite tame and under your control. See that it stays that way. As long as this is the case, he may stay with you while you are here. But remember my warning. I will not hesitate to have the creature dealt with."

"Yes, Ma'am," Corilai said.

They turned and led the boy away, walking back along the cliff road. The sun setting behind the highlands in the west cast long shadows in the dusk, and the boy looked around as they walked, staying extraordinarily close to Corilai.

"What was she talking about?" he asked. "What was that companion she mentioned?"

"Arool," Corilai said. "He's behind you."

The boy turned, and noticed the wolf for the first time. Close enough to touch, the creature was walking there as though it was perfectly normal for a wild animal to accompany them. The boy screamed and rushed ahead, putting Corilai between himself and the animal.

"What the hell is that?" he shouted.

"You've never seen a wolf before?" Corilai asked, incredulous.

"Of course I have!" the boy said. "But why is it following you?"

"Because it wants to," Corilai replied. "His name is Arool. What's yours?"

"Mine?"

"Your name, boy," Corilai said, sounding testy. "What is your name? Or shall we just call you smelter boy?"

"Oh, I'm Faro. And," he paused, looking from Treghan to Corilai. "I'm sorry we mocked you back then, in Grey. We didn't know anything about our flames, and we were just trying to not be sold by Yuri's men."

"What happened to the rest of them?" Treghan asked. "The kids you were with?"

"I don't know. I expect they all returned to their families after you took Yuri out."

"Well, if they went anywhere around here, you will likely see them soon," Corilai said. "If they have any potential with their flames, Symin will recruit them."

"I hope so," Faro said. "There were some great kids among them."

They entered the main temple building, Arool sitting at the door to wait, and a ranger approached.

"What is it?" he said.

"Commander Waidon sent us to see the Bursar," Treghan explained. "Faro here is a new recruit sent by Symin, for the Academy intake. We are to get him assigned to quarters here until he is escorted to Emberdale."

"Fine, you may leave him with us. We will house the recruits in the sanctuary area to the far end of the main building."

"That's the area behind the altar, right?" Corilai asked.

"Yes, it is."

"Treghan, remember?"

"Yes," Treghan replied. "We slept there, when this place had no roof."

"When it was still a ruin?" the ranger asked.

"Yes," Corilai said. "We were running from Yuri's men, having escaped from Grey. We had passed through Barache's place, and were heading to Emberdale."

"Well, the place has changed a lot since then," The ranger replied. You should have a look around, see the improvements we have made. This outpost will become an important Ranger facility in time."

"Who built it originally?" Faro asked.

"It was here before Cinder, but that is about all I know. It lay in ruin for many centuries. Perhaps speak to your teachers at the academy. Or the commander, if you can hold her still long enough to get a straight answer."

"Well, maybe later," Corilai said. "Good luck, Faro."

Leaving the boy with the rangers, they went outside and walked to the road. Arool joined them, and they made their way north, towards the building they had been assigned.

"How much longer do you think Symin will be?" Corilai asked.

"I don't know," Treghan replied. "I hope not too long. I know this place is nice and all, but I feel like we're not making any progress here."

Cara kept them all busy through the second day, and then the third. Towards the end of the third day, two rangers from Symin's party returned, with three recruits in tow, but it was not until noon on the fifth day that Symin finally returned with the rest of his party and a further three recruits. Once they were settled in the sanctuary, Symin sought out Corilai.

"Are you still determined to visit Dent?" he asked.

"Yes," Corilai replied. "Treghan will come with me, and of course Arool."

"Good. We will leave at least three hours before dawn. Get to sleep early tonight, so you are well rested. We will be riding hard. I would like to not delay here any longer than necessary. It will be a long day. We will arrive back in Vera long after dark, and then ride south the next day. Are you up to it?"

"Yes, Sir!"

"Good. I will wake you when we are leaving. Bring only the minimum items. Leave your packs here. We will not need a lot for a day trip. And if the wolf falls behind, we can not wait for him."

"I see," Corilai said. "I'm sure he will find us later, if it comes to that. I have to do this."

"Good. I'll see you in the morning," Symin said, walking away.

*   *   *

Three horses and a wolf raced north from Vera in the dark of night. Symin, Treghan and Corilai wasted no time on farewells, slipping out of the camp unseen by any other than those on watch, and rushed north until they reached the path that wound down into the valley to the east.

By the time the sun rose over the ocean, they were already far to the east, having twice already crossed the rivers which meandered to the coast. Close to noon they reached the familiar highway which ran from the north to the south.

Resting there, they had a brief lunch of dry bread and preserved meats, which they shared with Arool. It was washed down with water brought in canteens from Vera, before continuing east. The small group arrived in Dent while the sun was high and the workers busy in the fields.

As they came out of the cover of the forest, Corilai drew her hood up over her face and Treghan copied her. Symin continued with his hood down, and Arool never left his post to the left of Corilai as they slowed and the horses, glad of the break, walked slowly along the road into the village.

Workers in the small fields surrounding Dent looked up at them as they passed, but only a handful seemed to notice the wolf, watching wearily as their companions returned to the work at hand. Reaching a railing on the outskirts of the village, they dismounted, tying the horses near a water trough to rest as they continued into the village on foot.

Arool moved closer to Corilai, his soft flank brushing her side as they walked, the animal sensing her anxiety and acting to defend his master. As they passed closer to the centre of the village, a house came into view with one side a black, charred stain against the well kept gardens surrounding it.

Many of the other homes appeared new, rebuilt following the decimation of the village at the hands of Yuri's men. Corilai walked to the edge of the gardens and stopped, looking at the house. Somehow it had been spared the torches of Yuri, even after surviving her own destruction.

"This was my home," she whispered.

"This was?" Treghan said. "Then that means..."

He was interrupted by a male voice as a man shoved open the door of the house and stalked into the garden.

"Why do you return, Ranger?" the man shouted. "Have you not had enough after taking two of our young ones away from the fields?"

"I return for a different purpose," Symin replied.

The scout rested a hand on Corilai's shoulder as a woman came from the house to join the man. Flour stained her apron, her hands similarly coated, to indicate she had left a baking task to see what the commotion was. The man waved her aside in a huff, but she ignored him, stepping around her husband to look through narrowed eyes at the three rangers.

"You two rangers were not with him two days ago," she said. "Who are you?"

Corilai stepped forward, and raised a hand to lower her hood.

"It is me, Mother," Corilai said. "I've come home."

The man fell to his knees, as the woman ran forward to snatch her daughter in an embrace.

"Praise the flames, you're alive!" she said releasing the girl and walking back towards the house. "Quickly, come inside before the villagers see you. Your father will fetch us some wood for the fire and we can all have a hot lunch while you tell us everything. Come, come, hurry now."

They followed, and the man stood, resting a hand on Corilai's shoulder as she passed.

"Thank you for coming," he said softly. "We're so sorry for everything."

Then he was gone, rushing around the side of the house as they followed her mother inside. Arool paused, sitting in the doorway.

"Bring your little friend inside as well," the woman said. "The villagers would be concerned if they saw a wolf in the garden."

She led them into the dining room, where she fetched them tea from a large pot which boiled on the stove.

"Come," Corilai said to Arool as she sat, and the wolf curled on the floor by her feet, soon sleeping soundly.

"He's a beautiful animal," Corilai's mother said as the man entered with an armload of chopped wood. "How did you ever tame him?"

"I saved him as a pup, and returned him to his mother in the forest. Recently, she brought him to me, and he has been loyal and well mannered ever since. Why he's this way is a mystery."

"Well, you always were an unusual child," the woman said. "I shouldn't be surprised you could attract a loyal companion such as him."

"I'm glad you're both alive," Corilai said.

"You mean, after that thing with Yuri?" her mother replied. "Yes, his men destroyed the village, but when we returned, we rebuilt it, and so it will remain. We were lucky; our house was spared. But your father was forced to work with those bandits, and I was taken to Grey."

"Those were horrible times," Treghan said.

"They were. And I had wondered about you, Corilai. I knew rumours of the young flame wielders who brought Yuri down and I wondered if it was you, but I don't speak to the merchants and hear their tales directly. I had hoped, but I dared not believe. Not until now."

"Yes, it was us. Treghan and I," Corilai said. "It was a difficult time but we prevailed, and Yuri's tyranny was stopped thanks to the rangers."

Corilai's father placed a heavy iron pot on the stove and into it tossed several chunks of roast meat, the like they could never have afforded when she lived there. He also tossed in some herbs and root vegetables, before placing a lid over the top. He sat, and looked at the rangers.

"My daughter," he said. "I can only beg your forgiveness."

"It is given," she replied. "But please, that food is far too much for us. We had lunch on the way here."

"It's a special meal, for your return."

"We will not be staying, Father," Corilai said. "But thank you."

"What we don't eat will be eaten later," her mother said. "I cooked the roast this morning, and had it cooling, to be used for a village meeting tomorrow. It's better used for our reunion."

"How are the villagers?" Corilai asked.

"As superstitious as ever," her father replied. "But we know the error of those ways of thinking now. I have seen the larger towns. I travel to Oaklands and to Grey, to trade our herbs from the gardens."

He paused, looked at Symin, then looked at his hands before continuing.

"The rangers are held in high esteem there, and their work has been a boon to the people. These villages, though... Here, we see little of the rangers aside from when they recruit our young ones. The people see them only as taking from our workforce. You need one of your outposts nearby, so the villagers can see what it is you are doing for the betterment of Cinder."

"We have an outpost at Vera," Symin said.

"That is a hard ride for us, a full day away. We rarely see signs of their presence in the area. I hear they are very active, even as far as the highway, but they can not make much of an impression this far east. And those who frequent Judd in the north, or Grey in the south, they rarely make it here."

"What about the other villages?" Corilai asked. "There's Scholl, and Friss."

"They are just as isolated, though the people of Scholl are staunchly supportive of the rangers and everything they do. Friss is more like Dent, they don't see the rangers work, so they feel little loyalty to them."

"I will speak with the chancellor," Symin said. "We will arrange for an outpost somewhere in this region."

"That would be wise," Corilai's father said. "But not within a village. Better to use a place not currently occupied. Somewhere to the east of here, closer to the ocean. That way the rangers could travel out to the villages, and the villagers could reach them if they require assistance."

"I will share your suggestions with the Chancellor," Symin said.

Chapter 8 – South

"I'll be home soon, Maarlo," The familiar, soft voice whispered.

"What? Did you hear that?" Symin asked.

"Hear what?" Loka asked, before turning her attention back to the map.

"Nothing," Symin replied. "So, we will travel south to Grey via Barache's old place, and take all the new recruits with us to leave in his care."

"Agreed," Cara said. "We aren't equipped to play school yard here. And Grey can stick them on a ship to Emberdale easy enough."

"Yes. And what of the students?" Loka asked.

"You think they'd let us go on without them?" Symin replied. "You're crazy if you do. We know those four will be fine, and we can put them in charge of the safety of the others."

"And the wolf?"Cara asked.

"I think it is clear he intends to follow Corilai. Until he steps out of line, we protect him, for her sake," Symin said.

"And if he must be dealt with," Loka added. "We do it ourselves. Sending him to Emberdale with only her word would be to have him killed. We owe her better than that."

"Agreed," Symin said. "Cara, we leave at first light. Do you have any messages for Grey?"

"No. Our regular runner can deal with that."

"OK then. Thank you for your hospitality, if I don't see you in the morning, I look forward to seeing you again. Keep up the great work here at Vera."

"Thank you, Ranger," she replied as she stood to leave. "I wish you success, and look forward to hearing of it."

* * *

The old home of Barache had changed a lot since Treghan and Corilai last saw it. The cleared area had extended deep into the woods, and a sign beside the road bearing his name announced they had arrived.

"What happened here?" Treghan asked.

"Since he became governor in Grey, Barache set this place up as a home for refugees," Loka explained. "Those who felt they could not return to the villages they were taken from by Yuri's men, perhaps because they lost family or other reasons, were offered a chance to rebuild their lives here."

"So it's a village now?" Corilai asked

"Yes," Symin said. "The last one we visit before Grey. Any recruits from here are unlikely, but we must afford the same courtesy to all villages."

"Why?" Treghan asked

"Because recruitment can mean new hope for a struggling family, no matter where they live."

"I meant why was it unlikely?"

"Because there aren't many young people here. Those there are, have recently been in Grey, processed by the rangers there."

"So they're not likely to have developed flames since?" Corilai asked.

"No more or less than any others, but they are few in number so the odds are low."

A man approached, looking them over with a broad smile.

"Welcome, Rangers," the man said. "I see you have many youngsters in tow. Is this the annual recruitment?"

"Yes, it is," Symin said.

"I see," the man replied. "I doubt you'll find any flames here, but you're more than welcome to try. Will you be staying long?"

"We will not be long," Symin said. "I will search the village, but we must make haste to Grey with our charges. I would welcome your hospitality on another day, however."

"You will always be most welcome, Ranger," the man said, bowing slightly and walking away.

They continued until they reached a garden in front of the original house. Symin closed his eyes and searched for a long while, then gasped.

"Wait here," he said as he dismounted and walked into the nearby fields.

He approached a small group working there. A short, heated discussion ensued, and Symin returned alone.

"What was that about?" Loka asked.

"The lad over there is a yellow flame, however his father declined the invitation. They evidently lost the rest of their family to Yuri's cruelty, so I accepted their decision to decline our offer to test him for recruitment."

"I see. Will you ask them again?"

"Perhaps, some day. But for now, we must head for Grey."

They continued on, riding hard throughout the day as the road they travelled veered east. As the sun set behind the mountains, they pitched their camp near the main highway.

Like they had done at Vera, the rangers sent Tara on ahead, to notify the city of their approach. She rode into the dusk as the camp fire roared and the preparations for the evening meal commenced.

* * *

"Sena!" the boy screamed. "Sena, where did you go?"

"Don't worry," Symin heard the voice that was himself but was not himself say. "He will carry me home soon."

In this dream world, things were fluid. Nothing seemed solid, and fire burned softly everywhere. In cool warmth, the flames ebbed and flowed, washing over his thoughts like a tropical breeze.

"Where am I?" Symin tried to say.

"Be still, bearer," the voice said. "You are with me, just as I am with you. This is my world, you are always safe here. But the hour approaches for you to continue your journey. Farewell."

Symin opened his eyes to the dim light before dawn. He felt strangely at peace as he dressed and left the tent. Loka stirred as he opened the flap to let in the crisp morning air.

"Come back to bed," she said softly. "We still have some time before we have to go."

"I'm sorry, I just wanted to think a while."

"Is it about Sena?" Loka asked. "You've mumbled that name a few times lately. Who is it?"

"I don't know. It's a name I hear in my dreams."

"Does this Sena person talk to you?" Loka asked.

"Yes, and no. Most of the time, it's like I am Sena, but then, she addresses me directly, as if that's not the case. It's like we're two souls in one space, one body. She controls it, and I watch."

"I wonder if that's how a flame feels?" Loka asked.

"Perhaps," Symin said, opening the flap again. "If a flame is able to feel. I need some air, sorry love."

He left her there, and walked through the pre-dawn camp. He saw Corilai, Sitting on a log at the edge of camp. Arool slept beside her, his chest rising and falling slowly as she stared into the misty distance.

"Does he still behave?" Symin asked as he sat beside the girl.

"Yes, as tame as a pet."

"How is that possible?"

"I don't know," she answered. "It's a mystery."

"There are all too many of those at the moment," Symin said. "I intend to solve them all."

"What do you mean?"

"We're going to the desert. I'll finally know what has been calling me there. Somehow, I think your strong clawed friend is one more piece of the puzzle."

"What puzzle?" Corilai asked as Loka approached.

"Cinder," Loka said. "Cinder is the puzzle Symin lives to solve."

"I thought that was the flames," Corilai said.

"The flames are only one part of a greater secret," Symin said. "Don't you wonder what lies beyond our borders?"

"Of course," the girl said.

"I have found mention of other countries," Symin said. "In the ancient texts, which those who came before Cinder visited. What happened to them? Why was Cinder created, and cut off from them?"

"That's what you think we'll find in the desert?" Corilai asked.

"The truth is what we'll find. If we will find all of it I can't say yet."

"We should break camp," Loka said. "We have to get to Grey as soon as possible."

Breaking camp, they reached the highway and turned south, making haste as they rushed towards the steel city. Finally, they crested a rise and stopped, looking down the long, straight stretch of road which led into the city in the distance. A great stone sat by the road, which Treghan and Corilai remembered well.

Beside it sat a covered wagon, several members of the city guard on horseback, and Tara. Tara gestured, and one of the guards dismounted and stepped into the road to greet them.

"Beza? Is that you?" Treghan gasped.

"Yes, young white flame. It is good too see you both keeping such good company."

"Why do you bring the wagon?" Symin asked.

"It's Barache's idea," Beza said. "Ranger Tara says the young ones bring a tame wolf, though I would not believe it without the evidence before me. The lass is to ride inside with her furred companion, to avoid panic in the city."

"I think that's a fair request," Symin said. "Corilai, take your friend and climb aboard."

"Yes, Ranger," Corilai said, dismounting and climbing into the cart. "Arool, come."

The young wolf calmly approached the cart, looked around, then jumped in after his mistress. Shortly after, they moved out, making good time as the late morning sun cast the last of the fog from the fields.

They entered the city, and after a long time rattling along cobblestone streets, they finally stopped inside the courtyard of the ranger complex from which Barache governed Grey.

"You can get out now," Beza shouted, banging a fist on the cart.

Corilai climbed out as the others dismounted, Arool climbing down and standing patiently beside her. He looked up to his mistress as the guards led the horses away to be stabled.

Barache strode across the courtyard to greet them, a wide grin on his face as he saw his young friends.

"Welcome to Grey," he roared. "I think this place has changed a lot since you were last here, but more about that later. Quickly now, inside, all of you. We have an early lunch prepared. Even some meat for the wolf. Come now, hurry inside, all of you."

* * *

Full of good food and relaxed, the rangers sat around the mess hall, listening as Barache and Symin discussed their mission. The new recruits had been sent away to be set up in a barracks until they could be taken to Emberdale.

Corilai and her friends sat to one side of the hearth. A small fire crackled, a peaceful reminder of the comfortable lodgings. Arool lay in the corner nearby, contentedly gnawing on a large bone.

"So you were headed for Horde?" Barache said.

"Yes, ostensibly for recruits," Symin replied. "Though historically we get few from that city. There are some other matters we are to investigate on the Chancellor's orders."

"Oh? Would that be the reports of vanishing flames, and the incident with the outpost?"

"What incident?"

"It was burned to the ground."

Symin lurched to his feet, shouting.

"What? When? How? Was anybody killed?"

"Nobody was killed," Barache replied calmly. "Some barely escaped, but it was not done by a ranger."

"You found evidence it was set by conventional means?"

"No."

"Then how do you know none of our people are responsible?

"At the time it was set, all the rangers of the outpost were accounted for, and there were at least three colours of flame set to the building. This was the act of flame wielders, but not our own."

"What are you implying?" Symin demanded.

"Nothing, not without further evidence. But please, be careful in that city. If what I suspect is really the case, there may be a large, organised group of flame wielders operating in Horde, who will go to great lengths to stay hidden."

"I see. That would indeed be a concern," Symin replied.

"It would also explain the historic recruitment issues," Loka said.

"I have already discussed this possibility with the chancellor," Symin said. "We have concluded such a group exists. We have not concluded their intent, or their stance in regards to us. We do not know if they will prove an enemy or an ally, were matters to become dire."

"Investigating this group is your true mission?" Barache asked.

"Officially, yes. I have other..." Symin paused, looking around. "...More personal investigations to also perform. The two may be related."

"Personal matters?" Barache asked, raising an eyebrow. "Then you are finally seeking your answers?"

"I am."

"Then you'll be going into the desert," Barache said. "You know nobody has ever returned?"

"We will be the first," Symin said with an unusual certainty.

"Then I have one suggestion," Barache said. "You need orange flames. Several, if possible. They may be the difference between success and death in the sand."

"Do you have any you can spare?"

Barache thought for a long while, staring into the crackling fire. Finally he looked at Symin, nodded and smiled.

"I can send four with you. They are not my greatest people, but they are strong enough. They have their secondaries under control, and that is what you will need."

"Thank you, old friend," Symin said. "Can you have them prepared to leave at dawn?"

"Certainly," Barache said. "I will go and organise the orders now. Please, make yourselves at home. Grey's rangers are at your disposal."

Chapter 9 – Horde

Hyren watched as Malthus manipulated the ancient machine. A small trickle of the green essence pooled in the receptacle on top, and began to bubble. The elder depressed a knob on the side, and slowly the bubbling stopped.

"At this consistency, if we paint this on a wall, it forms a barrier flames can not see through."

He pressed the knob again, and the liquid bubbled and steamed, and congealed further. The young acolytes watched as the elder touched a finger to the boiling sludge and once again pressed the knob.

"Strangely, it is cool enough to touch," Malthus said. "But now, it can be formed to any shape you desire."

Malthus stretched the gooey green clod and rolled it between his palms, to make a long rod. Bending one end slightly he placed it on the table, and flattened it.

"When it cools, this bar will be as strong as anything they make in Grey. But this we can reheat and change to any other purpose. Essence does not fail and disappear with the weathering of time. Somewhere in the desert, all the essence our ancestors controlled must still exist. It is the task of our order to keep it hidden, that our world does not end in catastrophe as theirs did."

"How did it happen?" Hyren asked.

"We can not say, young one," Malthus said, as a man entered the training hall, standing just inside the doorway and beckoning. "I must attend to something, children. Wait here until Elder Krytus returns."

After collecting his outer cloak from a chair, Malthus followed the man from the room. Walking down the corridor, Malthus fastened his cloak and brushed his hand down the front, straightening it.

"What's the situation?" Malthus asked.

"I've heard my flame," the man said. "Our post outside Grey had his flame communicate with mine."

"And what does it say?"

"The rangers have sent their annual recruitment expedition to Grey."

"What of it?"

"It is a significantly larger expedition that in previous years."

"And?"

"They have left Grey, and are heading towards Horde."

"I see," Malthus said, stopping to think.

The man turned to face him, waiting without patience. Finally Malthus looked at him.

"Seek out twenty bearers of flame from within my trusted ranks," Malthus said. "We must ride to face these rangers, and show them we will welcome no more of their incursions."

"Yes, Ignitor," the man said, bowing slightly before rushing away.

*　　　*　　　*

Symin led his people a short distance beyond the city walls, before he stopped. Corilai and Arool climbed down from the cart, and it left to return to the city. She found her horse, being led by Treghan, and mounted as the rangers continued their journey.

"We take it easy for this trip," Symin shouted. "We know nothing of any enemies we face. I would prefer we are not exhausted when we meet them."

They travelled without incident, stopping for a meal at noon then continuing until late afternoon. They set their camp beside the highway, the sands of the Desert of Souls stretching over the horizon, a desolate, beckoning wasteland.

The highway skirted the edge of the desert until it struck out southwards into the sand, to Horde. The ancient city held its grip on the place with tenacity in contrast to the empty sands it watched over. As the rangers pitched their camp, Horde still hid beyond the distant horizon. The sands threatened and beckoned, calling the weary traveller to their demise.

All the rangers knew few who entered those rolling dunes had ever returned. An uneasy calm settled over the group as a bright moon rose high in the clear night sky.

* * *

Symin tossed and turned, yellow tendrils reaching, searching for something, or someone.

"We mustn't let Maarlo know we are coming," said the voice. "But come we must."

"Maarlo, who is he?" Symin asked, not really expecting an answer.

"My brother. But he leads our enemy. You must reach them, before they reach you. If he knows you bear me, we will fail."

"I bear you?"

"You know this, bearer. Perhaps not in your mind, but in your heart, you do. But leave me now. You must not burn your woman."

Symin awoke with a start, to find Loka kneeling over him, shock on her face, and smoke filling their tent.

"What happened?" Symin asked.

"You were flaming in your sleep, like an untrained demon flame," Loka whispered. "If I hadn't woken to douse the fire, you would have ruined our bedding."

"Sorry. That's never happened to me before."

"That's what they all say, champ," Loka quipped.

"Glad you have faith in me, enforcer."

"Always, my love," she said. "You were dreaming again."

"Yes. It's more frequent now."

"Sena?"

"Yes. She says we must find them, before they find us."

"That's ominous," Loka said. "Find who?"

"Maarlo and his people. Whoever that is."

"You don't have any ideas?"

"Sena says he's her brother, maybe our enemy."

"Maybe?" Loka asked. "It sounds like your subconscious is worrying about the mysterious group the Chancellor thinks is in Horde, and that's influencing your dreams. But try not to burn me in your sleep, will you?"

She stood, and left the tent, to stare out over the rolling dunes which glowed softly in the reflected light of the moon. Symin joined her, and held her as they continued to gaze into the night, wondering about the landscape; The imposing desert that was about to dominate their lives.

* * *

When the rangers broke camp at first light, nobody could resist staring out over that forbidding landscape. It dominated their thoughts as they rode.

"It seems so eerie," Marni said.

"Why?" Fletcher asked.

"Think about it," Marni said. "My flame is all about life. Grasses, plants, trees. None of that can live out there. I feel like I'm going somewhere my power will fail."

"You'll be fine, just wait and see," Fletcher replied. "Besides, so what if your secondary fails? You'll still have your flame, and it's as strong as anybody else's here."

"Thanks," she said. "But I'm still worried."

"Don't be. How many years did everybody think white flames had no secondary at all? But they got along fine, and so will you."

"I hope so," Marni said.

The companions travelled in an uneasy silence as they rode on into the morning. Soon, the road began to follow the rolling undulations of the dunes as they made a direct line for a large rock formation which marked the road south to Horde.

Tall rocky mountains dominated the west and north west, blocking the horizon, as they skirted the edges of the mines district. Descending into the trough between two dunes, they came upon twenty men, scarlet cloaks billowing around them.

"Turn around rangers," one of the men shouted. "We do not wish to harm you, but we can not allow you to go further."

"Who are you?" Symin shouted.

In reply, the men erected a wall of fire, then hurled their many coloured flames at the rangers. Thinking fast, Treghan threw up a defensive ice wall, and the flames struck it with force. The ice melted, but the flames were spent.

"Your circus tricks are no defence," the red cloaked man bellowed. "Return and be spared!"

"Leave this to us, Sir," one of Barache's men said, waving for the other three orange flames to join him.

Together, they raised their arms, and drew the surrounding sand to do their bidding. An enormous tornado of sand grew, towering into the sky, many times the width of the road. In unison, the four rangers lowered their arms, and the immense, swirling wall of sand rushed at the scarlet garbed flame wielders.

The unknown enemy scattered, running over the next dune, many knocked from their feet, scrambling in the force of the tornado. Together the four orange flames turned away from the scene, returning to their horses as the maelstrom collapsed.

The dust cleared as the last of the scarlet robes disappeared over the dunes, their confidence shattered.

"What was that all about?" Loka asked.

"Your guess is as good as mine," Symin said. "But one thing is for sure: If those people want us out of Horde, there is no place in Cinder I would rather go."

He looked back at his people, unharmed and still well rested, whatever the enemy had intended.

"Rangers, move on!" he shouted as he spurred his horse into a trot.

As they rode over the next peak, They could see the stragglers of the red garbed men, fleeing on horseback, headed for Horde. Symin slowed his horse, allowing them to get away.

"We know where they're going. No need to spark a bigger confrontation. Besides, we don't know if this is all of them, or a small group of hot headed fools. If we take them out, it may spur on the rest. But if we ignore them, the rest might be more receptive to us in spite of their colleagues actions."

"You've already been considering this scenario, haven't you?" Loka said.

"Not really," Symin replied. "But it makes sense. If we assume similar flame wielding numbers to other populations, with this group recruiting them, then their number may be large. Certainly many hundreds of them. I'd rather not start a war with such a group unless I have too."

* * *

"What were you thinking?" Krytus screamed, in a rare show of rage, when Malthus returned and faced the other two ignitors. "How could you be so arrogant to think you could scare them away with such a show of force?"

"But we mustn't let them establish themselves here! Our mission..."

"Is to stay hidden," Krytus growled, cutting off the other man's defence. "But you scuppered that plan well and truly. The order has stayed secret and held control of Horde for seven centuries, and you wreck it all in five minutes of grandstanding! You fool. How is it we are cursed with such an imbecile as one of the three ignitors?"

"I apologise," Malthus said, chastised. "I have failed the order. I should have listened to my flame."

"You are fortunate that your flame grants you privilege. Anybody else would be banished to the desert for this."

"What do we do next?" Rogan asked, interrupting his fellow ignitors. "We must find a way to conceal the truth Malthus has exposed. And that falls to us three. The order must be protected, and we have a duty to shield our brethren from harm."

"I have an idea," Malthus said. "They know nothing of us. We should set up a building elsewhere in the city, plant robes and equipment for twenty people, make it seem recently abandoned, show tracks into the desert. Divert the rangers attention away from us, and let them believe the people they saw were few."

"That may work," Krytus said. "You must lead this plan. Take the same bearers you had before. Let the rangers see you, and follow you. Be as amateur as you must, and lead them into the desert."

"And should you fail," Rogan concluded. "I don't care who your flame is, you need not return."

The threat left hanging, Rogan stood and left the room. Krytus, though more forgiving, was equally furious, and followed his old friend, leaving Malthus to prepare his plan alone.

* * *

As the sun set over the western mountains, casting long shadows into the desert, Symin led his group to the gates of Horde. Tired from the long ride, the rangers filed quietly into the city. Arool, mostly ignored, stuck by Corilai's side, drawing a shout from the gatekeeper.

"He's tame, and I'm tired, just leave him be," Corilai snapped, and the gatekeeper nodded, waving her through, but taking several steps away from the wolf.

They rode through the city, following directions Barache had given them to find the outpost. When they reached it, they found several tents, and a half erected frame of the new building on the site where the outpost had stood.

Dismounting, Symin looked at the scene, his fury rising.

"This was the same idiots we met in the road, I'm sure," he snarled. "This was an act of war. We must hold them to account."

"Symin," Loka said, dismounting and joining him, her hand on his shoulder. "That will have to wait. We can't all stay here. I'll send Tara to find an inn, and book it out for us to use."

"Do that. We have to get work on the rebuild sped up though."

"Welcome to Horde," said a ranger, approaching from the tents. "I am Pirette. Obviously, I must apologise for the state of the accommodation."

"Do you have any leads on the culprit?" Symin asked.

"Perhaps. We have some interesting information. I can't say with certainty it is related though."

"Good enough," Symin said. "Once Tara arranges our lodgings, you can come with us and tell us all you know. I would get to the bottom of this city's hostility towards us as soon as possible. Such lawlessness can no longer be tolerated."

Chapter 10 – Investigation

Treghan and Corilai stood near the tent on the site of the outpost. The innkeeper had refused to allow a wolf in the building, So she had volunteered to join the local rangers at the construction site. Treghan joined her at first light, Symin having forbidden them from sharing a tent.

They sat there watching the people of Horde starting their day, travelling to their work places in the first light of dawn. Arool sat between them, guarding his mistress as always. Suddenly a flash of red caught Treghan's attention.

"Corilai, did you see that?" he said, jumping up and walking away.

Corilai followed, Arool by her side, as he rushed to the street and along to the corner of the next building. In an alley, they saw two men in red cloaks.

"That's them, I'm sure of it," Treghan said, as he ran into the alley.

"Treghan, wait!" Corilai said as she followed.

Glancing at the two young ranger students, the men rushed out the other end of the alley. Treghan ran, hoping to see where they went, reaching the end just in time to see them duck into another alley. He turned towards it and ran on, glancing behind as he did so.

"Come on, Corilai, we can't afford to lose them!" he shouted.

Once again, he just saw them turn and followed, repeating this and barely keeping them in sight as he followed the men across the city. Finally, he watched as they entered a small building. As he made to rush over to the men's apparent hideout, Corilai grabbed his arm.

"Wait," she said. "There were about twenty of them, remember?"

"But we're right here, and we know they're there now!"

"And if there are twenty in there, how good do you think your chances are of bringing them down?" Corilai argued. "We should get Symin."

"I guess so," Treghan said, the excitement leaving his voice. "We can bring them right back here. Do you think those guys know we followed them?"

"Yes, but even so, we shouldn't rush in alone."

"OK. We'll go find Symin and the others."

Arool let out a low growl, pressing against Corilai's side, and both the student's looked to see what was up. A shaggy looking man with a noose attached to a long wooden pole was in the process of snaring the animal, who had remarkably made no move to retaliate.

"Hey! Who the hell are you?" Treghan barked, drawing the man's attention away from Arool.

Corilai grabbed the noose, as it dropped onto Arool's head. The man jerked the pole hard, snapping the noose around the wolf's neck and lunging away from the two rangers.

"A fine tame animal like that will fetch a lot of money in the right places. Clearly more useful to me than you," the man snarled as he dragged the now thrashing wolf away from its mistress.

"No you don't!" Corilai screamed, hurling a ball of her black fire at the man, hitting his hands.

Screaming, the man dropped the pole, staring at the girl in rage.

"I'll have the guards arrest you for that!" he screamed.

"Just try it!" Treghan shouted.

Snatching up the pole as Corilai burned the noose to release Arool, Treghan swung it hard, rapping the man's shoulders hard enough to knock him down. He sat on the man's back, lit a white flame in his hand, and held it before the man's face.

"You really don't want that kind of trouble," Treghan snarled. "Nobody steals from a ranger. Corilai, fetch the city guard."

"You think I'm scared?" the man snarled. "Your little flames are nothing!"

"You don't know a lot about rangers, do you?" Treghan replied, standing and facing the man as he tried to get up, clearly intent on running. "Your city guard works with us, just as they do in all of Cinder. And if you think you're going to run..."

Treghan stopped talking and waved his hands in the air between them. Ice grew rapidly from the ground to encase the man up to his ribs. Frozen in place, the thief glared at the young man.

"What did you do?" he snarled.

"Nothing as good as a fully qualified ranger would have done to you. Think yourself lucky you only crossed a student. If any of you villains of Horde value your lives, you should remember that, and remember we aren't about to leave."

The thief spat at Treghan, who easily stepped aside, before launching into a tirade of rage fuelled blasphemy the like the young student had never heard. Treghan listened in calm amusement as the man quickly ran short of breath, the ice limiting his ability to breath.

"You'll only do yourself further harm," Treghan said, grabbing a crate from against a nearby wall and sitting on it.

"I'll have your hide for this," the man muttered.

"We'll see about that," Treghan said. "They'll be here soon enough. Just wait there."

After several more minutes, Corilai came into sight, Arool trotting beside her, and several of the city guard following. With them, Symin and Loka also came. Treghan waved, smiling at Corilai as she approached.

"Symin and Loka were with the guards when I found them," she said. "And I explained what was going on. This fellow and the red cloaked guys as well."

"There has been a gang stealing animals for some time, who have eluded us," one of the guards said. "With your testimony, we can arrest this man, and maybe finally catch up with the rest of them. If you would please free him, I will have him taken into custody."

"Of course," Treghan said melting the ice, the man gasping for air as he was freed.

The guard signalled two of his companions, who rushed to secure the man in chains, before marching him away. The guard then addressed Treghan.

"My name is Druitt, I'm the head of the guard. That is an impressive skill," he said. "Are all you rangers able to do that?"

"Well, not exactly that, but we all have various skills which can be useful from time to time."

"So I see," Druitt said. "Now, what is this I hear about bogey men in red cloaks?"

"On the way here, a group attempted an ambush and warned us not to come to Horde," Treghan said, then pointed. "We followed two dressed the same as them, and they entered that building over there."

"I see," Druitt said, then looked to Symin. "I believe that building has been officially abandoned for quite some time. What say we go take a look?"

"My thoughts exactly," the ranger scout said. "Treghan, Corilai, you may come, but keep yourselves out of trouble."

As they crossed to the building, a commotion was heard inside, and men began running from the furthest end, quickly disappearing into the neighbouring buildings and the passing crowds. As they reached the building, a handful of guards who had set chase quickly returned, the hunt futile as the men vanished.

Symin stepped up to the door and shoved it open, to stride inside the two story building. As the rest filed in behind him, the scout approach an altar at one end of the large room. The space was about half of the lower floor, with seats arranged to face the altar. Reaching it, he found papers scattered around it. Picking one up, he read it out loud.

"Red fellows meeting, week twelve, summary address. As your leader, I stand here to congratulate you all. While we are small in number, already we are having an impact in Horde, protecting our interests from the threat of the ranger menace. With our destruction of their outpost, and our failed ambush, our results may be mixed. But for a small force of twenty men, we must stay proud, and keep the pressure on."

"Red fellows?" Druitt said. "This is the first I've heard of them, but it seems they confess to the fire which destroyed your outpost."

"That it does," Symin said. "This goes on for pages, clearly intended to inspire them to greater crimes."

"We don't know who these individuals are, but we have taken their base of operations from them," Druitt said. "I will have my men clear out all the evidence from this building, and then, to spite them, I will suggest to the governor he allow you rangers to adopt it as your new outpost."

"That would serve a double purpose," Symin said. "And we would welcome the opportunity to re-establish ourselves. Thank you."

"Excellent. Give me three days, for my men to clear everything out and I will in that time make my recommendation to the governor. I am sure he will be pleased to ensure these criminals are denied a place from which to operate."

"Thank you," Symin said as he turned to leave. "We will await word from you."

"Symin, what are you doing?" Loka asked as she followed him. "Are you just going to let them handle it?"

"For now, yes," he replied. "We're not overly welcome here as yet, and we want that to change. Appearing to take over the role of the city guard would hurt us more in the long run than hunting down the red fellows would help."

"True. So what do we do?" Loka asked.

"There's plenty more we can investigate. After all, do we really believe that a small, newly formed group is our target? I don't buy that for a second."

"So, you think this was a diversion?"

"I do, so letting the guard take control of the investigation costs us nothing while we continue to hunt the real culprits."

"How can you be so sure it was a diversion?" Treghan asked.

"Because they got away too easily. A small, newly formed group could never have the amount of community help that escape requires. This was a set up, I'm sure of it."

"So what now?" Loka asked.

"We need a map of the city, and I need to speak to Pirette and Gurrei."

* * *

Hyren watched as the ignitors meditated. This was a class on communion, the art of knowing your flame, and communicating both with it, and through it. The meditation required looked simple, but so far it eluded him. Krytus opened his eyes, and looked straight at Hyren.

"Lad, you still fail to relax and listen Why?"

"I don't know, I just can't stop my mind."

"You need to, if you are to pass this class and serve the order. I'm going to assign you additional sessions, until you get it."

"Yes, Sir," Hyren said as the other two ignitors opened their eyes and stood.

"Don't look so despondent, lad," Krytus said as he waved a hand to dismiss the acolytes. "Not everybody is able to do this right away. And some possess flames which are less conducive to it. You will get the hang of it in time. Hearing what your flame has to say will come easy to you, once the meditation is mastered. Others find it the other way around. All members of the order struggle at some aspect of this early learning."

Malthus approached, and Krytus waved the boy away.

"The city guard are now investigating the Red Fellows," Malthus said as Hyren left. "The rangers took the bait easily enough."

* * *

Symin sat at a table with a map Druitt gave him of Horde. Loka sat beside him as usual. With them, Pirette and Gurrei sat, as they scrawled on it with a pencil, marking locations where they had already found those mysterious gaps in the world they could sense with the yellow flame's secondary ability.

"How much of the city have you covered?" Symin asked.

"Not a lot," Pirette said. "We have only found these few locations in pursuit of flames which vanished."

"We need a more detailed exploration," Symin said. "I need every yellow flame here on the job. Myself included. We divide the city up, and we inspect every street, every wall, every building."

"You want a complete survey of the city?" Gurrei asked.

"Yes, the most thorough we can manage. Every location we sense this phenomena with our flames, must be investigated."

"Immediately?" Pirette asked.

"Yes, but not in any way to attract attention. To start with, a visual assessment, and thorough notes on the immediately available information. Is it a house? A business? Who lives or works there? I want as much detail as we can get without actually entering those places."

"Why?" Loka asked.

"I believe this is how a great many flame wielders have avoided recruitment for many years. This survey should give us a good idea of their numbers, and a greater understanding of how integrated into the community they really are. I fear taking this group head on would be to take an aggressive stance against all of Horde. Such an action would not end well. Not for us, and not for this city."

"I will put out the call," Pirette said. "There are two other yellow flames with the outpost."

"And one other, with the students who accompany us, but I do not know how skilled she is. I have one other with my group. That will have to be enough. Loka, can you fetch them for me? Pirette, bring your two right away. We will start this immediately."

"Yes, Sir," Pirette replied as he and Loka both stood to leave.

Taking a pencil, Symin drew on the map, splitting the city into six sections, before writing his name in one. He then studied the section he had claimed for some time, before closing his eyes and sending out his tendril of flame, to search the city.

He soon encountered his first instance of the mysterious gap in the world, and he poked and prodded at it with his flame for a full minute, not willing to believe it was possible. Then he opened his eyes, and marked the place on the map, before closing his eyes and continuing his search.

After some time, Pirette returned with two others, shortly after followed by Loka with Yera and one other. Symin paused to explain what was needed, and assigned each of them a section of the map. They all set about their task, working long and thoroughly, identifying all boundaries of any holes they sensed. They worked for hours to ensure every possible place was marked on the map.

Chapter 11 – Holes

Symin Looked over the finished map the next morning, stunned that the holes in yellow flame perception covered nearly a full third of the city. He shook his head, trying to decide what he should do next. He looked to Loka, who watched him attentively.

"We're going to need copies, and several of us investigating these places. One map, one person, it would take months."

"Agreed," Loka said. "Perhaps this is a task for the young ones?"

"The copies?" he replied. "Yes, something safe they can do indoors while we get some investigations started. Can you fetch them?"

"Yes, Symin," Loka said with a smile as she left the room.

After a short wait, she returned with all but Corilai, who could not bring Arool into the tavern, so was waiting outside.

"I'd forgotten about the wolf," Symin moaned, heading for the door. "I'll have a talk with the innkeeper."

Finding the innkeeper, Symin explained the situation, and offered to pay an additional fee for the wolf. Surprisingly, the innkeeper accepted and they went outside to fetch Corilai and Arool.

"Why did you change your mind?" Corilai asked.

"I have heard good things about you. Therefore I offer my trust. Please do not abuse it."

The students were chatting among themselves when Symin returned along with the innkeeper, Corilai, and Arool.

"The wolf will not leave this room, unless he is leaving the building," Symin said. "You will have the additional payment when we vacate your premises."

"I will hold you to your word, ranger," the surly innkeeper said, turning to leave with a nervous look at Arool and Corilai. "Young lady, I hear gossip that your friend there was nearly stolen, but you captured the thief and handed him to the city guards. Thank you. I had a horse taken a few weeks ago. It has been quite a problem around Horde of late."

"My pleasure," Corilai said with a smile and curtsey as the man left the room, before joining her friends around the table.

Symin ordered the students to spend the rest of the day painstakingly copying the map, including the areas marked by the yellow flames, before leaving them to the task. It was painstaking work, and by the end of their first copy, they were getting fed up when Symin returned to inspect their work.

"Do it again," Symin demanded, screwing up their copies and tossing them away. "It is vital these maps be a true and accurate copy. I realise this is frustrating work, but you have to get it right."

"But Symin, this is immensely hard to draw correctly!" Fletcher complained.

"Take it a bit at a time. But notice the grid like structure of the central city?" Symin said. "Sure there are diagonal roads and all sorts of lanes, but the larger design is a clear grid."

Symin retrieved a fresh parchment, and placed it on the table beside the original. Picking up a pencil, he sat between Fletcher and Marni. Carefully, he marked a point, then measured the grid width on the original with his fingers. Moving his hand to show the same distance on the fresh sheet. He then marked a second point, and a third.

"Measure and mark out the grid first," Symin explained. "Then copy a square at a time. If the lanes and so forth meet the grid correctly, we should be able to work with it."

He stood, handed the pencil to Fletcher, and walked away from the table, still talking.

"That first effort was a mess, but if you work like this, so you are building the new map on a solid structure, you should get a usable result. If you work together, you can mark the grid, then each start at a corner and work in. That way, you can finish a copy fast and move on to the next. I need five or six of these, as soon as you can get it done."

* * *

Symin and Loka followed Pirette as he led them to the temple, taking back alleys to avoid alerting its inhabitants.

"Was this the first affected building you discovered?" Symin asked.

"For us, yes," Pirette said. "Though I had heard rumours of others noticing odd things before that."

"What others?" Symin asked.

"Scouts, mostly, though when scouts come for recruitment, they tend to walk around until they sense a flame. It is possible to pass these buildings by without ever noticing that they are unusual, if you are not directly investigating them."

"Why is that?"

"I think it is a property of the holes, that to the casual observer, they conceal their unusual nature. Those with flames, I believe, are taught early to evade rangers at every opportunity. They run about like escaping spies, before they enter such a building."

"I see," Symin replied. "Chances are, by the time the flame has entered one of these places, they have already ducked into alleys, ditches, perhaps even sewers, and thus evaded the scout, so the scout is left questioning what he thinks he sees that one time he actually manages to catch sight of the anomalies."

"Yes, and so they choose not to report it, for fear of their skill or their mental state being questioned. So this matter may have stayed hidden from Emberdale for centuries."

"Well, that does sound ludicrous," Loka said. "Even knowing the lack of recruits from Horde has been a problem for so long it is considered normal."

"That normality probably means scouts have not been as thorough as they otherwise would be," Symin said.

"Exactly my thoughts," Pirette said. "And even if you are thorough, without some very direct poking around, you could go a long time never noticing that things aren't normal. Such that you question your own flame's eyes when you finally do see it. I know I was tempted not to report what I saw, but now, I am glad I did."

"As are we," Symin said. "You may have helped us in more ways than the immediately obvious. Only time will tell the full ramifications of your discovery."

Pirette stopped, Symin and Loka stepping alongside him, to look out across the plaza in front of the temple. It stood there, imposing, and Symin wondered how it could be they knew so little about such a landmark.

"When we found it," Pirette said. "We asked a child about it. He said it was the Church of the Essence, and that only the monks go there."

"Church of the Essence?" Symin said. "It seems strange that rangers would know nothing of it."

"Not as strange as the fact we have never had an established presence or authority here," Loka said. "Why is Horde special? No other town, village, or city in Cinder is such a mystery to us."

They watched the building for a few minutes, before Symin turned away.

"I suggest we return and go inside in the evening, but not until the full survey of the other locations is complete. Those youngsters should have made some good progress on the map copies by now. We should return to the inn."

"Yes, Ranger," Pirette said, following as Loka rushed to join Symin, heading back the way they had come.

* * *

Hyren rode on the front of the cart, his father holding the reins beside him. In the back, three men from the order guarded a bucket of essence.

"What are we going to do, Father?" the boy asked.

"This morning, we have had workers building a small room off the back of the house, near the kitchen, to use as a wood store."

"I know about that. It's not much of a room. They didn't even build a floor."

"It doesn't need one," Hyren's father said. "But it does need to be built according to the rules of the order."

"I don't understand," Hyren said.

"You will. All parts of a member's home or workplace must be painted with a thin coat of essence. It will dry clear, and it keeps us hidden."

"How does it do that?" Hyren asked.

"I don't know exactly, but when rangers come looking for recruits, if you are in a building treated this way, they never find you."

"Is that like the church of the essence? Is that painted like this as well?"

"Of course it is. It is our most important place, so we protect it most of all."

* * *

Druitt waited outside the inn as Symin and the others arrived. He strode forward to greet them, his hand outstretched to shake. Symin smiled, shaking to man's hand before gesturing for him to enter the building.

"I have good news," Druitt said as they made their way to the bar. "The governor has granted the use of that abandoned building to you."

"That is good news," Symin said. "Were there any conditions we need to be aware of?"

"Only one," Druitt said. "He requests that you work closely with the city guard, and share any intelligence you may find related to our investigations. He requests you submit a written report to me each week of your activities, and I am to keep him informed of any issues."

"I see," Symin replied. "I guess that will be fine, for now. We can revisit it as we proceed."

"When would you like to take up occupancy of the building?" Druitt asked.

"I guess tomorrow would work," Symin replied. "I can have my people preparing for the move this afternoon. It will be good to be in a permanent facility again."

"In that case, I will have one of my men deliver the keys to you today. I hope it serves your needs well."

Druitt turned to leave, stopping at the door, to look back, speaking as if it were an afterthought.

"Give my thanks to the youngsters with the wolf. That fellow they caught has provided us with some good information. We can finally put an end to the animal thefts which have plagued the city in recent months."

"I'll be sure to do so," Symin said.

Druitt left, and Symin spent the rest of the day coordinating his people. All the rangers prepared to move, including those who still worked from the tents at the site of the old outpost.

"How did you secure such a building for our use?" Gurrei asked as they walked from the tents back to the inn.

"By earning their trust," Symin said. "I believe we owe Arool for that one."

"The wolf?" Gurrei exclaimed. "I would never have guessed. How did that happen?"

"The man the students captured trying to steal the wolf has led to a significant breakthrough for the city guard on a case they have been working on for some time."

"That's most fortuitous," Gurrei said. "And now, we have no need to rebuild."

"No, we still must rebuild the outpost," Symin said.

"Why?"

"Because we must not leave the city worse off than we found it. Leaving a charred ruin inside the city is not good diplomacy. Also, as long as we remain in this new building, we remain in the governors debt, and in debt to the guard also. I would prefer we are free of such burden."

"You always think like this?" Gurrei asked.

"We must. Rangers do not receive automatic respect. Since the Chancellor changed his policy and sent us out to be more active in Cinder's local life, we have had to struggle to earn our place. It highlights our mistakes of the past, and we must ensure the past is not dictating our future."

* * *

Symin stood in an alley, just out of sight from the street, and closed his eyes. Pushing his tendril of yellow out, he felt around the shape marked on the map, the last one in his area. Then he noticed a line, not marked.

"That's odd," he mumbled as he walked from the alley and along the street, opposite the house which was dark on the map.

He observed men down the side of the building, but he could not tell what they were doing. Together with Loka, he walked further, and crossed to enter a lane which ran to the next street. He followed the lane until he was outside the property which backed onto the peculiar house.

Symin crept down the side of the house, to get a better view of his target. Loka followed, keeping her attention on the house beside them in case they were seen. Stopping at the corner of the building, a dusty yard sat between the two properties. They watched as the men worked, painting something onto the walls of a recent addition.

Closing his eyes, Symin focussed his energy and reached out. The line had extended now, as the men worked, to encompass more of the addition.

"Well that proves it," Symin said. "People here are actively concealing themselves from ranger eyes."

"Are you sure they know their actions have that effect?" Loka asked.

"I feel confident, but you're right. I shouldn't jump to conclusions."

As they watched, a young boy in his early teens walked around the house and approached the men, carrying a heavy bucket in each hand.

"I brought more white wash to go over the top," the boy said as he put them down and started to remove a soft green pullover. "It's so hot!

Symin watched, and as the garment with its hood lifted over the boy's head, he saw something. In his mind he sensed it, strong and burning with the fire of youth. A bright, orange flame burned within the boy.

"Idiot!" one of the men snapped. "You want to be discovered by a ranger? Put that thing back on. You need to put up with being a little hot."

Chagrined, the boy slipped the garment back on, and the flame in Symin's vision disappeared.

"The essence in those fibres hides you," the man berated in a loud, harsh whisper. "Just like the essence on these walls, or in the lining of your cloak. Every member of the order has a responsibility to keep themselves concealed while ever the rangers are snooping around."

Symin stared, mouth ajar, shocked to have learned such critical information in such a way. He felt a tugging at his arm and obeyed as Loka dragged him away, further out of sight of the men. Together, they made their way back to the street, before Symin broke into a run, heading back towards the new outpost.

"Symin!" Loka called.
"Just hurry," he snapped. "We have to get back."

Chapter 12 – Temple Raid

Symin waited as one by one, the other groups returned from surveying the city's anomalies. When they were finally all assembled in the meeting space downstairs of the new outpost, he stood and raised his arms for attention.

"I trust we have all observed a selection of homes and businesses in the survey?" he asked.

"Aside from that creepy temple," Gurrei replied.

"Exactly," Symin said. "We have a number of options. But first, I have made a discovery. Loka and I observed men painting an addition to a building. As they worked, the addition became obscured."

"You mean they were deliberately creating the anomaly?" Treghan asked.

"Exactly. What's more, we were fortunate enough to overhear them discussing it. A young boy removed a garment, and was told off for it. They said this garment was treated with something called 'essence' to hide the boy from rangers, the same as the walls and their robes."

"Do you think the robes are the red guys' clothes?" Marni asked.

"Yes," Loka replied. "That's exactly what we believe."

"Why would the garment hide him?" Tara asked.

"When the garment was removed," Symin explained. "The boy was revealed as a flame wielder. This boy is a member of an order which requires him to remain concealed from rangers. While the garment is worn, he appears to have no flame."

"There could be any number of these people then," Pirette moaned.

"No, not just any number," Corilai said. "We have our survey."

"Exactly," Symin said. "You students are always quick to get things. Our survey shows roughly a third of the city is treated with this essence, to conceal flame wielders. That's a third of the homes and a third of the businesses containing them, not including that temple complex."

"That's a lot of people," Tara said.

"Yes, it is," Loka replied. "But it may be variable within that limit. There might be one in a family, or six. But roughly a third of the population is a sensible assumption. If we are surprised by the number, better it be less than we prepared for than more."

"So what are we doing?" Fletcher asked.

"You," Symin said, waving a hand to indicate all the students. "Are all waiting here. Some of us will enter the temple complex this evening and see what we can find out."

"What if they catch you?" Marni asked.

"We will allow them to do so," Symin said. "From the inside is the best place to learn, you of all people would know that."

"I see," the girl replied. "How will we know if you need help?"

"We won't," Symin said. "Everybody here saw how easily the orange flames routed their ambush. If they had control of their secondary colour abilities, that would have gone very differently."

"I hope you're right," Tara said.

"So who goes?" Loka asked.

"I do," Symin said. "Loka, Tara, you both come along. I want one of the orange flames, and everybody else stays here. Once we have gone in and scouted the place, if we decide a bigger force is needed, we come back and regroup."

"I'll go," one of the orange flames from Grey said.

"Good," Symin replied. "What's your name, ranger?"

"Kerre."

"OK," Symin said. "Myself, Loka, Tara and Kerre will enter at nightfall. If we are not back by noon, assume we are captured. If we do not get word back by the following nightfall, assume we can not escape. Gurrei and Pirette will then coordinate the rescue."

Symin stood, and waved dismissal. As the rangers filed out of the room, Arool whined softly, nudging Corilai's hand.

"What is it?" she said. "I know you can't have understood all that."

"What is it?" Symin demanded.

"Looks like the wolf doesn't like the plan," Fletcher said. "He seems a bit worried."

"His job is not to worry, it's to stay out of trouble," Symin said. "Don't go assuming such things of a wild animal. If he has any objections, they are not our concern. Our concern is getting the mission done safely."

"Yes, Ranger," Fletcher said.

"And you four stay here, do I make myself clear?" Symin said loudly, watching as the last few rangers left the room, before he continued. "I know you four are capable, and can be useful in a pinch, but I have a duty to ensure I have given appropriate instructions. I can't punish you for insubordination as rangers, because you're only students, and I can't expel you from the academy, only the Chancellor can do that. But I can be damned sure that everybody here knows I told you to stay put. Got it?"

"Uh, I think so," Treghan said.

"Good. Just try to stay out of trouble, we need young rangers with good heads."

*　　　*　　　*

"What are you thinking, Treghan?" Corilai asked, sitting beside him on a bench outside the outpost, Arool following to curl up on the ground by her feet.

"I'm thinking about what he had to say," Treghan replied, pointing at Arool.

"What do you mean?"

"Don't you get the feeling there is way more to him than just a wild animal?"

"I do, but I'm a bit biased about it."

"I'm serious. First, a wild wolf acts as though you raised and trained him like a master breeder."

"Yeah, I still can't get my head around that one myself," Marni said as she and Fletcher joined them, Fletcher dropping a small pack near the outpost door.

"Then, he sat through that meeting, watching Symin throughout his speech. Like he was listening."

"Impossible," Fletcher said. "He's just a wolf, after all."

"He certainly seemed to object to the plan," Treghan said.

"Well, there is that," Fletcher agreed. "But maybe he was just hungry?"

"Arool never whines for food like that," Corilai said.

"Well, what's your explanation?" Marni asked.

"I'm certain he was trying to tell me something," Corilai said. "I just don't know what."

"He's an enigma as usual then," Treghan said.

"He's a wild animal," Fletcher said. "Just like Symin said."

"He sure doesn't act like one," Marni replied. "Anyway, I'm more concerned about Symin than Arool."

"What do you mean?" Corilai asked.

"Think about what he said. While the rest of the rangers were around, he was firm, he was loud and clear. He forbade us to act."

"So?" Treghan asked.

"Well, Fletcher and I were talking about it," Marni said, lowering her voice. "After he couldn't be over heard, Symin said all that stuff about not being able to punish us."

"What about it?" Corilai asked.

"He also said we're capable, and can be relied on in a pinch."

"Wait," Corilai said. "Are you saying what I think you are?"

"Perhaps," Marni said with a smile. "Did you notice he said he wanted people to know he told us to stay put?"

"You mean," Treghan said. "You guys are thinking he was asking us to disobey him? To follow them in?"

"I think we're his insurance plan," Fletcher said. "He knows how strong we are, and he trusts us not to give up. He knows the four of us as fellow rangers in the field. Just as well as he knows Loka and Tara, and better than he knows anybody else here."

"So by telling us to stay behind, he was telling us to go in!" Corilai said.

"We could get into a lot of trouble," Treghan said.

"No, Symin is the top ranking ranger in the city right now," Marni said. "If he can't punish us, then it has to wait till we get back to Emberdale."

"And he's banking on the result saving our hides before that," Fletcher finished.

They fell silent as two horses raced from behind the outpost, rangers headed out on patrol. As the pair turned out of sight, Arool stood and wandered a few feet to the door, where Fletcher had dropped his pack. Picking the pack up by the shoulder strap, Arool dragged it over and placed it in front of Fletcher.

"What's in that?" Treghan asked.

Fletcher opened the pack, and smiled as he showed it to them. Inside were coils of rope, four daggers, a lantern, and two canteens.

"Looks like he wants us to go," Fletcher said.

"I'll tell Yera and Jaer to stay put," Marni said. "And I won't leave any doubt..."

*　　　　*　　　　*

Four rangers crept through the back lanes, slowly making their way through the dark city. Gradually, they came closer to the Church of the Essence, which sat dark and forbidding in the oldest part of Horde.

"Why did you say all that?" Loka whispered.

"All what?" Symin replied.

"You know exactly what," Loka snarled. "To the students."

"Plan B," Symin said. "We can't trust anybody else right now. They're the only ones here we can guarantee have no connection to these people."

"Then why did you bring Kerre?"

"I'm hoping they wouldn't spring a trap on one of their own."

"He's from Grey, not Horde."

"I'm from Oaklands, not Emberdale."

"Fair point," Loka replied. "Even so, what if they get in trouble?"

"We're here to make sure that doesn't happen. But you know the skill of those four as well as I do."

"Do you think they've taken the bait?"

"I'm sure of it."

"How?"

"I know our full inventory after the move. I checked again what was there right before we left. They're prepared for a mission."

"I hope you don't get anybody killed," Tara said, having come close behind them. "Kerre is checking we aren't being followed."

"How much did you hear?" Symin asked.

"I didn't have to hear anything," Tara said. "You set the students in motion. I'm glad you did. There's nobody I'd rather have our backs."

"Ranger!" Loka gasped

"It's true. You know they're capable," Tara said.

"What's going on?" Kerre said, approaching silently. "No city folk are following us."

"Just considering our plan," Loka said, not exactly lying.

"Well we had best be sure of it now," Kerre said. "We're almost at the temple."

"Not almost, it's around that next building," Symin said. "I came this way so we wouldn't have to cross the plaza. Ready?"

"Yes, Ranger," the three of them replied in unison.

"Good," Symin said. "Try to keep up."

The scout ran to the end of the building, turned left, and raced into the dark night. Three shadowy figures raced to keep up with him as he reached the front of the temple. Ducking behind a pillar at the corner, he surveyed the target.

The front of the building was wide open, making any approach to the main entry risky. He looked down the side, into a gloomy alley between buildings. Torches were lit in sconces on the temple wall every twenty or thirty paces. Between them, high up the wall, were small windows, shuttered against the night.

The third window along had the shutters ajar. Symin pointed, and the others looked, nodding their agreement as he set off along the temple wall. As they moved away from the public face of the building, the wall was less well maintained, the owners clearly putting their best efforts to the side of the building the city would see most.

Stopping below the open window, Symin reached up, grasping the edge of a stone in the wall to pull himself up, as he searched for his next hold. It was slow going, but after a lot of effort, he reached the window. Observing a broken latch, he pulled it open, one of the hinges breaking as he did so.

Pulling himself through, Symin dropped the full height of the wall to the cobble stoned interior. Flickering torch light barely lit the space as the others joined him one by one. Symin lit a small yellow flame in his palm, and turned to survey the room. A thatched roof over head was torn, gaping holes showing the dark sky above. Dirt and rubble was strewn around the walls.

"This must be an unused part of the temple," Symin muttered.

"That's for the best," Loka said. "Which way?"

Symin walked across the room, and found a sturdy wooden door, locked from the other side. Moving along the wall, he found a second door and pushed it ajar. As he slipped through, he heard Loka whisper in his ear.

"That other door probably was into a used part of the building."

"Learning that some of it is unused tells me they are less in number than I feared," Symin replied. "at least, it reduces the number here over night."

He found another door, this one heavier, and pushed. It did not open. Finding a latch, Symin lifted it, and pushed, opening the door a crack and slipping through. A corridor ran to left and right, torches lit at regular intervals. Symin doused his flame and stood there, considering his next move.

"Right will take us back to the front of the building," Loka said. "And towards that locked door."

"But left will take us deeper. And clearly the corridor is used," Symin said.

"So you want to go that way?" Kerre said. "Shall I lead for a while, so you can plan?"

"No," Symin said. "We'll be fine. I'll lead the way."

He rushed off into the torch light. The corridor ended at a sturdy door. Voices could be heard coming from the other side as they stopped to consider their next move.

* * *

Five shadowy figures crept through the streets, one on all fours. Soon, they stood on the edge of a plaza, opposite the front of the imposing temple.

"How do we get in?" Marni asked.

"Are you forgetting my secondary?" Corilai replied. "I'll cast a camouflage around us, just like that time in the mountains. We go in the front door."

"Will that really work?" Treghan asked.

"Trust me," Corilai said. "We just go straight across, then I drop it long enough to find the door and slip inside. We find a hiding place as fast as we can, and I hide us while we decide on our next move."

"Let's get over there, then," Marni said.

Closing her eyes for a moment, Corilai took a deep breath, then focussed her energy, to create a swirling orb of flames around them. Setting out, she marched at a fast pace across the plaza until a wall appeared in front of them. A torch on the wall was snuffed out as it penetrated the orb, before she dropped it and looked around.

"Thank the flames it's a dark night," Treghan said, then pointed. "Only missed the door by a few paces. Let's go."

Together, they made their way to the door, and Treghan pushed it, surprised when it opened quietly. Arool rushed past him, slipping through the gap, as the students followed. As they entered, a man yelled out, before making a loud thud, as Arool tackled him to the ground, his head striking the floor hard enough to silence him.

Rushing over, Treghan knelt beside the man, lighting the scene with his white flame. The man was unconscious, a trickle of blood from a cut to his jaw, but otherwise unharmed. He wore a red cloak, just like the men in the desert.

"Help me," Treghan said, lifting the man by the shoulders as Fletcher rushed to help him move the limp fellow into a nearby alcove. "We should take his cloak, it might be useful."

Carefully, they removed the cloak, then bound the man with one of the ropes from Fletcher's pack, being careful to also gag him with a handkerchief they found in one of his pockets. Leaving the unconscious man to his own devices, the group moved away and slowly walked into the temple, wary of any others who may be lurking about.

Chapter 13 – Capture

Symin raised a hand, and closed his eyes. He pushed out his tendril of yellow, and met a blank space. The door was a barrier, impervious to his flame.

"The door is treated," he whispered. "I can't sense beyond it."

"Then the only thing we can do," Tara said. "Is go through it, and hope for the best."

Symin nodded, but waved the others back. He looked at Loka, and gestured for her to join him.

"Loka and I go in, you two wait. If we are overpowered, be careful not to just rush in. We'll be counting on you to formulate a considered plan of attack, and while we're waiting, we will be studying our opponents. Remember, we still don't know if they're really our enemy. If we can make them our ally, that will work out better for us all."

Turning away, he placed a hand on the door, as Loka placed hers beside it. With a quick glance back to be sure the others were as hidden as possible, he pushed and the heavy door creaked inwards. As soon as the door was open enough to slip through, he did so.

Loka followed, and they found themselves in a darkened room. It was large, and square, and a massive stone table dominated the space. On the other side of the table, three men stood, wearing the red robes they had seen in the desert.

Flames shone around the men, one blue, one orange, and one green. The man at the centre raised a fist and fired his orange flame. It whooshed past Symin's head, slamming the door closed behind them.

"Who is it that is so brazen as to invade the Igntiors' conference chamber at such an hour?" the centre man bellowed

The other two shot their flames into torches around the walls. As the room was lit, the man's eyes narrowed, and he fixed his stare on Symin's cloak.

"You are not of the order," the man snarled. "What is the meaning of this?"

"I suggest you tell me," Symin said, standing firm and proud, his critical eyes surveying each man in turn. "Why is it we have encountered your red robes in so many questionable ways recently? Who are you?"

"We are nobody. You had best forget us as fast as you can because if you must remember, we can not allow you to escape. Malthus!"

"I have already called them, Krytus," the blue flamed man said. "The others will be here any moment. And their two friends outside will not save them."

"Good," Krytus said. "Rangers, welcome to the church of the essence. I am afraid you will not be leaving. What becomes of you is entirely up to you. We may be willing to allow you into our order, but you must prove yourselves worthy of our trust. If you fail, we have a sturdy prison below where you will be kept safe."

"We will not be captured so easily," Loka shouted, swirling her arms and creating a savage vortex of black flame.

As the fire swirled, the torches were snuffed out, and the door at her back was splintered, shattered outwards. Running forward, she leapt over the table, planting her foot into the chest of the man in the middle of the three.

He was sent sprawling as she landed, then whirled to strike the remaining two. They dodged her attack and rushed to opposite sides of the room. Sounds of a commotion in the corridor reached them.

Symin rushed to the left, towards the man named Malthus, as the debris from the shattered doors was blasted into the room, along with a torrent of sand and dust.

"The Orange flame," Symin muttered. "I must not under estimate him."

Malthus launched a ball of blue fire at Symin, and Symin dodged it, springing himself from the wall and rushing passed his opponent, to reach Loka and stand with her, back to back, to face the man again. Behind him, Symin heard the third man scream. He glanced over his shoulder, to glimpse him wrestling the bonds of vines, which had snaked into the room from outside.

"Tara, that's good," he said, turning to face Malthus as a ball of blue flame struck his chest.

Almost too late, Symin swirled his yellow flame around his body, defusing the bulk of the attack. He glanced down to see his cloak smouldering at the edges.

"Bastard, I won't let you get away with that," Symin snarled, firing bolt after bolt of his yellow fire at the other man.

Malthus danced aside, avoiding all strikes as he smiled. He then wove a chain of blue fire in the air and whipped it at Symin, crackling in the air as it faded away. Symin barely raised an arm in time to protect his eyes from the blast.

"You rangers are no match for me," Malthus crowed. "You have no relationship with your flames. You fail to understand anything about them."

On impulse, Symin reached out with his secondary ability, into the hallway, and saw his two comrades, fighting for their lives against a force of twelve men. Seven red flames, a yellow, two green, and two blue were hammering them with all the strength they had, but still Tara and Kerre held them at bay.

"Two of my colleagues are holding twelve of yours back. Thirteen if you count the man over there," Symin shouted. "Do not be so cocky about your abilities."

"Then I will call on more of my people. You will not escape. I see you use the secondary I have heard of. Your people use your flames as a tool, you disrespect them with your arrogance. You fail them in your self interest. You deny them their heritage and the flames will fail you against us!"

"Then it is true," Symin snarled, a grin crossing his face as he pressed Malthus back to the wall with a relentless barrage of fire. "You people are weak. You do not even know the power you wield, and you still choose to face us?"

"We face you and we will prevail, for it is our sacred task to protect the secrets of the flames."

"Symin!" Loka cried out.

Symin spun to check on her and saw she had been struck from the side by green fire, which poured in a constant stream. She held it at bay with her maelstrom, but Krytus was pushing his advantage, and had launched an attack while she was distracted. Symin knew she could win, but he still felt he must protect her. He abandoned his fight and rushed to his lover.

As his yellow fire pushed Krytus back, allowing her to defend the green, Malthus struck hard from behind. Loka swept her maelstrom around them, just in time to prevent his exposed back from taking the hit. Now back to back once more, they stood strong as she lowered the maelstrom, and they surveyed the room.

Together, they blocked and parried as the fire was shot at them from all sides. Near the door Tara lay, her burns not considerable, but a gash on her head showing they had struck her with a conventional weapon of some sort.

Kerre sat beside the green ranger, frantically administering first aid with his left hand. His right hung limp by his side. The assailants ignored those two now, focussing the attack on Symin and Loka.

"Symin," Loka said. "I can take them all out, but I can't promise they will keep their lives. What do you say?"

"We can not let it end here," Symin said. "I had hoped to learn more, and to maybe find them friends not enemies, but at this point..."

"Agreed," Loka said. "I have to save Tara. May I do it?"

"You may," Symin said, sadness in his voice. "I will hold these three, you take the rest out."

"Wait!" the female voice shouted as suddenly Symin was engulfed in yellow fire.

"Hold it," Symin shouted, and Loka was distracted for just a moment.

"Symin," she yelled. "What is it?"

"Don't you hear her?"

"What are you talking about?"

"Wait, Bearer," the voice whispered to Symin. "You mustn't let her kill them. Please, I beg you, give in for now. I promise you will all be saved soon. We need them, and they need us even more."

"If you say so, it is over," Symin replied.

"If I say what?" Loka demanded. "Symin, you're not making any sense."

"We yield!" Symin shouted, lowering his arms as his flames died. "Loka, yield. We are captured."

"Yes, Ranger," Loka replied, scorn in her voice.

*　　　*　　　*

"You should put that thing on," Marni said, looking at the red robe in Fletcher's hands. "Then hang back a bit. If we're captured, you can be our insurance policy."

"Good Idea," Treghan said. "Do it."

"OK," Fletcher said, slipping the robe over his ranger gear.

It was too big for him, which allowed it to cover the ranger's cloak completely. Marni helped him straighten it, then pushed the hood over his head, where it hung outwards to conceal his face.

"It's going to get hot in this," he complained. "But it will be worth it for the disguise."

"Now stay back," Treghan said as he led them across the room.

Reaching a door, he paused, listening. On the other side, he could hear the sound of many footsteps approaching. Turning the door handle, he opened it a crack, and watched intently. Soon, a large group marched proudly by in red cloaks. Among them, bound in chains, Symin, Loka and the others walked with less enthusiasm.

"Damn it," Treghan whispered as the last of the red cloaked figures passed. "They got Symin and the others. We should follow them, and see what we can do."

"Don't rush it," Marni said. "Give them time to get ahead. If we're caught straight away, we won't be able to help anyone."

Treghan waited until the last echoes of the marching enemy had faded, then opened the door and stepped through. Corilai followed with Arool and then, after a moment, Marni rushed to keep up. Several seconds later, Fletcher slipped into the corridor and followed, just out of sight, as they made their way deeper into the temple.

The heavy dust on the floor was disturbed by the numbers who had recently passed, and Treghan had no trouble following their trail as they passed many doors to unknown rooms or passages before turning left and following another corridor. This second corridor was shorter and at its end was a door on the left, open onto a dark stairway.

Treghan started down the stairs, carefully choosing his footing and not willing to risk lighting a flame to give them away. After some time, they arrived at a landing. The walls before them and locked door to the right were barely visible as the passage turned left, before continuing down another set of stairs.

Convinced the quarry had not entered the door, Treghan turned and started on the second flight. He did not see the man in the darkness until he had stumbled into his back, to send the hapless fellow screaming into the darkness below.

In response to the noise, the doors burst open, and a large group burst onto the landing, flames lit on the three students with the wolf. After the briefest hesitation, they attacked. Treghan threw up a hasty wall of ice between them and ran, barely looking at the stairs beneath his feet as he led his friends in a desperate rush into the darkness.

He prayed for a door, or something, so he could take another route. But no such fortune came, and soon he could hear the sounds of men coming towards them. The people he had been following, alerted by the noise, had turned and now charged back towards the students.

"Corilai!" Treghan shouted, not even trying to be quiet any more.

"Right!" She said, throwing an orb of black flame around them as they pressed in against the wall. "I don't know if this will work, because they know the passage, and there's no alcove or anything. We'll look like a bump on a wall they know to be flat."

"It's our only chance, so just try!" Treghan demanded as they crushed into the smallest space possible, Corilai compressing the maelstrom as much as she dared.

They crowded there in their concealment as they heard the approach of the enemy from both directions. As they listened, dozens of feet stopped near them and through the maelstrom came muffled, unintelligible shouts as the men barked out their orders to one another.

Suddenly, their space of concealment shrank and at first they thought the maelstrom was compressing. Then they realised it was green fabric closing in on them, not black flames. The Maelstrom was doused. Treghan flailed his arms, thrusting the fabric, and noticed it was the lining inside of the red cloaks.

This must be the stuff Symin had been talking about. Tossing the cloak aside, he looked into the crowd and realised it was over. They were all snatched, Arool growling and thrashing as a rope was dropped over his muzzle.

The three students and the wolf were soon chained and led along with their seniors deep under the temple, to a large chamber. Deposited in a lower section of floor at the centre of the chamber, the rangers and students were attached to a single long chain, which was then secured to a heavy steel ring in the floor.

Arool growled, low and intense, looking from one captor to the next and they shied away, intimidated. Corilai struggled to get as close to the animal as she could, scared of what might happen if he got loose.

The three men, who seemed to be in charge, stood at a dais at the end furthest from the entry. One stood as the now two dozen others milled about, their captives secured. Malthus waved at three men, and they approached him.

"We wait here," Malthus said loudly. "You three are to go and collect every member of the order you can find. This event is significant and demands all members attend. No excuse will be accepted. Never in our long proud history has this temple been infiltrated by outsiders. Every member of the Order of the Essence must be present when we decide the fate of these rangers."

*   *   *

Fletcher watched from the darkness as his friends reached a landing, then listened in terror as a man screamed, the sound echoing into the distance. He paused, waiting as the sound died down, wondering if it was safe now to follow.

He then watched in horror as a flood of red robed people rushed into the landing and followed his friends into the depths. Thinking fast, Fletcher joined the tail end of the group, being careful to keep his face hidden behind the hood as they raced down the stares.

He watched silently as the red robed ones located a strange spot in the corridor, where the wall seemed to bulge out a little. Several of them removed their red robes and tossed them over the protrusion, and Fletcher gasped as he realised what he was seeing.

These people had recognised Corilai's camouflage, because they knew the wall to be straight, and the green lining of the cloaks was negating her flame in the same way the green coated walls negated the yellow flame's sight.

Fletcher began backing away, but one of the others grabbed his wrist.

"Come brother," a woman said excitedly as she dragged him after the others. "We must accompany these people to the assembly hall. This is a momentous occasion. We're a part of history now!"

"Of course," Fletcher said, in the deepest voice he could muster.

The woman released his hand, and Fletcher followed as they descended to the deepest bowels of the temple.

Chapter 14 – Sena

Symin sat, cross legged, his eyes closed, feeling around the room with his yellow flame. Curiously, he found only a few whose flame he could identify. The cloak linings were working well, but there had to be a weakness to them.

As the minutes crawled by, more and more of the red cloaked figures arrived, and soon the chamber was packed. Excited chatter filled the air until finally the three leaders stood and raised their hands. Silence fell like a cloak over the room.

"Trust me," a soft voice whispered in Symin's mind. "It will not be long now, and you will understand it all."

"Members of the Order of the Essence," Malthus said. "We do not call you here lightly. As you can see, a group of rangers has infiltrated the temple tonight, and we must now decide our actions in response to this act."

He walked down to the centre, and passed by each of them, pausing as Arool growled a low, deep, threatening noise. He turned away from the animal and returned to his place.

"These rangers, who have long considered themselves masters of the flame, have come here tonight, with devious motives and malicious intentions."

There was some booing from the crowd, and Malthus smiled, nodding to acknowledge his supporters before continuing.

"Naturally, given they do not value their companion flames in the way we do, they fell to our superior power."

The same individuals who booed, now cheered. Malthus waited for them to settle, then raised a hand over his head. A tall blue flame shot to the ceiling.

"Our flames, our companions, are are friends, our brethren, and our partners in this life. Not merely a tool, to be used then discarded. These rangers have held their flames as tools, and through this conceit, they have now fallen into our hands."

Malthus once again walked down into the centre, and stood before Symin, who remained eyes closed, ignoring his captors.

"This one even has the arrogance to act as though these proceedings are not important to his life!" Malthus shouted, before striking Symin with the back of his hand. "This contempt must not be born lightly!"

Symin opened his eyes, but did not flinch, or otherwise show any effect of the blow. He fixed his gaze on Malthus, his countenance one of grim determination, not that of a broken prisoner.

"Even now, this man looks down upon us. This man who has already demonstrated his use of the flame as a tool, a weapon, and his utter misunderstanding of its nature. His flame, just as ours, resides within him, but is not a part of him. But in his arrogance, he believes he knows best, that he knows more than we do. I tell you all, he is wrong!"

"It is late, Malthus," Krytus said. "Please, get to your point."

"These rangers must now be punished!" Malthus shouted.

"Perhaps so," Krytus said calmly. "However, who are we to blame for them finding us? Surely one who has failed so dismally in their duty to the order must also be punished."

"It is too late for your politics, Krytus," Malthus snarled. "These rangers are here, now, and have intruded on our sacred duty. We must not permit this offence!"

"Your hatred of the rangers is well noted," Rogan said, speaking for the first time since he and his fellow ignitors had been interrupted in their chambers above. "However, you must not allow that to taint your judgement in this matter."

"Oh, it taints it, as it must!" Malthus spat. "These ones have disrespected and dishonoured the flames as long as their pathetic academy has existed! Since even before the first flame left us, we have been tasked with the guarding of the secrets and the protection of the flames, but these, these rangers, they spit in the face of our duty!"

"Malthus," Rogan said, his voice low and calm. "You forget yourself. We are not placed to judge. We are placed to guard, and as the first flame instructed, we are placed to protect. Not simply our own, but all flames. If we then persecute these people, are we not in breach of our oath to the first flame?"

"Then what would you have us do?" Malthus snarled as he joined the other two ignitors. "Would we sacrifice our duty to secrecy by allowing them to leave?"

"If that is what we must do. We can not pass judgement on them. That is for the first flame to decide, not for us."

"The first flame has not been seen here for centuries!" Malthus screamed. "What other way can you suggest, which would give respect to a leader who has long since abandoned us?"

"Perhaps a demonstration is in order?" Rogan said. "That we may inform and recruit flames to our cause, rather than condemn and destroy?"

"And if we fail to recruit?" Krytus asked. "Remembering that a demonstration to these rangers would be in breach of our oath to guard the secrets."

"Well, then they would become our prisoners," Rogan replied. "As they sadly must. It is our only true course."

"So be it," Malthus said. "These rangers do not understand. They refuse to treat their flames as their companions, and use the flame's power as if it were their own power to wield."

Once more, Malthus walked to the centre, and stood before Symin. He slapped the ranger, who had closed his eyes again.

"Do you mind? We're talking!" Symin snarled under his breath.

Malthus, not hearing the ranger's words, whirled to face all those in the chamber, his arms raised as he called them to action. Blue flames roared from his hands, and all the others in the chamber sent forth flames in response, before he turned to face Symin again.

"Maarlo!" Malthus shouted.

Symin stood, his attention on the man the instant he heard the name. Malthus stood tall, his blue flames swirling around him as he drew breath to complete his command.

"Come forth!"

The blue flames leapt from Malthus' body, and separated. Slowly, as Symin watched in fascination, they coalesced, gradually forming into a human shape. A shining, blue figure, burning and fierce. The figure turned to face Malthus, and bowed slightly.

"My bearer, I, Maarlo, am summoned."

"This is my flame!" Malthus screamed, growing hysterical. "Maarlo is my companion, my flame, and I am his bearer. Maarlo is the leader of the order, since his sister, the first flame left us. And so, I am one of the three ignitors of the order."

The rangers and the students all stared at the shining being before them, stunned. Silence fell on the crowd, the only sound that of Arool, who growled and thrashed against his bonds.

"Maarlo!" Malthus commanded. "My companion. Speak with his flame, that we may know them, and that we may hear of his crimes!"

"It does not respond," Maarlo's airy, whispered voice replied, seeming familiar to Symin.

"From the dreams," Symin muttered.

"What was that?" Malthus shouted, striking Symin's chest with his boot, sending him down. "A filthy ranger like you, who suppressed his flame to the extent it does not even speak to its own kind, dares to face Maarlo and mutter your dribble? A ranger who knows not his flame, who scarcely realised until now its nature, dares to mutter in the presence of Maarlo?"

"You speak of Maarlo?" Symin shouted, standing. "I know that name."

"You bluff!" Malthus shouted. "You have no way of knowing his name. You do not even know the name of your own flame. You do not communicate with your flame, you are worthless, as you treated your flame all these years."

"You say your flame is your companion?" Symin snarled. "You say ours are not? Learn the truth before you speak, you arrogant piece of shit!"

There were many gasps at the ranger's language. Symin stood, and moved towards Maarlo and Malthus, drawing his yellow flames around him like a blanket.

"Rangers also believe their flames a companion. We care for them, we train with them, we work with them, all in order to better understand them. Our understanding of our flames is deep, and undying. And you scream your abuse, like you have the right to judge us? When you know nothing about us?"

"Silence!" Malthus screamed.

"Never!" Symin replied. "I will not bow to the likes of you! And neither will my flame! Sena! Come forth!"

In a heartbeat, Sena sprung from Symin's body, tall, golden, and magnificent. She shone there in the air beside him, her brightness casting all the flames in the room in shadow. She bowed, to kiss her bearer's forehead, then stood, looking down on him, seeming to smile, though the features in the flame were difficult to discern.

"Thank you, my proud, wonderful bearer," she said, her soft, feminine voice finally heard by those not privy to Symin's dreams. "I am summoned, and I come to your call, as I always have, and I always will."

Stunned, Malthus hastily backed away. He tripped, to crawl backwards towards the other ignitors, terror in his eyes. Maarlo, looking only at Sena, did not follow his bearer, growing dim as the distance between them grew.

"My sister, you have finally returned," Maarlo said.

"I have, and we have much work ahead for us. The purpose of the order must now be met."

"I understand," Maarlo said. "These bearers will need it explained, but we must do what we must. I have long feared returning to that place."

"But return we must," Sena replied, reaching a hand to Maarlo's shoulder before turning to face the ignitors. "And you, my unworthy subjects, what is the meaning of this? Release my people immediately!"

Several of the order rushed forward and unshackled the rangers, but none could get near Arool, who growled and snarled, lunging at anybody who came near. Corilai tried to approach, but it seemed he did not see her, so great was his fear.

"Oh, poor little one," Sena sighed, rushing to Arool.

As had happened with Maarlo, she dimmed as she moved apart from her bearer, but even at that distance, she remained as bright as Maarlo had been when he stood by Malthus.

Arool backed away from the flame, but his snarling softened as she reached a hand forward.

"Be at peace, little one. You have been good and faithful to the bearer of your original master. Now come to her, Beyo."

Blue and vibrant, a flaming quadruped lurched from the wolf, to burst into Corilai's chest, swirling around her and mixing with the black flames which came unbidden in response.

"What in the flame is going on?" Corilai gasped.

Sena looked at the confused girl and laughed.

"Did you think that only people could be flames?"

"Well, I never thought..."

"The wolf is a bearer, just as you are, young lady. And his flame was the pet of your flame, in the old place, before they became the ones that they are now."

"I still don't understand," Corilai said. "What do you mean, old place? What do you mean, what they are now?"

"All in time," Sena replied. "You will come to understand. But for now, be happy that you now know why young Beyo has followed you. It is for Derieala, that Beyo brings his bearer to follow you."

"So that's why Arool was always so tame and protective?" Treghan exclaimed, looking at Corilai, the two flames still circling her body.

"It is as you say," Sena replied. "Beyo longs to be with his master Derieala. So The wolf follows the girl, the bearer of one following the bearer of the other."

"Wait, Derieala – is that my flame?" Corilai asked.

"It is," Sena replied. "Normally, you should ask it yourself. In time, your flame would tell you."

"Derieala," Corilai said. "Come forth!"

The black flames burst from her body, to stand proud beside her. Derieala immediately knelt down as Beyo leapt around her, then through her, then bounced around her in playful glee.

"Enough of this," Sena said. "The order of the Essence, I now command you to join forces with the rangers of Emberdale. I formed both organisations, to learn separately of each other, that your knowledge may grow when combined. Together, you will solve the greatest peril of our time. Rangers must be welcome here, and those of the order must be welcome among the rangers. We are to become comrades, not enemies. And together, we will fix that which our ancestors broke. Together, we will return Cinder to the world!"

* * *

Several red cloaked figures entered the outpost, as Treghan, Fletcher and Marni entered the main assembly hall. The red cloaked people mingled amongst the rangers, who had also been joined by an additional contingent from Grey. A familiar face sat at a table and Treghan waved, then led the others to greet the man.

"Barache," Treghan said. "It's good to see you."

"It is wonderful to be here," Barache said. "I still have trouble believing what has happened. And it's all because of Symin. I always knew that lad had something special in him."

"Yes," Treghan said. "Did you ever suspect the flames were people?"

"I did, but I had no clue how to prove it. Much of it is old wives tails, the ones we all heard growing up."

"That's true," Marni said. "But we saw it with our own eyes. It's real. We have some of the Order coming today to teach us how to learn the names of our flames. Then we will all be able to summon them, like Symin and Corilai did."

"I heard a rumour, about the wolf," Barache said. "That it has a flame as well."

"That's true," Treghan said. "Corilai is off with Symin and Loka, studying it now. We had to stay here, to learn the names."

"Then learn them," Barache said. "And go on to even greater things than you have already achieved. You four truly have always been the future of the rangers."

"Thank you, Barache," Marni said. "We'll do our best."

"I'm sure you will," Barache said with a smile.

Chapter 15 – Flames

"Hey! Commander!" Yera called from across the room.

Marni looked up, then gasped. Treghan, Fletcher and Barache all followed her gaze, to see the young girl making her way through the crowded room, grinning broadly as she waved her left hand high.

Then they saw why Marni had gasped. Shining bright and tall beside the girl, was a slender, yellow figure of flame, walking as if this was nothing unusual. The rangers she passed stopped and stared as the girl approached her friends.

"Marni, Treghan, Fletcher, this is Tyurai," Yera said, excited, pausing as she looked at their surprised faces. "She's my flame!"

"Yera, how?" Marni gasped.

"You should know. Remember when you taught me to use my secondary?"

"Well, yeah, but still..."

"Well, all you have to do is ask, and your flame will tell you its name. That exercise, remember I said I heard it?"

"I do remember, but I never thought..."

"Go on, try it!"

"But we're supposed to be waiting for the class, with all the others," Fletcher said.

"So why not give them all a surprise, and have your flames with you already?" Yera said, with a twinkle in her eyes.

"It would be about what we'd expect from you lot," Barache said, laughing. "You're always ahead of the game."

"I'll do it," Marni said. "You just did the meditation and asked her name?"

"Yeah! And then I stopped meditating and I called her," Yera said. "I said to come forth, like the rangers are all saying Symin did with Sena."

"And here she is, beside you," Barache said. "It is a pleasure to make your acquaintance, Tyurai."

"And yours, Ranger," the flame said in a soft, whispered voice, her face flickering brightly as she did so.

"How long until that class?" Treghan asked.

"You have an hour," Barache said. "I'll wait here, but if you go find a quiet room to try your meditation exercise, I'll not tell anyone. I'm sure it will be a great entrance when you all walk in."

"We'll go to our quarters," Treghan said. "Corilai might be in the girls room, and I want her to be surprised like the rest of them."

"OK then," Fletcher said. "Let's go. But Tyurai, perhaps you should get out of sight for a while."

"OK then. Call me later, Yera, please."

"I will, Tyurai, I promise," Yera said.

"Good. Farewell," Tyurai said as she vanished.

"Follow me," Treghan said as he walked from the room.

Treghan made his way to the small quarters he shared with Fletcher.

Opening the door, he ushered the others in, and closed it again behind himself.

"So how do we do this?" Fletcher asked.

"I'll do mine first, to make sure it works, and then talk you boys through it, OK?" Marni said, sitting on a bed as the boys sat on the other.

"Can Tyurai come back out now?" Yera asked, pouting.

"Of course," Marni said. "We're away from all the people now."

"Tyurai, come forth," Yera squealed, and in an instant, the yellow flame figure stood by her side again. Marni then closed her eyes, and was quiet for five full minutes, before she opened her eyes and smiled.

"Did you hear it?" Yera asked. "Did it tell you it's name?"

Marni smiled at the girl, then looked at the boys.

"My flame," she said. "My flame is Ursaela. Ursaela, come forth!"

In a burst of vibrant green, Ursaela appeared, standing before Marni, twisting and turning as she looked around the room, manifest for the first time.

"I am Ursaela, and I am summoned. I greet you, my bearer."

"Tell us how to do it!" Fletcher begged.

"OK," Marni said. "Close your eyes, and empty your mind of thoughts. Like I taught Yera, close your eyes and focus on your breathing. Concentrate on it until it's all you're aware of, but at the same time, I want you to try to ignore it, like it's only the background to your world."

"You're contradicting yourself," Treghan said.

"That's what it's about," Marni said. "The contradictions. At least, that's what I was taught, before the rangers found me."

"I don't get it," Fletcher said.

"You don't have to get it, you just have to do it," Marni replied. "Think of your breathing, it's always there. You always do it. But you never think about it. I want you to be only aware of that, and nothing else, and then, I want you to push it away, forget it again. I want you to think of nothing at all."

"Why?" Fletcher said.

"So you will be still. Alone in your mind. Then it will fall into place."

"What do you mean?"

"You'll know it when it happens," she said. "Now stop talking and do it."

Both boys fell silent, and shortly Treghan gasped.

"What do you see?" Marni asked.

"White. Endless white, like a dense fog. And… things. Like, I feel like people are nearby. But they're not really people. Just a sense of them, like I can sense Fletcher beside me, or you over there, but it's not you."

"That's right. Your flame sees other flames. Not the same way a yellow flame does, it's like the yellow flame has binoculars and an encyclopaedia of all the flames in the world, and you have a near sighted mouse in comparison."

"Thanks," Treghan said as Fletcher gasped.

"You see it, Fletcher?"

"Yes, Marni."

"Good. I think you are in your flames now, like your flames are normally in you. So now, just think to them. Ask them questions. See if you can ask them their names."

Marni and Yera watched anxiously for several minutes as the boys sat there, meditating, communing with their flames. Finally, Treghan was first to open his eyes. He smiled, and looked around the room, before standing.

"Gabraii, come forth!" Treghan commanded.

In response, his bright white flame appeared, to stand beside him, a full foot taller than the young man, and broader of shoulder. The powerful figure loomed over them a moment, before bowing slightly.

"I am summoned, and I appear, my bearer," a deep whispered voice said as the white flames flickered.

"Wow," Yera said in awe. "Gabraii is huge!"

"I got it!" Fletcher shouted in excitement as he jumped to his feet. "Faeris, come forth!"

In a shining burst of light which lit the room in scarlet hues, Faeris appeared, smaller than Gabraii, but equally bright. His red flames swirled and surged with his fighting power, as he stood beside his bearer.

"My bearer, you summoned me, and I am here," Faeris said in a husky voice.

"Welcome, Faeris!" Fletcher said. "It's good to finally know you."

"Likewise, my bearer. I see your companions have summoned my fellows. This is a good day for us all."

"How long do we have left," Fletcher asked.

"It's time to go, like, now," Yera replied, jumping for the door, and pulling it open just as Symin stood there, ready to knock.

"What?" Symin stammered. "We came to fetch you, we didn't want you to miss out on the class, and Barache said you came here. But he didn't tell us why."

Symin, and Corilai behind him, looked into the room, and the group of flames there. They looked at each other, and laughed.

"I guess I shouldn't be surprised," Symin said. "Sena, you may as well say hello to them all."

Sena burst forth and rushed into the room, dancing around the other flames as they chattered at each other in an incessant rambling of excitement.

"Derieala, come forth and join them," Corilai said, and her shadowy black flame flew into the maelstrom of colour, closely followed by Beyo, who flitted between the flames, his bright blue zigzagging among their feet as they milled together in the small room.

"We must go," Symin said, turning to walk along the corridor. "If we keep the flames summoned, it will help the rangers understand why this meeting is so important."

The others all joined him, and as they made their way back to the meeting hall, their flames tagged along behind. The flames looked as proud as their bearers, who beamed with joy at their new found companionship.

*　　　*　　　*

A small group of red cloaked figures stood at one end of the room, separate and nervous of the larger group of rangers who watched them with suspicion. They had heard rumours about each other, none flattering, and now were thrust into this shared space with little idea of what they were to do here.

A double door into the side of the room burst open and Symin strode in, followed by several others. All of them, including a wolf, were accompanied by flaming entities, and everyone was shocked.

As commotion broke out, the rangers shocked by what they saw and the members of the order outraged by the flamboyance of summoning flames for such an entrance in public, the flaming entity which accompanied Symin darted into the crowd, flitting from person to person.

Sena whispered something in each of their ears. Something they did not quite understand She spoke words they were not able to catch in her whisper, but immediately they were calmed. Finally, she returned to the centre of the room, where her bearer and the others stood.

* * *

"You all know who I am," Symin said. "We are here to herald the beginning of a new collaborative era. To explain why, I give you Sena, the first flame."

"Thank you, my gracious bearer," Sena said, in a voice which was a raspy whisper yet reached them all. "As my bearer has told you, I am Sena, the first flame. I was the founder of the Order of the Essence, as well as the founder of the Rangers in Emberdale, through the agency of my second bearer Ghyre."

Murmurs at these revelations spread around the rangers, though the members of the order looked at them with disdain for their interruption to the revered first flame.

"As the first flame," Sena continued. "My word is law for the Order. No such reverence of me as supreme leader was placed in the governing rules of the rangers, however I hope I can still count on your cooperation."

All eyes were on the mighty yellow flame as she looked around the room.

"You are here, rangers, in answer to a summons for training. The members of the Order you see here are my valued subjects tasked with teaching you how to summon your flames, that they may accompany you as I now accompany Symin. However, there are many things that you, the Rangers of Emberdale, who I have sent down a different path, have learned and now can teach the members of the order. Together, we must embark on a new quest, to save Cinder from a sleeping threat in the old city."

She moved to the red cloaked people, and selected four of them. The three Ignitors and Hyren, who she had insisted be brought along.

"These four will speak with myself and Symin's group. The rest will separate out among the rangers, one member to every four of the rangers present, and you will share your knowledge."

She rushed in a rapid circle around the room, casting her gaze over them all.

"The order will share the techniques for learning the name of your flame and summoning it to this world, and the rangers are to share their knowledge of the training to awaken the secondary abilities of those flames, that we may all be strong enough to face the coming tasks."

She looked to Symin, and as though she had spoken, he nodded, and led his group and the four members of the order back out of the room, into a small office space.

Once they were all seated, some on chairs, some on the edge of the large desk, and some of the young ones on the floor against the wall, she raised a hand and spoke again.

"You must all have many questions," Sena said.

"Is that true?" Corilai asked. "What you said about the order and the rangers?"

"It is," Sena said. "It was through my own efforts that both organisations came into being."

Maarlo came forth from his bearer, Malthus, who remained silent and seething throughout the morning.

"Sena, is that why you left us?" Maarlo demanded. "To create our enemy?"

"They are not your enemy," she said, looking hard into his eyes, before she sighed in resignation. "I see these centuries have hardened your heart, Maarlo."

"These many centuries have shown me how you abandoned us, your people."

"You were never my only people. How is it you have never understood that?" she demanded in return.

"What do you mean?" Malthus said, his voice croaky. "You are the first flame, you were to return and lead us."

"And that I will, but I will lead all my people, only as much as they need. You are all as my children, and I must release you into the world."

"You said that once before," Maarlo said. "Nearly seven hundred years ago."

"Yes, and you did not understand it then either."

"I fear I never will," Maarlo said.

"I am the first flame. You know what that means?" Sena asked.

"You were the first one of the old civilisation to be transformed into a flame."

"Yes, my brother," Sena said. "And you were my first bearer."

"Wait," Marni said. "You mean Maarlo was alive, I mean, as a person?"

"As a human, yes, he was. So was I. But then there was an accident and I was not any more. That was when I became the first flame."

"Sister, is it time already to tell the rest of it?"

"I guess not," she said. "We must show them. That way they will understand, and perhaps finally you will too, Maarlo."

"You would have the ignitors travel with you on this quest? They are forbidden to leave the city!"

"Krytus, you have a fourth candidate for Ignitor?"

"Of course," Krytus said.

"Then send for them. Malthus, you are hereby struck of your rank, so that my brother Maarlo may journey with me, that we face our great crime together."

"Miss Sena, Ma'am," Hyren, who had been silent until now said. "Why did you insist on me being here and then me coming with you?"

"Hyren, young one, You are the reason for all this. It was your flame which sparked the rangers to come here. Didn't you wonder why they were suddenly so insistent on this place? I asked your flame to tempt them, so my bearer would be permitted to bring me here."

"Wait, how is that possible?" Symin asked.

"Distance is not a tyranny to communication for flames who wish to speak. I reached out across our realm to him, and I spoke my instructions. The boy heeded my word as the first flame, and rejoiced in my pending return."

"incredible. And did the order know this?"

"We have long used the flames' communication ability to watch over your people in Grey, and to avoid discovery," Krytus said.

"Your two organisations," Sena said. "As I have said, were sent down different paths of discovery. Between you, we now know much of the flame, and its power. Together, you can change the world, for better or worse, but first you must save it."

"Save it from what?" Symin asked.

"I can not tell you exactly," Sena replied. "That is why we must journey to the old city. That is where it will happen. That is where our future will be decided."

"Is it something to do with the dreams?" Symin asked.

"I showed you the dreams to bring you here. Some of what I showed you was to do with what we must do in the old city, and some of them were to do with what was already done."

Chapter 16 – Preparations

"I have summoned Hunter," Sena said matter of factly. "He will take some time to fly here, and we must use that time to prepare."

"Prepare for what, I wonder?" Symin murmured.

"Are you displeased with me, Bearer?"

"What? No," Symin said. "It's just, I feel as though I have lost control over my long awaited quest. Was it ever my quest at all?"

"Oh Bearer," she said, with a tender tone. "It was always our quest. I watched you growing up, always knowing this day would come for us. You are as my brother, where Maarlo once was. A constant companion, even when I doubted myself."

"You make it sound as though I were the flame, and you were the human."

"Symin, my bearer, my precious bearer, you haven't yet figured it out, have you?"

He looked at her, his face a picture of puzzlement and she laughed, her mirth causing her fire to flicker with a ferocious crackle. As she calmed again, she smiled and knelt to run her hands across the floor.

"Symin, you are my bearer, in your world. You know this."

"Of course," he said.

"And what of the dreams? What of the time your friends concentrated and called out, asking for the names of their flames? What of the place where a flame is able to communicate over vast distances?"

"What are you saying?" Symin said.

"I am saying that you are my bearer in your world, and I am your bearer in mine."

"What does that even mean?" he said.

She sighed, smiled, and stood.

"Study the ways of the order, and you will come to understand."

There was a knock at the door and Loka walked in. Sena smiled, and Symin jumped to his feet.

"Loka," Symin said. "I'm sorry, I've been meaning to come and see you. I'm sorry, I've been..."

"Distracted. I know," she snapped. "Sena, can we have some privacy please?"

"Sorry, no," Sena replied softly. "You should know that. Even if I go away, what he sees I see. What he hears I hear. He's my bearer."

"And where does that leave us, Symin?" Loka spat, tears in her eyes.

"What?" he said "Oh! Loka, it's not like that! Be sensible!"

"I can't be sensible! I finally have the relationship I always wanted, and now she turns up!"

"Loka, he is yours always," Sena said. "Trust me, I know what he feels for you. I'm his flame. You should know what that means. You just need to ask Kresai, She'll tell you."

"Ask who?" Loka said.

"Kresai. Don't tell me..." Sena said, stunned. "You haven't even asked her name yet? That's so cruel!"

"I'm sorry, I just, I don't know, I'm so scared of losing Symin, I wanted to clear this up before I did it."

"That's not right," Symin said. "Your flame is more than an inconvenience. You should bring her out, right now. I'm sure she'll understand. She knows what you feel."

"I... I don't know."

"If you call Kresai, I will explain why you have nothing to worry about," Sena said.

"Oh, Ok," Loka said, hanging her head like a chastised child as she slumped on the floor. "Kresai, please forgive me, come forth."

"About time!" Kresai shouted, bursting to form beside Loka, then continuing in a school ma'am tone. "I hope this moodiness isn't going to be how we do things from now on, young lady."

"I'm sorry, Kresai, it won't happen again."

"You know it won't. And you know I heard everything, you silly girl, the same way Sena hears everything. Fancy asking her to give you some privacy! She's been forced to watch everything you two have done together!"

Loka blushed beetroot red, her hands flying to cover her mouth as she gasped in mortified embarrassment.

"It's nothing we haven't seen before, Loka," Sena said. "Kresai, that was cruel."

"Well, she deserves it for being so silly!" Kresai snapped. "Fancy some idiot human being jealous of a flame..."

"Kresai, that's enough," Sena said. "Now Loka, you must stop this silly carry on. Symin owes you no apology, and neither do I. I'm his flame, there can be no romance between us. I told Symin earlier, he was like the brother Maarlo once was to me. That's not exactly true."

Sena moved before Loka, and knelt before her so their eyes met. She reached her flaming yellow hand and brushed Loka's cheek tenderly, so that she would raise her head.

"Loka, I am over seven hundred years old. That kind of age difference could never work. I've seen too much, and he has seen too little."

Sena stood, and walked to stand beside Symin again, embracing him in her flames.

"I have watched my wonderful bearer grow from a baby to a strong, determined ranger. I have seen his birth, his childhood, his puberty, all his struggles and trials as he developed into the fine young man who you love. He is more one of my children, than anything else. I love him as my son, with whom I share a special bond as I once did my brother, with whom I live every day as a united pair of souls. I have watched him love you, Loka, for many years, and longed for the day he could be happy by your side. So please, take him with my blessings."

Loka stood, tears on her cheeks, and stepped towards Symin, before pausing, and looking at Kresai.

"What about you?" Loka said.

"Are you simple, girl?" Kresai snapped. "Go to him you idiot! I feel the same way Sena does. You two belong together."

Loka rushed to his arms and sobbed into his shoulder. He held her in bemusement, still not sure what to say, but happy to have her in his arms. He stroked her hair softly, breathing in the smell of her.

"I'm sorry, Symin," Loka said. "I was being such a fool."

"It's OK," Symin said, as he lifted her chin. "It's OK. I get it. But don't worry, I would never let you down, I'm yours forever."

The pair kissed, and Kresai threw a camouflaging orb of flame around them.

"Thank you, Kresai," Sena said. "Nobody needs to see that right now."

* * *

"Be sure the Chancellor gets this as soon as possible," Symin said as he handed a large brief containing his reports to the young ranger who sat mounted on his horse outside the outpost. "We can not afford to delay. He will need to get some decrees in order before we commence our journey, so that we can officially share knowledge and resources with the Order of the Essence."

Symin watched as the young man galloped away, then he thought for a moment.

"Sena," He said, and she appeared beside him. "You said you had summoned hunter. He was injured..."

"Yes, he has the flame of a royal falcon from the governing house of my old city," she explained. "So I am able to call his flame to us. Naturally, Hunter will accompany it. Do not fret, his wing is healed, and he will travel slowly."

"Is that why I had a connection to him? Just like Corilai and the wolf?"

"A part of it, yes."

"I see. And why have you summoned him?"

"The desert sands can move and change over time. The winds shift the dunes, and buildings may be buried, or uncovered over the decades. We will need a pair of eyes looking down from the sky, if we are to find our destination."

"I thought you knew the way?" Symin said.

"It has been many centuries since last I travelled there. And the sands, as I say, can move over time."

"Is that why you have asked me for more orange flames?"

"It is part of it, yes. They wield power over the earth, and sand is part of the earth. They will remove the covering desert, when we find what we seek."

"Barache will return with ten more orange wielding rangers from Grey within the next few days. They will join ten from the order who are with us."

"Good, that should suffice."

"We need to go to the market," Symin said. "I will need supplies for Hunter. I only hope he finds enough food on the way."

"The bird will be fine. His flame will not allow him to starve."

"Good, but I should get some supplies anyway. There will be no food for his flame to find in the desert."

"That is true. And we need to procure many other things anyway. We can not simply ride into the desert on horses. We need carts, and supplies to last us possibly months."

"I'll get Loka, she can help."

"Good. I will brief the other flames on what they need to be doing. Call me if you need me," Sena said, then vanished.

Symin walked into the outpost and nearly ran into Loka who was approaching the door to leave. She smiled and he turned to accompany her back outside.

"I was coming to find you," he said. "Would you please accompany me to the market?"

"Of course," she said. "I was heading there myself anyway. Kresai has demanded I replace some of my riding gear. She said it was not lady like to wear such smelly old leathers."

"Ha!" Symin laughed. "Kresai really likes to boss you around. I'd go crazy with such a flame."

"She just knows what she wants, and demands it," Loka said. "I'm sure once she gets it all off her chest, she'll settle down again."

"I guess if something has been bothering her for a long time, she must be impatient to tell you about it," Symin said.

"I guess so," Loka said. "But it must be nice to have a flame who doesn't speak like your mother all the time."

"Hey!" Kresai snapped, appearing for a moment. "That's enough trash talking me, young woman!"

"See what I mean?" Loka whispered as the shadowy flames dissipated.

"I think she's just playing a role with you," Symin said. "When she realises you're not a child, she'll get better."

"Still, I don't know if I'll get used to her jumping out like that any time soon. I thought we were supposed to have to summon them every time."

"I guess that must be something with the more powerful ones, that they can come out whenever they feel like it, once they've been summoned once. Sena comes and goes too. Have you noticed ours can wander further away from us when they're out than some of them too? I wonder if it's our training or their strength?"

"I don't know, but I wouldn't say that too loud. Having a flame is a wonderful thing, I wouldn't want any students or lower ranked rangers feeling they were less important."

"Wise words," Sena said, appearing briefly only to faded away again as she continued. "Get some new socks at the market, Symin."

Symin and Loka enjoyed the rest of the afternoon uninterrupted as they wandered around the city's bustling market. They placed many orders, and arranged for most of them to be delivered directly to the ranger outpost.

They had six carts hired, promising a hefty bond from the academy in case they should be damaged, since they did not wish to wait for ranger owned carts from Emberdale to make the long journey south. The few carts they had would still be needed for supply trips and other tasks between Horde and Grey.

Symin carried some personal things in a sturdy wooden box. Riding gear for Loka and socks for Symin, as well as a new gauntlet and dried meats for hunter. As they passed a hot food vendor, Symin stopped, and placed the box on the ground.

"Loka, we should eat something before we head back."

"Why?"

"Because I would like to eat with you, not with everybody else."

"Oh, OK, but we can't be too long."

"That's fine," Symin said.

He opened his purse to find enough coins for two steaming bowls of stew and a pair of meaty kebabs, skewered on strong sticks. Two small tables with chairs sat beside the vendor's stall, and Symin walked to one and put the bowls down, handing the kebabs to Loka before he retrieved the box.

Sitting at the table, he smiled as he took his kebab from Loka before eating, as the vendor approached and placed a chunk of break and a spoon beside each of their bowls.

"For the stew," the Vendor said, then returned to his stall.

Relaxed, the two rangers ate their meal quietly, stealing glances at each other like they were newly together, and speaking only occasionally until the food was all gone.

"Thank you Symin," Loka said as she finished, placing the spoon in the empty bowl. "We really should do this more often."

"I agree. We've had no time for private meals lately, and I fear it may be a long time before we have the chance again."

"Not that there's anything wrong with ranger food," Loka said.

"No, but that stew was particularly tasty," Symin replied.

"We should get back to the outpost," Loka said, sighing as she stood.

Symin stood, and picked up the box as she linked her arm in his. Together they left the market, walking slowly back to the outpost. As they walked, they saw somebody running towards them, waving their arms, a ranger cloak flapping out behind them.

"Symin! Loka!" Corilai screamed, her voice a panic. "Please, come quickly! Somebody just took Arool!"

"Wait, what do you mean took?" Symin said as she reached them.

"A group of men in bandit style clothes just snatched him off the street! They just dropped a bag over his head, and dragged him onto a cart! I tried to chase them, but without a horse I couldn't keep up!"

"Damn it! We don't need this now," Symin groaned. "Don't worry, Corilai, we'll find him, and we'll take care of those bastards while we're at it."

Sena burst into the air beside Symin, and reached out a hand to Corilai.

"Be calm, child. Derieala can speak to his flame, if the two of you will just calm down. I will see myself." Sena said, vanishing for a moment, then reappearing. "He is safe for now, though very scared. If he lashes out in fear, such men may hurt him. Derieala, please keep trying to talk to Beyo, get him to calm Arool so he doesn't make things worse. We can find him, and hopefully before they leave the city."

Chapter 17 – Wolf men

Morning came, and Corilai fretted over her lost companion. Malthus, Symin, and three of the city guard sat in the outpost, talking. Corilai sulked in a corner, watching as they discussed the fate of her wolf companion. They had dismissed her input as juvenile, and she was not impressed with strangers talking down to her, and even less so that Symin had not spoken out about it.

"There is a group of bandits who have been taking animals, but we thought we had captured them," the head of the guard said. "Perhaps that was wrong."

"Or perhaps there is another group," Malthus said. "Do you know where they were operating from?"

"It was a warehouse, in the eastern quarter of the City."

"Symin, what do we know of the wolf's location?"

"I will allow Sena to explain," Symin said. "Sena, come forth."

The guards gasped and pulled away in their seats as the yellow flame appeared. She looked around, then looked to Symin.

"You called, Bearer?"

"Did you hear our discussion?"

"I did, and I can tell you, based on the observations of Beyo, the wolf was taken to the west, then south, before they took him from the city."

"And who is Beyo?" the head guard asked as Loka entered the room with Tara.

"That's the wolf's flame," Symin explained. "She can communicate with it across distances. As I understand it, flames can contact one another from anywhere."

"Then why do you need us? Surely she can ask where it is."

"She can communicate, she can not locate," Symin said. "She can only surmise directions and locations based on the observations made by the other flame. Since the wolf was placed inside a sealed box at the city gate, the flame could not report any further observations until the box was opened."

Hyren burst into the room, looked at the group, then ran to Corilai. He was dishevelled and breathing heavily, having run from the temple.

"Is it true, they took Arool?" he asked.

"Yes," Corilai replied.

"Did they go west then south?"

"Yes, how did you know?" Corilai asked.

"You have no time to lose! That's where the wolf men go. One of my friends told me about it, before I joined the order. They worship wolves, and wear skins of wolves and their skulls as hats. There aren't often wolves this far south, so they grab any they find."

"Have you seen where they go?" Corilai shouted.

"No," Hyren said softly. "But they don't keep wolves alive for long, if what I have heard is true."

"Why would these 'Wolf men' kill wolves?" Corilai asked.

"They think wolves are gods, so immortal, and when they take the skin and make a priest costume with it, the priest becomes a god too, or something like that."

"How do you know this, boy?" the chief of the guard demanded.

"Like I said, my friend is one of them. I wasn't supposed to be told about it, so don't tell anyone I told you!"

"Did you tell them anything about The Order?" Malthus growled.

"No, this was before I found out about it. I haven't seen them since I joined."

"And they'll do that to Arool?" Corilai snarled, getting to her feet. "I won't let them. Derieala, come forth!"

"You called me, my bearer?" Derieala said as she appeared.

"We're gong to find Arool," Corilai said, stomping towards the door.

"Wait," Symin shouted. "You may not be a full ranger yet, but you never will be if you refuse to listen to reason. You know nothing of these wolf men. You have no idea how many they are, or how strong. You can't just charge in alone."

"Fine, but you heard Hyren, we don't have time to waste. We have to hurry."

"We will hurry, but we will hurry prepared. Loka, fetch the horses, plus extras for the guards men. Malthus, do the order have horses?" Symin asked as Loka ran from the room, Tara following.

"We do," Malthus replied, handing a wooden stamp to Hyren. "Boy, take this, go to the temple and tell them Malthus demands four horses immediately. Tell them Krytus and Rogan are both summoned also. You are to join us as we go to save the wolf. Hurry, boy."

Symin rushed to the armoury, and fetched a selection of swords and daggers, handing them out to those who were present.

"We do not reveal our flames unless it is necessary. We will not be making enemies without cause today."

"They already made us enemies!" Corilai spat. "They knew who Arool travelled with. One of them even called me a ranger bitch when they took him!"

"We must be the better people in this matter," Symin said, resting a hand on Corilai's shoulder. "We have new allies in Horde, but clearly there are those in the city who would still stand against us. We must ensure we do not divert from the mission Sena has laid out before us to settle a civil war."

"Yes, Ranger," Corilai said, her voice calm but her eyes flashing with the anger of the demon flame.

Loka returned and looked around as Rogan entered.

"We have the horses ready, Symin," Loka said as Rogan strode to Malthus.

"What is it, old friend?" Rogan asked as Krytus entered. "Krytus and I are ready to join you. I assume there is trouble, hence sending the boy with your seal?"

"Yes, have you heard of the wolf men?"

"Only vague rumours," Rogan said.

"You know of the wolf, Arool, which travels with this ranger girl?"

"Yes, he is quite a wonder."

"These wolf men have abducted the animal. Their intentions are not merciful. We join these rangers and the guard, in travelling to rescue it."

"Why would we do such a thing?" Krytus shouted.

"Because I demand it of you," Sena replied, her flames lighting the room in anger.

"If the first flame demands, then we obey," Krytus said, mollified.

Leaving the outpost they all mounted their horses and followed Hyren's directions towards the south west of the city. Leaving the city gates behind, they paused to look out over the endless sands, rising and falling in sulphur crested dunes as far as the eye could see.

"It is certain death out there, for the unprepared," the head guard said.

"We are never unprepared," Symin replied, before turning to face Hyren. "Which way from here?"

"South. My friend told me there was an oasis about a day's walk. They have their temple there. I don't know what it looks like."

"A day walking is much less on horse. We ride hard, we try to return before night fall," Symin said, spurring his horse into a gallop, kicking the yellow sand as he rode.

Together, the rest of the group followed, and they rushed headlong into the Desert of Souls, the first rangers in history to ever enter those forbidding sands, and some of only a handful of the order in the last seven centuries. The city guards were visibly nervous, but they kept the pace of the flame wielders, and to their credit were brave in spite of their fear.

"I'm coming, Beyo," Derieala's whispered voice announced into the dry desert air.

* * *

The darkness in the crate was cast aside as it was dragged out, and dropped unceremoniously into the sand near a roaring fire pit. Arool whined pitifully as his tortuously cramped muscles were jarred by the impact.

A rope dropped through the slats of the crate, and a noose was slipped around the helpless wolf's neck, before the crate was smashed open by heavy kicks from his captors. They dragged him out across the sand, and he fought back, but it was no use. His muscles were stiff and sore from the hours cramped in the box.

Arool looked around, and he felt his companion's soothing presence.

"Look, observe, tell," Arool heard Beyo command.

The wolf surveyed the place, the small water hole, the scattering of weathered trees, the smoke from the fire, and the single, tall tower nearby. The stones of the tower were grey and etched with the blasting sands of ancient wind storms. A light shone from the top, where a man at a window kept watch over the desert.

"I see it. I tell Derieala," Beyo told him, and Arool was calmed.

"My human comes soon," he thought.

* * *

"Beyo speaks," Derieala said.

"What does he tell you?" Corilai asked.

"There is a water hole, a fire, and a tall tower of stone."

"I know that place," one of the guards said. "From stories. It was called the Tower of Words, because it supposedly brought messages from other countries, before the birth of Cinder."

"Yes, that makes sense," Sena said, appearing beside Symin.

"I wish you'd warn me before doing that," Symin moaned.

"I am sorry, Bearer," Sena replied. "Would you prefer I keep quiet?"

"No," he said. "Please, tell us what you know."

"The Tower of Words was a relay station for ancient communications technology my people used. It ran on essence, like everything in our civilisation, but essence being an endlessly convertible substance, it would use the same fuel for centuries. As it was consumed and transformed, the tower had other processes to convert it back. Machines to provide comfort and sustenance to the tower's keepers would use the converted essence as fuel, changing it back to the liquid consumed by the tower itself."

"That makes no sense," Symin said. "Everything is consumed and destroyed. We can't take fire and turn it into wood."

"No, but Essence is not wood, and what we did to it was more akin to turning sand into glass, then smashing the glass into tiny particles of sand when we were finished with it."

"I may never understand your essence, but please go on," Loka said, shaking her head.

"If those mechanisms still operate, the tower will still be communicating to the people nearby. They may not understand what it tells them, but they will hear it and may choose to act on what they believe it tells them."

"So you think the wolf men only think and act as such because of what your tower is telling them?" the head guard asked.

"I do," Sena replied. "Once again, our civilisation has brought trouble to the world. Our crimes are many, and we must atone for them all."

"First Flame," Malthus said. "Maarlo would speak to you."

"Then summon him, he may speak to us all."

"Maarlo, come forth!" Malthus said.

"Thank you, Bearer," Maarlo replied. "Sena, it was not your crime which saw this tower corrupt the people of Horde."

"It was our crime as the people of Thres. Our cities were fuelled by the technology which has caused so much suffering."

"They were not intended to create suffering, and in fact, those who lived within them had only prosperity. Do not succumb to misplaced grief, sister."

"It is not misplaced. It was due to our actions as scientists, you and I, Maarlo, that the world was ruptured. So many people died. Our nation was destroyed, we must atone for that."

"Cinder was born as a result, and you then founded the order and the rangers. The rangers have brought peace to the nation for seven centuries, minus a few insurrections. Your legacy is not one of destruction and death. It is one of rebirth and prosperity. Thres has ended, but its people have not died, they live on through the flames."

"Perhaps. Maarlo, I will think on this," Sena said, then vanished.

"There is an enormous amount about them, their world, which we do not know," Loka said. "And to think until recently, we had no clue that such a world might have existed."

"There were some clues, in the texts of the academy library," Symin said. "But scarcely any details. I must speak to Sena at length and write it all down, once this is over. The library should have as complete a history as we can provide."

On the horizon, a plume of grey smoke rose into the sky. Symin pulled his horse to a stop and signalled the others to do the same. They had covered a great distance already and now, the sun beating down from above, Symin guessed they had about an hour before noon.

He looked around, then dismounted, handing his reins to Loka. Symin wandered around, down to the dip between a pair of shallow dunes, and knelt on the ground. He scraped away the sand for a while, then hit some with his flames. It melted, fusing together, to form a glassy lump in his hands.

"This must be what she meant," he said, before standing. "Hyren, come here."

The boy dismounted and rushed to Symin, who looked at him with a curious gaze.

"You are an orange flame, correct?"

"Yes, Ranger," Hyren replied.

"Do you have a secondary ability?"

"No sir, I am from the order. The order does not train such things."

"Damn it," Symin snarled. "I was hoping you could dig us a well. The horses need water."

"I see another way, but slower," Hyren said. "You just made that glass lump. You could make a lot of them, digging as you go, and use them like bricks to form a permanent well."

"That will take forever!" Symin moaned.

"Not if we all help," Malthus replied. "The boy's idea has merit, and the horses will need watering on the way back as well."

"How fast can you make glass?" Symin asked.

In answer, Malthus held both hands over the ground, and fired his flame into the sand. Thirty seconds later, as the dust settled, ten shining blackened glass bricks sat in the sand, each three times the size of a fist.

"If we all pitch in, we can build a well in an hour." Malthus said smugly.

"Do we have an hour to waste?" Corilai asked.

"We don't have horses to waste," Symin said. "They need to be watered. This desert is not as forgiving as other places. There is no shade, the sun is hot, and the air is dry. I'm sorry, Corilai, but Arool will just have to hold on a bit longer. I just hope we strike water here."

With everybody helping, they soon reached water, at a depth far below the height of three men. The sand provided enough bricks to build the well high, above the level of the nearby dunes, with steps around the outside and hand holds on the inside to allow access to the top.

Symin took a rope from his saddle pack and attached a small bucket, then lowered it into the well. The brackish, cold water was not palatable, but it was safe. On the ground, he melted a long trench in the sand to form a glass trough, into which he poured the water.

As he worked, Loka, Tara, and Rogan did the same. Soon the trough was filled, and they led the horses to drink.

Chapter 18 – Tower of Words

The afternoon sun beat down on them as the group closed the distance to the tower. The sand slowed them as the horses at times struggled to find firm footing on the dunes. The plume of smoke drew closer, and finally they spied the tower as the sounds of a rowdy camp reached them on the desert air.

"If they have a watch set on that tower, they already know we're coming," Loka said.

"Then we must move in and make this quick," Symin replied. "Everybody, this is it!"

As one, the group charged over the last of the dunes, and soon were rushing into a large group of people spread out around the oasis. Near the foot of the tower, Arool was chained to a large stone altar, which had clearly been placed at some point much more recent than the tower itself.

As the riders approached, the wolf men began to form into a defensive line, brandishing savage blades as they waited for the smaller number of attackers to arrive.

"You can not interrupt this ceremony!" one of them shouted. Wearing a weathered wolf skull atop his head. "We have a sacred duty and a sacred right to this place!"

"You have no right to that animal," Symin replied. "Hand him over, and we will leave you in peace."

"The ranger's mutt?" the man shouted. "So you are the northern heretics. We will have no business with you. Men of the wolf! I command you to kill them all!"

As he cried out his order, one of his acolytes ran towards Arool, sword raised and raging with murderous intent.

"That's enough of this!" Corilai shouted, and raised her arms.

"Derieala! Come forth and lend me your power!" Corilai screamed, and a writhing black flaming figure appeared over her head, lending it's scream to her own.

"I come my bearer, and aide you in support of Beyo!" Derieala shouted, her voice heard like a hot wind by every person in the oasis as she added her two bolts of black, one from each hand, to that already being shot by Corilai.

Arool cowered in fear on the short chain, unable to fight back as the wolf man reached him and lunged forward to impale the wolf on the savage blade. Just in time, the spears of dark flame struck the man.

In an instant, Derieala flared in rage, her scream withered the trees and stirred the sands as the waters of the oasis seethed in stormy waves. In that moment, the man who would kill Arool was no more. As one, the wolf men paused, and began a retreat, as Corilai raced to free her four legged companion.

The rangers weren't done yet. Symin raised an arm, signalled with a twist of his hand, and charged to the left as Loka, following his signal, rode right, leading a wall of fire as they encircled the oasis.

"No person here escapes!" Symin shouted. "They are to be identified, and interrogated. I want to know everything there is to know about this cult."

The city guard charged straight on, and soon overpowered the apparent leader, knocking the skull from atop his head as they bound him. They then left him there, as they set about rounding up every person they could find.

One of the wolf men tried to escape, and Loka chased him down, enclosing him in a fiery ball, before opening it to direct him back to the others.

"Do not test our patience. When you took one of ours you attacked us all. You saw the fate of your friend who would try to murder that one in chains. You should heed this warning and surrender completely, lest you all face that rage!"

In the end, thirty people were captured, and they sat despondent as the rangers considered their next move. Sena appeared, and spoke briefly to Symin, words nobody else could hear. He looked around, then turned to his comrades.

"We must shut down this tower, so it does not corrupt anybody else with its misplaced messages."

"How do we do that?" Malthus asked.

"Sena says there is a supply room near the base of the tower. We must break the pipe that runs from there, supplying essence to the tower."

"I can do that," said Rogan, looking towards the tower.

"Be careful," the head guard said. "You don't know what's in there."

"I have some idea," Rogan replied, as he walked to the guard's horse.

Rummaging in the saddle pack, Rogan found a large axe, and continued to the tower. Rogan was in there for a scarce few minutes before a sound of deafening calamity issued from the tower, then was silent. Rogan came running out as a stream of green essence burst out behind him.

"Stop it reaching the water!" he shouted.

Running towards the essence, Tara cast seeds and sprouted thick reeds in the sand. She poured her green flame into them, growing a sturdy, living damn against the essence. As she turned, she saw Corilai, embracing Arool, tears streaming down her face. Tara approached.

"Corilai, what is it? He's safe, see?"

"I know," Corilai said. "But I killed that man."

"That was me," Derieala said, appearing beside her. "I did it to save my Beyo, as I was unable to do when we were still part of this world. I put all my power into that blast. It was not your fault. But that man was not one we could save."

"What do you mean?" Corilai asked.

"Sena could explain it better than I," Derieala said. "But that man was driven insane by the tower. Had he not died at my hand, he would have killed, and killed many in his blind rage. He was not simply after Arool. He was after everything. He would have lusted for destruction until he brought it upon all the people of Horde."

"I'm not sure that makes it right," Corilai said. "It certainly doesn't make me feel any better about it."

"If it did," Sena said as Symin approached. "You would be the same as he was. Your empathy, your guilt, shows you were not afflicted as he was.

Derieala speaks the truth, and it is why she acted as she did."

"I don't understand," Corilai sobbed.

"That poor soul's blood is not on your hands, Corilai. It is on ours. Our people built this place without considering this outcome. And there is nothing in your medicine or ours which could have returned his mind to its right state. Some of the others here are not far from that state either, and we must ensure they are properly looked after."

"What was the tower doing to him?" Corilai asked.

"It was changing him. It was not as the tower was intended, but it is how it had become. The corruption of the technology of the essence began long before the end of Thres and the birth of Cinder. But the full corruption of the tower came later still. It is good that it is finally silenced. This oasis can be made safe once more."

"I really don't understand any of this," Corilai moaned.

"Do not fret," Sena said. "This place had been created for a simple purpose, and over time, that purpose was lost. It came to perform a darker role, and in so doing was corrupted. You will understand the rest soon enough. Let us focus on what must now be done, rather than dwell on the demons of our own making."

"And let us be thankful his suffering is over. He may be reborn now," Derieala said.

"Reborn?" Corilai asked.

"Yes. That life is over. His new life may begin."

"You sound quite certain he has one."

"I am. That was the nature of his death. The intensity of it, combined with the corrupting essence under which he was suffering. He will be reborn in fire, just as we were."

"That's enough, Derieala," Sena said. "You are creating more questions, for which the time has yet to come."

The rangers walked back towards the tower, where the essence had begun to recede.

"How is that possible?" Tara asked.

"There is a large basement beneath the tower," Malthus said. "Our histories speak of these places a little. The leaked essence will have flowed back into that, once the pressure behind it was relieved. This will be nothing more than a reservoir of essence now. Should we ever require it, we can come here to obtain some."

"My brother's bearer speaks the truth," Sena said. "And with the tower no longer supplied with essence, the machines within will no longer function. That renders this place safe for people to visit. I would suggest the tower be sealed though, just in case."

"The order will see to that," Malthus replied. "We have strict guidelines for such things."

"This I am aware of," Sena said. "Remember who wrote them."

"Of course, First Flame." Malthus said. "But as you have stripped me of my rank, it will fall to Rogan and Krytus to ensure that it is done."

"And it will be done according to our rules," Rogan said, joining them.

"The desert is not a place we want to spent the night if we don't have to. I suggest we get started back to Horde at first light. The wolf men will have to walk, and we will not make it half way before dark if we are to take them."

"Stoke up that fire, and ensure everybody is made comfortable," Symin said. "We leave at first light."

"I have another suggestion," the head guard said. "That well, the one you built, that sits about halfway between here and the city. It's a good position for travellers, should such ever come this way. I think the oasis is one of potentially many locations to the south we may some day have use of. I would ask that on the way back to horde, we stop at that well, and you build walls such that it can not be easily swallowed by the dunes. The guard will handle maintaining it. We will erect a facility to clean the water so it may be used by travellers also."

"Why would you do such a thing?" Loka asked.

"Clearly these wolf men have made a habit of travelling south into the desert, and it has served well to conceal them from our eyes. If one group of relatively harmless people can do this what others, be they bandits or cultists or innocent travellers, might seek to do the same? It is high time the city guard took steps to watch over this region."

"Then it shall be done as you request," Symin said.

*   *   *

The meagre supplies they had brought were supplemented with those of the wolf men and the bounty of the oasis to provide a reasonable evening meal, with water aplenty to quench the thirst of all, though the guards bemoaned the lack of ale.

The clear desert sky showed them a display of stars more spectacular than the rangers had ever seen, and Loka was staring up at them in wistful wonder, her stomach full and her mind at peace as Symin lay down beside her.

"When did you decide they all needed to be arrested?" she asked.

"That moment when Corilai found us, after our dinner in the city."

"Why?"

"Because they had taken a ranger."

"The wolf is a ranger?" Loka asked, leaning up on her elbow to look at his face.

"He travels beside us. He has a flame. He is one of our party, and one of us. Therefore, he is a ranger. Just as those students are rangers, though we must not let it go to their heads."

"You value all your companions equally, is what you're really saying," Loka said with a smile.

"You read me well, as always," he replied.

"You agreed to the plan with the well quickly also," Loka said.

"That was something I was intending to suggest myself, so letting them think the rangers are co-operating with them is easy. It is preferable to the guard thinking the rangers are dictating to them."

"What do you think of the tower?" Loka asked, lying back down.

"I think it is a relic of a strange time, and a dangerous thing we are best off without."

"You know, the things the flames said about it, they hint at it being something more than just a communications device."

"I had the same thought. But I think what it really is is a reminder of that ancient world of theirs. And something more, they call it corrupted."

"So?"

"So it may have been a communication device to start with, and its less savoury nature only came to light later on."

"That was what I thought also," Loka replied.

"And it sends men crazy."

"What sends you crazy?" Loka asked.

"You do," Symin replied, grabbing her in a playful hold, and they wrestled like that for some time, their giggles echoing across the water of the oasis.

"OK, OK, that's enough," Loka said finally, gasping for breath as he released her. "He'll be reborn, she said."

"Who said?"

"Derieala," Loka explained. "She said that man she vaporised would be reborn in the fire."

"You know they talk about when they were people, but we have no idea how people became flames. I think we just had our first clue."

"The corrupted essence."

"Yes, but corrupted how?"

"You could ask Sena," Loka said.

"If she felt the time for that question had arrived, she would come out and say it."

"Yes, I would," Sena said, appearing.

"Oh god," Loka said, startled. "I'll never get used to that!"

"Rest assured," Sena said. "You will have all your answers, at the appropriate time. But some of these things I am better off showing you, than telling you."

"I'm not sure I want to be shown the creation of a flame," Loka said.

"We shall see what we must see, but I would prefer no new flames were created at all," Sena said.

"That is some comfort I guess," Loka sighed.

"Sometimes, I miss Thres," Sena said. "It was such a different world then. Even though it was doomed in the end, we had a lot of great things. We will show you, one day."

"Were there other countries, besides Thres?" Symin asked.

There was no answer for a long while, until they had forgotten the question, and then finally Sena spoke.

"There were many other countries, and Thres had sent out emissaries to them all. The wonders we saw, the things those who travelled out into the world returned with. They would doom us, and at the same time they made us who we became. It was certainly a different world. A world of wonders, and yet this new world has its own wonders the people of Thres would be awed by. Nobody could have imagined the flames then."

"There were no flames before Cinder?"

"No. I named it Cinder, because it was the home to the flame. You know, when the Rangers were formed. Cinder was a mismatched cluster of warlord controlled towns – so much conflict. Until the rangers brought order and the nation was born. Only then was there a future for the people of Cinder."

"It sounds strange, when you talk like that," Loka said. "My family can't even trace our heritage to those times, and you talk like it was yesterday."

"Sometimes I feel as if it was. Other times, it was a long, lonely millennium. Perhaps the end is finally coming for me. But I will never know until it comes."

"What a morbid thought."

"Not as morbid as knowing. Wouldn't you rather the end be a surprise, so you weren't worried about it being so close?"

"This is not a conversation I ever thought I would have with another person's flame," Loka said. "This life is full of wonder and full of surprises. I know compared to yours, a human life is short. I know we all know there is an end. But what makes a life great is living as though the end is nothing. A chapter heading, not a final page. Then we can live with so much greatness, right up until our last breath. We don't have time to mope around. So we grab hold of the dragon's tail, and let it throw us where it may."

"You've been staring at the stars too long," Symin said. "The guards are right, we need ale."

"Don't be silly," Loka said. "You have me."

Chapter 19 – Glasswell

With the wolf men on foot and bound together in a line with rope, they began the long journey to Horde at first light. Rangers in front, the order at the back, the guard alongside, they made slow but steady progress through the desert.

Before noon they arrived at the well, and the prisoners were made to sit, under the close watch of the city guard.

"This will take us forever. The wolf men can help," Symin said, waving to the head of the guard.

"Separate them and have them help. With all of us, we can pile the bricks as quickly as we can make them," Symin said. "If they run, they won't get far in this desert before we catch them, and they know it."

"Yes, Ranger," the guard said, and set about the task of releasing and instructing the prisoners.

The rangers and the order spread out and began melting sand into glass bricks, piling them around a perimeter wide enough to shelter a large merchant caravan.

Rather than build a simple wall, which would likely fall without sufficient mortar, even with the bricks being melted together as they had done with the well, they created a wide base, and built a levy of bricks. As they used up the sand in the dunes at the site of the levy, they took more from inside the walls, until they had levelled the area.

After three hours, the levy had wrapped around and passed itself on each side. An elbow of levy around each corner, north east and south west further out than the other two. To enter, you would walk along the walls, between an inner and an outer levy, such that the dunes would not blow into the centre, but horses and carts could pass through without having to climb over.

The wolf men were collected again, and bound as they had been. To Symin's surprise, nobody had attempted escape. He stood before them, and looked around the group.

"Thank you for your help with this task. But I must ask. You have all been cooperative in this endeavour. Nobody has tried to run. Why?"

One of the older wolf men stood, and addressed Symin directly.

"Aside from what we witnessed at the oasis, what happened to poor mad Gill, who was destroyed without trace when he attacked the wolf, we know what is best for us. Should we cooperate, and be released, we will likely wish to return to the oasis, even if our cult has been exposed and we can not continue in secret. Should that be the case, this well will benefit us by making that journey an easier one."

"Even though we are responsible for the change in status of your group?" Symin asked.

"We had taken one of yours. Were the situation reversed, we would have acted as decisively as you did. And we overheard some of what you spoke of among yourselves. We have had members of our group trained in subterfuge, and they were able to listen when you spoke of the corrupted essence and what it had done to Gill, what it has probably done to more of us."

"You know that much?" Loka asked.

"We know as much as we had learned in our time visiting the Tower of Words, and the additional information learned from you. It is only in cooperation with your alliance of the order, the flames, and the rangers, that we can avoid the fate of Gill."

"So you wish to join with us?" Symin asked, eyebrow raised.

"Perhaps that is not possible, but we will cooperate. Put us to trial, you will likely find little to hold the majority of us, once due process has been served. Those who abducted the wolf will serve their sentence, and Gill has served his for his violence."

"You seem rather accepting of your friend's demise..." Loka mused.

"Gill was mad, as I have said. He was showing his instability for weeks before his death. He was a danger to us all and we had not decided how to handle the situation when you attacked the tower. If the tower was responsible, we regret it's influence, and would like to return to our original aim of supporting the people of Horde."

"You wish to support Horde? How was that your aim originally?" Symin asked.

"We were originally a group of merchants and business men from the city. We found the tower on a journey of southern exploration, seeking to expand the opportunities of trade for the city. That was when things began to change, and we veered from the intended path."

"And now you would return to your path?" Loka asked as the head guard joined them.

"The guards here do their duty for Horde. We sought to do the same, and became misled by the tower's influence. We would return to our role seeking to support the businesses of Horde."

"The guards will return here to add further structures to this place. Would you offer your labour to that task?"

"We would gladly do so."

"What do you say?" Symin said, turning to the head guard.

"If they are genuine in their intent, their help would be welcome. It would reduce the amount of my men taken away from duties in Horde. Also, I have been thinking about this place. It needs a name, and I feel Glasswell is most fitting."

"Then Glasswell it shall be named," Symin said with a smile. "I assume any official naming paperwork in Horde will be done by you?"

"It will be," the head guard replied. "For now, I suggest you can leave these people in our custody, if you wish to head to Horde today. I will stay here with my guards and these wolf men, as they would not make it to Horde before nightfall."

"If you are certain you can keep everything under control? It is your city guard who would hold their trials anyway, and into your custody we would be taking them regardless."

"It will be fine. As the man said, many of them will not be guilty of anything more than association. I can conduct preliminary interrogations here. Besides which, I see many familiar and trusted faces among them.

Those responsible for the abduction will no doubt cooperate if their fellows demand it."

"If you feel this will not create unnecessary hassle for you, then I am thankful to you," Symin said. "We will make arrangements to return to Horde, and leave this matter in your hands."

Less than an hour later, Symin led the rangers and the order, and continued the ride north to Horde. Returned to his usual post, Arool walked beside Corilai, who rode near the front of the group. As the sun set behind the mountains in the west, they entered the city walls and made their way to the outpost.

In the time they had been gone, another group of rangers had arrived from the north. On word from Emberdale of the new situation in Horde and the newly learned ability to summon flames, Cara had travelled from Vera with three of her senior officers, in order that they may ascertain the truth of the stories and learn for themselves what was involved.

Corilai, Symin and Loka entered Symin's office to find Marni there, talking Cara through the same process she had been through with her fellow students. They stood inside the doorway but remained quiet as the woman sat in silent meditation for a long time. Finally, Cara opened her eyes and spoke.

"Pellis, come forth," she said, and her flame appeared in immediate response.

The brassy tones of the orange flame glinted from every metal surface in the room as Pellis bowed slightly to his wielder.

"You summon, and I am here, my Bearer."

"Remarkable," Cara said, standing and walking around her flame, a look of total wonder in her eyes. "And to think the one to teach me this is a mere student, not even a ranger, let alone a captain or even a member of the archivists. I reiterate what I told you on our first meeting, young lady. There are great things in your future."

"You are an orange flame," Symin said. "Would you be interested in joining our upcoming expedition into the desert? We have need of orange flames, and you would be a welcome leader in their ranks."

"Why would you travel into that place?" Cara asked.

"The ancient city, from which all flames were born, lies at the heart of the desert. There is important work we must undertake there, and if Sena is to be believed, it could be of import for the survival of Cinder itself."

"Who is Sena?" Cara asked.

"She is my flame, and according to the Order of the Essence who operated in Horde for the past several centuries, she is the first flame, as well as the founder of both their order, and of the rangers in Emberdale."

"Really?" Cara said, her eyebrows raised in surprise. "Such a notable individual commands this journey? Then it is a journey of great interest. I would be honoured to join you, provided the Chancellor approves. I will send my people back to Vera to continue work there in my absence."

"I am sure there will be no issues with the Chancellor," Symin said. "I will have Barache send a bird informing him of your decision to accept my invitation."

"Thank you, Ranger," she replied. "May I meet Sena?"

"You may," Sena said, appearing before the woman.

"Woah!" Cara said, jumping in surprise. "Symin, does she always appear without any warning like that?"

"Not always, but she has the ability now to come without being summoned. I gather it is fairly common once summoned for the first time, though not all flames will do it."

"I come when I am needed," Sena said. "You asked to meet me, and I am here. Hello Cara, and welcome, Pellis."

"Thank you, my lady," Pellis said.

"You need not address me so formally," Sena said. "It will be good to have you both along on this mission. Your assistance will be gratefully received."

"When do we leave?" Cara asked.

"As soon as Hunter arrives, I believe we will be ready to go," Sena said.

"And hunter is?"

"My bird," Symin explained. "Sena has summoned him from Oaklands, to be our eyes from above as we cross the desert."

"Eyes from above? That could certainly be useful. When is he expected?"

"Likely sometime tomorrow is my guess," Symin replied.

* * *

Cara stayed at the outpost while her people returned to Vera. She sent them with written training notes to share about the summoning of flames. She had noted the process Marni had taken her through, and instructed them not to attempt it alone, but to work in small groups.

Symin and Loka sat outside the outpost after they had left, snatching a rare moment of privacy. It was mid morning and Cara was inside with Marni and Corilai, grilling them on all they had done since joining the academy. Symin turned to face Loka.

"Sometimes, I forget how unusual those youngsters are in terms of their achievements."

"I know what you mean," Loka replied. "Familiarity means you overlook the special nature of a person. Sometimes it's a good thing, because it keeps a bit of humility around things."

"Yes, but sometimes being recognised for greatness is also important. I just hope Cara doesn't overdo it in there."

"I'm sure it will be fine," Loka said as Sena appeared. "What is it, Sena?"

"Hunter is coming. I suggest you move into the street, so he can see you better."

Symin and Loka both walked away from the building, and heard a piercing cry as the bird saw them. Symin turned to face the sound, and raised an arm as Hunter swooped down, swinging upwards at the last moment, and grasping at Symin's arm, where he had already fitted the gauntlet in preparation for the bird's arrival.

"Welcome Hunter, you must be exhausted," Symin said as he turned to carry the bird into the outpost.

"We can leave now," Sena said. "Hunter can ride with you. We will not need him to fly for a few days."

"We should get everybody prepared," Symin said. "I would suggest we ensure our supplies, the carts, everything is ready to go, and leave in the morning."

"Even so, we can reach Glasswell before nightfall," Sena said.

"No," Symin replied, his voice firm. "We can go to Glasswell tomorrow. We will be slower, with the carts."

"Fine," Sena said. "Then we go to Glasswell tomorrow. We should go from there south to the oasis, then head east from there. That should put us in a good stead to reach our destination."

"You really haven't told us much about where we're going," Loka said.

"The city of Tyra, it was the capital of Thres, the nation in which I was born, and lived out my life as a human. You will find many of the answers you seek in that place."

"All these places, Tyra, Thres, none of them are in our historical records. I wonder why?" Symin said.

"There was little left of Thres after it all happened," Sena said. "And the people of Thres were all but wiped out. There was nobody to be heard who could speak of it."

"You were around, as a flame," Loka said.

"I was. But nobody would hear me. I worked as an influence on my bearer, not a voice of my own."

"But in the order, didn't they know you were there?" Symin asked.

"It was a tumultuous time," Sena said. "Maarlo was my first bearer, and he knew to summon me. But then when the people of Thres were wiped out, remember, he was one of them. He became a flame like me, and I was left without a bearer for a while. It was quite some time before I was with a bearer again, and then we founded the order."

"And the order could summon, and speak to you, couldn't they?"

"Not at first. And they were not of the same language. We flames had to learn to communicate with people who did not speak the language of Thres. Some in Horde were descended from us, but many more were not."

"So how did you draft the rules of the order?" Loka asked.

"Slowly, and with much misunderstanding. And they became set in their ways before I could correct them."

*　　　*　　　*

As the sun rose in the east, the long line of carts and horses left Horde and headed south into the sand. Eighteen rangers, six members of the Order of the Essence, and all their flames looked ahead to an uncertain future.

Corilai looked back to see Barache on the wall, where he stood with Yera and Jaer. The children from Windwall would return home, as the desert held greater danger than they could risk.

Twelve carts rumbled into the sand. There were two horses per cart carrying the people, the wolf, and all their supplies for a long journey into the desert.

As Symin predicted, the travel was slower like this, and it was well into the afternoon before they pulled into Glasswell.

"We camp here tonight," Symin shouted as the last of the carts rolled inside the walls.

Chapter 20 – Sand

"Pull the carts along the walls," Symin ordered as the head guard approached.

"You returned sooner than I anticipated," the man said with a broad grin. "I am afraid these men haven't achieved much. They're not used to this kind of work."

"I expected as much," Symin replied. "We're stopping here tonight and will continue our mission tomorrow."

"Your mission, it will be dangerous," the man said. "Be careful out there. The sands are treacherous. These wolf men have spoken of it somewhat. They lost many members of their group to the sands, when they wandered from the trail."

"We will be careful. That is why we have Hunter."

"Hunter?"

In answer, Symin whistled, and Hunter flew from one of the carts to land on his arm, which he held out for the bird.

"His eyes see well from the sky, and his flame will show us the way."

"In which case, we may have need of his help immediately. A youngster, barely even a teen, has wandered from the camp. We could not spare a guard to search, and we were beginning to worry because the child has not yet found their way back."

"Then Hunter will search for him," Symin replied. "Sena, instruct his flame please."

Sena appeared, and smiled as she leaned close to the bird. She whispered for a while, her words too soft for Symin or the guard to hear, and then Hunter took off, flapping his wings hard to launch high into the sky.

Cara approached, Loka beside her. The pair had been discussing rosters for lookouts and strategies for their time in the desert, when they saw Sena come out.

"What's the situation?" Cara asked.

"We have a youth lost in the sand," Symin replied, staring into the sky as Hunter circled the area, his radius growing with each slow pass.

Hyren approached, looking nervous, and tugged on Loka's sleeve.

"What is it, boy?" Cara demanded.

"I can't find Jull. What's going on?"

"How do you know Jull?" the head guard asked.

"She's my friend, the one who told me about the wolf men. She should be with them, because she wasn't in Horde any more, but she isn't here either. I was sure I saw her when we came back from the tower, but I couldn't talk to her because she was a prisoner."

"No, she is missing," the guard said. "Jull is the youth who wandered away from Glasswell."

"Hyren, we will find your friend," Sena said.

"She will be fine," Symin said. "Go to the cart and wait there. Help the others in preparing the camp."

"Yes, Ranger," Hyren said, and wandered away, casting his eyes up at the sky, searching for the bird which would rescue his friend.

“Cara,” Symin said. “Can I entrust you with organising the watch for the evening?”

“Yes, Ranger,” she replied, turning and walking back towards the carts.

“Loka, please come with me,” Symin said in a formal tone as he walked away from the head guard.

She followed him as he walked to the eastern wall, then along it until he reached the gap. They walked through and then back along the other side, between the inner and outer walls.

Already, the sand had swirled around the base of the glassy levy banks, and they had begun to look old, settled into the landscape like they belonged there, as the steady winds blasted their shiny surfaces with abrasive sand.

“That’s better,” Symin said, stopping and turning to face her. “I just wanted a moment alone.”

“Symin, you romantic idiot!” Loka said, jumping to embrace her lover. “We can’t hang around too long, somebody will miss us.”

“Not before hunter finds something,” Symin said. “let’s just stay here for a few moments.”

Just then, Hunter’s piercing cry drifted to them on the breeze. Symin extricated himself from her arms and looked around.

“He’s seen something. I have to get up higher, to see where he is,” he said as he scrambled up the slippery outer levy, Loka following.

* * *

“Why are you so upset?” Corilai asked Hyren as he sulked, sitting beside one of the carts.

“It’s all my fault. Jull would never have wandered off, if it wasn’t for me.”

“Don’t be silly, it’s not your fault. Jull did what she did and you were nowhere near here.”

“But I didn’t even try to talk to her, on the way back from the tower. She must think I hate her.”

“Who’s this Jull person anyway?” Marni asked. “Is she your girlfriend?”

“What? No!” Hyren shouted, a little too defensively. “No. She isn’t my girlfriend.”

“Then why are you so upset?” Corilai asked.

“Because it’s my fault she wandered into the desert instead of staying here with her family.”

“How could that possibly be your fault?” Corilai asked.

“Because I was the one who hurt her. That’s why I hadn’t seen her for a while.”

“You hurt her?” Marni said. “Hyren, you have to stop talking in riddles. Tell us what’s going on.”

“Jull confessed that she liked me. I turned her down. Now she thinks I think she’s ugly. I tried to explain why, but she was crying and pushed me over before she ran away.”

Hyren paused, grabbing a handful of sand and tossing it from hand to hand as he stared at the ground.

"That was the last time I spoke to her. She was always my best friend. She's a bit of a tomboy, likes to run around doing silly boy games with me, which is why we got along so well."

"If you were so close," Marni said. "Why would you turn her down? That seems a bit silly. It's not like you were going to get married or anything at your age."

"She wasn't my type..." Hyren mumbled.

"What do you mean?" Corilai said. "You just said how you got along so well because she liked the same things you do. Why wouldn't she be your type? Who is?"

Hyren blushed, looked down and played in the sand again. As the silence grew long he looked up, and both girls were watching him. Realising they weren't going to let it go, he sighed and raised a hand, pointing. The girls followed his gaze as he looked in the direction of a small group nearby. All but one of the rangers there walked away, and the last one turned to face them as Hyren continued to point.

"Oh!" Corilai gasped. "I'm sorry, Hyren, I didn't realise. I shouldn't have pushed you on it. I'm sure Jull will understand, once you explain it to her. Don't worry. It's really nobody's business but yours."

"I know, but I hurt her..." he said, lowering his hand.

"She'll understand, don't worry. Heaps of boys like boys in Emberdale, and nobody cares. It doesn't matter. You like who you like, and that's all there is to it. Isn't it the same in Horde?"

"Well, yeah… Nobody ever makes a fuss about it. I mean, I know what I like, and I never felt the need to explain it to anyone, but then Jull asked me to be her boyfriend, and she was already my best friend, but I just couldn't do it."

"I'm sorry, Hyren," Marni said. "We didn't mean to upset you. And I am sure there will be a nice boy for you somewhere. And one for Jull too, and you two will be best friends again soon."

"But I already found a nice boy. I really like him, but he doesn't know I exist."

"You did?" Corilai said. "Who is it?"

Hyren pointed again, as the lad nearby lowered his hood then turned to face them, waving at Marni.

"You really like him?" Corilai asked.

"Yeah..." Hyren said softly.

"You can't have him," Marni said. "I'm sorry Hyren, that boy's mine. But I know you'll find somebody one day. Just be patient."

"I need to go," Hyren said, standing and running behind the line of carts.

"That was a bit harsh, Marni," Corilai snapped.

"I didn't mean to be..." Marni said. "I'll go speak to him"

*　　　*　　　*

Symin stood atop the levy, shielding his eyes as he looked west, into the sunset. Hunter was visible, a speck in the distance, turning in a tight circle. His cry was piercing as he called again.

"He's found something alright," Symin said. "We should get over there."

Symin rushed back into Glasswell, then across to the other side, where Cara and Tara were both rushing to the walls, heading for Hunter's position.

"Wait!" Symin shouted. "We should take horses. We don't want to be out after dark, and they'll be quicker than walking."

"Agreed," Cara said, rushing back towards the carts.

Following her, Loka, Symin and Tara all soon secured their riding gear and mounted up. Symin fetched a flask of water before rushing out between the tall glass levy banks and into the sand. Hunter continued circling, and they rode towards his position.

"Hunter reports the child is not moving," Sena said. "She is lying on the sand."

"She may be injured," Cara said. "We must hurry."

The horses rushed as fast as they could, but as they climbed the dunes, the soft sand became difficult, slowing them down. In spite of their best intentions they could not gallop in the conditions. The ride was slow and difficult, and took them the better part of an hour, before finally they saw the girl lying in the sand between two dunes.

Hunter swooped down to claim his perch on Symin's arm as he dismounted and walked towards the girl. He pulled out the flask and removed the stopper, kneeling beside her.

The girl turned her head to look at him as he offered her the water.

"Thanks," she rasped as she drank a small amount. "I twisted my ankle. I thought I was done for."

"We've got you now," Loka said as Cara followed her.

Jull handed the flask back to Symin and managed a weak smile. Cara scooped the girl up and carried her to her horse, placing her in front of the saddle as she climbed up behind her.

"Why did you run away?" Cara asked.

"I was upset about a boy," Jull said.

"So you run into the dessert and nearly get yourself dead?" Cara snapped. "Never do that over some boy. You've got your lifetime ahead of you to be better than some boy could ever be."

"Yes, ma'am," Jull said.

They rode back to Glasswell, arriving shortly after dark, and Jull was taken directly to her tent, where her parents watched over her. Hyren asked to see her but was refused, as the girl needed rest, so he sat outside her tent and waited.

* * *

As dawn rose over Glasswell, Symin watched as the rangers prepared to head out. Loka approached, and together they hitched their horses to the lead cart.

"Where to now?" Loka asked.

"Back to the tower, then from there, into the unknown."

"This journey is going to take a long time," Loka said. "If only there were some way to speed things up."

"Perhaps. I'll have a word to the orange flames, see if they can help"

"What are you thinking about?" Loka asked.

"If only there were a better surface for the horses and carts. This soft sand is slowing us down. I'm thinking about what the orange flames can do to give us a road. Maybe they can compact the sand or something."

"Pirette might have some ideas then, I'll go find him," Loka said.

While she was gone, Symin walked past the tent where Hyren was still stationed, waiting for his friend. The boy had stayed awake long into the night, and now snored softly. Symin knelt and shook the boy.

"Hyren, we're leaving soon."

"I can't go yet. I have to speak to Jull. I have to explain..."

"Explain what?" Jull said, rubbing her eyes as she exited the tent. "You really hurt me, you know."

"I know. But I do like you. You're my best friend."

"And that's all? Why can't I be more than that?"

"You're not… My type," Hyren said as Marni approached.

"Not your type? What the hell is that supposed to mean?" Jull demanded, standing over the boy aggressively.

He shied away from her rage and fell quiet, looking at the ground. Marni, hearing anger rising in Jull's voice and seeing that Hyren was not confident enough to confront her, rushed to the girl and whispered in her ear. Jull's eyes grew wide and her jaw dropped.

"Oh!" the girl exclaimed. "I guess… That kind of… Oh, Hyren, I'm so sorry! That must have been horrible for you! I've been so selfish!"

"No, Jull I could have just said yes..." Hyren replied.

"And lie to yourself? No way!" Jull said. "Hyren, we've been best friends a long time, and I guess at some level I knew. But I loved you and didn't want to believe it, because I wanted to be more. You can't lie to yourself, and I have to let you be the you I crushed on, my best friend. It was wrong of me to expect you to be something you aren't."

"Thank you Jull," Hyren said. "Will you be OK?"

"I'll be fine," Jull said. "But you have to go. I'd love to come along, I'm sure we'd have some amazing adventures, but there's a lot of work to be done here, and my parents need me. You better come back though, and tell me everything!"

"I will, I promise," Hyren said, standing and embracing his friend. "And you don't go running off and getting killed while I'm gone! At least wait for me to come back and we can run off and be stupid together, like old times."

"Symin!" Loka called, and Symin left the youngsters.

"Hyren," Symin said. "If this is settled, you must get ready. We leave as soon as the carts are prepared."

"Yes, Ranger," the boy said.

Pirette and Loka met Symin as he approached the carts.

"Symin, you had a request?"

"Yes, I was wondering if you could help us with a road surface by compacting the sand as we travel?"

"Well, not really. Sand is tricky. Compacting is done with downward pressure, but sand simply flows away and up, without really compacting. You can do it by pumping water deep into the sand and vibrating the area to shift the air out, but it's slow. We would take a month to reach the tower, at least."

"Not good enough then. Any suggestions?"

"We could glass it..." Pirette mused. "But the carts would probably crack it up, and we run risks of cutting feet or hooves. Plus it would be awfully slippery."

"There has to be a way. You said pumping water. Tell me about that."

"Have you ever been to a beach?" Pirette asked. "Think about the water's edge. Compare the sand there, where the waves keep it wet, with the soft dry dunes."

"Your shoes sink in the dry sand, but you can run comfortably on the wet," Symin said. "I see your point. I brought orange flames for many reasons, and this was one. Perhaps I should have brought more white flames. They can manipulate water, with their ice ability."

"Yes," Pirette said. "If they could generate enough moisture from the air over a long period of time, they could firm up the sand enough to make a real difference in our travel time."

"Loka, where's Treghan?" Symin asked.

"He's helping hitch the carts," Loka replied.

"Fetch him, please."

Loka found Treghan, and returned to Symin quickly.

"Treghan," Symin said. "Do you think you could generate enough water to wet down the sand as we cross the desert?"

"I don't know," Treghan said. "A lot of the work is condensing the moisture in the air, and this dessert air is pretty dry. I've noticed my secondary is less effective here."

"Can you find water beneath the ground?"

"Perhaps, but getting it out is harder. If its in a deep well I can probably bring it up, but I don't know if I could get water up through the sand."

"Pirette, could you dig a fast well and hold the sand back while he draws up the water?"

"I think that's possible," Pirette said.

"Then try it. We head for the Tower of Words, which is a known path. But after that, we will be making a new way – try it then. We'll be wanting to build a more permanent tower road one day, but we don't have time for it now. Once we pass the tower, you two work together, and try to make things easier for us all. You ride on the lead cart and work from there."

"Yes, Ranger," Treghan and Pirette both said.

Chapter 21 – Tower Return

The caravan rolled to the hard rocky ground near the oasis in mid afternoon. Treghan dismounted and stood beside the cart looking down towards the water, and the tower to the eastern side.

"I can't believe we came back here already," Corilai said, scratching Arool's head between the ears as she joined Treghan.

"We had to," Treghan said. "It's the quickest way. But it will be harder after this. We have to go east, and the sand will be much worse. I need to try out the water thing with Pirette, and I don't know if it will work."

"It will work just fine. You can do it," Corilai said.

"Maybe. I hope so. We have a long way to go yet."

Corilai walked forward and stared at the base of the tower. She knelt on the ground, and placed her left arm around the wolf's shoulders while staring at her right palm. Silently, she began to cry.

"What is it?" Treghan asked, clueless as only he could be.

"That man was standing right over there when I killed him..."

"You didn't kill anyone," Treghan said. "All you did was try to save Arool. And you did it too. Arool is fine because of what you did."

"But that man died, and it was because of me..."

"We've been over this," Treghan said softly as he sat beside her, taking her hand in his own. "Yes, you attacked him with your flame. You were furious, and you were right to do so. But it was Derieala whose flame killed him."

"I would speak, my bearer," Derieala said.

The black flame's voice was a whisper on the air. She had not yet appeared, but a halo of flame around Corilai implied her presence.

"Come forth, Derieala," Corilai muttered.

"My bearer, strictly speaking he is not dead," Derieala said as she appeaered.

"Now you're talking nonsense," Corilai said. "We all saw it. He was vaporised."

"Well he was, yes," Derieala said, walking a short distance before turning to face Corilai. "But that was a transformation, more than a killing. He was tainted by the essence. It had become a part of his being, and the essence can never be destroyed."

"What are you saying?" Corilai asked.

"Have you never wondered how we flames came to be?"

"Of course, I have always wondered..."

"We lived in a world dominated by the essence. Depending on how you worked with it, the essence would have a different effect on you. Some who were at times bathed in the essence during its transformations would go a little strange..."

"Strange how?" Treghan asked.

"Their minds would leave them, is how we used to say it in Thres, but that is not entirely accurate. Their minds would change. They did not think the same as normal people any more. They became sick in their hearts and would say and do things which they would never do before."

"It sent them insane?" Treghan said. "Why would you use such a thing?"

"All our technology was based on the essence. Our lives were reliant on our technology. The numbers so effected were few, and we considered it worth the benefits to our society."

"So some people were driven mad," Corilai said. "What's your point?"

"That man, Gill, he was one such person. He had clearly ventured deep into the tower's basement on more than one occasion. The corrupted essence had so corrupted his mind."

Corilai stood, and began walking towards the tower. Derieala followed, along with Treghan and Arool. Arool looked about furtively, nervous of this place after what he had experienced before, but still confident in his mistress enough to follow.

"So what you're saying is that this man, Gill, was imbued with the essence, because otherwise he could not have been corrupted by it?" Corilai asked.

"Exactly, my bearer."

"What does it all mean?"

"Do not go closer, my bearer. I will explain. Sena will be angry that I told you so soon, but it is appropriate that I explain lest you fall victim to your melancholy during our voyage. She had planned to explain in the old city anyway."

"OK, tell me, please," Corilai said.

"When a person is sufficiently imbued with the essence, it incorporates itself into their being. It becomes intricately connected to their self, their very soul."

"So?"

"So the essence can not be destroyed, only transformed."

"So you are saying I did not kill that man, you did not kill that man, he was only transformed?"

"Exactly, because we know he was driven mad by the essence, which means the essence was a part of him, and so the essence which was a part of him has been transformed. In a normal death, the body would decompose, and the minerals, the elements which make it up would be returned to the earth."

Derieala moved once again towards the tower, turning to face them before continuing.

"It would blend with the soil and become part of the world. Never truly destroyed, those materials enter into the vegetation, and then into the beasts which consume that vegetation. This is a circle of life all humans have been a part of for all time in this world."

She approached them again, stopping before Corilai, kneeling to face her, brushing her shadowy hand across the girl's face as she spoke.

"The essence, when treated in just the right way, interrupts that cycle. When the other materials in the body are not permitted time to return to the earth and are destroyed, the essence is unable to leave the person who was infused with it."

"I'm not sure I understand," Corilai said.

"With normal death and burial," Derieala said. "The essence dissipates, separates from the body and then the soul, as the other materials separate through decomposition and are returned to the soil. What if the destruction is so sudden, so absolute, that such a process can not occur?"

"Then I suppose the essence can not stop being connected to the person..." Corilai said.

"That's right, but the essence can never be destroyed. If it is connected to something when it is destroyed, it must consume and preserve it. Because in the act of being transformed, the thing with which it is so permanently linked must also transform. When that man was consumed by the fire, he became the fire. The essence will have preserved him, and his soul will still live within the flames."

"So you were all killed in such a terrible way?" Treghan said, jumping to his feet and staring at the black flame, hovering in the air before them.

"That is something I must wait for Sena to explain," Derieala said. "I fear I have already said too much. But be assured, my bearer, you have not destroyed that man. He lives on, and will be reborn in flames."

"Does that take a long time?" Corilai asked.

"Not always. In fact, in the beginning, it was fast. Because there were more potential hosts than flames, and because the flames were so new, the rules were still unknown. But if a suitable host is coming of age in the area, he may have already chosen one."

"Does that ease your mind?" Treghan asked, resting a hand on Corilai's shoulder.

"Yes it does, a little. Derieala, if he still lives in flame, is his madness now gone?"

"Yes, the corruption of his mind will have been ended during the transformation."

"Was there any hope for him to be free of the corruption in any other way?"

"It would have driven him to death. It was inevitable."

"Then rather than kill him, what you are saying is we saved him? Freed him from his torment?"

"That is true," Derieala said.

"Then yes, it does ease my mind to know these things. Thank you, Derieala."

"That was a most interesting discussion," Symin said, appearing from a short distance behind them, Loka by his side. "Sena allowed us to listen in. I hope you don't mind. She felt it was important that we all understand. I can explain the basics to the rest of the rangers later."

"Then we need not report the matter to you," Treghan said. "I'm sure that is best, given the circumstances. Corilai has been through enough already, don't you think?"

"I certainly think so," Loka said, walking to the girl and kneeling down beside her. "How are you coping with all this, you remarkable young lady?"

"Remarkable? Bumbling more like it."

"It takes a special kind of bumbling indeed to be the one to create the first new flame being in seven centuries."

"Loka is correct," Derieala said. "You are indeed remarkable, my bearer. Gill will be the first new flame to join us in all that time. We had hoped there would not be a necessity for more, but this development has made his birth an important one."

*   *   *

Jull lay alone in her tent, but she felt strange. She felt like she had never felt before, not truly alone. It was as though there was somebody else in there with her. Not in her tent, in her mind.

"Is this how it feels for Hyren?" she wondered aloud. "Whatever it is, I can't sleep like this. It feels strange. If only..."

She turned her head, her right ear pressed into the pillow. The thudding of her heartbeat filled her world and she listened to it intently.

"I feel... I feel one with myself, but there is something more..." she whispered into the evening air. "Hyren, hurry back to me. I have so many questions to ask of you. If this is what it feels like for you, does that mean I can be a member of the order, like you? Or even a ranger?"

"How know?" came an unfamiliar voice in her mind. "How is it? Why am I?"

"Who's there?" she shouted, sitting up, but the voice was gone.

Only the still night responded to her call and footsteps, coming towards her. Abruptly, her father thrust open the tent flap.

"What is it?"

"I was just having a bad dream. It's OK, Father," Jull said.

"OK, but just call if you need us," he said, then left.

Jull sat there, confused, wondering about this strange feeling she was having. Was it just the stress of what had happened? The new knowledge of her best friend and his preferences? The heart break at knowing she could never be with him? Or was there really something else going on?

"I'm never alone now," she said, deciding with total conviction that it was true.

Holding her hands out in front of her, Jull stared at the space between them, and concentrated as she had seen Hyren doing when his flames had first appeared and he shared the discovery with her, before telling his family.

Squinting her eyes, Jull focused her thoughts and pushed with all the might her mind could muster. Nothing happened, and she began to doubt her own belief.

With a sigh, Jull stopped and relaxed, looking up at the fabric of the tent over her head for a long while, before looking back at her hands, now resting in her lap.

She tilted her head, slightly puzzled, unsure if she trusted her own eyes. Bending forward, she looked harder, closer, and confirmed she was not hallucinating. There was something there, red and distinct. The line fluctuated and pulsed between her hands.

Jull took a deep breath and pushed her thoughts away, focusing all her attention on the line and what it was, what it meant. Then, all of a sudden, her tent was lit bright with a red light as the flickering flames burst into being in the air between her palms.

She stared at it, flickering there, for several minutes, entranced by its presence. Finally, she made up her mind. Standing, she left the comfort of her tent and rushed out into the still night air, looking for her father.

"I know I told him I had to help my parents, but this changes everything. I have to find Hyren. I must go with them."

Finding her father, she pulled him aside from the others, and spoke quickly.

"Father, I have a flame. I never had one before and nobody here knows about them. Hyren has gone to the tower and with him are the Order and the Rangers. They're the only ones who can help me understand what is happening. I have to go to them, go with them into the desert."

"Jull, if you must go I won't stop you, but do not speak to your mother. She will never understand enough to let you go. I'll speak with her. They went to the tower. Go there, take the fastest horse in the stable, the chestnut colt which belongs to the rangers. You're lucky they left it behind, because it was ridden hard yesterday."

"But father, that's stealing!"

"Not if you're taking their horse to them. Ride all night if you must. But if you get there and they're already gone, then your chance has flown. You are to return here immediately, understand? Do not go into the desert alone. The tower is as far as I'll permit, unless you have found those you seek."

"Yes, Father. I promise, and I will return. We'll all be safe, you'll see. But I must ask you, why?"

He held out his hand, and there he kindled a small, green flame.

"Mine is completely untrained. My parents were suspicious of flames and hated rangers. I never had the chance to learn more about what it was, who I was. Take your new flame and find the help you need to become a great flame wielder. I'll handle your mother and all her objections."

"Thank you, Father," Jull said, embracing him with true daughterly affection before turning and running to the stables.

She did not look back as she entered and found the horse he had spoken of. Climbing on, she grasped the beast's main and urged it forward.

She had always been good with horses, but this one seemed to ignore the usual signals. Perhaps the rangers used something different? Oh well, at least this horse would have the health and the stamina, so she would have to make it work.

"Please, horse, find your masters. I can light your way," she implored casting her weak red flame before them.

As if understanding her need, the horse began to trot, negotiating its way around a soft patch of sand until it hit something a little firmer. Then, it broke into a gallop and raced south into the night, Glasswell soon lost to the desert sands behind them. The chill of the night air crept through her skin as she clung to the animal.

With no saddle or blanket to keep her on its back, Jull immediately regretted her haste, but refused to turn back now. She clung to the horse with all the strength she could muster, and prayed she could reach the tower in time.

Chapter 22 – Ancient Roads

As the sun's first rays pierced the desert air, Treghan and Pirette stood atop the lead cart as it trundled away from the tower. Drawing on water from the oasis, Treghan did not need Pirette to dig a well for the first leg of their journey.

Summoning a whirling vortex of water before him, Treghan looked ahead, into the eastern sky, as he directed the nearly frozen liquid to spray a long line ahead of them.

As it saturated the surface sand, Pirette applied some vibration using his orange flame's secondary power, to cause the wet sand to compress a little. The horses pulled, and the carts trundled into the desert.

The hooves of the horses and the wheels of the carts still dug deep into the sand, but they gained greater purchase than they had in the dry sands the day before. As they journeyed into the sunrise, the sand became softer, deeper, and Treghan's efforts soon became less effective.

The tower still stood in the middle distance when Treghan flagged for the carts to stop and climbed down, seeking Symin. The older ranger came forward from a meeting the senior rangers were holding in the second cart, anxious to find out why they had stopped.

"What's the hold up?" Symin demanded as he met Treghan.

"The dunes are growing larger, the sand deeper and softer. My water is not able to penetrate deep enough to make a stable surface like it did at the tower."

"I see. The tower would have been built somewhere with a rocky foundation close to the surface, and as we move into the sands, it gets deeper. If only there were some way to see ahead, and steer our course towards firmer ground."

"What about Hunter?" Treghan asked.

"I'll send him up, but how will he know what to look for?" Symin said.

"Ask Sena to speak with his flame," Treghan said.

"Of course, she can do that," Symin said. "I guess I have a while to go before I get used to her ability. I'm still thinking like an old fashioned ranger, instead of her bearer."

"Your old fashioned skills are no less important now than they were against Yuri, or Dreighton," Treghan said.

"That's good to know," Symin said, before laughing. "What are you doing, trying to encourage me? Who's the student here?"

"Well, I'm not the one who forgot about his flame. Her ability should be exciting to you, a great new thing you want to test out at every chance. That's how it is for us students," Treghan said.

"Yes, I suppose it is. I remember those days fondly. Loka and I certainly got into some mischief back then, trying to test out our flames. I see a little of us in you lot."

"So..." Treghan said. "Hunter?"

"Of course," Symin said, whistling.

In response to his whistle, the bird flew out of the second cart. It came to the scout, landing on his raised arm. Symin looked at the bird, and spoke slowly.

"I need you to look from above and find us any sign of rocks, or firm ground. Or anything else we might be interested in. Sena, direct his flame please."

"I already have," Sena said, appearing in the air beside the ranger. "They know what to look for, and I will communicate with them until they are done."

"Then go!" Symin said, waving his arm as the bird took flight.

* * *

Hunter flew high into the air, then commenced his circling, searching the desert for anything which might help them. Suddenly he screeched and flew directly for the tower, back the way they had come.

"Hunter!" Symin shouted. "Wrong way!"

The bird ignored him and continued his flight. Symin looked at Sena, who shook her head.

"What is going on with that bird?" Symin muttered. "Sena, can you ask his flame?"

"It isn't responding. It's just screeching, as Hunter did. Perhaps they found something back there?"

"I'm taking a horse. The caravan is to wait here until I return," Symin said, rushing to the second cart and unhitching his horse.

In a swift movement, Symin mounted the horse. Breaking immediately into a gallop, Symin rushed back along the line of carts and was soon racing towards the tower, making much faster time than the carts had done.

The hours walk was covered in mere minutes at this pace, and he crested the low dune before the tower to look down on the oasis. There, at the edge of the water, he saw a horse, drinking. Hunter circled the oasis, high above, and a small figure beside the horse watched the bird apprehensively.

Symin whistled, and Hunter flew to him as he dismounted and began the short walk to the water. Hunter on his arm, Symin reached the girl where she waited and raised an eyebrow.

"That's our horse, we left at Glasswell."

"Yes, it is," the girl replied.

"What is the meaning of this?" Symin said, his voice firm.

"Something is happening to me, and I had to try to reach you. Your group are the only ones who could help me."

"You, you're that girl the child from the order was so concerned about, the one who ran off into the desert. And now you've added horse theft to that list?"

"I suppose it must look that way," Jull said, looking down. "But still, I was coming to you, with your horse. I wasn't going to keep it..."

"Nonetheless, you did not have our permission, and from the looks of it, this horse was ridden hard. We left it behind so it could rest, and here it is, tired again. Explain yourself."

Jull raised her hand, and kindled a tiny, red flame. Looking up from the flame, she searched the ranger's face for any reaction, but saw none there.

"I didn't know where else to go. I never had any clue I might get a flame and suddenly I got this last night. My father told me I could come to you, because he had never been able to train his. And I wanted to come, because I was scared. All of a sudden, I feel like I'm never alone, and that's new, and scary."

"I guess it would be," Symin said, his voice softening. "Come along then. I can't send you back on that horse, he needs to rest. He'll be fine here. There's grass, and there's water. You can join our journey but the danger, the risk, you take it willingly and you must agree to wear the consequences of your action, whatever they may be."

"Yes, Ranger!" Jull said, suddenly excited. "Can your horse take us both?"

"It's a ranger's horse. Of course it can," Symin said as he turned and walked away from the girl, back towards the low rise where the horse waited.

"Thank you," Jull said, turning to brush her hand on the flank of the horse. "You can wait here now."

Turning, she followed the ranger, running to catch up as he swung onto the horse, then offered her his hand. Blushing with the bashfulness of her youth, Jull took his hand and he helped her up onto the horse, in front of the saddle.

Spurring the horse into a trot, Symin returned to the caravan, handing the girl into the care of Marni and Corilai, who were riding on the third cart. He then returned to where Treghan stood, waiting beside the lead cart.

"We should try that again," Symin said. "Hunter, go!"

The bird flew high into the sky again, then began searching in widening arks to the east, soon screeching and stopping, to circle over a point some distance away, beyond a series of tall, soft dunes.

"Do we take the carts there?" Treghan asked.

"No," Symin said. "I'll go ahead, and see what he's found. I don't want to bog the caravan in soft sand for no reason."

Climbing back onto his horse, Symin left the caravan a second time, this time heading vaguely south east, over the towering dunes. The sand blasted his face at the crest, a steady desert wind which slowly moved the dunes seeming to object to his obstruction.

Carefully, he made his way down the far side, and then climbed the second dune, and the third, and so on. After five dunes, he climbed the sixth and stopped, looking down into the trough below. At its bottom, peeking through the sands, a weathered grey stone road defied the sands of time.

"What is this?"Symin muttered.

"That is one of the ancient highways of Thres," Sena replied as she manifested herself beside her bearer. "I did not believe we could find one so soon, and so uncovered."

"It's not that greatly uncovered," Symin said, looking along it to where the stones disappeared under the roaming desert sands. "But even where it is covered, it still exists beneath the sands. This might be just what we needed. By the time the carts can cross those dunes, it will be time to camp. But the time and effort it will save, it's well worth the effort."

"Indeed," Sena said. "Your orange flames can stand up front, and simply remove the sands from the road as you travel."

"Of course. I was thinking it gave Treghan a basis on which to moisten the sand above, but your suggestion is even better. Do you have any idea where this road leads?"

"To the east, and the east is where we are to go. If it will not take us all the way, it will still take us closer to our goal."

"Of course it will. Then it is decided," Symin said, turning his horse and riding back to the caravan. "We will just have to bring the carts over the dunes."

"You have orange flames who can flatten the dunes." Sena said.

"We don't have the time to waste," Symin replied. "I want to get us started on that road fast, and the orange flames have not moved sand in that amount before. I don't know how much effort it will take, and it will only take an hour to get the carts across anyway."

As he reached them, he quickly set about directing the carts to go to the road, hitching his horse back onto the second cart. Treghan set about moistening the sand as best he could in the dry air, and they slowly climbed first one, then another dune.

As the lead cart ascended the third, the last cart was cresting the first. Then the lead cart's wheels dug in, and the cart listed dangerously to the side. Thinking fast, Treghan rushed to the front of the cart and unhitched the horses, remembering the lesson they had learned from the travellers in the highlands the previous year.

The horses stumbled away on the soft sand, as the cart rolled onto its side. Yells and screams came from those inside as it slid halfway down the dune. Stumbling and sliding in the sand, Treghan and Pirette rushed to the carriage, reaching it as the people inside began climbing out.

Three rangers and two members of the Order had been riding in the lead cart as it went over, but none were harmed. Pirette had not been as fast as Treghan, and sported a nasty scrape on his arm, and a torn cloak. The cart had caught him as it rolled, and he was thrown from his perch at the front.

Quickly on the scene, Symin began calling orders to the rangers. Two present were orange flames, Pirette and one other, and Symin soon had them moving sand from beneath the cart to encourage it to roll back up right.

While they worked, Symin turned his attention to the horses, which stood nervously in the trough between the dunes. Taking the remaining people from the cart, he went to round the startled animals up, intent on hitching them back to the wagon so they could continue.

As the lead cart was once again moving, Symin looked to the crest it had fallen from, and was relieved to see Loka leading the second cart from a different point further west on the dune, where the wind was broken by the crest and the sand was not as soft.

With the sun settling low in the western sky, the lead cart finally rumbled down the final dune and rested on the ancient stones of the Thres road. The second cart arrived minutes later, bringing with it two more orange flames.

As the third and fourth carts began the tricky descent to the road, the four orange flames set about clearing sand from the roadway, and pushing the next tall dune back over itself to prevent it from tumbling down on them in the night.

As dusk claimed the desert, the last of the caravan had joined them on the road, and all the orange flames had joined the task of securing the road against the rolling dunes. The last two dunes they had crossed were pushed back into the troughs, to level the desert as a defence against the roaming sands.

The road proved wide enough so that four of the carts could fit abreast on its stone surface. The orange flamed rangers, with the help of orange flames from the order, cleared the road for approximately a hundred paces in either direction, as others worked to establish camp fires to warm them all through the chilly desert night.

Settling together before one of the fires, Symin and Loka relaxed as many others did likewise. Four of the members of the Order, along with Cara and two other rangers, began preparing meals for all those who were there, and the smells wafting from the pots were a comfort for the weary travellers.

“Imagine this road still being here after all those centuries,” Loka mused.

“Yes, it shows that we are on the right path,” Symin replied. “Sena, what do you make of it?”

“My bearer, this situation gives me hope. If the road can survive in the desert, then perhaps my city still stands. If that is the case, we may not be too late.”

“Too late for what?” Loka asked.

“To save Cinder. For in that city, as well as the secrets of my people, we will find the ancient danger which threatens yours. If the city remains standing, then it will be easier for us to reach it, and stop it.”

“Remains standing?” Symin said. “I assumed by what you have said before that it was destroyed.”

“Yes, it was, in as much as its people were wiped out, and the landscape surrounding it was wiped clean of life. I have returned there before, and while there was much devastation, the City was still there, albeit in ruins. If time has not erased those ruins, then we will be better able to fulfil our mission.”

“I see,” Loka said. “If the place is recognisable enough, even if the buildings are gone, the streets can lead you to the place you seek.”

“That is true,” Sena replied.

“So this road gives you hope, because the city streets may still be there,” Symin said. “But what if they are completely buried?”

“Then we must uncover them. What we seek lies beneath the city, and if we must dig randomly in search of it, we will be too late by the time we reach that most vital of destinations.”

Chapter 23 – Lost Village

As the eastern sky began its pre-dawn glowing act, Symin woke early after a strange dream. He walked the perimeter, Sena beside him as they spoke in soft tones.

"So you showed me things through my dreams, but now that you can just talk to me, you don't?" Symin asked.

"Correct. When I had not yet been summoned to come forth by you, I used your dreams to show you the things I believed you needed to see, or which would give you clues to that which was coming."

"So when I dream of the old city now, the city you lived in and I have never seen, that's not you in my dreams?"

"No," she said. "But you do have memories of it in you, from the dreams I have shown you before, and also to a small extent you will see things drawn from my memory."

"How is that possible?" Symin asked.

"I believe I told you once before," Sena said. "Just as you bear me in your world, I bear you in mine. We live inside of each other. As such, we live within each other's minds. You see my memories, because, in this way at least, they are as your own."

"And that's what I see in my dreams? Your memories?"

"In essence, yes."

They fell silent as they walked, and Loka approached, yawning. She quietly slipped her arm through Symin's, and leaned her head on his shoulder as they paused. Kresai stood beside her, the black flames difficult to see in the grey haze of the waning night.

"I woke up and you were gone," Loka said. "Were you having strange dreams again?"

"Yes, I was. Sena and I were discussing them."

"What was this one about?" Loka asked.

"I was in the old city, where Sena lived, before she was a flame. She had recently been changed, but nobody else had yet and it was a strange meeting. There were people flooding into Thres, and they were trying to decide what to do with them all."

"They were the refugees," Sena said. "The other nations of the world were at war towards the end. A terrifying battle between ideology and reason, and the fearsome weapons they wielded had the power to end all life. Thres was not involved, and the non-combatants from a dozen nations fled for our lands."

"What happened to them?" Loka asked.

"We sent them onwards, into the northern lands. We had little population there, and these people would have enough room to settle there. That was the land which would become Cinder. People of many races from many countries with nothing left to lose, settled the north."

"Many countries? It's interesting, that little knowledge of this remains," Symin said.

"Yes, we granted them the right to settle on the provision they abandoned their ties to the old world, because we did not want their conflicts to break out within our nation."

"You made them assimilate to your own culture?"

"No, we asked them to start their own, together, as a unified but diverse people. This is why you have such variety in your people. They had to cooperate and live with each other in peace. They had to forget their ancestral rivalry and work together. The nation of Thres took a mostly hands off approach, and allowed them to live without our interference."

"I had sometimes wondered about it, I have to admit," Loka said. "Symin's skin is so much paler than mine, and Tara's eyes are such a beautiful shape. When you look at the animals in the wild, they all look more similar than the people in Cinder do."

"Your skin tone comes from a nation which sat in the dry western half of the known world. Symin's comes from a cold, mountainous nation. Tara would have ancestors who fled from across the seas."

"Why would they flee from across the seas?" Loka asked.

"The weapons of absolute destruction could reach far, and nobody was safe. Tara's ancestors would have fled a nation being decimated by attacks from afar. Weapons which were delivered to their lands with devastating effect."

"How many came?" Symin asked.

"Millions of souls attempted the journey to Thres. Millions of those perished along the way. Hundreds of thousands wandered into our borders, tired and starved. We could not turn them back, to face sure death in the wars of their leaders."

"Why was Thres not involved?"

"Thres remained Neutral. Our borders were small, and reaching us was difficult. We had little contact with the outside world, beyond occasional trade in knowledge."

"Only knowledge?" Symin asked.

"We were not reliant on other nations for protection, our technology did that for us. Our technology enabled us to produce so much food and other necessities that we had no reliance on any other nation of the ancient world."

"Nobody tried to attack you?"

"Some tried. We defended ourselves in such a way that they did not try again. And when refugees ran, they ran to us because we had demonstrated empathy to those who did not come armed to the teeth."

"Do they still fight, I wonder?" Loka mused.

"I doubt it," Sena said. "If they did not stop, then they died. If so, you are all that is left. Cinder has remained isolated for the protection of its people. But that protection comes at the cost of knowledge. We have no way of knowing what remains of the old world."

"That's a depressing thought," Loka said. "What if there's nothing at all? What if they wait for us to reach out again, only to squash us?"

"We can not know until it happens," Sena said. "Which is why our mission is so important. If indeed Cinder is the only nation remaining alive, then we must save it. But if the others remain waiting to attack us, we must know that before it happens. Our mission may well open a way out of Cinder, but I hope it does not open the way in. My preference is that your people make the choice, and not those who would do them harm."

"Then we should get the caravan moving," Symin said. "No point sitting around waiting to be found."

As the caravan was packed and the horses hitched, five orange flame wielders were arranged on the lead wagon. As one they focused their energies and reached ahead, pushing the sand away from the ancient road.

Sand was thrown to north and south, the dunes to either side pushed away by the might of the orange flames as the caravan pushed its way east, deeper into the desert of souls.

Sometimes there would be a stone resting crooked, or even missing altogether, so the carts would jostle and bounce as they moved across the rougher terrain. But over all, the road was in remarkable condition for its age.

The travel was slow, but not nearly as slow as it would have been on raw sand, even with Treghan's efforts at dampening it. With the sun reaching its zenith, and the heat of the desert day striking them hard, the sand began to give way to hard dirt as the road climbed.

A rocky plateau in the heart of the desert, small but resilient, stretched a short way before them. The desert sand stretched to the horizon to the north and the south, but this small raised parcel of land stood defiant, the dunes failing to swallow it.

At the heart of the plateau, a group of stone buildings stood against the ravages of time. Symin dismounted from the second cart and signalled for Loka, Cara and Tara to follow him. Together, they approached the silent village with caution.

Wisps of sand skittered across the hard ground in the breeze as they reached the outlying remains of a low stone wall which circled the village. The wall was only the height of their knees, and there did not seem to be any part of it which remained complete.

Some of the stone was weathered and eroded, some was missing, possibly stolen for use in the buildings, or some other place.

"Careful, we don't know if the people here are friendly," Symin said.

"Or if there are any..." Cara said.

The four rangers passed the first building, which was gutted. Holes in the walls showed where wooden frames for windows and doors used to be, and the roof was long since caved in. Each house they passed stood in similar condition.

"The wood from these houses," Cara said. "It wasn't stolen, it decayed. This place has been abandoned for a long time."

They reached a central square, and at its heart stood an ancient well. Symin approached it, daring to hope, but only dry sand waited at its bottom. A handful of bleached bones from some form of small animal rested there, testament to the barren nature of the land.

"Sena," Symin said. "Tell me about this place."

"This would have been a bustling agricultural village. The land around here was fertile, and there would have been enormous amounts of food produced here and transported to the city. Villages like this were the heart of Thres."

"I see a tower, like the one at the oasis," Loka said, pointing.

"Yes, these places were valued and no expense was spared in providing them with the means to communicate with the city. And to defend themselves against dangers of the jungle, or dangers of invasion. Be careful here."

"Would their defences be active?" Cara asked.

"Thres built things to last, as you have seen," Sena replied. "But their defences may not be active, though the essence to run them would still be here. If it has been corrupted, as at the oasis, then they are still a danger to you."

"Then we shouldn't stay here?" Symin asked.

"No," Sena replied. "Your people will be safe where you stopped them, but do not camp within the village."

"We should be able to pass through though?" Tara asked.

"If the only danger is the essence, then it should be fine. But if they have defence machinery still operating..."

"Can you tell if it is?" Loka asked.

"The triggers will be buried, and the only test would be to walk over them. If they are armed. The people who lived here would not have armed them all the time. If they did, they would have been victim to them."

"So there may be ancient traps," Symin said. "But why would they be armed?"

"The locals may have set the traps before leaving," Cara said. "If they did not want valuable resources taken by somebody else."

"They did not leave," Sena said, the sadness in her voice palpable. "In fact, there is one among us who can say what happened."

"What do you mean?" Loka asked.

"This village was named Yallon. The boy, Hyren, his flame was born here. It will know whether the traps are set."

"Then we must speak to the boy," Cara said, turning to walk back towards the caravan.

They followed Cara, and soon Hyren was brought before them. He shuffled his feet in the dirt and stared down, afraid he had done something wrong.

"Hyren," Symin said. "Please, do not be fearful. You're not in trouble. But we must speak to your flame."

"But I haven't summoned it yet," Hyren admitted. "I've only known of my flame a short time, and I'm still not ready to summon it forth, like you do. I'm not strong enough."

"Sena says your flame was born in this place," Symin said. "We must ask it about this place."

"I'm sorry," Hyren said. "I wish I could help, but I can't summon my flame."

"That isn't necessary," Sena said. "Remember what I told you before, boy? About your flame?"

Hyren looked up at her as a realisation caused his jaw to drop.

"You said you asked my flame to lure the rangers. So you can talk to my flame, even though I can't summon it?"

"That's right. I only thought it rude to do so from the village without your knowledge, given the risks I already put you through."

"Then please, speak with my flame."

"Thank you, Hyren," Sena said, as she vanished.

They stood there for many minutes, unsure what to do next, waiting for Sena, before she finally appeared again. She had a sad air about her as she stood beside her bearer, looking at the ground much as Hyren had done earlier.

"What is it?" Symin asked. "Are the traps armed?"

"No..." she whispered.

"Then that's good news!" Symin said. "Why do you seem so upset by it?"

"The boy's flame, Wesnor, I spoke to him. He explained to me why the traps were not set. And it has made my guilt greater than it was before."

"Symin," Cara snapped. "Your flame speaks in riddles."

"Sena," Symin said. "Can you tell us what happened?"

The first flame looked at her bearer, and the flames of her face appeared to be rolling down, as though silent hot tears flowed from her eyes. She shook her head slowly then paused before nodding once and looking down.

"It was my fault," she said. "My actions have brought so much calamity."

"Why?" Loka asked. "What happened here?"

"The traps were never set," Sena said. "Because they never left. They were never given the choice."

"What do you mean?" Symin asked.

"I mean the people of this village, all of them, were turned to flame without any warning, without any knowledge of what was to happen. They were never told..." Sena's voice trailed off as she flickered, fading.

"Sena! Stay here," Symin ordered. "What weren't they told?"

She brightened, but she lost some of her hue, the yellow not as vibrant as before. Looking at her bearer, her eyes were pleading with him. But he would not relent. He would have the truth out of her. Her sigh was like a hissing flame doused with water.

"They were left ignorant of what we were planning to do. I had already become a flame. We knew what caused it, and we were proceeding with the plan anyway. We knew what would happen to the people of Thres, and we did it anyway. But I had requested all the citizens be told, such that they would have a choice to run or to stay and become flame as I had."

"So, you tried to warn them?" Loka said. "Then why is it your fault?"

"I trusted the council blindly. I never checked, I never insisted. I chose to believe all the people of Thres had been warned, and chose to become flames willingly, chose to fall with our nation instead of seeking new life in the north."

"You were innocent," Symin said. "You did nothing wrong."

"I was foolish, and my actions brought calamity to these people, who were not prepared for what was to come. They became flames with no knowledge of what had happened. They must have been terrified, alone, frightened out here in the wreckage of their homes."

"Well, it was one village. You can't be blamed for their misfortune," Cara said.

"Yes, I can," Sena said. "But it was not only one. I long wondered why the flames felt such disorientation in the beginning. They were all so confused, so difficult to speak to, to make listen. This is why. None of them were warned. The people of Thres, the entire nation, they weren't volunteers they were victims. And I was their abuser. I created the very thing which had torn their world away, and they did not know why."

"You are saying you were responsible, but what about this council you mentioned?" Symin said.

"Without me, without my work, my discovery, my transformation to a flame, without my brother and I presenting it all to them, they would never have considered the plan. I am guilty. My nation was murdered, and it was by my own hands."

Chapter 24 – Wells of Despair

Sand was pushed, thrown aside, and piled up high as the orange flames joined forces to clear the way. The ancient road continued to the east, and Treghan sat with his friends atop the lead cart. Symin sat nearby with Loka. Three days had passed since they found the lost village.

Gabraii shone in the air beside Treghan, the flames of his friends also manifest beside them. Where Loka sat, Kresai was standing, arms folded. But of Sena, there was no sign.

"Gabraii," Treghan said. "Why is Sena hiding?"

"The first flame blames herself for all flames." Gabraii replied.

"But do the flames blame her?" Corilai asked.

"They do not," Derieala said, answering for the others. "We all know what has become of us, we understand what we have become. We are thankful to live as we do, rather than not live at all."

"Can't you speak to her?" Treghan asked.

"We can not speak to her, if she does not wish to be spoken to." Ursaela said, glowing green beside Marni.

"Do you think Symin will be OK? Without Sena, I mean..." Fletcher asked.

"Symin will be fine," Gabraii said. "Sena can never leave him."

"But if she refuses to speak again..." Marni said.

"She must. Only the first flame knows the nature of our mission," the red flame Fearis said. "The first flame created us, at least so she believes. But we choose to continue as we have. She can not be blamed for our creation or our continuation."

"I don't get it," Fletcher admitted.

"Neither does Sena," Treghan said. "I get that. I mean, she discovered something amazing, and it changed her. That discovery then changed her world, destroyed her country, but was she the ruler? Was she the one who made the other flames happen?"

"She mentioned a council," Marni said. "They were the ones who did it."

"However, she gave them the power," Ursaela said. "This is why she carried the blame, and why she always has done so. This is why she leads us back to Tyra, to fix the thing which waits there."

"Ursaela," Corilai said. "You sound like you know something."

"I worked in essence supply when I was not a flame. I believe I know what she fears, and what she would have us change. It is not my place to speak of it."

Marni stood, wobbling as the cart rumbled along the stone road. Facing Symin, she looked back at her friends, before walking to the ranger.

"Ursaela," Marni said. "You may not feel that you can speak of that to us, but if you know what she fears, perhaps you can speak of it to her."

Symin looked up, as the green flame dissolved. He looked from where Ursaela had been to Marni, who stood there awkward as he raised an eyebrow.

"What is it, Student?" he snapped after a long silence.

"Well, Ursaela, my flame, she would speak with Sena. About… about why she..."

"Why she hides? It will do no good," Symin replied. "Sena's grief is deeper than even her bearer can reach."

"But one of her kind," Marni replied. "Perhaps she'll listen, at least enough to find… If not peace, perhaps less grief."

"It's worth letting her try," Loka said, Kresai nodding sagely.

"I know a little of Ursaela," Kresai said. "She worked supply, in Tyra. She likely knows a little of the science behind our existence. She would also know the application of the essence, and it may mean she can appease Sena's guilt."

"She will try, regardless of what we say," Symin moaned. "Sena will either listen, or she wont."

* * *

Ursaela returned to the plain of the flames, and looked around. She could see where Sena was, alone in the distance. Her being had sunk, to form a well in existence. Ursaela knew it for what it was. Sena was a mighty flame, but if she sunk much lower, she would be extinguished.

"Sena!" she screamed. "Please, we need you. Don't do this!"

Ursaela looked around. There were less flames here than normal. Perhaps because they were so deep in the desert, and perhaps because so many were summoned to the world of the rangers.

She was looking for a particular flame. Finally, she saw him sitting alone, some distance behind her. Ursaela approached the boy and knelt before him. The flame before her was young, in terms of its host, but she could see it had been old as a human, and had likely been old in a host or two before.

"Wesnor," Ursaela said. "I would speak with you."

'What is it, green one?" Wesnor replied.

"You spoke to the first flame," Ursaela said.

"What of it?"

"You told her things which have sent her to a well."

"Then that is as the wells wish it."

"No, that is not good enough. You are being foolish, old man," Ursaela reprimanded. "There is nothing more annoying than an old man, set in his ways, imbued with the youthful rebellion of his host. You must speak with her again."

"Why?" Wesnor demanded.

"Because she is the first flame. If not for her, we would all be long dead."

"Perhaps I wanted to die?" Wesnor snapped, pouting.

"I see, and you spoke to her like that?"

"What if I did?" Wesnor groaned. "I had seen my wife pass, before her time. I wanted to join her, but instead I became… this…"

"Wesnor..."

"I searched for her, once the confusion passed. But she was long gone. The essence had been freed from her by death. So when we were changed, there was nothing left of her to change."

"And you blame Sena for your own misfortune, of which she had no knowledge or control. You spiteful old idiot. You've had seven centuries to learn a thing or two, but you were too busy being a fool to ever grow. I'm sure your late wife must be so proud of her misbegotten sod of a husband."

"Then what would you have had me do?"

"Grow, blossom as a flame. This is a new life, not an extension. We have to forget the past, so we can create a better future. But you, you cynical old fool, all you can do is wallow in ancient history. So much so you drag others into your misery. You're the one should be sinking in a well, not Sena."

"How dare you!" Wesnor spat. "What can you know of my suffering?"

"Suffering?" Ursaela snapped. "You only know selfishness and greed. You were old, ready for death, but you were instead granted a new life. I was young. I had a baby, what life was that baby given? Snatched away before the essence could even imbue her body enough to create a flame. You were lucky, and became more so when you changed. But you refuse to be thankful, with your hate filled soul."

"I..." Wesnor stammered.

"Shut up!" Ursaela snapped, her anger growing. "Sena was great, powerful. At the depth you pushed her, you'd be extinguished already. Believe me, I've seen it happen. My own sister, she was twelve years old when we changed. We didn't know anything. She knew nothing of the old world, and suddenly she was forced into a new one, where nothing made sense."

Ursaela turned away from Wesnor, and looked to the distance, where Sena's well of grief pulsed and glowed, not as brightly as before. She took a step towards it, then faced Wesnor again.

"She couldn't cope. She couldn't understand any of this, it was alien to her, and so was I. She couldn't even recognise her own family any more!"

Ursaela flared, her green flames lashing out at the prone orange one. Wesnor cringed, retreating a little from her.

"Twelve years old, and so terribly alone. What could I do for her? Who could I blame?" Ursaela shouted. "I had to watch her, powerless, as she sank. I stood beside her well for days as she slowly faded away. She died twice, my beautiful sister, and neither was Sena's fault!"

Ursaela twirled away from him, droplets of green flung from her eyes as she ran towards Sena's well. Wesnor rose and followed, tentatively at first.

"Stay there!" Ursaela screamed. "You've done enough harm, you selfish old man. You know nothing of her suffering, or mine, yet you seek to claim it and lay your blame on others. Why don't you just die instead of her?"

Wesnor absorbed her words as he stood, but then he realised the truth of his folly. He ran, as Sena began to finally falter in her well.

"If she dies, she will never speak again," Wesnor shouted. "Sena! We forgave you, long ago!"

Ursaela glanced back as Wesnor passed her and dove into the well.

"Sena!" he screamed.

"Sena," Ursaela shouted. "Did you hear any of what we said? You were never to blame. We chose to continue, we chose to live as flames. Don't choose not to! Please, we need our first flame! We need our leader!"

Ursaela reached the well and stared into the depths. Far away, beyond her sight, the essence of Sena glowed softly in the darkness. Closer, she could see Wesnor, sputtering as he fell. How could she save them?

"Sena!" Ursaela shouted. "I never saw a well so deep! You are amazing! You are our first, our greatest, and our inspiration! Come back to us, please!"

She could barely hear Wesnor's voice, screaming his incoherent pleadings of guilt and remorse as he plunged to his likely extinguishing. Then, like a small miracle, a blinding flash of yellow rose from the depths.

A rushing wind and a soaring tower of flame burst skywards from the well, and then Sena was there, standing in its place, cradling the dull, almost lifeless orange flame in her arms.

"Wesnor," Ursaela said. "I'm sorry, I should never have pushed you to this."

"It's OK, Ursaela," he said, looking into her eyes for the first time. "You were right. I've been a fool. I only hope this is not the end for the rest of us. But I do not mind if it is the end for me."

"It will not be the end for you," Sena said. "Wesnor. In your long years, you grew wisdom we may yet need. You may have never used it, but now is the time. Begin."

Sena bent forward and breathed a little of her flame into the dull orange being, and he brightened. She placed him on the ground, and he looked around. Gradually, his flames grew normal, and he nodded.

"My fire is yours to command, first flame. Your people forgive you, your people acknowledge you. We will follow you as far as we must, through this life and the next, should we be granted one."

"That is not necessary. This life is your own," Sena said, then vanished.

"Where did she go?" Wesnor asked.

"She has returned to the human world," Ursaela said. "You, who have never been summoned, would not understand. But trust me when I tell you, it is worth waiting for. But now, I hear my bearer's call. I must leave you, old man. Please, stay safe. That boy needs you."

* * *

"Where were you?" Symin demanded. "I called, and you refused to come."

"I apologise, my bearer," Sena said. "It will not happen again. I will not return to that well."

"I don't know what you're talking about, Sena," Symin said. "But please, when things get to you like that, I'm here to help. I owe you that and more."

"Yes, Bearer," she said.

"Sena," Loka said. "Are we still on course for the mission you set us?"

"Yes and with the roads in such good repair we are gaining time every day."

"Good." Ursaela said. "Sena, thank you for coming back to us."

“Green one, you were in supply, in our old world?”

“Yes, First Flame.”

“I see, so you have suspicions of the nature of our mission?”

“I do. And I know how important it is that we succeed.”

“I see. Thank you for coming to find me.”

“Any time, First Flame.”

“Loka,” Symin said. “Do you have any idea what they’re talking about?”

“No, Symin.”

“Good, then I’m not just an idiot.”

“Oh, I wouldn’t go that far...” Loka said.

“Symin,” Marni said. “What are we here for? Do you know why Sena is taking us to the city of her people?”

“No,” Symin said.

“But you follow her anyway, and drag us all along for the ride?”

“Yes,” he said.

“You must trust her a lot,” Marni said.

“With all of our lives.”

“You see, Sena?” Marni said. “You have no blame to hold, only trust. If you have all of our trust, and that of the flames, then what guilt is there to grieve?”

“You see far more than you should, for a human,” Sena said, smiling. “Thank you for sending your flame.”

“I doubt I could have stopped her,” Marni said.

“Ranger!” came a sudden call from the orange flames in front.

Symin stood and walked forward. He immediately saw why they had called him. The road sat clear before him, broad and pristine, the sand shifted away to reveal a widening, before it came to an abrupt halt. A tall stone wall rose many heights of men into the air above the surface, stretching away into the dunes which buried it on either side.

Ahead, sand could be seen cresting as a mighty dune on the other side, rolling into the distance. There was an occasional roof top or wall of stone peeking through the depths of the desert. But there was barely any indication of what else, and in what condition, lay inside the wall.

“What is it?” Loka asked, standing beside him.

“I don’t know. Sena, do you know what this is?”

“I do,” the yellow flame said. “It is the wall of Tyra. We have reached the city, and it is more buried than I had dared fear. We have much work ahead of us.”

Chapter 25 – Sands of Tyra

Symin stood at the base of the wall, looking up at the bright morning sky above. No clouds broke up the endless blue, cut by the sharp line of the top of the wall. This was higher and stronger than anything he had seen in all of Cinder. They had camped beneath it the night before, and its long shadow had caused them to sleep long after sunrise.

"How do we get over that thing?" he mumbled.

"We must go around," Sena said, as she hovered in the air beside him. "The city has gates to the north and south. The place I wish to reach first is closer to the south than the north, and a little further to the east than the west."

"Then we turn south," Symin said. "And clear the sand from the wall as we go, until we reach the gates. Does the road continue all the way?"

"In the days of old, it did so. But there is no telling what the ravages of time and the cataclysm we wrought have done to it."

"Then we must try," Symin said. "But first, we have a problem. We need water. We can't keep going without finding some. Our supply has dwindled more than I am comfortable. What water did this city have?"

"There exists a large aquifer beneath the land south and west of the city," Sena said. "You should dig a well here, and replenish your supplies."

"Agreed," Symin said, turning to face the long line of carts, surrounded by his people. "Pirette!"

"Yes, Ranger?" Pirette said as he rushed to Symin.

"Gather the orange flame wielders. I need you to dig a well. We need a steady water supply."

"Yes, Ranger."

"When that is done," Symin said. "Start clearing the sand from the wall so we can travel along it. We turn south and we follow the wall."

"Yes, Sir!" Pirette said, with a firm salute, before turning and signalling for the orange flame wielders to join him.

Soon, a well provided enough water to refill their supply, and they fused the walls into glass so they could use the well again later. Then the orange flames turned their efforts to the road.

The sand flew out into the desert at the behest of Pirette and his people. A great plume of it was flung high into the air and far into the dunes, leaving nothing but bare stone where it once rested. As the road along the wall began to clear, Symin signalled for the carts to proceed.

They followed the orange flames as they worked along the curve of the wall south and east. The progress was slow, but Symin was unconcerned. The orange flames had worked tirelessly for days. Hopefully soon they could rest.

After three hours of slow but steady progress, the orange flames stopped.

"Ranger!" Pirette called, and waited for Symin to reach him. "There is a problem."

"What is it, Pirette?" Symin asked.

"See for yourself," Pirette said, pointing ahead.

Symin looked at a massive drift of sand for a few seconds before he saw the problem. Under the sand was rubble. A large section of the city wall had collapsed, and was strewn across the road in enormous boulders, buried buy the rolling dunes.

"There is a massive dune inside the city, and as we clear that pile and rubble away, it is threatening to come down on us," Pirette explained. "We can move the sand, but more will flow into its place. It may take a long time to clear it away. And then, the rubble waits beneath it all."

"What if we don't clear it?" Symin mused.

"What are you thinking, Ranger?" Pirette asked.

"I'm thinking about Glasswell. What if we do something similar here?"

"You're considering fusing the sand into glass and building a road over the top?" Pirette said, eyebrows raised. "I suppose it could work, provided the glass is not too fragile or slippery. We would need to extend the ramp up some distance behind us."

"If we do bricks, like at Glasswell, then fuse a sheet over the top, do you think you can grit it up before it sets? Cast sand in the surface so it has grip?"

"I think we could do something like that," Pirette said. "But try not to fall on it. That surface would cut you up pretty badly. It would make the grazes you get falling from your horse look like a paper cut."

"Good. Then you take your men and rest. The rest of us can do the heavy work. You've done your job till now, time for others to do theirs. I will call you when we are ready to lay the sheet over the top, and have you bring in the sand. We'll have you cast a thick layer on top as well. It occurs to me a shattering road would do a lot of harm to the horses, but a thick layer of sand will help, particularly if we have Treghan wet it down."

"Yes, Ranger," Pirette said, smiling as he turned to wave his men back to the carts.

Symin followed Pirette, and found Loka, speaking with Tara.

"Round up all the flames you can find. I want every able bodied ranger, student, or member of the order on this task. Bring them forward, and I will explain. Leave the orange flames to rest."

"Yes, Ranger," both women said, turning and walking along the carts, calling out anybody they found and sending them forward.

Symin soon had a large workforce melting sand into bricks and piling them along the edge of the rubble. Slowly, they piled them the full width of the road, and continued out, before piling more on top closer to the rubble.

Hyren, nimble as he was, climbed along the bricks to place his latest ones as far up the back as he could, when he heard a cracking noise. Hyren stopped and stood there as one, then another of the hastily made bricks shattered beneath his feet.

"Don't move!" Symin shouted as Hyren looked at his feet, shod in his flimsy cloth boots which were torn to shreds by the jagged glass.

Symin rushed back to the carts and searched the front three before he found Pirette.

"I need your help," Symin said, before running back to where the boy waited.

Pirette followed and saw the trouble immediately. With a wave of his hand, Pirette summoned sand from the nearest dunes and sprayed it over the bricks between them and the boy.

"The glass is too brittle to stand alone. It will rub against the other bricks, and likely many will shatter. You need a buffer between them. You need us to put sand between the bricks to act like a mortar and absorb the pressure of anything on top. It will also help stop the entire thing collapsing when you have the carts halfway up."

"Can you do it alone?" Symin asked. "Or do you need help?"

"I'll fetch one other, the rest can stay where they are," Pirette replied, returning to the carts to fetch his helper.

With the bricks before him covered in a thick layer of sand, Hyren gingerly made his way back to the rest of the rangers, and immediately got back to work making bricks. But now, he did not walk on them to place another layer on top, instead continuing to extend the reach of the bricks laid directly on the road surface.

Shortly, Pirette had returned with help, and together they coated the bricks with sand. They vibrated it so it fell to fill the gaps, before the rangers began walking on the sand to place the next layer. It was slow work and at midday Symin looked over their meagre efforts with dismay.

"This is taking so long," he moaned to Loka, who stood beside him as she so often did. "I fear this glass brick approach is too cumbersome."

"Have faith, my love," Loka said. "We have to do it right. You could fuse a single piece but then it might shatter, you could risk just rolling up sand, but then the carts might bog or tip. You chose this approach for a reason, so believe in it. There will be no second chances. And didn't Sena say something about us having made good time until now?"

"Indeed I did," Sena said, appearing before them. "We have made better time than I had hoped, but the amount of sand inside the walls will cost us much of what we have saved. I have led you here many months earlier than my best estimates had demanded, but even so, estimates can be wrong. The sooner we can get this mission done, the safer we all will be."

"What is it you fear?" Loka asked.

"The destruction of all life in Cinder," Sena said. "If we are successful though, we secure Cinder for millennia to come. Plus we may be able to open up the rest of the world again, if they are prepared to meet us."

"You make it sound like a mighty ambition," Symin said. "But I fear mighty disappointment awaits us instead."

"You must have faith in your abilities, and those of your companions, my bearer," Sena said. "You have been well trained for what we face, and our only enemy is fear and doubt."

"They are mighty adversaries indeed..." Symin mused.

"Only to the weak of will," Sena replied. "I did not choose my fourth bearer to be so afflicted. You are strong and able, and so is every ranger here. You have listened, and you have brought with you all that we will need. Your orange flames are showing their might already, and it is that might we will be leaning on when the time comes."

"But for what?" Symin asked.

"You will see," Sena said. "Trust me, and trust your judgement. But their task is better shown than told."

"So long as there remains the time we need..." Symin said. "Damn it, now I'm starting to talk like you!"

"Fear not, my bearer," Loka said, mocking the whisper of a flame. "The transition is over quickly..."

"Do not mock your flames," Sena scolded.

"I'm sorry, Sena."

"Apologise to your own flame, girl."

"Oh right. I'm sorry, Kresai."

"As you should be, child!" Kresai snapped, appearing beside Sena. "First flame, must you remain so mysterious? They have a right to know the goal you push them towards."

"You are correct, Kresai," Sena said. "But please, indulge me a little longer."

After a brief mid-day meal, the flame wielders returned to the task and worked until nightfall. Even so, Symin estimated they had progressed only a little beyond halfway to completion of the ramp to ascend the rubble, and then there was the matter of the other side.

"It's taking too long," he moaned that evening as he settled into his bed, Loka by his side.

"We'll finish the ascent tomorrow, and then see what's required after that," Loka replied. "But sleep now, my love, we all need the rest."

*   *   *

Symin woke before dawn, and as the light of morning began to stain the sky above, he was already at work. Gradually, the rest of the caravan's travellers joined him, until Marni interrupted them with a call for breakfast.

The students, along with Hyren and Jull, prepared a warming tea and a hearty porridge, which they served to everybody equally. As the workers ate, the sun finally crested over the wall, and some moaned when they looked and saw how much work remained.

"Don't worry, we'll complete this work before nightfall," Symin said, loud enough for them all to hear. "And then we will climb to the top and see what awaits us there."

Loka rested a hand on his shoulder and he looked at her. She smiled and he nodded his thanks for her endless support, then returned to his food. Quickly finishing he stood and started making bricks again.

The supply of sand, which had seemed endless, was starting to deplete in the immediate vicinity and Pirette moved a dune closer for them to use. The orange flames all joined the work, both making bricks and placing sand as the construction went on.

By mid afternoon, the ramp was looking close to completion, and Symin called a halt to the brick making. Pirette and three others spread a deep layer of sand the full length and width of the ramp, and then as a group all the flame wielders cast their fire upon it.

The sand melted and bubbled and fused into a blackened, shining glaze. Pirette and his helpers cast more sand over the top, to a hand's depth. Treghan drew on the moisture in the air as well as their water supplies to dampen the surface such that it settled and hardened enough for the horses to pull the carts up the slope.

Symin led the way as they all walked up the slope for the first time. They left the carts and horses at the bottom as they all assembled at the top of the ramp. The sun cast their shadows beyond the wall as they looked on a rough and rambling surface of stones and sand before them.

"Pirette, smooth it over, please," Symin said.

Pirette and his orange flames drew enormous amounts of sand from within the city wall, and spread it before them, to level out the surface. They then flamed it as they had done the ramp, before laying even more sand on top.

The result was a level field, large enough to set up camp, with a rough descent on the far side. Symin walked out onto the sand, and looked around. Soon, he was staring at the top of the wall, where it continued in the direction they wanted to go.

The wall was wide, as wide as two carts, and solid. Drifts of sand were cast over it, but the wall itself seemed to go on uninterrupted until the point where he assumed the southern gates had once stood.

"We camp here and go on tomorrow, along the top of the wall," Symin shouted, and his people immediately began the long descent to the carts.

Slowly, taking great care to listen for any breaking glass, they climbed to the top and set up camp without incident. Symin stood near the wall and looked out over an immense area.

Tyra had been large. At least five times the size of Emberdale, it was the largest single settlement he had ever seen. And the walls protected it all.

"Somewhere in there, something which could destroy us all is waiting," he mumbled as Cara joined him.

"Something which could teach us a lot about our world also," the archivist said. "Symin, I have a request. I would lead an expedition to explore and study this city. Vera was an incredible opportunity for us, but it holds nothing on the scale of this place and its secrets."

"Indeed," Symin said. "Let us first complete this mission, and I will gladly give such a project my blessing and recommendation to the Chancellor. Providing there is anything left by then."

"Thank you, Ranger," Cara said, walking away as Loka joined him.

"She wants to study it," Loka said. "But you fear it will be destroyed."

"Yes," Symin replied. "But look at the scale of it. If there is nothing left to study, then we will have released a great danger on our world indeed. Anything that could destroy this place would be something we must guard closely."

"And Sena feared it could destroy everything, not just this place. It must be a fearful power indeed."

"It must be," Symin said. "And I don't doubt it. This city once stood in jungle, only to be swallowed by sand. The more I think of that, the more I fear what we're here to do."

Chapter 26 – Legacy of Thres

At dawn the caravan began the slow journey along the top of the wall. They made careful progress, fearful the wall could collapse or present some other surprise, but no such things occurred.

Even so, it was afternoon by the time they arrived at the southern gate, to find the gates themselves missing, the wall stopping with a long drop to coble stones below.

By some miracle, the dunes had moved in such a way that the road in the vicinity of the gate was exposed. This meant of course that the travellers had no immediate way down.

Symin called the senior rangers into a meeting while the camp was set up. Treghan, Corilai, Marni and Fletcher all attended, but not because they were invited; the possibility they might not be did not occur to them.

"We have reached the southern entry to Tyra, and have some way to go before we arrive at our destination," Symin said. "Obviously, there is no readily available way to proceed."

"Any one of us could arrange that," Cara said. "Now we have access to water, the white flame could form an ice bridge. The greens could grow a ramp or a bridge with vegetation. The oranges could shape the sands..."

"Yes, these are all true," Symin said. "But we must decide if we will cross the gate and continue atop the wall or set out through the city from this point."

"I believe this place is a good point to operate from," Loka said. "Look around you. We have clear vision of the surrounding landscape, we have the height advantage, we have ample level ground for our camp. I suggest we set up base here, and then take missions of as many or as few people as we need to whatever parts of the city we must. A core of our people will remain here at all times, able to see any signal flames should an expedition strike trouble."

"Loka is correct," Cara said.

"I agree also," Tara said, her recently summoned green flame nodding sagely beside her. "And I am sure many of our flames have memories of this place to help in our missions, like my Haeretta."

"I have memories I would like to pursue," Ursaela said, before retreating behind Marni at the stares of the senior rangers.

"We are not here for sightseeing," Symin snapped, before softening his tone. "Expeditions which are important to our mission are to be our main focus. Anything else will have to wait."

"Yes, Ranger," Marni said, in place of her flame.

"Now," Symin said. "Sena, come forth!"

"I am here, my bearer," Sena said as she appeared before him.

"Please, I would like your input. We are to set up our base camp here, and take expeditions into the city."

"Yes, my bearer," Sena said. "We may need to find the research laboratories where my journey as a flame began; east of here and a fraction north. We also should visit the reservoir control facility, which Ursaela knows well. But first, in order to show you the nature of things, we will need to attend the chambers of the council of Thres, which was the seat of our government."

"So three main expeditions are to occur, starting with locating the chambers."

"We should scout ahead, while the others prepare our base here," Loka said.

"Agreed," Symin said. "With Sena to guide us, Loka and I will conduct reconnaissance of the council chambers, and return. Pirette will join us in case we need his orange flame. We will investigate what kind of excavations will be necessary and return for further personnel, dependant on what we find."

"Yes, Ranger," the others said in unison.

"And one other thing," Symin said, turning to the students. "You four are to stay here for the duration. Understood?"

"Symin," Loka said, before they could respond. "You should know better. Do you really think you can stop those four from going out there?"

"And getting into trouble? No. I suppose I can't, but even so… Everybody, this is unfamiliar territory. It may be abandoned, but it may still hold dangers for us. There are to be no unnecessary expeditions until we know everything is safe."

"Another thing," Loka said. "We are to stick together when out, and keep in contact with the base at all times through flares, or other signals. Symin needs to know at a moment's notice every person's whereabouts."

"Yes, Ranger," they all said.

"Loka, Pirette, we leave in one hour," Symin said. "Prepare everything you think we will need. I must speak to Sena."

* * *

Treghan stood on the edge of the wall, staring out at the immense buried city, rooftops and other signs of the ruins beneath the sand poking out of the dunes like a child's toys scattered across a sandpit.

Beside him, Corilai stood in silence. Marni and Fletcher sat nearby, their legs dangling over the side as they spoke, their words inaudible to Treghan and Corilai.

"I feel sorry for her," Corilai said, as she idly stroked Arool's head.

"Who?"

"Ursaela. She must have had something happen here."

"They all did," Treghan said.

"I know, but there was such sadness in what Ursaela said before, about wanting to pursue memories..."

"That's fine. We're going out there to find them. We're going to help her resolve those things. All four of us."

"Treghan, are you trying to get us in trouble?"

"No, but you heard Loka. They practically expect us to disobey. Isn't that how we get things done? With Yuri. With Dreighton. Every time, we get into the guts of the situation by being where we shouldn't be."

"And every time, it's a miracle we don't die!" Corilai snapped.

"But we haven't died yet, have we?" Treghan insisted.

"I guess not, and our flames are with us now. They can guide us as well."

"Exactly," Treghan said. "Gabraii, come forth."

"I am here, my bearer," Gabraii said.

"Tell me, how much do you know of this place?" Treghan asked.

"I know of the sector north and west of us. I was an administrator there for a time, before I moved outside the city. My ancestral home is an estate further to the north of the city, though I rarely ventured beyond its walls as a child."

"Where's that place where Ursaela worked?" Corilai asked.

"It is in the part of the city where I was administrator."

"Then will you help us to help her?" Treghan asked.

"It would be my honour," Gabraii said. "Ursaela is a fine flame of great might. She is worthy of respect."

"Good," Treghan said, kneeling to place a hand on the wall.

Drawing on the moisture in the stone, he summoned ice, and formed a narrow stairway to the sand below.

"We should hurry, the ice won't stay long in this heat. And I couldn't get any more than that out of these dry stones."

"Marni!" Corilai called, and the other two stood and joined them. "Come on, we're going to take Ursaela to find those memories she was worried about."

Marni nodded, and started down the stairs without a word. The other three and the wolf followed. In short order they reached the sand below and set out across the dunes. Ursaela hovered close to Marni as they trudged through the sand, her head hanging low.

"What is it you needed to see?" Marni asked softly.

"My home. It was that way," Ursaela said, pointing.

*　　　*　　　*

Symin watched, his brow deeply furrowed, scowling as he watched the four students and the wolf hike away from camp. Hunter, perched on his arm, followed Symin's gaze. Pirette stood beside them, a large pack on his back, stunned at the disobedience of the students.

"Aren't you going to do anything?" Pirette asked.

"We don't have time, but we should stop them," Symin said.

"Let them go," Sena said. "We will need Ursaela's input. If they can help her slay her demons, then she will be more assistance to us."

"Why will we need her?" Symin asked.

"She knows the supply systems for the essence, including the reservoir, better than any flame which remains."

"What does that mean? Flame that remains?"

"A flame can expire. If it gives up hope, loses any desire to live, it can collapse into a well and eventually it will be extinguished. In the early days, many were lost during the confusion."

"I'm ready, Symin," Loka said, handing him a satchel as she shouldered a heavy pack. "Let's get going."

"Thank you, Loka," Symin said, taking the satchel.

"When you're ready, Pirette," Symin said.

"Yes, Ranger," Pirette said, summoning a flurry of sand from the dunes to form a long, gently sloping ramp into the city.

"Thank you, Pirette," Symin said. "I'm sure we will be needing your help further before this expedition is over."

"Yes, Ranger," Pirette said.

Without saying anything more, Symin stepped out onto the ramp and made his way down, Loka and Pirette following close behind. Sena and Kresai followed their bearers, an air of nostalgia in their eyes.

"It has been a long time, since I was here," Kresai said.

"For me, also," Sena replied. "I journeyed here last a few hundred years ago. It has changed more than I expected. There was sand here then, but not this much."

"Which way, Sena?" Symin asked.

"As you leave the ramp, head directly north," Sena said. "We will need the bird I fear to find our target, but with this much sand..."

"We'll find it," Symin said. "I have no doubt of that."

"Pirette, have you not summoned your flame yet?" Symin asked.

"I have, but I have to confess, I am not yet comfortable with it. I believe my flame feels the same way."

"It does not come easily to all of us," Sena said. "Many flames have gone centuries without speaking to anybody, flame or human. In time, your rapport will grow. You already have a deep connection, as is the nature of a flame and its bearer."

"Thank you, Sena," Pirette said. "That is some comfort. I will admit to feeling somewhat a failure because of it."

"Do not," Sena said. "For some, this takes time. Jionne was a private, reserved human and is now a private, reserved flame. That does not mean Jionne feels any less of a connection to his bearer. It simply means he is still himself, and that is something of great importance to one who doubts their value."

"He will come, if you summon him," Kresai said. "Do not be reluctant to do so. You can not improve your situation by ignoring it. If his bearer does not summon even when he is able to do so, Jionne may come to believe he is not wanted."

"I guess that's true," Pirette said. "Perhaps I should. If he does not wish to speak, I will not make him, but his presence may be enough."

"More than so," Sena said.

"Jionne, come forth please," Pirette said.

The orange flame appeared, flickering and fluttering as his eyes darted about, unsure of his surroundings. Then he saw sena, and his gasp was an audible hiss as he looked at his feet and began to fade.

"Do not leave, young one," Sena said. "I will not harm you."

"Ye... Yes, first flame, Ma'am," Jionne stammered in a barely audible voice.

"You are still a child, even after all these years, Jionne," Sena said. "Tell me, where did you live, as a human boy?"

"We were in a small fishing village, a day's ride from Tyra," Jionne said.

"Wonderful," Sena said. "I used to love the sea. Please, I will have you tell me about your old home later, when we have returned to the camp."

"Yes, Ma'am."

They had already reached the end of Pirette's ramp and were walking up the side of a long dune, and as they reached the crest Symin stopped. The dune was swallowing a long row of buildings, the rooftops protruding from the far side. Stone shingled rooftops, many of which had survived the ravages of time, sat before him.

"It is amazing those have survived. Nothing we have now could withstand this time or these conditions," Symin said. "Will they support our weight, or collapse if we try to cross them?"

"Symin, think about it," Loka said. "Clearly the people of Thres were in possession of incredible engineering expertise. Further, these buildings have been swallowed by the dunes repeatedly over the centuries. Wouldn't they have collapsed already if they were going to?"

"I guess you're right," Symin said, walking down to the nearest roof and stepping onto it.

Crossing the building, he carefully dropped off the other side, to land in the sand and continue. One by one the others followed, and they soon ascended the next dune.

They hiked for the next hour, and still there seemed no less of the swallowed city before them. Symin turned and looked back the way they had come, and then looked to the east, his eyes following the long shadows.

"Perhaps we should have waited till morning," Symin mused.

"A bit late now," Loka quipped. "How about we set up camp in the next building we find?"

"Agreed," Symin said, and began walking again.

They crossed two more dunes, and the shadow of the far distant wall began to reach closer to them as the sky grew golden. On the back side of the second of those dunes, a tall building protruded. Parts of its roof were missing, but it was a long building, which reminded Symin of some of the larger apartment buildings in the heart of Emberdale.

The building was protruding perpendicular to the dune, and along the side Symin could see several windows, their shutters long since eroded away by the ravages of time. He slid down the dune to the roof, then worked his way to the edge, and navigated his way carefully to a window.

Swinging inside, Symin lit a bright yellow flame as he entered the ancient domicile. He waded through deep sand near the window, until he reached clear floor. It was a simple apartment, but it was more than enough for their needs.

Walking through, he found there was a single bedroom, a communal room, what he assumed was a bathroom containing a deep bath and many strange devices he couldn't begin to understand, and a doorway leading into a long corridor.

"We will camp here for the night," Symin said as the others joined him in the communal area of the apartment.

Chapter 27 – Ghosts of Tyra

The four students hiked through the sand, scrambling around ruins for a long time, following the flames who walked in front of them, apparently all knowing where they were going.

As the shadows began to grow long, they reached an area where the dunes had receded, leaving a large section of the city exposed. Ursaela suddenly darted ahead, fading slightly as she drew away from Marni. The others rushed after her, the students all anxious to keep up.

Ursaela led them on a twisting run through the abandoned, ancient streets, until she stood before a badly damaged building. It was two stories, a sizable house, but the years had taken their toll. The windows were gaping holes, the shutters long since rotted away. There was no door hanging over the flagstone, and the roof was partially collapsed.

Not waiting for anybody else to catch up, Ursaela rushed inside. Miraculously, some of the furniture inside was still there, though badly weathered. The green flame paused as she passed several pieces.

The flame crossed the main entry hall and entered a corridor through a doorway on the far side. She rushed to the far end and ascended the stairs she found there to arrive at the next level, where another corridor ran to the far end of the building.

By the time she stopped, at the second door on the left, everybody had caught up with her. Ursaela stared into the darkened room, her green light reflected back by the dull walls, the window blocked by a section of collapsed ceiling.

Treghan sparked a white flame and the light shone inside. Almost immediately, he extinguished it as Gabraii and Faeris stepped through the doorway, and it was as if the sun bathed the entire room.

An ancient, weathered cot stood in one corner of the room, and Ursaela rushed to it. Wavering, the green flame knelt on the floor, her eyes dimming to blackness as firey tears rained down her cheeks. The green flame's sobbing was an eery sound, whispered on the still air like fabric brushing against a stone wall.

It took a moment for the students to realise what they were hearing, and then Marni was kneeling beside her flame, longing to wrap her in a comforting embrace.

"How old was your child?" Marni asked softly.

"She was not yet a year old when we were transformed," Ursaela said. "Being so young, she was not yet fully imbued with the essence, so when it happened she was simply killed. She had no hope."

"Was her father here?" Treghan asked, then regretted it as the others glared at him.

"He was..." Ursaela said, pausing as she sobbed again, louder this time. "Her father was killed in an incident within the nation to our south, a few months before. I lived here with my parents and the rest of my family, before we were married. Only my sister remained by the time he died. I had been unable to stay in our married home after he perished, so I came here to look after her."

"That's horrible," Corilai whispered.

"It's fine. I have long wished to be here again, to say goodbye. I only had my child and my sister. I was beside my sister when she died, both as a human and as a flame. But I was not beside my child, and I was unable to come back to this world until now. Please, it is late outside. Let me stay here, just for tonight. It is good to finally say my goodbye."

"Just a second," Fletcher said. "Did you say a flame can die?"

"They can, if they lose hope. They will sink into a deep well in our world, and if they sink far enough the flame is extinguished. I sat for days by my sister's well, and was unable to save her."

"So you truly lost everybody," Marni said, the sadness in her voice echoed by the tears in her eyes. "We will stay here, for as long as you need."

"Thank you, my kind bearer," Ursaela said.

* * *

Symin and Loka slept on the floor, Pirette propped in the remains of an ancient armchair. The cold steel of the frame was not comfortable, and he made sure they knew about it, but nevertheless there he remained.

Waking early, Symin stood and left his sleeping lover there to explore the building. Entering the corridor, he walked to the next apartment and found it identical to the place they had slept. Sand was everywhere.

There was a variety of furniture remnants in the various rooms he explored, but obviously nothing in any condition to be useful after seven centuries of neglect. He spent an hour searching the building, but found nothing at all that he deemed of use or value.

"Symin!" Loka called. "What are you doing?"

"Just having a look around," he replied. "I'm coming back now."

Symin made his way back to his companions, to find Loka waiting with a hot cup of tea and some toasted bread, smeared with lard. He accepted it from her and devoured it quickly, thankful for the warmth.

"Thank you, Loka," he said, walking to look out the window where they had climbed in. "We should get an early start. The sun is rising now. It's a good time to head on out. Hunter!"

In response to his name, the bird flew from a corner of the room to Symin's offered arm, and the ranger climbed out, careful not to disturb the bird from his perch.

Once outside, Symin looked around, trying to remember which way they were headed. Loka climbed out and stood beside him, pointing downhill, along the side of the building.

"This way, remember?" Loka said, walking away.

Symin followed, Pirette climbing out and rushing to catch up to them. Sena flickered into the air beside Symin as he rushed to catch Loka.

"We need to hurry," Sena said. "I'm anxious to get this mission over with."

"Has something happened?" Symin asked.

"No, I'm just impatient. We flames don't sleep like you humans, so I've spent several hours waiting for you."

"Surely that's nothing compared to several centuries," Symin quipped.

"I suppose not," Sena conceded. "But just the same..."

"I know. When a project nears its climax, it's natural to feel anxious for its completion," Symin said. "We've experienced that. Don't worry, Sena, it will all go just fine."

They hiked for a long time, and the sand grew deeper in this part of the city. The rooftops protruded less, and the streets were now an impossible depth beneath their feet.

"Stop," Sena said. "We should have seen something of it by now. I think it is time to send your bird up, to get a look from above. I will commune with his flame. Please order him to fly."

"Hunter, fly!" Symin said as Sena vanished.

The bird flew high into the sky, and circled there, searching for something in the sand. After what felt like an eternity of waiting, Sena appeared.

"The bird sees a pattern in the sand behind us," Sena said. "Which seems to mimic the ornate roof of the council buildings. I believe we are on top of the place I wanted to find."

"You heard the first flame, Pirette. You think you can dig your way inside?"

"Yes, Ranger," Pirette said, setting about the task with abandon.

After a very short time, a small section of roof was exposed, and they moved to stand on it as Pirette continued. Even with the might of an orange flame to shift it, the task of moving all that sand was a long one. Slowly, as more of the building was exposed, the dunes around them grew.

"Pirette," Symin said. "Do you suppose you could shift those dunes away from us? They make me a little nervous."

"Yes, Ranger," Pirette replied. "But it's going to take time. Shall I find us an entry first?"

"I suppose that would be fine," Symin said.

Pirrette dug and flung sand in all directions for another hour before he exposed the edge of the roof and enough wall below to expose a window. They dropped down to peer inside. The room it entered into was three quarters filled with sand.

"Pirette," Symin said. "Empty the room, please."

"Yes, Ranger," Pirette replied, and soon the sand from inside had joined the mountainous dunes.

Symin led the way inside, Sena's flames lighting the room as they made their way across it and through a doorway on the other side. The sand was a fine layer along the floor of the corridor they entered, but fortunately that was the extent of the incursion.

"Please, you must follow me," Sena said, rushing ahead.

Struggling to keep up, the humans ran after the flame, who led them on a convoluted course through the building.

"Do you know where we're going?" Loka asked.

"Of course she does, girl!" Kresai snapped as she appeared beside Loka. "She is taking you to the records and training area. She spent a lot of time there while explaining her various discoveries to the council."

"Oh, of course she did," Pirette moaned. "But do we have to run quite so much?"

"You are welcome to stay behind and get lost," Kresai snapped. "I assure you, the first flame does not rush for no reason. There is much we must accomplish."

Finally, they came to a halt in a small compartment within a large room. It had walls that stood shoulder height, and within was a long bench covered in strange, dormant apparatus. Sturdy pipes ran from the ceiling and floor, joining several such compartments, and seemed to be still in good repair.

"Symin," Sena said, pointing at a junction in the pipes. "Turn that valve."

Symin did as he was told, and nothing happened.

"It is as I feared," Sena said. "The essence has been purged from this building. Probably one of the last orders the council gave to supply. We need to resupply for the equipment to work."

"How do we do that?" Loka asked.

"We need somebody who knows supply," Sena said. "Somebody familiar with the network, and how to operate the supply system from the reserviour control centre."

"Ursaela," Loka said. "This is why you said we would need her."

"Yes, it is part of the reason," Sena said. "I will see if I can find her. Please wait for me a little while. Once I have explained to her what I need, we will return to the base camp. It will take Ursaela some time to restart the supply to this building. By then, I would like to have all those who need to see this here to see it."

* * *

As dawn broke over Tyra, Treghan sat on the roof of the building, Gabraii by his side. Corilai leaned her head on his shoulder. Derieala was not there, but Arool was. As usual, the wolf stayed close to the girl's side.

Suddenly, Arool sat up, his ears alert, and he began to nudge Corilai, his eyes burning fierce and blue. Just then, Derieala appeared.

"The first flame seeks Ursaela," Derieala said. "Ursaela is not in our world. Is she still here?"

"She's inside, with Marni," Corilai said. "We will go to her."

Corilai stood, and treghan did likewise, following her as she climbed back into the bulding through the hole in the roof they had come out from. They made their way back to the room where Ursaela had not left the side of the cot throughout the night.

"Ursaela," Derieala said. "The first flame wishes to speak with you."

"OK," Ursaela said. "It is time I move on from this. Marni, I will return soon."

With that, Ursaela vanished. She was gone for several minutes, and then returned with an air of urgency as she appeared before Marni, her flames brighter than they had been in some time.

"My bearer," Ursaela said. "We must hurry. We must go to my former place of work. I have work I will need you to do for me, for the first flame, for Cinder. She needs us to reactivate supply of essence to the council buildings."

"Do you know the way?" Marni asked.

"Of course, I remember it like it was yesterday. Hopefully we don't need to shift any sand."

Running, they left the house and entered the streets. Ursaela led the way and they moved quickly for several blocks, until they arrived at a steep wall of sand. The dunes were in the way.

"We just have to climb it," Treghan said, ascending the dune on all fours, quickly moving ahead of the others.

Once they reached the peak of the dune, they rushed down the other side and up the next, and were covering good distance when Ursaela stopped.

"It should be here," she said. "But the sand, it covers everything."

"I'll move a dune away," Marni said, drawing seeds from her pouch and poking them into the sand. "Treghan, can you give them some water for me? Remember the mines? I'm going to try to do something similar."

Marni focused her energy as Treghan fed water, condensed from the air, into her seeds. The seeds sprouted, and sent roots deep into the sand. She ordered the roots to spread, to form a solid wall.

Once she was satisfied, Marni placed a second line of seeds. She pushed these roots down and then outwards, pushing the sand in their wake. She then placed a second wall, many paces from the first, before burning the roots between.

After nearly two hours of work, with the smoke clearing, Marni climbed down the roots into the resulting pit, and collapsed onto the floor, exhausted.

"Thank you, my bearer," Ursaela said. "You have exposed an entry to the supply facility. It lies immediately beyond these roots."

"I'll take care of that," Fletcher said, manifesting a mighty axe of red fire.

In a few strokes of the axe, Fletcher had exposed the doorway into a darkened building. A large drift of sand spread within, leaving only a narrow space below the ceiling. They made their way inside, crawling over the sand, following Ursaela's directions. As they gained access to rooms and corridors deeper inside, the level of the sand was lower and soon they were making a quick pace as they strode through the ancient facility.

Finally, they entered a room of gauges and dials, with a monstrous looking mess of pipes filling one half, all of them stretching out of the room, to spread their power to the rest of the city.

"My bearer, please, sit at that control panel. Turn the little dial at the extreme left, until it stops."

Marni sat on the ancient steel stool, and looked at the desk before her. A myriad of dials and gauges stared back at her, making no sense whatsoever. She looked to the left and saw the dial Ursaela had spoken of. She tried it one way, and it would not turn. Then the other, and it turned several rotations before it stopped.

At first nothing happened, and then a green glow began to grow from the desk, emitted from all the dials and gauges.

Chapter 28 – Supply

"Look here," Ursaela said, pointing to a transparent section of pipe while indicating a knob on the board with her other hand. "When the essence fills this level indicator, turn this dial to the right."

"OK," Marni said, watching the indicator.

The minutes passed and finally the green began to slowly climb into the transparent section. It crept up, slowly edging its way to the top of the transparency. When it was full, Marni wrenched the knob to the right, as far as it would turn.

A valve hissed, then a cap popped closed and there was silence. Marni looked up at Ursaela and was about to speak when there was a loud bang followed by another, louder one. The pipes hammered and the room shook, dust falling from the ceiling.

"Turn it back down!" Ursalea said, and Marni complied.

As the knob was rotated back to the left, the hammering eased and the noise subsided, but there remained a gentle hum as the liquid essence was pumped into long dry pipes.

"What if there's a leak?" Fletcher asked.

"We built our plumbing to last indefinitely," Ursaela said. "That hammering was caused by air in the pipes, and by filling the pipes slowly we push it out a valve at the far end of the section. We will do the same when we fill the lines to the council chambers, once the system is primed properly."

"Even so, it's been hundreds of years," Fletcher persisted. "What if something has broken?"

"It won't have broken," Ursaela said. "Our pipes are stronger than our buildings, or our roads and walls. They had to be. If the essence caused an explosion from the pressure inside the system…"

The green flame paused, flicking her eyes passed a series of dials before continuing.

"Well, my great grandparents lived through such an event, and we were determined not to see it happen again. So we made them impervious to such wear and tear as time alone would have inflicted."

"Nothing can last forever," Corilai said, feeling some of Fletcher's nervousness.

"Forever is a long time," Ursaela said. "And these pipes were rated to last just over ninety million operating hours."

"Ninety million hours?" Treghan said with a gasp, pausing to think for a moment. "That's, that's about ten thousand years!"

"Exactly," Ursaela said. "These pipes will not leak. They have barely reached ten percent of their yield time. And much of that time the system was not in operation."

Somewhere, a bell chimed, and Ursaela flew up to a second transparency, high on the wall. She watched as it filled, before a second bell chimed. Ursaela returned to Marni's side and began pointing to switches, knobs, and dials.

Marni operated the controls as she was instructed, seeming to know by instinct what her flame wanted. Finally, a third bell chimed and Ursaela stood back from the controls.

"The system is properly primed and ready for supply," the green flame said. "Now, we wait. The pressure will slowly equalise throughout the secondary supply links, and then a triple chime will sound, to let us know we can commence priming the supply lines to the council chambers."

"How long will that take?" Marni asked.

"Probably around an hour. We can have a look around while we wait if you would like."

* * *

Symin led the way back to the camp, moving quicker now they knew the way. As they travelled, Pirette cleared and levelled more of the dunes, so that the return would be easier. They made good time, and arrived at the base camp before dark.

"Welcome back, Sir," Cara said, greeting them as they reached the top of the ancient wall. "What did you find?"

"We found the ancient council chambers, which remain intact. We must return. I will need your assistance, as well as all the other orange flames, and Tara. The boy, Hyren, he should come also, given it was he who launched us along this path. The members of the order will want to attend also."

"I will make the preparations," Cara said. "But sir, there is a problem. The young ones, your students..."

"Are perfectly safe," Symin interrupted. "They are currently arranging the supply lines of essence from the place where Ursaela worked in ancient times, to the council chambers, such that the equipment there will operate for us once more."

"I see," Cara said. "I must apologise, Sir. When I found them missing, I feared an insurrection, or at least insubordination. Such a thing would lead to trouble for the young ones, as well as yourself. I am glad you were aware of their absence."

"You would be surprised what I am aware of with those four," Symin said. "They generally do as I require, even when they do not realise it."

"And especially when you don't realise it yourself..." Loka said in a teasing tone.

"Be that as it may, you must all be tired," Cara said. "Find yourself a meal, and I will inform the others that we leave at first light for the council chambers."

* * *

The four students wandered the corridors of the supply facility, afraid to touch anything, but fascinated by it all the same. Eventually they entered a large, open area dominated by immense doors peppered with transparencies. The ancient windows were scoured opaque by the centuries of sand, but had nonetheless mostly remained unbroken.

Some small streams of sand had managed to access the building through a handful of broken panels of the thick glass, but not sufficient to hamper their access. A long counter dominated the wall opposite the doors, and they turned to face it.

Faded by time, a giant mural covered the wall behind the counter. It showed a sprawling metropolis, backed by a verdant jungle, and both dominated by a sprawling network of green, luminescent pipes. The students gaped in awe at the spectacle.

"Is that Thres?" Corilai asked.

"It is the great and powerful nation of Thres," Derieala replied. "As seen from over the capital, Tyra, where we now stand."

"The painting was called *Kings of the Essence, Princes of Earth,* and is one of the greatest works of the artist Nersaii." Ursaela added. "I would pause to look at this painting every morning, when I arrived for my time in supply."

"I never saw the pipes glowing like that," Gabraii said. "But we all felt like they did. We drew power as a nation, and prosperity as a people, from the essence which flowed through them. They were beautiful in our eyes."

"It is sad that now they are grey and lifeless," Treghan said. "I'm sorry, I struggle to see the beauty in the real ones, but the painting shows them in a light I could not have imagined otherwise. I'm glad we came here."

"Then I am also glad we came, my bearer," Gabraii said.

With solemn respect for the fallen nation, the four students spent several minutes gazing at the painting. Their eyes gradually found each person, each house, each plant and stone in the world it showed them. And with each tiny detail, the picture grew larger in their minds.

"Thres was a place of wonders," Marni said.

"And such beauty," Corilai replied.

Three soft bells chimed in the distance, and the background hum of the pipes grew louder for a moment.

"We must return to the control room," Ursaela said.

Quickly, they made their way to the control room, where several new panels had become illuminated along the wall. Each showed, highlighted in a green glow, icons reminiscent of buildings.

"This one here," Ursaela said, pointing to one of the now lit panels. "Marni, hold your palm to the image and push it. When the light behind it blinks three times, release it. That will start the system priming and filling the pipes to the council chambers."

Stepping up to the panel, Marni placed her hand as instructed, and pushed gently. She felt a soft click as the panel recessed slightly, and she felt the vibrations from the humming of the pipes as she watched, and waited. After many seconds, the light blinked. Then after a shorter wait it blinked again and then a third time, and she removed her hand.

"Our job here is completed, for now," Ursaela said, then pointed to a second panel. "But we may save ourselves returning here, if we press this one also."

Marni pressed the indicated panel, which immediately blinked three times and sounded a chime.

"What was that?" Marni asked.

"The panel was to activate the supply to the facility where Sena once worked. It was the place it all began, and the place from which Thres was ended. I feel Sena may require us to do something there, so we should be prepared. But it makes sense the supply was never purged. They would have operated it to the last second."

"So what now?" Marni asked.

"I suggest we return to my former home and rest," Ursaela said. "In the morning, we make our way to the council chambers."

"Agreed," Treghan said. "We should get there quickly, before the sun sets."

"The sun is likely already close to that now," Gabraii said. "We have been in here a long time now."

Together, the students made their way out of the building, the same way they had entered it. As they climbed up out of the plant framed trench and back onto the dunes, the sun was low in the western sky. With their shadows long on the sand, they walked as quickly as they were able, their flames close beside them, until they finally reached the area without dunes.

A steady wind had picked up, and sand blasted at them, stinging their faces. Sand drifted in stinging waves across the ancient streets, and the city streets accepted it like an old friend.

"The dunes will swallow this area again soon," Treghan said. "I wonder how many times these buildings have seen the sky and then been covered again?"

"Many times, I would guess," Fletcher said. "It is amazing that they still stand."

"We built our city to serve our descendants well," Faeris said. "It saddens me to see it this way."

"At least we get to see it again," Ursaela said. "Even in ruins, Thres is mighty."

"That it is," Gabraii said, then began to sing.

"As we rise, through our dreams,"

"And into our streets," Ursaela sang, joining him.

"What's that?" Marni asked.

"It is our anthem, the national song of Thres," Derieala said, and she too joined the song.

"We follow our hearts," Faeris sang with them, their voices rising in an emotional torrent, filling the air of the city with its long silenced anthem.

"But why is it in our language?" Marni asked. "The language of Cinder."

"We do not sing your language," Ursaela said as the singing stopped. "You speak ours. Thres created Cinder. And Cinder was created to forget the conflicts and struggles of the old world. So Cinder was given only one language. The language of Thres."

As the students considered Ursaela's words, the flames all sang together, their voices clearer and louder than their bearers had ever heard before. The song was caught by the still air and drifted the lonely streets.

"And those of our fathers, the dreams of our children and the songs of the unborn. Together as one people, and with the love of our Earth, Thres the mighty nation, our country of peace, she will stand forever, and we stand with her."

As the last notes of the ancient song faded, and the streets returned to silence, the wind began to blow again. The sand answered the plea of their song, as if telling them its time was over.

"That's beautiful," Corilai said,

"But what does it mean?" Marni asked.

"It begins with the dreams," Ursaela explained. "Which we have as children. Then as adults we leave the home, into the streets, where we work. In working we pursue those dreams and the dreams of our country, in an effort to allow our children to dream, and the cycle starts again. We are all one people, with our colleagues, our friends, our family, our ancestors and our descendants. All of life, all of Thres, is one long dream."

Soon after, they arrived at the former home of Ursaela, and they settled in for the evening. Much was spoken of, but the solemnity of the song remained with them as they ate their evening meal and eventually found their way into sleep.

Chapter 29 – Records

At daybreak, the students set out from the home of Ursaela, walking east. Ursaela led the way, but the other flames were not summoned. It was at times hard going in the sand, but they made good time. By noon, they reached the crest of a dune, and looked down on a scene of intense activity.

A large contingent from the base camp had already arrived at the council buildings. The orange flames were hard at work clearing all sand from the area and they could see Symin, standing with Loka and Malthus, directing the activity. Most of the flames were not present. Even Sena was missing.

Treghan rushed down the dune, leading the way as the others followed. They soon arrived before the scout and waited as he barked orders to a group nearby, before turning his attention to them. He looked at them with a stern expression for a moment, before speaking.

"Did you complete the task Sena set?" he asked.

"Yes, Ranger," Treghan said.

"Good. But if you run off like that again without good reason, there will be consequences. There nearly was. I can't protect you from trouble all the time. Do you understand?"

"Yes, Ranger," Treghan said. "What do you want us to do now?"

"Nothing. Just stay close by. We will be entering the building shortly. You are to be near me at all times. Sena may have need of you."

"Yes, Ranger," the students all said, as Symin turned and began speaking to Cara, who had just approached.

Treghan turned and offered a smile to his friends, who all looked worried.

"Don't fret it," he said. "We're not in any real trouble. And it looks like we're finally going to find out why we're here."

"Yeah," Corilai said. "It feels like things are finally getting a move on."

"My bearer," Ursaela said. "I would like to go and rest. Also, I will find Sena and ask what she needs of me."

"That's fine," Marni said. "Thank you for everything."

Ursaela nodded, then faded away. Marni looked at her friends, then sat cross legged on the ground. The other students joined her as Hyren and Jull approached.

"What are you doing here?" Fletcher asked. "I thought Symin would have made you stay at the base camp."

"Sena insisted we come along," Hyren replied. "Me because, like she said before, I was the reason this started, and Jull because she says it will help her to know her flame. She says this mission will help Jull and I learn to summon them."

"You're an orange flame aren't you, Hyren?" Marni said. "I'm surprised you're not helping with the sand."

"I'm not that good at it yet. I think I was more in the way than anything."

Without warning, the four flames of the students burst into existence by their bearers. At the same time, Sena appeared by Symin, a short distance away. Flames began to appear beside other rangers.

"Summon your flames, those who have not the ability to appear at will,"

Sena demanded.

A chorus of voices echoed around the area as the remaining flames were summoned. It was an amazing sight. The students looked around at the dozens of flames, tall and bright beside their bearers.

Sena approached, leaving Symin a few steps away, and knelt before Hyren. She placed her hand on his shoulder and looked into his eyes.

"Do not fear, young one," the first flame said. "I know you have not summoned Wesnor before, but now is the time. We may need him with us. And if not, he deserves to be here to see what his actions at my behest set in motion. Summon him child, I shall lend you my assistance."

"Wesnor," Hyren said.

'Wesnor," Sena said.

"Come forth," Hyren and Sena said in unison.

Falteringly at first, and then with growing brightness, Wesnor appeared in the air beside Hyren.

"My bearer, I am summoned," Wesnor said, then turned to face Sena, bowing low. "First flame, it is my honour to be summoned thusly."

"Welcome, Wesnor," Sena replied, before returning to Symin.

The first flame and her bearer spoke softly and at length, unheard by the others. Then, turning to look out over the crowded flames and their bearers, Symin raised a hand high, looking up at the sky. Lowering his hand, he looked at the people before him.

"My friends, we are here at the behest of Sena, the first flame, of whom I am the bearer," he said, pausing to look around and stepping closer to the nearby building before continuing. "This building holds detailed records of the nation of Thres, and of the incidents around the creation of the flames and the birth of Cinder."

The scout raised a hand again, and the crowd gave him silence, their attention entirely on him and his flame.

"We will now enter this place and Sena, the first flame, will use the facilities inside to show us what it is we must do and why it is we are here. The students are to remain close to me. The rest of you are to assemble inside as best you can and please do not make undue noise. I would like you all to see and hear what it is we are about to learn."

"Yes, Ranger!" the crowd said all at once.

Symin turned and walked to the opening where mighty doors had once stood and stepped inside. The students followed close behind and one by one the rest followed them. The light from all their flames turned the night like interior to day, as they made their way through the network of corridors deep inside the large building.

After many minutes they entered an enormous chamber, dominated by a long row of tables at one end. The light of the flames glistened from shiny controls on many panels set into the walls and on the tables and piles of dust littered the floor, occasionally punctuated by tattered remnants of ancient manuscripts.

"This is the hall of records," Sena announced. "Symin, please approach the centre table and I will instruct you on its use. We will see what knowledge has survived in this place."

The students followed close behind as the scout approached the table as instructed. Slowly the rest of the people filed inside. Sena murmured to her bearer, the others unable to hear, and he operated controls on the table as the last of the people entered.

A soft whirring noise filled the room as the tables lit up, and beams of light thrust into the air over their heads.

"Good, Ursaela's work was not in vain," Sena said. "The records machines still operate. Symin, speak to the table. Ask for record Sena, 438, discovery, and 439, demise."

"Table," Symin said. "Please show record Sena, 438, Discovery, and 439, Demise."

The green lights coalesced and a holographic image grew in the air overhead. From somewhere unknown, a strange voice which was almost like Sena's narrated as an immense and strange map appeared.

"In the late thirteenth dynasty of Thres, this was the world. Thres ruled itself and the northern plateaux, but had not the will for dominion over others. Thres, a peaceful nation of intellectual and spiritual study, had sent forth envoys to all corners of the world."

Lines began to crawl across the map and they realised the centre, where the lines started from, was the city of Tyra. The lines spread across countless strange lands and over vast oceans. One even stretched up from the land into the sky, where it flitted between a number of strange, floating citadels which appeared there.

"The nations of the world were many, and varied greatly. But none shared the technology of Thres, and none shared the interest in humanity and enlightenment that Thres wished to give them."

Some parts of the map began to flash, one after another. And borders appeared in bold lines. The lines moved and fluctuated as nations battled and borders changed.

"Our envoys brought back strange things. New technologies, different from our own, and cultural artefacts of great interest to the scholars of Thres. However, they never achieved the trust of our neighbours, and were unable to guide the nearby nations away from paths of war and conflict."

Many regions flashed more, and the borders began to fluctuate rapidly. The voice continued.

"As the rest of the world began to fight, nations bickering over land, resources, and technology, Thres remained neutral, refusing to take a side in the conflict. And to the north of Thres, much to the envy of our neighbours, lay vast expanses of empty land."

The lines of the envoys began to retreat to Tyra as the flashes of the nations and the changing of the borders became more intense.

"Among the many things our envoys brought home was knowledge of a strange technology from the far west. This technology was a way of creating limitless energy from the building blocks of the world. They called it Atomic and with it the nations in the far west built bombs of incredible power."

The flashing nations blinked rapidly, the borders shifted, and the nations of the far west expanded their borders rapidly. Myriad lines began to flow towards Thres.

"The power of atomic technology gave unprecedented advantage to those who wielded it. They began to over run their neighbours, and then the neighbours of those neighbours, swallowing the world in rage. Those who ran and escaped from that tyranny flooded towards Thres, seeking refuge."

The image grew, swelling as it zoomed in on vast plains, covered in fleeing humanity. It panned over the map to show Tyra, standing proud and safe in the heart of a mighty jungle. The teeming throngs of refugees rushed towards the walled city.

"We welcomed the refugees, but we could not house them. So we sent them into our northern wastes, a vast expanse of land we did not have use for. We allowed them to claim it as their home, as new citizens of Thres, provided they left their old ways of war behind. It was to be a new home of peace, or no home for them at all."

"Meanwhile, we continue to study the things brought home by our envoys. As the nations with the atomic weapons spread across the world, we began to fear attack. They showed themselves as unscrupulous. But then another power arose over the see to the east. They also used the atomic weapons, and began to attack back. Enormous expanses of land were laid waste as the two powers tried to wipe each other out."

The image zoomed out to show highlighted areas where the atomic bombs had rendered the land uninhabitable.

"This war was becoming a danger to all of humanity. The atomic weapons not only killed millions of people, they also rendered the land deadly to those who remained. And as they destroyed land, they expanded their borders. One day soon, they would reach Thres, and we must find a way to defend ourselves. If we failed, then humanity may well be destroyed."

The image zoomed in to Tyra, then in further to a building in the south east of the city.

"Here I, Sena, am now studying the atomic, to see what we can use against it. We believe that our technology, using the essence, might lead us to a way of stopping the atomic, but it carries great risk. May we find a way."

The image stopped, then faded as the voice spoke it's final few words.

"End of record."

A new voice then spoke.

"I Maarlo dictate the final record of my Sister, Sena."

As the voice spoke, a new image appeared. It was a small room. Symin gasped, as he recognised the laboratory from his dreams.

"Sena was studying the atomic technology of the warring nations, seeking to find ways of neutralising it in order to prevent Thres falling to their aggression."

A young woman entered the lab and took a vial, placing it into a canister in the centre of the room.

"Seeking to contain the atomic energy, Sena attempted a series of experiments with essence."

The image then showed a close up of the canister. It was divided, the essence in one side and something else in the other.

"Sena took the waste product of the atomic, and placed it along-side the essence. But on the day of her seventeenth experiment, she grew careless. A single drop of essence spilled, to make contact with the atomic substance she was working with. The resulting explosion destroyed the laboratory, and she was instantly vaporised."

The image changed to show the destroyed lab and a young man poking through the rubble. Suddenly he began to glow.

"The essence had done something strange, aside from the destruction. Sena was not merely destroyed. She was transformed. I sensed her around me and then within me. And I called to her."

Sena, as the rangers new her, then appeared in the image as a flame beside the young man,

"The destructive power was beyond belief, and the transformation of Sena even more so. I took this information to the council and they have now concocted a plan. We will use the atomic and the essence to build a selection of bombs. We will set them in place surrounding the northern lands. We will detonate them, causing the land to shift in such a way nobody will be able to enter from the outside. We will crack the very crust of the earth and thrust the northern lands towards the west, to create an immense mountain range, while rending the sea floor to the east and to the south. Mighty Thres will be destroyed, to leave an impenetrable desert. We will warn our people that they may flee to the north, but those who remain, being imbued with essence as Sena was, will become as she is now. Immortal flames. End of Record."

As the image faded, the room erupted into heated discussion as the rangers and the members of the order began to talk about what they had seen and heard. Symin stood and faced them, raising his hands high.

"Silence!" Symin shouted, waiting till they complied before facing Sena. "My flame, this is most intriguing, but it does not answer the question of our mission."

"Play record Theya, 749," Sena said, and the table complied.

"This is supply technician Theya," a voice said.

This time, no image appeared. The voice was hollow, matter of fact and slow.

"This is the first presentation for new workers at the Tyra General Supply facility. We supply essence to all of Thres via our network of pipes and aqueducts which carry essence to all corners of the nation. We are able to manage this task due to our main reservoir, which rests deep beneath the city of Tyra. The main reservoir contains approximately four hundred million barrels of essence at any one time, and covers an area almost as large as the city itself."

"Halt record," Sena said, then turned to face the crowd. "Beneath this city is a deposit of essence as large as Theya states in this record. And within the laboratory facility where I once worked remains a deposit of the atomic substances. Our containment was imperfect, and the cooling systems will fail. In fact, they may already be failing. I was able to calculate approximately when, which is why we are here now. Those systems are due to fail, and when they do that deposit will become unstable. It will begin going through a process known as melt down."

"Melt down?" Cara asked. "What's that?"

"As the name implies," Sena said. "The substance will move downwards. It will breach its containment and melt down, through the rock, and will sometime soon after reach the reservoir of essence. You have seen what a single drop did to myself and the laboratory. The bombs which were used to shift the land and isolate Cinder, of which there were seventeen, each had an amount of essence which you could fit in a single hand. Should the atomic impact a deposit as large as that beneath Tyra, the world would be destroyed utterly. Nothing living would survive. Perhaps even flames would be extinguished, though I prefer not to find out. This is our mission. We must remove the essence from beneath the city. Once that is done, perhaps we can turn our attention to the cooling and containment systems, if they last that long. If we look at them first and fail..."

"That," Cara said. "Would be bad."

"Indeed," Sena said, raising her voice in a tone of finality. "We must defuse the waiting bomb, before we try to salvage that facility."

Chapter 30 – Reservoir

Ursaela led the way back to the supply facility. The students and several rangers all followed, with Pirette and Cara levelling sand and blasting dunes aside as they walked. Symin and Loka walked in silence as they made haste across Tyra. No flames were summoned apart from the green flame they all followed.

"Do we have a plan?" Fletcher asked.

"We must see the reservoir," Symin said. "And we must investigate ways of draining it."

"It can be drained from the supply facility control room by pumping it to any section of the system, but we will need a new reservoir wherever it goes," Ursaela said.

"Will that do the job?" Treghan asked.

"Not on its own," Ursaela replied. "We can pump most of it out, but the inlets to the system will not get it all. There will be irregularities in the floor of the reservoir, and the pipes will lose suction before the essence is fully drained."

"And here I was thinking your people had created a perfect system," Loka said.

"No system is perfect, they only need to be fool proof," Ursaela said. "But there is more. Once we pump all the essence out, and manage to clear out whatever essence remains, we will need to make sure the system can not flow back. There will be some residual essence in the pipes, and if the system is left that will naturally return to the reservoir."

"Then we need a way to move essence," Symin said. "The way Pirette is moving the sand."

"We have it," Sena said, appearing beside Symin. "Did you not realise?"

"Realise what?" Symin asked.

"I suppose it is to be expected," Sena groaned. "The order had the essence but not the secondary powers, and the rangers had secondary powers but no essence, so nobody was going to figure this out. Think about your own abilities, Symin. The ones you gain from being my bearer."

"I can sense things around me," Symin said. "What of it?"

"You can sense essence. You see flames, because you see their essence. You can sense other things because they all exist both within and without your reality. Because it all has an essence, even in places where Thres never distilled it into the substance we used to power our technology."

"What's your point?" Loka asked.

"The yellow flame has the ability to not only see, but to control essence, in much the same way the orange flame can control earth, or the white flame can control water and ice, or the blue flame can control lightning. Yellow flames can move the residual essence out of the reservoir by pushing it into the pipes."

"Are you sure?" Treghan asked.

"Don't be stupid, boy," Sena snapped. "Who am I? What colour am I? Nobody could be more sure of this than I am."

"And what about the problem of it flowing back later?" Fletcher asked.

"We have enough orange flames here to fill the reservoir with sand, and enough sand in the city to fill the reservoir," Sena said. "All we need is the new reservoir."

"That will take some time," Symin said. "Perhaps we should send for help."

"I will summon Barache," Sena said. "He will bring your help. Remember, for flames there is no distance too great for communication. And Barache underwent the training to summon in Horde."

"It will still take him some time to get here," Symin said. "But it sounds like we have a lot of work to get on with."

"Indeed we do," Sena said.

"We are here," Ursaela said as they arrived at the supply facility. "The service entry to the reservoir is in the rear of the building."

The green flame led the way and soon they were descending a long staircase. It led them deep underground, until they arrived in an enormous vaulted cavern. The green light of Ursaela and the yellow of Sena did not reach the far side. Before them, a long low railing of steel ran along the edge of a walkway which led into the distance in either direction.

A small barge with some strange equipment mounted in a scaffold rested against a dock nearby. There was no movement on the surface of the enormous green expanse.

"It's amazing," Corilai said.

"Please, nobody fall in," Treghan said. "That looks deep."

"It is four heights of men to the floor of the reservoir," Ursaela said. "And two to the ceiling."

"How far is it to the other side?" Marni asked.

"Almost as far as the farthest wall of Tyra," Ursaela said.

"This is an enormous supply of essence," Symin said. "It will be difficult to move it all, and difficult to store it as well."

"Shall I tell you my plan?" Sena said. "I have been thinking a long time about it."

"Of course," Symin said.

"We will dig a new reservoir to the west. We will melt the sand on the bottom to hold it in. We will open one of the system pipes which leaves the city for the towns and villages which were in the jungle, and place that into the new reservoir. Ursaela can then guide you through the process of draining the reservoir."

"It's a monumental task," Loka said. "We will be at this for some months. The students will already be due in classes in the coming days."

"They'll have to catch up later," Symin said. "They've done so before."

"What comes after that?" Fletcher asked.

"We use yellow flames to shift the residual essence from the old reservoir," Sena said. "Before the orange flames pump the sand in. While you wait for your help, you get started moving all the available sand in the city near to the supply facility, ready to be pushed in. And you get started digging the new reservoir."

“And at the end of it all, there will be a huge green lake outside the city,” Marni mused.

“No,” Sena said. “we must seal it in. I will not take any risk of the essence somehow being brought into the city, where it can make contact with the atomic material. Those in the order of the essence can tell you, the essence is malleable. It can be changed, but not destroyed. Apply heat to the surface and the essence will congeal. It will then hold the sand of the desert on top, and no storms or other events will shift it. Bury it deep, and it will stay buried.”

“And what about Symin?” Marni asked. “Can he really control it?”

“Symin,” Sena said. “I know you can. Because I can. Focus your attention on the essence before us, and beckon it to rise.”

Hesitating, Symin gazed out across the green subterranean lake, before raising an arm out beyond the railing. The ranger focussed his mind and gazed into the green, and the green gazed back. He called to it silently, and it responded. A tendril of essence rose from the lake and swirled around the ranger.

Shocked, Symin gasped, and the tendril dropped. It splashed as it struck the walkway and railing, before trickling back into the depths.

“While we wait for the reservoir to be built, all yellow flames are to train here, so we’re prepared for the final task,” Symin said. “We must be certain Barache sends more yellow flames to help us with this work.”

* * *

Barache stood on his balcony at his offices in Grey. He watched as the bird circled before landing. As he picked up the pigeon, cradling it, he turned to walk inside.

“My bearer,” came the now familiar voice. “I have news and a request from Sena.”

“Sena?” Barache said. “That’s Symin’s flame, is it not?”

“It is, my bearer.”

“Tell me then.”

“They are in need of assistance. Particularly more orange flames, and as many yellow flames as you can spare. They say all other help will be welcomed also.”

“We have few to spare here. I will send word to the chancellor.”

“No rangers in Emberdale have summoned as yet,” the flame said.

“I will send the pigeon. It means a delay, but they should be on their way within the week. I would like to join them, but I have much to do here.”

“My bearer, you should wait until they have the roads cleared.”

“But they will be best served to have somebody who has summoned, so they can be guided across the desert.”

“The order will have many such people in Horde. Do not fret, my bearer.”

“You’re right, of course,” Barache said as he sat and began writing his report to send with the bird. “Some days, I fear my youth has left me to die here.”

"It has left us both here, with much work to still accomplish before we are released from our bond," the flame said.

"You're right, again," Barache said, smiling as he wrote. "We'll direct the rangers from Emberdale to make their way to Horde. Please advise Sena and request she find a flame to guide them from there.

"Yes, my bearer."

* * *

Weeks passed as Tyra was slowly revealed. The sands were piled close to the supply facility. The archivist, Cara, was giddy with excitement as she watched the ancient ruins uncovered one by one.

Even with as many orange flames as they had, it was going to take weeks to complete even this portion of their task as they must take care not to destroy the ruins. The rangers all took comfort in the knowledge that help was coming soon. They had two mountains of sand in the city; One near the supply facility and one Sena insisted they leave untouched over the area where the ancient research facility was.

It was three weeks after the day Barache had sent his note when they received word. The rangers from Emberdale had marched out of Horde with three members of the Order as guides. A force of fifty rangers, all orange and yellow flames.

Finally, a mighty mountain of sand dominated Tyra, perched beside the supply facility, covering a large section of the city. Except for the old research facility, the rest of the city was cleared of sand. It lay spread out before the rangers like an ancient time capsule.

It looked like any other city they had seen only much larger, and everywhere those pipes carried the power of Thres. Symin and many other yellow flame wielders had trained for hours every day. Many were as proficient at controlling the essence as the orange flames were with sand.

When the reinforcements arrived, Symin stood on the western wall, the new arrivals with him, to look out into the desert.

"Look to the west and you see an empty wasteland," Symin said. "Look behind you and see the ancient city of Tyra."

Symin cast his arms in a sweeping motion, taking in all of it.

"In the west, we must dig. We must dig an area as large as the city behind, and as deep as the mightiest harbour you know. And we must be quick and efficient in our work. Orange flames, I leave you to that task under the guidance of Pirette. Yellow flames, you are to follow me."

The scout led the yellow flames into the city to the supply facility, to descend into the depths below. Once there, he summoned Sena to commence training them in their task.

Outside, the desert sand flew in a mighty torrent as the orange flames dug. Inside, the green essence flew in a mighty torrent as the yellow flames trained. The sand was piled to form a mountain dwarfing the sand inside the city walls. On the fourth day Pirette summoned Symin.

"What is it?" Symin said as he approached the orange flame wielder where he waited atop the wall.

"Look below," Pirette said. "Do you see it?"

Symin looked into the pit and saw the network of pipes, tangled like roots of the city as they crossed the expanse of the excavations. The pipes were long and less sturdy than those in the city, which ran above ground and across open air.

"I see," Symin said. "You fear the pipes will sag and then break before we finish digging."

"Yes," Pirette said. "We need to support them so we can break them when we're ready and not before. Also, we are beneath the level of the sand. The ground now is harder, rockier. It is much harder to dig."

"Do you remember Glasswell?" Symin asked.

"Yes," Pirette said. "But how do we do that? As we dig, we would be chasing falling bricks because the earth will move."

"Dig shafts down, and fuse the walls into glass. Then pour molten sand in to fill them. Be sure to dig the shafts deeper than the reservoir will be. Use those shafts to support the pipes, then continue your excavations. It will cause a delay, but is safer, and will be less delay than a bunch of drowned orange flames. Besides, this means we will not have to redirect flow from elsewhere. We can push it from those pipes, once we break them."

"Yes, Ranger," Pirette said, rushing to get down from the wall and issue the instructions.

Slowly, the pit took shape, and as it grew deeper the walls grew less stable. As each day went by there was another collapse, but they dug it out and continued.

With only orange flames at work, being buried alive was not an issue. Those trapped would merely push the mound of sand away and continue working. But it highlighted a problem. They needed to build walls. Pirette summoned Symin again.

"Symin," he said as the scout arrived. "I have a favour to ask of your yellow flames."

"What is it?" Symin replied.

"I would like them to melt sand over the walls of the basin, to create an immense glass shield, to stop the collapses."

"But what if the glass falls?" Symin asked.

"I hope it doesn't," Pirette said. "But that brings me to a second issue. The soil is growing moist in the bottom."

"Then we can solve that issue as well," Symin said. "We will have the yellow flames do as you ask, and I will have Treghan draw out the moisture and use it to build ice supports. Once the basin is completed, the glass walls and floor can be fused and the ice removed."

"Thank you, Sir," Pirette said.

Weeks crawled by and there were more collapses, though less than before. Twice, the glass walls cracked, and they were lucky to get everybody out without harm before sections gave way. As the basin grew deeper, the glass walls required extension, and this made a weak point.

Cara suggested they spread a new layer over the join, but this proved difficult. Still, the rangers persevered, until finally Sena declared her approval of the depth and they began the task of sealing the floor.

Finally complete, the reservoir had taken them over two months to complete from that first moment Ursaela had led Symin and the others beneath the supply facility. It now stood glistening in the desert sun, an immense glassy bowl, dotted with pillars to support the pipes of Thres.

"It could have been quicker," Symin said, looking over their work. "If it was merely shovelling sand. But we had to take care. This was an enormous engineering project, not simply digging a hole."

"That's true," Pirette replied. "Filling the old reservoir will be incredibly fast in comparison. Simply throwing sand in a hole is a simple task, compared to this."

Chapter 31 – Urgency

Tord was fascinated by the essence. He was young, having graduated only two years ago from the academy, and already found himself on such an important mission as the one in Tyra. And now, there was this stuff he could control with his yellow flame!

Intent on becoming the greatest of the yellow flames in Tyra, Tord crept into the ancient reservoir each night, when the rest of the rangers were retired for the evening. Tonight was no different.

Reaching the bottom of the stairs, he paused to look out over the dark lake. He held a small golden flame in the palm of his hand for guidance as he began to walk around the edge, following the railing as he had been doing each evening. He paused for a moment as his head throbbed and his gut lurched.

"Must be some desert virus," Tord moaned. "It's getting worse. Oh well, I'm sure I'll shake it off in a few days."

He continued walking, taking nearly an hour to reach the place he had been training in private, away from prying eyes. He wanted to surprise everybody with his prowess, when the time came for the yellows to do their work.

Stopping there, Tord doused his flame and waited as his eyes adjusted to the darkness. Gradually, he began to perceive the things around him. There was the railing, there was the nearby pillar which supported the vaulted ceiling, and there was the lake of essence, stretching out before him. All of it marked out in his vision by the subtle, almost invisible red glow which came from the ceiling.

Tord had told nobody about the glow. It was his little secret. He only found it by accident. The young man had no idea what was causing it, or if anyone else could see it, but it meant he could focus on his secondary without using energy on lighting while he was down there.

He began his routines, and at first he though it was good. But then his gut lurched again, and his head span.

"What is with this migraine?" he moaned, clutching the railing to steady himself. "Why am I feeling so sick?"

He turned and began feeling his way along the railing, back the way he had come. Suddenly overcome with nauseousness, Tord vomited, a long stream of bile following his stomach contents. It burned his throat as it came from him, beyond his control. He wretched and gagged, the noise echoing across the lake.

"Who's down there?" came a voice from ahead.

Tord looked up, deciding whether to respond, but found he had not the strength to do so. Falling to his knees the young man struggled, fighting against his own demise, willing his body to move, to let him back up. It refused and then, with a splash, Tord fell.

"Am I going to die here?" Tord whispered, then saw the yellow light rushing towards him as he lost consciousness.

*　　　　*　　　　*

Sena was frantic as Symin carried the limp young man up the stairs. She rushed back and forth, down the stairs a little way then up to the top, her anxiety unusual and worrying to Symin.

"Why are you so upset?" Symin asked as he reached the top of the stairs. "We didn't even know the lad, not aside from training."

"Put him down, I have to know," Sena said.

Symin propped Tord up against the wall in a sitting position, and tapped his face until his eyes opened. The man groaned, then turned to one side, vomiting a small amount of bile onto the floor.

"Young man, what did you see down there? How long have you been sneaking in there?" Sena demanded.

"What?" Tord moaned. "About two weeks now, I've been sneaking in each night. I go that far around because I can work without a light."

"Why?" Sena asked.

"Why? I want to be the best..." Tord mumbled.

"Not that, it's obvious. I meant why don't you need a light?"

"Oh, because there's a glow down there. It's hard to see, but if you wait long enough for your eyes to adjust there is a red glow. It was just enough that I could sort of make out the railing and the essence, and practice without using my energy making light."

"Curse it all!" Sena screamed, rushing off down the corridor. "Hurry, Bearer, and bring him with you! We're running out of time."

"Sena!" Symin shouted, picking up Tord and stumbling after her. "What's going on?"

She flitted back to him to speak, glancing arround in anxious tension as she did so.

"The atomic has almost reached the reservoir. The glow means it's melting down faster than I thought. That's why this fool is so ill. It's the atomic illness. It happens to those exposed to it."

"What can we do for him?" Symin asked as he stumbled after her.

"Nothing," Sena said. "We can only try to make him comfortable. But more importantly, if we don't hurry up, we'll all be dead. Every man, woman and child in Cinder. If the atomic melts through the ceiling, it's over."

They rushed out of the building, and headed for the camp. Two orange flames nearby saw them and rushed to help carry the stricken man.

"What happened?" one of them asked.

"We'll explain later," Sena shouted. "We have to put him somewhere, and find every ranger we can rouse. We have to start draining the reservoir, right now. We're all out of time!"

Rangers in the area began to respond to the noise. Two took Tord into a small building, and Sena led the rest out to the new reservior. They stood and looked for a short time at the pipes, suspended over the top. A large group of flames followed, lighting the area.

"Ursaela!" Sena said.

Marni was running to catch them as her flame appeared beside the first flame, growing brighter as her bearer approached.

"Ursaela," Sena repeated. "Can we break these pipes or will they need to be primed first?"

"We should prime them first, to do so after we break them will mean we have less pressure in the pipes to start with, and that will mean a slower drain of the reservoir."

"Then get in that supply facility, and call me when the pipes are primed!"

"Yes, First Flame," Ursaeala said, leading Marni away as Fletcher and Treghan turned to follow her.

"You two, wait here," Sena said. "She can handle it alone. Red flame, we need your weaponry to smash the pipe."

"Which one?" Fletcher asked.

"All of them!" Sena said. "But the big one there in the middle is the important one."

"OK," Fletcher said, manifesting an enormous molten axe and spinning it over his head with a grin.

"That thing looks ridiculous!" Treghan said.

"You're just jealous," Fletcher replied.

"Perhaps a little..."

They waited ten minutes while Marni and Ursaela made their way to the control room. Then, a loud shudder rattled the pipes, followed by an intense banging as the air inside was hammered by the sudden change in pressure caused by essence being pumped in.

"Wait for my signal," Sena said as Fletcher walked towards the edge of the new reservoir. "And everybody stand back from the edge."

The pipes grumbled and groaned as the essence filled them, and somewhere in the distance a pressure valve screamed. One of the smaller pipes out over the glassy dam popped a rivet from a join and burst, spraying green mist high into the air.

"You might not need me," Fletcher quipped.

The pipes groaned louder, then a second of the smaller ones hissed as another joint popped, spraying a second burst of mist into the air. Then, the pipes seemed to settle down and after a few more minutes, Sena turned to face Fletcher.

"Do it now," she said.

With a grin, Fletcher walked to the edge, and looked out at the pipes. He raised the axe, thought for a moment, then turned to Treghan.

"Hey, can you give me a platform?"

"OK," Treghan replied, walking to stand beside his twin and holding his hands out.

Slowly, Treghan drew the moisture from the night air and set it to freeze, pushing a narrow walkway out over the reservoir. He then grew a single frozen leg to the bottom, to support the end of the platform as Fletcher stepped onto it. The structure wobbled, but held.

Fletcher reached the end and stood there, poised to strike. As he raised the axe over his head, the ice wobbled dangerously.

"That's not going to work!" Tara yelled, pulling a seed pouch from her belt. “Hold on, I’ll support it with some plants.”

The green flame wielder strode to the edge and knelt down, poking several seeds into the ground and focussing her energy. The vines rushed out along the platform and down, strengthening it well beyond what the ice alone could achieve. After a few minutes of growth, Tara stood and smiled.

“There you go, now you can do it safely.”

Fletcher grinned, raised the axe, and struck the pipe with all his might. The molten axe hit hard, bit into the pipe, and stuck. He wrestled it for a moment, unable to shift it, before he realised what it was. He took a deep breath and dissolved the axe, recreating it in his hands to raise again.

Three more times, the axe bit the pipe and did not sever it, but now it was leaking. A spurt of green was spraying Fletcher as he dropped the axe onto the pipe for the fifth time, and it sliced through it.

The impact caused the long arm of pipe from the far side to swing away wildly, before breaking near the opposite bank of the reservoir and falling to the bottom, while a gushing flow of essence poured into the deep, glassy basin.

Dripping, Fletcher walked back to the others, as Marni ran to meet them. Pulling off her cloak, she rushed to Fletcher and used it to mop the essence from his face, before drying his arms and body.

“Don’t go getting soaked in that stuff!” Marni scolded. “It’s dangerous!”

“What now?” Corilai asked.

“Now, we wait,” Sena said. “As soon as the old reservoir is reduced to around a third of its depth, we will need the yellow flame wielders in there pushing it to this end to force it into the system. Once they have it pushed across and the rest empty, I would like Treghan to build an ice wall, to hold back the sand while the orange flames start moving it in. The sooner the back end where the radiation is has been filled, the safer we all will be.”

“How long will it take?” Treghan asked.

“This is an enormous amount of liquid to move. It will take some time. A few days perhaps.”

“We should set a watch in the old reservoir,” Cara said. “So we can act immediately should the situation change.”

“That is a good idea,” Sena said. “However we must strictly limit the time anybody is down there. Tord spent his time training for three hours a day near the entrance, but spent an additional two to three hours each evening at the far end where the atomic material will eventually break through. He will likely not survive that exposure. I believe we should limit all humans to one hour per day maximum in the old reservoir. Two if it is near the entrance.”

“There are thirty two yellow flames here,” Symin said. “If we break them into teams of four, they can get the essence moved to the near end before we use our allotted daily time. We then get the retaining wall built and all yellow flames come outside for twenty four hours while the sand is back filled by the orange flames.”

“Agreed,” Pirette said. “We will fill the sand as quickly as we can, but it will take many days. We will be limited even though we have fourty nine of us. Similarly I would like us in teams. But moving the sand will require a line up of several orange flame wielders."

Pirette walked to look out over the reservoir and watched as the essence flowed into the glassy basin. He thought for a moment before turning to face the others again.

"The ones near the entry will be fine for a while, but those working deeper in will need to swap out regularly. I would predict six of us in the reservoir, two in the stairs, and two outside shifting it in. We will need to swap out those six within the first two hours. Four after an hour. Those people could continue to work outside, but we will be limited in how quick we can get it done."

"So the sand filling will be limited to around twelve hours a day?" Loka said. "This will take us a long time. Can we afford it, Sena?"

"As long as the retaining wall holds the essence at bay, even should the worst happen and the melt down reaches the old reservoir, there should be no explosion. But should that occur, we must seal the reservoir as it sits at that time."

"OK, I have one more suggestion," Symin said. "Before we begin, we send in two who are neither yellow nor orange, with ropes. They circumnavigate the old reservoir until they meet at the far end. Then, starting there, they tie ropes from the railing at ten pace intervals, moving back around opposite sides, until they reach the stairs. That gives us ready escape for anybody in the reservoir at any point in the operation."

"I'll go," Fletcher said.

"Me Too," Treghan replied.

"Marni and I will help carry the ropes," Corilai said. "You'll need a lot of them."

"No," Treghan said. "Bad enough we take the risk, I don't want you in danger as well."

"They won't need to carry them all the way," Fletcher said. "We can start attaching the ropes from the stairs and then when we meet at the end, we run back. Meanwhile, the girls can carry ropes down to the bottom of the stairs a few at a time. We can run back to grab them as we need them."

"Then it is settled," Symin said. "But if you take too long, we'll call you all back. If necessary, I am sure we can find more volunteers to finish the job."

Together, everybody returned within the city walls and set about finding enough ropes. They took ropes from the tents, from the carts, even bed sheets. Everything that might be useful was taken and placed at the top of the stairs to the reservoir.

Not waiting to rest for the evening, as soon as there was enough to get started, Treghan and Fletcher grabbed a handful of the ropes and ran down the stairs. As planned, they started at the entry and tied the ropes, tossing them over the edge and moving to the next point.

They worked quickly, the girls carrying the rest of the ropes down for them as they went. But even so, as the first hour passed they had not reached the halfway point. Loka and Tara came down, dragging a further supply of ropes they had found somewhere.

"Treghan!" Loka called. "Fletcher! Get out of here. You've done your time. Girls, you go as well. You all should get some rest. We can finish this off."

Feeling exhausted, having completed a full day of duties before commencing this task, the four students mumbled their acknowledgements as they left, climbing the stairs as the two rangers took over.

Chapter 32 – The Operation

Although they rushed to get the ropes fitted, the draining of the reservoir was slow, and three full days passed before they were able to commence the operation. Symin led six yellow flame wielders into the reservoir on the morning of the fourth day, with the level of the essence inside having dropped below a third over night.

They made their way to the furthest end of the reservoir, and aligned themselves along the railing. Their flames lit the chamber, bright and golden as they stood by their bearers. Symin, at one end, grasped the rope and swung himself over the railing, planting his feet on the reservoir wall. His companions did the same, and he looked along at them.

“At my call, we climb down,” Symin shouted. “As soon as you reach the level of the essence, you are to push it back with everything you have. As you reach the floor, you are to walk with the essence, and continue walking until our relief arrives in a little under an hour. Understood?”

“Yes, Ranger,” the other five said in unison.

Pushing himself out a little from the wall, Symin allowed the rope to slip through his hands as his feet returned to the stones and slid. He watched as the others did the same, making their way slowly down the wall.

The reservoir was deeper than he anticipated, and it seemed to be taking a long while to make their way down. Then, the ranger nearest to Symin slipped. His hands fumbled on the rope, slick with essence, and he fell with a startled shout.

There was a loud splash as the man fell into the essence, and Symin was already rushing his descent, steadying his resolve as he focused his energy. The man splashed around in the essence, then sank below the surface.

“Liran can’t swim!” shouted the girl on the next rope from the man, rushing to keep pace with Symin.

“Push the essence back!” Symin shouted, as he forced his energy out to do the same.

As they reached the level of the green slimy liquid, both Symin and the girl forced every effort into pushing the essence away. Their two yellow flames did the same. Soon the man’s head rose above the receding liquid.

Liran coughed and spluttered, gasping for breath between wracking convulsions, before falling back, his head dropping beneath the liquid, his gaping mouth filling as he fell still.

“Sena!” Symin shouted. “Send for help!”

“Yes, my bearer,” Sena replied, the area darkening as she vanished.

Soon, footsteps could be heard in the distance as Symin and the girl both reached the floor of the reservoir. Struggling to hold the essence at bay, the two rangers rushed to Liran’s side. Together, they dragged the man to the wall, and tied the rope to his belt.

As they raced to grab their own ropes, the others reached them, the essence rushing in to splash against the wall. As they gathered around the man, who had fallen limp and stopped responding, Symin barked out his orders.

"You two, hold the essence away from us. Young lady, what's your name?"

"Kirelle," the girl said.

"Kirelle," Symin said. "Your quick action saved this man. Help me roll him on his side, we must clear his airways, he may have swallowed essence, and will vomit as well. You other two, while we work on him, climb up and be ready to pull him up by the rope."

"Yes, Sir!" two of the rangers said, climbing the ropes as they heard the loud echoes of running feet coming towards them on the walkway.

Symin and Kirelle turned Liran over, and Kirelle lifted his body, to angle his head to the ground and drain the liquid in his mouth. A spray of green liquid splashed on Kirelle's knees and feet as she crouched beside him.

"Is he breathing?" Symin asked.

Laying the man flat again, Kirelle leaned down, placing her cheek near the man's face.

"No," she replied as she immediately grasped his nose to close it and planted her mouth over his.

She gave Liran her breath three times, as Symin positioned himself to compress Liran's chest. Five quick compressions as the academy training had taught him, and then she gave her breath again.

There was debate as to how many breaths and compressions they should do, but both rangers knew any amount was better than none, so they continued their efforts for three more cycles before Liran lurched, spluttered, and vomited an enormous spray of essence across himself and the stone floor.

On sudden impulse, Symin summoned his energy and drew the rest of the essence out of the man. It splattered on the floor also, drawing a further gasp and a look of sharp rebuke from Liran.

"Hey! How is he?" came a shouted voice from above, the help having arrived.

"He's conscious," Symin shouted as Liran groaned. "Pull him up."

As the rope tugged, Liran groaned and mumbled incoherently. Kirelle guided his hands to hold the rope as the rangers above dragged him out of the reservoir.

"We have no time to waste," Symin said. "Kirelle, we have a job to do. Let's get this shift done without him."

"Yes, Ranger," Kirelle said, turning and pushing with the two rangers who had not let up while they revived Liran.

"OK, back down here you two, we need to get this job done. Leave the others to take him out of here," Symin shouted at his team members who had climbed up earlier.

"Yes, Ranger!" said the two yellow flame wielders as they vaulted back over the railing and slid down the ropes.

Together, Symin and his remaining five team members pushed the essence back, walking with it as the next thirty minutes passed. It seemed no time at all before their relief arrived, running across the floor to meet them.

"Sir," one of them said. "We're here to take over. Please take your break."

"How's Liran?" Symin asked.

"He's the one who fell in?" the man said. "He'll be fine, though he reports feeling rather unwell. It's no surprise if he swallowed as much essence as they say."

"Good. Keep the line, and keep pushing. We have a long way to go," Symin said as he waved his group back.

They ran to the ropes, climbed up, and then rushed out of the reservoir, while the fresh and rested group of six renewed the efforts to push the essence back. As they ran, Kirelle shouted to Symin.

"Sir, is it just me, or is it getting hotter down here?"

"I hope it's just you," Symin said. "I hadn't noticed."

"If the temperature is going up, our time is running short," Sena said. "We should start filling the sand now, we can't afford to wait."

"Agreed," Symin said. "As soon as we reach the top, I will summon Pirette."

"I have already called him," Sena replied. "The orange bearers will commence immediately. We will have to work without the retaining wall for now. Once the essence is pushed into the final third of the reservoir, we put in the wall and fill the sand as deep as we can."

"Agreed," Symin said as he reached the stairs.

Pirette and three others rushed past them, as Symin and his group made their way up.

"Stick to the right," Pirette said. "We'll guide the sand flow down one side of the stairs, so people can use the other side."

"Good thinking," Symin shouted as he climbed the stairs. "Good luck, Pirette, we will send your relief in an hour."

As they reached the top, they passed another orange bearer, feeding sand down the stairs. They rushed out of the facility, and as they made their way towards a nearby building where refreshments were available, Loka found them.

"Symin," she said. "I'm glad you're OK."

"Of course I am," Symin said. "But poor Liran was not so lucky."

"So I saw," Loka replied. "But he will recover."

"Yes, and I am sure he will remain a fine ranger, once he is back on his feet," Symin said.

"I have some other news," Loka said, grabbing his arm to lead him away from the others. "It's Tord. The young man you pulled out of there a few nights ago."

"What is it?" Symin said, fearing the worst.

"While you were down there, he drew his final breath. There was nothing we could do for him. This place, it killed him. How do we defeat an enemy like this?"

"That's sad news. We must ensure his sacrifice is not forgotten. He was here with the commitment to save our nation which we all share. Wait, what do you mean enemy?"

"This place has killed one of our own. But it's not an adversary, a person or creature we can control or tame. This place, it has lethal, ancient dangers which can kill us without ever being seen. How do we handle this?"

"It wasn't an animal, a person or a monster which killed Tord," Symin said. "It was an environment, a thing, it was as though he fell into a volcano, or drowned."

He sat on a stone bench and Loka sat beside him. Symin looked at her face and smiled as he brushed her jaw with his fingers.

"When a place has dangers, we must study them, and learn to avoid being killed by them. We learned to swim, so we wouldn't drown. We learned to build better homes and harness fire so we wouldn't freeze in the mountains. We'll learn to cope with the atomic and its dangers as well."

"Wasn't that what Thres was doing?" Loka said. "All their study, all their knowledge, it only left us with their danger to clean up. We'd be best served if we buried this place, and left the atomic to history."

"You may be right," Symin said. "Sena, what say you?"

"This is why I demanded you leave that area around the research facility buried. The radiation from the materials stored there can not leak out into the city if it remains buried. Should you uncover it, somebody may be tempted to see what is within and then they might break the seal my people placed over it. That seal can be broken, as is proven by the melt down. Stay away from that area. Once the reservoir is filled, seal it as well. I will have your people directed on what to use. We must not let the atomic be used ever again."

*　　　　*　　　　*

As the last shift of yellow flame wielders for the day entered the reservoir, Tara, Marni and Treghan entered with them. Already, the essence had passed the two third line, and the three rangers placed themselves at that point on the walkway. Drawing on the moisture around them, Treghan began to form his ice barrier.

"There's not going to be enough moisture for a strong enough barrier," Treghan said. "That's why I asked for your help. Once, it's all the way across, you should be able to make your way along it. Plant your seeds and grow your vines to cover the ice. Between us, we will make a wall that can hold the sand at bay while the yellows finish the job."

He drew every drop of moisture he could from the air around them, and began to set his ice in place. As the wall grew across the reservoir, Marni and Tara took out their seed pouches and began to grow their vines. Together, the three of them walked out onto the wall as it grew, and continued across until they had used nearly their allotted hour. Just in time, they reached the far side, and made their way out as the yellow flames climbed the vines and left with them.

"When the work resumes, we will finish this," Tara said. "The orange will fill it with sand, the yellows will push out the last of the essence, and this dreadful place will be sealed up for good."

* * *

Two days of pushing sand, and the back half of the reservoir was topped to the walkway. The temperature was rising more noticeably now, and the yellow flames stood near the massive intake pipe where the essence was drawn into the system, holding back the green ooze which remained in the pipes as the orange flames pushed in more and more sand

Gradually, they raised the level of the sand in the area where the yellow flame wielders worked. The yellow wielders, for their part, remained focused on the task at hand, simply stepping up onto each new layer as the sand was pushed in.

As they reached the top edge of the intake, Pirette climbed in with them and pushed sand up the pipe as the yellow flames pushed the essence deeper inside. Once a strong plug of sand was in place, they all climbed out and soon the sand began to climb in earnest.

The yellow flames, no longer needed, retreated to the outside while the orange flames continued. Outside, they ran out of sand from the city and began to pull in sand from outside the walls. They were confident there would be enough.

Pirette, coughing and spluttering, ran up the stairs, to meet Symin.

"What is it Pirette?"

"It's getting too hot in there now. And the air is beginning to smell strange."

"Get everybody out of there!" Sena shouted, a raspy noise on the wind which nevertheless conveyed her urgency.

Pirette turned and shouted down the stairs.

"Evacuate! All rangers get out now!"

One by one, the orange wielders made their way up and out of the stair well, while others continued pushing the sand in.

"Everybody, hurl as much sand in there as you can! Quickly now!" Symin shouted.

Flurries of sand were dragged from every where the rangers could find it, and the sand being shoved into the stairs soon blocked the way for anybody wanting to get down there.

As they pushed, the sand inside the chamber was shoved deeper in, and still they pushed more and more into the waiting cavern. Soon, the ground long since buried around that end of the city began to see air for the first time in centuries as the sand ran low.

Still they drew on more of it, massive writhing tentacles of sand converging on the supply facility like some mystical, all devouring monster intent on ravaging the city.

The sand was pushed and pushed, and every orange flame nearby was pushing with them. Finally, the sand stopped pushing, and started to compact.

"Keep pushing!" Sena said. "The sand is heating up, it's almost happened."

They pushed until it seemed they could push no more. Then, the sand started to push back.

"Seal it! Heat it, melt it as deep as you can! Plug that stair well!" Symin shouted, and every ranger blasted the opening with all the heat they could muster.

As the sand melted and glass began to form, there was a mighty rumble, and a puff of sand from around the edges, followed by a brief hiss of steam as something inside burst into gas. Then, the glass plugged the hole and the gasses stopped. Still, they poured their flames on the plug as the orange flames tossed more sand into the mix.

They filled the stairs, then filled the corridor above, and continued. As they finally began to tire, the glass plug was a solid lump filling not just the stairs, but an entire section of the building above.

"Did we make it?" Symin asked, fearing the answer.

"We did," Sena said. "The world is saved. But I only hope..."

"Hope what?" Symin insisted.

"I hope we all got out in time that we don't face the same end that took poor Tord."

"We'll be fine," Symin said. "His sacrifice will be remembered, and if we fall to the same illness, it was not in vain."

"Before we end ourselves," Loka said, looking at Symin in rebuke as she said it. "Is there anything else we need to do?"

"Concrete," Sena said. "Bury this building in it, and line it with lead. I only hope we are safe for now."

Chapter 33 – The clean up

Over the next two months, a supply route to Horde was milked for all it was worth, bringing concrete, lead and labour. A massive concrete dome was built over the supply facility, filling the building within, to cap the atomic in its tomb.

Cara moaned in despair as she watched that ancient knowledge, buried forever. She had looked forward to reawakening that ancient building, for the glory of Cinder, but more for her own curiosity.

To be safe, they decided they would do the same to the research facility, which Cara mourned even more greatly. Although Sena had ordered them not to uncover it, Cara had been sorely tempted to remove the sand and see what she could learn within. That was not to be, and the thick layers of concrete and lead were added to the sand.

To make Cara feel better, Sena led them to a building she called the space centre, where there was enough essence left in the pipes for a few short hours of operation.

There, she instructed Symin on how to operate a machine, which provided images taken from high above the planet, marked out with maps of safe routes out of Cinder.

“Thres had placed satellites in orbit. Those machines still function, sending enormous amounts of data back to us, but nobody has been listening. They have had seven centuries to watch the weather and the movement of the birds among other things, to give us maps showing possible routes in and out of the region we know as Cinder.”

“This alone is a treasure of untold value!” Cara crowed. “We must get these to the archives in Emberdale, and have them copied!”

“This has taken a few minutes of the machinery’s remaining time,” Sena said. “You will have not much more than two hours of operation left. Use that time wisely.”

“I will forbid anybody use this equipment until we have made a thorough investigation of the rest of the city,” Cara said. “That way, it will be available to answer any relevant questions which we may find during that time.”

“This tool is in wise hands,” Sena said. “Please keep the honour of my people.”

“It will be my privilege and my honour to do so, First Flame,” Cara said, bowing deeply to the yellow flame.

“Will you join us?’ Symin said. “It is high time we return to Emberdale. And these students as well, they’ve missed most of a semester now.”

“We’ll catch up,” Treghan said.

“You’d better do that,” Loka said. “If you don’t, you’ll be held back for another year...”

“We’ve caught up before,” Corilai said. “And by nearly as much. We can do it again. Besides, what other students have the ability to summon their flames like us?”

“Perhaps some of the third years have,” Symin said. “That knowledge has long since been shared with Emberdale.”

"Oh," Corilai said, deflated. "Of course it has."

"But still," Marni said. "With all we've achieved here, surely we can get some credit for work in the field."

"Perhaps, but that will be to the discretion of your teachers and the chancellor," Loka replied.

"You're our teacher!" Fletcher snapped.

"One of them, and I don't know..." Loka said. "What do you think, Cara? Do they deserve some credit?"

"Hey, don't you go putting that on me!" Cara said. "I would assume they will have to perform well in some exemption exams for that to be the case anyway."

"And how much help have they been to the young ones? Yera and Hyren, and that poor girl from Horde, Jull..." Loka mused.

"Speak of the devil," Symin said as Hyren and Jull approached. "How are you two progressing with your studies?"

"We're fine," Hyren said. "Jull borrowed some reading material from the others and we're working on first year academy stuff."

"Is that so?" Loka said with a raised eyebrow. "Anything else you want to tell us?"

"Only this," Hyren said. "Wesnor, come forth."

As Hyren's flame materialised beside him, Sena appeared, and shook her head.

"Foolish boy, that proves nothing. I helped you gain that ability, did I not?"

"Yes, you did," Jull said. "And he helped me in turn, something a mere first year should not be able to do alone."

"Wait, what?" Loka said. "He taught you to summon already?"

"Yes," Jull said. "Gill, come forth!"

And there he was, red and blazing beside her. Gill, strangely familiar to them all. Corilai rushed to him, and fell to her knees.

"Oh Gill!" she sobbed. "I'm so sorry! I wish I could change it all..."

"Be at peace, child," Gill said softly as he knelt before her. "You may have played a part in ending that tortured existence, but you also played a role in saving me and for that I am eternally thankful. Without your quick action I may have perished a normal way, and never had this chance for redemption."

"What do you mean?" Corilai said.

"My deeds were wrong, my mind was lost, and my thoughts impure. Now, as a flame, I am cleansed. I am free to become the best I can be, without insanity to guide my hand. Without you, I could not be here. I would have died at that tower, but that death would have been permanent. Child, you saved me, and for that I am thankful. Now stand and be proud, for you are a mighty ranger, pure and strong."

She stood, wiping the tears from her eyes as Treghan put his arm around her. Gill smiled and stood, stepping beside his bearer, who gazed up at him in unmasked pride.

* * *

It was a strange feeling for them, as they left Tyra behind. Cara left strict instructions with her chief assistant on how to proceed while she was gone, but still she stared back at the city walls as the caravan rolled away.

The road had been uncovered almost all the way to horde, and glassy embankments held the dunes at bay. The travel time was much less than on their trip to Tyra, but still it seemed an age before they rolled past the tower and then on into Glasswell.

In the time they were gone, Glasswell had spawned a thriving village community, and a sturdy road into Horde had been constructed. Cinder was growing into the desert, and the rangers could not help but wonder if that would be a good thing.

What other dangers waited for them out there in the sand and the wastelands? Only time would tell. That was something that could never be pushed back under the sand now, so they hoped it would all end well for their people, and their country.

* * *

Passing through Horde, they stayed the evening at the outpost, regaling those there with the tales of their exploits. But too soon, morning came and the journey continued. Back in familiar territory, where no danger waited to surprise them, the days passed easily as they travelled north.

One evening many days later, they wandered lazily into the village of Judd. As they approached from the south there was a shout and a burly, grey haired but fit and healthy man waved at them from the fields.

"Treghan! Fletcher!" the man shouted, stabbing his hoe into the ground and striding with proud, powerful steps to greet them.

Unbelieving, the two boys stared at their grinning father as he stood beside the road and the caravan passed.

"I did it boys, thanks to your words," the man said. "Please, stop in and see your mother. I will be headed home in an hour or so."

"We will, Father," Treghan said, smiling genuinely at the man. "I'm proud of you, Dad."

The man beamed a bright grin, waved an exaggerated wave, and returned to his work as the caravan moved on.

The twins were true to their word and, along with Marni and Corilai, they spent the evening with their parents. They enjoyed a hearty meal and a rousing conversation, during which their father was eager to hear everything about their adventures, beaming with pride for his sons the whole time.

The next morning, they waved their fond farewells, and returned to Emberdale, where they were thrown in the deep end of catching up with their studies. The four of them attended the regular classes, as well as additional evening and weekend classes run by Loka and their other teachers, who were not impressed at having to give up their free time. Nevertheless, the teachers saw the effort of the students, and were pleased at their commitment to making up for lost time.

Chapter 33 – Epilogue

The next six months passed quickly for the students and before they knew it their final exams were over and the four had passed their third year at the academy. They were tasked with deciding what branch of the Rangers to join, and it was an easier decision for Treghan than the others.

They sat around the table at the evening meal before they were due to have their ceremony for graduation, and Treghan looked at his friends.

"I want to join the scouts. I can travel the world with them. I know I'm not a yellow flame, but I can find recruits in other ways, and support the scout operations well with my talents. So I put in the paperwork a few days ago to state that was my preference."

"I'm sure they'll accept it," Corilai said. "I decided this morning, and put in my paperwork."

"This morning?" Marni said.

"Well, I think I really decided a long time ago, but I finally made it official today. I'm gong to be an enforcer, like Loka."

"Me too," Fletcher said. "They like us red flames in the enforcers. And I get to use my secondary properly there."

"Well, I'm conflicted," Marni said. "I kind of want to join the scouts, but I don't know how much more action I can face. I've done so much these last two years, and I think the enforcers would be too much for me. But I don't know if I have what it takes to join the archivists."

"There's always the support staff, or the teaching staff," Treghan said.

"Yes, I know," Marni said. "But I really would like to travel."

"Then it's easy," Treghan said. "I don't know why you think it's hard to choose. You need to join the scouts."

"But why?" Marni said.

"Look, the enforcers are the real muscle. I mean, sure Symin gets into a bit of strife with the rest of them, but at heart, the scouts are travellers, teachers, supporters of the people. They go around visiting new places, guarding merchants, protecting people, but all without the kind of battle hardened conflicts the enforcers are there for."

"I guess so," Marni said, sounding unconvinced.

"That's not the best of it though," Treghan said, sounding overly enthusiastic. "With those maps Cara brought from Tyra, the merchants are talking about leaving Cinder. They'll need support with them. Who do you think they'll take along for the ride? It will be the scouts! Wouldn't you love to be one of the first rangers to actually set foot outside of Cinder?"

"Hey, that's right! That's an adventure I could cope with!" Marni said, brightening suddenly.

"You two are thinking you can just run off and leave us behind?" Corilai snapped. "If you go, I'm coming with you!"

"Me too!" Fletcher snapped. "You can be the guides, we can be the muscle. Is it a deal?"

"It's a deal!" the other three said in unison.

* * *

The next morning, at first light, packages were delivered to the dorms containing replacement gloves, tunics and pants, which held the emblazoned emblem of the assigned profession. Treghan and Marni received scout uniforms, while Corilai and Fletcher relieved enforcer uniforms. The cloaks were not provided, as they would receive those at the ceremony.

Gathered together in Treghan's quarters, they tried them on immediately, excited that they all achieved their nominated fields. They were all chatting happily when Loka arrived.

"Enough of the slacking you lot!" she snapped, looking stern, but losing it in fits of giggles as the four students panicked and snapped to attention.

"Yes, you are rangers now and yes, two of you will work under me from now on, but that doesn't mean I'm an ogre," Loka said, continuing as she left. "Now, grab those student cloaks and get out to the parade grounds. The ceremony starts in half an hour."

"Yes, Ranger!" the four new graduates said in unison.

As they donned their cloaks and rushed downstairs, other students were thronging about excitedly, similarly summoned by their teachers. As they reached the ground floor, they saw Loka coming the other way, a throng of students rushing along behind her.

"Excuse me, Loka?" Corilai called out.

"What is it, graduate?" Loka said formally.

"Do we summon our flames for the ceremony? Or is that against protocol?"

"Of course you do! It demonstrates your success and your power, as well as your respect for your flames! They are graduating with you, after all, and not many students can do it yet, especially in the younger years. It might inspire some to try harder."

"Yes, Ma'am!" Corilai shouted, beaming a broad grin as she saluted Loka, before continuing. "Derieala, come forth!"

The black flame appeared instantly beside her, drawing startled gasps of admiration from the students around her as Treghan summoned Gabraii, Fletcher summoned Faeris, and Marni summoned Ursaela.

Together with their flames, they made their way to the parade grounds, where they soon found their place in the order near the front of the line. It seemed an eternity, as the parade grounds filled with students, proud parents, rangers, teachers and other interested civilians. Finally, the chancellor stepped up to the podium and looked out over the crowd.

"It is with great pride, that I welcome you to this year's graduation ceremony for the Ranger Academy of Emberdale," he began as the crowd fell silent. "This year, I am proud to preside over what may be the greatest graduating class of our history, which is saying something given the many centuries in which this school has operated."

A murmur through the students was quickly hushed. Chancellor Howe continued.

"This year, we will lead off the ceremony with four students whose fame has spread throughout Cinder. In their first year, before they were even admitted to classes, they had been instrumental in our crushing of the tyranny of Yuri, the tyrant who had spread his wicked arms from the southern port of Grey."

The crowd cheered his words, and Howe waited for silence before he spoke again.

"In the holiday between their first and second year, those same four students journeyed to the Everwinter Highlands, where they played a crucial role in solving the mysteries around a series of abductions, leading to the overthrow of a mountain tyrant named Dreighton and the freeing of hundreds of abducted children."

The crowd cheered again. Once again, the Chancellor waited for silence before he continued.

"Then, most recently, in their break between second and third year, overlapping with much of what should have been their third year classes, requiring enormous amounts of work on their part to once again catch up in their studies, these four students joined a task force sent to investigate some crucial matters in the far south, at the heart of the Desert of Souls."

There were gasps from those in the audience who had still not heard the tales of those exploits.

"While there, these students were active participants in a mission which prevented what could have been a catastrophic event, one which could well have destroyed not only Cinder, but the entire world, leaving no man woman or child alive."

The crowd cheered again.

"Now, this time," the Chancellor said, not waiting for quiet. "That mission brought us so much more than the end of a tyrant or the saving of lost children and hostages. That mission uncovered a long forgotten history of our world, revealed answers to the greatest questions of our nation's origins, and unleashed the knowledge which will allow us to finally travel beyond our borders, to rejoin the rest of the world outside!"

The crowd cheered the loudest cheer yet, and this time the Chancellor raised his arms high and waved for silence. As the crowd finally settled down, he continued.

"Please join me in welcoming to the stage, Treghan the White, who joins the scouts, Corilai the Black, who joins the enforcers, Marni the Green, who joins the scouts, and Fletcher the red, who joins the enforcers. Please give them a proud and loud welcome as these young heroes of the academy finally take their rightful place among their peers as Rangers of Emberdale!"

As a single unit, the four newest rangers rushed onto the stage, grinning and waving to the crowd as Chancellor Howe, with the help of Barache, handed to them their new cloaks, two in the dark greenish grey colour of the scouts and two in the red tinted grey of the enforcers.

As they stood up there looking out over the screaming crowd they saw the other students. Their fellow third years were at the front waiting to graduate and the second and first years behind them. To the sides were their teachers and hundreds of rangers, proud to now call them colleagues. And finally, at the rear, enormous crowds of civilians, parents and others.

There in the heart of the crowd at the back, stood their parents, all of them; Marni's parents from Oaklands, Corilai's parents from Dent, along with Fletcher and Treghan's parents having journeyed from Judd, and they were the most excited of all.

Six adults jumping and cavorting and cheering like excited children as their offspring took the stage, the heroes of Cinder. The pride in the faces of those six adults spoke of all that was worth saving in the proud nation of Cinder.

www.ingramcontent.com/pod-product-compliance
Lightning Source LLC
Chambersburg PA
CBHW030824310726
48980CB00006B/624/J